Angels of Darkness

Angels
of Darkness

Tales of Troubled
and Troubling Women

Selected and Edited
by Marvin Kaye
With an Introduction by Paula Volsky

GUILDAMERICA
B O O K S ®

Doubleday Book & Music Clubs, Inc.
Garden City, New York

To Toni Broaca
A Connecticut Yankee
and a friend

PUBLISHED BY GUILDAMERICA® BOOKS,
an imprint and a registered trademark of
Doubleday Book & Music Clubs, Inc.,
Department GB, 401 Franklin Avenue,
Garden City, New York 11530

GUILDAMERICA® is a registered trademark of
Doubleday Book & Music Clubs, Inc.

Acknowledgments on page 529

Book design by Paul Randall Mize

ISBN 1-56865-116-3

Contents

DISTAFF DARKNESS

Preface

Angels of Darkness, my fifteenth and perhaps most personal anthology, peers into the darker sides of womanhood and femininity, concepts no longer synonymous in the war of intolerance waged by many allegedly "liberated" Americans.

My initial intention was to prepare a collection of tales concerning threatened and/or threatening women created exclusively by female writers, an impulse stemming from what might glibly be labeled getting in phase with the feminine side of my psyche . . . except for the fact that I never lost touch with it.

My earliest memories are of a World War II household full of coddling women: mother, sisters, aunts whose absent husbands were soldiers or sailors. But there was a dark side to some of the distaff affection so readily bestowed. I got to hear oh, so many things wrong with men ("Oh, he's too little to know what we're talking about . . .") that I grew up saddled with the need to prove myself the shining exception to that sexist calumny that little boys mainly consist of frogs, snails and puppy-dog tails.

Yet in spite of this lifelong albatross around my neck, I soon saw the necessity of broadening the scope of *Angels of Darkness.* For one thing, many of the right-on-theme stories I found were by men (especially Bob Sheckley's "Love Song from the Stars"). This should not have surprised me; the best "women's lib" play ever written is inarguably James M. Barrie's 1910 comedy *The Twelve-Pound Look*.

As I searched my library, I also realized that there are more aspects to *Angels of Darkness* than could be captured adequately under the headings of "Women in Danger" and "Dangerous Women," so I added a comparatively gentler subsection, "Women Troubled and Troubling," as well as a final sequence of disturbing nonpareils composed exclusively by women and called "Distaff Darkness."

For anyone who insists on counting, the final tally turns out exactly equal, twenty-four contributors of each gender. (Vernon Lee, Maurice Level and one other byline are pseudonyms.) To offset this brief preface and keep the count fully egalitarian, I am pleased to include an incisive introduction by Paula Volsky, one of America's most important fantasists (*Illusion, The Luck of Relian Kru, The Sorcerer's Curse, The Wolf in Winter* among others).

As always in my anthologies, each author has been restricted to a single entry and less-familiar stories by well-known writers are given the spotlight. Several appear here in print for the first time.

The title derives from *Angels of Darkness,* an unpublished manuscript by Arthur Conan Doyle. Uh-oh, another *man* . . .

—MARVIN KAYE
New York, 1994

Introduction

The feminist movement of the last three decades redefined and clearly re-expressed the position of women in society, didn't it? A woman's proper place is—anywhere she wants to be (up to and including the men's locker room). Her appropriate role—whatever she chooses (with the possible exception of biological father). That was surely clear enough, admitting of little confusion—wasn't it? I confess, I used to think so.

How wrong I was.

In an era to which the label "postfeminist" is already being applied, confusion is rife as never before. How are women to be regarded at home and in the workplace? How should they be spoken to/whistled at, looked at/leered at, touched/not touched, included/excluded, respected/pedestaled/despised? How are the observable differences in brain structure and brain chemistry between the sexes to be reconciled with ideal notions of perfect equality? The legal ramifications of these questions have jammed the courts in recent years, and the social tensions have sent susceptible souls literally fleeing for the shelter of the deep woods and the sylvan comforts of campfires, tom-toms and all-male enclaves.

Amid disgruntled masculine queries (What do women WANT?) and peevish feminine rejoinders (MEN JUST DON'T GET IT!), there's no dearth of nostalgia for the golden past, wherein gender roles were well defined, and comprehended if not fully accepted by one and all. Back then, whenever *then* was, there were basically two varieties of women. There were the morally and emotionally sound ones content with their traditional femininity; the virgins/dutiful daughters/faithful wives/selfless mothers—sometimes spirited and willful, even occasionally rebellious, but never "masculine." Never seriously competitive with males, much less dominant. These fair creatures merited approval, support and protection. Then there were the others—the witches and bitches, the hags and seductresses, the schemers, screamers and apple-offering troublemakers—so often cursed with an unwomanly lust for power, independence and autonomy. These twisted sisters deserved whatever they got, and what they got sometimes beggars description.

Like it or not, fair or unfair, at least things were clear and definite—back then.

Only they weren't. Not then, not now, probably not ever. Feminine ambiguity is eternal, as the stories in Marvin Kaye's diabolically disturbing anthology amply demonstrate. The reader searching for clarification between these covers had best look elsewhere. *Angels of Darkness* offers a study in contrasts far more likely to raise questions than to answer them.

Assembled here is a highly unconventional collection of tales both old and new, guaranteed to rattle convictions, to confound expectation, and above all, to entertain. Here, we confront a sinister survey of feminine possibility, an examination of women's roles ranging from the literally angelic (see Jane Yolen's moral paradox, "Angelica") to the dreadful and demonic (too many to name), with numerous stops in between, including a few that nearly defy definition. The variety is impressive, the tone is almost consistently dark, and the one reliable constant is originality.

One of the most enduring and perversely compelling of traditionally female roles is that of temptress—the man-eating bombshell armed with all the power of raw sexuality, and quite willing to use it. She usually comes to a bad end, often suffering the vengeance of the society whose codes she has outraged, or, more likely, suffering the vengeance of the discarded male victim whose ego she has outraged—but while she lasts, she is the most enviably liberated and potent of females. No new variations possible on that ancient theme? The classic temptress—the irresistible, wildly desirable Cleopatra whose embrace is paradise, whose allure leads men to doom, for whom the world is accounted well-lost—is present among these pages in the guise of a Renaissance femme fatale whose

Amour is Dure. But Vernon Lee's Italian siren differs from others of her ilk in that she happens to be dead, an attribute linking her to the far gentler, possibly imaginary but no less consuming lady shade of Henry James's noncommittal "The Friends of the Friends." Likewise unconventional—the literally painted hussy of Morgan Llywelyn's "Untitled"; a devouring personification of unbridled lust, a red-hot, destroying Galatea whose luckless Pygmalion dies young but very happy (perhaps he's not so luckless at that).

Does the aptly-named White Fell of "The Were-Wolf," Clemence Housman's splendid tale of love and self-sacrifice, also qualify as an atypical temptress? Yes, in a sense, but it seems an oversimplification to label her as such, when she is clearly much more. Like many of the complex, unforgettable women haunting these pages, White Fell defies conventional categorization. Does she symbolize the seductive glamour of evil? Is she an earthly demon, her destruction a Christian triumph? Or is she a solitary, exotic creature, some evolutionary cousin to man, living as her nature dictates, and no more subject to humanity's moral standards and judgments than a she-wolf? The reader may judge. (I personally would have enjoyed seeing a portion of that story written from *her* point of view. But then, perhaps it's best after all that she retain her mystery.)

Most archetypal of feminine roles is the maternal, and Mother figures prominently among Kaye's dark angels. Here, however, Mother appears in unaccustomed guises. She is a mindless revenant, an eerily poignant memento mori, in Dan Simmons's melancholy "The River Styx Runs Upstream." She may be soulless as a hologram, she may be a zombie, a walking vacancy—but, for the desperate, she is still better than nothing. And there are many desperate.

Sad ghastliness aside, at least Simmons's strolling corpse is recognizably human. But what of the near-unimaginable maternal existence implied by the eponymous womblike space of Tanith Lee's "A Room with a Vie"? Does anyone really want to know Her?

Temptress, Mother—those are the oldest and most evocative of feminine roles, but many others, of far less traditional flavor, are represented here. There is the bewildering Woman as villainess/victim, tainted yet pitiable, exemplified by the wretched recipient of Maurice Level's "The Last Kiss," whose psychic blindness foreshadows her impending fate. (This is one of the few stories I've encountered whose dreadful effect depends less on surprise than on confirmation of gruesome expectation. The reader sees what's coming a mile off. The victim doesn't. The reader's increasingly urgent, telepathically shrieked warnings fail to reach her. The frustration is stupendous.)

Venturing on into ever stranger terrain, we encounter Jessica Amanda Salmonson's strangely voyaging Dr. Morbid, a kindly feminine angel of death. There is Robert Sheckley's nameless Andaran alien who knows just how to keep her man barefoot and pregnant. There is Zenna Henderson's fantastically beautiful and inexplicable Aunt Daid, whose dreams may perhaps shape the reality of our universe. There are innocently profane priestesses, juvenile undertakers, empath-telepath destiny-dabblers, and others of equally exotic description. There are wonders aplenty, heroines and sinners, whores and horrors, myths and monsters —everything imaginable except clichés.

The diverse dark angels, fallen and otherwise, inhabiting these stories are not always pleasant company. Many will bedevil the imagination, and a few are likely to kindle nightmares. Their society, however, is always stimulating, and their combined power nothing less than extraordinary. They are not easily forgotten.

Let the reader beware.

—PAULA VOLSKY
March 1994

Women in Danger

I watch my sister in the moonlight,
Rose-tipped like the Judas tree
Whose blossoms I must never finger.
— *Patterned on a haiku by Prince Yuhara*
   (Seventh Century)

The Last Kiss

Maurice Level

A romanticist might call love one of the gentler emotions, but not MAURICE
LEVEL *(1875–1926). The titanic passion in her lead-off tale is typical of this
unremittingly grisly French short story writer who, according to the Library
of Congress, was really Madame Jeanne Mareteux-Level. A play version of
"The Last Kiss" was once adapted for Paris's horrific Grand Guignol theatre.*

"FORGIVE ME . . . Forgive me."
His voice was less assured as he replied:
"Get up, dry your eyes. I, too, have a good deal to reproach myself
with."
"No, no," she sobbed.
He shook his head.
"I ought never to have left you; you loved me. Just at first after it all
happened . . . when I could still feel the fire of the vitriol burning my
face, when I began to realize that I should never see again, that all my
life I should be a thing of horror, of Death, certainly I wasn't able to
think of it like that. It isn't possible to resign oneself all at once to such a
fate . . . But living in this eternal darkness, a man's thoughts pierce far
below the surface and grow quiet like those of a person falling asleep,
and gradually calm comes. To-day, no longer able to use my eyes, I see
with my imagination. I see again our little house, our peaceful days, and
your smile. I see your poor little face the night I said that last good-bye.

The judge couldn't imagine any of that, could he? And it was only fair
to try to explain, for they thought only of your action, the action that
made me into . . . what I am. They were going to send you to prison
where you would slowly have faded . . . No years of such punishment
for you could have given me back my eyes . . . When you saw me go
into the witness-box you were afraid, weren't you? You believed that I
would charge you, have you condemned? No, I could never have done
that, never . . ."

She was still crying, her face buried in her hands.

"How good you are! . . ."

"I am just . . ."

In a voice that came in jerks she repeated:

"I repent, I repent; I have done the most awful thing to you that a
woman could do, and you—you begged for my acquittal! And now you
can even find words of pity for me! What can I do to prove my sorrow?
Oh, you are wonderful . . . wonderful . . ."

He let her go on talking and weeping; his head thrown back, his
hands on the arms of his chair, he listened apparently without emotion.
When she was calm again, he asked:

"What are you going to do now?"

"I don't know . . . I shall rest for a few days . . . I am so tired
. . . Then I shall go back to work. I shall try to find a place in a shop or
as a mannequin."

His voice was a little stifled as he asked:

"You are still as pretty as ever?"

She did not reply.

"I want to know if you are as pretty as you used to be?"

She remained silent. With a slight shiver, he murmured: "It is dark
now, isn't it? Turn on the light. Though I can no longer see, I like to feel
that there is light around me . . . Where are you? . . . Near the
mantelpiece? . . . Stretch out your hand. You will find the switch
there."

No sense even of light could penetrate his eyelids, but from the sudden sound of horror she stifled, he knew that the lamp was on. For the
first time she was able to see the result of her work, the terrifying face
streaked with white swellings, seamed with red furrows, a narrow black
band round the eyes. While he had pleaded for her in court, she had
crouched on her seat weeping, not daring to look at him; now, before

this abominable thing, she grew sick with a kind of disgust. But it was without any anger that he murmured:

"I am very different from the man you knew in the old days—I horrify you now, don't I? You shrink from me? . . ."

She tried to keep her voice steady.

"Certainly not. I am here, in the same place . . ."

"Yes, now . . . and I want you to come still nearer. If you knew how the thought of your hands tempt me in my darkness. How I should love to feel their softness once again. But I dare not . . . And yet that is what I wanted to ask you: to let me feel your hand for a minute in mine. We, the blind, can get such marvelous memories from just a touch."

Turning her head away, she held out her arm. Caressing her fingers, he murmured:

"Ah, how good. Don't tremble. Let me try to imagine we are lovers again just as we used to be . . . but you are not wearing my ring. Why? I have not taken yours off. Do you remember? You said, 'It is our wedding-ring.' Why have you taken it off?"

"I dare not wear it . . ."

"You must put it on again. You will wear it? Promise me."

She stammered:

"I promise you."

He was silent for a little while; then in a calmer voice:

"It must be quite dark now. How cold I am! If you only knew how cold it feels when one is blind. Your hands are warm; mine are frozen. I have not yet developed the fuller sense of touch. It takes time, they say . . . At present I am like a little child learning."

She let her fingers remain in his, sighing:

"Oh, *Mon Dieu . . . Mon Dieu . . .*"

Speaking like a man in a dream, he went on:

"How glad I am that you came. I wondered whether you would, and I felt I wanted to keep you with me for a long, long time: always . . . But that wouldn't be possible. Life with me would be too sad. You see, little one, when people have memories like ours, they must be careful not to spoil them, and it must be horrible to look at me now, isn't it?"

She tried to protest; what might have been a smile passed over his face.

"Why lie? I remember I once saw a man whose mistress had thrown vitriol over him. His face was not human. Women turned their heads away as they passed, while he, not being able to see and so not knowing, went on talking to the people who were shrinking away from him. I must be, I am like that poor wretch, am I not? Even you who knew me as I used to be, you tremble with disgust; I can feel it. For a long time you will be haunted by the remembrance of my face . . . it will come in between you and everything else . . . How the thought hurts . . . but don't let us go on talking about me . . . You said just now that you were going back to work. Tell me your plans; come nearer, I don't hear as well as I used to . . . Well?"

Their two armchairs were almost touching. She was silent. He sighed:

"Ah, I can smell your scent! How I have longed for it. I bought a bottle of the perfume you always used, but on me it didn't smell the same. From you it comes mixed with the scent of your skin and hair. Come nearer, let me drink it in . . . You are going away, you will never come back again; let me draw in for the last time as much of you as I can . . . You shiver . . . am I then so horrible?"

She stammered:

"No . . . it is cold . . ."

"Why are you so lightly dressed? I don't believe you brought a cloak. In November, too. It must be damp and dreary in the streets. How you tremble! How warm and comfortable it was in our little home . . . do you remember? You used to lay your face on my shoulder, and I used to hold you close to me. Who would want to sleep in my arms now? Come nearer. Give me your hand . . . There . . . What did you think when your lawyer told you I had asked to see you?"

"I thought I ought to come."

"Do you still love me? . . ."

Her voice was only a breath:

"Yes . . ."

Very slowly, his voice full of supplication, he said:

"I want to kiss you for the last time. I know it will be almost torture for you . . . Afterwards I won't ask anything more. You can go . . . May I? . . . Will you let me? . . ."

Involuntarily she shrank back; then, moved by shame and pity, not daring to refuse a joy to the poor wretch, she laid her head on his shoulder, held up her mouth and shut her eyes. He pressed her gently to him, silent, prolonging the happy moment. She opened her eyes, and seeing the terrible face so near, almost touching her own, for the second time she shivered with disgust and would have drawn sharply away. But he pressed her closer to him, passionately.

"You would go away so soon? . . . Stay a little longer . . . You haven't seen enough of me . . . Look at me . . . and give me your mouth again . . . more of it than that . . . It is horrible, isn't it?"

She moaned:

"You hurt me . . ."

"Oh, no," he sneered, "I frighten you."

She struggled.

"You hurt me! You hurt me!"

In a low voice he said:

"Sh-h. No noise; be quiet. I've got you now and I'll keep you. For how many days have I waited for this moment . . . Keep still, I say, keep still! No nonsense! You know I am much stronger than you."

He seized both her hands in one of his, took a little bottle from the pocket of his coat, drew out the stopper with his teeth, and went on in the same quiet voice:

"Yes, it is vitriol; bend your head . . . there . . . You will see; we are going to be incomparable lovers, made for each other . . . Ah, you tremble? Do you understand now why I had you acquitted, and why I made you come here to-day? Your pretty face will be exactly like mine. You will be a monstrous thing, and like me, blind! . . . Ah, yes, it hurts, hurts terribly."

She opened her mouth to implore. He ordered:

"No! Not that! Shut your mouth! I don't want to kill you, that would make it too easy for you."

Gripping her in the bend of his arm, he pressed his hand on her mouth and poured the acid slowly over her forehead, her eyes, her cheeks. She struggled desperately, but he held her too firmly and kept on pouring as he talked:

"There . . . a little more . . . you bite, but that's nothing . . . It hurts, doesn't it? It is Hell . . ."

Suddenly he flung her away, crying:

"I am burning myself."

She fell writhing on the floor. Already her face was nothing but a red rag.

Then he straightened himself, stumbled over her, felt about the wall to find the switch, and put out the light. And round them, as in them, was a great Darkness . . .

A Bride for the Devil

Stuart Palmer

"A Bride for the Devil" appeared in 1949 in the premiere issue of The Magazine of Fantasy, *which added* and Science Fiction *to its title with its second number.* STUART PALMER *(1905 1968), past president of the Mystery Writers of America, is best known for his Hildegarde Withers whodunits and for his Sherlock Holmes pastiches "The Adventure of the Marked Man" and "The Adventure of the Remarkable Worm."*

JUST AS A CURIOSITY," insisted Dr. Baynard, "I assure you that it is a very great bargain, even at the price."

"Perhaps," murmured Emily Parkinson slowly. Her crimson-tipped fingers stroked the yellowed sheet of parchment. "But the price does seem exorbitant, just for some faded old lettering that I can't even read."

"I have every reason to believe," the doctor continued, "that it is made of real human skin."

"How simply terrible!"

Dr. Baynard knew that Mrs. Parkinson was going to buy it, and she knew it also. This hesitation and haggling was a little game that she liked to play before squandering her husband's money on antiques or colored glass or primitive paintings. She was a handsome, Junoesque person, with smooth, suspiciously yellow hair, fine teeth, and the general appearance of a woman ten years her junior. Her record of three husbands and two divorces indicated that she was at the very least somewhere in her forties, but expensive beauty treatments had kept her plump face smooth as a girl's.

Her warm, enfolding smile, her full breasts, her ample femininity, had since her schooldays held out a promise unfulfilled to her husbands or for that matter to anyone else. Her current spouse, Frederic Parkinson, kept himself nowadays almost entirely to his Wall Street office, his club, and to a succession of pretty little secretaries, models, and chorus girls, from whom according to rumor he received whatever warmth and happiness can be purchased for spot-cash. He was represented in Emily Parkinson's life mainly by the large checkbook which now lay before her on the Sheraton desk in the big, heavily-draped library of the Park Avenue apartment.

"I assure you, dear lady," Dr. Baynard was saying, "that this is in all ways a most unusual sheet of parchment. Any collector of *curiosa*—"

"But what is so curious about a page torn from a volume written only three hundred years ago? It's handwritten, too, and most books were set in type by then, weren't they?"

Dr. Baynard, steadying himself by gripping the edge of the desk, bowed creakily. "This page," he explained, "comes from the notorious *Ausgeburten des Menschenwahns* of Benedict Koenig, a factual account of the torments of the inquisition in early Germany. A very grim, almost sadistic work, although supposedly set down for the glory of God and the edification of the public, in very primitive black-letter German. However, it is well-known among students that manuscript paper or parchment was very scarce at certain periods, particularly in the monasteries of Germany and France. The good monks were forced to make inroads, out of pious zeal, upon their own libraries. They carefully bleached out the previous, older writings in order to provide blank space for their own compositions. It was thus, we are told, that almost all of the poems of Sappho were lost."

Mrs. Parkinson toyed with her fountain pen. "Yes, doctor?"

"That is what evidently happened in this case. The writer ran short of paper and used a parchment, a most unusually fine and soft parchment, for the last page of the sixteenth chapter of his manuscript. It is interesting, of course, to conjecture as to the ancient volume from which the sheet was taken, and how such a thing happened to be in a monastery at all. However, I digress. The point is that the advances of modern science, particularly in chemistry and in fluoroscopic and infra-red lighting, can bring back the ancient writings even though they are, as in this case, invisible to the naked eye." Here Dr. Baynard smiled, showing all his yellowed bridgework.

"The original volume was sent to a colleague of mine for appraisal. In assisting him, I chanced to notice the unusual texture of this page, and took the liberty of removing it. Under the magic lights, dear lady, there appeared words, and then complete sentences, set down in a crabbed Latin hand. It must date back another six or seven hundred years, at the least. I happen to have with me a literal translation of the first few paragraphs. Read, dear lady, for yourself."

He offered a typewritten sheet, which Mrs. Parkinson accepted with a gracious bow. She opened a gold case, removed her pince-nez, and began to read. After a moment her mouth began to drop open, and her naturally hyperthyroid eyes bulged even more.

"Good heavens!" she cried. When she had finished there was a marked flush on her face and neck. "It's very specific, isn't it?"

After a moment she put down the sheet and reached for the checkbook. "I really shouldn't," she said. "But I'll make it a birthday present to myself, ahead of time."

Dr. Baynard looked extremely pleased, a smile showing faintly through his wispy Van Dyke. "I am very gratified, dear lady, and not only because of the slight commission involved. It is naturally not at all the sort of thing which could be offered to the regular dealers in the usual way."

"But one must be broad-minded, mustn't one?" Mrs. Parkinson blotted the check carefully. "I think it is perfectly fascinating. You will, of course, continue with the translation for me?"

"It will be a pleasure, madam."

"Because the most wonderful idea has just come to me!"

Dr. Baynard, folding up the check lovingly before tucking it away in his thin leather billfold, suddenly caught his breath. "My dear lady! You're not thinking of trying it?"

She nodded brightly. "Just as an adventure, of course. After all, the thing is really a ritual, is it not—combined with a very clear and detailed recipe?"

"But—some of the ingredients—"

"Yes, of course, doctor. The corpse-fat, and the unicorn's horn, and the blood of still-born babes. We may not be able to get everything, but

one can make substitutions. After all, the medical profession used to
laugh at the Chinese herb-doctors who prescribed the ground-up heads
of toads for heart trouble, until it was discovered that digitalis was
contained in them. What we shall aim at is the spirit, if not the letter, of
the list of ingredients. You will help me, doctor?"

Dr. Baynard had had two glasses of excellent sherry, and Mrs. Parkinson's eyes were very large and warm and compelling. "Why, I could
hardly refuse, dear lady. One cannot be, however, too hopeful about any
possible results—"

"Naturally. But we must not forget that where there is so much
smoke, there might be fire. After all, at some of the seances last year I
very definitely felt *something*. There are more things in Heaven and
earth, you know. Besides, it is really a scientific experiment."

Out of this beginning was born the Satanist Society, with Emily Parkinson as its president and prime-mover, and Dr. Baynard as secretary
and master of ceremonies. Mrs. Parkinson felt very daring, devilish even,
as she explained to her little group of kindred spirits the adventure that
lay before them. There were a dozen or so, almost all wealthy, idle
women who had long since passed over to others the care of their homes,
their husbands, and their children. Not that many of them had ever
cared to risk the travail and responsibility of having children in the first
place.

Some of the ladies had been with Mrs. Parkinson through her Ve-
danta era, through Dr. Coué, the Oxford Movement, Yoga, Christian
Science, and a few of the most daring had even followed her into a brief
and unsatisfying series of Black Masses under the guidance of a de-
frocked Roman Catholic priest.

They had sat through endless seances led by a succession of mediums,
including the famous Margery of Boston. They had heard horns blown,
tambourines pounded, and had felt the wet touch of ectoplasm—or wet
cheese-cloth—in the darkness.

They had tried numerology, during which many of them changed the
spelling of their first names. They had for a time trusted themselves to
the guidance of the stars, with individual horoscopes prepared by the
best and most expensive astrologers, and had shivered with delicious
apprehension when their sign was in the wrong house or under a baleful
influence.

But there had never been anything like this. The ladies of the group lived in a veritable frenzy of excitement during the weeks—and there were many many weeks—while Dr. Baynard was translating the rest of the invocation, and painstakingly assembling the necessary ingredients.

"Let us take as our slogan that Nothing Is Impossible!" Mrs. Parkinson had said.

It was surprising, really, how much could be done with the lavish backing of the Parkinson checkbook. Of course there were a number of substitutions that had to be made, for the original manuscript had been couched in the most archaic and almost fantastic language that could be imagined. It was Dr. Baynard who secured powdered unicorn's horn by bribing a zoo attendant to supply him with a bit of a rhinoceros's tusk—for what was the fabled beast but the result of garbled tales brought back to Europe from Africa by someone who had met someone who had seen a rhino?

Grave-robbing was avoided by the simple means of making an arrangement with the service staff of a large hospital, where still-born babes were nothing out of the way. And as for the venom of an adder, Dr. Baynard discovered that cobra venom was available in small quantities at most medical supply houses.

So it was that slowly, one by one, the long list of necessaries was at last completed, in the spirit if not completely in the letter of the formula. It was Mrs. Parkinson who insisted upon waiting until St. John's Eve for the actual ceremony. There might be nothing to the ancient tradition, but again there might. "What is most important is to place ourselves as much as is possible in tune, in harmony, with the forces that we hope to evoke."

The day finally arrived, and the ladies gathered at Mrs. Parkinson's big white country house on the north shore of Long Island. The hour had first been set at midnight, but after some research by the doctor it had been changed to moon-rise, which was due to occur shortly after eight in the evening. It was a full, round moon that hung over the Sound like a worn copper coin.

For some time the big house had been closed, which made it all the better. Mrs. Parkinson wanted no servants around to gossip and pry. With the help of the doctor, who was fairly trembling at the weight of his responsibility, the unused ballroom was made ready. There were folding chairs to be set up, lighting to be arranged, and the skylight opened so that the moonlight could enter.

There was a twitter of delighted apprehension among the ladies as they saw the stage, which had originally been the musicians' stand. It was bare now, covered only with a dark carpet on which had been traced, in various-colored chalks, a five-sided figure, with beautifully drawn devices in its corners.

This pentacle was illuminated only by one shaded bulb from the side, but a deeper, eerie light was beginning to shine from the brim of an iron pot which hung from a tripod set within the pentacle, and into which Dr. Baynard was from time to time throwing bits of unmentionable material, or pouring little gouts of liquid from an assortment of bottles, all the while referring constantly to a list in his hand.

Mrs. Parkinson stood beside him on the platform, as was her right. She was, the other ladies had to admit, looking her very best, in an evening gown of black and crimson which made the most of her fine shoulders and bust. "Please sit down, ladies," she announced. "In a very few minutes the time will be ripe. I must ask that we all maintain the most rigorous silence during this—this experiment. We must concentrate, and hold the thought!" She glared at one of the guests in the back row. "There will be no smoking please!"

The ladies settled themselves with a hushing, whispering buzz and rustle, and then all was silence. Mrs. Parkinson watched, nodding her approval, as Dr. Baynard tossed in a few more herbs and potions, and the pot flared higher. She then backed away to where a big radio-phonograph stood, and touched a switch. In a moment the room was filled with the powerful though diminished music of the "Danse Macabre."

The house lights were completely dark now, and in that darkness the ladies sat still, and held the thought. It is true that no two of them held the same thought, for their conceptions of His Satanic Majesty were all very different, based upon folklore, dimly remembered religious education, and literature. One lady in the front row, who had once been an avid reader of James Branch Cabell, visioned the Adversary as a neat, respectable tradesman in a brown velveteen jacket. Her neighbor, more in the classical tradition, saw Him as Lucifer, Son of the Morning—a beautiful, proud, fallen angel, a little like Rudolph Valentino only with more character in His face.

To some of the others, He was Mephistopheles, the swaggering Gallic devil with waxed moustaches and a pointed beard, wily yet polite, with a contract ready for signature and a promise of all the riches of this world. Yet again, there were ladies in the audience who confused Him with Pan, thinking of the cloven hoof, the shaggy dancing goat legs, the classic profile and the pipe of reeds that blew such strange sweet over-powering tunes. . . .

Oddly enough, each one of them had retained an idea of the Prince of Darkness, out of the illustrations seen in childhood, out of folklore and literature, when all the other concepts of religion had been long since eaten away. The villain of the piece is easier to remember, when the curtain has fallen. Who was it who trapped Fagin, who battled with Quasimodo, who sought to drive the stake through Dracula?

Not that anyone was going to let herself be disappointed when noth-ing happened. The experiment was of course doomed to failure, but even in its failure it would prove something. And it was all terribly terribly thrilling.

Sober and unsmiling, his manner somehow reverent, Dr. Baynard tossed another handful of ingredients into the pot, and then he began to read aloud from the paper he held in his hand. "Belphegor—Asmodeus—Beelzebub—"

The list of names was very long indeed, and the doctor's voice was thin and weak.

One of the ladies began to titter, in pure nervousness, and Mrs. Par-kinson glared, with her finger to her lips, until there was silence again. Now the incense was pouring out of the brazier, a pillar of thick brown-ish smoke streaked with flashes of reddish fire.

"Aeshma Devi!" cried Dr. Baynard, still following his text. "Azazel—Achitophel—Zita—Istar—Arcade! Princes, Principalities, Powers, Thrones and Dominions!"

Here he tossed a handful of whitish powder into the fire, which immediately erupted with a blaze of greenish-yellow flame.

Dr. Baynard cleared his throat, and began: "Amen forever glory the and power the is Thine for—"

"It's backwards!" explained a lady in the audience to her next neigh-bor.

"—forgive and bread daily our day this us give—"

His voice was fading. Mrs. Parkinson peered at him, wondering if they really ought to go any farther. Something had gone wrong with the record, too, for it was going around and around in the same groove.

"Doctor, are you all right?" she whispered.

". . . heaven in is it as even earth on, done be will Thy, come kingdom Thy, name Thy be hallowed—" The doctor was speaking faster and faster now ". . . heaven-in-art-whoFatherOur!"

Then there was a long and agonizing pause, during which the only sound in the room was Dr. Baynard's labored breathing and the monotonous repetition of the record. Mrs. Parkinson shut it off, and turned to the audience. Her poise had never deserted her, and she was quite evidently prepared for even such an anticlimax as this. "Ladies!" she cried. "I am sure that we all—I mean, I myself felt something, there at the end, a very definite *something* in the room."

Her voice died away in her throat as she saw the faces of the ladies in the audience, the bloated, terror masks that yammered and goggled up at her. She turned, to see Dr. Baynard kneeling within the pentacle.

Then she looked behind her. She shrieked, with all the power of her lungs, "Retro mas, Satanas!"

What happened after that is to some extent a matter for conjecture, as the accounts of eyewitnesses differ. Each of the ladies in the panic-stricken audience carried away with her on her mad flight a vision of a squat, anthropomorphic entity which had taken shape on the platform.

It stood there for a moment, surprised and blinking, crouched on its thick, bowed legs. Its body was toadlike, scabrous, and oily with a glistening, dripping ichor, and the scent which pervaded the room was by no means the comparatively clean reek of sulphur and brimstone.

It turned first toward Dr. Baynard, but halted at the edge of the pentacle. Then its reddish, mad little eyes opened wider and a hellish grin illumined its face.

By that time the room was almost emptied, except for the doctor, now completely collapsed within his chalk-drawn zone of safety. One or two of the ladies, more curious or less agile than the rest, saw in a quick glance over her shoulder a horrifying view of the demon as it seized delightedly upon Emily Parkinson.

With its thick legs clamped about her neck, its clawlike paws tangled in her yellow hair, its heavy hairless tail lashing her across the flanks, the thing rode Mrs. Parkinson as a rodeo performer rides a bucking horse, rode her around and around the platform and then off through the air and out the skylight into the night. Her shrill neighing screams died in the distance.

Nothing further was ever heard of Emily Parkinson, unless it could have been her bright yellow hair which appeared here and there in the fine elms of that part of Long Island, woven neatly into the nests of the robins.

The Unspeakable Betrothal

Robert Bloch

H. P. Lovecraft, the writer most often associated with Weird Tales *magazine, wrote a famous series of stories in which a panoply of ghastly entities
lurking in a dimension near ours seeks opportunities to claim us singly and/or
collectively. Writers as diverse as August Derleth, Frank Belknap Long and
even Stephen King have added chapters to Lovecraft's "Cthulhu mythos."
Now here is such a tale from* ROBERT BLOCH, *the award-winning author of
numerous horrific stories and novels, including "Enoch," "The Sorcerer's
Apprentice," "Yours Truly, Jack the Ripper" and especially* Psycho.

AVIS KNEW she wasn't really as sick as Doctor Clegg had said. She
was merely bored with living. The death-impulse, perhaps; then
again, it might have been nothing more than her distaste for clever
young men who persisted in addressing her as "*O rara Avis.*"

She felt better now, though. The fever had settled until it was no
more than one of the white blankets which covered her—something she
could toss aside with a gesture, if it weren't so pleasant just to burrow
into it, to snuggle deeply within its confining warmth.

Avis smiled as she realized the truth; monotony was the one thing that
didn't bore her. The sterility of excitement was the really jading routine,
after all. This quiet uneventful feeling of restfulness seemed rich and
fertile by comparison. Rich and fertile—creative—womb.

The words linked. Back to the womb. Dark room, warm bed, lying doubled up in the restful, nourishing lethargy of fever.

It wasn't the womb, exactly; she hadn't gone back that far, she knew. But it did remind her of the days when she was a little girl. Just a little girl with big round eyes, mirroring the curiosity that lay behind them. Just a little girl, living all alone in a huge old house, like a fairy princess in an enchanted castle.

Of course her aunt and uncle had lived here too, and it wasn't a really truly castle, and nobody else knew that she was a princess. Except Marvin Mason, that is.

Marvin had lived next door and sometimes he'd come over and play with her. They would come up to her room and look out of the high window—the little round window that bordered on the sky.

Marvin knew that she was a sure enough princess, and he knew that her room was an ivory tower. The window was an enchanted window, and when they stood on a chair and peeked out they could see the world behind the sky.

Sometimes she wasn't quite sure if Marvin Mason honest and truly saw the world beyond the window; maybe he just said he did because he was stuck on her.

But he listened very quietly while she told him stories about that world. Sometimes she told him stories she had read in books, and other times she made them up out of her very own head. It was only later that the dreams came, and she told him *those* stories, too.

That is, she always started to, but somehow the words would go wrong. She didn't always know the words for what she saw in those dreams. They were very special dreams; they came only on those nights when Aunt May left the window open, and there was no moon. She would lie in the bed, all curled up in a little ball, and wait for the wind to come through the high, round window. It came quietly, and she would feel it on her forehead and neck, like fingers stroking. Cool, soft fingers, stroking her face; soothing fingers that made her uncurl and stretch out so that the shadows could cover her body.

Even then she slept in the big bed, and the shadows would pour down from the window in a path. She wasn't asleep when the shadows came, so she knew they were real. They came on the breeze, from the window, and covered her up. Maybe it was the shadows that were cool and not the wind; maybe the shadows stroked her hair until she fell asleep.

But she would sleep then, and the dreams always came. They followed the same path as the wind and the shadows; they poured down from the sky, through the window. There were voices she heard but could not understand; colors she saw but could not name; shapes she glimpsed but which never seemed to resemble any figures she found in picture books.

Sometimes the same voices and colors and shapes came again and again, until she learned to recognize them, in a way. There was the deep, buzzing voice that seemed to come from right inside her own head, although she knew it really issued from the black, shiny pyramid-thing that had the arms with eyes in it. It didn't look slimy or nasty, and there was nothing to be afraid of—Avis could never understand why Marvin Mason made her shut up when she started telling about those dreams.

But he was only a little boy, and he got scared and ran home to his Mommy. Avis didn't have any Mommy, only Aunt May; but she would never tell Aunt May such things. Besides, why should she? The dreams didn't frighten her, and they were so very real and interesting. Sometimes, on gray, rainy days when there was nothing to do but play with dolls or cut out pictures to paste in her album, she wished that night would hurry up and come. Then she could dream and make everything real again.

She got so she liked to stay in bed, and would pretend to have a cold so she didn't have to go to school. Avis would look up at the window and wait for the dreams to come—but they never came in the daytime; only at night.

Often she wondered what it was like *up there.*

The dreams must come from the sky; she knew that. The voices and shapes *lived* way up, somewhere beyond the window. Aunt May said that dreams came from tummy-aches, but she knew that wasn't so.

Aunt May was always worried about tummy-aches, and she scolded Avis for not going outside to play; said she was getting pale and puny.

But Avis felt fine, and she had her secret to think of. Now she scarcely ever saw Marvin Mason any more, and she didn't bother to read. It wasn't much fun to pretend she was a princess, either. Because the dreams were ever so much realer, and she could talk to the voices and ask them to take her with them when they went away.

She got so she could almost understand what they were saying. The shiny thing that just hung through the window now—the one that looked like it had so much more to it she couldn't see—it made music inside her head that she recognized. Not a real tune; more like words in a rhyme. In her dreams she asked it to take her away. She would crawl up on its back and let it fly with her up over the stars. That was funny, asking it to fly; but she knew that the part beyond the window had wings. Wings as big as the world.

She begged and pleaded, but the voices made her understand that they couldn't take little girls back with them. That is, not entirely. Because it was too cold and too far, and something would change her.

She said she didn't care how she changed; she wanted to go. She would let them do anything they wanted if only they would take her: it would be nice to be able to talk to them all the time and feel that cool softness; to dream forever.

One night they came to her and there were more things than she had ever seen before. They hung through the window and in the air all over the room—they were so funny, some of them; you could see through them and sometimes one was partly inside another. She knew she giggled in her sleep, but she couldn't help it. Then she was quiet and listening to them.

They told her it was all right. They would carry her away. Only she musn't tell anyone and she musn't be frightened; they would come for her soon. They couldn't take her as she was, and she must be willing to change.

Avis said yes, and they all hummed a sort of music together, and went away.

The next morning Avis was really and truly sick and didn't want to get up. She could hardly breathe, she was so warm—and when Aunt May brought in a tray she wouldn't eat a bite.

That night she didn't dream. Her head ached, and she tossed all night long. But there was a moon out, so the dreams couldn't get through anyway. She knew they would be back when the moon was gone again, so she waited. Besides she hurt so that she didn't really care. She had to feel better before she was able to go anywhere.

The next day Dr. Clegg came to see her. Dr. Clegg was a good friend of Aunt May's and he was always visiting her because he was her guardian.

Dr. Clegg held her hand and asked her what seemed to be the matter with his young lady today?

Avis was too smart to say anything, and besides there was a shiny thing in her mouth. Dr. Clegg took it out and looked at it and shook his head. After a while he went away and then Aunt May and Uncle Roscoe came in. They made her swallow some medicine that tasted just awful.

By this time it was getting dark and there was a storm coming outside. Avis wasn't able to talk much, and when they shut the round window she couldn't ask them to please leave it open tonight because there was no moon and they were coming for her.

But everything kept going round and round, and when Aunt May walked past the bed she seemed to flatten out like a shadow, or one of the things, only she made a loud noise which was really the thunder outside and now she was sleeping really and truly even though she heard the thunder but the thunder wasn't real; nothing was real except the things that was it nothing was real any more but the things.

And they came through the window it wasn't closed after all because she opened it and she was crawling out high up there where she had never crawled before but it was easy without a body and soon she would have a new body they wanted the old one because they carried it but she didn't care because she didn't need it and now they would carry her *ulnagr Yuggoth farnomi ilyaa. . .*

That was when Aunt May and Uncle Roscoe found her and pulled her down from the window. They said later she had screamed at the top of her voice, or else she would have gone over without anyone noticing.

After that Dr. Clegg took her away to the hospital where there were no high windows and they came in to see her all night long. The dreams stopped.

When at last she was well enough to go back home, she found that the window was gone, too.

Aunt May and Uncle Roscoe had boarded it up, because she was a somnambulist. She didn't know what a somnambulist was, but guessed it had something to do with her being sick and the dreams not coming any more.

For the dreams stopped, then. There was no way of making them come back, and she really didn't want them any more. It was fun to play outside with Marvin Mason now, and she went back to school when the new semester began.

Now, without the window to look at, she just slept at night. Aunt May and Uncle Roscoe were glad, and Dr. Clegg said she was turning out to be a mighty fine little specimen.

Avis could remember it all now as though it were yesterday. Or today. Or tomorrow.

How she grew up. How Marvin Mason fell in love with her. How she went to college and they became engaged. How she felt the night Aunt May and Uncle Roscoe were killed in the crash at Leedsville. That was a bad time.

An even worse time was when Marvin Mason had gone away. He was in the service now, overseas. She had stayed on all alone in the house, for it was her house now.

Reba came in days to do the housework, and Dr. Clegg dropped around, even after she turned 21 and officially inherited her estate.

He didn't seem to approve of her present mode of living. He asked her several times why she didn't shut up the house and move into a small apartment downtown. He was concerned because she showed no desire to keep up the friendships she had made in college; Avis was curiously reminded of the solicitude he had exhibited during her childhood.

But Avis was no longer a child. She proved that by removing what had always seemed to her a symbol of adult domination; she had the high round window in her room unboarded once more.

It was a silly gesture. She knew it at the time, but somehow it held a curious significance for her. For one thing it re-established a linkage with her childhood, and more and more childhood came to epitomize happiness for her.

With Marvin Mason gone, and Aunt May and Uncle Roscoe dead, there was little enough to fill the present. Avis would sit up in her bedroom and pore over the scrapbooks she had so assiduously pasted up as a girl. She had kept her dolls and the old fairy tale books; she spent drowsy afternoons examining them.

It was almost impossible to lose one's time-sense in such pastimes. Her surroundings were unchanged. Of course, Avis was larger now and the bed wasn't quite as massive nor the window as high.

But both were there, waiting for the little girl that she became when, at nightfall, she curled up into a ball and snuggled under the sheets—snuggled and stared up at the high, round window that bordered the sky.

Avis wanted to dream again

At first, she *couldn't.*

After all, she was a grown woman, engaged to be married, she wasn't a character out of *Peter Ibbetson.* And those dreams of her childhood had been silly.

But they were *nice.* Yes, even when she had been ill and nearly fallen out of the window that time, it had been pleasant to dream. Of course those voices and shapes were nothing but Freudian fantasies—everyone knew that.

Or did they?

Suppose it was all real? Suppose dreams are not just subconscious manifestations; caused by indigestion and gas pressure.

What if dreams are really a product of electric impulse— or planetary radiations—attuned to the wave-length of the sleeping mind? Thought is an electrical impulse. Life itself is an electrical impulse. Perhaps a dreamer is like a spiritualist medium; placed in a receptive state during sleep. Instead of ghosts, the creatures of another world or another dimension can come through, if the sleeper is granted the rare gift of acting as a *filter.* What if the dreams feed on the dreamer or substance, just as spirits attain ectoplasmic being by draining the medium of energy?

Avis thought and thought about it, and when she had evolved this theory, everything seemed to fit. Not that she would ever tell anyone about her attitude. Dr. Clegg would only laugh at her, or still worse, shake his head. Marvin Mason didn't approve, either. Nobody wanted her to dream. They still treated her like a little girl.

Very well, she would be a little girl; a little girl who could do as she pleased, now. She would dream.

It was shortly after reaching this decision that the dreams began again; almost as though they had been waiting until she would fully accept them in terms of their own reality.

Yes, they came back, slowly, a bit at a time. Avis found that it helped to concentrate on the past during the day; to strive to remember her childhood. To this end, to this end she spent more and more time in her room, leaving Reba to tend housework downstairs. As for fresh air, she

always could look out of her window. It was high and small, but she
would climb on a stool and gaze up at the sky through the round
aperture; watching the clouds that veiled the blue beyond, and waiting
for night to come.

Then she would sleep in the big bed and wait for the wind. The wind
soothed and the darkness slithered, and soon she could hear the buzzing,
burring voices. At first only the voices came back, and they were faint
and far away. Gradually they increased in intensity and once more she
was able to discriminate, to recognize individual intonations.

Timidly, hesitantly, the figures re-emerged. Each night they grew
stronger. Avis Long (little girl with big round eyes in big bed below
round window) welcomed their presence.

She wasn't alone any more. No need to see her friends, or talk to that
silly old Dr. Clegg. No need to waste much time gossiping with Reba, or
fussing over meals. No need to dress or venture out. There was the
window by day and the dreams by night.

Then all at once she was curiously weak, and this illness came. But it
was all false, somehow, this physical change. Her mind was untouched.
She knew that. No matter how often Dr. Clegg pursed his lips and
hinted about calling in a "specialist," she wasn't afraid. Of course Avis
knew he really wanted her to see a psychiatrist. The doddering fool was
filled with glib patter about "retreat from reality" and "escape mecha-
nisms."

But he didn't understand about the dreams. She wouldn't tell him,
either. He'd never know the richness, the fullness, the sense of comple-
tion that came from experiencing contact with other worlds.

Avis knew *that* now. The voices and shapes that came in the window
were from other worlds. As a naive child she had invented them by her
very unsophistication. Now, striving consciously to return to the childlike attitude, she again admitted them.

They were from other worlds; worlds of wonder and splendor. Now
they could meet only on the plane of dreams, but someday; someday
soon, she would bridge the gap.

They whispered about her body. Something about the trip, making
the "change." It couldn't be explained in *their* words. But she trusted
them, and after all, a physical change was of slight importance contrasted with the opportunity.

Soon she would be well again, strong again. Strong enough to say "yes." And then they would come for her when the moon was right. Until then, she could strengthen the determination, and the dream.

Avis Long lay in the great bed and basked in the blackness; the blackness that poured palpably through the open window. The shapes filtered down, wriggling through the warps, feeding upon the night; growing, pulsing, encompassing all.

They reassured her about the body but she didn't care and she told them she didn't care because the body was unimportant and yes, she would gladly consider it an exchange if only she could go and she knew she belonged.

Not beyond the rim of the stars but between it and amongst substance dwells that which is blackness in blackness for Yuggoth is only a symbol no that is wrong there are no symbols for all is reality and only perception is limited ch'yar ul'nyar shaggornyth . . .

It is hard for us to make you understand but I do understand *you can not fight it* I will not fight it *they will try to stop you* nothing shall stop me for *I belong yes you belong* will it be soon *yes it will be soon* very soon *yes very soon* . . .

Marvin Mason was unprepared for this sort of reception. Of course, Avis hadn't written, and she wasn't at the station to meet him—but the possibility of her being seriously ill had never occurred to him.

He had come out to the house at once, and it was a shock when Dr. Clegg met him at the door.

The old man's face was grim, and the tenor of his opening remarks still grimmer.

They faced each other in the library downstairs; Mason self-consciously diffident in khaki, the older man a bit too professionally brusque.

"Just what is it Doctor?" Mason asked.

"I don't know. Slight, recurrent fever. Listlessness. I've checked everything. No TB, no trace of lowgrade infection. Her trouble isn't—organic."

"You mean something's wrong with her mind?"

Dr. Clegg slumped into an armchair and lowered his head.

"Mason, I could say many things to you; about the psychosomatic theory of medicine, about the benefits of psychiatry, about—but never mind. It would be sheer hypocrisy.

"I've talked to Avis; rather, I've tried to talk to her. She won't say much, but what she does say disturbs me. Her actions disturb me even more.

"You can guess what I'm driving at, I think, when I tell you that she is leading the life of an eight-year-old girl. The life she *did* lead at that age."

Mason scowled. "Don't tell me she sits in her room again and looks out of that window?"

Dr. Clegg nodded.

"But I thought it was boarded up long ago, because she's a somnambulist and—"

"She had it unboarded, several months ago. And she is not, never was, a somnambulist."

"What do you mean?"

"Avis Long never walked in her sleep. I remember the night she was found on that window's edge; not ledge, for there is no ledge. She was perched on the edge of the open window, already halfway out; a little tyke hanging through a high window.

"But there was no chair beneath her, no ladder. No way for her to climb up. She was simply *there*."

Dr. Clegg looked away before continuing.

"Don't ask me what it means. I can't explain, and I wouldn't want to. I'd have to talk about the things she talks about—the dreams and the presences that come to her; the presences that want her to go *away*. Mason, it's up to you. I can't honestly move to have her committed on the basis of material evidence. Confinement means nothing to *them;* you can't build a wall to keep out dreams. But you love her. You can save her. You can make her well, make her take an interest in reality. Oh, I know it sounds mawkish and stupid, just as the other sounds wild and fantastic. Yet it's true. It's happening right now, to her. She's asleep up in her room at this very moment. She's hearing the voices—I know that much. Let her hear your voice."

Mason walked out of the room and started up the stairs.

"But what do you mean you, you can't marry me?"

Mason stared at the huddled figure in the swirl of bedclothes. He tried to avoid the direct stare of Avis Long's curiously childlike eyes; just as he avoided gazing up at the black, ominous aperture of the round window.

"I can't, that's all," Avis answered. Even her voice seemed to hold a childlike quality. The high piercing tones might well have emanated from the throat of a little girl; a tired little girl, half-asleep and a bit petulant about being abruptly awakened.

"But our plans—your letters—"

"I'm sorry, dear. I can't talk about it. You know I haven't been well. Dr. Clegg is downstairs, he must have told you."

"But you're getting better," Mason pleaded. "You'll be up and around again in a few days."

Avis shook her head. A smile—the secret smile of a naughty child—clung to the corners of her mouth.

"You can't understand, Marvin. You never *could* understand. That's because you belong here." A gesture indicated the room. "I belong somewhere else." Her finger stabbed, unconsciously, towards the window.

Marvin looked at the window now. He couldn't help it. The round black hole that lead to nothingness. Or—something. The sky outside was dark, moonless. A cold wind curled about the bed.

"Let me close the window for you, dear," he said, striving to keep his voice even and gentle.

"No."

"But you're ill—you'll catch cold."

"That isn't why you want to close it." Even in accusation, the voice was curiously piping. Avis sat bolt upright and confronted him.

"You're jealous, Marvin. Jealous of me. Jealous of *them*. You would never let me dream. You would never let me go. And I want to go. They're coming for me. I know why Dr. Clegg sent you up here. He wants you to persuade me to go away. He'd like to shut me up, just as he wants to shut the window. He wants to keep me here because he's afraid. You're all afraid of what lies—out there. Well, it's no use. You can't stop me. You can't stop *them!*"

"Take it easy, darling—"

"Never mind. Do you think I care what they do to me, if only I can go? I'm not afraid. I know I can't go as I am now. I know they must alter me. There are certain parts they want for reasons of their own. You'd be frightened if I told you. But I'm not afraid. You say I'm sick and insane; don't deny it. Yet I'm healthy enough, sane enough to face them and their world. It's you who are too morbid to endure it all."

Avis Long was wailing now; a thin, high-pitched wail of a little girl in a tantrum.

"You and I are leaving this house tomorrow," Mason said. "We're going away. We'll be married and live happily ever after—in good old storybook style. The trouble with you, young lady, is that you've never had to grow up. All this nonsense about goblins and other worlds—"

Avis screamed.

Mason ignored her.

"Right now I'm going to shut that window," he declared.

Avis continued to scream. The shrill ululation echoed on a sustained note as Mason reached up and closed the round pane of glass over the black aperture. The wind resisted his efforts, but he shut the window and secured the latch.

Then her fingers were digging into his throat from the rear, and her scream was pouring down his ear.

"I'll kill you!" she wailed. It was the wail of an enraged child.

But there was nothing of the child, or the invalid, in the strength behind her clawing fingers. He fought her off, panting.

Then, suddenly, Dr. Clegg was in the room. A hypodermic needle flashed and gleamed in an arc of plunging silver.

They carried her back to the bed, tucked her in. The blankets nestled about the weary face of a child in sleep.

The window was closed tightly now.

Everything was in order as the two men turned out the light and tiptoed from the room.

Neither of them said a word until they stood downstairs once again.

Facing the fireplace, Mason sighed.

"Somehow I'll get her out of here tomorrow," he promised. "Perhaps it was too abrupt—my coming back tonight and waking her. I wasn't very tactful. But something about her; something about that room, frightened me."

Dr. Clegg lit his pipe. "I know," he said. "That's why I couldn't pretend to you that I completely understand. There's more to it than mere hallucination."

"I'm going to sit up here tonight," Mason continued. "Just in case something might happen."

"She'll sleep," Dr. Clegg assured him. "No need to worry."

"I'll feel better if I stay. I'm beginning to get a theory about all this talk—other worlds, and changes in her body before a trip. It ties in with the window, somehow. And it sounds like a fantasy on suicide."

"The death-impulse? Perhaps. I should have thought of that possibility. Dreams foreshadowing death—on second thought, Mason, I may stay with you. We can make ourselves comfortable here before the fire, I suppose."

Silence settled.

It must have been well after midnight before either of them moved from their place before the fire.

Then a sharp splinter of sound crashed from above. Before the tinkling echo died away, both men were on their feet and moving towards the stairway.

There was no further noise from above, and neither of them exchanged a single word. Only the thud of their running footsteps on the stairs broke the silence. And as they paused outside Avis Long's room, the silence seemed to deepen in intensity. It was a silence palpable, complete, accomplished.

Dr. Clegg's hand darted to the doorknob, wrenched it ineffectually. "Locked!" he muttered. "She must have gotten up and locked it." Mason scowled.

"The window—do you think she could have—?"

Dr. Clegg refused to meet his glance. Instead he turned and put his massive shoulder to the door panel. A bulge of muscle ridged his neck. Then the panel splintered and gave way. Mason reached around and opened the door from inside.

They entered the darkened room, Dr. Clegg in the lead, fumbling for the light-switch. The harsh, electric glare flooded the scene.

It was a tribute to the power of suggestion that both men glanced, not at the patient in the bed, but at the round window high up on the wall.

Cold night air streamed through a jagged aperture, where the glass had been shattered, as though by the blow of a gigantic fist.

Fragments of glass littered the floor beneath, but there was no trace of any missile. And obviously, the glass had been broken from the outer side of the pane.

"The wind," Mason murmured, weakly, but he could not look at Dr. Clegg as he spoke. For there was no wind, only the cold, soft breeze that billowed ever so gently from the night sky above. Only the cold, soft breeze, rustling the curtains and prompting a sarabande of shadows on the wall; shadows that danced in silence over the great bed in the corner.

The breeze and the silence and the shadows enveloped them as they stared now at the bed.

Avis Long's head was turned towards them on the pillow. They could see her face quite plainly, and Dr. Clegg realized on the basis of experience what Mason knew instinctively—Avis Long's eyes were closed in death.

But that is not what made Mason gasp and shudder—nor did the sight of death alone cause Dr. Clegg to scream aloud.

There was nothing whatsoever to frighten the beholder of the placid countenance turned towards them in death. They did not scream at the sight of Avis Long's face.

Lying on the pillow of the huge bed, Avis Long's face bore a look of perfect peace.

But Avis Long's body was . . . gone.

Am I Insane?

Guy de Maupassant

One of 1952's most popular songs was Georgia Gibbs's "Kiss of Fire," an example of "hurt-me-till-I-notice" love that the musical satirist Tom Lehrer later lampooned in "The Masochism Tango." In this vein [sic] is the following less-familiar conte cruelle *by* Guy de Maupassant *(1850–1893), the great French naturalist whose numerous novels and stories include such masterpieces as "Boule de suif," "The Horla" and "The Necklace," which appears in my 1993 GuildAmerica® Books anthology,* Masterpieces of Terror and the Unknown.

AM I INSANE or jealous? I know not which, but I suffer horribly. I committed a crime it is true, but is not insane jealousy, betrayed love, and the terrible pain I endure enough to make anyone commit a crime, without actually being a criminal?

I have loved this woman to madness—and yet, is it true? Did I love her? No, no! She owned me body and soul, I was her plaything, she ruled me by her smile, her look, the divine form of her body. It was all those things that I loved, but the woman contained in that body, I despise her; hate her. I always have hated her, for she is but an impure, perfidious creature, in whom there was no soul; even less than that, she is but a mass of soft flesh in which dwells infamy!

The first few months of our union were deliciously strange. Her eyes were three different colors. No, I am not insane, I swear they were. They were gray at noon, shaded green at twilight, and blue at sunrise. In moments of love they were blue; the pupils dilated and nervous. Her lips trembled and often the tip of her pink tongue could be seen, as that of a reptile ready to hiss. When she raised her heavy lids and I saw that ardent look, I shuddered, not only for the unceasing desire to possess her, but for the desire to kill this beast.

When she walked across the room each step resounded in my heart. When she disrobed and emerged infamous but radiant from the white mass of linen and lace, a sudden weakness seized me, my limbs gave way beneath me, and my chest heaved; I was faint, coward that I was!

Each morning when she awakened I waited for that first look, my heart filled with rage, hatred, and disdain for this beast whose slave I was; but when she fixed those limpid blue eyes on me, that languishing look showing traces of lassitude, it was like a burning, unquenchable fire within me, inciting me to passion.

When she opened her eyes that day I saw a dull, indifferent look; a look devoid of desire, and I knew then she was tired of me. I saw it, knew it, felt right away that it was all over, and each hour and minute proved to me that I was right. When I beckoned her with my arms and lips she shrank from me.

"Leave me alone," she said. "You are horrid!"

Then I became suspicious, insanely jealous; but I am not insane, no indeed! I watched her slyly; not that she had betrayed me, but she was so cold that I knew another would soon take my place.

At times she would say:

"Men disgust me!" Alas! It was too true.

Then I became jealous of her indifference, of her thoughts, which I knew to be impure, and when she awakened sometimes with that same look of lassitude I suffocated with anger, and an irresistible desire to choke her and make her confess the shameful secrets of her heart took hold of me.

Am I insane? No.

One night I saw that she was happy. I felt, in fact I was convinced, that a new passion ruled her. As of old, her eyes shone, she was feverish and her whole self fluttered with love.

I feigned ignorance, but I watched her closely. I discovered nothing, however. I waited a week, a month, almost a year. She was radiantly, ideally happy; as if soothed by some ephemeral caress.

At last I guessed. No, I am not insane, I swear I am not. How can I explain this inconceivable, horrible thing? How can I make myself understood? This is how I guessed.

She came in one night from a long ride on horseback and sank exhausted in a seat facing me. An unnatural flush tinted her cheeks and her eyes—those eyes that I knew so well—had such a look in them. I was not mistaken, I had seen her look like that; she loved! But whom? What? I almost lost my head, and so as not to look at her I turned to the window. A valet was leading her horse to the stable and she stood and watched him disappear; then she fell asleep almost immediately. I thought and thought all night. My mind wandered through mysteries too deep to conceive. Who can fathom the perversity and strange caprices of a sensual woman?

Every morning she rode madly through hills and dales and each time she came back languid; exhausted. At last I understood. It was of the horse I was jealous—of the wind which caressed her face, of the drooping leaves and of the dewdrops, of the saddle which carried her! It was all those things which made her so happy and brought her back to me satiated; exhausted! I resolved to be revenged. I became very attentive. Every time she came back from her ride I helped her down and the horse made a vicious rush at me. She would pat him on the neck, kiss his quivering nostrils, without even wiping her lips. I watched my chance.

One morning I got up before dawn and went to the path in the woods she loved so well. I carried a rope with me, and my pistols were hidden in my breast as if I were going to fight a duel. I drew the rope across the path, tying it to a tree on each side, and hid myself in the grass. Presently I heard her horse's hoofs, then I saw her coming at a furious pace; her cheeks flushed, an insane look in her eyes. She seemed enraptured; transported into another sphere.

As the animal approached the rope, he struck it with his forefeet and fell. Before she had struck the ground I caught her in my arms and helped her to her feet. I then approached the horse, put my pistol close to his ear, and shot him—as I would a man.

She turned on me and dealt me two terrific blows across the face with her riding whip which felled me, and as she rushed at me again, I shot her!

Tell me, am I insane?

Game for Motel Room

Fritz Leiber

FRITZ LEIBER *(1910–1992) was one of America's all-time grand masters of science fiction and fantasy. Winner of the Hugo, Nebula and other prestigious awards, Leiber is fondly remembered for his amusing swords and sorcery (a phrase Leiber himself coined) stories of Fafhrd and the Grey Mouser, and for novels like* Destiny Times Three, Gather, Darkness!, The Green Millennium *and the thrice-filmed* Conjure Wife. *"Game for Motel Room," from the March 1963 issue of* The Magazine of Fantasy and Science Fiction, *is a cynical reminder that illicit love, wherever it rears its lubricious head, can be extremely dangerous.*

SONYA MOVED around the warm, deeply carpeted motel room in the first gray trickle of dawn as if to demonstrate how endlessly beautiful a body can be if its owner will only let it. Even the body of a woman in, well, perhaps, her forties, Burton judged, smiling at himself in lazy reproof for having thought that grudging word "even." It occurred to him that bodies do not automatically grow less beautiful with age, but that a lot of bodies are neglected, abused and even hated by their owners: women in particular are apt to grow contemptuous and ashamed of their flesh, and this always shows. They start thinking old and ugly and pretty soon they look it. Like a car, a body needs tender constant care, regular tune-ups, an occasional small repair and above all it needs to be intimately loved by its owner and from time to time by an admiring second party, and then it never loses beauty and dignity, even when it corrupts in the end and dies.

Oh, the dawn's a cold hour for philosophy, Burton told himself, and somehow philosophy always gets around to cold topics, just as love-making and all the rest of the best of life make one remember death and even worse things. His lean arm snaked out to a bedside table, came back with a cigarette and an empty folder of matches.

Sonya noticed. She rummaged in her pale ivory traveling case and tossed him a black, pear-shaped lighter. Burton caught the thing, lit his cigarette, and then studied it. It seemed to be made of black ivory and shaped rather like the grip of a revolver, while the striking mechanism was of blued steel. The effect was sinister.

"Like it?" Sonya asked from across the room.

"Frankly, no. Doesn't suit you."

"You show good taste—or sound instinct. It's a vacation present from my husband."

"He has bad taste? But he married you."

"He has bad everything. Hush, Baby."

Burton didn't mind. Not talking let him concentrate on watching Sonya. Slim and crop-haired, she looked as trimly beautiful as her classic cream-colored, hard-topped Italian sportscar, in which she had driven him to this cosy hideaway from the bar where they'd picked each other up. Her movements now, stooping to retrieve a smoke-blue stocking and trail it across a chair, momentarily teasing apart two ribs in the upward-slanting Venetian blinds to peer at the cold gray world outside, executing a fraction of a dance figure, stopping to smile at emptiness . . . these movements added up to nothing but the rhythms and symbolisms of a dream, yet it was the sort of dream in which actor and onlooker might float forever. In the morning twilight she looked now like a schoolgirl, now like a witch, now like an age-outwitting ballerina out for her twenty-fifth season but still in every way the *premiere danseuse*. As she moved she hummed in a deep contralto voice a tune that Burton didn't recognize, and as she hummed the dim air in front of her lower face seemed to change color very faintly, the deep purples and blues and browns matching the tones of the melody. Pure illusion, Burton was sure, like that which some hashish-eaters and weed-smokers experience during their ecstasy when they hear words as colors, but most enjoyable.

To exercise his mind, now that his body had had its fill and while his eyes were satisfyingly occupied, Burton began to set in order the reasons why a mature lover is preferable to one within yoohooing distance of twenty in either direction. Reason One: she does quite as much of the approach work as you do. Sonya had been both heartwarmingly straightforward and remarkably intuitive at the bar last night. Reason Two: she is generally well equipped for adventure. Sonya had provided both sportscar and motel room. Reason Three: she does not go into an emotional tailspin after the act of love even if her thoughts trend toward death then, like yours do. Sonya seemed both lovely and sensible—the sort of woman it was good to think of getting married to and having children by.

Sonya turned to him with a smile, saying in her husky voice that still had a trace of the hum in it, "Sorry, Baby, but it's quite impossible. Especially your second notion."

"Did you really read my mind?" Burton demanded. "Why couldn't we have children?"

Sonya's smile deepened. She said, "I think I will take a little chance and tell you why." She came over and sat on the bed beside him and bent down and kissed him on the forehead.

"That was nice," Burton said lazily. "Did it mean something special?"

She nodded gravely. "It was to make you forget everything I'm going to tell you."

"How—if I'm to understand what you tell?" he asked.

"After a while I will kiss you again on the forehead and then you will forget everything I have told you in between. Or if you're very good, I'll kiss you on the nose and then you'll remember—but be unable to tell anyone else."

"If you say so," Burton smiled. "But what is it you're going to tell me?"

"Oh," she said, "just that I'm from another planet in a distant star cluster. I belong to a totally different species. We could no more start a child than a Chihauhau and a cat or a giraffe and a rhinoceros. Unlike the mare and the donkey we could not even get a cute little sterile mule with glossy fur and blue bows on his ears."

Burton grinned. He had just thought of Reason Four: a really grown-up lover plays the most delightfully childish nonsense games.

"Go on," he said.

"Well," she said, "superficially of course I'm very like an Earth woman. I have two arms and two legs and *this* and *these* . . ."

"For which I am eternally grateful," he said.

"You like them, eh?"

"Oh yes—especially *these.*"

"Well, watch out—they don't even give milk, they're used in esping. You see, inside I'm very different," she said. "My mind is different too. It can do mathematics faster and better than one of your electric calculating machines—"

"What's two and two?" Burton wanted to know.

"Twenty-two," she told him, "and also one hundred in the binary system and eleven in the trinary and four in the duodecimal. I have perfect recall—I can remember every least thing I've ever done and every word of every book I've leafed through. I can read unshielded minds—in fact anything up to triple shielding—and hum in colors. I can direct my body heat so that I never really need clothes to keep me warm at temperatures above freezing. I can walk on water if I concentrate, and even fly—though I don't do it here because it would make me conspicuous."

"Especially at the present moment," Burton agreed, "though it would be a grand sight. Why *are* you here, by the way, and not behaving yourself on your home planet?"

"I'm on vacation," she grinned. "Oh yes, we use your rather primitive planet for vacations—like you do Africa and the Canadian forests. A little machine teaches us during one night's sleep several of your languages and implants in our brains the necessary background information. My husband surprised me by giving me the money for this vacation —same time he gave me the lighter. Usually he's very stingy. But perhaps he had some little plot—an affair with his chief nuclear chemist, I'd guess—of his own in mind and wanted me out of the way. I can't be sure though, because he always keeps his mind quadruple-shielded, even from me."

"So you have husbands on your planet," Burton observed.

"Yes indeed! Very jealous and possessive ones, too, so watch your step, Baby. Yes, although my planet is much more advanced than yours we still have husbands and wives and a very stuffy system of monogamy— *that* seems to go on forever and everywhere—oh yes, and on my planet we have death and taxes and life insurance and wars and all the rest of the universal idiocy!"

She stopped suddenly. "I don't want to talk about that any more," she said. "Or about my husband. Let's talk about you. Let's play truths, deep-down truths. What's the thing you're most afraid of in the whole world?"

Burton chuckled—and then frowned. "You really want me to give you the honest answer?" he asked.

"Of course," she said. "It's the first rule of the game."

"Well," he said, "I'm most afraid of something going wrong with my brain. *Growing* wrong, really. Having a brain tumor. That's it." He had become rather pale.

"Oh Poor Baby," Sonya said. "Just you wait a minute."

Still uneasy from his confession, Burton started nervously to pick up Sonya's black lighter, but its black pistol-look repelled him.

Sonya came bustling back with something else in her right hand. "Sit up," she said, putting her left arm around him. "No, none of *that*—this is serious. Pretend I'm a very proper lady doctor who forgot to get dressed."

Burton could see her slim back and his own face over her right shoulder in the wide mirror of the dresser. She slipped her right hand and the small object it held behind his head. There was a click.

"No," said Sonya cheerily. "I can't see a sign of anything wrong in your brain or likely to grow wrong. It's as healthy as an infant's. *What's the matter, Baby?"*

Burton was shaking. "Look," he gasped reproachfully, "it's wonderful to play nonsense games, but when you use magic tricks or hypnotism to back them up, that's cheating."

"What do you mean?"

"When you clicked that thing," he said with difficulty, "I saw my head turn for a moment into a pinkish skull and then into just a pulsing blob with folds in it."

"Oh, I'd forgotten the mirror," she said, glancing over her shoulder. "But you were really just imagining things. Or having a mild optical spasm and seeing colors.

"No," she added as he reached out a hand, "I won't let you see my little XYZ-ray machine." She tossed it across the room into her traveling case. "It would spoil our nonsense game."

As his breathing and thoughts quieted, Burton decided she was possibly right—or at least that he'd best pretend she was right. It was safest and sanest to think of what he'd glimpsed in the mirror as an illusion, like the faint colors he'd fancied forming in front of her humming lips. Perhaps Sonya had an effect on him like hashish or some super-marijuana—a plausible enough idea considering how much more powerful drug a beautiful woman is than any opiate or resin. Nevertheless—

"All right, Sonya," he said, "what's *your* deepest fear?"

She frowned. "I don't want to tell you."

"*I* stuck to the rules."

"Very well," she nodded, "it's that my husband will go crazy and kill me. That's a much more dreadful fear on my planet than yours, because we've conquered all diseases and we each of us can live forever (though it's customary to disintegrate after forty to fifty thousand years) and we each of us have tremendous physical and mental powers—so that the mere thought of any genuine insanity is dreadfully shocking. Insanity is so nearly unknown to us that even our advanced intuition doesn't work on it—and what is unknown is always most frightening. By insanity I don't mean minor irrationalities. We have those, all right—my husband for instance, is bugged on the number 33, he won't begin any important venture except on the thirty-third day of the month—and me, I have a weakness for black-haired babies from primitive planets."

"Hey, wait a minute," Burton objected, "you said the thirty-third day of the month."

"On my planet the months are longer. Nights too. You'd love them—more time for demonstrating affection and empathy."

Burton looked at her broodingly. "You play this nonsense game pretty seriously," he said. "Like you'd read nothing but science fiction all your life."

Sonya shrugged her lovely shoulders. "Maybe there's more in science fiction than you realize. But now we've had enough to that game. Come on, Black-Haired Baby, let's play—"

"Wait a minute," Burton said sharply. She drew back, making a sulky mouth at him. He made his own grim, or perhaps his half-emerged thoughts did that for him.

"So you've got a husband on your planet," he said, "and he's got tremendous powers and you're deathly afraid he'll go crazy and try to kill you. And now he does an out-of-character thing by giving you vacation money and—"

"Oh yes!" she interrupted agitatedly, "and he's such a dreadful mixed-up superman and he always keeps up that permissible but uncustomary quadruple shield and he looks at me with such a secret gloating viciousness when we're alone that I'm choke-full of fear day and night and I've wished and wished I could really get something on him so that I could run to an officer of public safety and have the maniac put away, but I can't, I can't, he never makes a slip, and I begin to feel *I'm* going crazy—*I,* with my supremely trained and guarded mind—and I just *have* to get away to vacation planets and forget him in loving someone else. Come on, Baby, let's—"

"Wait a minute!" Burton commanded. "You say you've insurance on your planet. Are you insured for much?"

"A very great deal. Perfect health and a life-expectancy of fifty thousand years makes the premiums cheap."

"And your husband is the beneficiary?"

"Yes, he is. Come on, Burton, let's not talk about him. Let's—"

"No!" Burton said, pushing her back. "Sonya, what does your husband do? What's his work?"

Sonya shrugged. "He manages a bomb factory," she said listlessly and rapidly. "I work there too. I told you we had wars—they're between the league our planet belongs to and another star cluster. You've just started to discover the super-bombs on Earth—the fission bomb, the fusion bomb. They're clumsy oversize toys. The bombs my husband's factory manufactures can each of them destroy a planet. They're really fuses for starting the matter of the planet disintegrating spontaneously so that it flashes into a little star. Yet the bombs are so tiny you can hold one in your hand. In fact, this cigarette lighter is an exact model of one of them. The models were for Cosmos Day presents to top officials. My husband gave me his along with the vacation money. Burton, reach me one of your foul Earth cigarettes, will you? If you're going to refuse the other excitements, I've got to have something."

Burton automatically shook some cigarettes from his pack. "Tell me one more thing, Sonya," he rapped out. "You say you have a perfect memory. How many times have you struck that cigarette lighter since your husband gave it to you?"

"Thirty-one times," she answered promptly. "Counting the one time you used it."

She flicked it on and touched the tiny blue flame to her cigarette, inhaled deeply, then let the tiny snuffer snap down the flame. Twin plumes of faint smoke wreathed from her nostrils. "Thirty two now," She held the black pear-shaped object towards him, her thumb on the knurled steel-blue trigger. "Shall I give you a light?"

"NO!" Burton shouted. "Sonya, as you value your life and mine—and the lives of three billion other primitives—don't work that lighter again. Put it down."

"All right, all right, Baby," she said smiling nervously and dropping the black thing on the white sheet. "Why's Baby so excited?"

"Sonya," Burton said, "Maybe *I'm* crazy, or maybe you *are* only playing a nonsense game backed up with hypnotism—but . . ."

Sonya stopped smiling. "What is it, Baby?"

Burton said, "If you really do come from another planet where there is almost no insanity, homicidal or otherwise, what I'm going to tell you will be news. Sonya, we've just lately had several murders on Earth where a man plants a time-bomb on a big commercial airplane to explode it in the air and kill all its passengers and crew just to do away with one single person—generally for the sake of collecting a big life-insurance policy. Now if an Earth-murderer could be cold-blooded or mad enough to do that, why mightn't a super-murderer— "

"Oh no," Sonya said slowly, "not blow up a whole planet to get rid of just one person—" She started to tremble.

"Why not?" Burton demanded. "Your husband is crazy, only you can't prove it. He hates you. He stands to collect a fortune if you die in an accident—such as a primitive vacation planet exploding. He presents you with money for a vacation on such a planet and at the same time he gives you a cigarette lighter that is an exact model of—"

"I can't believe it," Sonya said very faintly, still shaking, her eyes far away. "Not a whole planet . . ."

"But that's the sort of thing insanity can be, Sonya. What's more, you can check it," Burton rapped out flatly. "Use that XYZ-ray gadget of yours to look through the lighter."

"But he *couldn't*," Sonya murmured, her eyes still far away. "Not even *he* could . . ."

"Look through the lighter," Burton repeated.

Sonya picked up the black thing by its base and carried it over to her traveling case.

"Remember not to flick it," Burton warned her sharply. "You'd told me he was bugged on the number thirty-three, and I imagine that would be about the right number to allow to make sure you were settled on your vacation planet before anything happened."

He saw the shiver travel down her back as he said that and suddenly Burton was shaking so much himself he couldn't possibly have moved. Sonya's hands were on the other side of her body from him, busy above her traveling case. There was a click and her pinkish skeleton showed through her. It was not quite the same as the skeleton of an Earth human—there were *two* long bones in the upper arms and upper legs, fewer ribs, but what looked like two tiny skulls in the chest.

She turned around, not looking at him.

"You were right," she said.

She said, *"Now I've got the evidence to put my husband away for ever! I can't wait!"*

She whirled into action, snatching articles of clothing from the floor, chairs and dresser, whipping them into her traveling case. The whole frantic little dance took less than ten seconds. Her hand was on the outside door before she paused.

She looked at Burton. She put down her traveling case and came over to the bed and sat down beside him.

"Poor Baby," she said. "I'm going to have to wipe out your memory and yet you were so very clever—I really mean that, Burton."

He wanted to object, but he felt paralyzed. She put her arms around him and moved her lips towards his forehead. Suddenly she said, "No, I can't do that. There's got to be some reward for you."

She bent her head and kissed him pertly on the nose. Then she disengaged herself, hurried to her bag, picked it up, and opened the door.

"Besides," she called back. "I'd hate you to forget any part of me."

"Hey," Burton yelled, coming to life. "You can't go out like that!"

"Why not?" she demanded.

"Because you haven't a stitch of clothes on!"

"On my planet we don't wear them!"

The door slammed behind her. Burton sprang out of bed and threw it open again.

He was just in time to see the sportscar take off—straight up.

Burton stood in the open door for half a minute, stark naked himself, looking around at the unexploded Earth. He started to say aloud, "Gosh, I didn't even get the name of her planet," but his lips were sealed.

Porphyria's Lover

Robert Browning

The rain set early in to-night,
    The sullen wind was soon awake,
It tore the elm-tops down for spite,
    And did its worst to vex the lake:
    I listened with heart fit to break.
When glided in Porphyria; straight
    She shut the cold out and the storm,
And kneeled and made the cheerless grate
    Blaze up, and all the cottage warm;
    Which done, she rose, and from her form
Withdrew the dripping cloak and shawl,
    And laid her soiled gloves by, untied
Her hat and let the damp hair fall,
    And, last, she sat down by my side
    And called me. When no voice replied,
She put my arm about her waist,
    And made her smooth white shoulder bare,
And all her yellow hair displaced,
    And, stooping, made my cheek lie there,
    And spread, o'er all, her yellow hair,
Murmuring how she loved me—she
    Too weak, for all her heart's endeavour,
To set its struggling passion free

From pride, and vainer ties dissever,
  And give herself to me for ever.
But passion sometimes would prevail.
  Nor could to night's gay feast restrain
A sudden thought of one so pale
  For love of her, and all in vain:
  So, she was come through wind and rain.
Be sure I looked up at her eyes
  Happy and proud; at last I knew
Porphyria worshipped me; surprise
  Made my heart swell, and still it grew
  While I debated what to do.
That moment she was mine, mine, fair,
  Perfectly pure and good: I found
A thing to do, and all her hair
  In one long yellow string I wound
  Three times her little throat around,
And strangled her. No pain felt she;
  I am quite sure she felt no pain.
As a shut bud that holds a bee,
  I warily oped her lids: again
  Laughed the blue eyes without a stain.
And I untightened next the tress
  About her neck; her cheek once more
Blushed bright beneath my burning kiss:
  I propped her head up as before,
  Only, this time my shoulder bore
Her head, which droops upon it still:
  The smiling rosy little head,
So glad it has its utmost will,
  That all it scorned at once is fled,
  And I, its love, am gained instead!
Porphyria's love: she guessed not how
  Her darling one wish would be heard.
And thus we sit together now,
  And all night long we have not stirred,
  And yet God has not said a word!

The Peace that Crusheth Understanding

Julia L. Keefer

JULIA L. KEEFER, PH.D., *wears many hats. She is an actor/comic, a professor at New York University, a playwright whose play* Through the Broken Glass *was produced in New York a few years ago and author of "A Secret," which appeared in the 1992 GuildAmerica Books anthology* Lovers & Other Monsters. *"The Peace that Crusheth Understanding" was inspired by Dr. Keefer's research on death row and her many appearances on Court TV and NBC's* Dateline, *where she spoke out against child abuse and capital punishment.*

SHE LOVED THE SOUND her voice made, resonating in the space around her, singing like a bird that could never be captured. Her coloratura gave the simple service a grandeur that transcended the drab location and its pathetic participants. Everyone said she might even have made it to the Metropolitan Opera, but Fate had locked her into this windowless interrogation room, made "holy" by a gunmetal crucifix and a chalice of wilted gladioli. After the service, everyone gathered round while Angela sang. Her repertory consisted of everything from folk songs, blues, gospel and quiet church music to grand opera. She let each person choose a favorite song, allowing them all to relax and reminisce as her own lungs filled with air enough to breathe for everyone.

Though her voice soared freely through space, Angela's hands were shackled behind her back, a reminder that freedom was not hers, life, in fact, was not hers. Her voice was the best and only thing she could offer others. When they left the prison chapel, everyone seemed more peaceful, soothed if not blessed by Angela's radiant presence.

Only the guard was impatient.

"Mamacita, we are already behind schedule."

They walked quickly back to her cell, avoiding the embarrassed, frightened glances of the other prisoners.

"Caramba! Ju can eat off dees floor—ees so clean."

She had cleaned it up only because she did not want the next prisoner to think she was a slob. The guard disappeared for a few minutes to get her dinner. Angela requested fresh fruit and yogurt—simple, natural foods that reminded her of the trees and plants she had not seen for years. They had tried to grow melons in the muddy courtyard, but their jaundiced color, pungent odor and deformed shape convinced the prisoners that Justice had also deprived them of Nature's generosity.

She bit the cool crust of the watermelon, filling her mouth with its sweet, succulent juices. When she was little, Daddy had let her carry the huge green melons down the hill to their picnics. She liked to feel important.

Alan never really needed her as much, but he did remind her of her father in the way that he planned everything so carefully that night. He said if she really loved him, she'd do anything for him.

Her teeth chipped on the seed of a plum. She spit it out and decided to slow down. She mixed the tangerine slices with the yogurt, savoring each spoonful until her tongue tasted the cold stainless steel. She took it out and popped some purple grapes into her mouth. That was less messy.

If it weren't for Alan, she would not be here. It might never have happened. She remembered the first time they made love, how different it was, how his massive muscles softened to weave themselves around her, to satisfy her in a way she had not thought possible. Their love had been enough of a miracle for her, but Alan wanted more. He was much stronger than her Dad because he was young and tough, and because he did not care what anyone thought about him.

Angela treasured that last dinner with her father because it was just like old times, with champagne and candles and fresh flowers. While he was in the basement getting another bottle of champagne, she let Alan into his bathroom. As they sat drinking by the fire, she knew she could still stop it, that they didn't have to kill him; but she was afraid Alan would get angry and call her a traitor. She never forgot her father's last words:

"I'll just wash up so I can spend some special time with my little angel."

She watched him enter the bathroom and stared at the closed door. She heard nothing. It took only a few minutes before Alan came out.

Angela choked on her food. She had seen that image every night for the past four years. . . . She had never realized a man that powerful could be so still, so quiet, so peaceful. . . .

Alan wanted her to leave right away, but she had to look again to make sure he wasn't just sleeping. She wanted to be alone with her father. Alan left to stage the burglary. Angela crept into the bathroom and shut the door. She clutched the kitchen knife desperately, as if she still had to protect herself. She turned him over. The bath towel fell away, revealing his naked body. His penis looked limp, but she didn't trust it. So many times it had stiffened against her delicate pleas, rising defiantly to humiliate and wound her. Surely it had a power that could transcend death. She plunged the knife into his testicles. The blood spurted ferociously all over her face, covering the full-length mirror with her father's final signs of life. Even in death his passion was stronger than hers. Now his groin was as open and vulnerable and bloody as a— vagina.

She had finally mutilated the organ that had controlled and given her life, but his huge shadow darkened her existence with memories. He was still inside her. She had disappointed him again. She wanted him to forgive her. As she bent down to kiss his purple face, Alan placed his hand on her shoulder and said angrily, "Gimme the knife and get the hell outta here. I'll finish up. God, you're one fuckin' sick broad."

Her father's blood mingled with her own salt tears as she ran out of the house and through the woods to the stream. It took Alan at least half an hour to join her. He buried the knife and the bloodstained clothes, covered her in a warm blanket and drove her back to the dorm. She had enough time to dry her hair and get into bed before the inevitable phone call came from the police. She didn't even need an alibi. She didn't have to fake tears. No one suspected her.

. . . .

The last piece of fruit, a mushy, overripe banana, dissolved in her mouth. She caressed the slope of the empty bowl. It was nice of them to give her such a large portion. Angela asked the guard if she could have a shower before they took her down.

"Of course, mamacita. I will do everyteeng to make ju"—she hesitated as she struggled with the word—"as tranquila as possible. I wish all dee prisoners were as obediente as ju."

Angela mumbled half to the guard, half to herself, "They say it's the most humane way to die—painless, peaceful . . . like going to sleep . . . you don't know when you begin or end. . . ."

The guard tried to hide her own fear as she accompanied her to the shower. This time Angela did not mind the gnats and roaches, the stench of the urine mixed with stagnant water, the menacing glare of an exposed light bulb. She let the spray of lukewarm water slide all over her body. There was no soap, but if the water ran long enough, surely she'd get clean.

When she was twelve years old, she let the bathtub overflow. That was the last time Dad spanked her, only because she never made him angry again. She also tried to avoid fights with Alan. After all, he had done it for their future.

Alan was surprised she wasn't happier. Yet every night her father invaded her dreams, his powerful crotch rising from the blood and tissue to mount her again with a vengeance that made her wake up screaming. Alan kept her close at night, cradling her in his arms, shielding her from thoughts that were as violent as the fluids that gushed from her father's groin.

Nothing bothered Alan. Unfortunately, he did not have the same attention to detail as her dad. Alan's alibi fell through when a "friend" said they had not gone to the movies. The coroner found his fingerprints on the corpse because he had used so much force to strangle him that he ripped one of his gloves. The knife and clothes were discovered by a police dog. Alan became a defendant. They said he had no choice. He got life in exchange for implicating Angela.

At first she felt free in jail. For once she could think what she wanted. She was so protective of her newly found privacy that she did not confide in her attorney. She vowed she'd never reveal her father's secrets or Alan's dreams. She just answered questions politely. Everything was so civil that she was almost convinced she might be acquitted—except for the photos that the prosecution had blown up for the jury. It seemed strange to immortalize her father in this brutal but brief state between death and decomposition.

Angela was too weak to take the stand, was unable to explain her abuse or justify her actions. They wanted nothing but the truth, but not the whole truth because Justice permits you only to answer questions, not throw up disorganizing secrets. All the jury saw was a mane of black hair covering her face, hiding her life—until Alan took the stand. He testified that she did not want to wait for her father's estate, that she had masterminded the murder and then performed a brutal castration which disturbed Alan's sensibilities. Even the judge looked horrified. Angela was too hurt to refute him, and too weak not to forgive him. As the court became inundated with incriminating evidence and testimony, Angela sank lower in her chair; her falling head stifled her breathing; her features retreated inside her face, squelching emotions too volcanic to be owned, much less expressed. She felt they would despise her if they found out what really happened. She certainly hated herself more for those eternal evenings of quiet, lethal sex than the quick butchery of the castration.

Angela suddenly jolted as the first spurt of the evening's hot water scalded her body. She turned on both faucets all the way. Her breathing quickened as she recalled the closing statements of the prosecutor who resembled Alan, Dad and God rolled into a vociferous rumble of threatening accusation.

The jury deliberated for only an hour. The judge said he did not want any inappropriate displays of emotion when the verdict was read. She wondered what he thought was an appropriate display of emotion. She was almost relieved when they convicted her of first degree murder with special circumstances.

Sentencing cost three hours of their time. Angela froze into her own twilight while her lawyers fraternized with the prosecution, joking and chatting as if they were relaxing after a squash tournament. There had been no family or friends to make the jury cry for her. A few professors had spoken of her talent and academic excellence, but no one could make her appear—human. The expert witness concluded she must be a sociopath.

Angela scrubbed her body with her nails, washing off the dead skin.

It was strange how one's right to live could be decided by three simple questions:

"Is the convicted a threat to society? Did she *intend* to kill? Are there mitigating circumstances that would warrant life imprisonment?"

Society is always threatened by people it does not understand. She *intended* to do only what Alan said, but the court had proven her premeditation and malice aforethought. There was no reason that she should be a burden to taxpayers for what promised to be a long life. Her attorney and the guards kept her standing as her legs softened beneath her. She heard only a few phrases of the judge's monotonous drawl:

"The court has deemed your punishment to be death by lethal injection . . . before sunrise at a date to be determined by the court. . . ."

His words trailed off. The important thing was that she was to know the exact hour of her execution, the minute she would be extinguished.

She turned off the faucets and dried her body with a fresh towel the guard gave her, just like Daddy used to do. She quickly hid her nakedness in the prison jump suit so she would not have to feel a sensuality that could still be aroused. As the guard brought her back to her cell, Angela laughed out loud, a strange, raucous, defiant guffaw so unlike her usual gentle, angelic demeanor that the guard was startled. She watched her prisoner closely as she packed. She was allowed only a Bible, a ball-point pen, stationery, a change of panties, a toothbrush and toothpaste. The guard looked away as Angela made a joke: "Guess they don't want us to die with bad breath."

Or shitty underpants, she thought to herself. Well, she would not lose control. She was ready for this. She had prepared herself.

The guard felt uncomfortable as she shackled Angela.

"Qué pena! Ju are such a good girl. Ju always do what ju are told. . . . Deez handcuffs are just routine."

As routine as her death, she thought. Yes, it was just another job, but she would not want to be the one who prepared the solution, deciding how much sodium pentathol was needed to make one lose consciousness, how much pancuronium bromide would paralyze the diaphragm and how much potassium chloride would stop the heart. She was so healthy, she might need an extra dosage—she might even cost the state more than the usual $71.51 they paid for the injection. She would not want to be the guard who tied her to the gurney, or the nurse who swabbed her

skin with alcohol to "prevent infection," or the doctor who pronounced
her dead, or the Judge who made sure Justice was served.

She hated being the person who had disappointed her father and
Alan.

They had to walk outside through the courtyard to the death house
where she would be sequestered before the execution. Even the moon
was too ashamed to light up the violet blackness of the night. The guard
let her stop to stroke the backs of her shackled hands against the bark of
a tree, the only tree strong enough to grow in such a wretched place.
The wind lifted the leaves lightly so as not to unravel the stillness of
night with too wild a rush of energy. She felt like the air—silenced by
huge shadows, protected by a vague emptiness. She asked the guard to
pick a leaf from the tree for her to keep until . . .

This cell was smaller than the other one, about five feet by eight feet
with a bed, toilet and washstand. It was immaculate, as if the space had
been cleansed of any residual pain, anaesthetized so that its occupants
would also contain themselves. Angela felt nauseated. Her slight frame
quivered as the two women embraced. Then she collapsed on the bed.
The guard covered her gently with the blanket and kissed her forehead
as if she were putting a young child to sleep. She locked the cell with
tears in her eyes, blinded by a sense of Justice even she could not understand.

The state must have anticipated Angela's loneliness. The chaplain
soon arrived to invade the privacy of her final thoughts.

"I am here for you, my child, if you want to confess, read the scrip-
tures or just sit in silence with a member of the church."

She had pretended to be religious so she could sing for everyone in the
chapel, but now she was free to fear the God who said that anyone who
strikes or even scorns a parent should be put to death; to despise the God
who had given and was about to take her life. God reminded her of her
father's smug satisfaction when he bragged about his accomplishments,
controlling light or darkness the way her father had turned her bedroom
switch off and on.

She couldn't help it. She pulled her hand away from his. "Leave me
alone . . ." She started screaming. "No, no, no . . ."

The chaplain looked sadly at the huge eyes that ignited the pasty
prison-white face with a lethal mixture of fury and fear. The darkness of

her eyes and the thick black hair that refused to stop growing made her less fragile, as if God had found a way to cloak an otherwise delicate image in evil.

"I'll come back with the guards for your last rites."

As his footsteps faded away, she felt a silence she had never known on this earth.

No, no, no, she said. No . . . for the first time . . . and he left her alone, alone, it seemed impossible that it was so easy to be alone she flushed the toilet so hard so hard it kept flushing gushing rushing until it became ice cold brimming with water clean enough to drink she jiggled the handle but it wouldn't stop it was stuck so the water kept flowing nothing so irritating and wasteful as a toilet that won't stop flushing like Chinese water torture but she couldn't tell anyone no never tell because they won't do anything I mean what could they do call a plumber to come to a death house at midnight or take her back to wait in the prison or postpone the execution or turn off the water or turn off yes they might even execute her earlier so they wouldn't have to think about it because people hate to think about nasty, dirty things like toilets or incest or but she could block it out close her eyes and pretend she was at Niagara Falls yes the mind can imagine anything she could be a honeymooner listening to the deafening cascades of the waterfalls instead of a noisy toilet in a death house for the damp air made her skin smooth and she did not feel the insect bites she had gotten in the shower or the cramps in her abdomen . . . no no the toilet would not ruin her last night on earth . . . no no no she would drown the noise with her voice yes she let it loose to vibrate in space making sounds that did not conform to the arrangement of songs sounds that pierced through the thickness of the world puncturing her secrecy coloring the vast expanse of her loneliness . . . she sang for hours unaware of the time that was draining away from her . . . water draining away . . . blood was draining away from her . . . she touched her crotch—warm red blood . . . a womb crying for life yes nature wanted her to live even though man sentenced her to die but he said it was humane she would die like Pumpkin yes she had kissed and stroked Pumpkin's fur as he fell asleep in her arms cradled in her love just like Daddy had done kissed and stroked and cradled her in his love yes to tell the truth she had liked it that's why she couldn't tell because it was the only way she could be loved by Daddy Daddy loved her voice too so strong and clear and heavenly it could drown out the sound of any toilet he said she sang like an angel the blood was coming down in clots she had not brought napkins the toilet paper was so thin too thin for all the blood pouring out of her no no no there was too much blood now her crotch was bloody like Daddy's when he lay dying on the bathroom floor no, she said, no, it will not happen again never neverNEVER. . . .

They used to kill at dawn, but guilt pushed them deeper into midnight. Her voice was so eerie and exquisite that the warden stood waiting outside the bars until the guards came with the chaplain and the other officials. They wanted her to stop singing. Music makes one too emotional.

No no she screamed they could not make her stop singing she'd never stop but they said her song would soon end that these sounds would no longer exist once she stopped breathing for they were going to poison her lungs any minute now no no she couldn't let them because it would destroy her voice no no she couldn't let them kill her eyes because she wanted to see the mountains and forests that had vanished from her life and her hands no no because she wanted to touch the bark of the trees the petals of the flowers because she wanted to touch herself her beautiful young strong body yes she was part of nature and if she died nature would disappear because she could no longer feel her . . .

Suddenly she wanted to live. Her voice grew more strident, shrieking like a tortured bird. She burst away from the sleepy guards with an electric force that propulsed her down the corridor. She thought she could make it outside, where she'd climb a tree or hide or maybe fly away like a bird soaring above the prison the cities the oceans higher than the clouds higher than Justice the Peace that Crusheth Understanding for there were so many beautiful things in the universe she wanted to see she could get there if she were given a few more minutes. Her body reared up like a wild, angry stallion explosive in its desire to fight, and therefore to live.

They had seen this before. They cornered and handcuffed her at the end of the hall. She had surprised them, but no one had ever escaped at this stage.

Her terror was pouring out of her pouring out like the burning blood so sticky and rancid and lethal and the tears that stung her face and the piss that soiled her panties she couldn't help it when she saw the gurney no no she pleaded they mustn't tie her up like that no no the Judge was reading the order of execution they wiped her skin and attached the IV just a few more minutes the chaplain mumbled "Take eat this in remembrance of me" no no she did not want to eat or to be taken or to remember she screamed NoNoNo LEAVE ME ALONE!

"This is the way Daddy tied me up so he could have his way."

Lovedeath

Marvin Kaye

Thanks to Jessica Amanda Salmonson, whose own story appears later on, for publishing the next selection in the eleventh issue of Fantasy Macabre *magazine. A revised version of "Lovedeath" constitutes the opening chapter of* Fantastique, *my 1992 novel from St. Martin's Press.*

BITCH!"
       She screamed as Carl flung her naked to the floor and mounted her. Shoving her legs apart, he tore into her body, strove to, could not climax, filled her with darkness.

d

ede

vedea

ovedeat

—she could not remember yesterday or sunset or the last five minutes, but every man who hurt her in the name of love stained her memory like secret blood; each was named Carl, a four-letter-word synonymous with shame, all except the first Carl, the only gentle Carl, yet she could hardly recall him, he died too soon, but the Carl who followed and every brutal Carl who came next compelled her to submit to the most degrading acts before abandoning her to pain and anger and self-loathing—

ede

vedea

ovedeat

Lovedeath

Suddenly, she was in a nearly empty diner. There was a henna-haired waitress behind the long service counter gossiping with a tall, morose policeman sitting on a red-leatherette swivel stool. At the cash register, a man with a straggly brown mustache read a newspaper and picked his nose. None of them paid any attention to her or to another woman wearing a slip and stretched out on her side on the countertop, face turned away from the man slumbering restlessly at the opposite end.

Carl?

She was sitting in one of the diner booths.

Why? How did I get here?

Staring down at the greasy surface of the table, she was surprised to see her own hands clutching a coffee cup half-filled with liquid too tepid to warm her chilly fingers.

When did I order it? When did I drink half? What am I doing here? And who—

"LOOK AT ME, BITCH!"

Icy dread gripped her; she glanced up and saw Carl framed in the doorway. He moved towards her in the half-crouch of a predator stalking its kill. The waitress disappeared, the policeman vanished, the cashier was gone, the restless slumberer faded away, the corner booths winked out. Her memory flooded back: this was the only reality she knew, a cycle of pain, a closed repeating loop of rape and humiliation.

"BITCH!"

She screamed as Carl flung her naked to the floor, shoved her legs apart, tore into her body, strove to climax, ripped her with one last despairing thrust as she cried out again and again in pain. Darkness filled her.

vedea

ovedeat

Lovedeath

Lovedeath

—no longer trusted tenderness or yesterday or the closed repeating loop of sunset, but she could not forget that agony called love by those angry Carls who defiled her in repeated despairing attempts to satisfy unappeasable passion before abandoning her, all except the first Carl, the only gentle Carl, the Carl who died too soon—

ovedeat

Lovedeath

L o v e d e a t h

L o v e d e a t h

A diner. A waitress gossiping with a policeman. A woman with her face turned away from a restless slumberer. At the cash register, a man reading a newspaper.

She was sitting in a booth.

Why?

Staring down at the tabletop, surprised to see her own hands clutching a coffee cup.

Why? When did I order it? And who am—

"Look at me . . . please?"

Carl was sitting across the booth from her. His voice was soft. He reached out to touch her. Memory made her flinch, but the only thing he did was lightly and reassuringly stroke the back of her hand. It ended the closed, repeating pattern. She wondered why at first, but then as she stared into his longing, lonely eyes, she thought she recognized the answer: *This is the first Carl, the only gentle Carl, the Carl who never hurt or had me. The Carl who died.*

Lovedeath

L o v e d e a t h

L o v e d e a t h

L o v e d e a t h

—although she no longer trusted sunset or the closed repeating loop of Carls who raped her in the name of love, now she knew the truth: all those brutal Carls were nothing more than obscene nightmares, they no longer existed, only the first Carl who died too soon, the gentle Carl was real—

L o v e d e a t h
L o v e d e a t h
L o v e d e a t h
L o v e d e a t h

He sat gazing at her in wonder, the Carl who truly loved her, *who never died at all* and now as he brought her hand to his lips and kissed her fingertips, for the very first time she felt wholly and gloriously alive. The room, the restless slumberer faded away. They were alone in hazy wilderness touched with morning as they clasped and kissed each other naked in a perfect union of flesh and harmony and flame.

L o v e d e a t h
L o v e d e a t h
L o v e d e a t h
L o v e d e a t h

—but because she still could not trust the sunset some call love, something shimmered beyond the rosy barriers of romance and she was distressingly aware once more that she could not remember yesterday or the last five minutes or anything but the closed repeating loop of memory that she had no memory—

Then WHO AM I?

L o v e d e a t h
L o v e d e a t h
L o v e d e a t h
L o v e d e a t h

As he whispered *I love you,* he parted her legs, gently entered her and swiftly climaxed, but even as her lips and tongue and teeth and breasts and limbs and hands and hips and heart crushed urgently against him, she shuddered in the agony of sudden truth as reality seized and cancelled her, but . . .

L o v e d e a t h
L o v e d e a t h
L o v e d e a t h
L o v e d e a t h

. . . just before she ended, a thought wholly and independently her own darkened her dying mind.

Tenderness is the worst rape of all.

$$
\begin{array}{l}
L\ o\ v\ e\ d\ e\ a\ t\ h \\
L\ o\ v\ e\ d\ e\ a\ t\ h \\
L\ o\ v\ e\ d\ e\ a\ t\ h \\
L\ o\ v\ e\ d\ e\ a\ t\ h \\
L\ o\ v\ e\ d\ e\ a\ t\ h \\
L\ o\ v\ e\ d\ e\ a\ t\ h \\
L\ o\ v\ e\ d\ e\ a\ t\ h \\
Lovedeath \\
ovedeat \\
vedea \\
ede \\
d
\end{array}
$$

7:01 A.M.

She was, waking or slumbering, the most beautiful woman he'd ever seen, but now he could not clearly picture her exquisite features; the harder he tried, the further she fled from memory. He cursed the radio-alarm that woke him playing Wagner's *Prelude and Lovedeath.*

Across the hall, Carl's wife stirred in sleep.

The Countess Kathleen O'Shea

A Folk Tale Retold
by W. B. Yeats

There are dangers and dangers; the countess Kathleen has more than her share, but fortunately she is woman enough for the challenge! This version of a Celtic legend is retold by W. B. YEATS *(1865–1939), a Dublin-born nationalist whose poetry, plays and studies of Irish legends and folklore won him the Nobel Prize for Literature in 1923.*

A VERY LONG TIME AGO, there suddenly appeared in old Ireland two unknown merchants of whom nobody had ever heard, and who nevertheless spoke the language of the country with the greatest perfection. Their locks were black, and bound round with gold, and their garments were of rare magnificence.

Both seemed of like age; they appeared to be men of fifty, for their foreheads were wrinkled and their beards tinged with grey.

In the hostelry where the pompous traders alighted it was sought to penetrate their designs; but in vain—they led a silent and retired life. And whilst they stopped there, they did nothing but count over and over again out of their money-bags pieces of gold, whose yellow brightness could be seen through the windows of their lodging.

"Gentlemen," said the landlady one day, "how is it that you are so rich, and that, being able to succour the public misery, you do no good works?"

"Fair hostess," replied one of them, "we didn't like to present alms to the honest poor, in dread we might be deceived by make-believe paupers. Let want knock at our door, we shall open it."

The following day, when the rumour spread that two rich strangers had come, ready to lavish their gold, a crowd besieged their dwelling; but the figures of those who came out were widely different. Some carried pride in their mien; others were shame-faced.

The two chapmen traded in souls for the demon. The soul of the aged was worth twenty pieces of gold, not a penny more; for Satan had had time to make his valuation. The soul of a matron was valued at fifty, when she was handsome, and a hundred when she was ugly. The soul of a young maiden fetched an extravagant sum; the freshest and purest flowers are the dearest.

At that time there lived in the city an angel of beauty, the Countess Kathleen O'Shea. She was the idol of the people and the providence of the indigent. As soon as she learned that these miscreants profited by the public misery to steal away hearts from God, she called to her butler.

"Patrick," said she to him, "how many pieces of gold in my coffers?"

"A hundred thousand."

"How many jewels?"

"The money's worth of the gold."

"How much property in castles, forests, and lands?"

"Double the rest."

"Very well, Patrick; sell all that is not gold; and bring me the account. I only wish to keep this mansion and the demesne that surrounds it."

Two days afterwards the orders of the pious Kathleen were executed, and the treasure was distributed to the poor in proportion to their wants. This, says the tradition, did not suit the purposes of the Evil Spirit, who found no more souls to purchase. Aided by an infamous servant, they penetrated into the retreat of the noble dame, and purloined from her the rest of her treasure. In vain she struggled with all her strength to save the contents of her coffers; the diabolical thieves were the stronger. If Kathleen had been able to make the sign of the Cross, adds the legend, she would have put them to flight, but her hands were captive. The larceny was effected.

Then the poor called for aid to the plundered Kathleen, alas, to no good: she was able to succour their misery no longer; she had to abandon them to the temptation.

Meanwhile, but eight days had to pass before the grain and provender would arrive in abundance from the western lands. Eight such days were an age. Eight days required an immense sum to relieve the exigencies of the dearth, and the poor should either perish in the agonies of hunger, or, denying the holy maxims of the Gospel, vend, for base lucre, their souls, the richest gift from the bounteous hand of the Almighty. And Kathleen hadn't anything, for she had given up her mansion to the unhappy. She passed twelve hours in tears and mourning, rending her sun-tinted hair, and bruising her breast, of the whiteness of the lily; afterwards she stood up, resolute, animated by a vivid sentiment of despair.

She went to the traders in souls.

"What do you want?" they said.

"You buy souls?"

"Yes, a few still, in spite of you. Isn't that so, saint, with the eyes of sapphire?"

"To-day I am come to offer you a bargain," replied she.

"What?"

"I have a soul to sell, but it is costly."

"What does that signify if it is precious? The soul, like the diamond, is appraised by its transparency."

"It is mine."

The two emissaries of Satan started. Their claws were clutched under their gloves of leather; their grey eyes sparkled; the soul, pure, spotless, virginal of Kathleen—it was a priceless acquisition!

"Beauteous lady, how much do you ask?"

"A hundred and fifty thousand pieces of gold."

"It's at your service," replied the traders, and they tendered Kathleen a parchment sealed with black, which she signed with a shudder.

The sum was counted out to her.

As soon as she got home she said to the butler, "Here, distribute this: with this money that I give you the poor can tide over the eight days that remain, and not one of their souls will be delivered to the demon."

Afterwards she shut herself up in her room and gave orders that none should disturb her.

Three days passed; she called nobody, she did not come out.

When the door was opened, they found her cold and stiff; she was dead of grief.

But the sale of this soul, so adorable in its charity, was declared null by the Lord; for she had saved her fellow-citizens from eternal death.

After the eight days had passed, numerous vessels brought into famished Ireland immense provisions in grain. Hunger was no longer possible. As to the traders, they disappeared from their hotel without anyone knowing what became of them. But the fishermen of the Blackwater pretend that they are enchained in a subterranean prison by order of Lucifer, until they shall be able to render up the soul of Kathleen, which escaped from them.

Centaurus Changeling

Marion Zimmer Bradley

MARION ZIMMER BRADLEY, *perhaps the only American woman to have a genre magazine named after her* (Marion Zimmer Bradley's Fantasy), *is author of the best-selling series of* Darkover *science fiction novels as well as other books, tales and works of nonfiction, including* The Door Through Space, Hunters of the Red Moon, *and* Men, Halflings and Hero-Worship. *In "Centaurus Changeling," Ms. Bradley's first published story (1954), the dangers of childbirth are nightmarishly compounded and intertwined with, of all things, interplanetary politics!*

". . . the only exception to the aforesaid policy was made in the case of Megaera (Theta Centaurus IV) which was given full Dominion status as an independent planetary government; a departure almost without precedent in the history of the Terran Empire. There are many explanations for this variation from the usual practice, the most generally accepted being that which states that Megaera had been colonized from Terra only a few years before the outbreak of the Rigel-Procyon war, which knocked out communications in the entire Centaurus sector of the Galaxy and forced the abandonment of all the so-called Darkovan League colonies, including Megaera, Darkover, Samarra and Vialles. During these Lost Years, as they were called, a period embracing, in all, nearly 600 years . . . the factors of natural selection, and the phenomenon of genetic drift and survival mutation observed among isolated populations, permitted these "lost" colonies to develop along scientific

*and social lines which made their reclamation by the Terran Empire an
imperative political necessity. . . ."*

> From J. T. Bannerton: A COMPREHENSIVE HISTORY
> OF GALACTIC POLITICS, *Tape* IX.

The Official Residence of the Terran Legate on Megaera was not
equipped with a roofport for landing the small, helicopter-like carioles.
This oversight, a gesture of bureaucratic economy from the desk of some
supervisor back on Terra, meant that whenever the Legate or his wife
left the Residence, they must climb down four flights of stairs to the level
of the rarely used streets, and climb again, up the endless twisting stairs,
to the platform of the public skyport a quarter of a mile away.

Matt Ferguson swore irritably as his ankle turned in a rut—since no
Centaurian citizen ever used the streets for walking if he could help it,
they were not kept in condition for that purpose—and took his wife's
arm, carefully guiding her steps on the uneven paving.

"Be careful, Beth," he warned. "You could break your neck without
half trying!"

"And all those stairs!" The girl looked sulkily up at the black shadow
of the skyport platform, stretched over them like a dark wing. The street
lay deserted in the lurid light of early evening; red Centaurus, a hovering
disk at the horizon, sent a slanting light, violently crimson, down into
the black canyon of the street, and the top-heavy houses leaned down,
somber and ominous. Wavering shadows gloomed down over them, and
a hot wind blew down the length of the street, bearing that peculiar,
pungent, all-pervasive smell which is Megaera's atmosphere. A curious
blend, not altogether unpleasant, a resinous and musky smell which was
a little sickish, like perfume worn too long. Beth Ferguson supposed that
sooner or later she would get used to Megaera's air, that combination of
stinks and chemical emanations. It was harmless, her husband assured
her, to human chemistry. But it did not grow less noticeable with time;
after more than a year, Terran Standard time, on Megaera, it was still
freshly pungent to her nostrils. Beth wrinkled up her pretty, sullen
mouth. "Do we have to go to this dinner, Matt?" she asked plaintively.

The man put his foot on the first step. "Of course, Beth. Don't be
childish," he remonstrated gently. "I told you, before we came to
Megaera, that my success at this post would depend mostly on my informal relations—"

"If you call a dinner at the Jeth-sans informal—" Beth began petulantly, but Matt went on, "—my informal relations with the Centaurian members of the government. Every diplomatic post in the Darkovan League is just the same, dear. Rai Jeth-san has gone out of his way to make things easy for both of us." He paused, and they climbed in silence for a few steps. "I know you don't like living here. But if I can do what I was sent here to do, we can have any diplomatic post in the Galaxy. I've got to sell the Centaurian Archons on the idea of building the big space station here. And, so far, I'm succeeding at a job no other man would take."

"I can't see why you took it," Beth sulked, snatching pettishly at her nylene scarf, which was flapping like an unruly bird in the hot, grit-laden wind.

Matt turned and tucked it into place. "Because it was better than working as the assistant to the assistant to the under-secretary of Terran affairs attached to the Proconsul of Vialles. Cheer up, Beth. If this space station gets built, I'll have a Proconsulship myself."

"And if it doesn't?"

Matt grinned. "It will. We're doing fine. Most Legates need years to find their way around a difficult post like Megaera." The grin melted abruptly. "Rai Jeth-san is responsible for that, too. I don't want to offend him."

Beth said, and her voice was not very steady, "I understand all that, Matt. But I've been feeling—ah, I hate to be always whining and complaining like this—"

They had reached the wide, flat platform of the skyport. Matt lighted the flare which would attract a cariole, and sank down on one of the benches. "You haven't whined," he told her tenderly. "I know this rotten planet is no place for a Terran girl." He slipped an arm around his wife's waist. "It's hard on you, with other Terran women half a continent away, and I know you haven't made many friends among the Centaurians. But Rai Jeth-san's wives have been very kind to you. Nethle presented you to her Harp Circle—I don't suppose any Terran woman for a thousand years has even seen one, let alone been presented—and even Cassiana—"

"Cassiana!" said Beth with a catch of breath, picking at her bracelet.

"Yes, Nethle's almost too sweet, but she's in seclusion, and until her baby is born, I won't see her. And Wilidh's just a child! But Cassiana—I can't *stand* her! That—that *freak*! I'm afraid of her!"

Her husband scowled. "And don't think she doesn't know it! She's telepathic, and a rhu'ad—"

"Whatever *that* is," Beth said crossly. "Some sort of mutant—"

"Still, she's been kind to you. If you were friends—"

"Ugh!" Beth shuddered. "I'd sooner be friends with—with a Sirian lizard-woman!"

Matt's arm dropped. He said coldly, "Well, please be polite to her, at least. Courtesy to the Archon includes all his wives—but particularly Cassiana." He rose from the bench. "Here comes our cariole."

The little skycab swooped down to the skyport. Matt helped Beth inside and gave the pilot the address of the Archonate. The cariole shot skyward again, wheeling toward the distant suburb where the Archon lived. Matt sat stiffly on the seat, not looking at his young wife. She leaned against the padding, her fair face sulky and rebellious. She looked ready to cry. "At least, in another month, by their own stupid customs, I'll have a good excuse to stay away from all these idiotic affairs!" she flung at him. "I'll be in seclusion by then!"

It hadn't been the way she'd wanted to tell him, but it served him right!

"Beth!" Matt started upright, not believing.

"Yes! I *am* going to have a baby! And I'm going into seclusion just like these silly women here, and not have to go to a single formal dinner, or Spice Hunt, or Harp Circle, for six cycles! So there!"

Matt Ferguson leaned across the seat. His fingers bit hard into her arm and his voice sounded hoarse. "Elizabeth! Look at me—" he commanded. "Didn't you *promise*—haven't you been taking your anti shots?"

"N-no," Beth faltered, "I wanted to—oh, Matt, I'm alone so much, and we've been married now almost four years—"

"Oh, my God," said Matt slowly, and let go her arm. "Oh, my God!" he repeated, and sank back, the color draining from his face.

"Will you stop saying that!" Beth raged. "When I tell you a thing like—" her voice caught on the edge of a sob, and she buried her face in her scarf.

Matt's hand was rough as he jerked her head up, and the gray pallor around his mouth terrified the girl. "You damn little fool," he shouted, then swallowed hard and lowered his voice. "I guess it's my fault," he muttered. "I didn't want to scare you—you promised to take the shots, so I trusted you—like an idiot!" He released her. "It's classified top-secret, Beth, but it's why this place is closed to colonization, and it's why Terran men don't bring their wives here. This damned, stinking, freak atmosphere! It's perfectly harmless to men, and to most women. But for some reason, it plays hell with the female hormones if a woman gets pregnant. For 60 years—since Terra set up the Legation here—not one Terran baby has been born alive. Not *one*, Beth. And eight out of ten women who get pregnant—oh, God, Betty, I trusted you!"

She whispered "But this—this was a Terran colony, once—"

"They've adapted—maybe. We've never found out why Centaurian women go into seclusion when they're pregnant, or why they hide the children so carefully."

He paused, looking down at the thinning jungle of roofs. There would not be time to explain it all to Beth. Even if she lived—but Matt did not want to think about that. They never *sent* married men to this planet, but Centaurian custom could not admit a single man to be mature enough to hold a place in government. He had succeeded at this post where single men, twice his age, had been laughed at by the Archons. But what good was that now?

"Oh, God, Beth," he whispered, and his arms went out blindly to hold her close. "I don't know what to do—"

She sobbed softly, scared, against him. "Oh, Matt, I'm afraid! Can't we go home—home to Terra? I want—I want to go home—to go home—"

"How can we?" the man asked drearily. "There won't be a star-ship leaving the planet for three months. By that time, you wouldn't be able to live through blastoff. Even now, you couldn't pass a physical for space." He was silent for minutes, his arms strained around her, and his eyes looked haunted. Then, almost visibly, he managed to pull himself together.

"Look, the first thing tomorrow, I'll take you to the Medical HQ. They've been working on it. Maybe—don't worry, darling. We'll get along." His voice lapsed again, and Beth, wanting desperately to believe him, could find no reassurance in the words. "You're going to be all right," he told her again. "Aren't you?" But she clung to him and did not answer. After a long, strained silence, he roused a little, and let her go, glancing from the windbreak of the cariole cabin.

"Beth, darling, fix your face—" he urged her gently. "We'll be late, and you can't go down looking like that—"

For a minute Beth sat still, simply not believing that after what she had told him, he would still make her go to the detested dinner. Then, looking at his tensed face, she suddenly knew it was the one thing on earth—no, she corrected herself with grim humor, the one thing on Theta Centaurus IV, Megaera, that she *must* do.

"Tell him not to land for a minute," she said shakily. She unfastened her wrist compact, and silently began to repair the wreckage of her cosmetics.

Above the Archonate, the cariole maneuvered frantically for place with another careening skycab, and after what seemed an imminent clash of tangled gyroscopes, slid on to the skyport only seconds before it. Beth shrieked, and Matt flung the door open and abused the pilot in choice Centaurian.

"I compliment you on your perfect command of our language," murmured a soft creamy voice, and Matt flushed darkly as he saw the Archon standing at the very foot of the roofport. He murmured confused apology; it was hardly the way to begin a formal evening. The Archon lipped a buttery smile. "I pray you do not think of it. I disregard speech of yours. It is again not spoken." With an air of esthetic unconcern, he gestured welcome at Beth, and she stepped down, feeling clumsy and awkward. "I stand where you expect me not, only because I think Senior Wife mine in cariole this one," the Archon continued. Out of courtesy to his guests, he was speaking a mangled dialect of Galactic Standard; Beth wished irritably that he would talk Centaurian. She understood it as well as Matt did. She also had the uncomfortable feeling that the Archon sensed her irritation and that it amused him; a sizable fraction of the Megaeran population was slightly telepathic.

"You must excusing Cassiana," the Archon offered languidly as he conducted his guests across the great open skycourt which was the main room of a Centaurian home. "She went to the City, one of our families visiting, for she is rhu'ad, and must be ever at their call when she is needed. And Second Wife is most fortunately in seclusion, so you must excusing her also," he continued as they approached the lighted penthouse. Beth murmured the expected compliments on Nethle's coming child. "Youngest wife then be our hostess, and since she not used to formal custom, we be like barbarian this night."

Matt gave his wife a vicious nudge in the ribs. "Cut that out," he whispered, savagely, and with an effort that turned her face crimson, Beth managed to suppress her rising giggles. Of course there was nothing even faintly informal in the arrangement of the penthouse room into which they were conducted, nor in the classic and affected poses of the other guests. The women in their stiff metallic robes cast polite, aloof glances at Beth's soft drapery, and their greetings were chilly, musical murmurs. Under their slitted, hostile eyes, Beth felt despairingly that she and Matt were intruders here, barbaric atavisms; too big and muscular, too burned by a yellow sun, blatantly and vulgarly colorful. The Centaurians were little and fragile, not one over five feet tall, bleached white by the red-violet sun, their foamy, blue-black hair a curious metallic halo above stiff classicized robes. Humans? Yes—but their evolution had turned off at right angles a thousand years ago. What had those centuries done to Megaera and its people?

Swathed in a symbolic costume, Rai Jeth-san's youngest wife Wilidh sat stiffly in the great Hostess Chair. She spoke to the guests formally, but her mouth quirked up at Beth in the beginnings of a giggle. "Oh, my good little friend," she whispered in Galactic Standard, "I *die* with these formals! These are Cassiana's friends, and not mine, for no one knew she would not be here tonight! And they laugh at me, and stick up their backs, all stiff, like this—" she made a rude gesture, and her topaz eyes glinted with mischief. "Sit here by me, Beth, and talk of something very dull and stupid, for I *die* trying not to disgrace me by laughing! When Cassiana comes back—"

Wilidh's mirth was infectious. Beth took the indicated seat, and they talked in whispers, holding hands after the fashion of Centaurian women. Wilidh was too young to have adopted the general hostility toward the Terran woman; in many ways, she reminded Beth of an eager school girl. It was hard to remember that this merry child had been married as long as Beth herself; still more incredible that she was already the mother of three children.

Suddenly Wilidh turned color, and stood up, stammering confused apologies. "Forgive me, forgive me, Cassiana—"

Beth also rose, but the Archon's Senior Wife gestured for them to

resume their seats. Cassiana was not dressed for formal dining. Her gray
street wrap was still folded over a plain dress of dark thin stuff, and her
face looked naked without cosmetics, and very tired. "Never mind,
Wilidh. Remain hostess for me, if you will." She smiled flittingly at
Beth. "I am sorry I am not here to greet you." Acknowledging their
replies with a weary politeness, Cassiana moved past them like a wraith,
and they saw her walking across the skycourt, and disappearing down
the wide stairway that led to the lower, private parts of the house.

She did not rejoin them until the formal dinner had been served,
eaten and removed, and the soft-footed servants were padding around
the room with bowls and baskets of exotic fruit and delicacies and gilded
cups of frosty mountain nectar. The penthouse shutters had been thrown
wide, so that the guests could watch the flickering play of lightning from
the giant magnetic storms which were almost a nightly occurrence on
Megaera. They were weirdly beautiful and the Centaurians never tired
of watching them, but they terrified Beth. She preferred the rare calm
nights when Megaera's two immense moons filled the sky with uncanny
green moonlight; but now thick clouds hid the faces of Alecto and
Tisiphone, and the jagged bolts leaped and cast lurid shadows on the
great massy clouds. Through the thunder, the eerie noise which passed,
on Megaera, for music, was wailing from the slitted walls. In its shadow,
Cassiana ghosted into the room and sat down between Beth and Wilidh.
She did not speak for minutes, listening with evident enjoyment to the
music and its counterpoint of thunder. Cassiana was somewhat older
than Beth, small and exquisite, a filigree dainty woman fashioned of
gilded silver. Her ash blonde hair had metallic lights, and her skin and
eyes had almost the same hue, a gold-cream, smudged with gilt freckles,
and with a sort of luminous, pearly glow . . . the distinguishing mark
of a curious mutation called rhu'ad. The word itself meant only *pearl;*
neither Beth nor any other Terran knew what it implied.

The servants were passing around tiny baskets, curiously woven of
reeds from the Sea of Storms. Deferentially, they laid a basket before the
three women. "Oh, *sharigs!*" Wilidh cried with a childish gusto. Beth
glanced into the basket at the wriggling mass of small, greenish-gold
octopods, less than three inches long, writhing and struggling in their
nest of odorous seaweed and striking feebly at each other with the
stumps of claws they did not know had been snapped off. The sight
disgusted Beth, but Wilidh took a pair of tiny tongs and picked up one

of the revolting little creatures, and as Beth watched with fascinated horror, thrust it whole into her mouth. Daintily, but with relish, her sharp small teeth crunched the shell; she sucked, and fastidiously spat the empty shell into her palm.

"Try one, Beth," Cassiana suggested kindly. "They are really delicious."

"N—no, thank you," Beth said weakly—and suddenly disgraced herself and all her conditioning by turning aside and being very completely and excruciatingly sick on the shimmering floor. She barely heard Cassiana's cry of distress, although she was conscious of a prim offended murmur, and knew she had outraged custom beyond all credibility. Through helpless spasms of retching, she was conscious of hands and voices. Then she was picked up in strong familiar arms, and heard Matt's worried "Honey, are you all right?"

She knew she was being carried across the skycourt and into a lower room, and opened her eyes sickly to see Cassiana and Matt standing over her. "I'm—I'm so sorry—" she whispered. Cassiana's thin hand patted hers, comfortingly. "Do not think of it," she reassured, "Legate Furr-gasoon, your wife will be well enough, you may return to the other guests," she said, gently, but in a tone that unmistakably dismissed him. There was no polite way to protest. Matt went, looking back doubtfully. Cassiana's strange eyes looked rather pitying. "Don't try to talk," she admonished. Beth felt too sick and weak to move and being alone with Cassiana terrified her. She lay quiet on the big divan, tears slipping weakly down her face. Cassiana's hand still clasped hers; in a kind of childish petulance, Beth pulled her hand away, but the slender fingers only closed more tightly around Beth's wrist. "Be still," said Cassiana, not unkindly, but in a tone of absolute command, and she sat there, looking down at Beth with a staring intensity, for some minutes. Finally she sighed and freed Beth's hand.

"Do you feel better now?"

"Why—yes!" said Beth, surprised. Quite suddenly, the nausea and the pain in her head were altogether gone. Cassiana smiled. "I am glad. No —lie quiet. Beth, I think you should not ride in cariole tonight, why not stay here? You can visit Nethle—she has missed you since she went into seclusion."

Beth almost cried out with surprise. This *was* rare—for an outsider to be invited into a Centaurian house any further than the skycourt and penthouse reserved for social affairs. Then, with a stab of frightened memory, she recalled the reason for Nethle's seclusion—and her own fears. Nethle was her friend, even Cassiana had shown her kindness. Perhaps in a less formal atmosphere she might be able to ask something about the curious taboo which surrounded the birth of children on Megaera, perhaps learn some way of averting her own danger . . . she closed her eyes and leaned against the cushions for a moment. If nothing else, it meant reprieve. For a little while she need not face Matt's gallantly concealed fear, his reproach. . . .

Matt, returning with Cassiana, quickly gave consent. "If that's what you really want, honey," he said gently. As she looked up into his tense face, Beth's impulse suddenly changed. She wanted to cry out "No— don't leave me here, take me home—" a night here in this strange place, alone with Centaurian women who were, however friendly they might be, entirely alien, seemed a thing too fearful to contemplate. She felt inclined to cry. But Cassiana's eyes on her proved rather steadying, and Beth's long conditioning in the ceremonial life necessary on Megaera triumphed over emotions she knew to be irrational.

Her husband bent and kissed her lightly. "I'll send a cariole for you tomorrow," he promised.

The lower portions of a Centaurian home were especially designed for a polygamous society in harmony with itself. They were carefully compartmented, and the only entrance from one to the other was from the great common stairway which led to the roof and skycourt. Roughly a third of the house was sectioned off for the habitation of Rai Jeth-san and his seasonal consort. The remainder was women's quarters, and the Archon himself might not enter them without specific invitation. In effect, Megaera's polygamous society was a rotational monogamy, for although Rai Jeth-san had three wives—the legal maximum was five— he had only one at a time and their alteration was strictly regulated by tradition. The surplus women lived together, always on terms of the most cordial friendship. Cassiana took precedence over the others, by custom, but there was the closest affection among all three—which had surprised Beth at first, especially when she found out that this was by no means rare; the bond between the wives of one man was traditionally the strongest family tie in existence, far stronger than the tie between natural sisters.

Beth had discovered long ago that she was not alone in her awe of Cassiana, who was one of the peculiar patriciate of the planet. Men and women fought for the privilege of serving the rhu'ads; Beth, relaxing into the almost sybaritic luxury of the women's quarters, wondered again—what was Cassiana's strange power over the Centaurians? She knew Cassiana was one of the rare telepaths who were found in the Darkovan planets, but that alone would not have explained it, nor would Cassiana's odd beauty. On Megaera there were perhaps 10,000 women like Cassiana: curiously beautiful, more curiously revered. There were no male rhu'ad. Beth had seen both men and women throw themselves to the ground in a burst of spontaneous emotion as one of the small, pearl-colored women passed, but had never understood, or dared to ask.

Cassiana asked her, "Would you like to see Nethle before you sleep— and our children?"

This was, indeed, a strange relaxation of tradition; Beth knew no Terran had ever seen a Centaurian child. Astonished, she followed Cassiana into a lower room.

It seemed full of children. Beth counted; there were nine, the youngest only a baby in arms, the oldest about ten. They were pale, pretty children, like hothouse flowers reared in secret. Seeing the stranger, they clustered together, whispering to each other timidly, staring with wide eyes at her strange hair and curious garments.

"Come here, my darlings," said Cassiana in her soft pleasant voice. "Don't stare." She was speaking in Centaurian, a further gesture of friendliness.

One little boy—the rest of the children were all girls—piped up valiantly, "Is she another mother for us?"

Cassiana laughed. "No, my son. Aren't three mothers enough?"

Nethle rose from a cushiony chair and came to Beth, her hands outstretched in welcome. "I thought you had forgotten me! Of course, you poor Terran women, only one wife to look after a husband, I cannot see how you ever have time for *anything!*"

Beth blushed—Nethle's outspoken references to Beth's "unhappy" state as a solitary wife, always embarrassed her. But she returned Nethle's greeting with genuine pleasure—Nethle Jeth-san was perhaps the only Centaurian whom Beth could tolerate without that sense of uneasy dislike.

She said, "I've missed you, Nethle," but secretly she was dismayed at the change in her friend. Since Nethle had gone into seclusion, months ago, she had changed frighteningly. In spite of the distortion of pregnancy, Nethle seemed to have lost weight, her small face looked haggard, and her skin was a ghastly color. She walked shakily, and sat down almost at once after greeting Beth, but her gay manner and brilliant joyous eyes belied her illness. She and Beth talked quietly, about inconsequential things—Centaurian custom almost outlawed serious conversation—while Cassiana curled up, kittenlike, in a nest of soft pillows, picking up the littlest baby.

Two toddlers came and tried to crawl up on her knees at once, so Cassiana laughed and slid down on the floor, letting the children climb all over her, snuggle against her shoulder, tug at her garments and her elaborately arranged hair. She was so tiny that she looked like a little girl with a lapful of dolls. Beth asked her—hesitantly, for she did not know if it was polite to ask—"Which are your children, Cassiana?"

Cassiana glanced up. "In a way, all, and in another way, none," she said curtly and Beth thought she had trespassed on courtesy; but Nethle put her hand on the solitary boy's head. "Cassiana has no children, Beth. She is rhu'ad, and rhu'ad women do not bear children. This is my son, and the oldest girl, and the girl with long hair. Those," she indicated the twin toddlers and the baby in Cassiana's lap, "are Wilidh's. The rest are Clotine's. Clotine was our sister, who died many cycles ago."

Cassiana gently put the children aside and came to Beth. She looked at one of the little girls playing in the corner. She made no sound, but the child turned and suddenly ran to Cassiana, flinging her arms around the rhu'ad. Cassiana hugged her, then let her go, and—to Beth's surprise —the tiny girl came and tugged at Beth's skirt, clambering into her lap. Beth put an arm around her, looking down in astonishment.

"Why, she—" she broke off, not knowing, again, whether she should remark on the extraordinary likeness. The tiny girl—she seemed about four—had the same, pearly, lustrous skin; her hair was a silvery eiderdown, pallid and patrician. Cassiana noted her discomfiture and laughed gaily. "Yes, Arli is rhu'ad. She is mine."

"I thought—"

"Oh, Cassiana, stop it," Nethle protested, laughing. "She doesn't understand!"

"There are many things she does not understand," said Cassiana abruptly, "but I think she will have to learn to understand them. Bet', you have done a terribly unwise thing. Terran women *cannot* have children here in safety!"

Beth could only blink in amazement. The self test taken the day before had shown her pregnancy to be less than a month advanced. "How *ever* did you know?" she asked.

"Your poor husband," Cassiana's voice was gentle. "I felt his fear like a gray murk, all evening. It is not pleasant to be telepath, sometimes. It is why I try not to go in crowds, I cannot help invading the privacy of others. Then, when you were so sick, I knew."

Nethle seemed to freeze, to go rigid. Her arms fell to her sides. "So that is it!" she whispered almost inaudibly. Then she burst out, "And that is the way with the women of Terra! That is why your Earthmen will never take this planet! As long as they despise us and come as conquerors, they cannot come here where their women—die!" Her eyes glared. She rose and stood, heavy, distorted, menacing, over Beth, her lips drawn back in an animal snarl, her arm raised as if to strike. Cassiana gasped, sprang up, and with a surprising strength, she pushed Nethle back into her chair.

"Bet', she is raving—even women here, sometimes—"

"Raving!" Nethle said with a curl of her lip. "Wasn't there a day when our women and their unborn children died by the hundreds because we did not know the air was poison? When women died, or were kept in airtight rooms and given oxygen till their children were born, and then left to die? When men married a dozen wives to be sure of one living child? Did the Terrans help us then, when we begged them to evacuate the planet? No! They had a war on their hands—for 600 years they had a war on their hands! Now they've finished their private wars, they try to come back to Megaera— "

"Nethle! Be quiet!" Cassiana commanded angrily. Beth had sunk into the cushions, but through her cupped hands she saw that Nethle's face blazed, a contorted mask of fury. "Yes, yes, Cassiana," her voice was a mocking croon, "Bet' condescends to make friends with me—and now she will see what happens to the women of Terra who mock our customs instead of finding out why we have them!" The wildness of her hysteria beat and battered at Beth. "Oh, yes, I liked you," she snarled, "but could you really be friends with a Centaurian woman? Don't you think I know you mock our rhu'ad? Could you live equal to us? Get out!" she shouted. "Get off our world! Go away, all of you! Leave us in peace!"

"Nethle!" Cassiana grasped the woman's shoulders and shook her, hard, until the wildness went out of her face. Then she pushed Nethle down in the cushions, where she lay sobbing. Cassiana looked down at her sorrowfully. "You hate worse than she hates. How can there ever be peace, then?"

"You have always defended her," Nethle muttered, "and she hates you worst of all!"

"That is exactly why I have more responsibility," Cassiana answered. She went to the curtained door at the end of the room. At her summons, a servant came and began unobtrusively to shepherd the children out of the room. They went obediently, the older ones looking scared and bewildered, glancing timidly at the weeping Nethle; the little ones reluctant, clinging to Cassiana, pouting a little as she gently pushed them out the door. Cassiana drew the curtain firmly down behind them; then went back to Nethle and touched her on the shoulder. "Listen," she said.

Then Beth had the curious feeling that Nethle and Cassiana were conversing through some direct mental exchange from which she was excluded. Their changing expressions, and faint gestures, told her that, and a few emphatic, spoken words seemed to give point to the soundless conversation—it made Beth's flesh crawl.

"My decisions are always final," Cassiana stated.

Nethle muttered ". . . cruel of you . . ."

Cassiana shook her head.

After long minutes of speech-silence, Cassiana said aloud, quietly, "No, I have decided. I did it for Clotine. I would do it for you—or for Wilidh, if you were fool enough to try what Bet' has done."

Nethle flared back, "I wouldn't *be* fool enough to try to have a baby *that way*—"

Cassiana checked her with a gesture, rose, and went to Beth, who was still lying huddled in the pillows of the big divan. "If I, who am rhu'ad, do not break the laws," she said, "then no one will ever dare to break them, and our planet will stagnate in dead traditions. Bet', if you can promise to obey me, and to ask me no questions, then I, who am rhu'ad, promise you this: you may have your child without fear, and your chance of life will be—" she hesitated, "equal to a Centaurian woman's."

Beth looked up, speechless, her eyes wide. A dozen emotions tangled in some secret part of her mind, fear, distrust—anger. Yet reason told her that Cassiana was showing disinterested kindness in the face of what must certainly have been obvious to her, Beth's own dislike. At the moment Beth was unaware that proximity to the telepath was sharpening her own sense perceptions, but for the first time in months she was thinking reasonably, unblurred by emotion.

Cassiana insisted, "Can you promise? Can you promise, especially, not to ask me questions about what I have to do?"

And Beth nodded soberly. "I'll promise," she said.

The pale pink, watery sunlight looked feeble and anachronistic on the white, sterile, characteristically Terran walls, floors and furnishings of the Medical HQ; and the white indoor face of the old doctor looked like some sun-sheltered slug.

"He's lived here so long, he's half Centaurian himself," Matt Ferguson thought irrelevantly, and threw down the chart in his hand. "You mean there's nothing to be done!" he said bluntly.

"We never say that in my profession," Dr. Bonner told him simply. "While there's life, and all the rest of it. But it looks bad. You never should have left it up to the girl to make sure she took her anti shots. Women aren't reliable about that kind of thing—not normal women. A woman's got to be pretty damned abnormal, to be conscientious about contraceptives." He frowned. "You know, it's not a question of adapting, either. If anything, the third, fourth, fourteenth generations are more susceptible than the first. The planet seems so perfectly healthy that women simply don't believe it until they *do* get pregnant, and then it's too late."

"Abortion?" Matt suggested, lowering his head. Dr. Bonner shrugged. "Worse yet. Operative shock on top of the hormone reaction would just kill her now, instead of later." He leaned his head on his hands. "Whatever it is in the air, it doesn't hurt anybody until we get the flood of female hormones released in pregnancy. Then it starts reacting, and we get a kind of internal explosion. We've tried everything—manufacturing our own air—chemically pure, but we can't get that stink out of it, and we can't keep it pure. There's just something linked into the atomic structure of the whole damned planet. It doesn't bother test animals, so we can't do any experimenting. It's just the human, female hormones of pregnancy. We've even tried locking the women in airtight domes, and giving them pure oxygen, the whole nine months. But we get the same reaction. Pernicious vomiting, weight loss, confusion of the balance centers, convulsions—and if the foetus isn't aborted, it's oxygen-starved and a monster. I've lived on Megaera 40 years, Matt, and I haven't delivered a live baby yet."

Matt raged, "Then how do the Centaurians manage? They have children, all right!"

"Have you ever seen one?" asked Dr. Bonner tersely. At Matt's denial, he continued, "Neither have I—in 40 years. For all I know, Centaurian women cultivate their babies in test tubes. Nobody's ever seen a pregnant Centaurian woman, or a child under about ten years old. But one of our men—ten, twelve years ago—got a Centaurian girl pregnant. Of course, her family threw her out—right in the damn street. Our man married the girl—he'd wanted to, anyhow. The man—I won't tell you his name—brought her in to me. I thought maybe—but the story was just *exactly* the same. Nausea, pernicious vomiting—all the rest. You wouldn't believe the things we tried to save that girl. I didn't know I had so much imagination myself." He dropped his eyes, bitter with an old failure. "But she died. The baby lived. It's up in the incurable ward."

"Jesus!" Matt shuddered uncontrollably. "What can I *do?*"

Dr. Bonner's eyes were very sorrowful. "Bring her in, Matt, right away. We'll do our damnedest for her." His hand found the younger man's shoulder as he rose, but Matt was not conscious of the touch. He never knew how he got out of the building, but after a reeling walk through streets that twisted around his bleared eyes, he heard the buzz of a descending cariole, and Cassiana Jeth-san's level voice.

"Legate Furr-ga-soon?"

Matt raised his head numbly. She was about the last person he cared to see. But Matt Ferguson was a Legate of the Terran Empire, and had undergone strenuous conditioning for this post. He could no more have been rude to anyone to whom courtesy was required, than he could have thrown himself from a moving cariole. So he said with careful graciousness, "I greet you, Cassiana."

She signalled the pilot to set the hovering skycab down. "This meeting is fortunate," she said quietly. "Get into this cariole, and ride with me."

Matt obeyed, mostly because he lacked, at the moment, the ingenuity to form an acceptable excuse. He climbed in; the skycab began to ascend again over the city. It seemed a long time before Cassiana said, "Bet' is at the Archonate. I have made a finding the most unfortunate. Understand me, Legate, you are in situation of the baddest."

"I know," Matt said grimly. His wife's dislike of Cassiana suddenly became reasonable to him. He had never been alone with a telepath before, and it made him a little giddy. There was almost a physical vibration in the small woman's piercing gaze. Cassiana's mangling of Galactic Standard—she spoke it better than her husband, but still abominably— was another irritation which Matt tried to hide. As if in answer to his unspoken thought, Cassiana switched to her own language. "Why did you come to Megaera?"

What a fool question, Matt thought irritably. Why did any man take a diplomatic post? "My government sent me."

"But not because you liked Megaera, or us? Not because you wanted to live here, or cared about Terrans and Centaurians getting along? Not because you cared about the space station?"

Matt paused, honestly surprised. "No," he said, "I suppose not." Then annoyance triumphed. "How *can* we live together? Your people don't travel in space. Ours can't live in health or ordinary comfort on this— this stinking planet! How can we do anything but live apart and leave you to yourselves?"

Cassiana said slowly, "We wanted, once, to abandon this colony. For all Terra cared, we could live or die. Now they have found out their lost property might be worth—"

Matt sighed. "The Imperialists who abandoned Megaera have all been dead for hundreds of years," he pointed out wearily. "Now, we have to have some contact with your planet, because of the political situation. You know that. No one is trying to exploit Megaera."

"I know that," she admitted. "Perhaps 50 other people on the whole planet realize that. The rest are one seething mass of public opinion, and under the anti-propaganda laws, we can't change that." She stopped. "But I didn't want to talk politics. Why did you bring Bet' here, Legate?"

Matt bit his lip. Under her clear eyes he told the truth. "Because I knew a single man couldn't succeed at this post."

Cassiana mused. "It's a pity. It's almost certain that this affair will close out the Legation here. No married man will want to come, and we cannot accept a single man in such an important position. It is against our most respected tradition for a man to remain single after he is mature. Our only objection to your space station is the immense flood of unattached personnel who will come here to build it—drifters, unmarried men, military persons—such an influx would throw Megaera into confusion. We would be glad to accept married colonists who wanted to settle here."

"You *know* that's impossible!" Matt said.

"Maybe," Cassiana said thoughtfully. "It *is* a pity. Because it is obvious that the Terrans need Megaera, and Megaera needs some outside stimulus. We're turning stagnant." She was silent for a minute. Then she continued, "But I'm talking politics again. I suppose I wanted to see if it was in you to be honest. Perhaps, if you had grown angry sooner, been less concerned with polite formalities—angry men are honest men. We like honesty, we rhu'ad."

Matt's smile was bitter. "We are conditioned in courtesy. Honesty comes second."

"A proof that you are not suited to a society where any fraction of the population is telepathic," said Cassiana bluntly. "But that is not important. This is—Bet' is in very real danger, Legate. I promise nothing— even we Centaurians die sometimes—but if you will let her live at the Archonate for three, maybe four of your months—I think I can promise you she'll live. And probably the baby, too."

Hope seethed in Matt. "You mean—go into seclusion—"

"That, and more," said Cassiana gravely. "You must not attempt to see her yourself, and you must keep your entire Legation from knowing where she is, or why. That includes your personal friends and your officials. Can you do this? If not, I promise nothing."

"But that isn't possible—"

Cassiana dismissed the protest. "It is your problem. I am not a Terran, I don't know how you will manage it."

"Does Beth want to—"

"At this moment, no. You are her husband, and it is your child's life at stake. You have authority to order her to do it."

"We don't think of things that way on Terra. I don't—"

"You are not on Terra now," Cassiana reminded him flatly.

"Can I see Beth before I decide? She'll want to make arrangements, pack her things—"

"No, you must decide here, now. It may already be too late. As for her 'things'," the pearly eyes held delicate scorn, "she must have nothing from Terra near her."

"What kind of rubbish is that?" Matt demanded. "Not even her clothes?"

"I will provide anything she needs," Cassiana assured him. "Believe me, it is necessary. No—don't apologize. Anger is honesty."

"Look," Matt suggested, still trying to compromise acceptably. "I'll want her to see a Terran doctor, first, the authorities—"

Without warning, Cassiana lost her temper.

"You Terrans," she exploded, in a gust of fury that was like a physical blow. "You stupid lackwit from a planet of insane authoritarians, I *told* you, you must say nothing to anyone! This isn't a political matter, it's her *life*, and your child's! What can your so-called *authorities* do?"

"What can *you* do?" Matt shouted back. Protocol went overboard. The man and woman from two alien star systems glared at each other across a thousand years of evolution.

Then Cassiana said coldly, "That is the first sensible question you have asked. When our planet was—jettisoned as useless—we had to acquire certain techniques the hard way. I can't tell you exactly what. It isn't allowed. If that answer is not adequate, I am sorry. It is the only answer you will ever get. Wars have been fought on Megaera because the rhu'ad have refused to answer that question. We've been hounded and stoned, and sometimes worshipped. Between science and religion and politics, we've finally worked out the answer, but I have never told even my husband. Do you think I would tell a— a bureaucrat from Terra? You can accept my offer or refuse it—now."

Matt looked over the windbreak of the cariole at the wide-flung roofs of the city. He felt torn with terrible indecision. Reared in a society of elaborately delegated responsibilities, it went against all his conditioning —how could one man make a decision like this? How could he explain Beth's absence? What would his government say, if they discovered that he had not even consulted the medical authorities? Still, the choice was bald—Bonner had made it very clear that he had no hope. It was: trust Cassiana, or watch Beth die.

And the death would be neither quick nor easy.

"All right," he said, pressing his lips together. "Beth—Beth doesn't like you, as you probably know, and I'll be—I'll be everlastingly damned if I know why you are doing this! But I—I can't see any other way out.

This isn't a very polite way to put it, but it was you who insisted on honesty. Go ahead. Do what you can. I—" his voice suddenly strangled, but the little rhu'ad did not take the slightest notice of his losing struggle for self-control. With an air of remote detachment, she directed the driver of the cariole to set him down before the Residence.

During the brief ride there, she did not speak a word. Only when the cariole settled on the public skyport did she raise her head. "Remember," she said quietly, "you must not call at the Archonate, or attempt to see Bet'. If you have business with the Archon, you must arrange to meet him elsewhere. That will not be easy."

"Cassiana—what can I say—"

"Say nothing," she advised, not smiling, but there was a glint in the pearly eyes. In a less reserved face, it might have been friendly amusement. "Sometimes men are more honest that way."

She left him staring dumbly upward as the cariole climbed the sky once more.

When Cassiana—no longer friendly, but reserved and rigid—had brought the news that Matt had commanded her to stay, Beth had disbelieved—had shouted her hysterical disbelief and terror until Cassiana turned and walked out, locking the door behind her. She did not return for three days. Beth saw no one but an old lady who brought her meals and was, or pretended to be, deaf. In that time, Beth lived through a million emotions; but at the end of three days, when Cassiana came back, she looked at Beth with approval.

"I left you alone," she explained briefly, "to see how you reacted to fear and confinement. If you could not endure it, I could have done nothing for you. But I see you are quite calm."

Beth bit her lip, looking down at the smaller woman. "I was angry," she admitted. "I didn't think it was necessary to treat me like a child. But somehow I don't think you would have done it without good reason."

Cassiana's smile was a mere flicker. "Yes. I can read your mind a little —not much. I'm afraid you will be a prisoner again, for some time. Do you mind much? We'll try to make it easy for you."

"I'll do whatever you say," Beth promised calmly, and the rhu'ad nodded. "Now, I think you mean that, Bet'."

"I meant it when I said it before!" Beth protested.

"Your brain, and your reason, said it. But a pregnant woman's reasoning faculties aren't always reliable. I had to be certain that your emotions would back up your reason in the event of a shock. Believe me, you'll get some shocks."

But so far there had been none, although Cassiana had not exaggerated in the slightest when she said Beth would be a prisoner. The Terran woman was confined closely in two rooms on the ground floor—a level rarely used in a Centaurian house—and saw no one but Cassiana, Nethle and a servant or two. The rooms were spacious—even luxurious—and the air was filtered by some process which—while it did not diminish the distinctive smell—was somehow less sickening, and easier to breathe. "This air is just as dangerous, chemically, as that outdoors," Cassiana cautioned her. "Don't think that this, alone, makes you safe. But it may make you a little more comfortable. Don't go outside these rooms."

But she kept her promise to make imprisonment easy for Beth. Nethle, too, had recovered from her hysterical attack, and was punctiliously cordial. Beth had access to Cassiana's library—one of the finest tape collections on the planet—although, from a little judicious searching—Beth decided that Cassiana had removed tapes on some subjects she thought the Terran woman should not study too closely—and when Cassiana learned that Beth knew the rather rare art of three-dimensional painting, she asked her guest to teach her. They made several large figures, working together. Cassiana had a quick, artistic sensitivity which delighted Beth, and she swiftly mastered the complicated technique. The shared effort taught them a good deal about each other.

But there was much inconvenience which Cassiana's kindness could not mitigate. With each advancing day, Beth's discomfort became more acute. There was pain, and sickness, and a terrible feeling of breathlessness—for hours she would lie fighting for every breath. Cassiana told her that her system, in the hormone allergy, had lost the ability, in part, to absorb oxygen from the bloodstream. She broke out in violent rashes which never lasted more than a few hours, but recurred every few days. The ordinary annoyances of early pregnancy were there, too, magnified a hundred times. And during the electric storms, there was a strange reaction, a taut pain as if her body were a conductor for the electricity itself. She wondered if this pain were psychosomatic or genuinely symptomatic, but she never knew.

For some reason, the sickness receded when Cassiana was in the room, and as the days slid past, Cassiana was with her almost constantly, once or twice even sleeping in the same room, on a cot pushed close to Beth's. Unexpectedly, one day, Beth asked her, "Why do I always feel better when you are in the room?"

Cassiana did not answer for a minute. All the morning, they had been working on a three-dimensional painting. The floor was scattered with eyepieces and pigments, and Cassiana picked up an eyepiece and scanned a figure in the foreground before she even turned around to Beth. Then she disengaged her painting cone, and began to refill it with pigment.

"I wondered when you would ask me that. A telepath's mind controls her body, to some extent—that's a very rough way of putting it, but you don't know enough about psychokinetics to know the difference. Well— when we are working together, as we have been today, your mind is in what we telepaths call vibratory harmony with mine, and you are able to pick up, to a very slight degree, my mental projections. And they, in turn, react on your body."

"You mean you control your body by *thinking?*"

"Everybody does that." Cassiana smiled faintly. "Yes, I know what you mean. I can, for instance, control reflexes which are involuntary in —in normal people. Just as easily as you would flex or relax a muscle in your arm, I can control my heartbeat, blood pressure, uterine contrac- tions—" she stopped abruptly, then finished, "and I can control gross reflexes, such as vomiting, in others—if they come within the kinetic field." She put down the spinning-cone. "Look at me, and I'll show you what I mean."

Beth obeyed. After a moment, Cassiana's gilt hair began to darken. It grew darker, darker, till the shining strands were the color of clear honey. Cassiana's cheeks seemed to lose their pearly luster, to turn pinker. Beth blinked and rubbed her eyes. "Are you controlling my mind so I think your skin and hair are changing color?" she asked suspiciously.

"You overestimate my powers! No, but I concentrated all the latent pigment in my skin into my hair. We rhu'ad can look almost as we choose, within certain limits—I couldn't, for instance, make my hair as dark as yours. There simply isn't enough melanin in my pigment. Even this much color wouldn't last, unless I wanted to alter my adrenalin balance permanently. I could do that, too, but it wouldn't be sensible. My hair and skin will change back to rhu'ad during the day—we keep our distinctive coloring, because it's a protection against being harmed or injured accidentally. We are important to Megaera—" abruptly she stopped again, and a mask of reticence slid down on her face. She re-engaged the spinning-cone and began to weave a surface pattern in the frame.

Beth persisted. "Can you control my body too?"

"A little," said Cassiana shortly. "Why do you think I spend so much time with you?"

Snubbed, Beth took up her spinning-cone and began to weave depth into Cassiana's surface figure. After a minute, Cassiana relented and smiled. "Oh, yes, I enjoy your company too—I did not at first, but I do now."

Beth laughed, a little shamefacedly. She had begun to like Cassiana very much—once she had grown accustomed to Cassiana's habit of an-swering what Beth was thinking, instead of what she had said.

Weeks slid into months. Beth had now lost all desire to go out of doors, although she dutifully took what slight exercise Cassiana required of her. The rhu'ad now remained with her almost continually. Although Beth was far too ill to study Cassiana, it finally became apparent even to her that Cassiana herself was far from well. The change in the rhu'ad was not marked; a tenseness in her movements, a pallor—Beth could not guess the nature of her ailment. But in spite of this, Cassiana watched over Beth with careful kindliness. Had she been Cassiana's own child, Beth thought, the rhu'ad could not have cared for her more solicitously.

Beth did not know that she was so dangerously ill as to shock Cas-siana out of her reserve. She could not walk more than a step or two without nausea and a shooting, convulsive pain. The nights were a hor-ror. She knew faintly that they had given her oxygen several times, and even this had left her half asphyxiated. And although it was now past the time when her child should have quickened, she had felt no stir of life.

Half the time she was dizzy, as if drugged. In her rare moments of lucidity, it disturbed her that Cassiana should spend her strength in tending her. But when she tried to voice this, Cassiana returned only a terse, hostile, "You think of yourself and I will take care of myself, and you too."

But once, when Cassiana thought Beth asleep, Beth heard her mutter aloud, "It's too slow! I can't wait much longer—I'm afraid!"

No news from the Terran sector penetrated her seclusion. She missed Matt, and wondered how he had managed to conceal her long absence. But she did not spend much time wondering; life, for her, had been stripped bare of everything except the fight for survival in each successive day. She had slipped so far down into this vegetable existence that she actually shuddered when Cassiana asked her one morning, "Do you feel well enough to go out of doors?" She dressed herself obediently, but roused a little when Cassiana held a heavy bandage toward her. There was compassion in her eyes.

"I must blindfold you. No one may know where the kail' rhu'ad is. It is too holy."

Beth frowned pettishly. She felt horribly ill, and Cassiana's mystical tone filled her with disbelieving disgust. Cassiana saw, and her voice softened.

She said persuasively, "You must do this, Bet'. I promise I will explain everything some day."

"But why blindfold me? Won't you trust me not to tell, if it's secret?"

"I might trust you and I might not," Cassiana returned coldly. "But there are 10,000 rhu'ad on Megaera, and I am doing this on my single responsibility." Then suddenly her hands clenched so tightly on Beth's that the Terran woman almost cried out with pain, and she said harshly, "I can die too, you know! The Terran women who have died here, don't you think anyone ever tried—" her voice trailed off, indistinct, and suddenly she began to cry softly.

It was the first time since Beth had known her that the rhu'ad had betrayed any kind of emotion. Cassiana sobbed, "Don't fight me, Bet', don't! Both our lives may depend on your personal feelings about me in the next few days—I can't reach you when you're hating me! Try not to hate me so much—"

"I don't hate you, Cassiana," Beth breathed, shocked, and she drew the Centaurian girl close and held her, almost protectively, until the stormy weeping quieted and Cassiana had herself under control again.

The rhu'ad freed herself from Beth's arms, gently, her voice reserved again. "You had better calm yourself," she said briefly, and handed Beth the scarf. "Tie this over your eyes. I'll trust you to do it securely."

.   .   .   .

Sometimes Beth tried to remember in detail what happened after Cassiana removed the blindfold, and she found herself in a vast, vaulted room of unbelievable beauty. The opalescent dome admitted a filtered, frosty glimmer of pallid light. The walls, washed in some light pigment which both absorbed and reflected colors too vague to be identified, drifted with hazy shadows. Beth was oblivious to the emotional appeal of the place—she was too alien for that—but the place was unmistakably a temple, and Beth began to be afraid. She had heard about some of the extra-terrestrial religions, and she had always suspected that the rhu'ad filled some religious function. But the beauty of the place touched even her, and gradually she became conscious of a low vibration, almost sound, pervading the entire building.

Cassiana whispered, "That's a telepathic damper. It cuts out the external vibrations and allows the augmentation of others."

The vibration had a soothing effect. Beth sat quietly, waiting, and Cassiana was altogether silent, her eyes closed, her lips moving as if she prayed, but Beth realized afterward that she was simply conversing telepathically with some unseen person. Later, she arose and led Beth through a door which she carefully closed and fastened behind them.

This inner chamber was smaller, and was furnished only with a few immense machines—Beth assumed they were machines, for they were enclosed anonymously in metallic casings, and dials and controls and levers projected chastely from a covering of gray paint—and a few small couches, arranged in pairs. Here three rhu'ad were waiting—slight patrician women who ignored Beth entirely and only glanced at Cassiana.

Cassiana told Beth to lie down on one of the couches, and, leaving her there, went to the other rhu'ad. They stood, their hands laced together, for minutes. Beth, by now habituated to Cassiana's moods, could guess that her friend was disturbed, even defiant. The others seemed equally disturbed; they shook their heads and made gestures that looked angry, but finally Cassiana's fair face looked triumphant and she came back to Beth.

"They are going to let me do what I planned. No, lie still—" she instructed, and to Beth's surprise, Cassiana lay down on the other couch of the pair. This one was located immediately beneath one of the big machines; the control panel was located in such a way that Cassiana could reach up and manipulate the dials and levers. This she proceeded to do, assuring herself that all were within easy reach; then reached across and touched Beth's pulse lightly. She frowned.

"Too fast—you're excited, or frightened. Here, hold my hand for a minute." Obediently Beth closed her hand around the one Cassiana extended. She forced back her questions, but Cassiana seemed to sense them. "Ssssh. Don't talk, Beth. Here, where the vibrations are dampered, I can control your involuntary reactions too." And, after a few minutes, the Terran woman actually felt her heartbeat slowing to normal, and knew that her breathing was quiet and natural again.

Cassiana took her hand away, reached upward, and began to adjust a dial, her delicate fingers feeling for a careful calibration. "Just lie quietly," she warned Beth, but Beth felt not the slightest desire to move. Warmth and well-being held her lapped in comfort. It was not a perceptible thing, but an intangible vibration, almost but not quite sensible to her nerves. For the first time in months, she was wholly free of discomfort.

Cassiana was fussing with the dials, touching one control, discarding another, playing the vibration now upward until it was almost visible, now downward until it disappeared into sound. Beth began to feel a little dizzy. Her senses seemed augmented, she was so wholly conscious of every nerve and muscle in her body that she could *feel* Cassiana's presence, a few feet away, through the nerves of her skin. The particular sensation identified Cassiana as completely as her voice. Beth even felt it —an odd little coldness—when one of the other rhu'ad approached the couch . . . and when she moved away again.

I suppose, she thought, this is what it feels like to be telepathic. And Cassiana's thoughts seemed to penetrate her brain like so many tiny needles: *Yes, almost like that. Actually, it's just the electrical vibration of your body being put into phase with mine. That's a kind of short-term telepathy. Each individual has his own personal wave-length. We're tuned in to each other now. We used to have to do this telepathically, and it was a horrible ordeal. Now we use the dampers, and it's easy.*

Beth seemed to float somewhere, weightless, above her body. A rhu'ad had walked through the edge of the vibratory field; Beth felt the shock of their out-of-phase bodies, as a painful electric jolt which gradually lessened as they adjusted into the vibration. Then she smelled a sharp-sweet smell, and with her augmented consciousness knew it was a smell of anesthetic—*what were they going to do?* In a spasm of panic she began to struggle; felt steady hands quieting her, heard strange voices—

Her body exploded in a million fragments of light.

The room, the machines and the rhu'ad were gone. Beth was lying on a low, wide shelf, built into the wall of a barren cubicle. She felt sick and breathless, and tried to sit up, but pain shot through her body and she lay still, blinking back tears of agony. She lay gasping, feeling the weight of her child holding her like a vise of iron.

As details came back to her clearing sight, she made out a second shelf across the room. What she had at first taken for a heap of padding was the body of a woman—it was Cassiana—sprawled face downward in an attitude of complete exhaustion. As Beth looked, the rhu'ad turned over and opened her eyes; they looked immense and bloodshot in the whiteness of her face. She whispered hoarsely, "How—do you—feel?"

"A little sick—"

"So do I." Cassiana struggled upright, got to her feet, and walked, with heavy deliberation, toward Beth. As she approached, Beth felt a sort of echo of the soothing vibration, and the pain slackened somewhat. Cassiana sat down on the edge of the shelf, and said quietly, "We are not out of danger. There is still to be—" she paused, seeking a word, and finally used the Galactic standard term, "still to be *allergic reaction*. We have to stay close together—in same kinetic field—days till the reaction is desensitized, and our body develop tolerance to the grafted—" she stopped and said sharply in Centaurian, "I have told you you must not ask me questions! You want your baby to live, don't you? Then just do as I say! I—I am sorry, Bet'—I do not mean to be angry, I do not feel very well either."

Beth knew already that Cassiana never exaggerated, but even knowing this she had not expected the violence of the next few hours. After they reached the Archonate, the world seemed to dissolve around her in a burning fever, a nausea and pain that made her previous illness seem like comfort by comparison. Cassiana, deathly pale, her hands as hot as Beth's own, did not leave her for an instant. They seemed unable to remain apart for an instant. When they were very close together, Beth felt a brief echo of the miasmic vibration which had eased her in the room of the machines; but at best this was faint, and when Cassiana drew away from her, by even a few feet, a vague, all-over trembling began in every nerve of her body, and the spasms of sickness were aggravated unbearably. The critical distance seemed about twelve feet; at that distance, the pain was almost intolerable. For hours, Beth was too miserable to notice, but it finally dawned on her that Cassiana was actually sharing this same torture. She clung to Beth in a kind of dread. Had they been less ill, Beth thought, they might have found it funny. It was a little like having a Siamese twin. But it was not funny at all. It was a grim business, urgent as survival.

They slept that night on the narrow cots pushed close together. Half a dozen times in her fitful sleep Beth woke to find Cassiana's hand nestled into hers, or the rhu'ad girl's arm flung over her shoulder. Once, in a moment of intimacy, she asked, "Do all women suffer like this—here?"

Cassiana sat up, and pushed back her long pale hair. Her smile was wry and the drawn face, in the flicker of lurid lightning that leaped and danced through the shutters, looked bitter and almost old. "No, or I fear there would be few children. Although, I'm told, when Megacra was first colonized, it was pretty bad. More than half the—the normal women died. But we found out that sometimes a normal woman could go through a pregnancy, if she was kept close to a rhu'ad constantly. I mean *constantly*. Almost from the minute of conception, she had to stay close to the rhu'ad who was helping her. It was confining for both of them. If they didn't like each other to start with—" suddenly, softly, Cassiana chuckled. "You can imagine, the way you used to feel about me!"

"Oh, Cassiana, *dear*—" Beth begged.

Cassiana went on laughing. "When they didn't hate us, they worshipped us, and that was worse. But now—well, a woman will have a little discomfort—inconvenience—you saw Nethle. But you—if I had not taken you to the kail' rhu'ad when I did, you would have died very soon. As it was I delayed almost too long, but I had to wait, because my child was not—"

"Cassiana," Beth asked her in sudden understanding, "are you going to have a baby too?"

"Of course," Cassiana said impatiently. "How could I help you if I wasn't?"

"You said, rhu'ad don't—"

"They don't usually, it's a waste of time," said Cassiana unguardedly. "Married rhu'ad are not allowed to go through a pregnancy, for now, during all the six cycles of my pregnancy and two more while I recover, no woman in our family group can have a child—" suddenly her anger came back and closed down like a black cloud between their brief intimacy. "Why do you torment me with questions?" she flung furiously at Beth. "You know I mustn't answer them! Just let me alone, let me alone, let me alone!"

She threw up her arm over her eyes, turned on her side and lay without speaking, her back to Beth; but the other, sinking into a restless doze, heard through her light sleep the sound of stifled crying. . . .

Beth thought it was the next day—she had lost consciousness of time—when she started out of sleep with the vague, all-over pain that told her Cassiana was not close to her. Voices filtered through a closed door; Cassiana's voice, muted and protesting, and Wilidh's high childish treble.

". . . but to suffer so, Cassiana, and for *her!* Why?"

"Perhaps because I was tired of being a freak!"

"Freak?" Wilidh cried, incredulous. "Is that what you call it?"

"Wilidh, you're only a child," Cassiana's voice sounded inexpressibly tender. "If you were what I am, you would know just how much we hate it. Wilidh—since I was younger than you, I have had the burden of four families on my head. In all my life, am I not to do one thing, just one, because I myself wished for it? You have had children of your own. Can't you try to understand me?"

"You have Arli—" Wilidh muttered, sulky.

"She isn't mine—not as Lassa and the twins are yours. Do you know what it's like to carry a child—to watch it die—" Cassiana's voice broke. The voices sank, were indistinct—then there was a sudden sound like a slap, and Cassiana cried out furiously, "Wilidh, tell me what Nethle has done! I'm not *asking* you, I am ordering you to tell—"

Beth heard Wilidh stammering something—then there was a stifled scream, a wailing sound, and Cassiana, her face drained of color, pushed the door and came with groping steps to Beth's side. "Bet'—wake up!"

"I'm awake—what's happened, Cassiana?"

"Nethle—*false friend, false sister*—" Cassiana's voice failed her. Her mouth moved, but no words came. She looked ghastly, sick and worn, and she had to support herself with one hand against the frame of Beth's cot. "Listen—there are—Terrans here, looking for you. They are looking for you—days now—your husband could not lie well enough, and Nethle told—" she clutched at Beth's hand. "You *cannot* leave here now. We might both die—" she stopped, her face gone impassive. There was a knock on the door.

Beth lay quiet, her eyes burning, as the door swung wide. Cassiana, a stony, statue-still figure of offended tradition, stared coldly at the two intruders who crossed the threshold. In 600 years no man had penetrated these apartments. The Terrans stood ill at ease, knowing they violated every tradition, law, custom of the planet.

"Matt!" Beth whispered, not believing.

In two strides he was beside her, but she drew away from his arms. "Matt, you promised!" she said unsteadily.

"Honey, honey—" Matt moaned. "What have they *done* to you here?" He looked down, tormented, at her thinner cheeks, and touched her forehead with disbelieving dismay. "Good God, Dr. Bonner, she's burning with fever!" He straightened and whirled on the other. "Let's get her out of here, and talk afterward. She belongs in a hospital!"

The doctor thrust the protesting Cassiana unceremoniously aside. "I'll deal with you later, young woman," he said between his teeth. He bent professionally over Beth; after a moment he turned on Cassiana again. "If this girl dies," he said slowly, "I will hold you personally responsible for denying her competent medical attention. I happen to know she hasn't been near any practitioner on the planet. If she dies, I will haul you into court if I have to take it to Galactic Center on Rigel!"

Beth pushed Matt's hand away. "Please—" she begged. "You don't realize—Cassiana's been good to me, she's tried to—" she sat up, clutching her night robe—one of Nethle's, a little too small for her—about her bare shoulders. "If it hadn't been for her—"

"Then why all this secrecy?" the doctor asked curtly. He thrust a message capsule into Cassiana's hands. "Here. This will settle it." Like a sleepwalker, Cassiana opened it, drew out the slip of flexible plastic, stared, shrugged and tossed it to Beth. Incredulous, Beth Ferguson read the legal words. Under the nominal law of the Terran Empire, they could be enforced. But this—to the wife of the Chief Archon of Megaera —she opened her mouth in silent indignation.

Matt said quietly, "Get dressed, Betty. I'm taking you to the hospital. No—" he checked her protest, "don't say a word. You aren't capable of making decisions for yourself. If Cassiana meant you any good, there wouldn't be all this business of hiding you."

Cassiana caught Beth's free hand tight. She looked desperate—trapped. "Leave her with me for three days," she made a final appeal. "She'll die if you take her away now!"

Dr. Bonner said tersely, "If you can give me a full explanation of that statement, I'll consider it. I'm a medical man. I think I'm a reasonable man." Cassiana only shook her head silently. Beth blinked hard, almost crying. "Cassiana! Can't you *tell* them—"

"Leave her with me for three days—and I'll try to get permission to tell you—" Cassiana begged helplessly. Before her despairing eyes, Matt lowered his own. "Look, Doc, we could be making a big mistake—"

"We're only delaying," the doctor said tersely. "Come on, Mrs. Ferguson, get dressed. We're taking you to the Medical HQ. If we find that this—this delay hasn't really hurt you any—" he turned and glared at Cassiana, "then maybe we'll do some apologizing. But unless you can explain—"

Cassiana said bitterly, "I am sorry, Bet'. If I were to tell now, without permission, I would not live till sunset. And neither would anyone who heard what I said."

"Are you threatening us?" Matt asked ominously.

"Not at all. Only stating a fact." Cassiana's eyes held cold contempt.

Beth was sobbing helplessly. Dr. Bonner rasped, "Pull yourself together! You'll go, or be carried. You're a sick girl, Mrs. Ferguson, and you'll do as you're told."

Cassiana said softly, "Leave her alone with me for just a few minutes, at least, while I get her dressed—"

Matt started to leave the room, but the doctor put a hand on his shoulder. "Stay with your wife. Or I will."

"Never mind," said Beth wearily, and began to get out of bed. Cassiana hovered near her, not speaking, her face sick with despair, while the Earth-woman managed to dress herself after a fashion. But as Beth, still protesting helplessly, leaned on Matt, Cassiana suddenly found her voice.

"You will do justice to remember," she said, very low, "that I have warn' you. When there come thing which you do not understand, remember. Bet'—" she looked up imploringly, then without warning she broke down and collapsed, a limp rag, on the tumbled bed. The servant women, spitting Centaurian curses, hastened to her. Beth struggled to free Matt's hands, but the two men carried her from the room.

It was like dying. It was like being physically pulled into pieces. Beth clawed and fought, knowing in some subconscious, instinctive way that she was fighting for her life, feeling strength drain out of her, second by second. The world dissolved in red fog, and she slumped down fainting in her husband's arms.

Time and delirium passed over her head. The white sterile smells of the Medical HQ surrounded her, and the screens around her bed bounded her sight except when Matt or a puzzled doctor bent over her. She was drugged, but through the sedatives there was pain and a fearful sickness and she cried and begged Matt incoherently, "Cassiana—I had to be near her, can't you understand—" and Matt only patted her hand and whispered gentle words. She dived down deep into delirium again, feeling her body burning, while faces, familiar and strange, multiplied around her, and once she heard Matt shouting in a voice that cracked like a boy's, "Damn it, she's worse than she was when we found her, *do* something, can't any of you *do* anything?"

Beth knew she was dying, and the idea seemed pleasant. Then quite suddenly, she came up to the surface of her fogged dreams to see the pallid stern face of a rhu'ad above her.

Beth's eyes and brain cleared simultaneously. The room was otherwise empty. Pinkish sunlight and a cool, pungent breeze filled the white spaces, and the rhu'ad's face was colorless and alien but full of reserved friendliness. Not only the room but the whole building seemed oddly silent; no distant voices, no hurrying footsteps, nothing but the distant hum of skycabs outside the windows, and the faint rustle of the ventilators. Beth felt a sort of drowsy, lazy comfort. She smiled, and said without surprise, "Cassiana sent you."

The rhu'ad murmured, "Yes. She nearly died too, you know. Your Terrans are—" she used a word which did not appear in Megaerean dictionaries "—but she did not forget you. I have done a fearful thing, so you must promise not to tell anyone that I've been here. I brought a damper into the building and hypnotized all the nurses on this floor. I've got to leave before they wake up. But you will get well now."

Beth pleaded, "Why is this secrecy so necessary? Why can't you just tell them what you've done? I know they didn't think I'd live, the fact that I feel better should be enough proof!"

"They would try to make me tell them, and then they would not believe me. After they see your baby, they will believe it. Then we will tell them."

Beth asked her, "Who are you?"

The rhu'ad smiled faintly and mentioned the name of one of the most important men on Megaera. Her eyes twinkled at Beth's astonishment. "They sent me rather than an unknown —in the event I *am* found here, your Terrans might hesitate to cause an international incident. But just the same I don't intend to let them see me."

"But what was the matter with me?"

"You developed an allergy to the baby. Alien tissue—blood types that didn't mix—but you'll be all right now. I haven't time to explain it," the rhu'ad finished impatiently and turned, without another word, and hurried out of the room.

Beth felt free and light, her body in comfort, without a trace of sickness or pain. She lay back on her pillows, smiling, feeling the faint stir and quickening of the child within her, then adjusted the smile to the proper angle as a nurse—one of Dr. Bonner's hard-faced old Darkovan assistants—tiptoed in, her face sheepish, and peered round the corner of the screen. Beth had to force back a spontaneous laugh at the change which came over the old lady's face as she gasped, "Oh—Mrs. Ferguson —you—you *do* look better this morning, don't you? I—I—I think Dr. Bonner had better have a look at you—" and she turned and actually ran out of the cubicle.

"But what did they *do* to you? Surely you must know what they did to you," Dr. Bonner protested tiredly for the hundredth time. "Just tell me what you remember. Even if it doesn't make sense to you."

Beth felt sorry for the old man's puzzlement. It couldn't be pleasant for him, to admit he'd failed. She said gently, "I've told you everything." She paused, trying to put it into words he could accept; she had tried to tell him about the manner in which Cassiana's physical presence had soothed her, but he had shrugged it off angrily as delirium.

"This place where they took you. Where was it?"

"I don't know. Cassiana blindfolded me." She paused again. From prolonged mental contact with Cassiana, she had come from the kail' rhu'ad with a subdued sense of having taken part in a religious ritual, but it meant nothing to her as religion, and she could only give incoherent scraps of her impressions. "A big domed room—and a room full of machines—" at his request, she described the machines in as much detail as she could remember, but he shook his head. Trying to help, she ventured, "Cassiana called one of them a telepathic damper—"

"Are you *sure?* Those things are made on Darkover, and their export is generally discouraged—even the Darkovans won't talk about them very much. The other thing could have been a Howell C-5 Electropsychometer. It must have been a special hopped-up model, though, if it could put your cell waves into phase with a telepath's!" His eyes were thoughtful. "I wonder what they did that for? It must have hurt like hell!"

"Oh, no!" Beth tried to explain just how it had felt, but he only shrugged and looked dissatisfied again. "When I examined you," he told her, and glanced sidewise at Matt, "I found an incision, about four inches long, in the upper right groin. It was almost healed over, and they'd pulled it together with a cosmetic lacquer—even under a magnifying glass, it was hard to see."

Beth said, struggling for a dim memory, "Just as I was going under the anesthetic, one of the rhu'ad said something. It must have been a technical term, because I didn't understand it. *Aghmara kedulhi varrha.* Does that mean anything to you, Dr. Bonner?"

The man's white head moved slightly. "The words mean, *placenta graft.* Placenta graft," he repeated, slowly. "Are you absolutely certain those were the words?"

"Positive."

"But that doesn't make sense, Mrs. Ferguson. Even a partial detachment of the human placenta would have caused miscarriage."

"I definitely haven't miscarried!" Beth laughed, patting her swollen body.

The old man smiled with her. "Thank God for that!" he said sincerely. But his voice was troubled. "I wish I was sure of those words."

Beth hesitated, "Maybe it was—*Aghmarda kedulhiarra va?*"

Bonner shook his head, almost smiling. "*Kedulhi*—placenta—is bad enough," he said. "*Kedulhiarra*—who ever heard of grafting a baby? No, you must have had it right the first time, I guess. Maybe they grafted, subcutaneously, some kind of placental tissue from a Centaurian. That would even explain the allergy. Possibly Mrs. Jeth-san acted as the donor?"

"Then why did she have the allergy too?" Beth asked. Dr. Bonner's heavy shoulders lifted and dropped. "God knows. All I can say is that you're a lucky, lucky girl, Mrs. Ferguson." He looked at her in unconcealed wonder, then turned to Matt. "You might as well take your wife home, Legate. She's perfectly all right. I've never seen a Terran woman look so healthy on Megaera. But stay close to home," he advised her. "I'll come over and have a look at you now and then. There must be some reason why the Centaurians go into seclusion. We'll try it with you—no sense in taking chances."

But Beth's sickness did not return. Contentedly secluded in the Residence, as snugly celled as a bee in her hive, she made tranquil preparations for the birth of her child. Nature has a sort of anesthesia for the pregnant woman; it smoothed Beth's faint disquiet about Cassiana. Matt was tender with her, refusing to discuss his work, but Beth detected lines of strain in his face and voice, and after a month of this she asked him point-blank, "Is something wrong, Matt?"

Matt hesitated—then exploded. "Everything's gone wrong! Your friend Cassiana has really messed us up properly with Rai Jeth-san! I'd counted on his cooperation, but now—" he gave a despondent shrug. "He just says, in that damned effeminate voice of his," Matt's husky baritone rose to a thin mocking echo of the Archon's accent, "peaceful settlement is what we want. Terran colonists with their wives and children we will accept, but on Megaera we will not accept floods of unmarried and unattached personnel to disturb the balance of our civilization." Matt made a furious gesture. "He knows Terrans can't bring their women here! The hell with this place, Betty—space station and all! They can blow the planet into the Milky Way, for all I care! As soon as Junior is born, and you're clear for space, I'm going to throw this job right in the Empire's face! I'll take a secretaryship somewhere—we'll probably have to go out on the fringe of the Galaxy—but at least I've got you!" He bent down to kiss his wife. "It serves me right for bringing you here in the first place!"

Beth hugged him, but she said in a distressed tone, "Matt, Cassiana saved my life! I simply can't believe that she'd turn the Archon against you. We don't deserve what Cassiana did for me—the Empire's been treating Megaera like a piece of lost-and-found property!"

Matt laughed, guilty. "Are you going in for politics?"

Beth said hotly, "You have authority to make recommendations, don't you? Why not, once, just once, do what's fair, instead of what the diplomatic manual recommends? You *know* that if you resign now, Terra will close out the Legation here, and put Megaera under martial law as a slave state! I know, the official term is protectorate satellite, but it means the same thing! Why don't you make a formal recommendation that Megaera be given dominion status, as an independent, affiliated government?"

Matt began, "To achieve that distinction, a planet has to make some important contribution to Galactic Civilization—"

"Oh, comet dust!" Beth snapped. "The fact of their survival proves that their science is ahead of ours!"

Matt said dubiously, "The Empire might agree to an independent buffer state in this end of the Galaxy. But they've been hostile to the Empire—"

"They sent a petition to Terra, 600 years ago," Beth said quietly. "Their women died by thousands while the petition was being pigeon-holed. I think they'd die all over again before they asked anything of Terra. It's Terra's turn to offer something. The Empire owes them something! Independence and affiliation—"

"Cassiana's certainly got *you* sold on Megaeran politics," Matt said sourly.

"Politics be damned!" Beth said with such heat that her husband stared. "Can't you *see* what it means, idiot—what Cassiana did? It proves that Terran women *can* come here in safety! It means that we *can* send colonists here for peaceful settlement! Can't you see, you half-wit, that's the opening Rai Jeth-san was leaving for you? Cassiana's proved a concession on their side—it's up to Terra to make the next move!"

Matt stared at her in blank surprise.

"I hadn't thought of it that way. But, honey, I believe you're right! I'll put through the recommendation, anyway. The planet's almost a dead loss now, things couldn't be worse. We've nothing to lose—and we might gain a good deal."

Beth's baby was born at the Residence—the Medical HQ did not have maternity ward facilities, and Dr. Bonner thought Beth would be more comfortable at home—on the first day of the brief Megaeran winter. She came, alert and awake, out of a brief induced sleep, and asked the usual questions.

"It's a girl." Dr. Bonner's lined old face looked tired and almost angry. "A little over three pounds, in this gravity. Try to rest, Mrs. Ferguson."

"But is she—is she all right?" Beth caught weakly at his hand. "Please tell me—please, please let me see her—"

"She's—she's—" the old doctor stumbled over a word, and Beth saw him blink hard. "She's—we're giving her oxygen. She's perfectly all right, it's just a precaution. Go to sleep, like a good girl. You can see her when you wake up." Abruptly, he turned his back and walked away.

Beth struggled against the lassitude that forced her head back. "Dr. Bonner—please—" she called after him weakly. The nurse bent over and there was the sharp prick of a needle in her arm. "Go to sleep, now, Mrs. Ferguson. Your baby's all right. Can't you hear her squalling?"

Beth sobbed, "What's the matter with him? *Is there something wrong with my baby?*" The nurse could not hold her back. Before her fierce maternity the old woman hesitated, then turned and crossed the room. "All right, I guess one look won't hurt you. You'll sleep better if you've seen her." She picked up something and came back to the bed. Beth reached out hungrily, and after a minute, smiling faintly, the Darkovan woman put the baby down on the bed beside Beth.

"Here. You can hold her for a minute. The men don't understand, do they?"

Beth smiled happily, folding back the square of blanket that lay lapped over the small face. Then her mouth fell open and she uttered a sharp cry.

"This isn't my baby! It's not—she isn't, you don't—" her eyes blurred with panicky tears. Rebelliously, scared, she looked down in terror at the baby she held.

The infant was not red or wrinkled. The smooth soft new skin was white—a shining, lustrous, *pearly* white. The tight-screwed eyes were a slaty silver, and a pallid, gilt-colored down already curled faintly on the little round head.

Perfect. Healthy. But—a rhu'ad.

The nurse dived for the baby as Beth fainted.

· · · ·

It was nearly a month before Beth was strong enough to get up during the day. Shock had played vicious havoc to her nerves, and she was very ill indeed. Her mind acquiesced, and she loved her small perfect daughter, but the unconscious conflict forced itself inward, and took revenge on every nerve of her body. The experience had left a hidden wound, too raw to touch. She sheltered herself behind her weakness.

The baby—over Matt's protest, Beth had insisted on calling the child Cassy—was more than a month old when one afternoon her Centaurian servant came into her room and announced, "The Archon's wife has come to visit you, Mrs. Legate Furr-ga-soon."

Beth had forced the memory so deep that she only thought that Nethle or Wilidh had come to pay a formal call. She sighed and stood up, sliding her bare feet into scuffs, and padding across to her dressing panel. She twisted buttons, playing out lengths of billowing nylene to cover her short indoor chemise, and slid her head into the brusher which automatically attended to her short hair. "I'll go up. Take Cassy down to the nursery, will you?"

The Centaurian girl murmured, "She has her baby—with her."

Beth stared in stupefaction. No wonder the servant girl had seemed thunderstruck. A baby outside its own home, on Megaera?

"Bring her down here, then—" she directed. But that did not dull her surprise when a familiar, lightly moving form shrouded in pale robes, ghosted into the room.

"Cassiana!" she said tremulously.

The ruh'ad smiled at her affectionately as they clasped hands. Then suddenly Beth threw her arms around Cassiana and broke down in a tempest of stormy crying.

"Don't, don't—" Cassiana pleaded, but it was useless. All the suppressed fear and shock had broken loose at once, and Cassiana held her, awkwardly, as if unused to this kind of emotion, trying to comfort, finally bursting into tears herself. When she could speak again steadily, she said, "Can you believe me, Beth, if I say I know how you are feeling? Look, you must try to pull yourself together, I have promised I'd explain to you—"

She freed herself gently, and from the servant's arms she took a bundle, carefully shielded in tough, transparent plastic, with double handles for carrying. She opened the package carefully and from the depths of this ingenious cradle she lifted a wrapped baby, held it out and put it into Beth's arms.

"This is my little boy—"

Beth finally raised her eyes to Cassiana, who was standing, fascinated, by Cassy's crib. "He—he—he looks like—" Beth faltered, and Cassiana nodded. "That's right. He is a Terran child. But he's mine. Rather—he's ours." Her earnest eyes rested on the other in something like appeal. "I promised to explain—*Dhe mhári*, Bet', don't start to cry again. . . ."

"We rhu'ad would probably have been killed, anywhere except on Megeara," Cassiana began, a few minutes later, when they had settled down together on a cushioned divan, the babies snuggled down in pillows between them. "Here, we saved the colony. Originally, I think, we were a cosmic ray mutation. We were part of the normal population then. We hadn't adapted quite so far." She paused. "Do you know what Genetic Drift is? In an isolated population, hereditary characteristics just drift away from normal. I mean—suppose a colony had, to begin with, half blonde people, and half brunette. In a normal society, it would stay distributed like that—about 50-50 per cent. But in one generation, just by chance, it might vary as far as 60-40. In the next generation, it could go back to normal, or—the balance once having been changed—it could keep drifting, and there would be 70 per cent of blondes and only 30 per cent of brunettes. That's oversimplified, of course, but if that keeps up for eight or ten generations, with natural selection working hard too, you get a distinct racial type. We had two directions of drifting, because we had the normal population, and—we had the rhu'ad. Our normal women were dying—more in every generation. The rhu'ad could have children safely, but somehow, we had to preserve the normal type."

She picked up Cassy and snuggled her close. "Did you name her for me, then?" she asked. "Well—I started to explain. A rhu'ad is human, and perfectly normal, except—they will find it out about Cassy some day —we have, in addition to our other organs, a *third* ovary. And this third ovary is parthenogenetic—self-reproducing. We could have perfectly human, normally sexed children, either male or female, who would breed true to the normal human type. They were even normally susceptible to the poisonous reaction in this air. These normal children were carried, in the normal way, except that a rhu'ad mother was immune to the hormone reaction, and could protect a normal child. Or, a rhu'ad woman could, from the *third* ovary, *at her own will*—we have control over all our reflexes, including conception—have a *rhu'ad*, female child. Any rhu'ad can reproduce, duplicate herself, without male fertilization. I never had a father. No rhu'ad does."

"Is *Cassy*—"

Cassiana paid no attention to the interruption. "But the mutation is female. While the normal women were dying, and only the rhu'ad could have children—and even these children died when they grew up—we were afraid that in three or four generations we would end with an all-female, parthenogenetic, all-rhu'ad society. No one wanted that. Least of all the rhu'ads themselves." She paused. "We have all the instincts of normal women. I *can* have a child without male fertilization," she looked searchingly at Beth, "but that does not change the fact that I—I love my husband and I want *his* children—like any other woman. Perhaps more—being telepathic. That's an emotional problem, too. We have done our part for Megaera, but we—we want to be women. Not sexless freaks!"

She paused, again, then continued, evidently searching for words. "The rhu'ad are almost completely adaptable. We tried implanting rhu'ad gametes—ova—from our normal ovaries, into normal women. It didn't work, so finally they evolved the system we have today. A rhu'ad becomes pregnant in the normal way—" for the first time Beth saw her blush slightly, "and carries her child for two, maybe three months. By that time, the unborn child builds up a *temporary* immunity against the toxins released by the hormone allergy. Then they transfer this two-month embryo into the host mother's womb. The immunity lasts long enough that the baby can be carried to full term, and birthed. Then, of course, there's no more danger at all, for a male child—or, for a female child, no more danger until she grows up and herself becomes pregnant.

"Another thing: After a woman has her first child like that, she also builds up a very slight immunity to the hormone reaction. For a woman's second child, or third, or more, it is sufficient to transplant a fertilized ovum of six or seven days . . . provided that there is a rhu'ad within immediate call, to stabilize the chemistry in case anything goes wrong. One or more of my families always has a woman who is pregnant, so I must be continuously available."

"Isn't that terribly hard on you?" Beth asked.

"Physically, no. We've done what they do with prize cattle all over the

Empire—hyperovulation. At certain days in each cycle, rhu'ads are given particular hormone and vitamin substances, so that we release not one ovum, but somewhere between four and twelve. Usually they can be transferred about a week later, and the operation is almost painless—"

"Then *all* the children in your four—families, are *yours*, and your husband's?"

"Why, no! Children belong to the woman who bears them and gives birth to them—and to the man who loves that woman, and mates with her!" Cassiana laughed. "Oh, I suppose all societies adapt their morals to their needs. To me, it's a little—nasty, for man to have just one wife, and live with her all year. And aren't you terribly lonely, with no other women in your house?"

It was Beth's turn to blush. Then she asked, "But you said those were normal children. Cassy—Cassy is a rhu'ad—"

"Oh yes. I couldn't do with you what I'd have done with a Centaurian. You had no resistance at all, and you were already pregnant. Women *do* become pregnant sometimes, in the ordinary way, on Megaera—we are strict about contraceptive laws, but nothing is entirely reliable—and when they do, they die, unless a rhu'ad will take for them the risk I took for you. I had done it once before, for Clotine, but the baby I had died—well, during those three days while you were shut up alone, I went to the kail' rhu'ad, and put myself under a damper—and became pregnant. By myself."

A thousand tiny hints were suddenly falling into place in Beth's mind. "Then you did graft—"

Cassiana nodded. "That's right. When we went together to the kail' rhu'ad, the dampers put us into phase—so the cellular wave lengths wouldn't vary enough to throw the babies into shock—and just exchanged the babies."

Beth had been expecting this; but even so, Cassiana's casual tone was a shock. "You really—"

"Yes. My little boy is—by heredity alone—your child and the Legate's. But he is mine. He lived because I—being rhu'ad—could carry him in safety, and manage to stabilize his reactions to the hormone allergy with the atmosphere. There was no question of Cassy's safety: a rhu'ad baby, even a rhu'ad embryo, is perfectly adaptable, even to the alien environment of a Terran body. The first few days were so crucial because you and I both developed allergies to the grafted alien tissue; our bodies were fighting the introduction of a foreign kind of substance. But once we mother-hosts began to develop a tolerance, I could stabilize myself, and my little boy, and you—and when you were taken from me too soon, I could send another rhu'ad to complete the stabilization. There was no need to worry about Cassy; she simply adapted to the poisonous condition which would have killed a normal child."

She picked up Cassy and rocked her almost wistfully. "You have a most unusual little daughter, Bet'. A perfect little parasite."

Beth looked down at Cassiana's little boy. Yes, she could trace in his face a faint likeness to the lines of Matt's, and yet—hers? No. Cassy was hers, borne in her body—she wanted to cry again.

Cassiana leaned over and put an arm around her. "Bet'," she said quietly, "I have just come from the Legation HQ, where—with full permission of the Council of Rhu'ad—I have laid before them a complete, scientific account of the affair. I have also been allowed to assure the Terran authorities that when Terran colonists come here to build the Space Station, their women will be safe. We have suggested that colonists be limited to families who have already had children, but we will give assurance that an accidental pregnancy need not be disastrous. In return I received assurance, forwarded from Galactic Center, that Megaera will receive full dominion status as an independent planetary government associated with the Empire. And we are being opened to colonization."

"Oh, how wonderful!" Beth cried impulsively. Then doubt crept into her voice. "But so many of your people hate us—"

The rhu'ad smiled. "Wait until your women come. Unattached men, on Megaera, could only make trouble. Men have so many different basic drives! An Empire man from Terra is nothing like a Centaurian from Megaera, and a Darkovan from Thendara is different from either—take ten men from ten different planets, and you have ten different basic drives—so different that they can only lead to war and ruin. But women —all through the Galaxy, Terran, Darkovan, Samarran, Centaurian, Rigelian—women are all alike, or at least they have a common basic area. A baby is the passport to the one big sorority of the universe. And admission is free to every woman in the Galaxy. We'll get along."

Beth asked numbly, "And you were convinced enough of that to risk your life for a Terran who—hated you? I'm ashamed, Cassiana."

"It wasn't entirely for you," Cassiana admitted. "You and your husband were Megaera's first and last chance to avoid being a backwater of the Galaxy. I planned this from the minute I first saw you. I—I wasn't your friend, either, at first."

"You—you *couldn't* have known I'd get pregnant—"

Cassiana looked shamed and embarrassed. "Bet'. I—I planned it, just as it happened. I'm a telepath. It was my mental command that made you stop taking your anti shots."

Beth felt a sudden surge of anger so great that she could not look at Cassiana. She had been manipulated like a puppet—

She felt the rhu'ad's thin hand on her wrist. "No. Only a fortuitous accident in the way of destiny. Bet', look at them—" Her free hand touched the two babies, who had fallen asleep, cuddled like two little animals. "They are sister and brother, in more than one way. And perhaps you will have other children. You belong to us, now, Bet'."

"My husband—"

"Men will adapt to anything, if their women accept it," Cassiana told her. "And your daughter is a rhu'ad—who will grow up in a Terran home. There will be others like her. In her turn she will help the daughters of Terran families who come here, until science finds a new way and each woman can bear her own children again—or until Centaurians take their place, moving out into the Galaxy with the rest—"

And Beth knew in her heart that Cassiana was right.

Snow

C. H. Sherman

It is always a pleasure to feature a new story by C. H. SHERMAN, *who, under another name, is a TV and theatre actor. Alternately tender and (in this case, literally) chilling Sherman tales such as "Doll-Baby," "Kaena Point," "Teacher" and "In the Valley of the Shades" have appeared, respectively, in* GuildAmerica Books *collections* Witches & Warlocks, Haunted America, Lovers & Other Monsters *and* Masterpieces of Terror and the Unknown.

IT'S ONE FORTY-FIVE in the morning. I'm sorry my handwriting is so bad but truly my fingers are frozen. Literally. Well, almost. In fact, that's why I'm writing this. I'm afraid my fingers will freeze to the point where I can't hold the pen and I want to write down what happened in case I forget later. Mike is asleep in the back seat. The map light in the glove compartment gives me enough light to see without waking him up. I'm writing in my psych notebook since no way can I even think about working on my paper (which I was supposed to have finished over the weekend). Mike and I are trying not to use up all our gas and we don't want to wear out the battery either so we're not running the car much at all. My feet are getting so cold.

I know we left too late last night. We should have spent the night but we wanted to get back in time for Mike's football practice, which is probably cancelled now, isn't it? Dad was right. The storm turned out to be a bruiser. But we have front-wheel-drive and we've gotten through some pretty rough storms in the past so we didn't think we'd have too big a problem. Actually, we made pretty good time considering the condition of the roads. The snow was heavy but there wasn't any ice and not too many other cars were out so we made it to exit 24 by twelve-thirty. I wanted to get off and look for a motel but Mike said we only had three exits to go. He's a good driver so we kept going.

The wind started kicking up maybe a mile past the exit and suddenly we couldn't see the road or anything. It was a white-out. Remember how I always said I thought a white-out would be exciting? Wrong. It's one of the most frightening things I've ever been through in my life. We couldn't even see the reflection of our headlights. Just a white wall, nothing else. And there was no sound either except for the windshield wipers even though they weren't doing any good at all. The defroster melted the snow on the windshield just enough to ice it up so that the newer snow froze. The wipers finally got stuck halfway. We couldn't even tell if we were still on the road.

Mike is very smart, you know, because he turned off the lights and the wipers so we wouldn't drain the battery. They weren't doing us any good anyway. We kept the radio and the heater on, though, because we decided to keep going until we got to the next exit. Then we'd find a motel so we could watch movies on cable for two days while they plow the roads. If the coffee shop workers couldn't get in we'd fix our own food and make food for everybody in the motel. It would be like a big party or going away to camp except we'd have a nice room and a TV.

Mike did a good job, Mom and Dad. He drove carefully and not too fast but it was just impossible to see the road. Then the snow suddenly stopped and so did the wind. Mike stuck his head out of the window and realized that we must be under the Route 63 overpass. So we decided to stop. We figured we'd be protected from the snow for a while. And we'd be warm because the tunnel would be like a burrow. He told me he wanted to make sure I'd be safe. So that's where we've stopped to wait out the storm.

I've got to warm up my fingers. I'll write again in a little while.

It's now two-twenty. Thank you, thank you, thank you, Mom, for the chocolate-chip cookies and the oranges! I was surprised how hungry we are since we haven't been on the road that long. We've decided to ration our food in case we have any trouble once the snow stops. Which could be hours from the look of things. I'm eating my cookies one bite at a

time so they'll last longer. I think Mike is planning on sleeping through
this whole thing. He's like a big old bear hibernating through the winter. I'm glad he filled the tank after we left the house. He said he wanted
to make sure we didn't run out of gas since it might take us a little
longer to get back to school. What an understatement, huh? When we
stopped Mike said that it would be smarter to turn off the car so we
don't use up all our gas. And we don't want to choke to death on carbon
monoxide either. But that also means no heat.

It's surprising that everything is sort of grey in the car even though
the little map light is the only thing on. I guess the whiteness of the snow
keeps it from being totally dark. We're not keeping the radio on either
because Mike is still worried about the battery. I tried getting in the back
seat too so that we could snuggle together for warmth (very romantic
but NOTHING HAPPENED, DAD) and we fell asleep for awhile.

I can't seem to sleep for very long at all. I don't know whether it's
because it's so cramped in the backseat or that Mike snores a little. Not a
lot but enough to keep waking me up. When you use your coat for a
blanket instead of a coat it's much warmer than when it's a coat, did you
know that? We put Mike's coat on the seat and mine on top of us like a
sandwich and we slept like Hansel and Gretel in the oven. Wait a
minute, they didn't actually sleep in the oven, did they? It's funny, but I
can't remember what happens to them.

This is really kind of an adventure, the sort of story we can tell our
grandchildren some day. Not that Mike has asked me to marry him or
anything. Who knows, maybe he'll ask me while we're *butt*—stuck in
this snowstorm. What a romantic ending, huh?

I'm sorry we missed seeing Gina and Carl. I know they were probably
smart not to come over on Thanksgiving since he had the flu. I'm sorry
he was sick but I wish Gina could have come by herself, you know, just
for the day. She could have brought back some turkey and stuff for him.
It's been a long time since I've seen her. I miss her.

I'm going to try to take another little nap. My fingers are stiff and
hurting. I've got to stop again. Now I know what it must be like for old
people with arthritis.

4:25 A.M. I woke up freezing. Mike had one of the front windows
open. He said he was going to climb out and go for help. I went crazy. I
started screaming at him and punching him. I didn't want him to leave
me. He was so calm. He asked if I wanted to come along. I started to cry

and I couldn't stop. Mom, what would you have done? He made a lot of sense but why leave the car where we're safe and we're together? I told him it was just a matter of time before we get rescued. Finally he yelled at me—which he never does—and said that he had to at least try to find help. He made me promise not to run the car unless the cold is unbearable because he said you can't smell carbon monoxide. I told him I'd promise to only run it for ten minutes at a time if he'd promise not to forget me. Then he said the sweetest thing. He said he could never forget the woman he was going to marry. Then he kissed me good-bye and climbed out the window. There was so much snow in the car that it was freezing again. When I finally got the window rolled up I couldn't even see where he had gone.

It's so quiet.

5:05 A.M. What if Mike doesn't come back for me? I might die here waiting for him. When he left I told myself if he wasn't back in two hours I'd better save myself and climb out the window too. It shouldn't be too hard to get to a motel or a gas station since we're right at Route 63. But now I'm not sure what to do. Maybe I should just wait here for him. I know he loves me and he'd never just leave me. That's why he left. To get help. But what if he can't find anybody to help him? What if he can't find the car again? I don't want to die here alone. Mom, what should I do?

8:13. Please, please help me. Mike's gone. I can't   8:33. Trying to stop shaking. Be calm. The heater doesn't seem to be working very well. I've got it on high but still freezing. Lucky I got the car started at all. My clothes are wet and I lost one of my gloves. Please don't be mad at me. I'm trying to take deep breaths so I can write down what happened. I tried to help Mike but I couldn't. I tried to get out. Please come get me. I want to go home.

I left Mike a note telling him that I'd gone just in case he couldn't find me. So he wouldn't worry. I opened the window and started digging my way out. The snow was heavier than I thought it would be. I braced my feet on the bottom of the open window and dug upwards so that I could stand on top of the car to get my bearings. I figured it would just take me a few minutes but it was harder than I expected and I had trouble breathing. I wanted to rest but it was so cold I dug as hard as I could.

Suddenly there he was. Just as I was trying to find him, he was coming back for me. I grabbed his hand as hard as I could to let him know that I was all right. I waited for him to pull me up but the snow was so heavy that I thought it would be easier for me to climb up to him. My face stung and I kept getting snow in my mouth. I was crying because he had come back to save me after all. My body felt like it weighed a ton. It took me forever to get face to face. I kissed him as hard as I could.

I can't stop crying. He looked so

8 something. The radio station isn't coming in at all now. Maybe we broke the antenna but also the tunnel maybe might be keeping out the signal so I don't know if it's stopped snowing yet. So cold. You're coming to get me, though, aren't you? Mike's not here now so I need you to take me home. I'm in the car under the underpass at route 6 you know, what is it route 65? 63? You know, near That's where I am because I've only got one more orange and I didn't stay in the car like Mike told me to. I'm so scared, Mom and Dad. Mike tried but the snow froze him. I'm still here though because I love him so much and I love you so much, Mom and Daddy, and I'm starting to get afraid because it's really cold. He was floating. All blue. I'm alone and I don't feel very good right now. He couldn't save me and I couldn't save him. Am I sweating because I ate so much snow? I rolled the window back up but there's a lot of snow in the car. I think I'll take nap first then when I wake up I'll wake him up Mike and we can swimming together unless we just stay maybe would be better idea if you just wake up wake wake us up when you get here sleep well and dont forget I love you mom and love you Dad don't forge to wake m

Dangerous Women

Let no man after me
Be forced to follow
The path of love I trod.
  —*Patterned on a haiku by Hitomaro*
  (c. A.D. 760)

Lydia's Season

Patricia Mullen

PATRICIA MULLEN *divides her time between writing and the stage. Affiliated with New York University and Manhattan's prestigious Circle-in-the-Square theatre company, Pat has recently completed an epic fantasy,* The Stone Movers, *to be published in 1995 by Warner Aspect Books. An earlier tale, "The Curse of the Wandering Gypsy," appeared in my GuildAmerica Books anthology* Witches & Warlocks.

IF NEIGHBORS WONDER about Lydia Barkley, or worry about what she's done, a glance at her rose garden reassures them. Lydia owns the house down at the end of the block. It's the small Victorian with the gingerbread facade and narrow side yard, right across from the railroad tracks. On either side of the brick walkway, her floribundas flood the yard with shades of red and yellow. Around back, the old-fashioned parlor and the big kitchen form an el, making a sunny nook where white climbing roses cascade from a weathered trellis. The whole yard is edged by the pink rose called Betty Prior. It's Lydia's favorite: a simple, six-petaled tea rose, a bit old fashioned, like Lydia herself. It's a pretty place, neat and well kept up. Most folks figure that things are just as they seem. Or so you would think. Maybe they are.

The street that runs past the house has no sidewalks, so in winter the snow plow piles up drifts as high as your head in the front yard. It's right in front of Lydia's parlor where the drifts get the highest, so that some winters you can't see into her windows and she can't see out. Come spring, the drifts are the last things to melt, so when roses are blooming on the south side of the house, there's still six inches of grimy snow down by the mailbox.

In winter, neighbors all along the street savor their seed and rose catalogs so, come spring, they can wage their friendly competitions over who's got the first crocus or liveliest forsythia. In the rose category, Lydia's big floribunda rosebush in front of the window is almost always the first to bloom in the spring. In the fall her Betty Priors are often the last flowers anywhere along the street. The reason is that she tends them. Like lots of things in a person's life, they want time. From the first leaf after she's raked back the mulch, to the last petals when the winds have gotten cold and it's time to prune back, Lydia's yard is an orderly riot of color.

Winters you can't do much outdoors in this part of Massachusetts except shovel snow. Hidden by snowdrifts, Lydia puts her time into her kitchen instead of the garden. There's always a wonderful smell of baking from her place on Saturday mornings. At Sunday church socials she comes with cakes and pies and even dainty pastries that nobody else has the nerve to try, let alone show in public.

A while back on weekday mornings, early, you'd see Lydia briskly walking the eight blocks to her job at the plant. It's a big plant in the old mill building on River Street, and it needs a big switchboard for all its departments. Lydia used to run that switchboard, placing all the incoming calls with the right people. When she couldn't find someone where he ought to be, it was her voice you heard over the PA system, pleasantly tracking them down. Although lots of folks from work knew her voice and the neighbors knew her roses and had tasted her cakes and pies, not many saw the inside of her house until Charlie Broome came back to town.

Charlie and Lydia had probably seen each other in high school, but she'd been shy then, and plain, too. Charlie was a couple of years ahead of her, which in high school is as good as a generation gap, so he'd never noticed her. He'd married a pretty girl he met in college, joined the sales force at the plant right out of school and gotten transferred to a branch office in the Mid-West. He'd done well over the years and now he was back, Vice-President In Charge of Sales. That had been his ambition when he was young, but it seemed like nothing now. He was a widower and childless, quite a bit heavier and redder in the face than he used to be. He'd had a heart attack the year before. It had frightened him, so he was trying to stop smoking and to lose weight.

Charlie was lonely. He didn't like New England as well as he'd liked the Mid-West, and being Vice-President wasn't nearly as challenging as being a salesman had been. All his old high school friends had become strangers. Alone in the bedroom of his hotel suite, he couldn't remember his dead wife's face without the help of a photograph.

Age is a great equalizer in women. Pretty ones lose their bloom and, if life is hard enough, their plain sisters can develop character. Lydia had pretty much lost her shyness listening to her own voice in the PA system over the years, and anyone who grows roses in defiance of New England winters is bound to grow character.

With nothing else to do, Charlie often worked late. It was Lydia's custom to work until the last calls were made. Sometimes she and Charlie would talk while he placed his many long distance calls, and before long he began lingering by the switchboard in the evenings. One miserable, sleet-pounded autumn night, he drove her home. The next day she brought a small, lemon-frosted cake to the office as thanks. The weather was clear and cold that day, but he drove her home again, anyway. This time she invited him in, and they talked for a while.

Lydia's home was bright and spotless inside. She kept her glass and china bric-a-brac dusted and shiny in her mother's cherry wood sideboard. Her African violets prospered in the north light of the kitchen where she baked cakes in a large, old-fashioned oven. Charlie seemed interested in everything and the third time he drove her home she even showed him her travel brochure collection. Lydia had collected brochures of almost every part of the world. When Charlie began dropping by regularly, Lydia went out and bought delicate little ash trays.

She had two cats, an ancient grey Persian and a scruffy tabby tom. The cats didn't like Charlie. They were used to napping in the evenings while Lydia read or worked in the kitchen. Whenever Charlie lit up a cigarette, the tabby would leave the room. He started looking scruffy and staying out at night. The old Persian established himself years before on the floral slip-covered chair, the best chair in the living room. Now he made hostile humming sounds when Charlie dislodged him to sit down. The cat scratched Charlie's hand one evening, and after that Lydia closed him in the bedroom whenever Charlie came over. You could hear him calling in high-pitched, kitten-like mews from half-way down the block. On evenings when Charlie stayed late, the tabby tom sometimes came home and sat glaring from the middle of the parlor rug.

Lydia was surprised at how much she enjoyed Charlie's company. He had a salesman's ability to talk about what interested the other person most, and Lydia found that she could talk to him about gardens and traveling. She discovered his favorite pastries and loved to surprise him with them. She was pleased with the admiration he showed at her careful frosting decorations. She was flattered by his astonishment that she had canned the peaches in the upside-down cake herself.

Lydia's life changed upside-down when Charlie came into it. Her few friends had long since given up trying to introduce her to what they considered a suitable match. With Charlie, she discovered for the first time the subtle esteem a woman acquires from being in the company of a successful man. Neighbors no longer called on her just to ask her to donate at the next church social or to help arrange the Washington's Birthday supper at the Community Hall. Now they asked her and Charlie to their homes for dinner. At the plant, when someone needed Charlie, they were just as likely to drop by the switchboard and ask Lydia where he was. And she was just as likely to know.

At Christmas, Charlie drove Lydia and some other ladies to the children's ward of the county hospital where great quantities of toys, cookies and candy were given as gifts. At Lydia's suggestion, Charlie had gone out and bought gifts of his own the week before. He'd bought half a dozen cap pistols for the boys and some toy irons for the girls because he didn't know what else girls would like. He'd started to wrap them himself, but he was all thumbs. He finally stopped in exasperation and paid the maid at the hotel to do it. Lydia said the packages were beautiful and the children would love them. Charlie didn't tell her that he hadn't done it himself.

But he told friends later that when he saw the children and the way that Lydia laughed and talked with them, he was stirred. When he stood beside the tree singing Silent Night, looking at Lydia as she held a sad-eyed three-year-old in her arms, he nearly cried for the sheer aching joy of giving Christmas to someone else.

No one was surprised (except perhaps Lydia) when Charlie asked her to marry him. She asked for time to consider it and called a friend who immediately told every other mutual acquaintance in town. The proposal was gravely discussed for an entire week, everyone assuming the final result but enjoying the speculation. When Lydia finally said yes, Charlie announced that he had already decided to take two weeks off in March for their honeymoon. A neighbor agreed to take care of the cats and the African violets while they were away.

They were married on a blustering, cold Massachusetts morning, and that afternoon they boarded a plane for a flight to Florida. Charlie had arranged their honeymoon to include Disneyworld and side trips to many of the places his bride had studied for years in her travel brochures. But Lydia worried about the cats, and they returned a few days early. Florida had been rainy. Lydia was reluctant to hurt Charlie's feelings, but she didn't really like the confusion of traveling. She found palm trees ugly. She much preferred the graceful maples that lined the street at home.

Charlie went back to work while Lydia stayed at home, making the house pleasant for him to come home to. As she learned more about his heart condition and aware of cholesterol, she changed the way she cooked. She served more vegetables at dinner. She baked less, and when she did, she used substitutes for butter. Her cakes no longer had the subtle richness that had made them the most sought after in the church bazaars, but she was making Charlie healthier, so she didn't mind.

At the plant, they were busy upgrading the phone system. Charlie told her funny stories about how the new system constantly fouled things up. "But it's all automation, now," he told her, "you married me just in time. You would have been out of a job!"

The tabby tom, who had taken to staying out more and more, didn't come home one morning. Lydia was upset and searched the neighborhood. Even Charlie went out that evening to look for him. He told a neighbor that he felt like an idiot calling "Tom! Here kitty, kitty, kitty!" but he was a good sport about it. If he was secretly relieved when there was no sign of the tom, he never said a word. Lydia went on searching for days, but it didn't seem likely that a cat could survive the blizzard that blew up.

Lydia was sad and quiet for a while after that. To cheer her up, Charlie stopped at a shop and bought a German shepherd puppy to take the place of the tom. The grey Persian, old as he was, instantly terrorized the puppy, who wet on the carpet as soon as Charlie set him down. Lydia was moved that Charlie had meant to cheer her up, but she'd never owned a dog and seemed a little more surprised than pleased. Charlie reassured her that puppies are easy to love. He mopped up all the spots on the rug, and even took the puppy for walks in the evening so Lydia wouldn't be bothered with him.

Lydia's cooking and the puppy's demands for exercise did wonders for Charlie. His spirits soared, his midriff shrank and a plan slowly formed in his mind. On Lydia's birthday in April, he told her of his life's dream and that he had decided to make it a reality for them both.

To prepare for his announcement, he bought Lydia a huge birthday cake, far more than the two of them could eat alone. On the way home he stopped off at the car dealer to pick up the new recreational vehicle he'd ordered. It would sleep two and had a small kitchen and a large lounge with a TV. It wouldn't fit in the narrow driveway, so he parked it in the street in front of the house. Attracted by the commotion, the puppy barked and whined, running to Charlie as Lydia opened the door to see what was happening. Charlie pushed the dog aside and kissed his astonished wife. He said Happy Birthday and told her his plan.

He had already handed in his resignation at the plant. He was past retirement age and his pension would be generous. Their car had been the down payment for the RV and he had put the house on the market. With what they had in the bank, they would have enough financial security to travel all over the country for the rest of their lives. Or, if they saw the right place, they were free to settle down wherever they liked. He'd always wanted to see the coast of Northern California—or maybe Mexico. They'd see it all and pick the choicest spot for themselves. Above all, they would lead the active life-style his doctors recommended.

Lydia was too overwhelmed to say anything but "Oh, Charlie." The old Persian scratched the puppy's nose and retreated under the couch, humming ominously. Charlie crawled under and got him, stuck him out on the back porch, and took Lydia out to dinner.

In the restaurant, they met some friends from the plant. The man who would be replacing Charlie told them about the Pueblos of the Southwest. Someone else talked about trout fishing in a certain stream in northern Michigan that was beloved of Hemingway and known to only a few enthusiasts. Before the evening was over, he'd drawn a map for Charlie.

The RV wasn't as big as it looked at first, but Charlie seemed to delight in organizing ways of packing things to save room. "Like a ship," he said enthusiastically. "We'll keep it spanking clean and neat, just like a ship's galley." He was just as careful about choosing the clothes that Lydia and he would need on their travels. If Lydia seemed disappointed at the space in the RV, she didn't come right out and say it. She was never outspoken, and some of her old shyness had come back since she'd left her job.

There were three generations of accumulated treasures in the attic to be disposed of. Charlie tried to help, but Lydia spent so much time just reading letters of her mother's—even trying on her grandmother's bridal dress—that nothing got done. He noticed that she'd been so tired lately that sometimes she didn't cook dinner, just went to bed early. Finally he had a couple of hired men come in to clear out the attic while he took her out to celebrate.

As the final day of his retirement approached, Charlie also took to washing dishes for her in the evening or early mornings before he went down to the plant. He couldn't figure where all the pots and dishes were stored, so he put them away wherever he could, and made a mental note to pick up a lightweight set of cookware for the RV.

The puppy was gaining weight and asserting himself. The grey Persian stayed in the bedroom more and more, leaving only when Charlie nudged him off the bed at night. One morning the shepherd raided the cat's food dish. The cat protested for a moment but then retreated, sick at his stomach the rest of the day. Charlie said he probably had hair balls.

They left in early May. Lydia had raked the mulch off the roses the day before and dug in fertilizer. She'd locked the dog on the back porch while the grey Persian rolled on his back in the sunshine and chased last fall's leaves beside her as she worked.

Charlie was sorry he'd never seen her roses bloom, for he'd met her the autumn before, after the frost had set in. But mostly he was excited about the trip. He'd stored everything so well that they had a little extra space, and he seemed not to notice when Lydia packed a small cardboard box with garden things they'd never need. While Charlie walked the dog around the neighborhood for final goodbyes, Lydia stayed in the house waiting for a friend who was going to take the African violets and some of the kitchen things.

Charlie said he wanted to see that stream in Michigan first. It was on a dirt road deep in the woods, miles from the nearest house. It was as beautiful as he'd been told, and twice as wild. He let the dog run loose in the woods and told Lydia that for the first time in his life he felt totally free. Since the kitchen in the RV was too small to be comfortable, he did most of the cooking over the campfire. The larder was well stocked and when he didn't catch trout in the stream, he heated up something from a can.

Lydia asked him once or twice over beans and franks if he didn't miss her cooking and baking. He hugged her and said he never wanted her to work that hard again. She tried to say that baking had never been work, she had loved doing it, but Charlie laughed and said his waistline had loved it, too. Maybe too much.

Saturday, he and Lydia dressed up and drove into town to a movie. On Sunday, he took a long hike with the dog. Although he tried to get Lydia to come, she wanted to stay behind and straighten the RV. The woods were beautiful and Charlie decided to stay on another week. That was the joy of traveling this way, he told her. Things could be flexible.

The next day the accident happened. The dog, who had taken to teasing the old Persian whenever he had nothing better to do, prowled the area of the RV all morning, ambushing the cat at unexpected moments. The Persian beat retreat after retreat, spitting, hounded, always in search of a private place to recover his dignity. Lydia tried to stop it, but the cat was miserable shut up in the stuffy RV and Charlie wouldn't hear of tying up the dog in country like this. He said he thought the Persian was really playing as much as the dog was. They needed to have time to get used to each other.

Just before lunch, the dog charged again and the cat bolted in panic. The first car to come down the road in a week swerved to avoid the barking dog and struck the cat instead. The Persian's back was broken and he moaned in stunned agony as the dog seized him and shook him roughly from side to side in his jaws.

Lydia screamed at the dog as she tore the dying cat away, cradling him in her arms. The Persian was past caring. Charlie took him gently from her and carried him out of earshot to put him out of his misery. When he finally returned to the clearing, Lydia still wept, but silently, her shoulders shaking. Charlie reassured her that he had buried the cat in a lovely forest glade and placed a pine bough over his grave.

After the first shock, Lydia just stared at Charlie in a wild way he had never seen before. She said little the rest of the afternoon, puttering in the RV, packing and unpacking the garden things she'd brought along in the cardboard box. Her eyes were red-rimmed, and she spent a long time fondling the senseless things she'd brought, like the old rose shears and the can of pesticide. But she roused enough to cook dinner that night.

About an hour later, Charlie began to feel ill. There was no phone, of course, and Lydia couldn't drive, so she had to leave him to walk out and get help. It took hours. By the time she returned with a doctor, Charlie was dead.

She stayed for the inquest. Everyone was very considerate. Given Charlie's medical history and the doctor's testimony, the coroner ruled it was a heart attack. There was no autopsy. Lydia had his body cremated and shipped to the Mid-West to be buried beside his first wife. Within a week of Charlie's death, the dog ran away and Lydia found a buyer for the RV. Since the house hadn't sold, she took it off the market and moved back in. Charlie's insurance made it possible for her not to have to go back to work, and the first roses bloomed shortly after she got back.

Lydia spent the rest of the summer spraying and tending her flowers. Although she hadn't been there to tend them that spring, they'd never bloomed as beautifully as they did that year. In the fall she found a stray kitten, and at Christmas she went with the other ladies to the county hospital with gifts and cookies for the children.

Spirits

Ivan Turgenev

Though many 1990s movies, books and TV programs focused on the theme of love beyond death, there is nothing new about the idea. One of its oddest variations was penned over one hundred years ago by IVAN TURGENEV *(1818–1883), the first Russian author to attain European success with such novels as* On the Eve *and* Fathers and Sons *and his 1850 play,* A Month in the Country. *"Spirits" was translated in 1897 by Constance Garnett, who called it "Phantoms," but according to my colleague Jessica Amanda Salmonson, " 'Spirits' strikes me as better. Rather than being about a phantom, the tale seems to embody the spirit of love."*

FOR A LONG TIME I could not get to sleep, and kept turning from side to side. 'Confound this foolishness about table-turning!' I thought. 'It simply upsets one's nerves.' . . . Drowsiness began to overtake me at last. . . .

Suddenly it seemed to me as though there were the faint and plaintive sound of a harp-string in the room.

I raised my head. The moon was low in the sky, and looked me straight in the face. White as chalk lay its light upon the floor. . . . The strange sound was distinctly repeated.

I leaned on my elbow. A faint feeling of awe plucked at my heart. A minute passed, another. . . . Somewhere, far away, a cock crowed; another answered still more remote.

I let my head sink back on the pillow. 'See what one can work oneself up to,' I thought again, . . . 'there's a singing in my ears.'

After a little while I fell asleep—or I thought I fell asleep. I had an extraordinary dream. I fancied I was lying in my room, in my bed—and was not asleep, could not even close my eyes. And again I heard the sound. . . . I turned over. . . . The moonlight on the floor began softly to lift, to rise up, to round off slightly above. . . . Before me, impalpable as mist, a white woman was standing motionless.

'Who are you?' I asked with an effort.

A voice made answer, like the rustle of leaves: 'It is I . . . I . . . I . . . I have come for you.'

'For me? But who are you?'

'Come by night to the edge of the wood where there stands an old oak-tree. I will be there.'

I tried to look closely into the face of the mysterious woman—and suddenly I gave an involuntary shudder: there was a chilly breath upon me. And then I was not lying down, but sitting up in my bed; and where, as I fancied, the phantom had stood, the moonlight lay in a long streak of white upon the floor.

II

The day passed somehow. I tried, I remember, to read, to work . . . everything was a failure. The night came. My heart was throbbing within me, as though it expected something. I lay down, and turned with my face to the wall.

'Why did you not come?' sounded a distinct whisper in the room.

I looked round quickly.

Again she . . . again the mysterious phantom. Motionless eyes in a motionless face, and a gaze full of sadness.

'Come!' I heard the whisper again.

'I will come,' I replied with instinctive horror. The phantom bent slowly forward, and undulating faintly like smoke, melted away altogether. And again the moon shone white and untroubled on the smooth floor.

III

I passed the day in unrest. At supper I drank almost a whole bottle of wine, and all but went out on to the steps; but I turned back and flung myself into my bed. My blood was pulsing painfully.

Again the sound was heard. . . . I started, but did not look round. All at once I felt that someone had tight hold of me from behind, and was whispering in my very ear: 'Come, come, come.' . . . Trembling with terror, I moaned out: 'I will come!' and sat up.

A woman stood stooping close to my very pillow. She smiled dimly and vanished. I had time, though, to make out her face. It seemed to me I had seen her before—but where, when? I got up late, and spent the whole day wandering about the country. I went to the old oak at the edge of the forest, and looked carefully all around.

Towards evening I sat at the open window in my study. My old housekeeper set a cup of tea before me, but I did not touch it. . . . I kept asking myself in bewilderment: 'Am I not going out of my mind?' The sun had just set: and not the sky alone was flushed with red; the whole atmosphere was suddenly filled with an almost unnatural purple. The leaves and grass never stirred, stiff as though freshly coated with varnish. In their stony rigidity, in the vivid sharpness of their outlines, in this combination of intense brightness and death-like stillness, there was something weird and mysterious. A rather large grey bird suddenly flew up without a sound and settled on the very window sill. . . . I looked at it, and it looked at me sideways with its round, dark eye. 'Were you sent to remind me, then?' I wondered.

At once the bird fluttered its soft wings, and without a sound—as before—flew away. I sat a long time still at the window, but I was no longer a prey to uncertainty. I had, as it were, come within the enchanted circle, and I was borne along by an irresistible though gentle force, as a boat is borne along by the current long before it reaches the waterfall. I started up at last. The purple had long vanished from the air, the colours were darkened, and the enchanted silence was broken. There was the flutter of a gust of wind, the moon came out brighter and brighter in the sky that was growing bluer, and soon the leaves of the trees were weaving patterns of black and silver in her cold beams. My old housekeeper came into the study with a lighted candle, but there was a draught from the window and the flame went out. I could restrain myself no longer. I jumped up, clapped on my cap, and set off to the corner of the forest, to the old oak-tree.

IV

This oak had, many years before, been struck by lightning; the top of the tree had been shattered, and was withered up, but there was still life left in it for centuries to come. As I was coming up to it, a cloud passed over the moon: it was very dark under its thick branches. At first I noticed nothing special; but I glanced on one side, and my heart fairly failed me —a white figure was standing motionless beside a tall bush between the oak and the forest. My hair stood upright on my head, but I plucked up my courage and went towards the forest.

Yes, it was she, my visitor of the night. As I approached her, the moon shone out again. She seemed all, as it were, spun out of half-transparent, milky mist,—through her face I could see a branch faintly stirring in the wind; only the hair and eyes were a little dark, and on one of the fingers of her clasped hands a slender ring shone with a gleam of pale gold. I stood still before her, and tried to speak; but the voice died away in my throat, though it was no longer fear exactly I felt. Her eyes were turned upon me; their gaze expressed neither distress nor delight, but a sort of lifeless attention. I waited to see whether she would utter a word, but she remained motionless and speechless, and still gazed at me with her deathly intent eyes. Dread came over me again.

'I have come!' I cried at last with an effort. My voice sounded muffled and strange to me.

'I love you,' I heard her whisper.

'You love me!' I repeated in amazement.

'Give yourself up to me,' was whispered me again in reply.

'Give myself up to you! But you are a phantom; you have no body even.' A strange animation came upon me. 'What are you—smoke, air, vapour? Give myself up to you! Answer me first, Who are you? Have you lived upon the earth? Whence have you come?'

'Give yourself up to me. I will do you no harm. Only say two words: "Take me."'

I looked at her. 'What is she saying?' I thought. 'What does it all mean? And how can she take me? Shall I try?'

'Very well,' I said, and unexpectedly loudly, as though some one had given me a push from behind; 'take me!'

I had hardly uttered these words when the mysterious figure, with a sort of inward laugh, which set her face quivering for an instant, bent forward, and stretched out her arms wide apart. . . . I tried to dart away, but I was already in her power. She seized me, my body rose a foot from the ground, and we both floated smoothly and not too swiftly over the wet, still grass.

V

At first I felt giddy, and instinctively I closed my eyes. . . . A minute later I opened them again. We were floating as before; but the forest was now nowhere to be seen. Under us stretched a plain, spotted here and there with dark patches. With horror I felt that we had risen to a fearful height.

'I am lost; I am in the power of Satan,' flashed through me like lightning. Till that instant the idea of a temptation of the evil one, of the possibility of perdition, had never entered my head. We still whirled on, and seemed to be mounting higher and higher.

'Where will you take me?' I moaned at last.

'Where you like,' my companion answered. She clung close to me; her face was almost resting upon my face. But I was scarcely conscious of her touch.

'Let me sink down to the earth, I am giddy at this height.'

'Very well; only shut your eyes and hold your breath.'

I obeyed, and at once felt that I was falling like a stone flung from the hand . . . the air whistled in my ears. When I could think again, we were floating smoothly once more just above the earth, so that we caught our feet in the tops of the tall grass.

'Put me on my feet,' I began. 'What pleasure is there in flying? I'm not a bird.'

'I thought you would like it. We have no other pastime.'

'You? Then what are you?'

There was no answer.

'You don't dare to tell me that?'

The plaintive sound which had awakened me the first night quivered in my ears. Meanwhile we were still, scarcely perceptibly, moving in the damp night air.

'Let me go!' I said. My companion moved slowly away, and I found myself on my feet. She stopped before me and again folded her hands. I grew more composed and looked into her face; as before it expressed submissive sadness.

'Where are we?' I asked. I did not recognise the country about me.

'Far from your home, but you can be there in an instant.'

'How can that be done? by trusting myself to you again?'

'I have done you no harm and will do you none. Let us fly till dawn, that is all. I can bear you away wherever you fancy—to the ends of the earth. Give yourself up to me! Say only: "Take me!"'

'Well . . . take me!'

She again pressed close to me, again my feet left the earth—and we were flying.

VI

'Which way?' she asked me.

'Straight on, keep straight on.'

'But here is a forest.'

'Lift us over the forest, only slower.'

We darted upwards like a wild snipe flying up into a birch-tree, and again flew on in a straight line. Instead of grass, we caught glimpses of tree-tops just under our feet. It was strange to see the forest from above, its bristling back lighted up by the moon. It looked like some huge slumbering wild beast, and accompanied us with a vast unceasing murmur, like some inarticulate roar. In one place we crossed a small glade; intensely black was the jagged streak of shadow along one side of it. Now and then there was the plaintive cry of a hare below us; above us the owl hooted, plaintively too; there was a scent in the air of mushrooms, buds, and dawn-flowers; the moon fairly flooded everything on all sides with its cold, hard light; the Pleiades gleamed just over our heads. And now the forest was left behind; a streak of fog stretched out across the open country; it was the river. We flew along one of its banks, above the bushes, still and weighed down with moisture. The river's waters at one moment glimmered with a flash of blue, at another flowed on in darkness, as it were, in wrath. Here and there a delicate mist moved strangely over the water, and the water-lilies' cups shone white in maiden pomp with every petal open to its full, as though they knew their safety out of reach. I longed to pick one of them, and behold, I found myself at once on the river's surface . . . The damp air struck me an angry blow in the face, just as I broke the thick stalk of a great flower. We began to fly across from bank to bank, like the water-fowl we were continually waking up and chasing before us. More than once we chanced to swoop down on a family of wild ducks, settled in a circle on an open spot among the reeds, but they did not stir; at most one of them would thrust out its neck from under its wing, stare at us, and anxiously poke its beak away again in its fluffy feathers, and another faintly quacked, while its body twitched a little all over. We startled one heron; it flew up out of a willow bush, brandishing its legs and fluttering its wings with clumsy eagerness: it struck me as remarkably like a German. There was not the splash of a fish to be heard, they too were asleep. I began to get used to the sensation of flying, and even to find a pleasure in it; any one will understand me, who has experienced flying in dreams. I proceeded to scrutinise with close attention the strange being, by whose good offices such unlikely adventures had befallen me.

VII

She was a woman with a small un-Russian face. Greyish-white, half-transparent, with scarcely marked shades, she reminded one of the alabaster figures on a vase lighted up within, and again her face seemed familiar to me.

'Can I speak with you?' I asked.

'Speak.'

'I see a ring on your finger; you have lived then on the earth, you have been married?'

I waited . . . There was no answer.

'What is your name, or, at least, what was it?'

'Call me Alice.'

'Alice! That's an English name! Are you an Englishwoman? Did you know me in former days?'

'No.'

'Why is it then you have come to me?'

'I love you.'

'And are you content?'

'Yes; we float, we whirl together in the fresh air.'

'Alice!' I said all at once, 'you are perhaps a sinful, condemned soul?'

My companion's head bent towards me. 'I don't understand you,' she murmured.

'I adjure you in God's name . . .' I was beginning.

'What are you saying?' she put in in perplexity. 'I don't understand.'

I fancied that the arm that lay like a chilly girdle about my waist softly trembled . . .

'Don't be afraid,' said Alice, 'don't be afraid, my dear one!' Her face turned and moved towards my face. . . . I felt on my lips a strange sensation, like the faintest prick of a soft and delicate sting. . . . Leeches might prick so in mild and drowsy mood.

VIII

I glanced downwards. We had now risen again to a considerable height. We were flying over some provincial town I did not know, situated on the side of a wide slope. Churches rose up high among the dark mass of wooden roofs and orchards; a long bridge stood out black at the bend of a river; everything was hushed, buried in slumber. The very crosses and cupolas seemed to gleam with a silent brilliance; silently stood the tall posts of the wells beside the round tops of the willows; silently the straight whitish road darted arrow-like into one end of the town, and silently it ran out again at the opposite end on to the dark waste of monotonous fields.

'What town is this?' I asked.

'X . . .'

'X . . . in Y . . . province?'

'Yes.'

'I'm a long distance indeed from home!'

'Distance is not for us.'

'Really?' I was fired by a sudden recklessness. 'Then take me to South America!'

'To America I cannot. It's daylight there by now.'

'And we are night-birds. Well, anywhere, where you can, only far, far away.'

'Shut your eyes and hold your breath,' answered Alice, and we flew along with the speed of a whirlwind. With a deafening noise the air rushed into my ears. We stopped, but the noise did not cease. On the contrary, it changed into a sort of menacing roar, the roll of thunder . . .

'Now you can open your eyes,' said Alice.

IX

I obeyed . . . Good God, where was I?

Overhead, ponderous, smoke-like storm-clouds; they huddled, they moved on like a herd of furious monsters . . . and there below, another monster; a raging, yes, raging, sea . . . The white foam gleamed with spasmodic fury, and surged up in hillocks upon it, and hurling up shaggy billows, it beat with a sullen roar against a huge cliff, black as pitch. The howling of the tempest, the chilling gasp of the storm-rocked abyss, the weighty splash of the breakers, in which from time to time one fancied something like a wail, like distant cannon-shots, like a bell ringing—the tearing crunch and grind of the shingle on the beach, the sudden shriek of an unseen gull, on the murky horizon the disabled hulk of a ship—on every side death, death and horror . . . Giddiness overcame me, and I shut my eyes again with a sinking heart . . .

'What is this? Where are we?'

'On the south coast of the Isle of Wight opposite the Blackgang cliff where ships are so often wrecked,' said Alice, speaking this time with peculiar distinctness, and as it seemed to me with a certain malignant pleasure . . .

'Take me away, away from here . . . home! home!' I shrank up, hid my face in my hands . . . I felt that we were moving faster than before; the wind now was not roaring or moaning, it whistled in my hair, in my clothes . . . I caught my breath . . .

'Stand on your feet now,' I heard Alice's voice saying. I tried to master myself, to regain consciousness . . . I felt the earth under the soles of my feet, and I heard nothing, as though everything had swooned away about me . . . only in my temples the blood throbbed irregularly, and my head was still giddy with a faint ringing in my ears. I drew myself up and opened my eyes.

X

We were on the bank of my pond. Straight before me there were glimpses through the pointed leaves of the willows of its broad surface with threads of fluffy mist clinging here and there upon it. To the right a field of rye shone dimly; on the left stood up my orchard trees, tall, rigid, drenched it seemed in dew . . . The breath of the morning was already upon them. Across the pure grey sky stretched like streaks of smoke, two or three slanting clouds; they had a yellowish tinge, the first faint glow of dawn fell on them; one could not say whence it came; the eye could not detect on the horizon, which was gradually growing lighter, the spot where the sun was to rise. The stars had disappeared; nothing was astir yet, though everything was already on the point of awakening in the enchanted stillness of the morning twilight.

'Morning! see, it is morning!' cried Alice in my ear. 'Farewell till to-morrow.'

I turned round . . . Lightly rising from the earth, she floated by, and suddenly she raised both hands above her head. The head and hands and shoulders glowed for an instant with warm, corporeal light; living sparks gleamed in the dark eyes; a smile of mysterious tenderness stirred the reddening lips. . . . A lovely woman had suddenly arisen before me. . . . But as though dropping into a swoon, she fell back instantly and melted away like vapour.

I remained passive.

When I recovered myself and looked round me, it seemed to me that the corporeal, pale-rosy colour that had flitted over the figure of my phantom had not yet vanished, and was enfolding me, diffused in the air. . . . It was the flush of dawn. All at once I was conscious of extreme fatigue and turned homewards. As I passed the poultry-yard, I heard the first morning cackling of the geese (no birds wake earlier than they do); along the roof at the end of each beam sat a rook, and they were all busily and silently pluming themselves, standing out in sharp outline against the milky sky. From time to time they all rose at once, and after a short flight, settled again in a row, without uttering a caw. . . . From the wood close by came twice repeated the drowsy, fresh chuck-chuck of the black-cock, beginning to fly into the dewy grass, overgrown by brambles. . . . With a faint tremor all over me I made my way to my bed, and soon fell into a sound sleep.

XI

The next night, as I was approaching the old oak, Alice moved to meet me, as if I were an old friend. I was not afraid of her as I had been the day before, I was almost rejoiced at seeing her; I did not even attempt to comprehend what was happening to me; I was simply longing to fly farther to interesting places.

Alice's arm again twined about me, and we took flight again.

'Let us go to Italy,' I whispered in her ear.

'Wherever you wish, my dear one,' she answered solemnly and slowly, and slowly and solemnly she turned her face towards me. It struck me as less transparent than on the eve; more womanlike and more imposing; it recalled to me the being I had had a glimpse of in the early dawn at parting.

'This night is a great night,' Alice went on. 'It comes rarely—when seven times thirteen . . .'

At this point I could not catch a few words.

'To-night we can see what is hidden at other times.'

'Alice!' I implored, 'but who are you, tell me at last?'

Silently she lifted her long white hand. In the dark sky, where her finger was pointing, a comet flashed, a reddish streak among the tiny stars.

'How am I to understand you?' I began, 'Or, as that comet floats between the planets and the sun, do you float among men . . . or what?'

But Alice's hand was suddenly passed before my eyes . . . It was as though a white mist from the damp valley had fallen on me . . .

'To Italy! to Italy!' I heard her whisper. 'This night is a great night!'

XII

The mist cleared away from before my eyes, and I saw below me an immense plain. But already, by the mere breath of the warm soft air upon my cheeks, I could tell I was not in Russia; and the plain, too, was not like our Russian plains. It was a vast dark expanse, apparently desert

and not overgrown with grass; here and there over its whole extent
gleamed pools of water, like broken pieces of looking-glass; in the distance could be dimly descried a noiseless motionless sea. Great stars
shone bright in the spaces between the big beautiful clouds; the murmur
of thousands, subdued but never-ceasing, rose on all sides, and very
strange was this shrill but drowsy chorus, this voice of the darkness and
the desert . . .

'The Pontine marshes,' said Alice. 'Do you hear the frogs? do you
smell the sulphur?'

'The Pontine marshes . . .' I repeated, and a sense of grandeur and
of desolation came upon me. 'But why have you brought me here, to this
gloomy forsaken place? Let us fly to Rome instead.'

'Rome is near,' answered Alice. . . . 'Prepare yourself!'

We sank lower, and flew along an ancient Roman road. A bullock
slowly lifted from the slimy mud its shaggy monstrous head, with short
tufts of bristles between its crooked backward-bent horns. It turned the
whites of its dull malignant eyes askance, and sniffed a heavy snorting
breath into its wet nostrils, as though scenting us.

'Rome, Rome is near . . .' whispered Alice. 'Look, look in
front. . . .'

I raised my eyes.

What was the blur of black on the edge of the night sky? Were these
the lofty arches of an immense bridge? What river did it span? Why was
it broken down in parts? No, it was not a bridge, it was an ancient
aqueduct. All around was the holy ground of the Campagna, and there,
in the distance, the Albanian hills, and their peaks and the grey ridge of
the old aqueduct gleamed dimly in the beams of the rising moon. . . .

We suddenly darted upwards, and floated in the air before a deserted
ruin. No one could have said what it had been: sepulchre, palace, or
castle. . . . Dark ivy encircled it all over in its deadly clasp, and below
gaped yawning a half-ruined vault. A heavy underground smell rose in
my face from this heap of tiny closely-fitted stones, whence the granite
facing of the wall had long crumbled away.

'Here,' Alice pronounced, and she raised her hand: 'Here! call aloud
three times running the name of the mighty Roman!'

'What will happen?'

'You will see.'

I wondered. *'Divus Caius Julius Caesar!* I cried suddenly; *'divus Caius Julius Caesar!* I repeated deliberately; *'Caesar!'*

XIII

The last echoes of my voice had hardly died away, when I heard . . .

It is difficult to say what I did hear. At first there reached me a confused din the ear could scarcely catch, the endlessly-repeated clamour of the blare of trumpets, and the clapping of hands. It seemed that somewhere, immensely far away, at some fathomless depth, a multitude innumerable was suddenly astir, and was rising up, rising up in agitation, calling to one another, faintly, as if muffled in sleep, the suffocating sleep of ages. Then the air began moving in dark currents over the ruin. . . . Shades began flitting before me, myriads of shades, millions of outlines, the rounded curves of helmets, the long straight lines of lances; the moonbeams were broken into momentary gleams of blue upon these helmets and lances, and all this army, this multitude, came closer and closer, and grew, in more and more rapid movement. . . . An indescribable force, a force fit to set the whole world moving, could be felt in it; but not one figure stood out clearly. . . . And suddenly I fancied a sort of tremor ran all round, as if it were the rush and rolling apart of some huge waves. . . . *'Caesar, Caesar venit!'* sounded voices, like the leaves of a forest when a storm has suddenly broken upon it . . . a muffled shout thundered through the multitude, and a pale stern head, in a wreath of laurel, with downcast eyelids, the head of the emperor, began slowly to rise out of the ruin. . . .

There is no word in the tongue of man to express the horror which clutched at my heart. . . . I felt that were that head to raise its eyes, to part its lips, I must perish on the spot! 'Alice!' I moaned, 'I won't, I can't, I don't want Rome, coarse, terrible Rome. . . . Away, away from here!'

'Coward!' she whispered, and away we flew. I just had time to hear behind me the iron voice of the legions, like a peal of thunder . . . then all was darkness.

XIV

'Look round,' Alice said to me, 'and don't fear.'

I obeyed—and, I remember, my first impression was so sweet that I could only sigh. A sort of smoky-grey, silvery-soft, half-light, half-mist, enveloped me on all sides. At first I made out nothing: I was dazzled by this azure brilliance; but little by little began to emerge the outlines of beautiful mountains and forests; a lake lay at my feet, with stars quivering in its depths, and the musical plash of waves. The fragrance of orange flowers met me with a rush, and with it—and also as it were with a rush—came floating the pure powerful notes of a woman's young voice. This fragrance, this music, fairly drew me downwards, and I began to sink . . . to sink down towards a magnificent marble palace, which stood, invitingly white, in the midst of a wood of cypress. The music flowed out from its wide open windows, the waves of the lake, flecked with the pollen of flowers, splashed upon its walls, and just opposite, all clothed in the dark green of orange flowers and laurels, enveloped in shining mist, and studded with statues, slender columns, and the porticoes of temples, a lofty round island rose out of the water. . . .

'Isola Bella!' said Alice. . . . 'Lago Maggiore. . . .'

I murmured only 'Ah!' and continued to drop. The woman's voice sounded louder and clearer in the palace; I was irresistibly drawn towards it. . . . I wanted to look at the face of the singer, who, in such music, gave voice to such a night. We stood still before the window.

In the centre of a room, furnished in the style of Pompeii, and more like an ancient temple than a modern drawing-room, surrounded by Greek statues, Etruscan vases, rare plants, and precious stuffs, lighted up by the soft radiance of two lamps enclosed in crystal globes, a young woman was sitting at the piano. Her head slightly bowed and her eyes half-closed, she sang an Italian melody; she sang and smiled, and at the same time her face wore an expression of gravity, almost of sternness . . . a token of perfect rapture! She smiled . . . and Praxiteles' Faun, indolent, youthful as she, effeminate, and voluptuous, seemed to smile back at her from a corner, under the branches of an oleander, across the delicate smoke that curled upwards from a bronze censer on an antique tripod. The beautiful singer was alone. Spell-bound by the music, her beauty, the splendour and sweet fragrance of the night, moved to the heart by the picture of this youthful, serene, and untroubled happiness, I utterly forgot my companion, I forgot the strange way in which I had become a witness of this life, so remote, so completely apart from me, and I was on the point of tapping at the window, of speaking . . .

I was set trembling all over by a violent shock—just as though I had touched a galvanic battery. I looked round. . . . The face of Alice was —for all its transparency—dark and menacing; there was a dull glow of anger in her eyes, which were suddenly wide and round. . . .

'Away!' she murmured wrathfully, and again whirling and darkness and giddiness. . . . Only this time not the shout of legions, but the voice of the singer, breaking on a high note, lingered in my ears. . . .

We stopped. The high note, the same note was still ringing and did not cease to ring in my ears, though I was breathing quite a different air, a different scent . . . a breeze was blowing upon me, fresh and invigorating, as though from a great river, and there was a smell of hay, smoke and hemp. The long-drawn-out note was followed by a second, and a third, but with an expression so unmistakable, a trill so familiar, so peculiarly our own, that I said to myself at once: 'That's a Russian singing a Russian song!' and at that very instant everything grew clear about me.

XV

We found ourselves on a flat riverside plain. To the left, newly-mown meadows, with rows of huge hayricks, stretched endlessly till they were lost in the distance; to the right extended the smooth surface of a vast mighty river, till it too was lost in the distance. Not far from the bank, big dark barges slowly rocked at anchor, slightly tilting their slender masts, like pointing fingers. From one of these barges came floating up to me the sounds of a liquid voice, and a fire was burning in it, throwing a long red light that danced and quivered on the water. Here and there, both on the river and in the fields, other lights were glimmering, whether close at hand or far away, the eye could not distinguish; they shrank together, then suddenly lengthened out into great blurs of light; grasshoppers innumerable kept up an unceasing churr, persistent as the frogs of the Pontine marshes; and across the cloudless, but dark lowering sky floated from time to time the cries of unseen birds.

'Are we in Russia?' I asked of Alice.

'It is the Volga,' she answered.

We flew along the river-bank. 'Why did you tear me away from there, from that lovely country?' I began. 'Were you envious, or was it jealousy in you?'

The lips of Alice faintly stirred, and again there was a menacing light in her eyes. . . . But her whole face grew stony again at once.

'I want to go home,' I said.

'Wait a little, wait a little,' answered Alice. 'To-night is a great night. It will not soon return. You may be a spectator. . . . Wait a little.'

And we suddenly flew across the Volga in a slanting direction, keeping close to the water's surface, with the low impetuous flight of swallows before a storm. The broad waves murmured heavily below us, the sharp river breeze beat upon us with its strong cold wing . . . the high right bank began soon to rise up before us in the half-darkness. Steep mountains appeared with great ravines between. We came near to them.

'Shout: "Lads, to the barges!" ' Alice whispered to me. I remembered the terror I had suffered at the apparition of the Roman phantoms. I felt weary and strangely heavy, as though my heart were ebbing away within me. I wished not to utter the fatal words; I knew beforehand that in response to them there would appear, as in the wolves' valley of the Freischütz, some monstrous thing; but my lips parted against my will, and in a weak forced voice I shouted, also against my will: 'Lads, to the barges!'

XVI

At first all was silence, even as it was at the Roman ruins, but suddenly I heard close to my very ear a coarse bargeman's laugh, and with a moan something dropped into the water and a gurgling sound followed. . . . I looked round: no one was anywhere to be seen, but from the bank the echo came bounding back, and at once from all sides rose a deafening din. There was a medley of everything in this chaos of sound: shouting and whining, furious abuse and laughter, laughter above everything; the plash of oars and the cleaving of hatchets, a crash as of the smashing of doors and chests, the grating of rigging and wheels, and the neighing of horses, and the clang of the alarm bell and the clink of chains, the roar and crackle of fire, drunken songs and quick, gnashing chatter, weeping

inconsolable, plaintive despairing prayers, and shouts of command, the
dying gasp and the reckless whistle, the guffaw and the thud of the
dance . . . 'Kill them! Hang them! Drown them! rip them up! bravo!
bravo! don't spare them!' could be heard distinctly; I could even hear the
hurried breathing of men panting. And meanwhile all around, as far as
the eye could reach, nothing could be seen, nothing was changed; the
river rolled by mysteriously, almost sullenly, the very bank seemed more
deserted and desolate—and that was all.

I turned to Alice, but she put her finger to her lips. . . .

'Stepan Timofeitch! Stepan Timofeitch is coming!' was shouted noisily all round; 'he is coming, our father, our ataman, our breadgiver!' As
before I saw nothing but it seemed to me as though a huge body were
moving straight at me. . . . 'Frolka! where art thou, dog?' thundered
an awful voice. 'Set fire to every corner at once—and to the hatchet with
them, the white-handed scoundrels!'

I felt the hot breath of the flame close by, and tasted the bitter savour
of the smoke; and at the same instant something warm like blood
spurted over my face and hands. . . . A savage roar of laughter broke
out all round. . . .

I lost consciousness, and when I came to myself, Alice and I were
gliding along beside the familiar bushes that bordered my wood, straight
towards the old oak. . . .

'Do you see the little path?' Alice said to me, 'where the moon shines
dimly and where are two birch-trees overhanging? Will you go there?'

But I felt so shattered and exhausted that I could only say in reply:
'Home! home!'

'You are at home,' replied Alice.

I was in fact standing at the very door of my house—alone. Alice had
vanished. The yard-dog was about to approach, he scanned me suspiciously—and with a bark ran away.

With difficulty I dragged myself up to my bed and fell asleep without
undressing.

XVII

All the following morning my head ached, and I could scarcely move my
legs; but I cared little for my bodily discomfort; I was devoured by
regret, overwhelmed with vexation.

I was excessively annoyed with myself. 'Coward!' I repeated incessantly; 'yes—Alice was right. What was I frightened of? how could I miss such an opportunity? . . . I might have seen Cæsar himself—and I was senseless with terror, I whimpered and turned away, like a child at the sight of the rod. Razin, now—that's another matter. As a nobleman and landowner . . . though, indeed, even then what had I really to fear? Coward! coward!' . . .

'But wasn't it all a dream?' I asked myself at last. I called my housekeeper.

'Marfa, what o'clock did I go to bed yesterday—do you remember?'

'Why, who can tell, master? . . . Late enough, surely. Before it was quite dark you went out of the house; and you were tramping about in your bedroom when the night was more than half over. Just on morning —yes. And this is the third day it's been the same. You've something on your mind, it's easy to see.'

'Aha-ha!' I thought. 'Then there's no doubt about the flying. Well, and how do I look to-day?' I added aloud.

'How do you look? Let me have a look at you. You've got thinner a bit. Yes, and you're pale, master; to be sure, there's not a drop of blood in your face.'

I felt a slight twinge of uneasiness . . . I dismissed Marfa.

'Why, going on like this, you'll die, or go out of your mind, perhaps,' I reasoned with myself, as I sat deep in thought at the window. 'I must give it all up. It's dangerous. And now my heart beats so strangely. And when I fly, I keep feeling as though some one were sucking at it, or as it were drawing something out of it—as the spring sap is drawn out of the birch-tree, if you stick an axe into it. I'm sorry, though. And Alice too. . . . She is playing cat and mouse with me . . . still she can hardly wish me harm. I will give myself up to her for the last time—and then. . . . But if she is drinking my blood? That's awful. Besides, such rapid locomotion cannot fail to be injurious; even in England, I'm told, on the railways, it's against the law to go more than one hundred miles an hour. . . .'

So I reasoned with myself—but at ten o'clock in the evening, I was already at my post before the old oak-tree.

XVIII

The night was cold, dull, grey; there was a feeling of rain in the air. To my amazement, I found no one under the oak; I walked several times round it, went up to the edge of the wood, turned back again, peered anxiously into the darkness. . . . All was emptiness. I waited a little, then several times I uttered the name, Alice, each time a little louder, . . . but she did not appear. I felt sad, almost sick at heart; my previous apprehensions vanished; I could not resign myself to the idea that my companion would not come back to me again.

'Alice! Alice! come! Can it be you will not come?' I shouted, for the last time.

A crow, who had been waked by my voice, suddenly darted upwards into a tree-top close by, and catching in the twigs, fluttered his wings. . . . But Alice did not appear.

With downcast head, I turned homewards. Already I could discern the black outlines of the willows on the pond's edge, and the light in my window peeped out at me through the apple-trees in the orchard—peeped at me, and hid again, like the eye of some man keeping watch on me—when suddenly I heard behind me the faint swish of the rapidly parted air, and something at once embraced and snatched me upward, as a buzzard pounces on and snatches up a quail. . . . It was Alice sweeping down upon me. I felt her cheek against my cheek, her enfolding arm about my body, and like a cutting cold her whisper pierced to my ear, 'Here I am.' I was frightened and delighted both at once. . . . We flew at no great height above the ground.

'You did not mean to come to-day?' I said.

'And you were dull without me? You love me? Oh, you are mine!'

The last words of Alice confused me. . . . I did not know what to say.

'I was kept,' she went on; 'I was watched.'

'Who could keep you?'

'Where would you like to go?' inquired Alice, as usual not answering my question.

'Take me to Italy—to that lake, you remember.'

Alice turned a little away, and shook her head in refusal. At that point I noticed for the first time that she had ceased to be transparent. And her face seemed tinged with colour; there was a faint glow of red over its misty whiteness. I glanced at her eyes . . . and felt a pang of dread; in those eyes something was astir—with the slow, continuous, malignant movement of the benumbed snake, twisting and turning as the sun begins to thaw it.

'Alice,' I cried, 'who are you? Tell me who you are.'

Alice simply shrugged her shoulders.

I felt angry . . . I longed to punish her; and suddenly the idea occurred to me to tell her to fly with me to Paris. 'That's the place for you to be jealous,' I thought. 'Alice,' I said aloud, 'you are not afraid of big towns—Paris, for instance?'

'No.'

'Not even those parts where it is as light as in the boulevards?'

'It is not the light of day.'

'Good; then take me at once to the Boulevard des Italiens.'

Alice wrapped the end of her long hanging sleeve about my head. I was at once enfolded in a sort of white vapour full of the drowsy fragrance of the poppy. Everything disappeared at once; every light, every sound, and almost consciousness itself. Only the sense of being alive remained, and that was not unpleasant.

Suddenly the vapour vanished; Alice took her sleeve from my head, and I saw at my feet a huge mass of closely-packed buildings, brilliant light, movement, noisy traffic. . . . I saw Paris.

XIX

I had been in Paris before, and so I recognised at once the place to which Alice had directed her course. It was the Garden of the Tuileries with its old chestnut-trees, its iron railings, its fortress moat, and its brutal-looking Zouave sentinels. Passing the palace, passing the Church of St. Roche, on the steps of which the first Napoleon for the first time shed French blood, we came to a halt high over the Boulevard des Italiens, where the third Napoleon did the same thing and with the same success. Crowds of people, dandies young and old, workmen in blouses, women in gaudy dresses, were thronging on the pavements; the gilded restaurants and cafés were flaring with lights; omnibuses, carriages of all sorts and shapes, moved to and fro along the boulevard; everything was bustle, everything was brightness, wherever one chanced to look. . . . But, strange to say, I had no inclination to forsake my pure dark airy height. I had no inclination to get nearer to this human ant-hill. It seemed as though a hot, heavy, reddish vapour rose from it, half-fragrance, half-stench; so many lives were flung struggling in one heap together there. I was hesitating. . . . But suddenly, sharp as the clang of iron bars, the voice of a harlot of the streets floated up to me; like an insolent tongue, it was thrust out, this voice; it stung me like the sting of a viper. At once I saw in imagination the strong, heavy-jawed, greedy, flat Parisian face, the mercenary eyes, the paint and powder, the frizzed hair, and the nosegay of gaudy artificial flowers under the high-pointed hat, the polished nails like talons, the hideous crinoline. . . . I could fancy too one of our sons of the steppes running with pitiful eagerness after the doll put up for sale. . . . I could fancy him with clumsy coarseness and violent stammering, trying to imitate the manners of the waiters at Véfour's, mincing, flattering, wheedling . . . and a feeling of loathing gained possession of me. . . . 'No,' I thought, 'here Alice has no need to be jealous. . . .'

Meanwhile I perceived that we had gradually begun to descend. . . . Paris was rising to meet us with all its din and odour. . . .

'Stop,' I said to Alice. 'Are you not stifled and oppressed here?'

'You asked me to bring you here yourself.'

'I am to blame, I take back my word. Take me away, Alice, I beseech you. To be sure, here is Prince Kulmametov hobbling along the boulevard; and his friend, Serge Varaksin, waves his hand to him, shouting: "Ivan Stepanitch, *allons souper,* make haste, zhay angazha Rigol-bouche itself!" Take me away from these furnished apartments and *maisons dorées,* from the Jockey Club and the Figaro, from close-shaven military heads and varnished barracks, from sergents-de-ville with Napoleonic beards, and from glasses of muddy absinthe, from gamblers playing dominoes at the cafés, and gamblers on the Bourse, from red ribbons in button-holes, from M. de Four, inventor of "matrimonial specialities," and the gratuitous consultations of Dr. Charles Albert, from liberal lectures and government pamphlets, from Parisian comedies and Parisian operas, from Parisian wit and Parisian ignorance. . . . Away! away! away!'

'Look down,' Alice answered; 'you are not now in Paris.'

I lowered my eyes. . . . It was true. A dark plain, intersected here and there by the whitish lines of roads, was rushing rapidly by below us, and only behind us on the horizon, like the reflection of an immense conflagration, rose the great glow of the innumerable lights of the capital of the world.

XX

Again a veil fell over my eyes. . . . Again I lost consciousness. The veil was withdrawn at last. What was it down there below? What was this park, with avenues of lopped lime-trees, with isolated fir-trees of the shape of parasols, with porticoes and temples in the Pompadour style, with statues of satyrs and nymphs of the Bernini school, with rococo tritons in the midst of meandering lakes, closed in by low parapets of blackened marble? Wasn't it Versailles? No, it was not Versailles. A small palace, also rococo, peeped out behind a clump of bushy oaks. The moon shone dimly, shrouded in mist, and over the earth there was, as it were spread out, a delicate smoke. The eye could not decide what it was, whether moonlight or fog. On one of the lakes a swan was asleep; its long back was white as the snow of the frost-bound steppes, while glow-worms gleamed like diamonds in the bluish shadow at the base of a statue.

'We are near Mannheim,' said Alice; 'this is the Schwetzingen garden.'

'We are in Germany,' I thought, and I fell to listening. All was silence, except somewhere, secluded and unseen, the splash and babble of falling water. It seemed continually to repeat the same words: 'Aye, aye, aye, for aye, aye.' And all at once I fancied that in the very centre of one of the avenues, between clipped walls of green, a cavalier came tripping along in red-heeled boots, a gold-braided coat, with lace ruffs at his wrists, a light steel rapier at his thigh, smilingly offering his arm to a lady in a powdered wig and a gay chintz. . . . Strange, pale faces. . . . I tried to look into them. . . . But already everything had vanished, and as before there was nothing but the babbling water.

'Those are dreams wandering,' whispered Alice; 'yesterday there was much—oh, much—to see; to-day, even the dreams avoid man's eye. Forward! forward!'

We soared higher and flew farther on. So smooth and easy was our flight that it seemed that we moved not, but everything moved to meet us. Mountains came into view, dark, undulating, covered with forest;

they rose up and swam towards us. . . . And now they were slipping by beneath us, with all their windings, hollows, and narrow glades, with gleams of light from rapid brooks among the slumbering trees at the bottom of the dales; and in front of us more mountains sprung up again and floated towards us. . . . We were in the heart of the Black Forest.

Mountains, still mountains . . . and forest, magnificent, ancient, stately forest. The night sky was clear; I could recognise some kinds of trees, especially the splendid firs, with their straight white trunks. Here and there on the edge of the forest, wild goats could be seen; graceful and alert, they stood on their slender legs and listened, turning their heads prettily and pricking up their great funnel-shaped ears. A ruined tower, sightless and gloomy, on the crest of a bare cliff, laid bare its crumbling turrets; above the old forgotten stones, a little golden star was shining peacefully. From a small almost black lake rose, like a mysterious wail, the plaintive croak of tiny frogs. I fancied other notes, long-drawn-out, languid like the strains of an Eolian harp. . . . Here we were in the home of legend! The same delicate moonlight mist, which had struck me in Schwetzingen, was shed here on every side, and the farther away the mountains, the thicker was this mist. I counted up five, six, ten different tones of shadow at different heights on the mountain slopes, and over all this realm of varied silence the moon queened it pensively. The air blew in soft, light currents. I felt myself a lightness at heart, and, as it were, a lofty calm and melancholy. . . .

'Alice, you must love this country!'

'I love nothing.'

'How so? Not me?'

'Yes . . . you!' she answered indifferently.

It seemed to me that her arm clasped my waist more tightly than before.

'Forward! forward!' said Alice, with a sort of cold fervour.

'Forward!' I repeated.

XXI

A loud, thrilling cry rang out suddenly over our heads, and was at once repeated a little in front.

'Those are belated cranes flying to you, to the north,' said Alice; 'would you like to join them?'

'Yes, yes! raise me up to them.'

We darted upwards and in one instant found ourselves beside the flying flock.

The big handsome birds (there were thirteen of them) were flying in a triangle, with slow sharp flaps of their hollow wings; with their heads and legs stretched rigidly out, and their breasts stiffly pressed forward, they pushed on persistently and so swiftly that the air whistled about them. It was marvellous at such a height, so remote from all things living, to see such passionate, strenuous life, such unflinching will, untiringly cleaving their triumphant way through space. The cranes now and then called to one another, the foremost to the hindmost; and there was a certain pride, dignity, and invincible faith in these loud cries, this converse in the clouds. 'We shall get there, be sure, hard though it be,' they seemed to say, cheering one another on. And then the thought came to me that men, such as these birds—in Russia—nay, in the whole world, are few.

'We are flying towards Russia now,' observed Alice. I noticed now, not for the first time, that she almost always knew what I was thinking of. 'Would you like to go back?'

'Let us go back . . . or no! I have been in Paris; take me to Petersburg.'

'Now?'

'At once. . . . Only wrap my head in your veil, or it will go ill with me.'

Alice raised her hand . . . but before the mist enfolded me, I had time to feel on my lips the contact of that soft, dull sting. . . .

XXII

'Li-i-isten!' sounded in my ears a long drawn out cry. 'Li-i-isten!' was echoed back with a sort of desperation in the distance. 'Li-i-isten!' died away somewhere far, far away. I started. A tall golden spire flashed on my eyes; I recognised the fortress of St. Peter and St. Paul.

A northern, pale night! But was it night at all? Was it not rather a pallid, sickly daylight? I never liked Petersburg nights; but this time the night seemed even fearful to me; the face of Alice had vanished completely, melted away like the mist of morning in the July sun, and I saw her whole body clearly, as it hung, heavy and solitary on a level with the

Alexander column. So here was Petersburg! Yes, it was Petersburg, no doubt. The wide empty grey streets; the greyish-white, and yellowish-grey and greyish-lilac houses, covered with stucco, which was peeling off, with their sunken windows, gaudy sign-boards, iron canopies over steps, and wretched little green-grocer's shops; the façades, inscriptions, sentry-boxes, troughs; the golden cap of St. Isaac's; the senseless motley Bourse; the granite walls of the fortress, and the broken wooden pavement; the barges loaded with hay and timber; the smell of dust, cabbage, matting, and hemp; the stony-faced dvorniks in sheep-skin coats, with high collars; the cab-drivers, huddled up dead asleep on their decrepit cabs—yes, this was Petersburg, our northern Palmyra. Everything was visible; everything was clear—cruelly clear and distinct—and everything was mournfully sleeping, standing out in strange huddled masses in the dull clear air. The flush of sunset—a hectic flush—had not yet gone, and would not be gone till morning from the white starless sky; it was reflected on the silken surface of the Neva, while faintly gurgling and faintly moving, the cold blue waves hurried on. . . .

'Let us fly away,' Alice implored.

And without waiting for my reply, she bore me away across the Neva, over the palace square to Liteiny Street. Steps and voices were audible beneath us; a group of young men, with worn faces, came along the street talking about dancing-classes. 'Sub-lieutenant Stolpakov's seventh!' shouted suddenly a soldier, standing half-asleep on guard at a pyramid of rusty bullets; and a little farther on, at an open window in a tall house, I saw a girl in a creased silk dress, without cuffs, with a pearl net on her hair, and a cigarette in her mouth. She was reading a book with reverent attention; it was a volume of the works of one of our modern Juvenals.

'Let us fly away!' I said to Alice.

One instant more, and there were glimpses below us of the rotting pine copses and mossy bogs surrounding Petersburg. We bent our course straight to the south; sky, earth, all grew gradually darker and darker. The sick night; the sick daylight; the sick town—all were left behind us.

XXIII

We flew more slowly than usual, and I was able to follow with my eyes the immense expanse of my native land gradually unfolding before me, like the unrolling of an endless panorama. Forests, copses, fields, ravines, rivers—here and there villages and churches—and again fields and forests and copses and ravines. . . . Sadness came over me, and a kind of indifferent dreariness. And I was not sad and dreary simply because it was Russia I was flying over. No. The earth itself, this flat surface which lay spread out beneath me; the whole earthly globe, with its populations, multitudinous, feeble, crushed by want, grief and diseases, bound to a clod of pitiful dust; this brittle, rough crust, this shell over the fiery sands of our planet, overspread with the mildew we call the organic, vegetable kingdom; these human flies, a thousand times paltrier than flies; their dwellings glued together with filth, the pitiful traces of their tiny, monotonous bustle, of their comic struggle with the unchanging and inevitable, how revolting it all suddenly was to me. My heart turned slowly sick, and I could not bear to gaze longer on these trivial pictures, on this vulgar show. . . . Yes, I felt dreary, worse than dreary. Even pity I felt nothing of for my brother men: all feelings in me were merged in one which I scarcely dare to name: a feeling of loathing, and stronger than all and more than all within me was the loathing—for myself.

'Cease,' whispered Alice, 'cease, or I cannot carry you. You have grown heavy.'

'Home,' I answered her in the very tone in which I used to say the word to my coachman, when I came out at four o'clock at night from some Moscow friends', where I had been talking since dinner-time of the future of Russia and the significance of the commune. 'Home,' I repeated, and closed my eyes.

XXIV

But I soon opened them again. Alice seemed huddling strangely up to me; she was almost pushing against me. I looked at her and my blood froze at the sight. One who has chanced to behold on the face of another a sudden look of intense terror, the cause of which he does not suspect, will understand me. By terror, overmastering terror, the pale features of Alice were drawn and contorted, almost effaced. I had never seen anything like it even on a living human face. A lifeless, misty phantom, a shade, . . . and this deadly horror. . . .

'Alice, what is it?' I said at last.

'She . . . she . . .' she answered with an effort. 'She.'

'She? Who is she?'

'Do not utter her name, not her name,' Alice faltered hurriedly. 'We must escape, or there will be an end to everything, and for ever . . . Look, over there!'

I turned my head in the direction in which her trembling hand was pointing, and discerned something . . . something horrible indeed.

This something was the more horrible that it had no definite shape. Something bulky, dark, yellowish-black, spotted like a lizard's belly, not a storm-cloud, and not smoke, was crawling with a snake-like motion over the earth. A wide rhythmic undulating movement from above downwards, and from below upwards, an undulation recalling the malignant sweep of the wings of a vulture seeking its prey; at times an indescribably revolting grovelling on the earth, as of a spider stooping over its captured fly. . . . Who are you, what are you, menacing mass? Under her influence, I saw it, I felt it—all sank into nothingness, all was dumb. . . . A putrefying, pestilential chill came from it. At this chill breath the heart turned sick, and the eyes grew dim, and the hair stood up on the head. It was a power moving; that power which there is no resisting, to which all is subject, which, sightless, shapeless, senseless, sees all, knows all, and like a bird of prey picks out its victims, like a snake, stifles them and stabs them with its frozen sting. . . .

'Alice! Alice!' I shrieked like one in frenzy. 'It is death! death itself!'

The wailing sound I had heard before broke from Alice's lips; this time it was more like a human wail of despair, and we flew. But our flight was strangely and alarmingly unsteady; Alice turned over in the air, fell, rushed from side to side like a partridge mortally wounded, or trying to attract a dog away from her young. And meanwhile in pursuit of us, parting from the indescribable mass of horror, rushed sort of long undulating tentacles, like outstretched arms, like talons. . . . Suddenly a huge shape, a muffled figure on a pale horse, sprang up and flew upwards into the very heavens. . . . Still more fearfully, still more desperately Alice struggled. 'She has seen! All is over! I am lost!' I heard her broken whisper. 'Oh, I am miserable! I might have profited, have won life, . . . and now. . . . Nothingness, nothingness!' It was too unbearable. . . . I lost consciousness.

XXV

When I came to myself, I was lying on my back in the grass, feeling a dull ache all over me, as from a bad bruise. The dawn was beginning in the sky: I could clearly distinguish things. Not far off, alongside a birch copse, ran a road planted with willows: the country seemed familiar to me. I began to recollect what had happened to me, and shuddered all over directly my mind recalled the last, hideous apparition. . . .

'But what was Alice afraid of?' I thought. 'Can she too be subject to that power? Is she not immortal? Can she too be in danger of annihilation, dissolution? How is it possible?'

A soft moan sounded close by me. I turned my head. Two paces from me lay stretched out motionless a young woman in a white gown, with thick disordered tresses, with bare shoulders. One arm was thrown behind her head, the other had fallen on her bosom. Her eyes were closed, and on her tightly shut lips stood a fleck of crimson stain. Could it be Alice? But Alice was a phantom, and I was looking upon a living woman. I crept up to her, bent down. . . .

'Alice, is it you?' I cried. Suddenly, slowly quivering, the wide eyelids rose; dark piercing eyes were fastened upon me, and at the same instant lips too fastened upon me, warm, moist, smelling of blood . . . soft arms twined tightly round my neck, a burning, full heart pressed convulsively to mine. 'Farewell, farewell for ever!' the dying voice uttered distinctly, and everything vanished.

I got up, staggering like a drunken man, and passing my hands several times over my face, looked carefully about me. I found myself near the high road, a mile and a half from my own place. The sun had just risen when I got home.

All the following nights I awaited—and I confess not without alarm —the appearance of my phantom; but it did not visit me again. I even set off one day, in the dusk, to the old oak, but nothing took place there out of the common. I did not, however, overmuch regret the discontinuance of this strange acquaintance. I reflected much and long over this inexplicable, almost unintelligible phenomenon; and I am convinced that not only science cannot explain it, but that even in fairy tales and legends nothing like it is to be met with. What was Alice, after all? An apparition, a restless soul, an evil spirit, a sylphide, a vampire, or what? Sometimes it struck me again that Alice was a woman I had known at some time or other, and I made tremendous efforts to recall where I had seen her. . . . Yes, yes, I thought sometimes, directly, this minute, I shall remember. . . . In a flash everything had melted away again like a dream. Yes, I thought a great deal, and, as is always the way, came to no conclusion. The advice or opinion of others I could not bring myself to invite; fearing to be taken for a madman. I gave up all reflection upon it at last; to tell the truth, I had no time for it. For one thing, the emancipation had come along with the redistribution of property, etc.; and for another, my own health failed; I suffered with my chest, with sleeplessness, and a cough. I got thin all over. My face was yellow as a dead man's. The doctor declares I have too little blood, calls my illness by the Greek name, 'anæmia,' and is sending me to Gastein. The arbitrator swears that without me there's no coming to an understanding with the peasants. Well, what's one to do?

But what is the meaning of the piercingly-pure, shrill notes, the notes of an harmonica, which I hear directly any one's death is spoken of before me? They keep growing louder, more penetrating. . . . And why do I shudder in such anguish at the mere thought of annihilation?

The Mystery
of Black Jean

Julian Kilman

One of the best of the earliest contributors to Weird Tales *was* JULIAN KILMAN, *who sold a handful of memorably horrifying stories to the magazine during its first year, and never again. "The Mystery of Black Jean," a nasty history of figurative and literal bestiality, appeared in the very first issue of* The Unique Magazine *in March 1923.*

AYE, SIR, since you have asked, there has been many a guess about where Black Jean finally disappeared to.

He was a French-Canadian and a weed of a man—six-feet-five in his socks; his eyes were little and close together and black; he wore a long thin mustache that drooped; and he was as hairy as his two bears.

He just drifted up here to the North, I guess, picking up what scanty living he could by wrestling with the bears and making them wrestle each other. 'Twas in the King William hotel that many's the time I've seen Black Jean drink whisky by the cupful and feed it to the bears. Yes, he was interesting, especially to us boys.

Along about the time the French-Canadian and his trick animals were getting to be an old story, there comes—begging your pardon—a Yankee, who said he would put up a windmill at Morgan's Cove if he could get the quicklime to make the mortar with.

Black Jean said he knew how to make lime and if they would give

him time he would put up a kiln. So the French-Canadian went to work
and built that limekiln you see standing there.

I was a youngster then, and I know how Black Jean, a little later, built
his cabin. I used to hide and watch him and his bears. They worked like
men together, with an ugly-looking woman that had joined them. They
put up the cabin, the bears doing most of the heavy lifting work.

The place he picked for the cabin—over there where that clump of
trees. . . . No, not that way—more to the right, half a mile about—
that place is called "Split Hill," because there is a deep crack in the rock
made by some earthquake. The French-Canadian built his cabin across
the crack, and as the woman quarreled with him about the bears sleeping in the cabin he made a trap-door in the floor of the building and
stuck a small log down it, so the bears could climb up and down from
their den below.

The kiln, you can see for yourself, is a pit-kiln, so called because it is
in the side of a hill and the limestone is fed from the top and the fuel
from the bottom. Like a big chimney it works, and when Black Jean got
the fire started and going good it would roar up through the stone and
cook it. You could see the blaze for a mile.

One day Black Jean came to the King William looking for that Yankee. Seems that individual hadn't paid for his lime. When Black Jean
didn't find him at the tavern he started for the Cove.

I have never known who struck first; but they say the Yankee called
Black Jean a damn frog-eater and there was a fight; and that afternoon
the French-Canadian came to the tavern with his bears and all three of
them got drunk. Black Jean used to keep a muzzle on the larger of the
bears, but by tilting the brute's head he could pour whisky down its
throat. They got pretty drunk, and then someone dared Black Jean to
wrestle the muzzled bear.

There was a big tree standing in front of the tavern, and close by was
a worn-out pump having a big iron handle. Black Jean and the bear
went at it under the tree, the two of them clinching and hugging and
swearing until they both gasped for air. This day the big bear was
rougher than usual, and Black Jean lost his temper. It was his custom
when he got in too tight a place to kick the bear in the stomach; and this
time he began using his feet.

Suddenly we heard a rip of clothing. The bear had unsheathed his
claws; they were sharp as razors and tore Black Jean's clothing into

shreds and brought blood. Black Jean broke loose, his eyes flashing, his teeth gritting. Like lightning, he grabbed his dirk and leaped at the brute and jabbed the knife into its eye and gave a quick twist. The eyeball popped out and hung down by shreds alongside the bear's jaw.

Never can I forget the human-sounding shriek that bear gave, and how my father caught me up and scrambled behind the tree as the bear started for Black Jean. But the animal was near blinded, and Black Jean had time to jerk the iron handle out of the pump; and then, using it as if it didn't weigh any more than a spider's thought, he beat the bear over the head. He knocked it cold.

Then my father said: "That bear will kill you some day, Jean."

Black Jean stuck the iron pump handle back into its place.

"Bagosh! you t'ink dat true?" he sneered. "Mebbe I keel *her,* eh?"

Our place was next to the piece where Black Jean lived, and it was only next morning we heard a loud yelling over at Split Hill. I was a little fellow but spry, and when I reached Black Jean's cabin I was ahead of my father. I saw the French-Canadian leaning against a stump all alone, the blood streaming from his face.

"By God, M'sieu!" he blurted, when my father came up. "She scrat' my eye out."

My father thought he meant the woman.

"Who did?" he asked.

"Dat dam' bear," said Black Jean. "She just walk up an' steeck her foots in my eye."

Father caught hold of Black Jean and helped him to the cabin.

"Which bear was it?" he asked.

Black Jean slumped forward without answering. He had fainted.

I helped father get him into the house—he was more than one man could carry—and just as we went inside there was a growling and snarling, and the big muzzled bear went sliding down that pole to her nest.

Well, we looked all around for the woman, expecting to get her help; but we couldn't find her, which was the first we knew that she had left Black Jean.

It took the French-Canadian's eye two or three months to heal, and then he came to our place to get something to wear over the empty socket. So father hammered out a circular piece of copper about twice the size of a silver dollar and bored a hole in opposite sides for a leather

thong to hold it in place. Black Jean always wore it after that. He seemed
vain of that piece of copper, for he used to keep it polished and shined
until it glowed on a bright day like a bit of fire.

That fall the settlers opened up the first school in the district and im-
ported a woman teacher from "The States."

I must tell you about that teacher. She was a thin, little mite of a thing
that you would think the wind would blow away. Some said she was
pretty and some that she wasn't. I could have called her pretty if her eyes
hadn't been so black—hereabouts you don't see many eyes that are black
—brown, maybe, and blue and gray, but not black. Fact is, there were
just two people in these parts having those black eyes: Black Jean and the
little mite of a school teacher.

Well she came. And she hadn't been here a month before it was
noticed that Black Jean was coming to town more regular. And, what is
more, he was coming down by the school and waiting around there with
his bears.

This went on. They say that at first she didn't pay any attention to
him, but I can't speak for that as I was too young. But in time there was
talk and it came to me; then I watched. And I remember one afternoon
after the teacher let us out we all went over to where the bears were.
The teacher followed.

Black Jean was grinning and showing his white teeth.

"Beautiful ladee," says he. "Sooch eyes, mooch black like the back of a
water-bug."

Teacher smiled and said something I couldn't understand. It must
have been French. I had never seen a Frenchman around women before,
and Black Jean's manners were new to me. Here was a big weed of a
man bowing and scraping and standing with his cap in his hand. We
boys laughed at that—holding his cap in his hand.

The long and short of it was the French-Canadian was sparking the
school teacher. And everybody talked about it, of course; they said it was
a shame; they said if she didn't have sense enough to see what kind of a
man he was, someone should tell her.

I have often wondered since what would have happened if anybody
had gone to that woman with stories of Black Jean. I know I'd never
dared to, because, without knowing why, I was afraid of her. I guess
maybe that is why the others didn't, either.

There was no mistaking she was encouraging to Black Jean. She didn't seem to object in the slightest to his attentions, and I can see them yet: her, little and pretty and in a white dress, and Black Jean lingering there with his bears, dirty, and towering head and shoulders above her.

Black Jean kept coming and people went on talking, and finally somebody said she had been to Split Hill.

And one day I began to understand it, too. It was the time she was punishing some pupils. Three of them were lined up before her, and she started along whacking the outstretched hands with a stout ruler. Right in front of where I was sitting stood Ben Anger. He was the smallest of the lot and was trembling like a leaf.

Her first clip at him must have raised a welt on his hands, because he whimpered. She hit him again, and he closed his fingers. At that she caught up the jackknife he'd been whittling at his desk with and pried at his fingers until the blood came.

Sitting where I was, I saw her face while she was at it. It had the expression of a female devil. I didn't say anything to my folks about that; but I wasn't surprised when word came next week that we were to have a new teacher—the little one had gone to live with Black Jean.

Well, there was more talk—talk of rail-riding the pair of them out of the district. But nothing was done, and one evening, a month later, there was a rap at our door and the French-Canadian staggered in. He was carrying the school teacher in his arms.

"What has happened?" my father demanded.

"Dat dam' leetle bear," snarled Black Jean—"She try to keel Madam."

He laid the woman on the bed. She looked pretty badly cut up, and we sent for the doctor. Mother would only let her stay in the house that night, being shocked at the way she was living with the French-Canadian.

It turned out she wasn't much hurt, and father kept trying to find out just what had happened. But he couldn't. *I* knew, however. Most of my time, when I wasn't in school or running errands for the folks, I was spending watching that couple, and only that afternoon I had seen her stick a hot poker into the side of the smaller bear and wind it up into his fur until he screamed. And the bear must have bided his time and gone for her—those brutes were just like folks.

Next morning Black Jean came and got his woman, and I stole out and followed. I knew there would be more to it. I was right. The two of them went into the cabin, and pretty soon I heard a rumpus and out comes Black Jean with the smaller bear and behind them the woman. She was carrying a cowhide whip.

The French-Canadian had a chain looped about each forepaw of the animal, and, pulling it under a tree, he tossed the free end of the chain over a stout branch and yanked the bear off his feet. Then he wound the end of the chain about the trunk of the tree and sat down. So the bear hung, his feet trussed, and squirming and helpless.

And there in that clear day and warm sunshine, the woman started at the bear with the whip. She lashed it until it cried like a child. Black Jean watched the proceedings and grinned.

"Bah!" he shouted, after the woman had begun to tire. "She t'ink you foolin'. Heet harder. Heet the eyes!"

Again the woman went at it and kept it up until the bear quit moaning, and its head drooped and its body got limp. I was feeling sick at the sight, and I stole away.

But next morning, when I crawled back, there was the bear still hanging. It was dead.

That woman was a fair mate for Black Jean.

She kept him working steady over here to this kiln—most any night you could see the reflection of the blaze—and it was something to watch Black Jean when he was feeding his fire with the light playing on that copper piece and making it look like a big red eye flashing in the night. I saw it many times.

And it was noticed that Black Jean wasn't getting drunk any more, and he wasn't wrestling the one-eyed bear any more. He had good reason for that. I began to believe Black Jean was afraid of that brute.

But he made it work for him in the kiln, using the whip, and it was a curious animal, growling and snarling most of the time, as it pulled and lifted big sticks of wood and lugged them to the kiln.

When Black Jean wasn't working he was over at the cabin where he would follow the woman around like a dog. She could make him do anything. She was getting thinner and crosser, and I was more afraid of her than ever I was of Black Jean.

Once she caught me watching her from my spying-place in a tree. She had been petting the one-eyed bear, rubbing his snout and feeding him sugar. She ran to the house and got a rifle and, my friends, I came down out of that tree lickety split.

When I reached the ground she didn't say a word—just let her eyes rest on mine. After that I was more careful.

Then something happened.

I was hoeing corn one afternoon in a field next the road when I spied a woman coming along from the village. She was big and blowsy and was wearing a shawl. I knew she was headed for Black Jean's, because she climbed through the fence on his side of the road.

Keeping her in sight, I followed along my side and crossed over when I came to a place where she couldn't see me. I followed her because I knew she was the woman who had come to Black Jean when he first landed in the district. She walked up to the cabin, and I was wondering who she would find home, when out comes Black Jean.

"*Sacre!*" he exclaimed, putting one hand to his eye. "Spik queeck! Ees it Marie?"

"Yes," the woman said. "I have come back."

Black Jean looked around fearfully.

"Wat you want?" he demanded.

"I'd like to know who knocked your eye out," she laughed.

Black Jean did not laugh.

"You steal hunder' dollar from me an' run 'way," he snarled. "*Bagosh!* You give me dat monee."

"You fool!" said the woman. "You think I don't know where you got that money? You killed—"

A sound of rustling leaves in the wood nearby interrupted.

"*Ssh!*" hissed Black Jean, his face blanching. "For de love o' God, nod so loud."

He listened a moment; then his expression grew crafty. His teeth showed, and he went close to the woman and said something and started into the cabin.

The next instant I knew someone else had seen them. It was no other than the little ex-school teacher—and she was running away! I lay still a moment, scared out of my wits. Then I went home.

"Did you see Black Jean's wife?" my mother asked.

"You mean the school teacher woman?" I said.

"Yes," my mother said. "Who else?"

"I did," I said, "a while ago."

"I mean just now," said my mother, breathing quick. "She rushed in here, right into the house, and before I could stop her she snatched your father's rifle from the wall and ran out."

I didn't wait to hear more.

I set off through the fields for Black Jean's. Before I had run half the distance, I heard shooting, and it was father's rifle—I knew the sound of her only too well.

When I got to my spying-place it was all quiet at Black Jean's. I could not see a thing stirring about the cabin.

Then I thought of mother and started home. Father had gone over to the Cove that morning, with a load of wheat for the Yankee's mill, and wasn't to get back until late. So mother and I waited.

It was nearly one o'clock in the morning when we heard father's wagon, and I rushed outside.

"Hello, son," he exclaimed. "You're up late. And here's mother, too."

Father listened to what we told him, without saying a word.

"Well," he said, when we had finished. "I don't really see anything to worry about. Black Jean can take care of himself. Look there!"

He was pointing over here to this limekiln.

"Jean's had her loaded for a week," said father, "waiting for better weather."

Later, in the house, my father said: "It is none of our business, anyway."

And in a little he added, as if worried some: "But I am going over there after my rifle."

The following Sunday—three days later—father and I went to Black Jean's to get the rifle.

The door of the cabin opened, and the little woman came out. She was carrying the rifle. Somehow, she looked thin and old and her hands were like claws. But her eyes were bright and as sharp as the teeth of a weasel trap.

"I suppose," she said, as cool as a cucumber and as sweet as honey, "you have come after the rifle."

"That is what," said my father, sternly.

She handed it over.

"Please apologize to your wife for me," she said, "for the sudden way I took it. I was in a hurry. I saw a deer down by the marsh."

"Did you get the deer?" I piped in.

"No," she said. "I missed it."

Father and I started away. But he stopped and called: "Where is Black Jean this morning?"

"Black Jean!" she laughed. "Oh, he's got another sweetheart. He has gone away with her."

"Good-day," said father.

"Good-day," said she.

And that was the end of that.

Neither Black Jean nor the big blowsy woman was ever seen again, nor hide nor hair of them. But there was lots of talk. You see, there hadn't been any deer in these parts for many years; and besides it just was not possible for so well known a character as Black Jean to vanish so completely, without leaving a single trace.

Well, finally someone laid information in the county seat and over comes a smart young chap. He questioned father and mother and made me tell him all I knew, and took it all down in writing; then he gets a constable and goes over and they arrest the little black-eyed woman.

There was no trouble about it. They say she just smiled and asked what she was being arrested for—and they told her for the murder of Black Jean. She didn't say anything to that; only asked that someone feed the big one-eyed bear during the time she was locked up.

Then the people started coming. They came on horseback, they came afoot, they came in canoes, they came in lumber wagons—no matter how far away they lived—and brought their own food along. I calculate near every soul in the district turned out and made it a sort of general holiday and lay-off, for certain it is that no one cared anything about Black Jean himself.

Every inch of the land hereabouts was searched; they poked along the entire length of that earthquake crack, and in the clearings, and in the bush, looking for fresh-turned earth. But they could not find a thing— not a thing!

Now you gentlemen know that you can't convict a person for murder unless you have got positive proof that murder's been done—the dead body itself. Which was the case here, and that smart youth from the county seat had to let the little woman go free. So she came back to the cabin, living there as quiet as you please and minding her own precise business.

Here is a pocket-piece I have had for some time. You can see for yourself that it is copper.

It is the thing my father made for Black Jean to wear over his bad eye. I found that piece of copper two years after the little woman died—near twelve years after Black Jean disappeared. And I found it in the ashes and stone at the bottom of the limekiln standing there, half-tumbled down.

A lot of people hereabouts say it doesn't follow that Black Jean's body was burned in the kiln—cremated, I guess you city chaps would call it. They can't figure out how the mischief a little ninety-pound woman could have lugged those two bodies after she shot them with my father's rifle, the distance from the cabin to the kiln—a good half mile and more.

They point out that the body of Black Jean must have weighed over two hundred pounds, not to mention that the other woman was big and fat. But they make me weary.

It is as simple as the nose on your face: The big one-eyed bear did the job for her!

Lady Eleanore's Mantle

Nathaniel Hawthorne

Leave it to NATHANIEL HAWTHORNE *(1804–1864), author of such brooding masterpieces as "Young Goodman Brown,"* The Scarlet Letter *and* The House of the Seven Gables, *to equate turpitude with communal infection. Perhaps only Hawthorne, the descendant of somber Puritan settlers, could conceive of a disquieting belle dame sans merci like Lady Eleanore.*

MINE EXCELLENT FRIEND, the landlord of the Province House, was pleased, the other evening, to invite Mr. Tiffany and myself to an oyster supper. This slight mark of respect and gratitude, as he handsomely observed, was far less than the ingenious taleteller, and I, the humble note-taker of his narratives, had fairly earned, by the public notice which our joint lucubrations had attracted to his establishment. Many a cigar had been smoked within his premises—many a glass of wine, or more potent aqua vitae, had been quaffed—many a dinner had been eaten by curious strangers, who, save for the fortunate conjunction of Mr. Tiffany and me, would never have ventured through that darksome avenue which gives access to the historic precincts of the Province House. In short, if any credit be due to the courteous assurances of Mr. Thomas Waite, we had brought his forgotten mansion almost as effectually into public view as if we had thrown down the vulgar range of shoe shops and drygoods stores, which hides its aristocratic front from Washington Street. It may be unadvisable, however, to speak too loudly of the increased custom of the house, lest Mr. Waite should find it difficult to renew the lease on so favorable terms as heretofore.

Being thus welcomed as benefactors, neither Mr. Tiffany nor myself felt any scruple in doing full justice to the good things that were set before us. If the feast were less magnificent than those same paneled walls had witnessed in a bygone century, if mine host presided with somewhat less of state than might have befitted a successor of the royal Governors, if the guests made a less imposing show than the bewigged and powdered and embroidered dignitaries who erst banqueted at the gubernatorial table, and now sleep, within their armorial tombs on Copp's Hill, or round King's Chapel—yet never, I may boldly say, did a more comfortable little party assemble in the Province House, from Queen Anne's days to the Revolution. The occasion was rendered more interesting by the presence of a venerable personage, whose own actual reminiscences went back to the epoch of Gage and Howe, and even supplied him with a doubtful anecdote or two of Hutchinson. He was one of that small, and now all but extinguished, class whose attachment to royalty, and to the colonial institutions and customs that were connected with it, had never yielded to the democratic heresies of aftertimes. The young queen of Britain has not a more loyal subject in her realm— perhaps not one who would kneel before her throne with such reverential love—as this old grandsire, whose head has whitened beneath the mild sway of the Republic, which still, in his mellower moments, he terms a usurpation. Yet prejudices so obstinate have not made him an ungentle or impracticable companion. If the truth must be told, the life of the aged loyalist has been of such a scrambling and unsettled character —he has had so little choice of friends and been so often destitute of any —that I doubt whether he would refuse a cup of kindness with either Oliver Cromwell or John Hancock, to say nothing of any democrat now upon the stage. In another paper of this series I may perhaps give the reader a closer glimpse of his portrait.

Our host, in due season, uncorked a bottle of Madeira, of such exquisite perfume and admirable flavor that he surely must have discovered it in an ancient bin, down deep beneath the deepest cellar, where some jolly old butler stored away the Governor's choicest wine, and forgot to reveal the secret on his deathbed. Peace to his red-nosed ghost, and a libation to his memory! This precious liquor was imbibed by Mr. Tiffany with peculiar zest; and after sipping the third glass, it was his pleasure to give us one of the oddest legends which he had yet raked from the storehouse where he keeps such matters. With some suitable adornments from my own fancy, it ran pretty much as follows.

Not long after Colonel Shute had assumed the government of Massachusetts Bay, now nearly a hundred and twenty years ago, a young lady of rank and fortune arrived from England, to claim his protection as her guardian. He was her distant relative, but the nearest who had survived the gradual extinction of her family; so that no more eligible shelter could be found for the rich and highborn Lady Eleanore Rochcliffe than within the Province House of a transatlantic colony. The consort of Governor Shute, moreover, had been as a mother to her childhood, and was now anxious to receive her, in the hope that a beautiful young woman would be exposed to infinitely less peril from the primitive society of New England than amid the artifices and corruptions of a court. If either the Governor or his lady had especially consulted their own comfort, they would probably have sought to devolve the responsibility on other hands; since, with some noble and splendid traits of character, Lady Eleanore was remarkable for a harsh, unyielding pride, a haughty consciousness of her hereditary and personal advantages, which made her almost incapable of control. Judging from many traditionary anecdotes, this peculiar temper was hardly less than a monomania; or, if the acts which it inspired were those of a sane person, it seemed due from Providence that pride so sinful should be followed by as severe a retribution. That tinge of the marvelous which is thrown over so many of these half-forgotten legends has probably imparted an additional wildness to the strange story of Lady Eleanore Rochcliffe.

The ship in which she came passenger had arrived at Newport, whence Lady Eleanore was conveyed to Boston in the Governor's coach, attended by a small escort of gentlemen on horseback. The ponderous equipage, with its four black horses, attracted much notice as it rumbled through Cornhill, surrounded by the prancing steeds of half a dozen cavaliers, with swords dangling to their stirrups and pistols at their holsters. Through the large glass windows of the coach, as it rolled along, the people could discern the figure of Lady Eleanore, strangely combining an almost queenly stateliness with the grace and beauty of a maiden in her teens. A singular tale had gone abroad among the ladies of the province that their fair rival was indebted for much of the irresistible charm of her appearance to a certain article of dress—an embroidered mantle—which had been wrought by the most skillful artist in London, and possessed even magical properties of adornment. On the present occasion, however, she owed nothing to the witchery of dress, being clad in a riding habit of velvet, which would have appeared stiff and ungraceful on any other form.

The coachman reined in his four black steeds, and the whole cavalcade came to a pause in front of the contorted iron balustrade that fenced the Province House from the public street. It was an awkward coincidence that the bell of the Old South was just then tolling for a funeral; so that, instead of a gladsome peal with which it was customary to announce the arrival of distinguished strangers, Lady Eleanore Rochcliffe was ushered by a doleful clang, as if calamity had come embodied in her beautiful person.

"A very great disrespect!" exclaimed Captain Langford, an English officer, who had recently brought dispatches to Governor Shute. "The funeral should have been deferred, lest Lady Eleanore's spirits be affected by such a dismal welcome."

"With your pardon, sir," replied Dr. Clarke, a physician, and a famous champion of the popular party, "whatever the heralds may pretend, a dead beggar must have precedence of a living queen. King Death confers high privileges."

These remarks were interchanged while the speakers waited a passage through the crowd which had gathered on each side of the gateway, leaving an open avenue to the portal of the Province House. A black slave in livery now leaped from behind the coach, and threw open the door; while at the same moment Governor Shute descended the flight of steps from his mansion, to assist Lady Eleanore in alighting. But the Governor's stately approach was anticipated in a manner that excited general astonishment. A pale young man, with his black hair all in disorder, rushed from the throng, and prostrated himself beside the coach, thus offering his person as a footstool for Lady Eleanore Rochcliffe to tread upon. She held back an instant, yet with an expression as if doubting whether the young man were worthy to bear the weight of her footstep, rather than dissatisfied to receive such awful reverence from a fellow mortal.

"Up, sir," said the Governor, sternly, at the same time lifting his cane over the intruder. "What means the bedlamite by this freak?"

"Nay," answered Lady Eleanore, playfully, but with more scorn than pity in her tone, "your Excellency shall not strike him. When men seek only to be trampled upon, it were a pity to deny them a favor so easily granted—and so well deserved!"

Then, though as lightly as a sunbeam on a cloud, she placed her foot upon the cowering form, and extended her hand to meet that of the Governor. There was a brief interval during which Lady Eleanore retained this attitude; and never, surely, was there an apter emblem of aristocracy and hereditary pride trampling on human sympathies and the kindred of nature than these two figures presented at that moment. Yet the spectators were so smitten with her beauty, and so essential did pride seem to the existence of such a creature, that they gave a simultaneous acclamation of applause.

"Who is this insolent young fellow?" inquired Captain Langford, who still remained beside Dr. Clarke. "If he be in his senses, his impertinence demands the bastinado. If mad, Lady Eleanore should be secured from further inconvenience by his confinement."

"His name is Jervase Helwyse," answered the doctor, "a youth of no birth or fortune, or other advantages, save the mind and soul that nature gave him; and being secretary to our colonial agent in London, it was his misfortune to meet this Lady Eleanore Rochcliffe. He loved her—and her scorn has driven him mad."

"He was mad so to aspire," observed the English officer.

"It may be so," said Dr. Clarke, frowning as he spoke. "But I tell you, sir, I could well-nigh doubt the justice of the Heaven above us if no signal humiliation overtake this lady, who now treads so haughtily into yonder mansion. She seeks to place herself above the sympathies of our common nature, which envelops all human souls. See if that nature do not assert its claim over her in some mode that shall bring her level with the lowest!"

"Never!" cried Captain Langford, indignantly—"neither in life, nor when they lay her with her ancestors."

Not many days afterwards, the Governor gave a ball in honor of Lady Eleanore Rochcliffe. The principal gentry of the colony received invitations, which were distributed to their residences, far and near, by messengers on horseback, bearing missives sealed with all the formality of official dispatches. In obedience to the summons, there was a general gathering of rank, wealth, and beauty; and the wide door of the Province

House had seldom given admittance to more numerous and honorable guests than on the evening of Lady Eleanore's ball. Without much extravagance of eulogy, the spectacle might even be termed splendid; for, according to the fashion of the times, the ladies shone in rich silks and satins, outspread over wide-projecting hoops; and the gentlemen glittered in gold embroidery, laid unsparingly upon the purple, or scarlet, or sky-blue velvet which was the material of their coats and waistcoats. The latter article of dress was of great importance, since it enveloped the wearer's body nearly to the knees, and was perhaps bedizened with the amount of his whole year's income, in golden flowers and foliage. The altered taste of the present day—a taste symbolic of a deep change in the whole system of society—would look upon almost any of those gorgeous figures as ridiculous; although that evening the guests sought their reflections in the pier glasses, and rejoiced to catch their own glitter amid the glittering crowd. What a pity that one of the stately mirrors has not preserved a picture of the scene, which, by the very traits that were so transitory, might have taught us much that would be worth knowing and remembering!

Would, at least, that either painter or mirror could convey to us some faint idea of a garment already noticed in this legend—the Lady Eleanore's embroidered mantle—which the gossips whispered was invested with magic properties, so as to lend a new and untried grace to her figure each time that she put it on! Idle fancy as it is, this mysterious mantle has thrown an awe around my image of her, partly from its fabled virtues, and partly because it was the handiwork of a dying woman, and, perchance, owed the fantastic grace of its conception to the delirium of approaching death.

After the ceremonial greetings had been paid, Lady Eleanore Rochcliffe stood apart from the mob of guests, insulating herself within a small and distinguished circle, to whom she accorded a more cordial favor than to the general throng. The waxen torches threw their radiance vividly over the scene, bringing out its brilliant points in strong relief; but she gazed carelessly, and with now and then an expression of weariness or scorn, tempered with such feminine grace that her auditors scarcely perceived the moral deformity of which it was the utterance. She beheld the spectacle not with vulgar ridicule, as disdaining to be pleased with the provincial mockery of a court festival, but with the deeper scorn of one whose spirit held itself too high to participate in the enjoyment of other human souls. Whether or no the recollections of those who saw her that evening were influenced by the strange events with which she was subsequently connected, so it was that her figure ever after recurred to them as marked by something wild and unnatural —although, at the time, the general whisper was of her exceeding beauty, and of the indescribable charm which her mantle threw around her. Some close observers, indeed, detected a feverish flush and alternate paleness of countenance, with a corresponding flow and revulsion of spirits, and once or twice a painful and helpless betrayal of lassitude, as if she were on the point of sinking to the ground. Then, with a nervous shudder, she seemed to arouse her energies and threw some bright and playful yet half-wicked sarcasm into the conversation. There was so strange a characteristic in her manners and sentiments that it astonished every right-minded listener; till looking in her face, a lurking and incomprehensible glance and smile perplexed them with doubts both as to her seriousness and sanity. Gradually, Lady Eleanore Rochcliffe's circle grew smaller, till only four gentlemen remained in it. These were Captain Langford, the English officer before mentioned; a Virginian planter, who had come to Massachusetts on some political errand; a young Episcopal clergyman, the grandson of a British earl; and, lastly, the private secretary of Governor Shute, whose obsequiousness had won a sort of tolerance from Lady Eleanore.

At different periods of the evening, the liveried servants of the Province House passed among the guests, bearing huge trays of refreshments and French and Spanish wines. Lady Eleanore Rochcliffe, who refused to wet her beautiful lips even with a bubble of champagne, had sunk back into a large damask chair, apparently overwearied either with the excitement of the scene or its tedium, and while, for an instant, she was unconscious of voices, laughter, and music, a young man stole forward, and knelt down at her feet. He bore a salver in his hand, on which was a chased silver goblet, filled to the brim with wine, which he offered as reverentially as to a crowned queen, or rather with the awful devotion of a priest doing sacrifice to his idol. Conscious that someone touched her robe, Lady Eleanore started, and unclosed her eyes upon the pale, wild features and disheveled hair of Jervase Helwyse.

"Why do you haunt me thus?" said she, in a languid tone, but with a kindlier feeling than she ordinarily permitted herself to express. "They tell me that I have done you harm."

"Heaven knows if that be so," replied the young man, solemnly. "But, Lady Eleanore, in requital of that harm, if such there be, and for your own earthly and heavenly welfare, I pray you to take one sip of this holy wine, and then to pass the goblet round among the guests. And this shall be a symbol that you have not sought to withdraw yourself from the chain of human sympathies—which whoso would shake off must keep company with fallen angels."

"Where has this mad fellow stolen that sacramental vessel?" exclaimed the Episcopal clergyman.

This question drew the notice of the guests to the silver cup, which was recognized as appertaining to the communion plate of the Old South Church; and, for aught that could be known, it was brimming over with the consecrated wine.

"Perhaps it is poisoned," half whispered the Governor's secretary.

"Pour it down the villain's throat!" cried the Virginian, fiercely.

"Turn him out of the house!" cried Captain Langford, seizing Jervase Helwyse so roughly by the shoulder that the sacramental cup was overturned, and its contents sprinkled upon Lady Eleanore's mantle. "Whether knave, fool, or bedlamite, it is intolerable that the fellow should go at large."

"Pray, gentlemen, do my poor admirer no harm," said Lady Eleanore, with a faint and weary smile. "Take him out of my sight, if such be your pleasure; for I can find in my heart to do nothing but laugh at him; whereas, in all decency and conscience, it would become me to weep for the mischief I have wrought!"

But while the bystanders were attempting to lead away the unfortunate young man, he broke from them, and with a wild, impassioned earnestness, offered a new and equally strange petition to Lady Eleanore. It was no other than that she should throw off the mantle, which, while he pressed the silver cup of wine upon her, she had drawn more closely around her form, so as almost to shroud herself within it.

"Cast it from you!" exclaimed Jervase Helwyse, clasping his hands in an agony of entreaty. "It may not yet be too late! Give the accursed garment to the flames!"

But Lady Eleanore, with a laugh of scorn, drew the rich folds of the embroidered mantle over her head, in such a fashion as to give a completely new aspect to her beautiful face, which—half hidden, half revealed—seemed to belong to some being of mysterious character and purposes.

"Farewell, Jervase Helwyse!" said she. "Keep my image in your remembrance, as you behold it now."

"Alas, lady!" he replied, in a tone no longer wild, but sad as a funeral bell. "We must meet shortly, when your face may wear another aspect—and that shall be the image that must abide within me."

He made no more resistance to the violent efforts of the gentlemen and servants, who almost dragged him out of the apartment, and dismissed him roughly from the iron gate of the Province House. Captain Langford, who had been very active in this affair, was returning to the presence of Lady Eleanore Rochcliffe, when he encountered the physician, Dr. Clarke, with whom he had held some casual talk on the day of her arrival. The doctor stood apart, separated from Lady Eleanore by the width of the room, but eying her with such keen sagacity that Captain Langford involuntarily gave him credit for the discovery of some deep secret.

"You appear to be smitten, after all, with the charms of this queenly maiden," said he, hoping thus to draw forth the physician's hidden knowledge.

"God forbid!" answered Dr. Clarke, with a grave smile; "and if you be wise, you will put up the same prayer for yourself. Woe to those who shall be smitten by this beautiful Lady Eleanore! But yonder stands the Governor—and I have a word or two for his private ear. Good night!"

He accordingly advanced to Governor Shute, and addressed him in so low a tone that none of the bystanders could catch a word of what he said, although the sudden change of his Excellency's hitherto cheerful visage betokened that the communication could be of no agreeable import. A very few moments afterwards, it was announced to the guests that an unforeseen circumstance rendered it necessary to put a premature close to the festival.

The ball at the Province House supplied a topic of conversation for the colonial metropolis for some days after its occurrence, and might still longer have been the general theme, only that a subject of all-engrossing interest thrust it, for a time, from the public recollection. This was the appearance of a dreadful epidemic, which, in that age and long before and afterwards, was wont to slay its hundreds and thousands on both sides of the Atlantic. On the occasion of which we speak, it was distinguished by a peculiar virulence, insomuch that it has left its traces—its pit marks, to use an appropriate figure—on the history of the country, the affairs of which were thrown into confusion by its ravages. At first, unlike its ordinary course, the disease seemed to confine itself to the higher circles of society, selecting its victims from among the proud, the well-born, and the wealthy, entering unabashed into stately chambers, and lying down with the slumberers in silken beds. Some of the most distinguished guests of the Province House—even those whom the haughty Lady Eleanore Rochcliffe had deemed not unworthy of her favor—were stricken by this fatal scourge. It was noticed, with an ungenerous bitterness of feeling, that the four gentlemen—the Virginian, the British officer, the young clergyman, and the Governor's secretary— who had been her most devoted attendants on the evening of the ball were the foremost on whom the plague stroke fell. But the disease, pursuing its onward progress, soon ceased to be exclusively a prerogative of aristocracy. Its red brand was no longer conferred like a noble's star, or an order of knighthood. It threaded its way through the narrow and crooked streets, and entered the low, mean, darksome dwellings, and laid its hand of death upon the artisans and laboring classes of the town. It compelled rich and poor to feel themselves brethren then; and stalking to and fro across the Three Hills, with a fierceness which made it almost a new pestilence, there was that mighty conqueror—that scourge and horror of our forefathers—the smallpox!

We cannot estimate the affright which this plague inspired of yore, by contemplating it as the fangless monster of the present day. We must remember, rather, with what awe we watched the gigantic footsteps of the Asiatic cholera, striding from shore to shore of the Atlantic, and marching like destiny upon cities far remote which flight had already half depopulated. There is no other fear so horrible and unhumanizing as that which makes man dread to breathe heaven's vital air lest it be poison, or to grasp the hand of a brother or friend lest the gripe of the pestilence should clutch him. Such was the dismay that now followed in the track of the disease, or ran before it throughout the town. Graves were hastily dug, and the pestilential relics as hastily covered, because the dead were enemies of the living, and strove to draw them headlong, as it were, into their own dismal pit. The public councils were suspended, as if mortal wisdom might relinquish its devices, now that an unearthly usurper had found his way into the ruler's mansion. Had an enemy's fleet been hovering on the coast, or his armies trampling on our soil, the people would probably have committed their defense to that same direful conqueror who had wrought their own calamity, and would permit no interference with his sway. This conqueror had a symbol of his triumphs. It was a blood-red flag, that fluttered in the tainted air over the door of every dwelling into which the smallpox had entered.

Such a banner was long since waving over the portal of the Province House; for thence, as was proved by tracking its footsteps back, had all this dreadful mischief issued. It had been traced back to a lady's luxurious chamber—to the proudest of the proud—to her that was so delicate, and hardly owned herself of earthly mold—to the haughty one, who took her stand above human sympathies—to Lady Eleanore! There remained no room for doubt that the contagion had lurked in that gorgeous mantle which threw so strange a grace around her at the festival. Its fantastic splendor had been conceived in the delirious brain of a woman on her deathbed, and was the last toil of her stiffening fingers, which had interwoven fate and misery with its golden threads. This dark tale, whispered at first, was now bruited far and wide. The people raved against the Lady Eleanore, and cried out that her pride and scorn had evoked a fiend, and that, between them both, this monstrous evil had been born. At times, their rage and despair took the semblance of grinning mirth; and whenever the red flag of the pestilence was hoisted over another and yet another door, they clapped their hands and shouted through the streets, in bitter mockery: "Behold a new triumph for the Lady Eleanore!"

One day, in the midst of these dismal times, a wild figure approached the portal of the Province House, and folding his arms, stood contemplating the scarlet banner which a passing breeze shook fitfully, as if to fling abroad the contagion that it typified. At length, climbing one of the pillars by means of the iron balustrade, he took down the flag and entered the mansion, waving it above his head. At the foot of the staircase he met the Governor, booted and spurred, with his cloak drawn around him, evidently on the point of setting forth upon a journey.

"Wretched lunatic, what do you seek here?" exclaimed Shute, extending his cane to guard himself from contact. "There is nothing here but Death. Back—or you will meet him!"

"Death will not touch me, the banner-bearer of the pestilence!" cried Jervase Helwyse, shaking the red flag aloft. "Death, and the Pestilence, who wears the aspect of the Lady Eleanore, will walk through the streets tonight, and I must march before them with this banner!"

"Why do I waste words on the fellow?" muttered the Governor, drawing his cloak across his mouth. "What matters his miserable life, when none of us are sure of twelve hours' breath? On, fool, to your own destruction!"

He made way for Jervase Helwyse, who immediately ascended the staircase, but, on the first landing place, was arrested by the firm grasp of a hand upon his shoulder. Looking fiercely up, with a madman's impulse to struggle with and rend asunder his opponent, he found himself powerless beneath a calm, stern eye, which possessed the mysterious property of quelling frenzy at its height. The person whom he had now encountered was the physician, Dr. Clarke, the duties of whose sad profession had led him to the Province House, where he was an infrequent guest in more prosperous times.

"Young man, what is your purpose?" demanded he.

"I seek the Lady Eleanore," answered Jervase Helwyse, submissively.

"All have fled from her," said the physician. "Why do you seek her now? I tell you, youth, her nurse fell death-stricken on the threshold of that fatal chamber. Know ye not that never came such a curse to our shores as this lovely Lady Eleanore? that her breath has filled the air with poison? that she has shaken pestilence and death upon the land, from the folds of her accursed mantle?"

"Let me look upon her!" rejoined the mad youth, more wildly. "Let me behold her, in her awful beauty, clad in the regal garments of the pestilence! She and Death sit on a throne together. Let me kneel down before them!"

"Poor youth!" said Dr. Clarke; and, moved by a deep sense of human weakness, a smile of caustic humor curled his lip even then. "Wilt thou still worship the destroyer and surround her image with fantasies the more magnificent, the more evil she has wrought? Thus man doth ever to his tyrants. Approach, then! Madness, as I have noted, has that good efficacy, that it will guard you from contagion—and perchance its own cure may be found in yonder chamber."

Ascending another flight of stairs, he threw open a door and signed to Jervase Helwyse that he should enter. The poor lunatic, it seems probable, had cherished a delusion that his haughty mistress sat in state, unharmed herself by the pestilential influence, which, as by enchantment, she scattered round about her. He dreamed, no doubt, that her beauty was not dimmed, but brightened into superhuman splendor. With such anticipations, he stole reverentially to the door at which the physician stood, but paused upon the threshold, gazing fearfully into the gloom of the darkened chamber.

"Where is the Lady Eleanore?" whispered he.

"Call her," replied the physician.

"Lady Eleanore! Princess! Queen of Death!" cried Jervase Helwyse, advancing three steps into the chamber. "She is not here! There, on yonder table, I behold the sparkle of a diamond which once she wore upon her bosom. There"—and he shuddered—"there hangs her mantle, on which a dead woman embroidered a spell of dreadful potency. But where is the Lady Eleanore?"

Something stirred within the silken curtains of a canopied bed; and a low moan was uttered, which, listening intently, Jervase Helwyse began to distinguish as a woman's voice, complaining dolefully of thirst. He fancied, even, that he recognized its tones.

"My throat! my throat is scorched," murmured the voice. "A drop of water!"

"What thing art thou?" said the brain-stricken youth, drawing near the bed and tearing asunder its curtains. "Whose voice hast thou stolen for thy murmurs and miserable petitions, as if Lady Eleanore could be conscious of mortal infirmity? Fie! Heap of diseased mortality, why lurkest thou in my lady's chamber?"

"O Jervase Helwyse," said the voice—and as it spoke the figure contorted itself, struggling to hide its blasted face—"look not now on the woman you once loved! The curse of Heaven hath stricken me, because I would not call man my brother, nor woman sister. I wrapped myself in pride as in a mantle, and scorned the sympathies of Nature; and therefore has Nature made this wretched body the medium of a dreadful sympathy. You are avenged—they are all avenged—Nature is avenged—for I am Eleanore Rochcliffe!"

The malice of his mental disease, the bitterness lurking at the bottom of his heart, mad as he was, for a blighted and ruined life, and love that had been paid with cruel scorn, awoke within the breast of Jervase Helwyse. He shook his finger at the wretched girl, and the chamber echoed, the curtains of the bed were shaken, with his outburst of insane merriment.

"Another triumph for the Lady Eleanore!" he cried. "All have been her victims! Who so worthy to be the final victim as herself?"

Impelled by some new fantasy of his crazed intellect, he snatched the fatal mantle and rushed from the chamber and the house. That night a procession passed, by torchlight, through the streets, bearing in the midst the figure of a woman, enveloped with a richly embroidered mantle; while in advance stalked Jervase Helwyse, waving the red flag of the pestilence. Arriving opposite the Province House, the mob burned the effigy, and a strong wind came and swept away the ashes. It was said that from that very hour, the pestilence abated, as if its sway had some mysterious connection, from the first plague stroke to the last, with Lady Eleanore's mantle. A remarkable uncertainty broods over that unhappy lady's fate. There is a belief, however, that in a certain chamber of this mansion a female form may sometimes be duskily discerned, shrinking into the darkest corner and muffling her face within an embroidered mantle. Supposing the legend true, can this be other than the once proud Lady Eleanore?

Mine host and the old loyalist and I bestowed no little warmth of applause upon this narrative, in which we had all been deeply interested; for the reader can scarcely conceive how unspeakably the effect of such a tale is heightened when, as in the present case, we may repose perfect confidence in the veracity of him who tells it. For my own part, knowing how scrupulous is Mr. Tiffany to settle the foundation of his facts, I could not have believed him one whit the more faithfully had he professed himself an eyewitness of the doings and sufferings of poor Lady Eleanore. Some skeptics, it is true, might demand documentary evidence, or even require him to produce the embroidered mantle, forgetting that—Heaven be praised—it was consumed to ashes. But now the old loyalist, whose blood was warmed by the good cheer, began to talk, in his turn, about the traditions of the Province House, and hinted that he, if it were agreeable, might add a few reminiscences to our legendary stock. Mr. Tiffany, having no cause to dread a rival, immediately besought him to favor us with a specimen; my own entreaties, of course, were urged to the same effect; and our venerable guest, well pleased to find willing auditors, awaited only the return of Mr. Thomas Waite, who had been summoned forth to provide accommodations for several new arrivals. Perchance the public—but be this as its own caprice and ours shall settle the matter—may read the result in another tale of the Province House.

The Thing at Ghent

Honoré de Balzac

"The Thing at Ghent" is a brief guignol by the French writer HONORÉ DE
BALZAC *(1799–1859), who wrote the* Comédie Humaine, *an interrelated
sequence of ninety-one novels and stories that, if Balzac had lived to complete
it, would have totaled 137 compositions. This English version was translated
in 1900 by—believe it or not!—Ellen Marriage.*

A PECULIAR THING took place at Ghent while I was staying
there. A lady ten years a widow lay on her bed attacked by mortal
sickness. The three heirs of collateral lineage were waiting for her last
sigh. They did not leave her side for fear that she would make a will in
favor of the convent of Beguins belonging to the town. The sick woman
kept silent, she seemed dozing and death appeared to overspread very
gradually her mute and livid face. Can't you imagine those three relations seated in silence through that winter midnight beside her bed? An
old nurse is with them and she shakes her head, and the doctor sees with
anxiety that the sickness has reached its last stage, and holds his hat in
one hand and with the other makes a sign to the relations, as if to say to
them: "I have no more visits to make here." Amid the solemn silence of
the room is heard the dull rustling of a snow storm which beats upon the
shutters. For fear that the eyes of the dying woman might be dazzled by
the light, the youngest of the heirs had fitted a shade to the candle which
stood near the bed so that the circle of light scarcely reached the pillow

of the death bed, from which the sallow countenance of the sick woman stood out like the figure of Christ imperfectly gilded and fixed upon a cross of tarnished silver. The flickering rays shed by the blue flames of a crackling fire were therefore the sole light of this somber chamber, where the dénouement of a drama was just ending. A log suddenly rolled from the fire onto the floor, as if presaging some catastrophe. At the sound of it the sick woman quickly rose to a sitting posture. She opened two eyes, clear as those of a cat, and all present eyed her in astonishment. She saw the log advance, and before any one could check an unexpected movement which seemed prompted by a kind of delirium, she bounded from her bed, seized the tongs and threw the coal back into the fireplace. The nurse, the doctor, the relations rushed to her assistance; they took the dying woman in their arms. They put her back in bed; she laid her head upon her pillow and after a few minutes died, keeping her eye fixed even after her death upon that plank in the floor which the burning brand had touched. Scarcely had the Countess Van Ostroem expired when the three co-heirs exchanged looks of suspicion, and thinking no more about their aunt, began to examine the mysterious floor. As they were Belgians their calculations were as rapid as their glances. An agreement was made by three words uttered in a low voice that none of them should leave the chamber. A servant was sent to fetch a carpenter. Their collateral hearts beat excitedly as they gathered round the treasured flooring, and watched their young apprentice giving the first blow with his chisel. The plank was cut through.

"My aunt made a sign," said the youngest of the heirs.

"No; it was merely the quivering light that made it appear so," replied the eldest, who kept one eye on the treasure and the other on the corpse.

The afflicted relations discovered exactly on the spot where the brand had fallen a certain object artistically enveloped in a mass of plaster.

"Proceed," said the eldest of the heirs.

The chisel of the apprentice then brought to light a human head and some odds and ends of clothing, from which they recognized the count whom all the town believed to have died at Java, and whose loss had been bitterly deplored by his wife.

The Sisters

Alfred, Lord Tennyson

We were two daughters of one race:
She was the fairest in the face:
    The wind is blowing in turret and tree.
They were together, and she fell;
Therefore revenge became me well.
    O the Earl was fair to see!

She died: she went to burning flame:
She mix'd her ancient blood with shame.
    The wind is howling in turret and tree.
Whole weeks and months, and early and late,
To win his love I lay in wait:
    O the Earl was fair to see!

I made a feast; I bade him come;
I won his love, I brought him home.
    The wind is roaring in turret and tree.
And after supper, on a bed,
Upon my lap he laid his head:
    O the Earl was fair to see!

I kiss'd his eyelids into rest:
His ruddy cheek upon my breast.
   The wind is raging in turret and tree.
I hated him with the hate of Hell,
But I loved his beauty passing well.
   O the Earl was fair to see!

I rose up in the silent night:
I made my dagger sharp and bright.
   The wind is raving in turret and tree.
As half-asleep his breath he drew,
Three times I stabb'd him thro' and thro'.
   O the Earl was fair to see!

I curl'd and comb'd his comely head,
He look'd so grand when he was dead.
   The wind is blowing in turret and tree.
I wrapt his body in the sheet,
And laid him at his mother's feet.
   O the Earl was fair to see!

Malevendra's Pool

Darrell Schweitzer

*Women are especially dangerous when they happen to be goddesses, as may be
seen in this dark tale from the prolific* DARRELL SCHWEITZER, *a Pennsylvania
editor and author of such imaginative fiction as "The Throwing Suit" (with
Jason Van Hollander), "The Adventure of the Death-Fetch," "Pennies from
Hell" and numerous other fantasy stories.*

We are all as cripples before the gods.
   —unknown

*I accept death as the necessary counterbalance to life, and sorrow as the
perpetual handmaiden of joy; for no victory comes without pain, and the gold
of glory is always tarnished.*
   —from the initiation oath of the Knights Inquisitor

You can hear the pretty stories: about Malevendra, the Goddess of
Spring, the Lady of the Flowers, who is also called the Mother of Sorrows. The priests will tell you. The poets will tell you, especially, how
she weeps with the realization that each living thing must die, how each
of her flowers will soon be brown and brittle; and they'll tell you of her
famed and mysterious pool, which is located in no specific place, but
appears to some men and not to others, whenever the inscrutable will of

the goddess causes it to appear. They say that it is formed out of a single tear.

That may well be so, but there is more. I know. I found that pool—of sorrow and forgetting and revelation—when I was still a child, and I saw my whole life unfold in its miraculous waters. It was from the waters of Malevendra's pool that I learned what it means to be a knight.

This is not a pretty story. It is merely true.

The first thirteen years of my life were filled with comings and goings, and the distant thunder of battles.

My very first memory is of riding in a crowded, covered wagon, held firmly on my mother's lap among silent strangers; riding past ruined farmhouses and empty fields. I could smell the burnt wood, the mud, and, I think, the fear of the other passengers.

Suddenly the road was filled with cavalry, hoofbeats thudding, armor and weapons jangling in the darkness as the horsemen streamed back the way we had come. I broke away from my mother. My father, sitting across from us, made a half-hearted grab for me and missed. I clambered to the end of the wagon, and stood clutching the tailgate, hoping for a glimpse of the knights in their golden armor, their tall plumes, their lances draped with pennons.

These men were fighters, not on parade. Their armor was tarnished. They carried no pennons.

I remember standing there, bewildered and disappointed, staring.

Then one of them turned back—a silver-bearded face—and our eyes met for an instant, and he seemed more astonished than I.

One more thing happened on that journey, just at dawn. Again we were alone on the road, and my parents hadn't bothered to retrieve me from the end of the wagon.

I was half asleep, leaning over the tailgate, gazing out at the empty fields beneath the greying sky.

A woman appeared from somewhere. She was running to keep up with us, begging to be let aboard. Somehow her gaunt, soot-streaked face frightened me, and I screamed.

Everyone was shouting. I was shoved back, and had to crawl back toward my mother between the legs of the adults. At the very last, the woman let out a hoarse cry and heaved a bundle into the wagon.

It was a baby, blue and dead. It landed on the floor in front of me. Father threw it out again.

My parents settled in a new town and set up a tavern there. So all my childhood was filled with the company of armored men, their songs, their oaths, their stories. There were few other travellers on the roads in those days, as the war sometimes drew so near that we could see the smoke from burning fields, then receded like a tide.

Soldiers filled our common room, rough men dressed in black leather and studs and mail; and sometimes barbarian mercenaries in skins, or just ragged, sullen strangers who would not be questioned. Only once in a great while did we host a true knight, and rarer still a Knight Inquisitor, one of those holy warriors of the Nine Gods, who did, indeed, wear beautifully decorated armor of silver or black plate and carry pennon-draped lances.

It seemed to me that there was no finer person in all the world than such a man, and from almost the first day of my life, I knew that I wanted to be one too, likewise to serve the Gods of Light and let my ears be filled with thunder as a hundred armies contended on the threshing-floor of nations.

"A strange ambition for a cripple," people said. They laughed, "Hail Sir Vynae Crooked Foot!"

It was so. I had been born with my right leg withered and twisted below the knee. I could walk easily enough with the aid of a stick, but I could not run, and was unpromising material for the Knights Inquisitor.

When I was ten, my mother went to the Gods. I wasn't allowed to see her for days. Father went up to her room, sometimes accompanied by a black-bearded man who wore a sable robe and a gold medallion.

"You wouldn't understand, child," this stranger replied, whenever I questioned him.

I think Father had told him I was "simple."

But I did understand. So many things are clear to children that are hidden from adults.

I understood the blue baby.

Then Mother came to me in the night, and her face was pale, yet shining, like a full moon seen through mist; and when she put her hand on my forehead, her touch was like winter's ice. Yet when I reached to touch her, she was gone.

I sat up in bed, alone in the darkness, listening to rain rattling on the roof and shutters, and to the creakings of the house.

Mother hadn't said anything. It hadn't been necessary.

So I clambered down the rope ladder out of my loft, shuffled across the common room where our poorer guests slept on tables and benches before the smoldering fireplace, then began to crawl up the stairs to my mother's room, my walking stick tucked under my belt, thumping against each step as I went.

Father was standing at the top of the stairs, a lamp in his hand, his head against the wall. He was crying. It was such an astonishing thing to see him cry that I just stood up and gaped.

He turned toward me, and I could see the sorrow on his face transformed so quickly into anger it was like flipping the page of a book.

"Father, what has happened—?"

"*You* are all I have left!" His sob became almost a scream. "Get out of here!"

He produced a stick from somewhere, and before I could even react, he struck me full in the face.

"*Get out!*"

I yelped and tumbled backwards down the stairs, spattering blood. Halfway down, I caught hold of the railing and hung there, awkwardly, almost on my knees.

"Father, please. I didn't do anything—"

"*Get out!*"

I slid my walking stick out of my belt and began to hop down the stairs, holding onto the railing with my other hand.

"That's right," Father called after me. "Scrape and scurry like a crab!"

In the darkness, I missed a step and tumbled once more.

A wad of spit splashed off the wall inches from my face.

"Useless thing," Father said.

And that night I went out, as my father had commanded me, terrified and grieving and bewildered, uncertain that I would ever be allowed to return. I must have splashed for hours through the muddy streets. Then I was in the forest, my head bent forward against the wind and rain, shivering beneath the scrap of an old blanket I wore as a cloak. All around me, the leafless trees rattled.

And on that night I discovered Malevendra's Pool, because my sorrows were sufficient to allow me to see it, for all I was only ten years old.

In the forest, I played a game to drive away my fear. I made a pretend-sword out of a branch, and did battle with shadows. I shouted my war cry into the storm. When I slipped and fell face down into mud, I rolled quickly onto my back and said, "Ha! You do not have me, sir! I shall not yield!" Then I sprang up again, my sword slicing off the heads and arms of enemy knights and giants and renegade gods, and twigs off bushes.

And for a long while, I merely wept. I threw my play-sword away. I think I was a little bit mad then.

But when I came to the cliffs and started to climb, I felt much better. I knew this forest, these cliffs, for all I could see almost nothing in the dark. I came here often. My hands were strong, and with two hands and one good leg I could climb better than I could walk. One of the mercenaries had once called me a little monkey. Then he had to explain what he meant. He came from a hot land, where they had monkeys. I decided he was correct. I was a three-limbed monkey who wanted to be a knight.

Silent for a while, then weeping again, then in frenzied desperation, I climbed the familiar hillside, over bare rock, up steep boulder-strewn slopes where pine trees clung at crazy angles. Often I lost my grip and slid down amid mud and needles, only to make my way back up again, clinging to roots.

At the top, the mountain rose above the last few gnarled trees, alone, like an island in a dark sea.

There I found the pool, perfectly round, perfectly still, glowing like white fire, its surface unrippled by the pouring rain. There had been no pool on the mountain before, of course.

Amazed, I sat down by the water's edge. I reached out to touch the surface, then thought better and drew my hand back.

I only watched. The fire diminished, and I seemed to be looking through a window, as if into a lighted room from the darkness outside. At first, near at hand, I saw myself staring back; but behind my reflection, in some impossible distance, there were many things, and my attention went to them, one after another. I forgot that I was sitting by the pool, and I was many places at once: charging across a field in the company of armored knights, on a ship, sitting on my horse in the middle of a burning town in a dusty land, where my comrades had crucified or impaled all the inhabitants. And I saw those comrades die, one by one, along roads, murdered in bed, in the rain on a beach in the winter, trampled under the horses of charging knights. I saw myself amid all these things, like a tiny chip of wood tossed in a storm.

I saw glory too. That was the alluring, terrible part. I saw the knights riding in triumph before the Master Inquisitor, and he sat above us on his golden throne, his robes a perfect white. My own armor was silver. I held my naked, beautiful sword across my saddle before me, and my heart was filled with pride.

At the very end, I think I glimpsed my own death, but my reflection let out a startled cry, and I turned aside.

When I looked again, a lady seemed to be rising toward me out of a great depth; a queen in flowing white and yellow and red; sometimes drifting like a thing of cloud, sometimes walking around and around on a spiral stairway I could not see; her face was pale, serene, yet filled with suffering beyond words to describe; and I knew her to be the Lady of Sorrows, Malevendra, whose pool this was.

I prayed to her then, in my grief, with fumbling words, and apologized that I had nothing to offer in sacrifice.

She spoke, and her voice was like the wind rattling through the branches, and she said only, "You have offered enough already. It is sufficient."

I thought I understood, but I did not. Then the goddess left me, and somehow I slept. My dreams were a continuation and repetition of what I had already seen.

I awoke at dawn on the mountaintop, cold and wet and stiff. The rain had diminished to a light spray. All around me clouds hugged the land, concealing the forest, and I was truly alone then on my little refuge of bare stone, shut off from the whole earth.

The pool was gone, of course. I did not expect to find it still there.

My life after that was mostly spent alone, waiting, remembering, my mind filled with the mysteries and miracles of the gods. Father would not speak to me, save to call me "crab" or "spider" or "useless thing," as if I had somehow caused Mother's death.

Then my time came and the waiting ended. I was thirteen.

It was another bitterly cold, late autumn day, the sky dark with rain. They say that the rain is the weeping of Malevendra, her tears so many because of all the sorrows of the world. But that is just another pretty story. It was raining, hard, the wind, which is the shouting of gods, howling down from the blue ice mountains of the far north.

I nudged open the door to the inn with my right knee and struggled inside, a bundle of firewood under my left arm. As soon as the door was closed and my eyes had adjusted to the gloom of the common room, I saw the stranger.

He was our only guest. The war hovered far away and the soldiers were elsewhere, but still the roads were not safe. There was little business for our inn that season.

But he wasn't a stranger. It was impossible, yet I knew him. In Malevendra's pool I had seen him, and I had ridden by his side into many battles. I had seen him, too, from the tailgate of the wagon, so many years before.

My glance took him in quickly: his thin, lined face, his silver beard, his tattered cloak and tarnished armor, the dented helm on the table before him, with one of its wing-ornaments snapped off, like a crippled bird.

He was alone, without retainers.

He studied me as quickly, and somehow I knew that he recognized me, too.

I dropped the firewood to my feet and said, stupidly, "Are you . . . a *knight?*"

He nodded.

"I want to be a knight too. I will be very brave."

I took one step toward him, my stick scraping on the floor.

He smiled slightly. "I'm sure you will."

Just then, the kitchen door burst open behind me, slamming into my back. Scalding soup splashed down my neck, and I tumbled forward, scattering logs, while my father cursed and tried to pick up bowls, and spilled more. Shrieking, he threw his tray aside, grabbed a stick, and swung at me. I rolled under a table. Father swung again, missing the side of my head by inches, and I rolled, then crawled beneath the knight's feet.

Father straightened up and said, "You have to understand, sir. He's an idiot. A verminous nuisance—"

He reached down and grabbed me by the ankle, hauling me out from under the table.

"Let the boy alone," said the knight firmly. "Let him stay with me."

Father let go, and I scrambled onto the bench opposite the knight.

"Fine. If you take a fancy to him, take him with you when you go. Of all the useless—"

He resumed piling spilled dishes on his tray. Muttering, he left the room.

I clung to the edge of the table. For an instant, it seemed, horribly, that I was going to be sick. So many conflicting emotions piled up within me—wonder and fear and grief and hope.

"Boy, what is your name?"

"Vynae, sir. People call me Vynae Crooked Foot."

"I will call you just Vynae. Do you know what it means to be a knight, Vynae?"

"Oh, yes, sir! It means *fighting* and *battles* and killing *monsters!*"

He folded his hands on the tabletop and gazed down at them.

"It means all of those things, yes," he said slowly. "But it also means suffering and toil without end. It means your friends dying on battlefields with their guts pouring out. It means your life is sworn to the gods, to your lord, to your satrap, and to the emperor. It means you are a kind of slave. I should think you already knew that, Vynae."

For an instant I was terribly afraid, and his gaze seemed to penetrate every recess of my soul, as if he were some kind of god, who knew every moment of my life from start to finish.

I didn't know what to say, but at that moment my father came back with the knight's dinner, nodded, and left, acting as if I didn't exist.

The knight dipped a piece of bread into his stew, and handed it to me.

"Here. You look hungry."

"Yes, sir. Thank you, sir."

"But you want to hear about battles, don't you?"

I nodded, my mouth full.

So he told me of cities stormed, of great lines of horsemen crashing together like mountains falling; of how he and twenty brother knights held off a thousand in a ruined tower for weeks until the satrap could bring up the main army and destroy the enemy. In the end, only he and three companions were left alive.

I stared at him, wide-eyed, and just then I was thinking of my games in the forest, not of what I had seen in Malevendra's pool.

". . . but it isn't all like that. You must understand this, if you are to be a knight yourself one day."

The way he spoke, he was not mocking me.

"Much of it," he continued, "is . . . a lot more sordid."

"Surely you will slay any wicked knights!"

He handed me another piece of bread.

"Vynae, I will tell you another story. Once there was an order of knights, called the Fellowship of the Golden Forest, who lived in a warm land, where the trees were indeed golden, yet alive, as if the first days of autumn lingered forever and winter never came. It was a beautiful, bountiful place, where the common folk tilled rich fields, and the knights dwelt in a castle of shining white marble. It was a place of righteousness, too, where the Nine Gods of Light were held in great worship, and the dark titans of lust and wild rage were shunned.

"But one of the knights must have conversed with the titans of shadow, or seen them in his sleep, for he said, 'Enough of this. We are slayers of men, not herders of sheep. Let us go and fight and find glory.'

"The Fellowship sorrowed then, and the marble castle rang with arguments and pleadings, and, finally, commands. But a small band agreed with the rash knight, and, though the masters of the Fellowship had forbidden it, these few stole out into the darkness. They made their way to another country and burned a town, slaughtering the people there, not because they had any quarrel with them, but for glory.

"Some of them were ashamed at what they had done. They cast away their armor and forswore their knighthood, proclaiming themselves unworthy of the sword. They told the truth, but it was too late for any of them.

"One of the others, the bloodiest killer of the lot, found a woman alive in the ruins. Her former name is lost, but later she was called *Tanaeve Heda,* which merely means *ash;* for truly she had seen all her life reduced to ashes, her husband and children slain before her eyes.

"And Tanaeve Heda was a witch, but the knights did not know that, and it did not matter until later.

"They mocked her and each of them had their way with her, one after the other—"

I interrupted. "But surely," I said, afraid again and almost in tears, "surely these were evil, wicked knights. Surely you have slain them all with your own hands—"

But our guest merely waved me into silence.

"Peace, Vynae. This all happened long ago. Some of the knights were indeed killed. Some died in their beds. Ultimately it didn't matter, for this Tanaeve, the woman of ashes, spoke to Malevendra many times, and became the most intimate companion of the goddess, to whom she offered up her very pain in sacrifice.

"I think it was that same pain which animated the seed of the knights within her, so that she wandered over many lands in wretchedness, always great about the belly, giving birth to an endless stream of monsters, which she smothered and buried by roadsides and in desolate places, making those places accursed. I think that, in the end, the Lady of Ashes would have it no other way. It was her will, part of some infinitely complicated plan.

"At the very end, she spoke to Malevendra once more, and she found the pool of the goddess at last—on a mountaintop, so the story goes. Malevendra rose up to her, and her aspect was not a pleasing one. The goddess looked like a corpse, a thing of bones and rags. Malevendra and Tanaeve could have been sisters, twins. The goddess touched the woman where she was great about the waist, and said, *'Let this one live, for his name is Vengeance.'*

"It was so. There, by the pool, the woman and the goddess dwelt for many years, raising the child; and the monster became a beautiful youth, tall and strong and swift. They dressed him in golden armor. His visor was like a flower made of metal, and his eyes, peering out of the middle, were like malicious fire.

"When he was a man, he rode out into the world, and by his beauty, by his seeming gentleness, by the persuasion of his voice, he made men follow him. *You have been wronged,* he told them. *Rise up and slay, and seize what is justly yours.*

"When he came to the Kingdom of the Three Rivers, Tanaeve's native land, he told the folk, *Remember those who have perished.* And they remembered. To the Knights of the Golden Forest he whispered, *Honor, your honor as knights, above all things.*

"So the war began, and the people killed one another for generations, until both the Kingdom of the Rivers and the Golden Forest were made waste. At the end, the combatants no longer remembered why they were

fighting. It had gone on so long. And at the very end, no one remained
to mourn or to bury the dead."

The knight's dinner had grown cold as he told his story. He slid the tray
across to me. I picked at the stew, listlessly.

Then he laid his scabbard on the table before me, and slowly drew the
sword out.

I gasped in amazement. The blade was gleaming silver, almost blue,
and intricately carved. The grip was wound with golden wire, and the
pommel was shaped like a bird, with huge green gems for eyes. I had
never seen such a beautiful thing.

"Do you know what this is, boy?"

". . . a sword?"

I flinched. Father would have hit me for saying something so stupid.

The knight leaned forward and spoke intently, in a low voice, his tone
a mixture of anger and weariness.

"It is the sword of an initiate of the inmost circle of the Knights
Inquisitor, you young fool. It is a weapon of the most righteous, con-
secrated to the gods of light. Harken: the story I told you is entirely true.
I know. I lived it. I am Sir Vorleide, the last of the Knights of the
Golden Forest, who could neither mourn the dead nor bury them—"

"But you, sir, surely, you could stop all that killing before—"

He reached across the table and grabbed me by the front of my coat.
With a swift yank, he had me onto the tabletop, my face inches from his.

"Please. You're hurting me—"

"I could *not* stop it, for each death had to be avenged, and that
brought *more* death. When your comrades are slain, you don't just leave
them for the buzzards and forget. *That* is what it means to be a knight.
It is called honor."

He let go of me. I rolled off the table, onto the floor, with a thump,
scattering dishes. Then I groped for my stick and stood, steadying myself
against the edge of the table.

"Sit down, Vynae, who shall be a knight. I won't do that again. Upon
my honor."

He waved his hand. I sat.

"There is little more to tell," he said. "I am here for a purpose, Vynae.
Our lives, yours and mine, have been wound together like a braid. Don't
doubt that. It is one of the mysteries and miracles of the gods, who do

such things with us for their own reasons. Vynae, I have never told my story before, but I have told it to you, *because I know who you are.*"

"But . . . but, I'm just Crooked Foot, son of Kostan—that's my father, who owns this place. He doesn't like me—"

"No, child," said Sir Vorleide.

"That's all there is. I'm nobody. I don't matter."

"Vynae, you are lying. You know more. You are not telling me all."

"I—"

"Vynae, when I was in the far south, in the course of my wanderings, I consulted an oracle, an ancient Sybil who dwelt in a house like a huge spiderweb filled with bones. I asked her, *'Will my quest ever end?'* And she replied, *'It will, when the hobbled hero leads you to the goddess of endings.'* "

"What quest?"

"My life, Boy. That too is what it means to be a knight, to travel on the journey of this life without once knowing rest, no certain goal before you, your way filled with peril, the road never ending until you do. When the last castle of the Three River Kingdom was burnt and all the knights were dead, I thought my own quest was over. I did not understand. So I became a Knight Inquisitor, wielding the sword of righteousness to atone for my crimes. But the spirit of Vengeance dogs me still, murdering my companions, the few friends I have had in my life. Sometimes I am roused to madness, and I murder them. I have wrought as much evil as good. Malevendra drives me on, that I might feed her sorrows."

He paused, and I couldn't think of anything at all to say. I didn't want to hear any more. But I knew it would be useless to get up, to scurry away, for his words would follow me like the implacable golden knight called Vengeance.

"You can well imagine," he said, after a while, "that I could not remain among the Knights Inquisitor. They drove me out."

I gazed first at the long, beautifully-wrought sword before me, and then into Sir Vorleide's eyes, in which I recognized, indeed, madness.

"Will you . . . murder me too, in the end?"

Much to my surprise, the knight began to weep. It was only after several minutes that he could speak at all.

"I don't think so," he said. "I don't want to. Upon my honor, it is not my intention. But you must *help* me—"

I think that at that moment I would have done anything for him, even let him murder me.

"What must I do?"

"You must tell me the truth," he said. "Merely that. The entire truth."

So I told him of my wanderings in the darkness and rain three years previously, and how I had come to Malevendra's pool.

"It is so," he said. "I do not know why it is—just another mystery of the gods—but all my sufferings, all the sufferings of my fellow knights, were not sufficient to reveal that pool to me. Yet you, Vynae, have seen it. I think you have seen it for the reason the Sybil prophesied, that you might lead me to it. On the morrow, when I have rested, you shall take me there. That is my command. Then I shall do battle with the Lady of Ashes. I know she is there, within the pool, dwelling in the house of the goddess. When both of us have died, the balance of things shall be set right."

"Do you have to die?" I said.

"Yes. That is what it means to be a knight."

He dismissed me and lay down on a bench by the fire. For all he was a knight, he had not the coin to pay for a bed, and Father did not give him one.

I climbed into my loft.

"You climb like a monkey!" Sir Vorleide called after me, drowsily, almost merrily.

I lay in the darkness for a long time, absurdly trying to sleep, weeping softly for the death of all I had ever dreamed or hoped.

Then I sat up. I knew what I had to do. I wrapped myself in my torn blanket and, stealthily as I could, I climbed down into the common room where Sir Vorleide slept. Crawling on my hands and knees, I made my way silently to him.

I stole his sword. Every second thereafter was agony, every scrape, every creaking of the house a voice shouting in alarm. But, despite my terror, I made it out into the street. There I stood up, tucked the sword under my belt, and hurried toward the forest.

The rain was turned to sleet, the mud hardening into crusts of ice. My hands, my cheeks, were numb with the touch of the wind. More than once I stumbled and fell, once losing the sword, groping for it in the half-frozen mud, weeping, until I cut my hand on its blade.

The sleet rattled among the trees. The forest seemed alive, hostile, it too shouting in alarm as the thief of the holy Inquisitor's sword skulked by. When I came to the cliffs, the ice made the way more perilous than ever.

Despite my suffering, despite my fear, I continued without wavering, as a true knight would.

At last I reached the top, and stood on the dark summit. The pool of the Sorrowful Goddess lay before me, glaring up at the moon as if at its own reflection.

I touched the surface with the tip of the sword. Again, the water did not ripple. The blade merely slid beneath it, as if through colored air.

"Lady of Ashes," I said. "Come out."

Faint, glowing wisps rose up, and she came to me, that most blessed one of Malevendra, the mortal who had become the handmaiden of the goddess. She stood up out of the water, uncurling herself like a huge insect, skeletal, clad only in tatters of cloth, her eyes wild with pain and hatred. She opened her mouth, revealing teeth filed sharp as knives. Her hands were gnarled and sharp, like eagle's claws.

This had been a woman once, who had been wronged and deserving of pity, but her humanity was far behind her.

"I have come to kill you," I said.

"You have come to die."

How can I describe her voice? Like the shrieking wind among crags. Like the groaning of the very earth. Like death. If death had a voice, it was hers.

"Yes," I said. "I have come to die, too."

"You are not the *one*. You are not Vorleide of the Golden Forest."

I steadied my grip on my walking stick and hefted the silver sword clumsily.

"I'll have to do. He can't come. He has to live. He has to make his life right. So I'm his substitute. Take me instead."

"And you. What are you?"

"No one. Nothing. I don't matter."

"Then you are a poor substitute."

I hobbled to the edge of the pool and raised the sword to strike. She curled back like a huge centipede, impossibly jointed, hissing.

"Wait!"

I whirled about. The Ash Lady snarled.

Sir Vorleide was there, rushing upon me. He snatched the sword from my hand and shoved me back from the pool, ramming his elbow into my stomach.

"How *dare* you?" he screamed. "How *dare* you rob me of my death?"

I sat up, gasping, clutching where he had hit me.

"No! It isn't like that. I didn't want you to die—"

He turned toward me, furious. I was sure he was going to kill me, one final sacrifice to Vengeance.

"You want to be a *knight,* Boy? Yet you would steal my honor?"

"I didn't! It wasn't like that!" I rolled over, my face in the mud, sleet beating down around me, and wept.

Then, to my astonishment, he stood over me, prodding me with his sword.

"Get up," he said gently. "A true knight doesn't blubber like that. Be brave, as you already have been brave, beyond the ability of words to describe."

I lurched unsteadily to my feet. He caught me by the arm and led me to the edge of the pool. I shrank back from the apparition, but he bowed courteously and said, "Lady, I pray you, withdraw within. I have a small matter to attend to here."

The skeletal thing replied in a woman's voice, "Sir Knight, if you will join me in my domain, I shall withdraw."

"Momentarily," Sir Vorleide said. "Upon my honor."

The monster sank into the pool without a ripple and was gone, like a reflection vanishing from a glass.

Sir Vorleide sheathed his sword, then took hold of me under the arms and lifted me up, swinging me around, depositing me abruptly at the edge of the pool. My legs fell into the water.

I screamed, more out of surprise than pain. For an instant, the waters burned. Then they were so cold they burned again. Finally I felt nothing at all.

I sat unresistingly while he unwrapped the rags I wore instead of a shoe, then ripped my right trouser leg almost up to my waist, completely exposing my malformed leg. With his sword he cut a thin line the length of my leg, so that my blood mingled with the waters of the pool. And with his firm, mailed hands he shaped my flesh and bones like dough.

"I prayed many times," he said, as he worked, "that at the very end I should be allowed to perform some final act of goodness, that I would be worthy of some little miracle."

I felt dizzy and sick. I lay back and clutched at mud and ice.

Once more he lifted me up.

"Now stand."

Both my legs were numb, and I swayed so much he had to steady me, but I stood. My right leg had been made whole and straight.

"Say nothing. There is nothing you can say. Just give me your stick, as a gift."

I nodded, befuddled, and gave it to him.

He hefted it, slapping his mailed palm. "Ah, a stout cudgel is just what I need. Nothing more."

Then he pressed his sword into my hands. He took off his spurs and gave them to me also.

"You will find my horse at the foot of the cliff," he said. "I saw you coming here in a dream. That was how I followed you. But I also saw you riding my horse. Therefore take it, and, if you wish—for the choice is still yours to make—go into the many lands bearing this sword and wearing these spurs, and holding my shield upon your arm, and become known as a knight, Sir Monkey—"

He nudged me gently, and I dropped to my knees. He took the sword from me one last time, and touched me on either shoulder with the flat of the blade. Then he gave the weapon back to me, and, hesitating as if he'd forgotten something, took off his scabbard and belt, and gave me those also.

Without another word, he stepped into the water and sank down out of sight.

I knelt by that pool until dawn, oblivious to the cold, weeping, and watching the visions as they passed before me. I saw Sir Vorleide on a stairway, turning, my stick in his hand. Again, he was in a dark forest, battling three woman-headed dogs with the fangs of serpents. He smote them with his cudgel, and like a true knight, went on; fought again with black leopards like shapes of living metal; until at last a skeletal thing reared up before him out of a bed of ashes. It seemed he spoke courteously, and the monster replied. But I could not hear what they said.

For the first and last time, the surface of the pool rippled, and a single bubble rose and broke, darkness spreading over the whole surface, until the pool of Malevendra was the color of blood.

Once more I wept, and, as the sun rose, I knelt down and cupped my hands, and drank from the Pool of Sorrows, of the Waters Ending, and the taste was both bitter and sweet.

I did not return to the village, but rode through many lands, thinking of the glory of what I had seen; and I became a knight, and was called, as Sir Vorleide named me, Monkey. But not in jest. There was honor in that name.

You have heard of me. There are songs of my wars, my quests, my deeds. I have slain the foes of the Nine Gods, taken castles, dispelled the shadows from the Earth in the name of righteousness, all for the everlasting fame of the Knights Inquisitor.

But the poets, as always, tell only the pretty parts. They do not tell of the fields of crows, of the massacres and burnings, or even the deaths of brave comrades, as they really are—sloppy dyings under a bush, coughing up blood, when no one can remember what noble words they're supposed to say.

The poets do not tell of my crimes. And they do not tell how I came to a town in a dusty land, where my comrades had crucified or impaled all they had not slain outright, and a boy called down to me in his pain. Our eyes met for just an instant. To my astonishment, I thought I knew him. Before he could speak more, I ran him through with my spear, not out of mercy, but because I was afraid; to silence his accusations.

For Malevendra's pool shall always be filled with tears.

I know this, for I am her true servant.

That is what it means to be a knight.

Sylvia

Ira Levin

IRA LEVIN, *the popular dramatist and author of the best-selling horror novel* Rosemary's Baby, *told me that he has written only three short stories. The most obscure may well be "Sylvia," which first appeared in the April 1955 edition of* Manhunt *magazine. It asks the question What's a father to do when his poor daughter wears emotional blinders? The answer? Watch her closely.* . . .

SHORTLY BEFORE NOON on the day of his scheduled departure for the Italian Riviera, Lewis Melton searched his daughter's room for a letter she had received a few hours earlier. This secret violation of Sylvia's privacy was performed with reluctance. Like every act it was the result of a somewhat involved set of circumstances and motivations.

A month before, Sylvia had been granted a divorce. Her husband, Lyle Waterman, had been a fortune hunter—a fact which, though obvious to everyone else, had not been demonstrable to Sylvia until he was caught red-handed tracing her endorsement onto an intercepted dividend check. When this happened Melton made a bargain with his son-in-law; Melton would not press a charge of forgery and Waterman would not contest a Nevada mental cruelty divorce. Melton, who was retired, then accompanied Sylvia to a dude ranch outside Reno, where in the usual six weeks the divorce was accomplished.

Back again in Connecticut Melton succumbed to the idea of a few weeks on the Riviera, a suggestion of Sylvia's. The year before, returning from two months abroad to find Sylvia married to Waterman, Melton had been forced to recognize that despite her thirty-two years it was unwise to leave her alone for long periods of time, and he had resolved to avoid doing so in the future. But his relief at Sylvia's freedom, coupled with her expressed desire for solitude, had erased his resolution and lulled him into booking air passage, renewing his passport, contacting acquaintances in San Remo—and now, on the very day of departure, Mrs. Redden, bringing the coffee into his bedroom, had said, "Redden thinks I should tell you, sir, that Miss Sylvia just got a letter addressed in Mr. Waterman's handwriting"—and immediately the whole trip was subject to cancellation.

A letter from Lyle might be harmless; a request, perhaps, for the forwarding of some clothes he had left behind. But it might also be the first step in a brazen campaign to reestablish his influence over Sylvia, undertaken in the knowledge of Melton's planned absence. If that were the case the trip was certainly out of the question, for Sylvia was as easily led as a child's pony. Furthermore, Melton suddenly realized, her habitual demeanor of withdrawn silence, which had deepened since the moment when she learned the truth about Lyle, had effectually masked what emotions might lie within her, and he really had no way of knowing whether her love for Lyle had turned to bitterness, as he had assumed, or whether there might not linger an inclination to forgive, an eagerness to accept any explanation . . .

Desultorily he began his packing, almost certain that the suitcases would have to be unpacked before the day was over. At eleven-thirty, when Sylvia retired to her garden at the rear of the estate, Melton entered her room and began to search for the letter.

In the course of the search he came upon a gun. He had opened a quilted satin box in the top drawer of her dresser and had riffled the edges of the handkerchiefs stacked within it. They parted in mid-pile. He lifted off the upper stack and there it was; a small nickel-plated pistol with a black bakelite grip, incredible upon the soft cushion of Sylvia's flowered handkerchiefs. Melton looked at it, his right hand blindly depositing handkerchiefs on the dresser, thinking: *It must be a joke or a cigarette lighter or something.*

He picked it up. It was heavier than it looked; certainly no cigarette lighter. He held it disbelievingly on the flat of his palm. The bakelite grip was milled in a pattern of tiny diamonds. The short barrel gleamed with an oily sheen, smooth to the fingertips, the whole having an indefinable smell of newness. Where had she gotten it? Reno? The fool! a gun. . . . Events of the past month suddenly sprang into a new and frightening significance. "You really do need a rest," she had said. "The Mallinsons are still in San Remo, aren't they?"

"Well . . . yes. I suppose we *could* leave on the—"

"Not we. You go alone. Honestly, I think being here by myself for a while would be the best thing."

And he had let her talk him into it!

"About the Reddens," she had said later. "We might as well give them their vacation while you're away. I can fend for myself, and then you won't have to put up with a few weeks of canned food later on. I really think that being completely by myself . . ."

Knowing that each of his previous absences had been the occasion for some sort of irresponsible behavior on her part, he had still let her talk him into it! So lulled, so blind!

He found the way to open the gun; the bakelite plaque on the right side swung clockwise, revealing within the handle a vertical metal rack holding five small bullets ready to be pushed up in turn into the firing chamber. Melton shuddered and swung the plaque back down, wishing he could as easily replace Sylvia's mask of stolidity which, penetrated, had disclosed such unsuspected depth of feeling, love warped into such pathetically intense hatred.

The letter from Lyle . . . Melton set the gun carefully upon the dresser and, with an aggrieved headshake, returned his attention to the handkerchief box. He found the letter almost immediately; it was beneath the uppermost handkerchief, the one on which the gun had lain. The envelope, ripped open at one end, was addressed to Sylvia in Lyle's bold, affectedly masculine hand.

Melton drew out a single sheet of paper and unfolded it. It was the stationery of an unfamiliar hotel on West 54th Street in New York. Dated the day before, it read:

Syl darling,

How can I tell you how happy your sweet letter has made me? I can't —not on paper. But when I see you, darling!

Lewis's plane leaves at midnight, so I suppose the train you are driving

*him to will be the 9:01. I will take the 8:00 from N. Y. which will get
me into New Haven at 9:35, so you will only have to wait in the station
half an hour.*

  Until tomorrow night, darling—

*Always your loving
Lyle*

Melton read the letter twice, then folded it back into its envelope. He picked up the gun and stood with the letter in one hand and the gun in the other, staring at them, thinking that Lyle, poor Lyle, with his scheming and conniving, wasn't truly dangerous at all; but Sylvia, slow, quiet Sylvia . . .

He put the letter back on the handkerchiefs in the box, covered it with the single one, and put the gun on top of that. He replaced the other handkerchiefs, closed the box and closed the drawer. With his hands braced on the top of the dresser, he leaned forward, resting his suddenly tired weight upon them. Slow, quiet Sylvia . . .

He straightened up and stared unseeingly at his reflection in the mirror. After a moment he turned and walked quickly from the room.

He went back into his own room and to the telephone beside the bed. A call to Information supplied him with the number of the hotel on West 54th Street. He relayed it to the operator along with his own number and stood waiting, his eyes on Sylvia's photograph on the bedside table, until a female voice small in his ear slurred the name of the hotel into an unintelligible syllable.

"Lyle Waterman, please," Melton said. Again he waited, searching for words that would not sound melodramatic. After a moment there was the sound of a receiver being lifted and Lyle's voice said, "Hello?"— thick, cut out of a yawn.

"Lyle? This is Lewis."

"Well. What a *lovely* way to start the day."

"Lyle, I have to speak to you." There was a moment of silence. "You mustn't come up here tonight. Sylvia—"

Angrily Lyle said, "Been reading Sylvia's mail?"

"Lyle, she's—"

"Let me speak to Sylvia."

"She isn't in the house. She—"

Lyle hung up.

Melton jiggled the crossbar and got the operator back. He told her he had been disconnected and she put the call through again.

"Mr. Waterman doesn't answer," the girl in the hotel said.

"This is a matter of life and death," Melton said. "Literally of life and death."

"I'll try again," the girl said nervously.

She tried again, but there was no response. "Should I send one of the boys up?"

"No. Never mind." Melton hung up.

He rang for Redden and took off his sport shirt. He put on a white shirt and was knotting his tie when Redden came in. Melton told him to bring the Lincoln around front. He ran a comb through his white hair and took a tweed jacket from the closet.

When he descended the stairs into the hall, Mrs. Redden was on a stepladder polishing the mirror with a ball of wadded newspaper. Melton said, "Tell Sylvia I was called into New York on some business. I'll be back at five or so." He straightened his tie in the mirror. "I want you to take all the phone calls this afternoon, Mrs. Redden," he said. "If Mr. Waterman calls—you'll know his voice, won't you?"

"Yes, sir."

"Tell him that Sylvia's in New Haven. He's been bothering her."

"Yes, sir," Mrs. Redden said.

Melton went briskly out into the graveled drive, where Redden was holding open the driver's door of the Lincoln.

At a quarter past two Melton parked the car in a lot on West 53rd Street and walked around the block to Lyle's hotel. It was a shabby building with a blue neon sign—*Transients*—glowing dispiritedly in the bright sunlight. The lobby was dim, with sagging leather chairs and the smell of rubber floormats. There was a quarter-circle desk in one corner and behind it, in a nest of pigeonholes, a round-faced man with no facial hair whatsoever and an embarrassingly obvious wig. Melton asked him for Lyle Waterman.

"He's out," the man said.

"What room is he in?"

"Three-fourteen, but he's out. You can't go up."

"Did he tell you to say he was out?"

"He's out," the man said. He pointed to the 314 pigeonhole; a brick-colored key tag hung from it. "He went out about an hour ago."

"Did he leave any word as to when he'd be back?"

"No word," the man said. "He just went out."

Melton sat down in one of the leather club chairs, across from two dark-skinned men speaking machine gun Spanish. The chair was too deep for comfort and there was a fetid cigar butt in the pot of sand beside it. After a few minutes Melton pulled himself up, went to the newsstand and bought a *Journal-American*. In a different chair, which was just as bad, he sat skimming the newspaper, glancing up at each sibilant push of the revolving door.

Lyle came in at twenty after three, his finger hooking a paper-sheathed clothes hanger over his shoulder. Melton stood up. Lyle paused for a moment, staring at him, and then he continued on his way towards the desk, his lips clamped and his thick-lashed eyes narrowed, like a spoiled child going up to bed without his dinner. Melton intercepted him and caught his free arm, gripping it tight in a sudden burst of hatred. "Let go of me!" Lyle whispered.

Melton took a deep breath and, with urgent emphasis, said, "I have to speak to you."

"Let *go* of me."

Melton released his arm.

"Go on," Lyle said, not looking at Melton, "speak. I can hardly wait."

"Not here," Melton said.

"Look, if you—"

"I drove all the way for this, Lyle. Not for my sake; for yours."

Lyle's mouth worked peevishly, and finally he said, "Oh, hell," and went resignedly to the desk to collect his key. Melton followed him. Waiting for the elevator Melton saw that Lyle had just had a haircut; bits of black hair clung to the back of his shirt collar.

They rode up to the third floor and walked along a narrow corridor whose floor creaked under thin carpet. Lyle unlocked 314. "The presidential suite," he said wryly, pushing open the door and going in. Melton followed him and closed the door. Lyle hooked the clothes hanger on a partially opened closet door. *"House Beautiful* is taking pictures next Tuesday," he said.

The room was small and crowded. There were a bureau, a writing table and a sink squeezed together against one wall, and jutting at them from the wall opposite, twin beds separated by a night table with a spindly white lamp. The single window, in the central wall, had a buff shade and a green one, but no curtains. The beds were metal, painted to look like wood. On the one nearer the window lay a gray leather suitcase with white whipcord stitching and L.W. in small gold letters

Lyle sat down on the other bed, then swung himself out full length, his hands cupping his head on the pillow, his heels pushing ripples into the faded peach bedspread. He lay looking at the ceiling, blinking occasionally, as though he were completely alone.

Melton drew a chair from the writing table, turned it to face the beds, and sat down.

"Before I tell you what I have to tell you," he said, "I want you to bear in mind that Sylvia is thirty-three years old, that she was thirty-two when you married her, and that she had never been in love before."

Lyle closed his eyes.

"You should also know," Melton said, "that her face, when she was shown your little penmanship exercise on the back of her check, was not a very pleasant face to behold. It was like watching a human being turn into a statue. And she's remained that way. She holds a book in front of her but she doesn't read. Or she goes into her garden and presses earth around flowers that are already dead."

A deep breath lifted Lyle's chest and sighed out from his nostrils.

"I think she has it in her mind to kill you tonight," Melton said. "There's a gun in the top drawer of her dresser."

Lyle's eyes opened.

"I assume she bought it in Reno."

Lyle raised himself on his elbows and looked at Melton. After a moment he said, "You're making this up."

Sharply Melton said, "Oh, yes. I go around telling people that my daughter is contemplating murder." He stared contemptuously at Lyle, and then sank back in his chair. "This trip of mine," he said. "It was Sylvia's idea. And the Reddens are leaving for Vermont tonight. Immediately after dinner. That was Sylvia's idea too."

Lyle said, "She didn't tell me the Reddens would be away . . ." He swung his legs off the bed and sat leaning forward, his elbows on his knees and his hands clasped in space.

"What *did* she tell you?"

Lyle rubbed the heels of his clasped hands together.

Melton said, "For pity's sake, there's a *gun* in her dresser!"

Lyle unclasped his hands and sat up straight, palming his thighs rigidly. "I got a letter the day before yesterday," he said. He was trying to sound brisk and businesslike, but he sounded frightened. "She said she wanted to see me. She was driving you to New Haven and she wanted me to come up and meet her at the station after you left. Tonight. She wanted to give me a chance to explain. She told me—" his voice wavered—"she told me not to tell anyone where I was going because it might get back to you somehow and you might call off your trip."

Melton put his hands to his face and rubbed his eyelids with his fingertips. "Oh Lord," he said, "can you conceive of her plotting, planning . . ." He stood up and turned his chair back under the writing table. "It's my fault," he said. "I never should have let her talk me into taking the trip." He turned to the window and stared out into a gray courtyard. "Did she ever tell you about the gypsies?"

"Gypsies?"

"Eight, no, ten years ago. My wife was alive then. We went to South America for a couple of months. You would think you could leave a girl of twenty-three alone for two months, wouldn't you? With a houseful of servants? Well, we came back to find the servants gone—she'd paid them off and given them a holiday—and the house full of gypsies. Gypsies! She'd invited them in for tea, like a girl in a fairy tale." He shook his head dolefully. "There were two goats in the garage."

"Gypsies," Lyle said, smiling thinly.

"There are some people," Melton said, "who grow up without ever attaining a firm grasp on reality."

They fell silent for a moment.

"What are you going to do?" Lyle asked.

"I'm not sure," Melton said. "My trip is cancelled, of course. I'll tell her that there's been some trouble with my passport or something. I'd like to avoid humiliating her, manage somehow to smooth over this entire situation without ever letting her know I'm aware of its existence. I'll talk to her, tell her I can see she's still brooding about you. If I can make her realize you're best forgotten . . ."

Lyle said softly, "Good Lord, she actually wants to kill me . . ." He stretched out on the bed again. "Good Lord," he said wonderingly. There was a faint, flattered smile about his lips. It lingered for a moment, then dissolved, his eyes growing thoughtful. He glanced at Melton's back.

"What if you can't?" he said. He was speaking more slowly now. "What if you can't make her see the light? Suppose she takes her gun and comes after me. Don't you think it would be a good idea if I moved to a different hotel?"

"Yes," Melton said, "I suppose it would."

"The only trouble is," Lyle said, "I can't afford to move to a different hotel."

Melton turned from the window.

"I would even leave New York," Lyle said, "if I could afford to. Then you wouldn't have *any* worries about Sylvia getting herself into trouble."

Melton looked at him.

"Where would you go?" he said.

Lyle pondered.

"Dallas," he said. "Dallas, Texas." He thought for a moment. "Or is Houston the big city there? Oh well, Dallas or Houston."

Impassively Melton took out his wallet. Behind the bills he always kept a blank check.

Locked in the crawling traffic of the West Side Highway, Melton considered how best to temper Sylvia from her intended violence without revealing his own knowledge of it. He turned off onto the Merritt Parkway and as he did so he remembered that he had not eaten since breakfast. He stopped at a restaurant, ordered mechanically and ate without interest.

It was past seven o'clock when he guided the Lincoln between the stone posts and up the circular drive towards the front of the house. The Reddens' Plymouth was parked there, with Mrs. Redden in the act of pushing down the lid of the luggage compartment. Melton pulled up behind her and got out of the car.

"Good evening, sir," Mrs. Redden said a bit uncomfortably. "There's some dinner keeping warm on the stove."

"I ate on the road," Melton said.

Mrs. Redden brightened. "We offered to stay on till tomorrow, but Miss Sylvia insisted we shouldn't."

"Where is she?"

"Playing the piano."

Melton went up the steps and to the front door, stopping short as Redden came out with two umbrellas on his arm. "Oh, good evening," Redden said cheerfully. "I finished your packing and brought the suitcases down. There are two telegrams in your room."

"I . . . thanks." Melton caught the door, interrupting its slow swing closed.

"Bon voyage," Redden said.

"Yes, *bon voyage!"* Mrs. Redden called from the car.

"Thanks. Have a good trip." Melton stepped into the house and pulled the door shut after him. He heard Mrs. Redden call out something about Italian food.

His three aluminum suitcases, tagged and labeled, were lined up in a corner of the hall. He looked at them blankly. From the rear of the house came the skipping notes of *The Spinning Song.* Sylvia had been given lessons as a child, but *The Spinning Song* was the only piece she remembered now. She played it rarely and not well. Melton went to the stairs. He listened as he climbed, thinking of all the lessons and practicing that had gone to produce this one awkwardly played selection, and thinking, beneath that, of what he would say to Sylvia.

He went into his room and found the two telegrams. They were from friends, wishing him a safe flight and a pleasant stay on the Riviera. He tossed them on the bed and went into the bathroom.

When he had washed up he came down the stairs again. The piano was silent now. "Sylvia?" he called.

There was no answer. He went into the living room and through it to the music room. She was not there. He returned to the hallway and called her name up the stairs, thinking that perhaps she had gone into her bedroom while he was in the bathroom, but the only answer was silence.

She was in her garden, of course. Melton went down the hall, through the pantry, and into the kitchen. He opened the back door. The sun had gone from the sky and the first blue of dusk was falling. Melton peered across the expanse of lawn, searching for movement behind the high shrubbery that fronted the garden. He moved forward. How like Sylvia, he thought—a walled garden . . . Birds were calling from the woods beyond. Melton was halfway across the lawn when there was a flutter of movement in the shrubbery and Sylvia came out. She was wearing her gardening smock.

"Sylvia," Melton called.

She gave a little jump. "Oh, hello," she said, smiling. Her glasses were askew and as Melton drew nearer he saw drops of perspiration on her white forehead.

"Working hard?" he said.

"I was beginning to worry. You're late, aren't you? The Reddens have left already."

"I know."

She looked at his jacket. "You're going to change, aren't you?"

"No rush," Melton said. He went over to a wooden bench built around the trunk of an old oak and sat down.

Sylvia followed and stood before him, looking at her watch. "It's twenty of eight," she said.

"I'm afraid the trip is postponed," Melton said.

"What?" She was staring at him.

"There's been some trouble with my passport."

"How could there be trouble with your passport? They renewed it. You showed it to me. How could there be trouble?"

He took her hands and drew her gently to the seat beside him. "Well, as a matter of fact, there *hasn't* been trouble. It's because of you that I'm going to put it off."

"But you told everyone you're leaving!"

"So I'll call them tomorrow and tell them I'm not leaving."

"But why?" she said. "Why?"

"Because you're still brooding about Lyle," he said. "I can't leave you this way, Sylvia."

She managed a nervous laugh. "No," she said. "No, I'm not. Honestly I'm not."

"You are, Sylvia," he said. "You know you can't fool *me.*"

Her gaze dropped to her lap.

"He's not worth it, Sylvia," Melton said. "Believe me, he's not worth brooding over, not worth hating, not even worth thinking about."

She looked up, suddenly smiling. She took his hand. "Come look at the flowers," she said childishly.

"All right, Sylvia."

They rose and went to the shrubbery and the narrow path that penetrated it. Sylvia parted the branches with her free hand, holding them as she went through so they wouldn't spring back at Melton.

Once on the other side she released his hand and moved forward quickly to a hill of earth at the far side of the garden. She pointed to the ground beside it. "Look!" she said proudly.

Melton came forward and looked. There was a large rectangular hole, very long and quite deep. In the bottom of it, inexplicably, lay Melton's three aluminum suitcases.

He looked at Sylvia wonderingly.

The gun was in her hand. She pushed a wisp of hair up off her forehead. "You ruined my life," she said softly.

Melton stared at her.

"You did," she said. "Ruined it. Thirty-three years. Snooping, spying, arranging things behind my back. Do you think I'm some kind of idiot who can't comb her own hair?" Tears welled up behind her glasses. "That's all there is, a person's life. And you ruined mine!"

"Sylvia . . ."

"Thirty-three years!" It was a scream, cords stretching in her throat. "But no more! Not the rest of it! He's coming back!" Tears were rolling down her flushed cheeks. "Lyle's coming back! Tonight! And he still loves me and this time you're not going to send him away!"

The gun in her hand spat brightness and shot a bolt of heat into Melton's chest. "Sylvia!" he cried.

Melton swayed, trying to speak, trying to tell her that Lyle was no good, that Lyle had been bought off, that Lyle wasn't . . . He stood swaying, staring at her, his hands to his wet chest, and for the first time in his life he saw that her eyes, which had always seemed a dull and empty blue, could burst on occasion to a vivid, gemlike intensity.

"Oh my God," he said, tumbling forward to the ground.

Amour Dure:

Passages from the Diary of Spiridion Trepka.

Vernon Lee

VERNON LEE *was the pseudonym of Violet Paget (1856–1935), who spent most of her life in Italy, where she wrote approximately forty-five volumes of essays, novels, travel notes and powerful ghost stories like "Amour Dure."*

Part I

Urbania, August 20th, 1885.—I had longed, these years and years, to be in Italy, to come face to face with the Past; and was this Italy, was this the Past? I could have cried, yes cried, for disappointment when I first wandered about Rome, with an invitation to dine at the German Embassy in my pocket, and three or four Berlin and Munich Vandals at my heels, telling me where the best beer and sauerkraut could be had, and what the last article by Grimm or Mommsen was about.

Is this folly? Is it falsehood? Am I not myself a product of modern, northern civilisation; is not my coming to Italy due to this very modern scientific vandalism, which has given me a travelling scholarship because I have written a book like all those other atrocious books of erudition and art-criticism? Nay, am I not here at Urbania on the express understanding that, in a certain number of months, I shall produce just another such book? Dost thou imagine, thou miserable Spiridion, thou

Pole grown into the semblance of a German pedant, doctor of philosophy, professor even, author of a prize essay on the despots of the fifteenth century, dost thou imagine that thou, with thy ministerial letters and proof-sheets in thy black professorial coat-pocket, canst ever come in spirit into the presence of the Past?

Too true, alas! But let me forget it, at least, every now and then; as I forgot it this afternoon, while the white bullocks dragged my gig slowly winding along interminable valleys, crawling along interminable hillsides, with the invisible droning torrent far below, and only the bare grey and reddish peaks all around, up to this town of Urbania, forgotten of mankind, towered and battlemented on the high Apennine ridge. Sigillo, Penna, Fossombrone, Mercatello, Montemurlo—each single village name, as the driver pointed it out, brought to my mind the recollection of some battle or some great act of treachery of former days. And as the huge mountains shut out the setting sun, and the valleys filled with bluish shadow and mist, only a band of threatening smoke-red remaining behind the towers and cupolas of the city on its mountain-top, and the sound of church bells floated across the precipice from Urbania, I almost expected, at every turning of the road, that a troop of horsemen, with beaked helmets and clawed shoes, would emerge, with armour glittering and pennons waving in the sunset. And then, not two hours ago, entering the town at dusk, passing along the deserted streets, with only a smoky light here and there under a shrine or in front of a fruit-stall, or a fire reddening the blackness of a smithy; passing beneath the battlements and turrets of the palace. . . . Ah, that was Italy, it was the Past!

August 21st.—And this is the Present! Four letters of introduction to deliver, and an hour's polite conversation to endure with the Vice-Prefect, the Syndic, the Director of the Archives, and the good man to whom my friend Max had sent me for lodgings. . . .

August 22nd–27th.—Spent the greater part of the day in the Archives, and the greater part of my time there in being bored to extinction by the Director thereof, who to-day spouted Æneas Sylvius' Commentaries for three-quarters of an hour without taking breath. From this sort of martyrdom (what are the sensations of a former racehorse being driven in a cab? If you can conceive them, they are those of a Pole turned Prussian professor) I take refuge in long rambles through the town. This town is a handful of tall black houses huddled on to the top of an Alp, long

narrow lanes trickling down its sides, like the slides we made on hillocks
in our boyhood, and in the middle the superb red brick structure, turreted and battlemented, of Duke Ottobuono's palace, from whose windows you look down upon a sea, a kind of whirlpool, of melancholy grey
mountains. Then there are the people, dark, bushy-bearded men, riding
about like brigands, wrapped in green-lined cloaks upon their shaggy
pack-mules; or loitering about, great, brawny, low-headed youngsters,
like the parti-coloured bravos in Signorelli's frescoes; the beautiful boys,
like so many young Raphaels, with eyes like the eyes of bullocks, and the
huge women, Madonnas or St. Elizabeths, as the case may be, with their
clogs firmly poised on their toes and their brass pitchers on their heads,
as they go up and down the steep black alleys. I do not talk much to
these people; I fear my illusions being dispelled. At the corner of a street,
opposite Francesco di Giorgio's beautiful little portico, is a great blue
and red advertisement, representing an angel descending to crown Elias
Howe, on account of his sewing-machines; and the clerks of the Vice-
Prefecture, who dine at the place where I get my dinner, yell politics,
Minghetti, Cairoli, Tunis, ironclads, &c., at each other, and sing snatches
of *La Fille de Mme. Angot,* which I imagine they have been performing
here recently.

No; talking to the natives is evidently a dangerous experiment. Except
indeed, perhaps, to my good landlord, Signor Notaro Porri, who is just
as learned, and takes considerably less snuff (or rather brushes it off his
coat more often) than the Director of the Archives. I forgot to jot down
(and I feel I must jot down, in the vain belief that some day these scraps
will help, like a withered twig of olive or a three-wicked Tuscan lamp
on my table, to bring to my mind, in that hateful Babylon of Berlin,
these happy Italian days)—I forgot to record that I am lodging in the
house of a dealer in antiquities. My window looks up the principal street
to where the little column with Mercury on the top rises in the midst of
the awnings and porticoes of the market-place. Bending over the
chipped ewers and tubs full of sweet basil, clove pinks, and marigolds, I
can just see a corner of the palace turret, and the vague ultramarine of
the hills beyond. The house, whose back goes sharp down into the
ravine, is a queer up-and-down black place, whitewashed rooms, hung
with the Raphaels and Francias and Peruginos, whom mine host regularly carries to the chief inn whenever a stranger is expected; and surrounded by old carved chairs, sofas of the Empire, embossed and gilded

wedding-chests, and the cupboards which contain bits of old damask and embroidered altar-cloths scenting the place with the smell of old incense and mustiness; all of which are presided over by Signor Porri's three maiden sisters—Sora Serafina, Sora Lodovica, and Sora Adalgisa —the three Fates in person, even to the distaffs and their black cats.

Sor Asdrubale, as they call my landlord, is also a notary. He regrets the Pontifical Government, having had a cousin who was a Cardinal's train-bearer, and believes that if only you lay a table for two, light four candles made of dead men's fat, and perform certain rites about which he is not very precise, you can, on Christmas Eve and similar nights, summon up San Pasquale Baylon, who will write you the winning numbers of the lottery upon the smoked back of a plate, if you have previously slapped him on both cheeks and repeated three Ave Marias. The difficulty consists in obtaining the dead men's fat for the candles, and also in slapping the saint before he have time to vanish.

"If it were not for that," says Sor Asdrubale, "the Government would have had to suppress the lottery ages ago—eh!"

Sept. 9th.—This history of Urbania is not without its romance, although that romance (as usual) has been overlooked by our Dryasdusts. Even before coming here I felt attracted by the strange figure of a woman, which appeared from out of the dry pages of Gualterio's and Padre de Sanctis' histories of this place. This woman is Medea, daughter of Galeazzo IV Malatesta, Lord of Carpi, wife first of Pierluigi Orsini, Duke of Stimigliano, and subsequently of Guidalfonso II, Duke of Urbania, predecessor of the great Duke Robert II.

This woman's history and character remind one of that of Bianca Cappello, and at the same time of Lucrezia Borgia. Born in 1556, she was affianced at the age of twelve to a cousin, a Malatesta of the Rimini family. This family having greatly gone down in the world, her engagement was broken, and she was betrothed a year later to a member of the Pico family, and married to him by proxy at the age of fourteen. But this match not satisfying her own or her father's ambition, the marriage by proxy was, upon some pretext, declared null, and the suit encouraged of the Duke of Stimigliano, a great Umbrian feudatory of the Orsini family. But the bridegroom, Giovanfrancesco Pico, refused to submit, pleaded his case before the Pope, and tried to carry off by force his bride, with whom he was madly in love, as the lady was most lovely and of most cheerful and amiable manner, says an old anonymous chronicle.

Pico waylaid her litter as she was going to a villa of her father's, and carried her to his castle near Mirandola, where he respectfully pressed his suit; insisting that he had a right to consider her as his wife. But the lady escaped by letting herself into the moat by a rope of sheets, and Giovanfrancesco Pico was discovered stabbed in the chest, by the hand of Madonna Medea da Carpi. He was a handsome youth only eighteen years old.

The Pico having been settled, and the marriage with him declared null by the Pope, Medea da Carpi was solemnly married to the Duke of Stimigliano, and went to live upon his domains near Rome.

Two years later, Pierluigi Orsini was stabbed by one of his grooms at his castle of Stimigliano, near Orvieto; and suspicion fell upon his widow, more especially as, immediately after the event, she caused the murderer to be cut down by two servants in her own chamber; but not before he had declared that she had induced him to assassinate his master by a promise of her love. Things became so hot for Medea da Carpi that she fled to Urbania and threw herself at the feet of Duke Guidalfonso II, declaring that she had caused the groom to be killed merely to avenge her good fame, which he had slandered, and that she was absolutely guiltless of the death of her husband. The marvellous beauty of the widowed Duchess of Stimigliano, who was only nineteen, entirely turned the head of the Duke of Urbania. He affected implicit belief in her innocence, refused to give her up to the Orsinis, kinsmen of her late husband, and assigned to her magnificent apartments in the left wing of the palace, among which the room containing the famous fire-place ornamented with marble Cupids on a blue ground. Guidalfonso fell madly in love with his beautiful guest. Hitherto timid and domestic in character, he began publicly to neglect his wife, Maddalena Varano of Camerino, with whom, although childless, he had hitherto lived on excellent terms; he not only treated with contempt the admonitions of his advisers and of his suzerain the Pope, but went so far as to take measures to repudiate his wife, on the score of quite imaginary ill-conduct. The Duchess Maddalena, unable to bear this treatment, fled to the convent of the barefooted sisters at Pesaro, where she pined away, while Medea da Carpi reigned in her place at Urbania, embroiling Duke Guidalfonso in quarrels both with the powerful Orsinis, who continued to accuse her of Stimigliano's murder, and with the Varanos, kinsmen of the injured Duchess Maddalena; until at length, in the year 1576, the Duke of

Urbania, having become suddenly, and not without suspicious circumstances, a widower, publicly married Medea da Carpi two days after the decease of his unhappy wife. No child was born of this marriage; but such was the infatuation of Duke Guidalfonso, that the new Duchess induced him to settle the inheritance of the Duchy (having, with great difficulty, obtained the consent of the Pope) on the boy Bartolommeo, her son by Stimigliano, but whom the Orsinis refused to acknowledge as such, declaring him to be the child of that Giovanfrancesco Pico to whom Medea had been married by proxy, and whom, in defence, as she had said, of her honour, she had assassinated; and this investiture of the Duchy of Urbania on to a stranger and a bastard was at the expense of the obvious rights of the Cardinal Robert, Guidalfonso's younger brother.

In May 1579 Duke Guidalfonso died suddenly and mysteriously, Medea having forbidden all access to his chamber, lest, on his deathbed, he might repent and reinstate his brother in his rights. The Duchess immediately caused her son, Bartolommeo Orsini, to be proclaimed Duke of Urbania, and herself regent; and, with the help of two or three unscrupulous young men, particularly a certain Captain Oliverotto da Narni, who was rumoured to be her lover, seized the reins of government with extraordinary and terrible vigour, marching an army against the Varanos and Orsinis, who were defeated at Sigillo, and ruthlessly exterminating every person who dared question the lawfulness of the succession; while, all the time, Cardinal Robert, who had flung aside his priest's garb and vows, went about in Rome, Tuscany, Venice—nay, even to the Emperor and the King of Spain, imploring help against the usurper. In a few months he had turned the tide of sympathy against the Duchess-Regent; the Pope solemnly declared the investiture of Bartolommeo Orsini worthless, and published the accession of Robert II, Duke of Urbania and Count of Montemurlo; the Grand Duke of Tuscany and the Venetians secretly promised assistance, but only if Robert were able to assert his rights by main force. Little by little, one town after the other of the Duchy went over to Robert, and Medea da Carpi found herself surrounded in the mountain citadel of Urbania like a scorpion surrounded by flames. (This simile is not mine, but belongs to Raffaello Gualterio, historiographer to Robert II.) But, unlike the scorpion, Medea refused to commit suicide. It is perfectly marvellous how, without money or allies, she could so long keep her enemies at bay; and Gualterio attributes this to those fatal fascinations which had brought Pico and Stimigliano to their deaths, which had turned the once honest Guidalfonso into a villain, and which were such that, of all her lovers, not one but preferred dying for her, even after he had been treated with ingratitude and ousted by a rival; a faculty which Messer Raffaello Gualterio clearly attributed to hellish connivance.

At last the ex-Cardinal Robert succeeded, and triumphantly entered Urbania in November 1579. His accession was marked by moderation and clemency. Not a man was put to death, save Oliverotto da Narni, who threw himself on the new Duke, tried to stab him as he alighted at the palace, and who was cut down by the Duke's men, crying, "Orsini, Orsini! Medea, Medea! Long live Duke Bartolommeo!" with his dying breath, although it is said that the Duchess had treated him with ignominy. The little Bartolommeo was sent to Rome to the Orsinis; the Duchess, respectfully confined in the left wing of the palace.

It is said that she haughtily requested to see the new Duke, but that he shook his head, and, in his priest's fashion, quoted a verse about Ulysses and the Sirens; and it is remarkable that he persistently refused to see her, abruptly leaving his chamber one day that she had entered it by stealth. After a few months a conspiracy was discovered to murder Duke Robert, which had obviously been set on foot by Medea. But the young man, one Marcantonio Frangipani of Rome, denied, even under the severest torture, any complicity of hers; so that Duke Robert, who wished to do nothing violent, merely transferred the Duchess from his villa at Sant' Elmo to the convent of the Clarisse in town, where she was guarded and watched in the closest manner. It seemed impossible that Medea should intrigue any further, for she certainly saw and could be seen by no one. Yet she contrived to send a letter and her portrait to one Prinzivalle degli Ordelaffi, a youth, only nineteen years old, of noble Romagnole family, and who was betrothed to one of the most beautiful girls of Urbania. He immediately broke off his engagement, and, shortly afterwards, attempted to shoot Duke Robert with a holster-pistol as he knelt at mass on the festival of Easter Day. This time Duke Robert was determined to obtain proofs against Medea. Prinzivalle degli Ordelaffi was kept some days without food, then submitted to the most violent tortures, and finally condemned. When he was going to be flayed with red-hot pincers and quartered by horses, he was told that he might obtain the grace of immediate death by confessing the complicity of the

Duchess; and the confessor and nuns of the convent, which stood in the place of execution outside Porta San Romano, pressed Medea to save the wretch, whose screams reached her, by confessing her own guilt. Medea asked permission to go to a balcony, where she could see Prinzivalle and be seen by him. She looked on coldly, then threw down her embroidered kerchief to the poor mangled creature. He asked the executioner to wipe his mouth with it, kissed it, and cried out that Medea was innocent. Then, after several hours of torments, he died. This was too much for the patience even of Duke Robert. Seeing that as long as Medea lived his life would be in perpetual danger, but unwilling to cause a scandal (somewhat of the priest-nature remaining), he had Medea strangled in the convent, and, what is remarkable, insisted that only women—two infanticides to whom he remitted their sentence—should be employed for the deed.

"This clement prince," writes Don Arcangelo Zappi in his life of him, published in 1725, "can be blamed only for one act of cruelty, the more odious as he had himself, until released from his vows by the Pope, been in holy orders. It is said that when he caused the death of the infamous Medea da Carpi, his fear lest her extraordinary charms should seduce any man was such, that he not only employed women as executioners, but refused to permit her a priest or monk, thus forcing her to die unshriven, and refusing her the benefit of any penitence that may have lurked in her adamantine heart."

Such is the story of Medea da Carpi, Duchess of Stimigliano Orsini, and then wife of Duke Guidalfonso II of Urbania. She was put to death just two hundred and ninety-seven years ago, December 1582, at the age of barely seven-and-twenty, and having, in the course of her short life, brought to a violent end five of her lovers, from Giovanfrancesco Pico to Prinzivalle degli Ordelaffi.

Sept. 20th.—A grand illumination of the town in honour of the taking of Rome fifteen years ago. Except Sor Asdrubale, my landlord, who shakes his head at the Piedmontese, as he calls them, the people here are all Italianissimi. The Popes kept them very much down since Urbania lapsed to the Holy See in 1645.

Sept. 28th.—I have for some time been hunting for portraits of the Duchess Medea. Most of them, I imagine, must have been destroyed, perhaps by Duke Robert II's fear lest even after her death this terrible beauty should play him a trick. Three or four I have, however, been able

to find—one a miniature in the Archives, said to be that which she sent
to poor Prinzivalle degli Ordelaffi in order to turn his head; one a
marble bust in the palace lumber-room; one in a large composition,
possibly by Baroccio, representing Cleopatra at the feet of Augustus.
Augustus is the idealised portrait of Robert II, round cropped head, nose
a little awry, clipped beard and scar as usual, but in Roman dress. Cleopatra seems to me, for all her Oriental dress, and although she wears a
black wig, to be meant for Medea da Carpi; she is kneeling, baring her
breast for the victor to strike, but in reality to captivate him, and he
turns away with an awkward gesture of loathing. None of these portraits
seem very good, save the miniature, but that is an exquisite work, and
with it, and the suggestions of the bust, it is easy to reconstruct the
beauty of this terrible being. The type is that most admired by the late
Renaissance, and, in some measure, immortalised by Jean Goujon and
the French. The face is a perfect oval, the forehead somewhat over-
round, with minute curls, like a fleece, of bright auburn hair; the nose a
trifle over-aquiline, and the cheek-bones a trifle too low; the eyes grey,
large, prominent, beneath exquisitely curved brows and lids just a little
too tight at the corners; the mouth also, brilliantly red and most delicately designed, is a little too tight, the lips strained a trifle over the teeth.
Tight eyelids and tight lips give a strange refinement, and, at the same
time, an air of mystery, a somewhat sinister seductiveness; they seem to
take, but not to give. The mouth with a kind of childish pout, looks as if
it could bite or suck like a leech. The complexion is dazzlingly fair, the
perfect transparent roset lily of a red-haired beauty; the head, with hair
elaborately curled and plaited close to it, and adorned with pearls, sits
like that of the antique Arethusa on a long, supple, swan-like neck. A
curious, at first rather conventional, artificial-looking sort of beauty, voluptuous yet cold, which, the more it is contemplated, the more it trou-
bles and haunts the mind. Round the lady's neck is a gold chain with
little gold lozenges at intervals, on which is engraved the posy or pun
(the fashion of French devices is common in those days), "Amour Dure
—Dure Amour." The same posy is inscribed in the hollow of the bust,
and, thanks to it, I have been able to identify the latter as Medea's
portrait. I often examine these tragic portraits, wondering what this face,
which led so many men to their death, may have been like when it spoke
or smiled, what at the moment when Medea da Carpi fascinated her
victims into love unto death—"Amour Dure—Dure Amour," as runs

her device—love that lasts, cruel love—yes indeed, when one thinks of the fidelity and fate of her lovers.

Oct. 13th.—I have literally not had time to write a line of my diary all these days. My whole mornings have gone in those Archives, my afternoons taking long walks in this lovely autumn weather (the highest hills are just tipped with snow). My evenings go in writing that confounded account of the Palace of Urbania which Government requires, merely to keep me at work at something useless. Of my history I have not yet been able to write a word. . . . By the way, I must note down a curious circumstance mentioned in an anonymous MS. life of Duke Robert, which I fell upon to-day. When this prince had the equestrian statue of himself by Antonio Tassi, Gianbologna's pupil, erected in the square of the *Corte,* he secretly caused to be made, says my anonymous MS., a silver statuette of his familiar genius or angel—"familiaris ejus angelus seu genius, quod a vulgo dicitur *idolino"*—which statuette or idol, after having been consecrated by the astrologers—"ab astrologis quibusdam ritibus sacrato"—was placed in the cavity of the chest of the effigy by Tassi, in order, says the MS., that his soul might rest until the general Resurrection. This passage is curious, and to me somewhat puzzling; how could the soul of Duke Robert await the general Resurrection, when, as a Catholic, he ought to have believed that it must, as soon as separated from his body, go to Purgatory? Or is there some semipagan superstition of the Renaissance (most strange, certainly, in a man who had been a Cardinal) connecting the soul with a guardian genius, who could be compelled, by magic rites ("ab astrologis sacrato," the MS. says of the little idol), to remain fixed to earth, so that the soul should sleep in the body until the Day of Judgment? I confess this story baffles me. I wonder whether such an idol ever existed, or exists nowadays, in the body of Tassi's bronze effigy?

Oct. 20th.—I have been seeing a good deal of late of the Vice-Prefect's son: an amiable young man with a love-sick face and a languid interest in Urbanian history and archæology, of which he is profoundly ignorant. This young man, who has lived at Siena and Lucca before his father was promoted here, wears extremely long and tight trousers, which almost preclude his bending his knees, a stick-up collar and an eyeglass, and a pair of fresh kid gloves stuck in the breast of his coat, speaks of Urbania as Ovid might have spoken of Pontus, and complains (as well he may) of the barbarism of the young men, the officials who dine at my inn and howl and sing like madmen, and the nobles who drive gigs, showing almost as much throat as a lady at a ball. This person frequently entertains me with his *amori,* past, present, and future; he evidently thinks me very odd for having none to entertain him with in return; he points out to me the pretty (or ugly) servant-girls and dressmakers as we walk in the street, sighs deeply or sings in falsetto behind every tolerably young-looking woman, and has finally taken me to the house of the lady of his heart, a great black-moustachioed countess, with a voice like a fish-crier; here, he says, I shall meet all the best company in Urbania and some beautiful women—ah, too beautiful, alas! I find three huge half-furnished rooms, with bare brick floors, petroleum lamps, and horribly bad pictures on bright wash-ball-blue and gamboge walls, and in the midst of it all, every evening, a dozen ladies and gentlemen seated in a circle, vociferating at each other the same news a year old; the younger ladies in bright yellows and greens, fanning themselves while my teeth chatter, and having sweet things whispered behind their fans by officers with hair brushed up like a hedgehog. And these are the women my friend expects me to fall in love with! I vainly wait for tea or supper which does not come, and rush home, determined to leave alone the Urbanian *beau monde.*

It is quite true that I have no *amori,* although my friend does not believe it. When I came to Italy first, I looked out for romance; I sighed, like Goethe in Rome, for a window to open and a wondrous creature to appear, "welch mich versengend erquickt." Perhaps it is because Goethe was a German, accustomed to German *Fraus,* and I am, after all, a Pole, accustomed to something very different from *Fraus;* but anyhow, for all my efforts, in Rome, Florence, and Siena, I never could find a woman to go mad about, either among the ladies, chattering bad French, or among the lower classes, as 'cute and cold as money-lenders; so I steer clear of Italian womankind, its shrill voice and gaudy toilettes. I am wedded to history, to the Past, to women like Lucrezia Borgia, Vittoria Accoramboni, or that Medea da Carpi, for the present; some day I shall perhaps find a grand passion, a woman to play the Don Quixote about, like the Pole that I am; a woman out of whose slipper to drink, and for whose pleasure to die; but not here! Few things strike me so much as the degeneracy of Italian women. What has become of the race of Faustinas, Marozias, Bianca Cappellos? Where discover nowadays (I confess she haunts me) another Medea da Carpi? Were it only possible to meet a woman of that extreme distinction of beauty, of that terribleness of nature, even if only potential, I do believe I could love her, even to the Day of Judgment, like any Oliverotto da Narni, or Frangipani or Prinzivalle.

Oct. 27th.—Fine sentiments the above are for a professor, a learned man! I thought the young artists of Rome childish because they played practical jokes and yelled at night in the streets, returning from the Caffé Greco or the cellar in the Via Palombella; but am I not as childish to the full—I, melancholy wretch, whom they called Hamlet and the Knight of the Doleful Countenance?

Nov. 5th.—I can't free myself from the thought of this Medea da Carpi. In my walks, my mornings in the Archives, my solitary evenings, I catch myself thinking over the woman. Am I turning novelist instead of historian? And still it seems to me that I understand her so well; so much better than my facts warrant. First, we must put aside all pedantic modern ideas of right and wrong. Right and wrong in a century of violence and treachery does not exist, least of all for creatures like Medea. Go preach right and wrong to a tigress, my dear sir! Yet is there in the world anything nobler than the huge creature, steel when she springs, velvet when she treads, as she stretches her supple body, or smooths her beautiful skin, or fastens her strong claws into her victim?

Yes; I can understand Medea. Fancy a woman of superlative beauty, of the highest courage and calmness, a woman of many resources, of genius, brought up by a petty princelet of a father, upon Tacitus and Sallust, and the tales of the great Malatestas, of Cæsar Borgia and such-like!—a woman whose one passion is conquest and empire—fancy her, on the eve of being wedded to a man of the power of the Duke of Stimigliano, claimed, carried off by a small fry of a Pico, locked up in his hereditary brigand's castle, and having to receive the young fool's red-hot love as an honour and a necessity! The mere thought of any violence to such a nature is an abominable outrage; and if Pico chooses to embrace such a woman at the risk of meeting a sharp piece of steel in her arms, why, it is a fair bargain. Young hound—or, if you prefer, young hero—to think to treat a woman like this as if she were any village wench! Medea marries her Orsini. A marriage, let it be noted, between an old soldier of fifty and a girl of sixteen. Reflect what that means: it means that this imperious woman is soon treated like a chattel, made roughly to understand that her business is to give the Duke an heir, not advice; that she must never ask "wherefore this or that?" that she must curtsey before the Duke's counsellors, his captains, his mistresses; that, at the least suspicion of rebelliousness, she is subject to his foul words and blows; at the least suspicion of infidelity, to be strangled or starved to death, or thrown down an oubliette. Suppose that she know that her husband has taken it into his head that she has looked too hard at this man or that, that one of his lieutenants or one of his women have whispered that, after all, the boy Bartolommeo might as soon be a Pico as an Orsini. Suppose she know that she must strike or be struck? Why, she strikes, or gets some one to strike for her. At what price? A promise of love, of love to a groom, the son of a serf! Why, the dog must be mad or drunk to believe such a thing possible; his very belief in anything so monstrous makes him worthy of death. And then he dares to blab! This is much worse than Pico. Medea is bound to defend her honour a second time; if she could stab Pico, she can certainly stab this fellow, or have him stabbed.

Hounded by her husband's kinsmen, she takes refuge at Urbania. The Duke, like every other man, falls wildly in love with Medea, and neglects his wife; let us even go so far as to say, breaks his wife's heart. Is this Medea's fault? Is it her fault that every stone that comes beneath her chariot-wheels is crushed? Certainly not. Do you suppose that a woman like Medea feels the smallest ill-will against a poor, craven Duchess Maddalena? Why, she ignores her very existence. To suppose Medea a cruel woman is as grotesque as to call her an immoral woman. Her fate is, sooner or later, to triumph over her enemies, at all events to make their victory almost a defeat; her magic faculty is to enslave all the men who come across her path; all those who see her, love her, become her slaves; and it is the destiny of all her slaves to perish. Her lovers, with the exception of Duke Guidalfonso, all come to an untimely end; and in this there is nothing unjust. The possession of a woman like Medea is a happiness too great for a mortal man; it would turn his head, make him forget even what he owed her; no man must survive long who conceives himself to have a right over her; it is a kind of sacrilege. And only death, the willingness to pay for such happiness by death, can at all make a man worthy of being her lover; he must be willing to love and suffer and die. This is the meaning of her device—"Amour Dure—Dure Amour." The love of Medea da Carpi cannot fade, but the lover can die; it is a constant and a cruel love.

Nov. 11th.—I was right, quite right in my idea. I have found—Oh, joy! I treated the Vice-Prefect's son to a dinner of five courses at the Trattoria La Stella d'Italia out of sheer jubilation—I have found in the Archives, unknown, of course, to the Director, a heap of letters—letters of Duke Robert about Medea da Carpi, letters of Medea herself! Yes, Medea's own handwriting—a round, scholarly character, full of abbreviations, with a Greek look about it, as befits a learned princess who could read Plato as well as Petrarch. The letters are of little importance, mere drafts of business letters for her secretary to copy, during the time that she governed the poor weak Guidalfonso. But they are her letters, and I can imagine almost that there hangs about these mouldering pieces of paper a scent as of a woman's hair.

The few letters of Duke Robert show him in a new light. A cunning, cold, but craven priest. He trembles at the bare thought of Medea—"la pessima Medea"—worse than her namesake of Colchis, as he calls her. His long clemency is a result of mere fear of laying violent hands upon her. He fears her as something almost supernatural; he would have enjoyed having had her burnt as a witch. After letter on letter, telling his crony, Cardinal Sanseverino, at Rome his various precautions during her lifetime—how he wears a jacket of mail under his coat; how he drinks only milk from a cow which he has milked in his presence; how he tries his dog with morsels of his food, lest it be poisoned; how he suspects the wax-candles because of their peculiar smell; how he fears riding out lest some one should frighten his horse and cause him to break his neck— after all this, and when Medea has been in her grave two years, he tells his correspondent of his fear of meeting the soul of Medea after his own death, and chuckles over the ingenious device (concocted by his astrologer and a certain Fra Gaudenzio, a Capuchin) by which he shall secure the absolute peace of his soul until that of the wicked Medea be finally "chained up in Hell among the lakes of boiling pitch and the ice of Caina described by the immortal bard"—old pedant! Here, then, is the explanation of that silver image—*quod vulgo dicitur idolino*—which he caused to be soldered into his effigy by Tassi. As long as the image of his soul was attached to the image of his body, he should sleep awaiting the Day of Judgment, fully convinced that Medea's soul will then be properly tarred and feathered, while his—honest man!—will fly straight to Paradise. And to think that, two weeks ago, I believed this man to be a hero! Aha! my good Duke Robert, you shall be shown up in my history;

and no amount of silver idolinos shall save you from being heartily laughed at!

Nov. 15th.—Strange! That idiot of a Prefect's son, who has heard me talk a hundred times of Medea da Carpi, suddenly recollects that, when he was a child at Urbania, his nurse used to threaten him with a visit from Madonna Medea, who rode in the sky on a black he-goat. My Duchess Medea turned into a bogey for naughty little boys!

Nov. 20th.—I have been going about with a Bavarian Professor of mediæval history, showing him all over the country. Among other places we went to Rocca Sant' Elmo, to see the former villa of the Dukes of Urbania, the villa where Medea was confined between the accession of Duke Robert and the conspiracy of Marcantonio Frangipani, which caused her removal to the nunnery immediately outside the town. A long ride up the desolate Apennine valleys, bleak beyond words just now with their thin fringe of oak scrub turned russet, thin patches of grass sered by the frost, the last few yellow leaves of the poplars by the torrents shaking and fluttering about in the chill Tramontana; the mountain-tops are wrapped in thick grey cloud; to-morrow, if the wind continues, we shall see them round masses of snow against the cold blue sky. Sant' Elmo is a wretched hamlet high on the Apennine ridge, where the Italian vegetation is already replaced by that of the North. You ride for miles through leafless chestnut woods, the scent of the soaking brown leaves filling the air, the roar of the torrent, turbid with autumn rains, rising from the precipice below; then suddenly the leafless chestnut woods are replaced, as at Vallombrosa, by a belt of black, dense fir plantations. Emerging from these, you come to an open space, frozen blasted meadows, the rocks of snow clad peak, the newly fallen snow, close above you; and in the midst, on a knoll, with a gnarled larch on either side, the ducal villa of Sant' Elmo, a big black stone box with a stone escutcheon, grated windows, and a double flight of steps in front. It is now let out to the proprietor of the neighbouring woods, who uses it for the storage of chestnuts, faggots, and charcoal from the neighbouring ovens. We tied our horses to the iron rings and entered: an old woman, with dishevelled hair, was alone in the house. The villa is a mere hunting-lodge, built by Ottobuono IV, the father of Dukes Guidalfonso and Robert, about 1530. Some of the rooms have at one time been frescoed and panelled with oak carvings, but all this has disappeared. Only, in one of the big rooms, there remains a large marble fireplace, similar to those in the palace at Urbania, beautifully carved with Cupids on a blue ground; a charming naked boy sustains a jar on either side, one containing clove pinks, the other roses. The room was filled with stacks of faggots.

We returned home late, my companion in excessively bad humour at the fruitlessness of the expedition. We were caught in the skirt of a snowstorm as we got into the chestnut woods. The sight of the snow falling gently, of the earth and bushes whitened all round, made me feel back at Posen, once more a child. I sang and shouted, to my companion's horror. This will be a bad point against me if reported at Berlin. A historian of twenty-four who shouts and sings, and that when another historian is cursing at the snow and the bad roads! All night I lay awake watching the embers of my wood fire, and thinking of Medea da Carpi mewed up, in winter, in that solitude of Sant' Elmo, the firs groaning, the torrent roaring, the snow falling all round; miles and miles away from human creatures. I fancied I saw it all, and that I, somehow, was Marcantonio Frangipani come to liberate her—or was it Prinzivalle degli Ordelaffi? I suppose it was because of the long ride, the unaccustomed pricking feeling of the snow in the air; or perhaps the punch which my professor insisted on drinking after dinner.

Nov. 23rd.—Thank goodness, that Bavarian professor has finally departed! Those days he spent here drove me nearly crazy. Talking over my work, I told him one day my views on Medea da Carpi; whereupon he condescended to answer that those were the usual tales due to the mythopoeic (old idiot!) tendency of the Renaissance; that research would disprove the greater part of them, as it had disproved the stories current about the Borgias, &c.; that, moreover, such a woman as I made out was psychologically and physiologically impossible. Would that one could say as much of such professors as he and his fellows!

Nov. 24th.—I cannot get over my pleasure in being rid of that imbecile; I felt as if I could have throttled him every time he spoke of the Lady of my thoughts—for such she has become—*Metea,* as the animal called her!

Nov. 30th.—I feel quite shaken at what has just happened; I am beginning to fear that that old pedant was right in saying that it was bad for me to live all alone in a strange country, that it would make me morbid. It is ridiculous that I should be put into such a state of excitement merely by the chance discovery of a portrait of a woman dead these three hundred years. With the case of my uncle Ladislas, and other suspicions of insanity in my family, I ought really to guard against such foolish excitement.

Yet the incident was really dramatic, uncanny. I could have sworn that I knew every picture in the palace here; and particularly every picture of Her. Anyhow, this morning, as I was leaving the Archives, I passed through one of the many small rooms—irregular-shaped closets —which fill up the ins and outs of this curious palace, turreted like a French château. I must have passed through that closet before, for the view was so familiar out of its window; just the particular bit of round tower in front, the cypress on the other side of the ravine, the belfry beyond, and the piece of the line of Monte Sant' Agata and the Leonessa, covered with snow, against the sky. I suppose there must be twin rooms, and that I had got into the wrong one; or rather, perhaps some shutter had been opened or curtain withdrawn. As I was passing, my eye was caught by a very beautiful old mirror-frame let into the brown and yellow inlaid wall. I approached, and looking at the frame, looked also, mechanically, into the glass. I gave a great start, and almost shrieked, I do believe—(it's lucky the Munich professor is safe out of Urbania!). Behind my own image stood another, a figure close to my shoulder, a face close to mine; and that figure, that face, hers! Medea da Carpi's! I turned sharp round, as white, I think, as the ghost I expected to see. On the wall opposite the mirror, just a pace or two behind where I had been standing, hung a portrait. And such a portrait!—Bronzino never painted a grander one. Against a background of harsh, dark blue, there stands out the figure of the Duchess (for it is Medea, the real Medea, a thousand times more real, individual, and powerful than in the other portraits), seated stiffly in a high-backed chair, sustained, as it were, almost rigid, by the stiff brocade of skirts and stomacher, stiffer for plaques of embroidered silver flowers and rows of seed pearl. The dress is, with its mixture of silver and pearl, of a strange dull red, a wicked poppy-juice colour, against which the flesh of the long, narrow hands with fringe-like fingers; of the long slender neck, and the face with bared forehead, looks white and hard, like alabaster. The face is the same as in the other portraits: the same rounded forehead, with the short fleece-like, yellow-ish-red curls; the same beautifully curved eyebrows, just barely marked; the same eyelids, a little tight across the eyes; the same lips, a little tight across the mouth; but with a purity of line, a dazzling splendour of skin, and intensity of look immeasurably superior to all the other portraits.

She looks out of the frame with a cold, level glance; yet the lips smile. One hand holds a dull-red rose; the other, long, narrow, tapering, plays with a thick rope of silk and gold and jewels hanging from the waist; round the throat, white as marble, partially confined in the tight dull-red bodice, hangs a gold collar, with the device on alternate enamelled medallions, "AMOUR DURE—DURE AMOUR."

On reflection, I see that I simply could never have been in that room or closet before; I must have mistaken the door. But, although the explanation is so simple, I still, after several hours, feel terribly shaken in all my being. If I grow so excitable I shall have to go to Rome at Christmas for a holiday. I feel as if some danger pursued me here (can it be fever?); and yet, and yet, I don't see how I shall ever tear myself away.

Dec. 10th.—I have made an effort, and accepted the Vice-Prefect's son's invitation to see the oil-making at a villa of theirs near the coast. The villa, or farm, is an old fortified, towered place, standing on a hillside among olive-trees and little osier-bushes, which look like a bright orange flame. The olives are squeezed in a tremendous black cellar, like a prison: you see, by the faint white daylight, and the smoky yellow flare of resin burning in pans, great white bullocks moving round a huge millstone; vague figures working at pulleys and handles: it looks, to my fancy, like some scene of the Inquisition. The Cavaliere regaled me with his best wine and rusks. I took some long walks by the seaside; I had left Urbania wrapped in snow-clouds; down on the coast there was a bright sun; the sunshine, the sea, the bustle of the little port on the Adriatic seemed to do me good. I came back to Urbania another man. Sor Asdrubale, my landlord, poking about in slippers among the gilded chests, the Empire sofas, the old cups and saucers and pictures which no one will buy, congratulated me upon the improvement in my looks. "You work too much," he says; "youth requires amusement, theatres, promenades, *amori*—it is time enough to be serious when one is bald"— and he took off his greasy red cap. Yes, I am better! and, as a result, I take to my work with delight again. I will cut them out still, those wiseacres at Berlin!

Dec. 14th.—I don't think I have ever felt so happy about my work. I see it all so well—that crafty, cowardly Duke Robert; that melancholy Duchess Maddalena; that weak, showy, would-be chivalrous Duke

Guidalfonso; and above all, the splendid figure of Medea. I feel as if I were the greatest historian of the age; and, at the same time, as if I were a boy of twelve. It snowed yesterday for the first time in the city, for two good hours. When it had done, I actually went into the square and taught the ragamuffins to make a snow man; no, a snow woman; and I had the fancy to call her Medea. "La pessima Medea!" cried one of the boys—"the one who used to ride through the air on a goat?" "No, no," I said; "she was a beautiful lady, the Duchess of Urbania, the most beautiful woman that ever lived." I made her a crown of tinsel, and taught the boys to cry "Evviva, Medea!" But one of them said, "She is a witch! She must be burnt!" At which they all rushed to fetch burning faggots and tow; in a minute the yelling demons had melted her down.

Dec. 15th.—What a goose I am, and to think I am twenty-four, and known in literature! In my long walks I have composed to a tune (I don't know what it is) which all the people are singing and whistling in the street at present, a poem in frightful Italian, beginning "Medea, mia dea," calling on her in the name of her various lovers. I go about humming between my teeth, "Why am I not Marcantonio? or Prinzivalle? or he of Narni? or the good Duke Alfonso? that I might be beloved by thee, Medea, mia dea," &c. &c. Awful rubbish! My landlord, I think, suspects that Medea must be some lady I met while I was staying by the seaside. I am sure Sora Serafina, Sora Lodovica, and Sora Adalgisa—the three Parcæ or *Norns,* as I call them—have some such notion. This afternoon, at dusk, while tidying my room, Sora Lodovica said to me, "How beautifully the Signorino has taken to singing!" I was scarcely aware that I had been vociferating, "Vieni, Medea, mia dea," while the old lady bobbed about making up my fire. I stopped; a nice reputation I shall get! I thought, and all this will somehow get to Rome, and thence to Berlin. Sora Lodovica was leaning out of the window, pulling in the iron hook of the shrine-lamp which marks Sor Asdrubale's house. As she was trimming the lamp previous to swinging it out again, she said in her odd, prudish little way, "You are wrong to stop singing, my son" (she varies between calling me Signor Professore and such terms of affection as "Nino," "Viscere mie," &c.); "you are wrong to stop singing, for there is a young lady there in the street who has actually stopped to listen to you."

I ran to the window. A woman, wrapped in a black shawl, was standing in an archway, looking up to the window.

"Eh, eh! the Signor Professore has admirers," said Sora Lodovica.

"Medea, mia dea!" I burst out as loud as I could, with a boy's pleasure in disconcerting the inquisitive passer-by. She turned suddenly round to go away, waving her hand at me; at that moment Sora Lodovica swung the shrine-lamp back into its place. A stream of light fell across the street. I felt myself grow quite cold; the face of the woman outside was that of Medea da Carpi!

What a fool I am, to be sure!

Part II

Dec. 17th.—I fear that my craze about Medea da Carpi has become well known, thanks to my silly talk and idiotic songs. That Vice-Prefect's son—or the assistant at the Archives, or perhaps some of the company at the Contessa's, is trying to play me a trick! But take care, my good ladies and gentlemen, I shall pay you out in your own coin! Imagine my feelings when, this morning, I found on my desk a folded letter addressed to me in a curious handwriting which seemed strangely familiar to me, and which, after a moment, I recognised as that of the letters of Medea da Carpi at the Archives. It gave me a horrible shock. My next idea was that it must be a present from some one who knew my interest in Medea—a genuine letter of hers on which some idiot had written my address instead of putting it into an envelope. But it was addressed to me, written to me, no old letter; merely four lines, which ran as follows:—

"To Spiridion.—A person who knows the interest you bear her will be at the Church of San Giovanni Decollato this evening at nine. Look out, in the left aisle, for a lady wearing a black mantle, and holding a rose."

By this time I understood that I was the object of a conspiracy, the victim of a hoax. I turned the letter round and round. It was written on paper such as was made in the sixteenth century, and in an extraordinarily precise imitation of Medea da Carpi's characters. Who had written it? I thought over all the possible people. On the whole, it must be the Vice-Prefect's son, perhaps in combination with his lady-love, the Countess. They must have torn a blank page off some old letter; but that either of them should have had the ingenuity of inventing such a hoax, or the power of committing such a forgery, astounds me beyond measure. There is more in these people than I should have guessed. How pay them off? By taking no notice of the letter? Dignified, but dull. No, I will go; perhaps some one will be there, and I will mystify them in their turn. Or, if no one is there, how I shall crow over them for their imperfectly carried out plot! Perhaps this is some folly of the Cavalier Muzio's to bring me into the presence of some lady whom he destines to be the flame of my future *amori*. That is likely enough. And it would be too idiotic and professorial to refuse such an invitation; the lady must be worth knowing who can forge sixteenth-century letters like this, for I am sure that languid swell Muzio never could. I will go! By Heaven! I'll pay them back in their own coin! It is now five—how long these days are!

Dec. 18th.—Am I mad? Or are there really ghosts? That adventure of last night has shaken me to the very depth of my soul.

I went at nine, as the mysterious letter had bid me. It was bitterly cold, and the air full of fog and sleet; not a shop open, not a window unshuttered, not a creature visible; the narrow black streets, precipitous between their high walls and under their lofty archways, were only the blacker for the dull light of an oil-lamp here and there, with its flickering yellow reflection on the wet flags. San Giovanni Decollato is a little church, or rather oratory, which I have always hitherto seen shut up (as so many churches here are shut up except on great festivals); and situate behind the ducal palace, on a sharp ascent, and forming the bifurcation of two steep paved lanes. I have passed by the place a hundred times, and scarcely noticed the little church, except for the marble high relief over the door, showing the grizzly head of the Baptist in the charger, and for the iron cage close by, in which were formerly exposed the heads of criminals; the decapitated, or, as they call him here, decollated, John the Baptist, being apparently the patron of axe and block.

A few strides took me from my lodgings to San Giovanni Decollato. I confess I was excited; one is not twenty-four and a Pole for nothing. On getting to the kind of little platform at the bifurcation of the two precipitous streets, I found, to my surprise, that the windows of the church or oratory were not lighted, and that the door was locked! So this was the precious joke that had been played upon me; to send me on a bitter cold, sleety night, to a church which was shut up and had perhaps been shut up for years! I don't know what I couldn't have done in that moment of rage; I felt inclined to break open the church door, or to go and pull the Vice-Prefect's son out of bed (for I felt sure that the joke was his). I determined upon the latter course; and was walking towards his door, along the black alley to the left of the church, when I was suddenly stopped by the sound as of an organ close by; an organ, yes, quite plainly, and the voice of choristers and the drone of a litany. So the church was not shut, after all! I retraced my steps to the top of the lane. All was dark and in complete silence. Suddenly there came again a faint gust of organ and voices. I listened; it clearly came from the other lane, the one on the right-hand side. Was there, perhaps, another door there? I passed beneath the archway, and descended a little way in the direction whence the sounds seemed to come. But no door, no light, only the black walls, the black wet flags, with their faint yellow reflections of flickering oil-lamps; moreover, complete silence. I stopped a minute, and then the chant rose again; this time it seemed to me most certainly from the lane I had just left. I went back—nothing. Thus backwards and forwards, the sounds always beckoning, as it were, one way, only to beckon me back, vainly, to the other.

At last I lost patience; and I felt a sort of creeping terror, which only a violent action could dispel. If the mysterious sounds came neither from the street to the right, nor from the street to the left, they could come only from the church. Half-maddened, I rushed up the two or three steps, and prepared to wrench the door open with a tremendous effort. To my amazement, it opened with the greatest ease. I entered, and the sounds of the litany met me louder than before, as I paused a moment between the outer door and the heavy leathern curtain. I raised the latter and crept in. The altar was brilliantly illuminated with tapers and garlands of chandeliers; this was evidently some evening service connected with Christmas. The nave and aisles were comparatively dark, and about half-full. I elbowed my way along the right aisle towards the altar. When my eyes had got accustomed to the unexpected light, I began to look round me, and with a beating heart. The idea that all this was a hoax, that I should meet merely some acquaintance of my friend the Cavaliere's, had somehow departed: I looked about. The people were all wrapped up, the men in big cloaks, the women in woollen veils and mantles. The body of the church was comparatively dark, and I could not make out anything very clearly, but it seemed to me, somehow, as if, under the cloaks and veils, these people were dressed in a rather extraordinary fashion. The man in front of me, I remarked, showed yellow stockings beneath his cloak; a woman, hard by, a red bodice, laced behind with gold tags. Could these be peasants from some remote part come for the Christmas festivities, or did the inhabitants of Urbania don some old-fashioned garb in honour of Christmas?

As I was wondering, my eye suddenly caught that of a woman standing in the opposite aisle, close to the altar, and in the full blaze of its lights. She was wrapped in black, but held, in a very conspicuous way, a red rose, an unknown luxury at this time of the year in a place like Urbania. She evidently saw me, and turning even more fully into the light, she loosened her heavy black cloak, displaying a dress of deep red, with gleams of silver and gold embroideries; she turned her face towards me; the full blaze of the chandeliers and tapers fell upon it. It was the face of Medea da Carpi! I dashed across the nave, pushing people roughly aside, or rather, it seemed to me, passing through impalpable bodies. But the lady turned and walked rapidly down the aisle towards the door. I followed close upon her, but somehow I could not get up with her. Once, at the curtain, she turned round again. She was within a few paces of me. Yes, it was Medea. Medea herself, no mistake, no delusion, no sham; the oval face, the lips tightened over the mouth, the eyelids tight over the corner of the eyes, the exquisite alabaster complexion! She raised the curtain and glided out. I followed; the curtain alone separated me from her. I saw the wooden door swing to behind her. One step ahead of me! I tore open the door; she must be on the steps, within reach of my arm!

I stood outside the church. All was empty, merely the wet pavement and the yellow reflections in the pools: a sudden cold seized me; I could not go on. I tried to re-enter the church; it was shut. I rushed home, my hair standing on end, and trembling in all my limbs, and remained for an hour like a maniac. Is it a delusion? Am I too going mad? O God, God! am I going mad?

Dec. 19th.—A brilliant, sunny day; all the black snow-slush has disappeared out of the town, off the bushes and trees. The snow-clad mountains sparkle against the bright blue sky. A Sunday, and Sunday weather; all the bells are ringing for the approach of Christmas. They are preparing for a kind of fair in the square with the colonnade, putting up booths filled with coloured cotton and woollen ware, bright shawls and kerchiefs, mirrors, ribbons, brilliant pewter lamps; the whole turnout of the pedlar in "Winter's Tale." The pork-shops are all garlanded with green and with paper flowers, the hams and cheeses stuck full of little flags and green twigs. I strolled out to see the cattle-fair outside the gate; a forest of interlacing horns, an ocean of lowing and stamping: hundreds of immense white bullocks, with horns a yard long and red tassels, packed close together on the little piazza d'armi under the city walls. Bah! why do I write this trash? What's the use of it all? While I am forcing myself to write about bells, and Christmas festivities, and cattle-fairs, one idea goes on like a bell within me: Medea, Medea! Have I really seen her, or am I mad?

Two hours later.—That Church of San Giovanni Decollato—so my landlord informs me—has not been made use of within the memory of man. Could it have been all a hallucination or a dream—perhaps a dream dreamed that night? I have been out again to look at that church. There it is, at the bifurcation of the two steep lanes, with its bas-relief of the Baptist's head over the door. The door does look as if it had not been opened for years. I can see the cobwebs in the window-panes; it does look as if, as Sor Asdrubale says, only rats and spiders congregated within it. And yet—and yet; I have so clear a remembrance, so distinct a consciousness of it all. There was a picture of the daughter of Herodias dancing, upon the altar; I remember her white turban with a scarlet tuft of feathers, and Herod's blue caftan; I remember the shape of the central chandelier; it swung round slowly, and one of the wax lights had got bent almost in two by the heat and draught.

Things, all these, which I may have seen elsewhere, stored unawares in my brain, and which may have come out, somehow, in a dream; I have heard physiologists allude to such things. I will go again: if the church be shut, why then it must have been a dream, a vision, the result of overexcitement. I must leave at once for Rome and see doctors, for I am afraid of going mad. If, on the other hand—pshaw! there *is no other hand* in such a case. Yet if there were—why then, I should really have seen Medea; I might see her again; speak to her. The mere thought sets my blood in a whirl, not with horror, but with . . . I know not what to call it. The feeling terrifies me, but it is delicious. Idiot! There is some little coil of my brain, the twentieth of a hair's-breadth out of order—that's all!

Dec. 20th.—I have been again; I have heard the music; I have been inside the church; I have seen Her! I can no longer doubt my senses.

Why should I? Those pedants say that the dead are dead, the past is past. For them, yes; but why for me?—why for a man who loves, who is consumed with the love of a woman?—a woman who, indeed—yes, let me finish the sentence. Why should there not be ghosts to such as can see them? Why should she not return to the earth, if she knows that it contains a man who thinks of, desires, only her?

A hallucination? Why, I saw her, as I see this paper that I write upon; standing there, in the full blaze of the altar. Why, I heard the rustle of her skirts, I smelt the scent of her hair, I raised the curtain which was shaking from her touch. Again I missed her. But this time, as I rushed out into the empty moonlit street, I found upon the church steps a rose —the rose which I had seen in her hand the moment before—I felt it, smelt it; a rose, a real, living rose, dark red and only just plucked. I put it into water when I returned, after having kissed it, who knows how many times? I placed it on the top of the cupboard; I determined not to look at it for twenty-four hours lest it should be a delusion. But I must see it again; I must. . . . Good Heavens! this is horrible, horrible; if I had found a skeleton it could not have been worse! The rose, which last night seemed freshly plucked, full of colour and perfume, is brown, dry —a thing kept for centuries between the leaves of a book—it has crumbled into dust between my fingers. Horrible, horrible! But why so, pray? Did I not know that I was in love with a woman dead three hundred years? If I wanted fresh roses which bloomed yesterday, the Countess Fiammetta or any little sempstress in Urbania might have given them me. What if the rose has fallen to dust? If only I could hold Medea in my arms as I held it in my fingers, kiss her lips as I kissed its petals, should I not be satisfied if she too were to fall to dust the next moment, if I were to fall to dust myself?

Dec. 22nd, Eleven at night.—I have seen her once more!—almost spoken to her. I have been promised her love! Ah, Spiridion! you were right when you felt that you were not made for any earthly *amori*. At the usual hour I betook myself this evening to San Giovanni Decollato. A bright winter night; the high houses and belfries standing out against a deep blue heaven luminous, shimmering like steel with myriads of stars; the moon has not yet risen. There was no light in the windows; but, after a little effort, the door opened and I entered the church, the altar, as usual, brilliantly illuminated. It struck me suddenly that all this crowd of men and women standing all round, these priests chanting and moving about the altar, were dead—that they did not exist for any man save me. I touched, as if by accident, the hand of my neighbour; it was cold, like wet clay. He turned round, but did not seem to see me: his face was ashy, and his eyes staring, fixed, like those of a blind man or a corpse. I felt as if I must rush out. But at that moment my eye fell upon Her, standing as usual by the altar steps, wrapped in a black mantle, in the full blaze of the lights. She turned round; the light fell straight upon her face, the face with the delicate features, the eyelids and lips a little tight, the alabaster skin faintly tinged with pale pink. Our eyes met.

I pushed my way across the nave towards where she stood by the altar steps; she turned quickly down the aisle, and I after her. Once or twice she lingered, and I thought I should overtake her; but again, when, not a second after the door had closed upon her, I stepped out into the street, she had vanished. On the church step lay something white. It was not a flower this time, but a letter. I rushed back to the church to read it; but the church was fast shut, as if it had not been opened for years. I could not see by the flickering shrine-lamps—I rushed home, lit my lamp, pulled the letter from my breast. I have it before me. The handwriting is hers; the same as in the Archives, the same as in that first letter:—

"To SPIRIDION—Let thy courage be equal to thy love, and thy love shall be rewarded. On the night preceding Christmas, take a hatchet and saw; cut boldly into the body of the bronze rider who stands in the Corte, on the left side, near the waist. Saw open the body, and within it thou wilt find the silver effigy of a winged genius. Take it out, hack it into a hundred pieces, and fling them in all directions, so that the winds may sweep them away. That night she whom thou lovest will come to reward thy fidelity."

On the brownish wax is the device—

"AMOUR DURE—DURE AMOUR."

Dec. 23rd.—So it is true! I was reserved for something wonderful in this world. I have at last found that after which my soul has been straining. Ambition, love of art, love of Italy, these things which have occupied my spirit, and have yet left me continually unsatisfied, these were none of them my real destiny. I have sought for life, thirsting for it as a man in the desert thirsts for a well; but the life of the senses of other youths, the life of the intellect of other men, have never slaked that thirst. Shall life for me mean the love of a dead woman? We smile at what we choose to call the superstition of the past, forgetting that all our vaunted science of to-day may seem just such another superstition to the men of the future; but why should the present be right and the past wrong? The men who painted the pictures and built the palaces of three hundred years ago were certainly of as delicate fibre, of as keen reason, as ourselves, who merely print calico and build locomotives. What makes me think this, is that I have been calculating my nativity by help of an old book belonging to Sor Asdrubale—and see, my horoscope tallies almost exactly with that of Medea da Carpi, as given by a chronicler. May this explain? No, no; all is explained by the fact that the first time I read of this woman's career, the first time I saw her portrait, I loved her, though I hid my love to myself in the garb of historical interest. Historical interest indeed!

I have got the hatchet and the saw. I bought the saw of a poor joiner, in a village some miles off; he did not understand at first what I meant, and I think he thought me mad; perhaps I am. But if madness means the happiness of one's life, what of it? The hatchet I saw lying in a timber-yard, where they prepare the great trunks of the fir-trees which grow high on the Apennines of Sant' Elmo. There was no one in the yard, and I could not resist the temptation; I handled the thing, tried its edge, and stole it. This is the first time in my life that I have been a thief; why did I not go into a shop and buy a hatchet? I don't know; I seemed unable to resist the sight of the shining blade. What I am going to do is, I suppose, an act of vandalism; and certainly I have no right to spoil the property of this city of Urbania. But I wish no harm either to the statue or the city; if I could plaster up the bronze, I would do so willingly. But I must obey Her; I must avenge Her; I must get at that silver image which Robert of Montemurlo had made and consecrated in order that his cowardly soul might sleep in peace, and not encounter that of the being whom he dreaded most in the world. Aha! Duke Robert, you forced her to die unshriven, and you stuck the image of your soul into the image of your body, thinking thereby that, while she suffered the tortures of Hell, you would rest in peace, until your well-scoured little soul might fly straight up to Paradise—you were afraid of Her when both of you should be dead, and thought yourself very clever to have prepared for all emergencies! Not so, Serene Highness. You too shall taste what it is to wander after death, and to meet the dead whom one has injured.

What an interminable day! But I shall see her again to-night.

Eleven o'clock.—No; the church was fast closed; the spell had ceased. Until to-morrow I shall not see her. But to-morrow! Ah, Medea! did any of thy lovers love thee as I do?

Twenty-four hours more till the moment of happiness—the moment for which I seem to have been waiting all my life. And after that, what next? Yes, I see it plainer every minute; after that, nothing more. All those who loved Medea da Carpi, who loved and who served her, died: Giovanfrancesco Pico, her first husband, whom she left stabbed in the castle from which she fled; Stimigliano, who died of poison; the groom who gave him the poison, cut down by her orders; Oliverotto da Narni, Marcantonio Frangipani, and that poor boy of the Ordelaffi, who had never even looked upon her face, and whose only reward was that handkerchief with which the hangman wiped the sweat off his face, when he was one mass of broken limbs and torn flesh: all had to die, and I shall die also.

The love of such a woman is enough, and is fatal—"Amour Dure," as her device says. I shall die also. But why not? Would it be possible to live in order to love another woman? Nay, would it be possible to drag on a life like this one after the happiness of to-morrow? Impossible; the others died, and I must die. I always felt that I should not live long; a gipsy in Poland told me once that I had in my hand the cut-line which signifies a violent death. I might have ended in a duel with some brother-student, or in a railway accident. No, no; my death will not be of that sort! Death—and is not she also dead? What strange vistas does such a thought not open! Then the others—Pico, the Groom, Stimigliano, Oliverotto, Frangipani, Prinzivalle degli Ordelaffi—will they all be *there?* But she shall love me best—me by whom she has been loved after she has been three hundred years in the grave!

Dec. 24th.—I have made all my arrangements. To-night at eleven I slip out; Sor Asdrubale and his sisters will be sound asleep. I have questioned them; their fear of rheumatism prevents their attending midnight mass. Luckily there are no churches between this and the Corte; whatever movement Christmas night may entail will be a good way off. The Vice-Prefect's rooms are on the other side of the palace; the rest of the square is taken up with state-rooms, archives, and empty stables and coach-houses of the palace. Besides, I shall be quick at my work.

I have tried my saw on a stout bronze vase I bought of Sor Asdrubale;

and the bronze of the statue, hollow and worn away by rust (I have even noticed holes), cannot resist very much, especially after a blow with the sharp hatchet. I have put my papers in order, for the benefit of the Government which has sent me hither. I am sorry to have defrauded them of their "History of Urbania." To pass the endless day and calm the fever of impatience, I have just taken a long walk. This is the coldest day we have had. The bright sun does not warm in the least, but seems only to increase the impression of cold, to make the snow on the mountains glitter, the blue air to sparkle like steel. The few people who are out are muffled to the nose, and carry earthenware braziers beneath their cloaks; long icicles hang from the fountain with the figure of Mercury upon it; one can imagine the wolves trooping down through the dry scrub and beleaguering this town. Somehow this cold makes me feel wonderfully calm—it seems to bring back to me my boyhood.

As I walked up the rough, steep, paved alleys, slippery with frost, and with their vista of snow mountains against the sky, and passed by the church steps strewn with box and laurel, with the faint smell of incense coming out, there returned to me—I know not why—the recollection, almost the sensation, of those Christmas Eves long ago at Posen and Breslau, when I walked as a child along the wide streets, peeping into the windows where they were beginning to light the tapers of the Christmas-trees, and wondering whether I too, on returning home, should be let into a wonderful room all blazing with lights and gilded nuts and glass beads. They are hanging the last strings of those blue and red metallic beads, fastening on the last gilded and silvered walnuts on the trees out there at home in the North; they are lighting the blue and red tapers; the wax is beginning to run on to the beautiful spruce green branches; the children are waiting with beating hearts behind the door, to be told that the Christ-Child has been. And I, for what am I waiting? I don't know; all seems a dream; everything vague and unsubstantial about me, as if time had ceased, nothing could happen, my own desires and hopes were all dead, myself absorbed into I know not what passive dreamland. Do I long for to-night? Do I dread it? Will to-night ever come? Do I feel anything, does anything exist all round me? I sit and seem to see that street at Posen, the wide street with the windows illuminated by the Christmas lights, the green fir-branches grazing the window-panes.

Christmas Eve, Midnight.—I have done it. I slipped out noiselessly. Sor

Asdrubale and his sisters were fast asleep. I feared I had waked them, for my hatchet fell as I was passing through the principal room where my landlord keeps his curiosities for sale; it struck against some old armour which he has been piecing. I heard him exclaim, half in his sleep; and blew out my light and hid in the stairs. He came out in his dressing-gown, but finding no one, went back to bed again. "Some cat, no doubt!" he said. I closed the house door softly behind me. The sky had become stormy since the afternoon, luminous with the full moon, but strewn with grey and buff-coloured vapours; every now and then the moon disappeared entirely. Not a creature abroad; the tall gaunt houses staring in the moonlight.

I know not why, I took a roundabout way to the Corte, past one or two church doors, whence issued the faint flicker of midnight mass. For a moment I felt a temptation to enter one of them; but something seemed to restrain me. I caught snatches of the Christmas hymn. I felt myself beginning to be unnerved, and hastened towards the Corte. As I passed under the portico at San Francesco I heard steps behind me; it seemed to me that I was followed. I stopped to let the other pass. As he approached his pace flagged; he passed close by me and murmured, "Do not go: I am Giovanfrancesco Pico." I turned round; he was gone. A coldness numbed me; but I hastened on.

Behind the cathedral apse, in a narrow lane, I saw a man leaning against a wall. The moonlight was full upon him; it seemed to me that his face, with a thin pointed beard, was streaming with blood. I quickened my pace; but as I grazed by him he whispered, "Do not obey her; return home: I am Marcantonio Frangipani." My teeth chattered, but I hurried along the narrow lane, with the moonlight blue upon the white walls.

At last I saw the Corte before me: the square was flooded with moonlight, the windows of the palace seemed brightly illuminated, and the statue of Duke Robert, shimmering green, seemed advancing towards me on its horse. I came into the shadow. I had to pass beneath an archway. There started a figure as if out of the wall, and barred my passage with his outstretched cloaked arm. I tried to pass. He seized me by the arm, and his grasp was like a weight of ice. "You shall not pass!" he cried, and, as the moon came out once more, I saw his face, ghastly white and bound with an embroidered kerchief; he seemed almost a child. "You shall not pass!" he cried; "you shall not have her! She is mine, and mine alone! I am Prinzivalle degli Ordelaffi." I felt his ice-cold clutch, but with my other arm I laid about me wildly with the hatchet which I carried beneath my cloak. The hatchet struck the wall and rang upon the stone. He had vanished.

I hurried on. I did it. I cut open the bronze; I sawed it into a wider gash. I tore out the silver image, and hacked it into innumerable pieces. As I scattered the last fragments about, the moon was suddenly veiled; a great wind arose, howling down the square; it seemed to me that the earth shook. I threw down the hatchet and the saw, and fled home. I felt pursued, as if by the tramp of hundreds of invisible horsemen.

Now I am calm. It is midnight; another moment and she will be here! Patience, my heart! I hear it beating loud. I trust that no one will accuse poor Sor Asdrubale. I will write a letter to the authorities to declare his innocence should anything happen. . . . One! the clock in the palace tower has just struck. . . . "I hereby certify that, should anything happen this night to me, Spiridion Trepka, no one but myself is to be held . . ." A step on the staircase! It is she! it is she! At last, Medea, Medea! Ah! AMOUR DURE—DURE AMOUR!

NOTE.—Here ends the diary of the late Spiridion Trepka. The chief newspapers of the province of Umbria informed the public that, on Christmas morning of the year 1885, the bronze equestrian statue of Robert II had been found grievously mutilated; and that Professor Spiridion Trepka of Posen, in the German Empire, had been discovered dead of a stab in the region of the heart, given by an unknown hand.

The Were-Wolf

Clemence Housman

No one would cavil with the claim that Bram Stoker's Dracula *is and always will be the quintessential vampire novel, but no work of fiction is considered the last word on lycanthropy, though strong cases could be made for Rudyard Kipling's "The Mark of the Beast," Guy Endore's* The Werewolf of Paris, *or "The Were-Wolf," an unjustly obscure masterpiece by* CLEMENCE HOUS-MAN, *who fellow anthologist Alden H. Norton presumes to have been related to the poet A. E. Housman and his artist-brother Laurence Housman.*

THE GREAT FARM HALL was ablaze with the fire-light, and noisy with laughter and talk and many-sounding work. None could be idle but the very young and the very old—little Rol, who was hugging a puppy, and old Trella, whose palsied hand fumbled over her knitting. The early evening had closed in, and the farm servants had come in from the outdoor work and assembled in the ample hall, which had space for scores of workers. Several of the men were engaged in carving, and to these were yielded the best place and light; others made or repaired fishing tackle and harness, and a great seine net occupied three pairs of hands. Of the women, most were sorting and mixing eider feather and chopping straw of the same. Looms were there, though not in present use, but three wheels whirred emulously, and the finest and swiftest thread of the three ran between the fingers of the house mistress. Near her were some children, busy, too, plaiting wicks for candles and

lamps. Each group of workers had a lamp in its centre, and those farthest from the fire had extra warmth from two braziers filled with
glowing wood embers, replenished now and again from the generous
hearth. But the flicker of the great fire was manifest to remotest corners,
and prevailed beyond the limits of the lesser lights.

Little Rol grew tired of his puppy, dropped it incontinently, and made
an onslaught on Tyr, the old wolf-hound, who basked, dozing, whimpering and twitching in his hunting dreams. Prone went Rol beside Tyr,
his young arms round the shaggy neck, his curls against the black jowl.
Tyr gave a perfunctory lick, and stretched with a sleepy sigh. Rol
growled and rolled and shoved invitingly, but could gain nothing from
the old dog but placid toleration and a half-observant blink. "Take that,
then!" said Rol, indignant at this ignoring of his advances, and sent the
puppy sprawling against the dignity that disdained him as playmate.
The dog took no notice, and the child wandered off to find amusement
elsewhere.

The baskets of white eider feathers caught his eye far off in a distant
corner. He slipped under the table and crept along on all-fours, the
ordinary commonplace custom of walking down a room upright not
being to his fancy. When close to the women he lay still for a moment
watching, with his elbows on the floor and his chin in his palms. One of
the women seeing him nodded and smiled, and presently he crept out
behind her skirts and passed, hardly noticed, from one to another, till he
found opportunity to possess himself of a large handful of feathers. With
these he traversed the length of the room, under the table again, and
emerged near the spinners. At the feet of the youngest he curled himself
round, sheltered by her knees from the observation of the others, and
disarmed her of interference by secretly displaying his handful with a
confiding smile. A dubious nod satisfied him, and presently he proceeded with the play he had planned. He took a tuft of the white down,
and gently shook it free of his fingers close to the whirl of the wheel.
The wind of the swift motion took it, spun it round and round in
widening circles, till it floated above like a slow white moth. Little Rol's
eyes danced, and the row of his small teeth shone in a silent laugh of
delight. Another and another of the white tufts was sent whirling round
like a winged thing in a spider's web, and floating clear at last. Presently
the handful failed.

Rol sprawled forward to survey the room and contemplate another journey under the table. His shoulder thrusting forward checked the wheel for an instant; he shifted hastily. The wheel flew on with a jerk and the thread snapped. "Naughty Rol!" said the girl. The swiftest wheel stopped also, and the house mistress, Rol's aunt, leaned forward and sighting the low curly head, gave a warning against mischief, and sent him off to old Trella's corner.

Rol obeyed, and, after a discreet period of obedience, sidled out again down the length of the room farthest from his aunt's eye. As he slipped in among the men, they looked up to see that their tools might be, as far as possible, out of reach of Rol's hands, and close to their own. Nevertheless, before long he managed to secure a fine chisel and take off its point on the leg of the table. The carver's strong objections to this disconcerted Rol, who for five minutes thereafter effaced himself under the table.

During this seclusion he contemplated the many pairs of legs that surrounded him and almost shut out the light of the fire. How very odd some of the legs were; some were curved where they should be straight; some were straight where they should be curved; and as Rol said to himself, "They all seemed screwed on differently." Some were tucked away modestly, under the benches, others were thrust far out under the table, encroaching on Rol's own particular domain. He stretched out his own short legs and regarded them critically, and, after comparison, favorably. Why were not all legs made like his, or like his?

These legs approved by Rol were a little apart from the rest. He crawled opposite and again made comparison. His face grew quite solemn as he thought of the innumerable days to come before his legs could be as long and strong. He hoped they would be just like those, his models, as straight as to bone, as curved as to muscle.

A few moments later Sweyn of the long legs felt a small hand caressing his foot, and looking down met the up-turned eyes of his little cousin Rol. Lying on his back, still softly patting and stroking the young man's foot, the child was quiet and happy for a good while. He watched the movements of the strong, deft hands and the shifting of the bright tools. Now and then minute chips of wood puffed off by Sweyn fell down upon his face. At last he raised himself very gently, lest a jog should wake impatience in the carver, and crossing his own legs round Sweyn's ankle, clasping with his arms too, laid his head against the knee. Such an act is evidence of a child's most wonderful hero worship. Quite content was Rol, and more than content when Sweyn paused a minute to joke, and pat his head and pull his curls. Quiet he remained, as long as quiescence is possible to limbs young as his. Sweyn forgot he was near, hardly noticed when his leg was gently released, and never saw the stealthy abstraction of one of his tools.

Ten minutes thereafter was a lamentable wail from low on the floor, rising to the full pitch of Rol's healthy lungs, for his hand was gashed across and the copious bleeding terrified him. Then there was soothing and comforting, washing and binding, and a modicum of scolding, till the loud outcry sank into occasional sobs, and the child, tear-stained and subdued, was returned to the chimney-corner, where Trella nodded.

In the reaction after pain and fright, Rol found that the quiet of that fire-lit corner was to his mind. Tyr, too, disdained him no longer, but, roused by his sobs, showed all the concern and sympathy that a dog can by licking and wistful watching. A little shame weighed also upon his spirits. He wished he had not cried quite so much. He remembered how once Sweyn had come home with his arm torn down from the shoulder, and a dead bear; and how he had never winced nor said a word, though his lips turned white with pain. Poor little Rol gave an extra sighing sob over his own faint-hearted shortcomings.

The light and motion of the great fire began to tell strange stories to the child, and the wind in the chimney roared a corroborative note now and then. The great black mouth of the chimney, impending high over the hearth, received the murky coils of smoke and brightness of aspiring sparks as into a mysterious gulf, and beyond, in the high darkness, were muttering and wailing and strange doings, so that sometimes the smoke rushed back in panic, and curled out and up to the roof, and condensed itself to invisibility among the rafters. And then the wind would rage after its lost prey, rattling and shrieking at window and door.

In a lull, after one such loud gust, Rol lifted his head in surprise and listened. A lull had also come on the babble of talk, and thus could be heard with strange distinctness a sound without the door—the sound of a child's voice, a child's hands. "Open, open; let me in!" piped the little voice from low down, lower than the handle, and the latch rattled as though a tip-toe child reached up to it, and soft small knocks were struck. One near the door sprang up and opened it. "No one is here," he said. Tyr lifted his head and gave utterance to a howl, loud, prolonged, most dismal.

Sweyn, not able to believe that his ears had deceived him, got up and went to the door. It was a dark night; the clouds were heavy with snow, that had fallen fitfully when the wind lulled. Untrodden snow lay up to the porch; there was no sight nor sound of any human being. Sweyn strained his eyes far and near, only to see dark sky, pure snow, and a line of black fir trees on a hill brow, bowing down before the wind. "It must have been the wind," he said, and closed the door.

Many faces looked scared. The sound of a child's voice had been so distinct—and the words, "Open, open; let me in!" The wind might creak the wood or rattle the latch, but could not speak with a child's voice; nor knock with the soft plain blows that a plump fist gives. And the strange unusual howl of the wolf-hound was an omen to be feared, be the rest what it might. Strange things were said by one and other, till the rebuke of the house mistress quelled them into far-off whispers. For a time after there was uneasiness, constraint, and silence; then the chill fear thawed by degrees, and the babble of talk flowed on again.

Yet half an hour later a very slight noise outside the door sufficed to arrest every hand, every tongue. Every head was raised, every eye fixed in one direction. "It is Christian; he is late," said Sweyn.

No, no; this is a feeble shuffle, not a young man's tread. With the sound of uncertain feet came the hard tap tap of a stick against the door, and the high-pitched voice of eld, "Open, open; let me in!" Again Tyr flung up his head in a long doleful howl.

Before the echo of the tapping stick and the high voice had fairly died way, Sweyn had sprung across to the door and flung it wide. "No one again," he said in a steady voice, though his eyes looked startled as he stared out. He saw the lonely expanse of snow, the clouds swagging low, and between the two the line of dark fir trees bowing in the wind. He closed the door without word of comment, and recrossed the room.

A score of blanched faces were turned to him as though he were the solver of the enigma. He could not be unconscious of this mute eye-questioning, and it disturbed his resolute air of composure. He hesitated, glanced toward his mother, the house mistress, then back at the frightened folk, and gravely, before them all, made the sign of the cross. There was a flutter of hands as the sign was repeated by all, and the dead silence was stirred as by a huge sigh, for the held breath of many was freed as if the sign gave magic relief.

Even the house mistress was perturbed. She left her wheel and crossed the room to her son, and spoke with him for a moment in a low tone that none could overhear. But a moment later her voice was high-pitched and loud, so that all might benefit by her rebuke of the "heathen chatter" of one of the girls. Perhaps she essayed to silence thus her own misgivings and forebodings.

No other voice dared speak now with its natural fulness. Low tones made intermittent murmurs, and now and then silence drifted over the whole room. The handling of tools was as noiseless as might be, and suspended on the instant if the door rattled in a gust of wind. After a time Sweyn left his work, joined the group nearest the door, and loitered there on the pretence of giving advice and help to the unskillful.

A man's tread was heard outside in the porch, "Christian!" said Sweyn and his mother simultaneously, he confidently, she authoritatively, to set the checked wheels going again. But Tyr flung up his head with an appalling howl.

"Open, open; let me in!"

It was a man's voice, and the door shook and rattled as a man's strength beat against it. Sweyn could feel the planks quivering, as on the instant his hand was upon the door, flinging it open, to face the blank porch, and beyond only snow and sky, and firs aslant in the wind.

He stood for a long minute with the open door in his hand. The bitter wind swept in with its icy chill, but a deadlier chill of fear came swifter, and seemed to freeze the beating of hearts. Sweyn snatched up a great bearskin cloak.

"Sweyn, where are you going?"

"No farther than the porch, mother," and he stepped out and closed the door.

He wrapped himself in the heavy fur, and leaning against the most sheltered wall of the porch, steeled his nerves to face the devil and all his works. No sound of voices came from within; but he could hear the crackle and roar of the fire.

It was bitterly cold. His feet grew numb, but he fore-bore stamping them into warmth lest the sound should strike panic within; nor would he leave the porch, nor print a foot-mark on the untrodden snow that testified conclusively to no human voices and hands having approached the door since snow fell two hours or more ago. "When the wind drops there will be more snow," thought Sweyn.

For the best part of an hour he kept his watch, and saw no living thing—heard no unwonted sound. "I will freeze here no longer," he muttered, and reentered.

One woman gave a half-suppressed scream as his hand was laid on the latch, and then a gasp of relief as he came in. No one questioned him, only his mother said, in a tone of forced unconcern, "Could you not see Christian coming?" as though she were made anxious only by the absence of her younger son. Hardly had Sweyn stamped near to the fire than clear knocking was heard at the door. Tyr leaped from the hearth —his eyes red as the fire—his fangs showing white in the black jowl— his neck ridged and bristling; and overleaping Rol, ramped at the door, barking furiously.

Outside the door a clear, mellow voice was calling. Tyr's bark made the words undistinguishable.

No one offered to stir toward the door before Sweyn.

He stalked down the room resolutely, lifted the latch, and swung back the door.

A white-robed woman glided in.

No wraith! Living—beautiful—young.

Tyr leapt upon her.

Lithely she balked the sharp fangs with folds of her long fur robe, and snatching from her girdle a small two-edged axe, whirled it up for a blow of defence.

Sweyn caught the dog by the collar and dragged him off, yelling and struggling. The stranger stood in the doorway motionless, one foot set forward, one arm flung up, till the house mistress hurried down the room, and Sweyn, relinquishing to others the furious Tyr, turned again to close the door and offer excuses for so fierce a greeting. Then she lowered her arm, slung the axe in its place at her waist, loosened the furs about her face, and shook over her shoulder the long white robe—all, as it were, with the sway of one movement.

She was a maiden, tall and very fair. The fashion of her dress was strange—half masculine, yet not unwomanly. A fine fur tunic, reaching but little below the knee, was all the skirt she wore; below were the cross-bound shoes and leggings that a hunter wears. A white fur cap was set low upon the brows, and from its edge strips of fur fell lappet-wise about her shoulders, two of which at her entrance had been drawn forward and crossed about her throat, but now, loosened and thrust back, left unhidden long plaits of fair hair that lay forward on shoulder and breast, down to the ivory-studded girdle where the axe gleamed.

Sweyn and his mother led the stranger to the hearth without question or sign of curiosity, till she voluntarily told her tale of a long journey to distant kindred, a promised guide unmet, and signals and landmarks mistaken.

"Alone!" exclaimed Sweyn, in astonishment. "Have you journeyed thus far—a hundred leagues—alone?"

She answered "Yes," with a little smile.

"Over the hills and the wastes! Why, the folk there are savage and wild as beasts."

She dropped her hand upon her axe with a laugh of scorn.

"I fear neither man nor beast; some few fear me," and then she told strange tales of fierce attack and defence, and of the bold, free huntress life she had led.

Her words came a little slowly and deliberately, as though she spoke in a scarce familiar tongue; now and then she hesitated, and stopped in a phrase, as if for lack of some word.

She became the centre of a group of listeners. The interest she excited dissipated, in some degree, the dread inspired by the mysterious voices. There was nothing ominous about this bright, fair reality, though her aspect was strange.

Little Rol crept near, staring at the stranger with all his might. Unnoticed, he softly stroked and patted a corner of her soft white robe that reached to the floor in ample folds. He laid his cheek against it caressingly, and then edged close up to her knees.

"What is your name?" he asked.

The stranger's smile and ready answer, as she looked down, saved Rol from the rebuke merited by his question.

"My real name," she said, "would be uncouth to your ears and tongue. The folk of this country have given me another name, and from this"— she laid her hand on the fur robe—"they call me 'White Fell.' "

Little Rol repeated it to himself, stroking and patting as before. "White Fell, White Fell."

The fair face, and soft, beautiful dress pleased Rol. He knelt up, with his eyes on her face and an air of uncertain determination, like a robin's on a doorstep, and plumped his elbows into her lap with a little gasp at his own audacity.

"Rol!" exclaimed his aunt; but, "Oh, let him!" said White Fell, smiling and stroking his head; and Rol stayed.

He advanced farther, and, panting at his own adventurousness, in the face of his aunt's authority, climbed up on to her knees. Her welcoming arms hindered any protest. He nestled happily, fingering the axe head, the ivory studs in her girdle, the ivory clasp at her throat, the plaits of fair hair; rubbing his head against the softness of her fur-clad shoulder, with a child's confidence in the kindness of beauty.

White Fell had not uncovered her head, only knotted the pendant fur loosely behind her neck. Rol reached up his hand toward it, whispering her name to himself, "White Fell, White Fell," then slid his arms round her neck, and kissed her—once—twice. She laughed delightedly and kissed him again.

"The child plagues you?" said Sweyn.

"No, indeed," she answered, with an earnestness so intense as to seem disproportionate to the occasion.

Rol settled himself again on her lap and began to unwind the bandage bound round his hand. He paused a little when he saw where the blood had soaked through, then went on till his hand was bare and the cut displayed, gaping and long, though only skin-deep. He held it up toward White Fell, desirous of her pity and sympathy.

At sight of it and the blood-stained linen she drew in her breath suddenly, clasped Rol to her—hard, hard—till he began to struggle. Her face was hidden behind the boy, so that none could see its expression. It had lighted up with a most awful glee.

Afar, beyond the fir grove, beyond the low hill behind, the absent Christian was hastening his return. From day-break he had been afoot, carrying summons to a bear hunt to all the best hunters of the farms and hamlets that lay within a radius of twelve miles. Nevertheless, having been detained till a late hour, he now broke into a run, going with a long smooth stride that fast made the miles diminish.

He entered the midnight blackness of the fir grove with scarcely slackened pace, though the path was invisible, and, passing through into the open again, sighted the farm lying a furlong off down the slope. Then he sprang out freely, and almost on the instant gave one great sideways leap and stood still. There in the snow was the track of a great wolf.

His hand went to his knife, his only weapon. He stooped, knelt down, to bring his eyes to the level of a beast, and peered about, his teeth set, his heart beating—a little harder than the pace of his running had set it. A solitary wolf, nearly always savage and of large size, is a formidable beast that will not hesitate to attack a single man. This wolf track was the largest Christian had ever seen, and, as far as he could judge, recently made. It led from under the fir-trees down the slope. Well for him, he thought, was the delay that had so vexed him before; well for him that he had not passed through the dark fir grove when that danger of jaws lurked there. Going warily, he followed the track.

It led down the slope, across a broad ice-bound stream, along the level beyond, leading toward the farm. A less sure knowledge than Christian's might have doubted of it being a wolf track, and guessed it to be made by Tyr or some large dog; but he was sure, and knew better than to mistake between a wolf's and a dog's footmark.

Straight on—straight on toward the farm.

Christian grew surprised and anxious at a prowling wolf daring so near. He drew his knife and pressed on, more hastily, more keenly eyed. Oh, that Tyr were with him!

Straight on, straight on, even to the very door, where the snow failed. His heart seemed to give a great leap and then stop. There the track ended.

Nothing lurked in the porch, and there was no sign of return. The firs stood straight against the sky, the clouds lay low; for the wind had fallen and a few snowflakes came drifting down. In a horror of surprise Christian stood dazed a moment; then he lifted the latch and went in. His glance took in all the old familiar forms and faces, and with them that of the stranger, fur-clad and beautiful. The awful truth flashed upon him. He knew what she was.

Only a few were startled by the rattle of the latch as he entered. The room was filled with bustle and movement, for it was the supper hour, and all tools were being put aside and trestles and tables shifted. Christian had no knowledge of what he said and did; he moved and spoke mechanically, half thinking that soon he must wake from this horrible dream. Sweyn and his mother supposed him to be cold and dead-tired, and spared all unnecessary questions. And he found himself seated beside the hearth, opposite that dreadful Thing that looked like a beautiful girl, watching her every movement, curdling with horror to see her fondle Rol.

Sweyn stood near them both, intent upon White Fell also, but how differently! She seemed unconscious of the gaze of both—neither aware of the chill dread in the eyes of Christian, nor of Sweyn's warm admiration.

These two brothers, who were twins, contrasted greatly, despite their striking likeness. They were alike in regular profile, fair brown hair, and deep blue eyes; but Sweyn's features were perfect as a young god's, while Christian's showed faulty details. Thus, the line of his mouth was set too straight, the eyes shelved too deeply back, and the contour of the face flowed in less generous curves than Sweyn's. Their height was the same, but Christian was too slender for perfect proportion, while Sweyn's well-knit frame, broad shoulders and muscular arms made him pre-eminent for manly beauty as well as for strength. As a hunter Sweyn was without rival; as a fisher without rival. All the countryside acknowledged him to be the best wrestler, rider, dancer, singer. Only in speed could he be surpassed, and in that only by his younger brother. All others Sweyn could distance fairly; but Christian could out-run him easily. Ay, he could keep pace with Sweyn's most breathless burst, and laugh and talk the while. Christian took little pride in his fleetness of foot, counting a man's legs to be the least worthy of his limbs. He had no envy of his brother's athletic superiority, though to several feats he had made a moderate second. He loved as only a twin can love—proud of all that Sweyn did, content with all that Sweyn was, humbly content also that his own great love should not be so exceedingly returned, since he knew himself to be so far less loveworthy.

Christian dared not, in the midst of women and children, launch the horror that he knew into words. He waited to consult his brother; but Sweyn did not, or would not, notice the signal he made, and kept his face always turned toward White Fell. Christian drew away from the hearth, unable to remain passive with that dread upon him.

"Where is Tyr?" he said, suddenly. Then catching sight of the dog in a distant corner, "Why is he chained there?"

"He flew at the stranger," one answered.

Christian's eyes glowed. "Yes?" he said interrogatively, and, rising, went without a word to the corner where Tyr was chained. The dog rose up to meet him, as piteous and indignant as a dumb beast can be. He stroked the black head. "Good Tyr! Brave dog!"

They knew—they only—and the man and the dumb dog had comfort of each other.

Christian's eyes turned again toward White Fell. Tyr's also, and he strained against the length of the chain. Christian's hand lay on the dog's neck, and he felt it ridge and bristle with the quivering of impotent fury. Then he began to quiver in like manner, with a fury born of reason, not instinct; as impotent morally as was Tyr physically. Oh, the woman's form that he dare not touch! Anything but that, and he with Tyr, would be free to kill or be killed.

Then he returned to ask fresh questions.

"How long has the stranger been here?"

"She came about half an hour before you."

"Who opened the door to her?"

"Sweyn. No one else dared."

The tone of the answer was mysterious.

"Why?" queried Christian. "Has anything strange happened? Tell me?"

For answer he was told in a low undertone of the summons at the door, thrice repeated, without human agency; and of Tyr's ominous howls, and of Sweyn's fruitless watch outside.

Christian turned toward his brother in a torment of impatience for a word apart. The board was spread and Sweyn was leading White Fell to the guest's place. This was more awful! She would break bread with them under the roof tree.

He started forward and, touching Sweyn's arm, whispered an urgent entreaty. Sweyn stared, and shook his head in angry impatience.

Thereupon Christian would take no morsel of food.

His opportunity came at last. White Fell questioned of the landmarks of the country, and of one Cairn Hill, which was an appointed meeting place at which she was due that night. The house mistress and Sweyn both exclaimed.

"It is three long miles away," said Sweyn, "with no place for shelter but a wretched hut. Stay with us this night and I will show you the way tomorrow."

White Fell seemed to hesitate. "Three miles," she said, "then I should be able to see or hear a signal."

"I will look out," said Sweyn; "then, if there be no signal, you must not leave us."

He went to the door. Christian silently followed him out.

"Sweyn, do you know what she is?"

Sweyn, surprised at the vehement grasp and low hoarse voice, made answer:

"She? Who? White Fell?"

"Yes."

"She is the most beautiful girl I have ever seen."

"She is a were-wolf."

Sweyn burst out laughing. "Are you mad?" he asked.

"No; here, see for yourself."

Christian drew him out of the porch, pointing to the snow where the footmarks had been—had been, for now they were not. Snow was falling, and every dint was blotted out.

"Well?" asked Sweyn.

"Had you come when I signed to you, you would have seen for yourself."

"Seen what?"

"The footprints of a wolf leading up to the door; none leading away."

It was impossible not to be startled by the tone alone, though it was hardly above a whisper. Sweyn eyed his brother anxiously, but in the darkness could make nothing of his face. Then he laid his hands kindly and reassuringly on Christian's shoulders and felt how he was quivering with excitement and horror.

"One sees strange things," he said, "when the cold has got into the brain behind the eyes; you came in cold and worn out."

"No," interrupted Christian. "I saw the track first on the brow of the slope, and followed it down right here to the door. This is no delusion."

Sweyn in his heart felt positive that it was. Christian was given to day dreams and strange fancies, though never had he been possessed with so mad a notion before.

"Don't you believe me?" said Christian desperately. "You must. I swear it is sane truth. Are you blind? Why, even Tyr knows."

"You will be clearer-headed tomorrow, after a night's rest. Then come, too, if you will, with White Fell, to the Hill Cairn, and, if you have doubts still, watch and follow, and see what footprints she leaves."

Galled by Sweyn's evident contempt, Christian turned abruptly to the door. Sweyn caught him back.

"What now, Christian? What are you going to do?"

"You do not believe me; my mother shall "

Sweyn's grasp tightened. "You shall not tell her," he said, authoritatively.

Customarily Christian was so docile to his brother's mastery that it was now a surprising thing when he wrenched himself free vigorously and said as determinedly as Sweyn: "She shall know." But Sweyn was nearer the door, and would not let him pass.

"There has been scare enough for one night already. If this notion of yours will keep, broach it tomorrow." Christian would not yield.

"Women are so easily scared," pursued Sweyn, "and are ready to believe any folly without proof. Be a man, Christian, and fight this notion of a were-wolf by yourself."

"If you would believe me," began Christian.

"I believe you to be a fool," said Sweyn, losing patience. "Another, who was not your brother, might think you a knave, and guess that you had transformed White Fell into a were-wolf because she smiled more readily on me than on you."

The jest was not without foundation, for the grace of White Fell's bright looks had been bestowed on him—on Christian never a whit. Sweyn's coxcombry was always frank and most forgivable, and not without justifiableness.

"If you want an ally," continued Sweyn, "confide in old Trella. Out of her stores of wisdom—if her memory holds good—she can instruct you in the orthodox manner of tackling a were-wolf. If I remember aright, you should watch the suspected person till midnight, when the beast's form must be resumed, and retained ever after if a human eye sees the change; or, better still, sprinkle hands and feet with holy water, which is certain death! Oh, never fear, but old Trella will be equal to the occasion."

Sweyn's contempt was no longer good-humored, for he began to feel excessively annoyed at this monstrous doubt of White Fell. But Christian was too deeply distressed to take offence.

"You speak of them as old wives' tales, but if you had seen the proof I have seen, you would be ready at least to wish them true, if not also to put them to the test."

"Well," said Sweyn, with a laugh that had a little sneer in it, "put them to the test—I will not mind that, if you will only keep your notions to yourself. Now, Christian, give me your word for silence, and we will freeze here no longer."

Christian remained silent.

Sweyn put his hands on his shoulders again and vainly tried to see his face in the darkness.

"We have never quarreled yet, Christian?"

"I have never quarreled," returned the other, aware for the first time that his dictatorial brother had sometimes offered occasion for quarrel, had he been ready to take it.

"Well," said Sweyn, emphatically, "if you speak against White Fell to any other, as tonight you have spoken to me—we shall."

He delivered the words like an ultimatum, turned sharp round and re-entered the house. Christian, more fearful and wretched than before, followed.

"Snow is falling fast—not a single light is to be seen."

White Fell's eyes passed over Christian without apparent notice, and turned bright and shining upon Sweyn.

"Nor any signal to be heard?" she queried. "Did you not hear the sound of a sea-horn?"

"I saw nothing and heard nothing; and signal or no signal, the heavy snow would keep you here perforce."

She smiled her thanks beautifully. And Christian's heart sank like lead with a deadly foreboding, as he noted what a light was kindled in Sweyn's eyes by her smile.

That night, when all others slept, Christian, the weariest of all, watched outside the guest chamber till midnight was past. No sound, not the faintest, could be heard. Could the old tale be true of the midnight change? What was on the other side of the door—a woman or a beast— he would have given his right hand to know. Instinctively he laid his hand on the latch, and drew it softly, though believing that bolts fastened the inner side. The door yielded to his hand; he stood on the threshold; a keen gust of air cut at him. The window stood open; the room was empty.

So Christian could sleep with a somewhat lightened heart.

In the morning there was surprise and conjecture when White Fell's absence was discovered. Christian held his peace; not even to his brother did he say how he knew that she had fled before midnight; and Sweyn, though evidently greatly chagrined, seemed to disdain reference to the subject of Christian's fears.

The elder brother alone joined the bear hunt; Christian found pretext to stay behind. Sweyn, being out of humor, manifested his contempt by uttering not one expostulation.

All that day, and for many a day after, Christian would never go out of sight of his home. Sweyn alone noticed how he manoeuvred for this, and was clearly annoyed by it. White Fell's name was never mentioned between them, though not seldom was it heard in general talk. Hardly a day passed without little Rol asking when White Fell would come again; pretty White Fell, who kissed like a snowflake. And if Sweyn answered, Christian would be quite sure that the light in his eyes, kindled by White Fell's smile, had not yet died out.

Little Rol! Naughty, merry, fair-haired little Rol! A day came when his feet raced over the threshold never to return; when his chatter and laugh were heard no more; when tears of anguish were wept by eyes that never would see his bright head again—never again—living or dead.

He was seen at dusk for the last time, escaping from the house with his puppy, in freakish rebellion against old Trella. Later, when his absence had begun to cause anxiety, his puppy crept back to the farm, cowed, whimpering, and yelping—a pitiful, dumb lump of terror—without intelligence or courage to guide the frightened search.

Rol was never found, nor any trace of him. How he had perished was known only by an awful guess—a wild beast had devoured him.

Christian heard the conjecture, "a wolf," and a horrible certainty flashed upon him that he knew what wolf it was. He tried to declare what he knew, but Sweyn saw him start at the words with white face and struggling lips, and, guessing his purpose, pulled him back and kept him silent, hardly, by his imperious grip and wrathful eyes, and one low whisper. Again Christian yielded to his brother's stronger words and will, and against his own judgment consented to silence.

Repentance came before the new moon—the first of the year—was old. White Fell came again, smiling as she entered as though assured of a glad and kindly welcome; and, in truth, there was only one who saw again her fair face and strange white garb without pleasure. Sweyn's face glowed with delight, while Christian's grew pale and rigid as death. He had given his word to keep silence, but he had not thought that she would dare to come again. Silence was impossible—face to face with that Thing—impossible. Irrepressibly he cried out:

"Where is Rol?"

Not a quiver disturbed White Fell's face; she heard, yet remained bright and tranquil—Sweyn's eyes flashed round at his brother dangerously. Among the women some tears fell at the poor child's name, but none caught alarm from its sudden utterance, for the thought of Rol rose naturally. Where was Rol, who had nestled in the stranger's arms, kissing her, and watched for her since, and prattled of her daily?

Christian went out silently. Only one thing there was that he could do, and he must not delay. His horror overmastered any curiosity to hear White Fell's glib excuses and smiling apologies for her strange and uncourteous departure; or her easy tale of the circumstances of her return; or to watch her bearing as she heard the sad tale of little Rol.

The swiftest runner of the countryside had started on his hardest race —little less than three leagues and back, which he reckoned to accomplish in two hours, though the night was moonless and the way rugged. He rushed against the still cold air till it felt like a wind upon his face. The dim homestead sank below the ridges at his back, and fresh ridges of snowlands rose out of the obscure horizon level to drive past him as the stirless air drove, and sink away behind into obscure level again. He took no conscious heed of landmarks, not even when all sign of a path was gone under depths of snow. His will was set to reach his goal with unexampled speed, and thither by instinct his physical forces bore him, without one definite thought to guide.

And the idle brain lay passive, inert, receiving into its vacancy, restless siftings of past sights and sounds; Rol weeping, laughing, playing, coiled in the arms of that dreadful Thing; Tyr—O Tyr!—white fangs in the black jowl; the women who wept on the foolish puppy, precious for the child's last touch; footprints from pinewood to door; the smiling face among furs, of such womanly beauty—smiling—smiling; and Sweyn's face.

"Sweyn, Sweyn, O Sweyn, my brother!"

Sweyn's angry laugh possessed his ear within the sound of the wind of his speed; Sweyn's scorn assailed more quick and keen than the biting cold at his throat. And yet he was unimpressed by any thought of how Sweyn's scorn and anger would rise if this errand were known.

To the younger brother all life was a spiritual mystery, veiled from his clear knowledge by the density of flesh. Since he knew his own body to be linked to the complex and antagonistic forces that constitute one soul, it seemed to him not impossibly strange that one spiritual force should possess divers forms for widely various manifestation. Nor, to him, was it great effort to believe that as pure water washes away all natural foulness, so water holy by consecration must needs cleanse God's world from that supernatural evil Thing. Therefore, faster than ever man's foot had covered those leagues, he sped under the dark, still night, over the waste trackless snow ridges to the far-away church where salvation lay in the holy-water stoop at the door. His faith was as firm as any that wrought miracles in days past, simple as a child's wish, strong as a man's will.

He was hardly missed during these hours, every second of which was by him fulfilled to its utmost extent by extremest effort that sinews and nerves could attain. Within the homestead the while the easy moments went bright with words and looks of unwonted animation, for the kindly hospitable instincts of the inmates were roused into cordial expression of welcome and interest by the grace and beauty of the returned stranger.

But Sweyn was eager and earnest, with more than a host's courteous warmth. The impression that at her first coming had charmed him, that had lived since through memory, deepened now in her actual presence. Sweyn, the matchless among men, acknowledged in this fair White Fell a spirit high and bold as his own, and a frame so firm and capable that only bulk was lacking for equal strength. Yet the white skin was moulded most smoothly, without such muscular swelling as made his might evident. Such love as his frank self-love could concede was called forth by an ardent admiration for this supreme stranger. More admiration than love was in his passion, and therefore he was free from a lover's hesitancy, and delicate reserve and doubts. Frankly and boldly he courted her favor by looks and tones, and an address that was his by natural ease.

Nor was she a woman to be wooed otherwise. Tender whispers and sighs would never gain her ear; but her eyes would brighten and shine if she heard of a brave feat, and her prompt hand in sympathy fall swiftly on the axe haft and clasp it hard. That movement ever fired Sweyn's admiration anew; he watched for it, strove to elicit it and glowed when it came. Wonderful and beautiful was that wrist, slender and steel-strong;

the smooth shapely hand that curved so fast and firm, ready to deal instant death.

Desiring to feel the pressure of these hands, this bold lover schemed with palpable directness, proposing that she should hear how their hunting songs were sung, with a chorus that signalled hands to be clasped. So his splendid voice gave the verses, and, as the chorus was taken up, he claimed her hands, and, even through the easy grip, felt, as he desired, the strength that was latent, and the vigor that quickened the very finger tips, as the song fired her, and her voice was caught out of her by the rhythmic swell and rang clear on the top of the closing surge.

Afterward she sang alone. For contrast, or in the pride of swaying moods by her voice, she chose a mournful song that drifted along in a minor chant, sad as a wind that dirges:

> "Oh, let me go!
> Around spin wreaths of snow;
> The dark earth sleeps below.
>
> "Far up the plain
> Moans on a voice of pain:
> 'Where shall my babe be lain?
>
> "In my white breast
> Lay the sweet life to rest!
> Lay, where it can be best!
>
> " 'Hush! hush!' it cries;
> 'Tense night is on the skies;
> 'Two stars are in thine eyes.'
>
> "Come, babe away!
> But lie thou till dawn be gray,
> Who must be dead by day.
>
> "This cannot last;
> But, o'er the sickening blast,
> All sorrows shall be past;
>
> "All kings shall be
> Low bending at thy knee,
> Worshipping life from thee.

> "For men long sore
> To hope of what's before—
> To leave the things of yore.
>
> "Mine, and not thine,
> How deep their jewels shine!
> Peace laps thy head, not mine!"

Old Trella came tottering from her corner, shaken to additional palsy by an aroused memory. She strained her dim eyes toward the singer, and then bent her head that the one ear yet sensible to sound might avail of every note. At the close, groping forward, she murmured with the high pitched quaver of old age:

"So she sang, my Thora; my last and brightest. What is she like—she, whose voice is like my dead Thora's? Are her eyes blue?"

"Blue as the sky."

"So were my Thora's! Is her hair fair and in plaits to the waist?"

"Even so," answered White Fell herself, and met the advancing hands with her own, and guided them to corroborate her words by touch.

"Like my dead Thora's," repeated the old woman; and then her trembling hands rested on the fur-clad shoulders and she bent forward and kissed the smooth fair face that White Fell upturned, nothing loath to receive and return the caress.

So Christian saw them as he entered.

He stood a moment. After the starless darkness and the icy night air, and the fierce silent two hours' race, his senses reeled on sudden entrance into warmth and light and the cheery hum of voices. A sudden unforeseen anguish assailed him, as now first he entertained the possibility of being overmatched by her wiles and her daring, if at the approach of pure death she should start up at bay transformed to a terrible beast, and achieve a savage glut at the last. He looked with horror and pity on the harmless helpless folk, so unwitting of outrage to their comfort and security. The dreadful Thing in their midst, that was veiled from their knowledge by womanly beauty, was a centre of pleasant interest. There, before him, signally impressive, was poor old Trella, weakest and feeblest of all, in fond nearness. And a moment might bring about the revelation of a monstrous horror—a ghastly, deadly danger, set loose and at bay, in a circle of girls and women, and careless, defenceless men.

And he alone of the throng prepared!

For one breathing space he faltered, no longer than that, while over him swept the agony of compunction that yet could not make him surrender his purpose.

He alone? Nay, but Tyr also, and he crossed to the dumb sole sharer of his knowledge.

So timeless is thought that a few seconds only lay between his lifting of the latch and his loosening of Tyr's collar; but in those few seconds succeeding his first glance, as lightning-swift had been the impulses of others, their motion as quick and sure. Sweyn's vigilant eye had darted upon him, and instantly his every fiber was alert with hostile instinct; and half divining, half incredulous, of Christian's object in stooping to Tyr, he came hastily, wary, wrathful, resolute to oppose the malice of his wild-eyed brother.

But beyond Sweyn rose White Fell, blanching white as her furs, and with eyes grown fierce and wild. She leapt down the room to the door, whirling her long robe closely to her. "Hark!" she panted. "The signal horn! Hark, I must go!" as she snatched at the latch to be out and away.

For one precious moment Christian had hesitated on the half loosened collar; for, except the womanly form were exchanged for the bestial, Tyr's jaws would gnash to rags his honor of manhood. He heard her voice, and turned—too late.

As she tugged at the door, he sprang across grasping his flask, but Sweyn dashed between and caught him back irresistibly, so that a most frantic effort only availed to wrench one arm free. With that, on the impulse of sheer despair, he cast at her with all his force. The door swung behind her, and the flask flew into fragments against it. Then, as Sweyn's grasp slackened, and he met the questioning astonishment of surrounding faces, with a hoarse inarticulate cry: "God help us all!" he said; "she is a were-wolf!"

Sweyn turned upon him, "Liar, coward!" and his hands gripped his brother's throat with deadly force as though the spoken word could be killed so, and, as Christian struggled, lifted him clear off his feet and flung him crashing backward. So furious was he that, as his brother lay motionless, he stirred him roughly with his foot, till their mother came between, crying, "Shame!" and yet then he stood by, his teeth set, his brows knit, his hands clenched, ready to enforce silence again violently, as Christian rose, staggering and bewildered.

But utter silence and submission was more than he expected, and turned his anger into contempt for one so easily cowed and held in subjection by mere force. "He is mad!" he said, turning on his heel as he spoke, so that he lost his mother's look of pained reproach at this sudden free utterance of what was a lurking dread within her.

Christian was too spent for the effort of speech. His hard drawn breath labored in great sobs; his limbs were powerless and unstrung in utter relax after hard service. His failure in this endeavor induced a stupor of misery and despair. In addition was the wretched humiliation of open violence and strife with his brother, and the distress of hearing misjudging contempt expressed without reserve, for he was aware that Sweyn had turned to allay the scared excitement half by imperious mastery, half by explanation and argument that showed painful disregard of brotherly consideration.

Sweyn the while was observant of his brother, despite the continual check of finding, turn and glance where he would, Christian's eyes always upon him, with a strange look of helpless distress, discomposing enough to the angry aggressor. "Like a beaten dog!" he said to himself, rallying contempt to withstand compunction. Observation set him wondering on Christian's exhausted condition. The heavy laboring breath and the slack, inert fall of the limbs told surely of unusual and prolonged exertion. And then why had close upon two hours' absence been followed by manifestly hostile behavior toward White Fell? Suddenly, the fragments of the flask giving a clue, he guessed all, and faced about to stare at his brother in amaze. He forgot that the motive scheme was against White Fell, demanding derision and resentment from him; that was swept out of remembrance by astonishment and admiration for the feat of speed and endurance.

That night Sweyn and his mother talked long and late together, shaping into certainty the suspicion that Christian's mind had lost its balance, and discussing the evident cause. For Sweyn, declaring his own love for White Fell, suggested that his unfortunate brother with a like passion— they being twins in love as in birth—had through jealousy and despair turned from love to hate, until reason failed at the strain, and a craze developed, which the malice and treachery of madness made a serious and dangerous force.

So Sweyn theorized; convincing himself as he spoke; convincing afterward others who advanced doubts against White Fell; fettering his judgment by his advocacy, and by his staunch defence of her hurried flight, silencing his own inner consciousness of the unaccountability of her action.

But a little time and Sweyn lost his vantage in the shock of a fresh horror at the homestead. Trella was no more, and her end a mystery. The poor old woman crawled out in a bright gleam to visit a bed-ridden gossip living beyond the fir grove. Under the trees she was last seen halting for her companion, sent back for a forgotten present. Quick alarm sprang, calling every man to the search. Her stick was found among the brushwood near the path, but no track or stain, for a gusty wind was sifting the snow from the branches and hid all sign of how she came by her death.

So panic-stricken were the farm folk that none dared go singly on the search. Known danger could be braced, but not this stealthy Death that walked by day invisible, that cut off alike the child in his play and the aged woman so near to her quiet grave.

"Rol she kissed; Trella she kissed!" So rang Christian's frantic cry again and again, till Sweyn dragged him away and strove to keep him apart from the rest of the household.

But thenceforward all Sweyn's reasoning and mastery could not uphold White Fell above suspicion. He was not called upon to defend her from accusation, when Christian had been brought to silence again; but he well knew the significance of this fact, that her name, formerly uttered freely and often, he never heard now—it was huddled away into whispers that he could not catch.

For a time the twins' variance was marked on Sweyn's part by an air of rigid indifference, on Christian's by heavy downcast silence, and a nervous, apprehensive observation of his brother. Superadded to his remorse and foreboding, Sweyn's displeasure weighed upon him intolerably, and the remembrance of their violent rupture was ceaseless misery. The elder brother, self-sufficient and insensitive, could little know how deeply his unkindness stabbed. A depth and force of affection such as Christian's was unknown to him, and his brother's ceaseless surveillance annoyed him greatly. Therefore, that suspicion might be lulled, he judged it wise to make overtures for peace. Most easily done. A little kindliness, a few evidences of consideration, a slight return of the old brotherly imperiousness, and Christian replied by a gratefulness and relief that might have touched him had he understood all, but instead increased his secret contempt.

So successful was his finesse that when, late on a day, a message summoning Christian to a distance was transmitted by Sweyn no doubt of its genuineness occurred. When, his errand proving useless, he set out to return, mistake or misapprehension was all that he surmised. Not till he sighted the homestead, lying low between the night gray snow ridges, did vivid recollection of the time when he had tracked that horror to the door rouse an intense dread, and with it a hardly defined suspicion.

His grasp tightened on the bear-spear that he carried as a staff; every sense was alert, every muscle strung; excitement urged him on, caution checked him, and the two governed his long stride, swiftly, noiselessly to the climax he felt was at hand.

As he drew near to the outer gates, a light shadow stirred and went, as though the gray of the snow had taken detached motion. A darker shadow stayed and faced Christian.

Sweyn stood before him, and surely the shadow that went was White Fell.

They had been together—close. Had she not been in his arms, near enough for lips to meet?

There was no moon, but the stars gave light enough to show that Sweyn's face was flushed and elate. The flush remained, though the expression changed quickly at sight of his brother. How, if Christian had seen all, should one of his frenzied outbursts be met and managed—by resolution? by indifference? He halted between the two, and as a result, he swaggered.

"White Fell?" questioned Christian, breathlessly.

"Yes?" Sweyn's answer was a query, with an intonation that implied he was clearing the ground for action.

From Christian came, "Have you kissed her?" like a bolt direct, staggering Sweyn by its sheer, prompt temerity.

He flushed yet darker, and yet half smiled over this earnest of success he had won. Had there been really between himself and Christian the rivalry that he imagined, his face had enough of the insolence of triumph to exasperate jealous rage.

"You dare ask this!"

"Sweyn, O Sweyn, I must know! You have!"

The ring of despair and anguish in his tone angered Sweyn, misconstruing it. Jealousy so presumptuous was intolerable.

"Mad fool!" he said, constraining himself no longer. "Win for yourself a woman to kiss. Leave mine without question. Such a one as I should desire to kiss is such a one as shall never allow a kiss to you."

Then Christian fully understood his supposition.

"I—I—!" he cried. "White Fell—that deadly Thing! Sweyn, are you blind, mad? I would save you from her—a were-wolf!"

Sweyn maddened again at the accusation—a dastardly way of revenge, as he conceived; and instantly, for the second time, the brothers were at strife violently. But Christian was now too desperate to be scrupulous; for a dim glimpse had shot a possibility into his mind, and to be free to follow it the striking of his brother was a necessity. Thank God! he was armed, and so Sweyn's equal.

Facing his assailant with the bear-spear, he struck up his arms, and with the butt end hit so hard that he fell. Then the matchless runner leapt away, to follow a forlorn hope.

Sweyn, on regaining his feet, was as amazed as angry at this unaccountable flight. He knew in his heart that his brother was no coward, and that it was unlike him to shrink from an encounter because defeat was certain, and cruel humiliation from a vindictive victor probable. Of the uselessness of pursuit he was well aware; he must abide his chagrin until his time for advantage should come. Since White Fell had parted to the right, Christian to the left, the event of a sequent encounter did not occur to him.

And now Christian, acting on the dim glimpse he had had, just as Sweyn turned upon him, of something that moved against the sky along the ridge behind the home-stead, was staking his only hope on a chance, and his own superlative speed. If what he saw was really White Fell, he guessed she was bending her steps toward the open wastes; and there was just a possibility that, by a straight dash, and a desperate, perilous leap over a sheer bluff, he might yet meet her or head her. And then— he had no further thought.

It was past, the quick, fierce race, and the chance of death at the leap, and he halted in a hollow to fetch his breath and to look—did she come? Had she gone?

She came.

She came with a smooth, gliding, noiseless speed, that was neither walking nor running; her arms were folded in her furs that were drawn tight about her body; the white lappets from her head were wrapped and knotted closely beneath her face; her eyes were set on a far distance. Then the even sway of her going was startled to a pause by Christian.

"Fell!"

She drew a quick, sharp breath at the sound of her name thus mutilated, and faced Sweyn's brother. Her eyes glittered; her upper lip was lifted and showed the teeth. The half of her name, impressed with an ominous sense as uttered by him, warned her of the aspect of a deadly foe. Yet she cast loose her robes till they trailed ample, and spoke as a mild woman.

"What would you?"

Christian answered with his solemn, dreadful accusation:

"You kissed Rol—and Rol is dead! You kissed Trella—she is dead! You have kissed Sweyn, my brother, but he shall not die!"

He added: "You may live till midnight."

The edge of the teeth and the glitter of the eyes stayed a moment, and her right hand also slid down to the axe haft. Then, without a word, she swerved from him, and sprang out and away swiftly over the snow.

And Christian sprang out and away, and followed her swiftly over the snow, keeping behind, but half a stride's length from her side.

So they went running together, silent, toward the vast wastes of snow where no living thing but they two moved under the stars of night.

Never before had Christian so rejoiced in his powers. The gift of speed and the training of use and endurance were priceless to him now. Though midnight was hours away he was confident that go where that Fell Thing would hasten as she would, she could not outstrip him, nor escape from him. Then, when came the time for transformation, when the woman's form made no longer a shield against a man's hand, he could slay or be slain to save Sweyn. He had struck his dear brother in dire extremity, but he could not, though reason urged, strike a woman.

For one mile, for two miles they ran; White Fell ever foremost, Christian ever at an equal distance from her side, so near that, now and again, her outflying furs touched him. She spoke no word; nor he. She never turned her head to look at him, nor swerved to evade him; but, with set face looking forward, sped straight on, over rough, over smooth, aware of his nearness by the regular beat of his feet, and the sound of his breath behind.

In a while she quickened her pace. From the first Christian had judged of her speed as admirable, yet with exulting security in his own excelling and enduring whatever her efforts. But, when the pace increased, he found himself put to the test as never had been done before in any race. Her feet indeed flew faster than his; it was only by his length of stride that he kept his place at her side. But his heart was high and resolute, and he did not fear failure yet.

So the desperate race flew on. Their feet struck up the powdery snow, their breath smoked into the sharp, clear air, and they were gone before the air was cleared of snow and vapor. Now and then Christian glanced up to judge, by the rising of the stars, of the coming of midnight. So long —so long!

White Fell held on without slack. She, it was evident, with confidence in her speed proving matchless, as resolute to outrun her pursuer, as he to endure till midnight and fulfil his purpose. And Christian held on, still self-assured. He could not fail; he would not fail. To avenge Rol and Trella was motive enough for him to do what man could do; but for Sweyn more. She had kissed Sweyn, but he should not die, too—with Sweyn to save he could not fail.

Never before was such a race as this; no, not when in old Greece man and maid raced together with two fates at stake; for the hard running was sustained unabated, while star after star rose and went wheeling up toward midnight—for one hour, for two hours.

Then Christian saw and heard what shot him through with fear. Where a fringe of trees hung round a slope he saw something dark moving, and heard a yelp, followed by a full, horrid cry, and the dark spread out upon the snow—a pack of wolves in pursuit.

Of the beasts alone he had little cause for fear; at the pace he held he could distance them, four footed though they were. But of White Fell's wiles he had infinite apprehension, for how might she not avail herself of the savage jaws of these wolves, akin as they were to half her nature. She vouchsafed to them nor look nor sign; but Christian, on an impulse, to assure himself that she should not escape him, caught and held the back-flung edge of her furs, running still.

She turned like a flash with a beastly snarl, teeth and eyes gleaming again. Her axe shone on the upstroke, on the downstroke, as she hacked at his hand. She had lopped it off at the wrist, but that he parried with the bear-spear. Even then she shore through the shaft and shattered the bones of the hand, so that he loosed perforce.

Then again they raced on as before, Christian not losing a pace, though his left hand swung bleeding and broken.

The snarl, indubitably, though modified from a woman's organs; the vicious fury revealed in teeth and eyes; the sharp, arrogant pain of her maiming blow, caught away Christian's heed of the beasts behind, by striking into him close, vivid realization of the infinitely greater danger that ran before him in that deadly Thing.

When he bethought him to look behind, lo! the pack had but reached their tracks, and instantly slunk aside, cowed; the yell of pursuit changing to yelps and whines. So abhorrent was that fell creature to beast as to man.

She had drawn her furs more closely to her, disposing them so that, instead of flying loose to her heels, no drapery hung lower than her knees, and this without a check to her wonderful speed, nor embarrassment by the cumbering of the folds. She held her head as before; her lips were firmly set, only the tense nostrils gave her breath; not a sign of distress witnessed to the long sustaining of that terrible speed.

But on Christian by now the strain was telling palpably. His head weighed heavy, and his breath came laboring in great sobs; the bear-spear would have been a burden now. His heart was beating like a hammer, but such a dullness oppressed his brain that it was only by degrees he could realize his helpless state; wounded and weaponless, chasing that Thing, that was a fierce, desperate, axe-armed woman, except she should assume the beast with fangs yet more deadly.

And still the far, slow stars went lingering nearly an hour from midnight.

So far was his brain astray that an impression took him that she was fleeing from the midnight stars, whose gain was by such slow degrees that a time equalling days and days had gone in the race round the northern circle of the world, and days and days as long might last before the end—except she slackened, or except he failed.

But he would not fail yet.

How long had he been praying so? He had started with a self-confidence and reliance that had felt no need for that aid; and now it seemed the only means by which to restrain his heart from swelling beyond the compass of his body; by which to cherish his brain from dwindling and shriveling quite away. Some sharp-toothed creature kept tearing and dragging on his maimed left hand; he never could see it, he could not shake it off, but he prayed it off at times.

The clear stars before him took to shuddering and he knew why; they shuddered at sight of what was behind him. He had never divined before that strange Things hid themselves from men, under pretence of being snow-clad mounds of swaying trees; but now they came slipping out from their harmless covers to follow him, and mock at his impotence to make a kindred Thing resolve to truer form. He knew the air behind him was thronged; he heard the hum of innumerable murmurings together; but his eyes could never catch them—they were too swift and nimble; but he knew they were there, because, on a backward glance, he saw the snow mounds surge as they grovelled flatlings out of sight; he saw the trees reel as they screwed themselves rigid past recognition among the boughs.

And after such glance the stars for a while returned to steadfastness, and an infinite stretch of silence froze upon the chill, gray world, only deranged by the swift, even beat of the flying feet, and his own—slower from the longer stride, and the sound of his breath. And for some clear moments he knew that his only concern was to sustain his speed regardless of pain and distress, to deny with every nerve he had her power to outstrip him or to widen the space between them, till the stars crept up to midnight.

A hideous check came to the race. White Fell swirled about and leapt to the right, and Christian, unprepared for so prompt a lurch, found close at his feet a deep pit yawning, and his own impetus past control. But he snatched at her as he bore past, clasping her right arm with his one whole hand, and the two swung together upon the brink.

And her straining away in self-preservation was vigorous enough to counterbalance his headlong impulse, and brought them reeling together to safety.

Then, before he was verily sure that they were not to perish so, crashing down, he saw her gnashing in wild, pale fury, as she wrenched to be free; and since her right arm was in his grasp, used her axe left-handed, striking back at him.

The blow was effectual enough even so; his right arm dropped powerless, gashed and with the lesser bone broken that jarred with horrid pain when he let it swing, as he leaped out again, and ran to recover the few feet she had gained from his pause at the shock.

The near escape and this new, quick pain made again every faculty alive and intense. He knew that what he followed was most surely Death animate; wounded and helpless, he was utterly at her mercy if so she should realize and take action. Hopeless to avenge, hopeless to save, his very despair for Sweyn swept him on to follow and follow and precede the kiss-doomed to death. Could he yet fail to hunt that Thing past midnight, out of the womanly form, alluring and treacherous, into lasting restraint of the bestial, which was the last shred of hope left from the confident purpose of the outset.

The last hour from midnight had lost half its quarters, and the stars went lifting up the great minutes, and again his greatening heart and his shrinking brain and the sickening agony that swung at either side conspired to appal the will that had only seeming empire over his feet.

Now White Fell's body was so closely enveloped that not a lap nor an edge flew free. She stretched forward strangely aslant, leaning from the upright poise of a runner. She cleared the ground at times by long bounds, gaining an increase of speed that Christian agonized to equal.

He grew bewildered, uncertain of his own identity, doubting of his own true form. He could not be really a man, no more than that running Thing was really a woman; his real form was only hidden under embodiment of a man, but what it was he did not know. And Sweyn's real form he did not know. Sweyn lay fallen at his feet, where he had struck him down—his own brother—he; he stumbled over him and had to overleap him and race harder because she who had kissed Sweyn leapt so fast. "Sweyn—Sweyn—O Sweyn!"

Why did the stars stop to shudder? Midnight else had surely come!

The leaning, leaping Thing looked back at him a wild, fierce look, and laughed in savage scorn and triumph. He saw in a flash why, for within a time measurable by seconds she would have escaped him utterly. As the land lay a slope of ice sunk on the one hand; on the other hand a steep rose, shouldering forward; between the two was space for a foot to be planted, but none for a body to stand; yet a juniper bough, thrusting out, gave a handhold secure enough for one with a resolute grasp to swing past the perilous place, and pass on safe.

Though the first seconds of the last moment were going, she dared to flash back a wicked look, and laugh at the pursuer who was impotent to grasp.

The crisis struck convulsive life into his last supreme effort; his will surged up indomitable, his speed proved matchless yet. He leapt with a rush, passed her before her laugh had time to go out, and turned short, barring the way, and braced to withstand her.

She came hurling desperate, with a feint to the right hand, and then launched herself upon him with a spring like a wild beast when it leaps to kill. And he, with one strong arm and a hand that could not hold, with one strong hand and an arm that could not guide and sustain, he caught and held her even so. And they fell together. And because he felt his whole arm slipping and his whole hand loosing, to slack the dreadful agony of the wrenched bone above, he caught and held with his teeth the tunic at her knee, as she struggled up and wrung off his hands to overleap him victorious.

Like lightning she snatched her axe, and struck him on the neck—deep—once—twice—his life-blood gushed out, staining her feet.

The stars touched midnight.

The death scream he heard was not his, for his set teeth had hardly yet relaxed when it rang out. And the dreadful cry began with a woman's shriek, and changed and ended as the yell of a beast. And before the final blank overtook his dying eyes, he saw the She gave place to It; he saw more, that Life gave place to Death—incomprehensibly.

For he did not dream that no holy water could be more holy, more potent to destroy an evil thing than the life-blood of a pure heart poured out for another in willing devotion.

His own true hidden reality that he had desired to know grew palpable, recognizable. It seemed to him just this: a great, glad, abounding hope that he had saved his brother; too expansive to be contained by the limited form of a sole man, it yearned for a new embodiment infinite as the stars.

What did it matter to that true reality that the man's brain shrank, shrank, till it was nothing; that the man's body could not retain the huge pain of his heart, and heaved it out through the red exit riven at the neck: that hurtling blackness blotted out forever the man's sight, hearing, sense?

In the early gray of day Sweyn chanced upon the footprints of a man—of a runner, as he saw by the shifted snow; and the direction they had taken aroused curiosity, since a little farther their line must be crossed by the edge of a sheer height. He turned to trace them. And so doing, the length of the stride struck his attention—a stride long as his own if he ran. He knew he was following Christian.

In his anger he had hardened himself to be indifferent to the night-long absence of his brother; but now, seeing where the footsteps went, he was seized with compunction and dread. He had failed to give thought and care to his poor, frantic twin, who might—was it possible?—have rushed to a frantic death.

His heart stood still when he came to the place where the leap had been taken. A piled edge of snow had fallen, too, and nothing lay below when he peered. Along the upper edge he ran for a furlong, till he came to a dip where he could slip and climb down, and then back again on the lower level to the pile of fallen snow. There he saw that the vigorous running had started afresh.

He stood pondering; vexed that any man should have taken that leap where he had not ventured to follow; vexed that he had been beguiled to such painful emotions; guessing vainly at Christian's object in this mad freak. He began sauntering along half-unconsciously following his brother's track, and so in a while he came to the place where the footprints were doubled.

Small prints were these others, small as a woman's, though the pace from one to another was longer than that which the skirts of women allow.

Did not White Fell tread so?

A dreadful guess appalled him—so dreadful that he recoiled from belief. Yet his face grew ashy white, and he gasped to fetch back motion to his checked heart. Unbelievable? Closer attention showed how the smaller footfall had altered for greater speed, striking into the snow with a deeper onset and a lighter pressure on the heels. Unbelievable? Could any woman but White Fell run so? Could any man but Christian run so? The guess became a certainty. He was following where alone in the dark night White Fell had fled from Christian pursuing.

Such villainy set heart and brain on fire with rage and indignation— such villainy in his own brother, till lately loveworthy, praiseworthy, though a fool for meekness. He would kill Christian; had he lives as many as the footprints he had trodden, vengeance should demand them all. In a tempest of murderous hate he followed on in haste, for the track was plain enough; starting with such a burst of speed as could not be maintained, but brought him back soon to a plod for the spent, sobbing breath to be regulated.

Mile after mile he traveled with a bursting heart; more piteous, more tragic, seemed the case at this evidence of White Fell's splendid supremacy, holding her own so long against Christian's famous speed. So long, so long, that his love and admiration grew more and more boundless, and his grief and indignation therewith also. Whenever the track lay clear he ran, with such reckless prodigality of strength that it was soon spent, and he dragged on heavily, till, sometimes on the ice of a mere, sometimes on a wind-swept place, all signs were lost; but, so undeviating had been their line, that a course straight on, and then short questing to either hand recovered them again.

Hour after hour had gone by through more than half that winter day, before ever he came to the place where the trampled snow showed that a scurry of feet had come and gone! Wolves' feet—and gone most amazingly! Only a little beyond he came to the lopped point of Christian's bear-spear—farther on he would see where the remnant of the useless shaft had been dropped. The snow here was dashed with blood, and the footsteps of the two had fallen closer together. Some hoarse sound of exultation came from him that might have been a laugh had breath sufficed. "O White Fell, my poor brave love! Well struck!" he groaned, torn by his pity and great admiration, as he guessed surely how she had turned and dealt a blow.

The sight of the blood inflamed him as it might a beast that ravens. He grew mad with a desire to once again have Christian by the throat, not to loose this time till he had crushed out his life—or beat out his life —or stabbed out his life—or all of these, and torn him piecemeal likewise—and ah! then, not till then, bleed his heart with weeping, like a child, like a girl, over the piteous fate of his poor lost love.

On—on—on—through the aching time, toiling and straining in the track of those two superb runners, aware of the marvel of their endurance, but unaware of the marvel of their speed that in the three hours before midnight had overpassed all that vast distance that he could only traverse from twilight to twilight. For clear daylight was passing when he came to the edge of an old marlpit, and saw how the two who had gone before had stamped and trampled together in desperate peril on the verge. And here fresh blood stains spoke to him of a valiant defence against his infamous brother; and he followed where the blood had dripped till the cold had staunched its flow, taking a savage gratification from the evidence that Christian had been gashed deeply, maddening afresh with desire to do likewise more excellently and so slake his murderous hate. And he began to know that through all his despair he had entertained a germ of hope, that grew apace, rained upon by his brother's blood.

He strove on as best he might, wrung now by an access of hope—now of despair, in agony to reach the end however terrible, sick with the aching of the toiled miles that deferred it.

And the light went lingering out of the sky, giving place to uncertain stars.

He came to the finish.

Two bodies lay in a narrow place. Christian's was one, but the other beyond not White Fell's. There where the footsteps ended lay a great white wolf. At the sight Sweyn's strength was blasted; body and soul he was struck down groveling.

The stars had grown sure and intense before he stirred from where he had dropped prone. Very feebly he crawled to his dead brother, and laid his hands upon him, and crouched so, afraid to look or stir further.

Cold stiff—hours dead. Yet the dead body was his only shelter and stay in that most dreadful hour. His soul, stripped bare of all comfort, cowered, shivering, naked, abject, and the living clung to the dead out of piteous need for grace from the soul that had passed away.

He rose to his knees, lifting the body. Christian had fallen face forward in the snow, with his arms flung up and wide, and so had the frost made him rigid; strange, ghastly, unyielding to Sweyn lifting, so that he laid him down again and crouched above, with his arms fast round him and a low, heart-wrung groan.

When at last he found force to raise his brother's body and gather it in his arms, tight clasped to his breast, he tried to face the Thing that lay beyond. The sight set his limbs in a palsy with horror and dread. His senses had failed and fainted in utter cowardice, but for the strength that came from holding dead Christian in his arms, enabling him to compel his eyes to endure the sight, and take into the brain the complete aspect of the Thing. No wound—only blood stains on the feet. The great, grim jaws had a savage grin, though dead-stiff. And his kiss—he could bear it no longer, and turned away, nor ever looked again.

And the dead man in his arms, knowing the full horror, had followed and faced it for his sake; had suffered agony and death for his sake; in the neck was the deep death-gash, one arm and both hands were dark with frozen blood, for his sake! Dead he knew him—as in life he had not known him—to give the right meed of love and worship. He longed for annihilation, that so he might lose the agony of knowing himself so unworthy such perfect love. The frozen calm of death on the face appalled him. He dared not touch it with lips that had cursed so lately, with lips fouled by a kiss of the Horror that had been Death.

He struggled to his feet, still clasping Christian. The dead man stood upright within his arms, frozen rigid. The eyes were not quite closed; the head had stiffened, bowed slightly to one side; the arms stayed straight and wide. It was the figure of one crucified, the blood-stained hands also conforming.

So living and dead went back along the track, that one had passed in the deepest passion of love, and one in the deepest passion of hate. All that night Sweyn toiled through the snow, bearing the weight of dead Christian, treading back along the steps he before had trodden when he was wronging with vilest thoughts and cursing with murderous hate the brother who all the while lay dead for his sake.

The River Styx
Runs Upstream

Dan Simmons

Mother love can be joyous and sometimes sorrowful, but it took DAN SIM-
MONS, *popular author of* Hyperion, The Fall of Hyperion *and* Summer of
Night, *to think up its more sinister ramifications. From the first issue of*
Night Cry *magazine comes this memorably ghastly speculation about tomor-
row's family values.*

> What thou lovest well remains
> the rest is dross
> What thou lov'st well shall not be reft
> from thee
> What thou lov'st well is thy
> true heritage . . .
> —EZRA POUND, Canto LXXXI

I LOVED MY MOTHER very much. After her funeral, after the coffin was lowered, the family went home and waited for her return.

I was only eight at the time. Of the required ceremony I remember
little. I recall that the collar of the previous year's shirt was far too tight
and that the unaccustomed tie was like a noose around my neck. I
remember that the June day was too beautiful for such a solemn gathering. I remember Uncle Will's heavy drinking that morning and the

bottle of Jack Daniels he pulled out as we drove home from the funeral.
I remember my father's face.

The afternoon was too long. I had no role to play in the family's
gathering that day, and the adults ignored me. I found myself wandering from room to room with a warm glass of Kool-Aid, until finally I
escaped to the backyard. Even that familiar landscape of play and seclusion was ruined by the glimpse of pale, fat faces staring out from the
neighbors' windows. They were waiting. Hoping for a glimpse. I felt
like shouting, throwing rocks at them. Instead I sat down on the old
tractor tire we used as a sandbox. Very deliberately I poured the red
Kool-Aid into the sand and watched the spreading stain digging a small
pit.

They're digging her *up now.*

I ran to the swing set and angrily began to pump my legs against the
bare soil. The swing creaked with rust, and one leg of the frame rose out
of the ground.

*No, they've already done that, stupid. Now they're hooking her up to big
machines. Will they pump the blood back into her?*

I thought of bottles hanging. I remembered the fat, red ticks that
clung to our dog in the summer. Angry, I swung high, kicking up hard
even when there was no more height to be gained.

*Do her fingers twitch first? Or do her eyes just slide open like an owl
waking up?*

I reached the high point of my arc and jumped. For a second I was
weightless and I hung above the earth like Superman, like a spirit flying
from its body. Then gravity claimed me and I fell heavily on my hands
and knees. I had scraped my palms and put grass stain on my right knee.
Mother would be angry.

*She's being walked around now. Maybe they're dressing her like one of the
mannequins in Mr. Feldman's store window.*

My brother Simon came out to the backyard. Although he was only
two years older, Simon looked like an adult to me that afternoon. An old
adult. His blond hair, as recently cut as mine, hung down in limp bangs
across a pale forehead. His eyes looked tired. Simon almost never yelled
at me. But he did that day.

"Get in here. It's almost time."

I followed him through the back porch. Most of the relatives had left, but from the living room we could hear Uncle Will. He was shouting. We paused in the hallway to listen.

"For Chrissakes, Les, there's still time. You just can't do this."

"It's already done."

"Think of the . . . Jesus Christ . . . think of the kids."

We could hear the slur of the voice and knew that Uncle Will had been drinking more. Simon put his finger to his lips. There was a silence.

"Les, think about just the money side of it. What's . . . how much . . . it's twenty-five percent of everything you have. For how many years, Les? Think of the kids. What'll that do to—"

"It's *done,* Will."

We had never heard that tone from Father before. It was not argumentative—the way it was when he and Uncle Will used to argue politics late at night. It was not sad like the time he talked to Simon and me after he had brought Mother home from the hospital the first time. It was just final.

There was more talk. Uncle Will started shouting. Even the silences were angry. We went to the kitchen to get a Coke. When we came back down the hallway, Uncle Will almost ran over us in his rush to leave. The door slammed behind him. He never entered our home again.

They brought Mother home just after dark. Simon and I were looking out the picture window and we could feel the neighbors watching. Only Aunt Helen and a few of our closest relatives had stayed. I felt Father's surprise when he saw the car. I don't know what we'd been expecting—maybe a long black hearse like the one that had carried Mother to the cemetery that morning.

They drove up in a yellow Toyota. There were four men in the car with Mother. Instead of dark suits like the one Father was wearing, they had on pastel, short-sleeved shirts. One of the men got out of the car and offered his hand to Mother.

I wanted to rush to the door and down the sidewalk to her, but Simon grabbed my wrist and we stood back in the hallway while Father and the other grown-ups opened the door.

They came up the sidewalk in the glow of the gaslight on the lawn. Mother was between the two men, but they were not really helping her walk, just guiding her a little. She wore the light blue dress she had bought at Scott's just before she got sick. I had expected her to look all pale and waxy—like when I peeked through the crack in the bedroom door before the men from the funeral home came to take her body away —but her face was flushed and healthy, almost sunburned.

When they stepped onto the front stoop, I could see that she was wearing a lot of makeup. Mother never wore makeup. The two men also had pink cheeks. All three of them had the same smile.

When they came into the house, I think we all took a step back— except for Father. He put his hands on Mother's arms, looked at her a long time, and kissed her on the cheek. I don't think she kissed him back. Her smile did not change. Tears were running down Father's face. I felt embarrassed.

The Resurrectionists were saying something. Father and Aunt Helen nodded. Mother just stood there, still smiling slightly, and looked politely at the yellow-shirted man, as he spoke and joked and patted Father on the back. Then it was our turn to hug Mother. Aunt Helen moved Simon forward, and I was still hanging onto Simon's hand. He kissed her on the cheek and quickly moved back to Father's side. I threw my arms around her neck and kissed her on the lips. I had *missed* her.

Her skin wasn't cold. It was just *different.*

She was looking at me. Baxter, our German shepherd, began to whine and scratch at the back door.

Father took the Resurrectionists into the study. We heard snatches of conversation down the hall.

". . . if you think of it as a stroke . . ."

"How long will she . . ."

"You understand the tithing is necessary because of the expenses of monthly care and . . ."

The women relatives stood in a circle around Mother. There was an awkward moment until they realized that Mother did not speak. Aunt Helen reached her hand out and touched her sister's cheek. Mother smiled and smiled.

Then Father was back and his voice was loud and hearty. He explained how similar it was to a light stroke—did we remember Uncle Richard? Meanwhile, Father kissed people repeatedly and thanked everyone.

The Resurrectionists left with smiles and signed papers. The remaining relatives began to leave soon after that. Father saw them down the walk, smiling and shaking their hands.

"Think of it as though she's been ill but has recovered," said Father. "Think of her as home from the hospital."

Aunt Helen was the last to leave. She sat next to Mother for a long time, speaking softly and searching Mother's face for a response. After a while Aunt Helen began to cry.

"Think of it as if she's recovered from an illness," said Father as he walked her to her car. "Think of her as home from the hospital."

Aunt Helen nodded, still crying, and left. I think she knew what Simon and I knew. Mother was not home from the hospital. She was home from the grave.

The night was long. Several times I thought I heard the soft slap of Mother's slippers on the hallway floor and my breathing stopped, waiting for the door to open. But it didn't. The moonlight lay across my legs and exposed a patch of wallpaper next to the dresser. The flower pattern looked like the face of a great, sad beast. Just before dawn, Simon leaned across from his bed and whispered, "Go to sleep, stupid." And so I did.

For the first week, Father slept with Mother in the same room where they had always slept. In the morning his face would sag and he would snap at us while we ate our cereal. Then he moved to his study and slept on the old divan in there.

The summer was very hot. No one would play with us, so Simon and I played together. Father had only morning classes at the University. Mother moved around the house and watered the plants a lot. Once Simon and I saw her watering a plant that had died and been removed while she was at the hospital in April. The water ran across the top of the cabinet and dripped on the floor. Mother did not notice.

When Mother did go outside, the forest preserve behind our house seemed to draw her in. Perhaps it was the darkness. Simon and I used to enjoy playing at the edge of it after twilight, catching fireflies in a jar or building blanket tents, but after Mother began walking there, Simon spent the evenings inside or on the front lawn. I stayed back there because sometimes Mother wandered and I would take her by the arm and lead her back to the house.

Mother wore whatever Father told her to wear. Sometimes he was rushed to get to class and would say, "Wear the red dress," and Mother would spend a sweltering July day in heavy wool. She didn't sweat. Sometimes he would not tell her to come downstairs in the morning, and she would remain in the bedroom until he returned. On those days I tried to get Simon at least to go upstairs and look in on her with me; but he just stared at me and shook his head. Father was drinking more, like Uncle Will used to, and he would yell at us for nothing at all. I always cried when Father shouted; but Simon never cried anymore.

Mother never blinked. At first I didn't notice; but then I began to feel uncomfortable when I saw that she never blinked. But it didn't make me love her any less.

Neither Simon nor I could fall asleep at night. Mother used to tuck us in and tell us long stories about a magician named Yandy who took our dog, Baxter, on great adventures when we weren't playing with him. Father didn't make up stories, but he used to read to us from a big book he called Pound's *Cantos*. I didn't understand most of what he read, but the words felt good and I loved the sounds of words he said were Greek. Now nobody checked in on us after our baths. I tried telling stories to Simon for a few nights, but they were no good and Simon asked me to stop.

On the Fourth of July Tommy Wiedermeyer, who had been in my class the year before, drowned in the swimming pool they had just put in. That night we all sat out back and watched the fireworks above the fairgrounds half a mile away. You couldn't see the ground displays because of the forest preserve, but the skyrockets were bright and clear. First you would see the explosion of color and then, four or five seconds later, it seemed, the sound would catch up. I turned to say something to Aunt Helen and saw Mother looking out from the second-story window. Her face was very white against the dark room, and the colors seemed to flow down over her like fluids.

It was not long after the Fourth that I found the dead squirrel. Simon and I had been playing Cavalry and Indians in the forest preserve. We took turns finding each other . . . shooting and dying repeatedly in the weeds until it was time to start over. Only this time I was having trouble finding him. Instead, I found the clearing.

It was a hidden place, surrounded by bushes as thick as our hedge. I was still on my hands and knees from crawling under the branches when I saw the squirrel. It was large and reddish and had been dead for some time. The head had been wrenched around almost backward on the body. Blood had dried near one ear. Its left paw was clenched, but the other lay open on a twig as if it were resting there. Something had taken one eye, but the other stared blackly at the canopy of branches. Its mouth was open slightly, showing surprisingly large teeth gone yellow at the roots. As I watched, an ant came out of the mouth, crossed the dark muzzle, and walked out onto the staring eye.

This is what dead is, I thought.

The bushes vibrated to some unfelt breeze. I was scared to be there and I left, crawling straight ahead and bashing through thick branches that grabbed at my shirt.

In the autumn I went back to Longfellow School, but soon transferred to a private school. The Resurrectionist families were discriminated against in those days. The kids made fun of us or called us names and no one played with us. No one played with us at the new school either, but they didn't call us names.

Our bedroom had no wall switch but an old-fashioned hanging light bulb with a cord. To turn on the light I had to cross half the dark room and feel around in the dark room until I found the cord. Once when Simon was staying up late to do his homework, I went upstairs by myself. I was swinging my arm around in the darkness to find the string when my hand fell on Mother's face. Her teeth felt cool and slick. I pulled my hand back and stood there a minute in the dark before I found the cord and turned on the light.

"Hello, Mother," I said. I sat on the edge of the bed and looked up at her. She was staring at Simon's empty bed. I reached out and took her hand. "I miss you," I said. I said some other things, but the words got all mixed up and sounded stupid, so I just sat there, holding her hand, waiting for some returning pressure. My arm got tired, but I remained sitting there and holding her fingers in mine until Simon came up. He stopped in the doorway and stared at us. I looked down and dropped her hand. After a few minutes she went away.

Father put Baxter to sleep just before Thanksgiving. He was not an old dog, but he acted like one. He was always growling and barking, even at us; and he would never come inside anymore. After he ran away for the third time, the pound called us. Father just said, "Put him to sleep," and hung up the phone. They sent us a bill.

Father's classes had fewer and fewer students and finally he took a sabbatical to write his book on Ezra Pound. He was home all that year, but he didn't write much. Sometimes he would spend the morning down at the library, but he would be home by one o'clock and would watch TV. He would start drinking before dinner and stay in front of the television until really late. Simon and I would stay up with him sometimes; but we didn't like most of the shows.

Simon's dream started about then. He told me about it on the way to school one morning. He said the dream was always the same. When he fell asleep, he would dream that he was still awake, reading a comic book. Then he would start to set the comic on the nightstand, and it would fall on the floor. When he reached down to pick it up, Mother's arm would come out from under the bed and she would grasp his wrist with her white hand. He said her grip was very strong, and somehow he knew that she wanted him under the bed with her. He would hang onto the blankets as hard as he could, but he knew that in a few seconds the bedclothes would slip and he would fall.

He said that last night's dream had finally been a little different. This time Mother had stuck her head out from under the bed. Simon said that it was like when a garage mechanic slides out from under a car. He said she was grinning at him, not smiling but grinning real wide. Simon said that her teeth had been filed down to points.

"Do you ever have dreams like that?" he asked. I knew he was sorry he'd told me.

"No," I said. I loved Mother.

That April the Farley twins from the next block accidentally locked themselves in an abandoned freezer and suffocated. Mrs. Hargill, our cleaning lady, found them, out behind their garage. Thomas Farley had been the only kid who still invited Simon over to his yard. Now Simon only had me.

It was just before Labor Day and the start of school that Simon made plans for us to run away. I didn't want to run away, but I loved Simon. He was my brother.

"Where are we gonna go?"

"We got to get out of here," he said. Which wasn't much of an answer.

But Simon had set aside a bunch of stuff and even picked up a city map. He'd sketched out our path through the forest preserve, across Sherman River at the Laurel Street viaduct, all the way to Uncle Will's house without ever crossing any major streets.

"We can camp out," said Simon. He showed me a length of clothesline he had cut. "Uncle Will will let us be farmhands. When he goes out to his ranch next spring, we can go with him."

We left at twilight. I didn't like leaving right before it got dark, but Simon said that Father wouldn't notice we were gone until late the next morning when he woke up. I carried a small backpack filled with food Simon had sneaked out of the refrigerator. He had some stuff rolled up in a blanket and tied over his back with the piece of clothesline. It was pretty out until we got deeper into the forest preserve. The stream made a gurgling sound like the one that came from Mother's room the night she died. The roots and branches were so thick that Simon had to keep his flashlight on all the time; and that made it seem even darker. We stopped before too long, and Simon strung his rope between two trees. I threw the blanket over it and we both scrabbled around on our hands and knees to find stones.

We ate our bologna sandwiches in the dark while the creek made swallowing noises in the night. We talked a few minutes, but our voices seemed too tiny, and after a while we both fell asleep, on the cold ground with our jackets pulled over us and our heads on the nylon pack and all the forest sounds going on around us.

I woke up in the middle of the night. It was very still. Both of us had huddled down under the jackets, and Simon was snoring. The leaves had stopped stirring, the insects were gone, and even the stream had stopped making noise. The openings of the tent made two brighter triangles in the field of darkness.

I sat with my heart pounding.

There was nothing to see when I moved my head near the opening. But I knew exactly what was out there. I put my head under my jacket and moved away from the side of the tent.

I waited for something to touch me through the blanket. At first I thought of Mother coming after us, of Mother walking through the forest after us with sharp twigs brushing at her eyes. But it wasn't Mother.

The night was cold and heavy around our little tent. It was as black as the eye of that dead squirrel, and it wanted in. For the first time in my life I understood that the darkness did not end with the morning light. My teeth were chattering. I curled up against Simon and stole a little of his heat. His breath came soft and slow against my cheek. After a while I shook him awake and told him we were going home when the sun rose, that I wasn't going with him. He started to argue, but then he heard something in my voice, something he didn't understand, and he only shook his head tiredly and went back to sleep.

In the morning the blanket was wet with dew and our skins felt clammy. We folded things up, left the rocks lying in their rough pattern, and walked home. We did not speak.

Father was sleeping when we got home. Simon threw our stuff in the bedroom and then he went out into the sunlight. I went to the basement.

It was very dark down there, but I sat on the wooden stairs without turning on a light. There was no sound from the shadowed corners, but I knew that Mother was there.

"We ran away, but we came back," I said at last. "It was my idea to come back."

Through the narrow window slats I saw green grass. A sprinkler started up with a loud sigh. Somewhere in the neighborhood, kids were shouting. I paid attention only to the shadows.

"Simon wanted to keep going," I said, "but I made us come back. It was *my* idea to come home."

I sat a few more minutes but couldn't think of anything else to say. Finally I got up, brushed off my pants, and went upstairs to take a nap.

· · · · ·

A week after Labor Day, Father insisted we go to the shore for the weekend. We left on Friday afternoon and drove straight through to Ocean City. Mother sat alone in the rear seat. Father and Aunt Helen rode up front. Simon and I were crowded into the back of the station wagon, but he refused to count cows with me or talk to me or even play with the toy planes I'd brought along.

We stayed at an ancient hotel right on the boardwalk. The other Resurrectionists in Father's Tuesday group recommended the place, but it smelled of age and rot and rats in the walls. The corridors were a faded green, the doors a darker green, and only every third light worked. The halls were a dim maze, and you had to make two turns just to find the elevator. Everyone but Simon stayed inside all day Saturday, sitting in front of the laboring air conditioner and watching television. There were many more of the resurrected around now, and you could hear them shuffling through the dark halls. After sunset they went out to the beach, and we joined them.

I tried to make Mother comfortable. I set the beach towel down for her and turned her to face the sea. By this time the moon had risen and a cool breeze was blowing in. I put Mother's sweater across her shoulders. Behind us the midway splashed lights out over the boardwalk and the roller coaster rumbled and growled.

I would not have left if Father's voice hadn't irritated me so. He talked too loudly, laughed at nothing, and took deep drinks from a bottle in a brown bag. Aunt Helen said very little but watched Father sadly and tried to smile when he laughed. Mother was sitting peacefully, so I excused myself and walked up to the midway to hunt for Simon. I was lonely without him. The place was empty of families and children, but the rides were still running. Every few minutes there would be a roar and screams from the few riders as the roller coaster took its steepest plunge. I ate a hot dog and looked around, but Simon was nowhere to be found.

While walking back along the beach, I saw Father lean over and give Aunt Helen a quick kiss on the cheek. Mother had wandered away, and I quickly offered to go find her just to hide the tears of rage in my eyes. I walked up the beach past the place where the two teenagers had drowned the previous weekend. There were a few of the resurrected around. They were sitting near the water with their families; but no sight of Mother. I was thinking of heading back when I thought I noticed some movement under the boardwalk.

It was incredibly dark under there. Narrow strips of light, broken into weird sorts of patterns by the wooden posts and cross-braces, dropped down from cracks in the walkway overhead. Footsteps and rumbles from the midway sounded like fists pounding against a coffin lid. I stopped then. I had a sudden image of dozens of them being there in the darkness. Dozens, Mother among them, with thin patterns of light crossing them so that you could make out a hand or shirt or staring eye. But they were not there. Mother was not there. Something else was.

I don't know what made me look up. Footsteps from above. A slight turning, turning; something turning in the shadows. I could see where he had climbed the cross-braces, wedged a sneaker here, lifted himself there to the wide timber. It would not have been hard. We'd climbed like that a thousand times. I stared right into his face, but it was the clothesline I recognized first.

Father quit teaching after Simon's death. He never went back after the sabbatical, and his notes for the Pound book sat stacked in the basement with last year's newspapers. The Resurrectionists helped him find a job as a custodian in a nearby shopping mall, and he usually didn't get home before two in the morning.

After Christmas I went away to a boarding school that was two states away. The Resurrectionists had opened the Institute by this time, and more and more families were turning to them. I was later able to go to the University on a full scholarship. Despite the covenant, I rarely came home during those years. Father was drunk during my few visits. Once I drank with him and we sat in the kitchen and cried together. His hair was almost gone except for a few white stands on the sides, and his eyes were sunken in a lined face. The alcohol had left innumerable broken blood vessels in his cheeks, and he looked as though he were wearing more makeup than Mother.

Mrs. Hargill called three days before graduation. Father had filled the bath with warm water and then drawn the razor blade up the vein rather than across it. He had read his Plutarch. It had been two days before the housekeeper found him, and when I arrived home the next evening the bathtub was still caked with congealed rings. After the funeral I went through all of his old papers and found a journal he had been keeping for several years. I burned it along with the stacks of notes for his unfinished book.

Our policy with the Institute was honored despite the circumstances, and that helped me through the next few years. My career is more than a job to me—I believe in what I do and I'm good at it. It was my idea to lease some of the empty school buildings for our new neighborhood centers.

Last week I was caught in a traffic jam, and when I inched the car up to the accident site and saw the small figure covered by a blanket and the broken glass everywhere, I also noticed that a crowd of *them* had gathered on the curb. There are so many of them these days.

I used to have shares in a condominium in one of the last lighted sections of the city, but when our old house came up for sale I jumped at the chance to buy it. I've kept many of the old furnishings and replaced others so that it's almost the way it used to be. Keeping up an old house like that is expensive, but I don't spend my money foolishly. After work a lot of guys from the Institute go out to bars, but I don't. After I've put away my equipment and scrubbed down the steel tables, I go straight home. My family is there. They're waiting for me.

Women Troubled
and Troubling

There where we used to sleep
Something stabs my foot—
The comb of my late wife.
—*Patterned on a haiku by Taniguchi Buson
(1715–1783)*

Passeur

Robert W. Chambers

Though the American writer ROBERT W. CHAMBERS *(1865–1933) wrote more than seventy genre novels, he is chiefly remembered today for* The King in Yellow, *an 1895 collection of related short stories of psychological terror that influenced the work of H. P. Lovecraft. The following eerie reflection on deathless love, however, is not from that volume. According to scholar Sam Moskowitz, it appeared two years later in the October issue of* The English Illustrated Magazine.

WHEN HE HAD FINISHED HIS PIPE he tapped the brier bowl against the chimney until the ashes powdered the charred log smouldering across the andirons. Then he sat back in his chair, absently touched the hot pipe-bowl with the tip of each finger until it grew cool enough to be dropped into his coat pocket.

Twice he raised his eyes to the little American clock ticking upon the mantel. He had half an hour to wait.

The three candles that lighted the room might be trimmed to advantage; this would give him something to do. A pair of scissors lay open upon the bureau, and he rose and picked them up. For a while he stood dreamily shutting and opening the scissors, his eyes roaming about the room. There was an easel in the corner, and a pile of dusty canvases behind it; behind the canvases there was a shadow—that gray, menacing shadow that never moved.

When he had trimmed each candle he wiped the smoky scissors on a paint rag and flung them on the bureau again. The clock pointed to ten; he had been occupied exactly three minutes.

The bureau was littered with neckties, pipes, combs and brushes, matches, reels and flybooks, collars, shirt studs, a new pair of Scotch shooting stockings, and a woman's workbasket.

He picked out all the neckties, folded them once, and hung them over a bit of twine that stretched across the looking-glass; the shirt studs he shovelled into the top drawer along with brushes, combs, and stockings; the reels and fly-books he dusted with his handkerchief and placed methodically along the mantel shelf. Twice he stretched out his hand toward the woman's workbasket, but his hand fell to his side again, and he turned away into the room staring at the dying fire.

Outside the snow-sealed window a shutter broke loose and banged monotonously, until he flung open the panes and fastened it. The soft, wet snow, that had choked the window-panes all day, was frozen hard now, and he had to break the polished crust before he could find the rusty shutter hinge.

He leaned out for a moment, his numbed hands resting on the snow, the roar of a rising snow-squall in his ears; and out across the desolate garden and stark hedgerow he saw the flat black river spreading through the gloom.

A candle sputtered and snapped behind him; a sheet of drawing paper fluttered across the floor, and he closed the panes and turned back into the room, both hands in his worn pockets.

The little American clock on the mantel ticked and ticked, but the hands lagged, for he had not been occupied five minutes in all. He went up to the mantel and watched the hands of the clock. A minute—longer than a year to him—crept by.

Around the room the furniture stood ranged—a chair or two of yellow pine, a table, the easel, and in one corner the broad curtained bed; and behind each lay shadows, menacing shadows that never moved.

A little pale flame started up from the smoking log on the andirons; the room sang with the sudden hiss of escaping wood gases. After a little the back of the log caught fire; jets of blue flared up here and there with mellow sounds like the lighting of gas-burners in a row, and in a moment a thin sheet of yellow flame wrapped the whole charred log.

Then the shadows moved; not the shadows behind the furniture—

they never moved—but other shadows, thin, gray, confusing, that came and spread their slim patterns all around him, and trembled and trembled.

He dared not step or tread upon them, they were too real; they meshed the floor around his feet, they ensnared his knees, they fell across his breast like ropes. Some night, in the silence of the moors, when wind and river were still, he feared these strands of shadow might tighten—creep higher around his throat and tighten. But even then he knew that those other shadows would never move, those gray shapes that knelt crouching in every corner.

When he looked up at the clock again ten minutes had struggled past. Time was disturbed in the room; the strands of shadow seemed entangled among the hands of the clock, dragging them back from their rotation. He wondered if the shadows would strangle Time, some still night when the wind and the flat river were silent.

There grew a sudden chill across the floor; the cracks of the boards let it in. He leaned down and drew his sabots toward him from their place near the andirons, and slipped them over his chaussons; and as he straightened up, his eyes mechanically sought the mantel above, where in the dusk another pair of sabots stood, little slender, delicate sabots, carved from red beech. A year's dust grayed their surface; a year's rust dulled the silver band across the instep. He said this to himself aloud, knowing that it was within a few minutes of the year.

His own sabots came from Mort-Dieu; they were shaved square and banded with steel. But in days past he had thought that no sabot in Mort-Dieu was delicate enough to touch the instep of the Mort-Dieu passeur. So he sent to the shore lighthouse, and they sent to Lorient, where the women are coquettish and show their hair under the coiffe, and wear dainty sabots; and in this town, where vanity corrupts and there is much lace on coiffe and collarette, a pair of delicate sabots was found, banded with silver and chiselled in red beech. The sabots stood on the mantel above the fire now, dusty and tarnished.

There was a sound from the window, the soft murmur of snow blotting glass panes. The wind, too, muttered under the eaves. Presently it would begin to whisper to him from the chimney—he knew it—and he held his hands over his ears and stared at the clock.

In the hamlet of Mort-Dieu the panes sing all day of the sea secrets, but in the night the ghosts of little gray birds fill the branches, singing of the sunshine of past years. He heard the song as he sat, and he crushed his hands over his ears; but the gray birds joined with the wind in the chimney, and he heard all that he dared not hear, and he thought all that he dared not hope or think, and the swift tears scalded his eyes.

In Mort-Dieu the nights are longer than anywhere on earth; he knew it—why should he not know? This had been so for a year; it was different before. There were so many things different before; days and nights vanished like minutes then; the pines told no secrets of the sea, and the gray birds had not yet come to Mort-Dieu. Also, there was Jeanne, passeur at the Carmes.

When he first saw her she was poling the square, flatbottomed ferry-skiff from the Carmes to Mort-Dieu, a red skirt fluttering just below her knees. The next time he saw her he had to call to her across the placid river. "Ohe! Ohe! passeur!" She came, poling the flat skiff, her deep blue eyes fixed pensively on him, the scarlet skirt and kerchief idly flapping in the April wind. Then day followed day when the far call "Passeur!" grew clearer and more joyous, and the faint answering cry, "I come!" rippled across the water like music tinged with laughter. Then spring came, and with spring came love—love, carried free across the ferry from the Carmes to Mort-Dieu.

The flame above the charred log whistled, flickered, and went out in a jet of wood vapour, only to play like lightning above the gas and relight again. The clock ticked more loudly, and the song from the pines filled the room. But in his straining eyes a summer landscape was reflected, where white clouds sailed and white foam curled under the square bow of a little skiff. And he pressed his numbed hands tighter to his ears to drown the cry, "Passeur! Passeur!"

And now for a moment the clock ceased ticking. It was time to go—who but he should know it, he who went out into the night swinging his lantern? And he went. He had gone each night from the first—from that first strange winter evening when a strange voice answered him across the river, the voice of the new passeur. He had never heard *her* voice again.

So he passed down the windy wooden stairs, lantern hanging lighted in his hand, and stepped out into the storm. Through sheets of drifting snow, over heaps of frozen seaweed and icy drift he moved, shifting his lantern right and left, until its glimmer on the water warned him. Then he called out into the night, "Passeur!" The frozen spray spattered his face and crusted the lantern: he heard the distant boom of breakers beyond the bar, and the noise of mighty winds among the seaward cliffs.

"Passeur!"

Across the broad flat river, black as a sea of pitch, a tiny light sparked a moment. Again he cried, "Passeur!"

"I come!"

He turned ghastly white, for it was her voice—or was he crazy?—and he sprang waist deep into the icy current and cried out again, but his voice ended in a sob.

Slowly through the snow the flat skiff took shape, creeping nearer and nearer. But she was not at the pole—he saw that: there was a tall, thin man, shrouded to the eyes in oilskin; and he leaped into the boat and bade the ferryman hasten.

Halfway across he rose in the skiff, and called, "Jeanne!" But the roar of the storm and the thrashing of the icy waves drowned his voice. Yet he heard her again, and she called to him by name.

When at last the boat grated upon the invisible shore, he lifted his lantern, trembling, stumbling among the rocks, and calling to her, as though his voice could silence the voice that had spoken a year ago that night. And it could not. He sank shivering upon his knees, and looked out into the darkness, where an ocean rolled across a world. Then his stiff lips moved, and he repeated her name, but the hand of the ferryman fell gently upon his head.

And when he raised his eyes he saw that the ferryman was Death.

Putting the Devil into Hell

Giovanni Boccaccio

Since subtlety and erotic humor are seldom linked in today's frank market-place, it may come as a surprise that till recently English translations of the great Italian bawdy short story collection The Decameron *by* GIOVANNI BOCCACCIO *(1313–1375) always left the following droll tale in the original Latin with the mendacious excuse that "the language of magic" had grown too corrupt to render felicitously. To wax modern—not!*

IN THE CITY of Capsa in Barbary, there lived a very rich man who, among his other children, had a fair and winsome young daughter, by name Alibech. She, not being a Christian and hearing many Christians who abode in the town mightily extol the Christian faith and the service of God, one day questioned one of them in what manner one might avail to serve God with the least hindrance. The other answered that they best served God who most strictly eschewed the things of the world, as those did who had betaken them into the solitudes of the deserts of Thebaïs. The girl, who was maybe fourteen years old and very simple, moved by no ordered desire, but by some childish fancy, set off next morning by stealth and all alone to go to the desert of Thebaïs, without letting any know her intent. After some days, her desire persisting, she won, with no little toil, to the deserts in question and, seeing a hut afar off, went thither and found at the door a holy man, who marveled to see her there and asked her what she sought. She replied that, being inspired of God, she went seeking to enter into His service and was now in quest of one who should teach her how it behooved to serve Him.

The worthy man, seeing her young and very fair and fearing lest, an he entertained her, the devil should beguile him, commended her pious intent and, giving her somewhat to eat of roots of herbs and wild apples and dates and to drink of water, said to her, "Daughter mine, not far hence is a holy man, who is a much better master than I of that which thou goest seeking; do thou betake thyself to him;" and put her in the way. However, when she reached the man in question, she had of him the same answer and, faring farther, came to the cell of a young hermit, a very devout and good man, whose name was Rustico and to whom she made the same request as she had done to the others. He, having a mind to make a trial of his own constancy, sent her not away, as the others had done, but received her into his cell, and the night being come, he made her a little bed of palm fronds and bade her lie down to rest thereon. This done, temptations tarried not to give battle to his powers of resistance, and he, finding himself grossly deceived by these latter, turned tail, without awaiting many assaults, and confessed himself beaten; then, laying aside devout thoughts and orisons and mortifications, he fell to revolving in his memory the youth and beauty of the damsel and bethinking himself what course he should take with her, so as to win to that which he desired of her, without her taking him for a debauched fellow.

Accordingly, having sounded her with sundry questions, he found that she had never known man and was in truth as simple as she seemed. Wherefore he bethought him how, under color of the service of God, he might bring her to his pleasure. In the first place he showed her with many words how great an enemy the devil was of God, and afterwards gave her to understand that the most acceptable service that could be rendered to God was to put the devil into hell, whereto He had condemned him. The girl asked him how this might be done; and he, "Thou shalt soon know that; do thou but as thou shalt see me do." So saying, he proceeded to put off the few garments he had and abode stark naked, as likewise did the girl, whereupon he fell on his knees, as he would pray, and caused her abide over against himself.

Matters standing thus and Rustico being more than ever inflamed in his desires to see her so fair, there came the resurrection of the flesh, which Alibech observing and marveling, "Rustico," quoth she, "what is that I see on thee which thrusteth forth thus and which I have not?" "Faith, daughter mine," answered he, "this is the devil thereof I bespoke thee; and see now he giveth me such sore annoy that I can scarce put up with it." Then said the girl, "Now praised be God! I see I fare better than thou, in that I have none of yonder devil." "True," rejoined Rustico, "but thou hast otherwhat that I have not, and thou hast it instead of this." "What is that?" asked Alibech; and he, "Thou hast Hell, and I tell thee methinketh God hath sent thee hither for my soul's health, for that, whenas this devil doth me this annoy, an it please thee have so much compassion on me as to suffer me put him back into Hell, thou wilt give me the utmost solacement and wilt do God a very great pleasure and service, so indeed thou be come into these parts to do as thou sayst."

The girl answered in good faith, "Marry, father mine, since I have Hell be it whensoever it pleaseth thee;" whereupon quoth Rustico, "Daughter, blessed be thou; let us go then and put him back there, so he may after leave me in peace." So saying, he laid her on one of their little beds and taught her how she should do to imprison that accursed one of God. The girl, who had never yet put any devil in Hell, for the first time felt some little pain; wherefore she said to Rustico, "Certes, father mine, this same devil must be an ill thing and an enemy in very deed of God, for that it irketh Hell itself, let be otherwhat, when he is put back therein." "Daughter," answered Rustico, "it will not always happen thus;" and to the end that this should not happen, six times, or ever they stirred from the bed, they put him in Hell again, insomuch that for the nonce they so took the conceit out of his head that he willingly abode at peace. But, it returning to him again and again the ensuing days and the obedient girl still lending herself to take it out of him, it befell that the sport began to please her and she said to Rustico, "I see now that those good people in Capsa spoke sooth, when they avouched that it was so sweet a thing to serve God; for, certes, I remember me not to have ever done aught that afforded me such pleasance and delight as putting the devil in Hell; wherefore methinketh that whoso applieth himself unto aught other than God His service is a fool."

Accordingly, she came ofttimes to Rustico and said to him, "Father mine, I came here to serve God and not to abide idle; let us go put the devil in Hell." Which doing, she said whiles, "Rustico, I know not why the devil fleeth away from Hell; for, an he abode there as willingly as Hell receiveth him and holdeth him, he would never come forth therefrom." The girl, then, on this wise often inviting Rustico and exhorting him to the service of God, so took the bombast out of his doublet that he felt cold what time mother had sweated. Wherefore he fell to telling her that the devil was not to be chastised nor put into Hell, save whenas he should lift up his head for pride. "And we," added he, "by God's grace, have so baffled him that he prayeth our Lord to suffer him abide in peace;" and on this wise be for a while imposed silence on her. However, when she saw that he required her not of putting the devil into Hell, she said to him one day, "Rustico, even if thy devil be chastened and give thee no more annoy, my Hell letteth me not be. Wherefore thou wilt do well to aid me with thy devil in abating the raging of my Hell, even as with my Hell I have helped thee take the conceit out of thy devil."

Rustico, who lived on roots and water, could ill avail to answer her calls and told her that it would need overmany devils to appease Hell, but he would do what he might thereof. Accordingly, he satisfied her bytimes, but so seldom it was but casting a bean into the lion's mouth. Whereat the girl, believing she served not God as diligently as she would fain have done, murmured somewhat. Whilst this debate was going on between Rustico, his devil, and Alibech, her Hell, for overmuch desire on the one part and lack of power on the other, it befell that a fire broke out in Capsa and burnt Alibech's father in his own house, with as many children and other family as he had. By reason of this, she became heir to all his estate. Thereupon a young man called Neerbale, who had spent all his substance in gallantry, hearing that she was alive, set out in search of her. Finding her, before the court had laid hands upon her father's estate, to Rustico's great satisfaction but against her own will, he brought her back to Capsa, where he took her to wife and succeeded, in her right, to the ample inheritance of her father.

There, being asked by the women at what she served God in the desert, she answered (Neerbale having not yet lain with her) that she served Him at putting the devil in Hell and that Neerbale had done a grievous sin in that he had taken her from such service. The ladies asked, "How putteth one the devil in Hell?" And the girl, what with words and what with gestures, expounded it to them; whereat they set up so great a laughing that they laugh yet and said, "Give yourself no concern, my child; nay, for that is done here also and Neerbale will serve our Lord full well with thee at this." Therefore, telling it from one to another throughout the city, they brought it to a common saying there that the most acceptable service one could render to God was to put the devil in Hell, which byword, having passed the sea hither, is yet current here. Wherefore do all you young ladies, who have need of God's grace, learn to put the devil in Hell, for that this is highly acceptable to Him and pleasing to both parties and much good may grow and ensue therefrom.

The Lady in the Tower

Anne McCaffrey

Shakespeare admitted no impediments to the marriage of true minds, but his lovers were not telepaths stationed in deep space facing a hostile takeover by a race of aliens! ANNE MCCAFFREY *is the Hugo and Nebula award-winning author of the* Dragonflight *series of novels, the* Chronicles of Pern, *the* "Crystal Singer" *tales and a recent Tor Books novel,* The Girl Who Heard Dragons. *"The Lady in the Tower," from the April 1959 issue of* The Magazine of Fantasy and Science Fiction, *is the first story about characters and situations that she developed in three books:* Damia, Damia's Children *and* Lyon's Pride.

W HEN SHE CAME STORMING toward the station, its personnel mentally and literally ducked. Mentally because she was apt to forget to shield. Literally because the Rowan was apt to slam around desks and filing cabinets when she got upset. Today, however, she was in fair command of herself and merely stamped up the stairs into the tower. A vague rumble of noisy thoughts tossed around the first floor of the station for a few minutes, but the computer and analogue men ignored the depressing effects with the gratitude of those saved from greater disaster.

From the residue of her passage, Brian Ackerman, the stationmaster, caught the impression of intense purple frustration. He was basically only a T-9, but constant association with the Rowan had widened his

area of perception. Ackerman appreciated this side effect of his position
—when he was anywhere else but at the station.

He had been trying to quit Callisto for more than five years, with no
success. Federal Telepathers and Teleporters, Inc., had established a routine regarding his continuous applications for transfer. The first one
handed in each quarter was ignored; the second brought an adroitly
worded reply on how sensitive and crucial a position he held at Callisto
Prime Station; his third—often a violently worded demand—always got
him a special shipment of scotch and tobacco; his fourth—a piteous wail
—brought the Section Supervisor out for a face-to-face chat and, only
then, a few discreet words to the Rowan.

Ackerman was positive she always knew the full story before the
Supervisor finally approached her. It pleased her to be difficult, but the
one time Ackerman discarded protocol and snarled at her himself, she
had mended her ways for a whole quarter. It had reluctantly dawned on
Ackerman then that she must like him, and he had used this to advantage since. He had lasted eight years, as against five stationmasters in
three months before his appointment.

Each of the twenty-three station staff members had gone through a
similar shuffling until the Rowan had accepted them. It took a very
delicate balance of mental talent, personality and intelligence to achieve
the proper *gestalt* needed to move giant liners and tons of freight. Federal Tel and Tel had only five complete Primes—five T-1's—each strate-
gically placed in a station near the five major and most central stars to
effect the best possible transmission of commerce and communications
throughout the sprawling Nine-Star League. The lesser staff positions at
each Prime Station were filled by personnel who could only teleport, or
telepath. It was FT&T's dream to someday provide instantaneous transmission of anything anywhere, anytime. Until that day, FT&T was extremely careful with its five T-1's, putting up with their vagaries like the
doting owners of so many golden geese. If keeping the Rowan happy
had meant changing the entire lesser personnel twice daily, it would
probably have been done. As it happened, the present staff had been
intact for over two years and only minor soothing had been necessary.

Ackerman hoped that only minor soothing would be needed today.
The Rowan had been peevish for a week, and even he was feeling the
backlash. So far no one knew why the Rowan was upset.

READY FOR THE LINER, her thought lashed out so piercingly that Ackerman was sure everyone in the ship waiting outside had heard her. But he switched the intercom in to the ship's captain.

"I heard," the captain said wryly. "Give me a five-count and then set us off."

Ackerman didn't bother to relay the message to the Rowan. In her mood, she'd be hearing straight to Capella and back. The generator men were hopping around their switchboards, bringing the booster field up to peak, while she impatiently revved up the launching units to push-off strength. She was well ahead of the standard timing, and the pent-up power seemed to keen through the station. The countdown came fast as the singing power note increased past endurable limits.

ROWAN, NO TRICKS, Ackerman cautioned her.

He caught her mental laugh, and barked a warning to the captain. He hoped the man had heard it, because the Rowan was on zero before he could finish, and the ship was gone beyond radio transmission distance in seconds.

The keen of the dynamos lost only a minute edge of sharpness before they picked up to peak again. The lots on the launchers started snapping out into space as fast as they could be set up. Then loads came rocketing into receiving areas from other Prime Stations, and the ground crews hustled in and out with rerouting and hold orders. The power-note settled to a bearable hum as the Rowan worked out her mood without losing the efficient and accurate thrust that made her FT&T's best Prime.

One of the ground crew signalled a frantic yellow across the board, then red as ten tons of cargo from Earth settled on the Priority Receiving cradle. The waybill said Deneb VIII, which was at the Rowan's limit. But the shipment was marked Rush, Emergency—priority medicine for a virulent plague on the colony planet. And the waybill specified direct transmission.

WELL, WHERE'RE MY COORDINATES AND MY PLACEMENT PHOTO? snapped the Rowan. I CAN'T THRUST BLIND, YOU KNOW, AND WE'VE ALWAYS REROUTED FOR DENEB VIII.

Bill Powers was flipping through the indexed catalogue, but the Rowan reached out and grabbed the photo.

ZOWIE, DO I HAVE TO LAND ALL THAT MASS THERE MYSELF?

NO, LAZYBONES, I'LL PICK IT UP AT 24.578.82—THAT NICE LITTLE CONVE-

NIENT BLACK DWARF MIDWAY. YOU WON'T HAVE TO STRAIN A SINGLE CONVO-LUTION. The lazy, masculine voice drawled in everyone's mind.

The silence was deafening.

WELL, I'LL BE . . . came from the Rowan.

YOU'VE GOT NO CHOICE, SWEETHEART—JUST PUSH THAT NICE LITTLE PACK-AGE OUT MY WAY. OR IS IT TOO MUCH FOR YOU? the lazy voice drawled back.

YOU'LL GET YOUR PACKAGE! snapped the Rowan and the dynamos keened just once piercingly as the ten tons disappeared out of the cradle.

WHY, YOU LITTLE MINX . . . SLOW IT DOWN OR I'LL BURN YOUR EARS OFF!

COME OUT AND CATCH IT! the Rowan laughed, but her laughter broke off with a gasp of surprise and even Ackerman could feel her slamming up her shields.

I WANT THAT STUFF IN ONE PIECE, NOT SMEARED A MILLIMETER THIN ON THE SURFACE, DEARIE, the voice replied sternly. OKAY, I'VE GOT IT. THANKS. WE NEED THIS.

HEY, WHO THE BLAZES ARE YOU? WHAT'S YOUR PLACEMENT?

DENEB SENDER, DEAR GIRL, AND A BUSY LITTLE BOY. TA TA.

The silence was broken only by the whine of the dynamos dying to an idle hum.

Not a hint of what the Rowan was thinking came through, but Ackerman could pick up the aura of incredulity, shock, speculation and satisfaction that pervaded the thoughts of everyone else in the station. The Rowan had met her match. No one except a T-1 could have projected that far. There'd been no mention of another T-1 at FT&T and, as far as Ackerman knew, FT&T's five T-1's were the only ones known. Still, Deneb was now in its third generation, and colonial peculiarities had produced the Rowan in two.

"Hey, fellows," Ackerman cautioned the crew, "sock 'em up. She's not going to like your drift." Shields went up dutifully but the grins did not fade, and Powers even started to whistle.

Another yellow flag came up from a ground man at the Altair hurdle, and the waybill designated live shipment to Betelgeuse. The dynamos whined noisily and then the launcher was empty. Whatever might be going through her mind at the moment, the Rowan was still doing her work.

It was an odd day all told, and Ackerman didn't know whether to be thankful or not. He had no precedents to go on and the Rowan wasn't leaking any clues. She spun the day's lot in and out with careless ease. By the time Jupiter's big bulk had moved around to blanket out-System traffic, Callisto's day was over, and she still wasn't off-power as much as decibel one. The in-Sun traffic was finished with, Ackerman signed off for the day, and the computer banks and dynamos were slapped off . . . but the Rowan did not come down.

Ray Loftus came over to sit on the edge of Ackerman's desk. They took out smokes.

"I was going to ask her Highness to give me a lift home," Loftus said. "But I dunno, now. Got a date with—" He disappeared. A moment later, Ackerman could see him by a personnel carrier. Not only had he been set gently down but various small necessities, among them a shaving kit, floated out of nowhere to a neat pile in the carrier. Ray even had time to settle himself before the hatch sealed and he was whisked off.

Powers came over. "She's sure in a funny mood," he said. When the Rowan got peevish, few of the men at the station asked her to transport them to Earth. She was psychologically committed to staying planetbound, and resented the fact that lesser talents had the ability to be moved about through space without traumatic shock.

ANYONE ELSE?

Adler and Toglia spoke up, and promptly disappeared together.

Ackerman and Powers exchanged looks they hastily suppressed as the Rowan appeared before them smiling. It was the first time that particular expression had crossed her face in two weeks, and it was a welcome and totally unexpected relief to Ackerman.

She smiled, but she said nothing. She took a drag of Ackerman's cigarette and handed it back with a thank you.

The Rowan, for all her temperament, acted with propriety face-to-face. She had grown up with her skill, carefully taught by the old and original T-1, Siglen, the Altairan. She'd had it drilled into her that it might alienate the less gifted to be manhandled by her talent. She might cut corners by "reaching" things during business hours, but she refrained at other times.

"The big boys mention our Denebian friend before, ever?" she asked too casually.

Ackerman shook his head. "Those planets are three generations colonized, though. You came out from Altair in two."

"That could explain it. But there isn't even an FT&T station there."

"Not even a proposed one?" Powers asked in astonishment.

"Too far off the beaten track." She shook her head. "I checked it. All Center knows is they received an urgent call about a virus, giving a rundown on the syndrome and symptoms. Lab came up with a serum, batched it, and packed it. They were assured there was someone capable of picking it up and taking it the rest of the way past 24.578.82 if a Prime could get it there. And that's all anybody knows. After all, Deneb VIII isn't very big, yet."

OH, WE'RE BIG ENOUGH, SWEETHEART, drawled the voice again. SORRY TO GET YOU AFTER HOURS, OLD THING, BUT I CAN'T SEEM TO GET IN TO TERRA AND I HEARD YOU COLORING THE ATMOSPHERE.

WHAT'S WRONG? the Rowan shot back. DID YOU SMEAR YOUR SERUM AFTER ALL THAT BIG TALK?

SMEAR IT HELL, I'VE BEEN DRINKING IT. WE'VE GOT SOME ET VISITORS. THEY THINK THEY'RE EXTERMINATORS. LEASTWISE, WE'VE GOT THIRTY UFO HERE, PERCHED FOUR THOUSAND MILES UP. THAT BATCH OF SERUM YOU WAFTED OUT TO ME THIS MORNING WAS AN ANTIBIOTIC FOR THE SIXTH VIRUS WE'VE BEEN SOCKED WITH IN THE LAST TWO WEEKS. SOON AS OUR BOYS WHIP UP SOMETHING TO KNOCK OUT ONE, ANOTHER ONE TAKES ITS PLACE. IT'S ALWAYS WORSE THAN THE ONE BEFORE. WE'VE LOST 25% OF OUR POPULATION ALREADY, AND THIS LAST ONE WAS A BEAUT. I WANT TWO TOP GERMDOGS OUT HERE ON THE DOUBLE, AND ABOUT THREE PATROL SQUADRONS. WE'RE FLAT ON OUR BACKS NOW, AND OUR FRIENDS WON'T SETTLE FOR JUST HOVERING AROUND AND DOUSING US WITH NASTY BUGS MUCH LONGER. THEY'RE GOING TO START BLOWING HOLES IN US ANY MINUTE NOW. SO SORT OF PUSH THE WORD ALONG TO EARTH, WILL YOU, OLD THING?

I'LL RELAY, NATURALLY. DON'T YOU HAVE A PRIORITY CALL SIGNAL ASSIGNED TO YOU?

WHY SHOULD I? I'M NOT FT&T.

YOU WILL BE SOON, IF I KNOW MY BOSSES.

YOU MAY KNOW YOUR BOSSES, COOKIE, BUT YOU DON'T KNOW ME.

THAT CAN ALWAYS BE ARRANGED.

THIS IS NO TIME FOR FLIRTING. GET THAT MESSAGE THROUGH FOR ME LIKE A GOOD GIRL.

WHICH MESSAGE?

THE ONE I JUST GAVE YOU.

THAT OLD ONE? THEY SAY YOU CAN HAVE TWO GERMDOGS IN THE MORN-ING, AS SOON AS WE CLEAR JUPITER. BUT EARTH SAYS NO SQUADRONS. HAVE TO WAIT FOR ARMED ATTACK.

YOU CAN DOUBLE-TALK TOO, HUH? YOU'RE TALENTED. BUT THE MORNING DOES US NO GOOD. NOW IS WHEN WE NEED THEM. CAN'T YOU SLING THEM . . . NO, THEY MIGHT LEAVE A FEW IMPORTANT ATOMS OR SOMETHING IN JUPITER'S MASS. BUT I'VE GOT TO HAVE SOME PRETTY POTENT HELP. AND IF SIX VIRUSES DON'T CONSTITUTE ARMED ATTACK, I'M AT A LOSS FOR A DEFINITION OF WHAT WE'RE UNDER.

MISSILES CONSTITUTE ARMED ATTACK, recited the Rowan primly.

I'LL NOTIFY MY FRIENDS UP THERE. MISSILES WOULD BE PREFERABLE—THEM I CAN SEE. I NEED THOSE GERMDOGS *now*. CAN'T YOU TURN YOUR SWEET LITTLE MIND TO A SOLUTION?

AS YOU MENTIONED, IT'S AFTER HOURS.

BY THE HORSEHEAD, WOMAN! The drawl was replaced by a cutting roar. THIS IS DOUBLE CRASH PRIORITY!

LOOK, AFTER HOURS HERE MEANS WE'RE BEHIND JUPITER . . . BUT . . . WAIT . . . HOW DEEP IS YOUR RANGE?

I HONESTLY DON'T KNOW. And doubt crept into the bodiless voice in their minds.

"Ackerman," snapped the Rowan.

"I've been listening."

HANG ON, DENEB. I'VE GOT AN IDEA. I BELIEVE I CAN GET YOU YOUR GERMDOGS. OPEN TO ME IN HALF AN HOUR.

The Rowan whirled on Ackerman. "I want my shell." Her brilliant eyes were flashing and her face was alight. "Afra!"

The station's T-4, a yellow-eyed, handsome Capellan, raised his head from where he had been watching her quietly. Except for the Rowan herself, Afra was the staff's most talented member.

"Yes, Rowan."

The Rowan's brilliant eyes were flashing, her face alight as she charged into the problem. She frowned faintly as she realized the station men were grinning at her. But the dynamos were warming up, and her special shell was waiting on its launching rack. The miraculous smile that always shocked Ackerman with its hint of passion lit her sharp face as she looked over each of her team men.

"Launch me slow over Jupiter's curve, Afra. Then I'll want to draw heavy. Nice and real slow, friend," she cautioned. Like all Primes, she simply didn't have the fortitude to launch herself through space. Her one trip from Altair to Callisto had almost driven her mad. Only severe self-discipline had conditioned her even to riding a shell a short way off Callisto.

She gathered herself and disappeared to the launcher. In the shell, she settled daintily into the shock couch. The moment the lock whistle shut off she could feel the ship launching gently, gently away from Callisto. Only when the ship had swung into position over Jupiter's great curve did she answer the priority call coming in from Earth Central.

NOW WHAT THE BILLY BLAZES ARE YOU DOING, ROWAN? Reidinger, the FT&T Central Prime, cracked his voice across the void. HAVE YOU LOST WHAT'S LEFT OF YOUR PRECIOUS MIND?

SHE'S DOING ME A FAVOR, Deneb said crisply, joining them.

WHO'N HELL'RE YOU? snapped Reidinger. Then, in shocked surprise: DENEB! HOW'D YOU GET OUT THERE?

WISHFUL THINKING. HEY, PUSH ME OUT THOSE GERMDOGS TO MY PRETTY FRIEND HERE, HUH?

NOW, WAIT A MINUTE! YOU'RE GOING A LITTLE TOO FAR, DENEB. YOU CAN'T BURN OUT MY BEST GIRL WITH AN UNBASED SEND LIKE THAT.

OH, I'LL PICK IT UP MIDWAY, LIKE THOSE ANTIBIOTICS THIS MORNING.

DENEB, WHAT'S THIS BUSINESS WITH ANTIBIOTICS AND GERMDOGS? WHAT'RE YOU COOKING UP OUT THERE IN THAT HEATHENISH HOLE?

OH, WE'RE FIGHTING A FEW PLAGUES WITH ONE HAND AND KEEPING THIRTY BOGEY ET's UPSTAIRS. He gave them a look with his vision at an enormous hospital, with a continuous stream of airborne ambulances coming in; at crowded wards, grim-faced nurses and doctors, and uncomfortably high piles of sheeted, still figures.

WELL, I'M NOT SURPRISED YOU NEED HELP. ALL RIGHT. YOU CAN HAVE ANYTHING YOU WANT—WITHIN REASON. BUT I WANT A FULL REPORT.

WHAT ABOUT THOSE PATROL SQUADRONS.

NO! ABSOLUTELY NO PATROL SQUADRONS. IT DOESN'T LOOK TO ME LIKE THOSE ET's ARE GOING TO COME DOWN. THEY WERE HOPING FOR A SOFT TOUCH. YOU'RE SHOWING 'EM DIFFERENT. THEY'LL GIVE UP AND GET OUT, NOW.

WISH YOU WERE HERE WITH ME TO WAVE 'EM BYE-BYE, Deneb said.

Reidinger ignored him. GERMDOGS'RE SEALED, ROWAN. PICK 'EM UP AND THROW 'EM OUT, he said, and signed off.

Rowan—that's a pretty name, mused Deneb.

I'm working, boy, she said absently. She had followed along Reidinger's initial push, and picked up the two personnel carriers as they materialized beside her shell. She pressed into the station dynamos and gathered up strength. The generators whined, and she pushed out. The carriers disappeared.

They're coming in, Rowan. Thanks a lot.

A passionate and tender kiss was blown to her across eighteen light years of space. She tried to follow after the carriers and pick up his touch again, but he was no longer receiving.

She sank back in her couch. Deneb's sudden appearance had disconcerted her. All of the Primes were isolated by their high talents, but the Rowan was more alone than any of them.

Siglen, the Altairan Prime who had discovered her as a mere child and carefully nursed her talent into its tremendous potential, was the oldest Prime of all. The Rowan, a scant twenty-three now, had never gotten anything from Siglen to comfort her except old-maidish platitudes. Betelgeuse Prime David was madly in love with his T-2 wife and occupied with raising a brood of high-potential brats. Although Reidinger was always open to the Rowan, he also had to keep open every minute to all the vast problems of the FT&T system. Capella was also open, but so mixed up herself that her touch only distressed the Rowan to the point of madness.

Reidinger had tried to ease her devastating loneliness by sending up T-3's and T-4's like Afra, but she had never taken to any of them. The only male T-2 ever discovered in the Nine-Star League had been a confirmed homosexual. Ackerman was a nice, barely talented guy devoted to his wife. And now, on Deneb, a T-1 had appeared, out of nowhere—and so very, very far away.

Afra, take me home now, she said tiredly.

Afra brought the shell down with infinite care.

She lay for a while on her couch in the shell after the others had left. In her unsleeping consciousness, she was aware that the station was closing down, that Ackerman and the others had left for home until Callisto once more came out from behind Jupiter's titan bulk. Everybody had some place to go, except the Rowan, who made it all possible. The screaming, bitter loneliness that overcame her during her off hours

welled up—the frustration of being locked up out here, unable even to
steel herself to going off ground past Afra's sharply limited range—
alone, alone with her two-edged talent. Murky green and black
swamped her mind until she remembered the blown kiss. Suddenly,
completely, she fell into the first restful sleep of two weeks.

ROWAN. It was Deneb's touch that roused her. ROWAN, PLEASE WAKE UP
FROM THAT SLEEP, ROWAN.

HMMM? she murmured sleepily.

OUR GUESTS ARE GETTING ROUGHER . . . SINCE THE GERMDOGS . . .
WHIPPED UP A BROAD-SPECTRUM ANTIBIOTIC . . . THAT PHASE . . . OF
THEIR ATTACK . . . FAILED . . . SO NOW THEY'RE . . . POUNDING US . . .
WITH MISSILES . . . GIVE MY REGARDS . . . TO YOUR SPACE-LAWYER FRIEND
. . . REIDINGER.

AND YOU'RE PLAYING PITCH WITH THEM? The Rowan came awake hurriedly. She could feel Deneb's contact cutting in and out as he interrupted himself to catch incoming missiles and fling them back.

ONLY THING . . . TO DO.

THEN YOU'D BETTER TAKE SOME EVASIVE ACTION. IF THEY HAVE ANY TAL-
ENT AMONG THEM, THEY'LL SPOT YOU.

CAN'T BE HELPED . . . NO TIME TO . . . MOVE AROUND . . . I'M A
POGO-STICK . . . SWEETHEART . . . IS WHY I . . . NEED YOU HERE . . .
AND . . . ANY . . . TWIN . . . SISTERS . . . YOU HAPPEN . . . TO HAVE
HANDY.

THERE! BUT I CAN'T GO THERE!

WHY NOT?

I CAN'T—I CAN'T, moaned the Rowan, twisting against the web of the
couch.

BUT I'VE . . . GOT . . . TO . . . HAVE . . . HELP, he said and faded
away.

REIDINGER! the Rowan screamed.

ROWAN, I DON'T CARE IF YOU ARE A T-1. THERE ARE CERTAIN LIMITS TO MY
PATIENCE AND YOU'VE STRETCHED EVERY BLASTED ONE OF THEM, YOU LITTLE
WHITE-HAIRED APE!

His answer scorched at her. She blocked automatically, but clung to
his touch. SOMEONE HAS GOT TO HELP DENEB! she cried, transmitting his
message.

WHAT? HE'S JOKING.

How could he, about a thing like that?

Did you see the missiles? Did he show you what he was actually doing?

Well, no, but I felt him thrusting. And since when does one of us distrust another one when he asks for help—even if Deneb hasn't ever been in contact with us before.

Since when? Reidinger snapped. Since Eve handed Adam a rosy round fruit and said eat. And exactly since Deneb's never been integrated into the Prime network and none of us can be sure who or what he is—or even exactly where he is. I don't like this taking everything at his word. Try and get him back for me.

I can't reach him. He's too busy repelling missiles.

That's a hot one! Look, he can tap any other potentials on his own planet. That's all he needs.

But . . .

But me no buts and leave me alone. I've got a company—a League —to hold together. Reidinger signed off with a blacklash that stung. The Rowan lay in her couch, bewildered at Reidinger's attitude. He was always busy, always gruff. But he had never been this stupidly unreasonable. While out there, Deneb was growing weaker . . .

The station was operating again—that is, Callisto was clear of Jupiter, and the incoming cargoes were piling up at the launchers. But there was no outgoing traffic. Tension and worry hung over the station personnel.

"There must be something we can do for him . . . something," the Rowan said, choked with tears.

Afra looked at her sadly and compassionately. He patted her frail shoulder. "Nobody can help him. Not even you can reach all the way out to him. If he can't get enough help on his own planet, he's lost. Only some other Primes, right there on the spot with him, could help. And none of you can. You're all tied to your little worlds by your umbilical cords of space-fear. And it would take a normally powered ship eighteen years to reach him from here."

"I know—I know!" the Rowan wailed.

Kee-rist! The Radar Warning! It was Ackerman's shout in their minds. The Rowan linked her mind to his as he plunged toward the little-used radar screen. As she probed into space she found the intruder, a highly powered projectile arrowing in from behind Uranus. Guiltily, she flushed, for she ought to have detected it 'way beyond radar range.

IT'S A MISSILE! she cried out incredulously.

There was no time to run up the idle dynamos. The missile was coming in too fast.

I WANT A WIDE-OPEN MIND FROM EVERYONE ON THIS MOON! the Rowan broadcast loudly. She felt the surge of power as forty-eight talents on Callisto, including Ackerman's ten-year-old son, lowered their shields. She picked up their power—from the least 12 to Afra's sturdy 4—sent her touch racing out beyond Jupiter and picked up the alien bomb. She had to wrestle for a moment with the totally unfamiliar molecular arrangement of its substance. Then, with her augmented energy, it was easy enough to swerve the projectile down into Jupiter's seething mass. She deactivated the trigger and then scattered the fissionables from the warhead into the planet's deep crevasses.

She released the others who had joined her and fell back again on the couch.

"How in hell did that thing ever find us?" Afra asked from the chair where he had slumped.

She shook her head wearily. Without the dynamos, there was no surge of power to act as the initial carrier wave for her touch. Even with the help of the others—and all of them put together didn't add up to one-tenth of another Prime—it was hard launching her power. She thought of Deneb—alone—without an FT&T station to help him—doing it again, and again, and again—and her heart twisted.

WARM UP THE DYNAMOS, BRIAN—THERE'LL BE MORE OF THEM IN.

Afra looked up, startled.

PRIME ROWAN OF CALLISTO STATION ALERTING EARTH PRIME REIDINGER AND ALL OTHER PRIMES! PREPARE FOR POSSIBLE ATTACK BY FISSIONABLE PROJECTILES OF ALIEN ORIGIN. ALERT ALL RADAR WATCH STATIONS AND PATROL FORCES.

She lost her official calm and added hysterically: WE'VE GOT TO HELP DENEB NOW—WE'VE GOT TO! IT'S NO LONGER AN ISOLATED ATTACK ON AN OUTLYING COLONY. IT'S A CONCERTED ATTACK ON OUR HEART WORLD. IT'S AN ATTACK ON EVERY PRIME IN THE NINE-STAR LEAGUE!

ROWAN! Reidinger exploded, but before he could say any more, the Rowan opened her mind to him and showed him the five new projectiles driving on Callisto. FOR THE LOVE OF LITTLE APPLES! he exclaimed incredulously. WHAT HAS OUR LITTLE MAN BEEN STIRRING UP?

SHALL WE FIND OUT? Rowan asked with deadly sweetness.

Reidinger transmitted impatience, fury, misery, and then shock as he gathered her intention.

YOUR PLAN WON'T WORK. IT'S IMPOSSIBLE! WE CAN'T MERGE MINDS TO FIGHT THIS THING. ALL OF US ARE TOO EGOCENTRIC—TOO UNSTABLE. WE'D BURN OUT, FIGHTING EACH OTHER. FT&T WOULD COLLAPSE!

YOU, ME, ALTAIR, BETELGEUSE AND CAPELLA—WE CAN DO IT. IF I CAN DEACTIVATE ONE OF THOSE HELL MISSILES WITH ONLY FORTY-EIGHT MINOR TALENTS AND NO POWER FOR HELP, FIVE PRIMES PLUS FULL POWER OUGHT TO BE ABLE TO TURN THE TRICK. WE CAN KNOCK THE MISSILES OFF. AND WE CAN MERGE WITH DENEB TO HELP HIM. THAT'LL MAKE SIX OF US. SHOW ME THE ET WHO COULD STAND UP TO IT.

LOOK, GIRL, Reidinger pleaded, WE DON'T EVEN KNOW HIM! WE CAN'T JUST MERGE—HE COULD THROW US APART, OR WE COULD BURN HIM UP WITH OUR POWER. WE DON'T KNOW HIM! WE CAN'T GAUGE HIS STRENGTH.

YOU'D BETTER CATCH THAT MISSILE COMING AT YOU, she said calmly. I CAN'T HANDLE MORE THAN TEN AT A TIME AND KEEP UP A SENSIBLE CONVERSATION.

She felt Reidinger weakening. She went on: IF DENEB'S BEEN HANDLING A PLANET-WIDE BARRAGE, THAT'S A PRETTY GOOD INDICATION OF HIS STRENGTH. I'LL HANDLE THE EGO-MERGE BECAUSE I DAMNED WELL WANT TO. BESIDES, THERE ISN'T ANY OTHER COURSE OPEN TO US, IS THERE?

Their conversation was taking the briefest possible time, and yet more missiles were coming in. It was too late for the Patrol. And now all the Prime stations were under bombardment.

ALL RIGHT, Reidinger said.

"NO, NO, NO, NO! YOU'LL BURN HER OUT—BURN HER OUT, POOR THING! old Siglen babbled from Altair. LET US STICK TO OUR LAST—WE CAN DO THIS ALONE—ALONE AND SAFE—WE DARE NOT EXPOSE OURSELVES—NO, NO, NO!

SHUT UP, IRONPANTS, David said.

SHOULDER TO THE WHEEL, YOU OLD WART! Capella chimed in waspishly.

LOOK, ROWAN, Reidinger interjected suddenly. SIGLEN'S RIGHT. WE'RE GOING TO HAVE TO FOCUS THROUGH YOU TO REACH DENEB. YOU'RE THE ONLY ONE WHO KNOWS HIS TOUCH.

I KNOW THAT—I ALREADY SAID SO. I'LL TAKE MY CHANCES.

DAMN DENEB FOR STARTING ALL THIS! Reidinger muttered.

I'VE GOT TO DO IT was all the Rowan said.

Then the unleashed power of the other FT&T Primes, plus all the mechanical surge of the station generators, shot through her. She grew, grew, and only dimly saw the bombarding ET missiles wiped out like so many mayflies. She grew, grew until she felt like a colossus, larger than ominous Jupiter. Slowly, carefully, tentatively, because the massive power was braked only by her own slender conscious control, she reached out toward Deneb.

She spun on, in grandeur, astounded by the limitless force she had become. She passed the small black dwarf that was the midway point. Then she felt the mind she searched for; a tired mind, its periphery wincing, ready to cringe with weariness.

OH, DENEB, DENEB, YOU'RE STILL THERE! she cried out in relief and happiness, so grateful to find him still fighting his desperate battle that they had merged before her ego was even aware of what she was doing. She abandoned her most guarded self to him and, with that surrender, the massed power she held flowed into him. The tired mind of the man grew, healed, strengthened and blossomed until she was only a small part of it, lost in the greater part of this immense mental whole. Suddenly she saw with his eyes, heard with his ears and felt with his touch, aware of the titanic struggle.

The greenish sky above was pitted with mushroom puffs, and even the raw young hills around him were scarred with deflected missiles. Easily now, he was turning aside the rockets aimed at him.

LET'S GO UP THERE AND FIND OUT WHAT THEY ARE, Reidinger said. NOW.

Deneb took them up to the thirty mile-long ships. The massed minds took indelible note of intruders. Then, off-handedly, Deneb broke the hulls of twenty-nine of the ET ships, spilling their contents into space. To the occupants of the survivor, he gave a searing impression of the Primes and the indestructability of the worlds in this section of space. With one great heave, he threw the lone ship away from his exhausted planet, sent it hurtling farther than it had come, into uncharted black immensity.

THANK YOU FOR HELPING, he said to all the Primes. I HOPED YOU WOULD.

Then the Rowan felt the links dissolving. Deneb caught her fast to him and held her until the others had all retreated. When they were alone, he opened all his thoughts to her, so that now she knew him as intimately as he knew her.

DON'T GO YET, SWEET ROWAN. LOOK AROUND YOU. IT'LL TAKE A WHILE FOR MY HOME TO BE BEAUTIFUL AGAIN, BUT IT'LL BE LOVELIER THAN EVER. COME LIVE WITH ME, MY LOVE.

The Rowan's wracked cry of protest made him wince.

I CAN'T—I CAN'T! she cried, cringing against her own outburst and closing off her inner heart so he couldn't see the pitiful why. She retreated, in the moment of his confusion, back to her own frail body. She beat her fists hopelessly against her thighs.

ROWAN! came his cry. ROWAN, I LOVE YOU!

She closed even the outer fringe of her perception, and curled forward in her chair. Afra, who had watched patiently over her while her mind was far away, touched her shoulder.

OH, AFRA, AFRA! she moaned. IT MAY BE TRUE THAT DENEB AND I COULD LOVE EACH OTHER PERFECTLY, TOUCHING EACH OTHER'S WHOLE MINDS, KNOWING EACH OTHER COMPLETELY. BUT I'LL NEVER, NEVER BE ABLE TO HOLD HIM IN MY ARMS—NEVER KISS HIM—OH, DENEB, I LOVED YOU SO!

And the Rowan forced her bruised self into sleep. Afra picked her up gently and carried her to a bed in a room off the station's main level. He shut the door after he had put her down and tip-toed away, and sat down on watch in the corridor outside, his handsome face dark and inscrutable.

Afra and Ackerman reached the only possible decision. Rowan had burned herself out. They'd have to tell Reidinger. It was forty-eight hours since they'd had a single contact with her mind. She had ignored, or not heard, their tentative requests for help. Afra, Ackerman and the machines could handle some of the routine freighting, but two liners were due in and that required her. They knew she was still alive, but that was all. At first, Ackerman had assumed she was only resting. Only Afra knew better, and for forty-eight hours he'd hoped desperately that she would wake again.

"I'll run up the dynamos and we'll tell Reidinger," said Ackerman with a reluctant sigh.

WELL—WHERE'S ROWAN? Reidinger demanded. A moment's touch with Afra told him. He sighed. WE'LL JUST HAVE TO ROUSE HER, SOME WAY. BUT SHE ISN'T BURNED OUT. WE CAN BE GRATEFUL FOR THAT.

YOU OUGHT TO BE, Ackerman said bitterly. IF YOU'D PAID ANY ATTEN-
TION TO HER IN THE FIRST PLACE——

YES, I'M SURE, Reidinger cut him off brusquely. IF I'D GOTTEN HER
LIGHT OF LOVE HIS PATROL SQUADRONS WHEN SHE WANTED ME TO, SHE
WOULDN'T EVEN HAVE BEEN ABLE TO MERGE WITH HIM MENTALLY. I PUT AS
MUCH PRESSURE ON HER AS I DARED; BUT WHEN THAT COCKY YOUNG ROOSTER
ON DENEB STARTED LOBBING DEFLECTED ET MISSILES AT US TO GET US TO DO
SOMETHING, I HAD TO GIVE IN. SO I MANAGED TO GET THE ROWAN TO LEARN
TO CRAWL. He sighed. I WAS HOPING I COULD GET AT LEAST ONE PRIME WHO
COULD FLY.

WHA——AT! YOU MEAN THE BATTLE WASN'T REAL?

A LITTLE TOO REAL. ANOTHER FEW HOURS OF FENDING THOSE MISSILES
AWAY FROM HIS PLANET, AND DENEB WOULD HAVE BEEN COMPLETELY EX-
HAUSTED. THE ET'S WOULD HAVE WON. SO HE SPARED A LITTLE STRENGTH——
FROM SOMEWHERE——AND GOT US MOVING.

BUT YOU LET THINGS GO THAT FAR.

I SENT THE GERMDOGS. THAT STOPPED ANYONE'S DYING, AT LEAST UNTIL
DENEB'S MISSILE DEFENSE BROKE DOWN. LOOK——I WAS TRYING TO GET THE
ROWAN TO BREAK DOWN THIS FEAR PSYCHOSIS WE ALL HAVE. I WAS TRYING TO
GET HER TO GO TO HIM PHYSICALLY. SHE'S THE YOUNGEST ONE OF US ALL, AND
THE STRONGEST, EXCEPT FOR DENEB. I WAS HOPING——BUT, I FAILED. Rei-
dinger sounded resigned. I'M GETTING OLD. OLD AND DECREPIT. I'M TRYING
DESPERATELY TO GET SOME NEW PRIMES——I DON'T KNOW WHERE FROM. I'D
HOPED THAT SHE AND DENEB——

I WOULDN'T COUNT ON THAT NOW, Afra said.

NO. NOT IF SHE'S GIVEN HIM UP FOREVER . . .

They cut off abruptly as the door opened to admit the Rowan—a
wan, pale, very quiet Rowan.

She smiled apologetically. "I've been asleep a long time."

"You were mighty tired," Ackerman said.

She winced a little and then smiled at Ackerman's instant concern. "I
still am, a little." She frowned. "Didn't I hear you two talking to Reidinger, just now?"

"We got a little worried you'd never wake up," Ackerman admitted.
"There're two liners coming in, and Afra and I just plain can't handle
human cargo."

The Rowan smiled ruefully. "I'll do my best." She walked slowly up
the stairs to her tower.

Ray Loftus murmured sadly, watching her: "She sure has changed."

Her chastened attitude wasn't the relief her staff had once considered it would be. The work that day went on with monotonous efficiency, with none of the by-play and freakish temperament that had previously kept them on their toes. The men moved around automatically, saddened by this gently tragic Rowan. That might have been one reason why, toward the very end of the day, no one particularly noticed the young man come in. It was only when Ackerman got up from his desk for more coffee that he noticed him sitting there quietly.

"You new?"

"Well, yes. I was told to see Miss Rowan. Mr. Reidinger signed me on in his office late this morning." He spoke pleasantly, stood up, and then he smiled. Fleetingly, Ackerman was reminded of the miracle of the Rowan's sudden smiles which hinted at some secret of beauties. This man's smile was full of uninhibited vigor. The entire tanned face echoed the warmth of his expression. The brilliant blue eyes danced with good humor and friendliness.

Ackerman found himself grinning back like a fool and shaking the man's hand stoutly.

"Mighty glad to know you. What's your name?"

"Jeff Raven. I just got in from . . ."

"Hey, Afra, want you to meet Jeff Raven. Here, have a cup of coffee. A little raw on the walk up from the freighting station this morning, isn't it? Been on other Prime Stations?"

"Well, as a matter of fact . . ."

Toglia and Loftus had looked around from their computers toward the recipient of such unusual cordiality. They found themselves grinning as broadly and rushing up to welcome this magnetic stranger. Raven accepted the coffee graciously from Ackerman, who instantly proferred cigarettes. He had the feeling he must give this wonderful guy something else, it had been such a pleasure to serve him coffee.

Afra looked quietly at the stranger, his calm yellow eyes a little clouded. "Hello," he murmured ruefully.

Jeff Raven's cheeks flushed a little. "Hello," he said gently.

Before anyone in the station quite realized what was happening, everyone had left his post and gathered around Raven, chattering and grinning, using the simplest excuse to touch his hand or shoulder. He was genuinely interested in everything said, and although there were twenty-three people anxious to monopolize his attention, no one felt slighted. His attention seemed to envelop them all.

WHAT IN HELL IS HAPPENING DOWN THERE? demanded the Rowan with an echo of her familiar irritation. WHY . . .

Contrary to all her previously sacred rules, she appeared suddenly in the middle of the room, looking wildly around her. Raven touched her hand gently.

"Reidinger said you needed me," he said.

"Deneb?" she whispered. *"Deneb?* But—but you're *here*—you're *here!"*

He smiled tenderly and drew his hand across her shining hair.

The Rowan's jaw dropped and then she burst out laughing, the laughter of a supremely happy, carefree girl. Her laughter broke off into a gasp of pure terror.

HOW DID YOU GET HERE?

JUST CAME. YOU CAN TOO, YOU KNOW.

NO, NO—I CAN'T. NO T-1 CAN. Rowan tried to free herself from him as if he were suddenly repulsive.

I DID, THOUGH, he reminded her gently. IT'S ONLY A QUESTION OF RE-ARRANGING ATOMS. WHY SHOULD IT MATTER WHOSE THEY ARE?

OH, NO—NO—

"Did you know," Raven said conversationally, speaking for everyone's benefit, "that Siglen gets sick just going up and down stairs. Lives all on one floor and has furniture with short legs, doesn't she, Rowan?"

"Yes . . ."

"Ever stop to wonder what that might mean? I did a little digging. Siglen's middle ear reacts very badly to free fall. She was so miserably sick the first time she tried moving herself anywhere, she went into a trauma about it. Of course, it never occurred to her to find out *why*. So she went a little crazy on the subject; and *who* trained all the other Primes?"

"Siglen . . . Oh, Deneb, you mean . . . ?"

Raven grinned. "Yup. Passed it on to every one of you, of course. The Curse of Talent. The Great Fear. The Great Bushwah! It might have gone on forever—except Siglen never trained *me*." He laughed with wicked boyishness and opened his mind to the Rowan. Warmth and reassurance passed between them. Her careful conditioning withered in that warmth. Her eyes shone.

COME LIVE WITH ME NOW, MY ROWAN. REIDINGER SAYS YOU CAN COMMUTE FROM HERE TO DENEB EVERY DAY.

"Commute?" She said it aloud, conscious of the valuable parts of Siglen's training, reserving only their most private thoughts for the super-high channels of Prime communication.

"Certainly," he said, sharing her impulse. "You're still a working T-1 under contract to FT&T. And so, my love, am I."

"I guess I do know my bosses, don't I?" she giggled.

"Well, the price was right. Reidinger didn't haggle for a second after I walked into his private office at eleven this morning."

"Commuting to Callisto," the Rowan repeated dazedly.

"All finished here for the day?" Raven asked Ackerman, who shook his head after a glance at the launching racks.

"C'mon, gal. Take me to your ivory tower and we'll finish this up in a jiffy and then go home. I've got some patching up to do on some pretty mountains the ET's knocked down. You can help me with it." AND WHEN WE'VE FINISHED THAT . . .

Raven smiled wickedly at the Rowan and pressed her hand to his lips in the age-old gesture of courtliness. The Rowan's smile answered his with blinding joy.

Afra took the burning forgotten cigarette from between Ackerman's fingers and dragged on it. Afra was a colonial, his subtle drift away from Terrestrial human stock reflected in minute differences, such as his yellow eyes and his very faintly greenish skin. No one could understand why he smoked—tobacco made his eyes water badly, and brought out the greenish tint in his skin—but he always joined the rest of the staff in one cigarette at quitting time. His eyes were wet now, as the Rowan and her lover climbed the stairs to the tower.

The White Dog

Feodor Sologub

The bloodthirsty predator of Clemence Housman's "The Were-Wolf" (earlier this volume) has nothing in common with the pathetic protagonist of "The White Dog," which Weird Tales *published in February 1926 with a footnote that it was translated from the Russian, but the magazine provided no further information about the story's author or anonymous translator. However, my colleague David G. Hartwell reports that* FEODOR SOLOGUB *(1863–1927) was a popular Russian short story writer.* The Sweet-Scented Name, *a collection of his tales, was published in English in 1915.*

EVERYTHING WAS IRKSOME for Alexandra Ivanovna in the workship of this out-of-the-way town. It was the shop in which she had served as apprentice and now for several years as seamstress. Everything irritated Alexandra Ivanovna; she quarreled with everyone and abused the apprentices. Among others to suffer from her tantrums was Tanechka, the youngest of the seamstresses, who had only recently become an apprentice.

In the beginning Tanechka submitted to her abuse in silence. In the end she revolted, and, addressing her assailant, said quite calmly and affably, so that everyone laughed, "Alexandra Ivanovna, you are a dog!"

Alexandra Ivanovna scowled.

"You are a dog yourself!" she exclaimed.

Tanechka was sitting sewing. She paused now and then from her work and said, calmly and deliberately, "You always whine . . . you certainly are a dog . . . You have a dog's snout . . . And a dog's ears . . . And a wagging tail . . . The mistress will soon drive you out of doors, because you are the most detestable of dogs—a poodle."

Tanechka was a young, plump, rosy-cheeked girl with a good-natured face which revealed a trace of cunning. She sat there demurely, barefooted, still dressed in her apprentice clothes; her eyes were clear, and her brows were highly arched on her finely curved white forehead, framed by straight dark chestnut hair, which looked black in the distance. Tanechka's voice was clear, even, sweet, insinuating, and if one could have heard its sound only, and not given heed to the words, it would have given the impression that she was paying Alexandra Ivanovna compliments.

The other seamstresses laughed, the apprentices chuckled, they covered their faces with their black aprons and cast side glances at Alexandra Ivanovna, who was livid with rage.

"Wretch!" she exclaimed. "I will pull your ears for you! I won't leave a hair on your head!"

Tanechka replied in a gentle voice: "The paws are a bit short . . . The poodle bites as well as barks . . . It may be necessary to buy a muzzle."

Alexandra Ivanovna made a movement toward Tanechka. But before Tanechka had time to lay aside her work and get up, the mistress of the establishment entered.

"Alexandra Ivanovna," she said sternly, "what do you mean by making such a fuss?"

Alexandra Ivanovna, much agitated, replied, "Irina Petrovna, I wish you would forbid her to call me a dog!"

Tanechka in her turn complained: "She is always snarling at something or other."

But the mistress looked at her sternly and said, "Tanechka, I can see through you. Are you sure you didn't begin it? You needn't think that because you are a seamstress now you are an important person. If it weren't for your mother's sake—"

Tanechka grew red, but preserved her innocent and affable manner. She addressed her mistress in a subdued voice: "Forgive me, Irina Petrovna, I will not do it again. But it wasn't altogether my fault . . ."

. . . . . .

Alexandra Ivanovna returned home almost ill with rage. Tanechka had guessed her weakness.

"A dog! Well, then, I am a dog." thought Alexandra Ivanovna, "but it is none of her affair! Have I looked to see whether she is a serpent or a fox? It is easy to find one out, but why make a fuss about it? Is a dog worse than any other animal?"

The clear summer night languished and sighed. A soft breeze from the adjacent fields occasionally blew down the peaceful streets. The moon rose clear and full, that very same moon which rose long ago at another place, over the broad desolate steppe, the home of the wild, of those who ran free and whined in their ancient earthly travail.

And now, as then, glowed eyes sick with longing; and her heart, still wild, not forgetting in town the great spaciousness of the steppe, felt oppressed; her throat was troubled with a tormenting desire to howl.

She was about to undress, but what was the use? She could not sleep, anyway. She went into the passage. The planks of the floor bent and creaked under her, and small shavings and sand which covered them tickled her feet not unpleasantly.

She went out on the doorstep. There sat the *babushka* Stepanida, a black figure in her black shawl, gaunt and shriveled. She sat with her head bent, and seemed to be warming herself in the rays of the cold moon.

Alexandra Ivanovna sat down beside her. She kept looking at the old woman sideways. The large curved nose of her companion seemed to her like the beak of an old bird.

"A crow?" Alexandra Ivanovna asked herself.

She smiled, forgetting for the moment her longing and her fears. Shrewd as the eyes of a dog, her own eyes lighted up with the joy of her discovery. In the pale green light of the moon the wrinkles of her faded face became altogether invisible, and she seemed once more young and merry and light-hearted, just as she was ten years ago, when the moon had not yet called upon her to bark and bay of nights before the windows of the dark bathhouse.

She moved closer to the old woman, and said affably, *"Babushka* Stepanida, there is something I have been wanting to ask you."

The old woman turned to her, her dark face furrowed with wrinkles, and asked in a sharp, oldish voice that sounded like a caw, "Well, my dear? Go ahead and ask."

Alexandra Ivanovna gave a repressed laugh; her thin shoulders suddenly trembled from a chill that ran down her spine.

She spoke very quietly: *"Babushka* Stepanida, it seems to me—tell me is it true?—I don't know exactly how to put it—but you, *babushka,* please don't take offense—it is not from malice that I—"

"Go on, my dear, say it," said the old woman, looking at Alexandra Ivanovna with glowing eyes.

"It seems to me, *babushka*—please, now, don't take offense—as if you, *babushka,* were a crow."

The old woman turned away. She nodded her head, and seemed like one who had recalled something. Her head, with its sharply outlined nose, bowed and nodded, and at last it seemed to Alexandra Ivanovna that the old woman was dozing. Dozing, and mumbling something under her nose—nodding and mumbling old forgotten words, old magic words.

An intense quiet reigned out of doors. It was neither light nor dark, and everything seemed bewitched with the inarticulate mumbling of old, forgotten words. Everything languished and seemed lost in apathy.

Again a longing oppressed her heart. And it was neither a dream nor an illusion. A thousand perfumes, imperceptible by day, became subtly distinguishable, and they recalled something ancient and primitive.

In a barely audible voice the old woman mumbled, "Yes, I am a crow. Only I have no wings. But there are times when I caw, and I caw, and tell of woe. And I am given to forebodings, my dear; each time I have one I simply must caw. People are not particularly anxious to hear me. And when I see a doomed person I have such a strong desire to caw."

The old woman suddenly made a sweeping movement with her arms, and in a shrill voice cried out twice: "Kar-r, Kar-r!"

Alexandra Ivanovna shuddered, and asked, *"Babushka,* at whom are you cawing?"

"At you, my dear," the old woman answered. "I am cawing at you."

It had become too painful to sit with the old woman any longer. Alexandra Ivanovna went to her own room. She sat down before the open window and listened to two voices at the gate.

"It simply won't stop whining!" said a low and harsh voice.

"And uncle, did you see?" asked an agreeable young tenor.

Alexandra Ivanovna recognized in this last the voice of the curly-headed, freckled-faced lad who lived in the same court.

A brief and depressing silence followed. Then she heard a hoarse and harsh voice say suddenly, "Yes, I saw. It's very large—and white. It lies near the bathhouse, and bays at the moon."

The voice gave her an image of the man, of his shovel-shaped beard, his low, furrowed forehead, his small, piggish eyes, and his spread-out fat legs.

"And why does it bay, uncle?" asked the agreeable voice.

And again the hoarse voice did not reply at once.

"Certainly to no good purpose—and where it came from is more than I can say."

"Do you think, uncle, it may be a werewolf?" asked the agreeable voice.

"I should not advise you to investigate," replied the hoarse voice.

She could not quite understand what these words implied, nor did she wish to think of them. She did not feel inclined to listen further. What was the sound and significance of human words to her?

The moon looked straight into her face and persistently called her and tormented her. Her heart was restless with a dark longing, and she could not sit still.

Alexandra Ivanovna quickly undressed herself. Naked. all white. she silently stole through the passage: she then opened the outer door (there was no one on the step or outside) and ran quickly across the court and the vegetable garden, and reached the bathhouse. The sharp contact of her body with the cold air and her feet with the cold ground gave her pleasure. But soon her body was warm.

She lay down in the grass, on her stomach. Then, raising herself on her elbows, she lifted her face toward the pale, brooding moon, and gave a long-drawn-out whine.

"Listen, uncle, it is whining," said the curly-haired lad at the gate.

The agreeable tenor voice trembled perceptibly.

"Whining again, the accurst one!" said the hoarse, harsh voice slowly. They rose from the bench. The gate latch clicked.

They went silently across the courtyard and the vegetable garden, the two of them. The older man, black-bearded and powerful, walked in front, a gun in his hand. The curly-headed lad followed tremblingly, and looked constantly behind.

Near the bathhouse, in the grass, lay a huge white dog, whining piteously. Its head, black on the crown was raised to the moon, which pursued its way in the cold sky; its hind legs were strangely thrown backward while the front ones, firm and straight, pressed hard against the ground.

In the pale green and unreal light of the moon it seemed enormous. So huge a dog was surely never seen on earth. It was thick and fat. The black spot, which began at the head and stretched in uneven strands down the entire spine seemed like a woman's loosened hair. No tail was visible; presumably it was turned under. The fur on the body was so short that in the distance the dog seemed wholly naked, and its hide shone dimly in the moonlight, so that altogether it resembled the body of a nude woman who lay in the grass and bayed at the moon.

The man with the black beard took aim. The curly-haired lad crossed himself and mumbled something.

The discharge of a rifle sounded in the night air. The dog gave a groan, jumped up on its hind legs, became a naked woman, who, her body covered with blood, started to run, all the while groaning, weeping and raising cries of distress.

The black-bearded one and the curly-haired one threw themselves in the grass, and began to moan in wild terror.

The Visit

Carole Buggé

One of New York's most esteemed professional comedy improvisers and teachers, CAROLE BUGGÉ *is a playwright with one show currently under option; a composer with a new musical in progress; an award-winning poet and author of several unusual short stories, including* Laura, Miracle at Chimayo, A Day in the Life of Comrade Lenin *and a critically acclaimed Sherlock Holmes pastiche,* The Case of the Tongue-Tied Tenor, *included in the 1994 St. Martin's Press book* The Game Is Afoot. *Carole's writing is generally poignant, tender and quietly wry, but "The Visit" is an exception: a wildly irreverent diatribe against sheep-mindless folk (you know a few, don't you?) who claim religion's comforts without shouldering its concomitant responsibilities.*

MY SISTER told me on the phone the other day that she has invited Christ into her life. My first thought was: how can He fit it into His busy schedule, but then I figured he's *Christ;* He can create another day of the week just for my sister if He wants to. *And on the eighth day he visited Kelly.* Then I thought: how would Miss Manners suggest you treat a visit from Christ? For instance, what would you serve Him? Bread and wine were out; it would just bring up painful memories. You could serve Him water, but then He might think you were hinting that you wanted a miracle and were too cheap to go out and *buy* wine. Dairy products were probably out, too, because a lot of

Mediterranean people are lactose intolerant. Goat's milk would work, but that would involve a lot of shopping, and my sister lives in the suburbs. I would guess, too, that Christ probably doesn't eat red meat—even if He did *then* He's probably given it up by now. (You have to think He reads *Prevention,* or at least the *Berkeley Wellness Letter.)* He might like fish, but then you run into that whole miracle thing again: would Christ think you wanted to feed the whole neighborhood and—maybe without even asking—start multiplying the fish right there in your kitchen, so that when you came in to toss the salad you would find the entire room full of sea bass, flopping around on your linoleum? When you finally did sit down to dinner, should you ask Him to say grace, or would He rather be allowed to relax for a change?

Even if you could solve the food problem, what kind of cocktail conversation can you have with Christ? The weather would bore Him, certainly, though He would be too polite to say so. Omniscience is a cool thing to possess, but it does limit dinner talk. In fact, *any* talk of the future would probably bore Him, since He is by definition all-knowing and all-powerful. But if you talked about history, full of wars and plagues and famines, I would think Christ might regard that as a criticism. After all, He presumably could have changed all that. It would in fact be very tempting to point out that He could have prevented the invasion of Poland and the rise of the Khmer Rouge; He could have stopped Ronald Reagan before he even became president of the Screen Actors Guild. As for a discussion of the current state of the world, which frankly is a mess, where would Christ stand on, say, the Middle East? It would probably be best to just steer clear of that subject. Maybe you could talk about TV shows—Christ might like *Seinfeld,* for example. Even a guy who is all-knowing needs a good belly laugh once in a while, and He might find it easy to relate to Kramer.

Also, when Christ arrived at your house, would you be expected to wash His feet, or should you just delicately show Him the way to the bathroom? Would He bring any disciples along—should you just go ahead and set the table for twelve? Should you invite the rest of his family; if so, what kind of food do you serve the Holy Ghost, assuming you could even see it? It's also hard to know which of your friends to invite. Your Jewish friends might think you were rubbing their noses in some ancient accusation of racial guilt; your agnostic friends would treat Him just like any other guy, which He might resent; your atheist friends might pretend He wasn't even there and talk around Him. Your Buddhist and Hindu friends might keep calling Him by the wrong name. You could invite your other friends who had also invited Christ into their lives, but what if He hadn't had time yet to reply to their invitation —Christ must get more mail than Oprah. Your friends would show up and feel hurt that He'd come to see you before them.

And then how *do* you address Him? "Mr. Christ"? "Jesus" would imply a first-name basis and might be too familiar on the first visit, but did He even have a last name? In the Bible He was Jesus of Nazareth: "Mr. Nazareth" seems too weird. "Your Holiness" has already been taken by the Pope, and "Your Omnipotence" seems a bit of a tongue-twister and might come out as "Your Impotence" or something.

I didn't say any of this to my sister, of course; I just murmured something about it being nice and hung up. Later I thought: what if Christ *doesn't always wait for an invitation;* what if He sometimes shows up unannounced, to keep people on their toes? That got me really scared, and I thought he might drop in on *me* sometime, on the spur of the moment, without even calling ahead first. Then, after I thought about it, I relaxed a little. Christ isn't going to visit me: I live in New York City.

The Friends of the Friends

Henry James

American-born, European in spirit, HENRY JAMES (1843–1916) wrote some two dozen novels, essays, plays and nearly one hundred short stories, many of them occult. One of the most famous and controversial ghost stories in English letters is James's "The Turn of the Screw." Scholars passionately wrangle over whether its ghastly events "really happened" or were lewd by-products of its female narrator's self-deluding imagination. Little has been said, though, about the following story, which James wrote only a few months before "The Turn of the Screw." Its sequence of odd, ultimately supernatural events told by a neurotic young woman whose motives we come to distrust makes "The Friends of the Friends" a less ambiguous and therefore potentially enlightening companion piece to "The Turn of the Screw."

I FIND, as you prophesied, much that's interesting, but little that helps the delicate question—the possibility of publication. Her diaries are less systematic than I hoped; she only had a blessed habit of noting and narrating. She summarised, she saved; she appears seldom indeed to have let a good story pass without catching it on the wing. I allude of course not so much to things she heard as to things she saw and felt. She writes sometimes of herself, sometimes of others, sometimes of the combination. It's under this last rubric that she's usually most vivid. But it's not, you'll understand, when she's most vivid that she's always most publishable. To tell the truth she's fearfully indiscreet, or has at least all

the material for making *me* so. Take as an instance the fragment I send
you after dividing it for your convenience into several small chapters. It's
the contents of a thin blank-book which I've had copied out and which
has the merit of being nearly enough a rounded thing, an intelligible
whole. These pages evidently date from years ago. I've read with the
liveliest wonder the statement they so circumstantially make and done
my best to swallow the prodigy they leave to be inferred. These things
would be striking, wouldn't they? to any reader; but can you imagine for
a moment my placing such a document before the world, even though,
as if she herself had desired the world should have the benefit of it, she
has given her friends neither name nor initials? Have you any sort of
clue to their identity? I leave her the floor.

I know perfectly of course that I brought it upon myself; but that doesn't
make it any better. I was the first to speak of her to him—he had never
even heard her mentioned. Even if I had happened not to speak some
one else would have made up for it: I tried afterwards to find comfort in
that reflexion. But the comfort of reflexions is thin: the only comfort that
counts in life is not to have been a fool. That's a beatitude I shall
doubtless never enjoy. "Why you ought to meet her and talk it over" is
what I immediately said. "Birds of a feather flock together." I told him
who she was and that they were birds of a feather because if he had had
in youth a strange adventure she had had about the same time just such
another. It was well known to her friends—an incident she was constantly called on to describe. She was charming clever pretty unhappy;
but it was none the less the thing to which she had originally owed her
reputation.

Being at the age of eighteen somewhere abroad with an aunt she had
had a vision of one of her parents at the moment of death. The parent
was in England hundreds of miles away and so far as she knew neither
dying nor dead. It was by day, in the museum of some great foreign
town. She had passed alone, in advance of her companions, into a small
room containing some famous work of art and occupied at that moment
by two other persons. One of these was an old custodian; the second,
before observing him, she took for a stranger, a tourist. She was merely
conscious that he was bareheaded and seated on a bench. The instant her
eyes rested on him however she beheld to her amazement her father,
who, as if he had long waited for her, looked at her in singular distress

and an impatience that was akin to reproach. She rushed to him with a bewildered cry, "Papa, what *is* it?" but this was followed by an exhibition of still livelier feeling when on her movement he simply vanished, leaving the custodian and her relations, who were by that time at her heels, to gather round her in dismay. These persons, the official, the aunt, the cousins, were therefore in a manner witnesses of the fact—the fact at least of the impression made on her; and there was the further testimony of a doctor who was attending one of the party and to whom it was immediately afterwards communicated. He gave her a remedy for hysterics, but said to the aunt privately: "Wait and see if something doesn't happen at home." Something *had* happened—the poor father, suddenly and violently seized, had died that morning. The aunt, the mother's sister, received before the day was out a telegram announcing the event and requesting her to prepare her niece for it. Her niece was already prepared, and the girl's sense of this visitation remained of course indelible. We had all, as her friends, had it conveyed to us and had conveyed it creepily to each other. Twelve years had elapsed, and as a woman who had made an unhappy marriage and lived apart from her husband she had become interesting from other sources; but since the name she now bore was a name frequently borne, and since moreover her judicial separation, as things were going, could hardly count as a distinction, it was usual to qualify her as "the one, you know, who saw her father's ghost."

As for him, dear man, he had seen his mother's—so there you are! I had never heard of that till this occasion on which our closer, our pleasanter acquaintance led him, through some turn of the subject of our talk, to mention it and to inspire me in so doing with the impulse to let him know that he had a rival in the field—a person with whom he could compare notes. Later on his story became for him, perhaps because of my unduly repeating it, likewise a convenient worldly label; but it hadn't a year before been the ground on which he was introduced to me. He had other merits, just as she, poor thing, had others. I can honestly say that I was quite aware of them from the first—I discovered them sooner than he discovered mine. I remember how it struck me even at the time that his sense of mine was quickened by my having been able to match, though not indeed straight from my own experience, his curious anecdote. It dated, this anecdote, as hers did, from some dozen years before —a year in which, at Oxford, he had for some reason of his own been

staying on into the "Long." He had been in the August afternoon on the
river. Coming back into his room while it was still distinct daylight he
found his mother standing there as if her eyes had been fixed on the
door. He had had a letter from her that morning out of Wales, where
she was staying with her father. At the sight of him she smiled with
extraordinary radiance and extended her arms to him, and then as he
sprang forward and joyfully opened his own she vanished from the
place. He wrote to her that night, telling her what had happened: the
letter had been carefully preserved. The next morning he heard of her
death. He was through this chance of our talk extremely struck with the
little prodigy I was able to produce for him. He had never encountered
another case. Certainly they ought to meet, my friend and he; certainly
they would have something in common. I would arrange this, wouldn't
I?—if *she* didn't mind; for himself he didn't mind in the least. I had
promised to speak to her of the matter as soon as possible, and within the
week I was able to do so. She "minded" as little as he; she was perfectly
willing to see him. And yet no meeting was to occur—as meetings are
commonly understood.

That's just half my tale—the extraordinary way it was hindered. This
was the fault of a series of accidents; but the accidents, persisting for
years, became, to me and to others, a subject of mirth with either party.
They were droll enough at first, then they grew rather a bore. The odd
thing was that both parties were amenable: it wasn't a case of their being
indifferent, much less of their being indisposed. It was one of the caprices of chance, aided I suppose by some rather settled opposition of
their interests and habits. His were centred in his office, his eternal
inspectorship, which left him small leisure, constantly calling him away
and making him break engagements. He liked society, but he found it
everywhere and took it at a run. I never knew at a given moment where
he was, and there were times when for months together I never saw
him. She was on her side practically suburban: she lived at Richmond
and never went "out." She was a woman of distinction, but not of
fashion, and felt, as people said, her situation. Decidedly proud and
rather whimsical, she lived her life as she had planned it. There were
things one could do with her, but one couldn't make her come to one's
parties. One went indeed a little more than seemed quite convenient to
hers, which consisted of her cousin, a cup of tea and the view. The tea

was good; but the view was familiar, though perhaps not, like the cousin —a disagreeable old maid who had been of the group at the museum and with whom she now lived—offensively so. This connexion with an inferior relative, which had partly an economic motive—she proclaimed her companion a marvellous manager—was one of the little perversities we had to forgive her. Another was her estimate of the proprieties created by her rupture with her husband. That was extreme—many persons called it even morbid. She made no advances; she cultivated scruples; she suspected, or I should perhaps rather say she remembered, slights: she was one of the few women I've known whom that particular predicament had rendered modest rather than bold. Dear thing, she had some delicacy! Especially marked were the limits she had set to possible attentions from men: it was always her thought that her husband only waited to pounce on her. She discouraged if she didn't forbid the visits of male persons not senile: she said she could never be too careful.

When I first mentioned to her that I had a friend whom fate had distinguished in the same weird way as herself I put her quite at liberty to say, "Oh bring him out to see me!" I should probably have been able to bring him, and a situation perfectly innocent or at any rate comparatively simple would have been created. But she uttered no such word; she only said: "I must meet him certainly; yes, I shall look out for him!" That caused the first delay, and meanwhile various things happened. One of them was that as time went on she made, charming as she was, more and more friends, and that it regularly befell that these friends were sufficiently also friends of his to bring him up in conversation. It was odd that without belonging, as it were, to the same world or, according to the horrid term, the same set, my baffled pair should have happened in so many cases to fall in with the same people and make them join in the droll chorus. She had friends who didn't know each other but who inevitably and punctually recommended *him*. She had also the sort of originality, the intrinsic interest, that led her to be kept by each of us as a private resource, cultivated jealously, more or less in secret, as a person whom one didn't meet in society, whom it was not for every one—whom it was not for the vulgar—to approach, and with whom therefore acquaintance was particularly difficult and particularly precious. We saw her separately, with appointments and conditions, and found it made on the whole for harmony not to tell each other. Somebody had always had a note from her still later than somebody else.

There was some silly woman who for a long time, among the un-privileged, owed to three simple visits to Richmond a reputation for being intimate with "lots of awfully clever out-of-the-way people."

Every one has had friends it has seemed a happy thought to bring together, and every one remembers that his happiest thoughts have not been his greatest successes, but I doubt if there was ever a case in which the failure was in such direct proportion to the quantity of influence set in motion. It's really perhaps here the quantity of influence that was most remarkable. My lady and my gentleman each pronounced it to me and others quite a subject for a roaring farce. The reason first given had with time dropped out of sight and 50 better ones flourished on top of it. They were so awfully alike: they had the same ideas and tricks and tastes, the same prejudices and superstitions and heresies; they said the same things and sometimes did them; they liked and disliked the same persons and places, the same books, authors and styles; there were touches of resemblance even in their looks and features. It established much of a propriety that they were in common parlance equally "nice" and almost equally handsome. But the great sameness, for wonder and chatter, was their rare perversity in regard to being photographed. They were the only persons ever heard of who had never been "taken" and who had a passionate objection to it. They just *wouldn't* be—no, not for anything any one could say. I had loudly complained of this; him in particular I had so vainly desired to be able to show on my drawing-room chimney-piece in a Bond Street frame. It was at any rate the very liveliest of all the reasons why they ought to know each other—all the lively reasons reduced to naught by the strange law that had made them bang so many doors in each other's face, made them the buckets in the well, the two ends of the see-saw, the two parties in the State, so that when one was up the other was down, when one was out the other was in; neither by any possibility entering a house till the other had left it or leaving it all unawares till the other was at hand. They only arrived when they had been given up, which was precisely also when they de-parted. They were in a word alternate and incompatible; they missed each other with an inveteracy that could be explained only by its being preconcerted. It was however so far from preconcerted that it had ended —literally after several years—by disappointing and annoying them. I don't think their curiosity was lively till it had been proved utterly vain. A great deal was of course done to help them, but it merely laid wires for them to trip. To give examples I should have to have taken notes; but I happen to remember that neither had ever been able to dine on the right occasion. The right occasion for each was the occasion that would be wrong for the other. On the wrong one they were most punctual, and there were never any but wrong ones. The very elements conspired and the constitution of man reenforced them. A cold, a headache, a bereavement, a storm, a fog, an earthquake, a cataclysm, infallibly intervened. The whole business was beyond a joke.

Yet as a joke it had still to be taken, though one couldn't help feeling that the joke had made the situation serious, had produced on the part of each a consciousness, an awkwardness, a positive dread of the last accident of all, the only one with any freshness left, the accident that *would* bring them together. The final effect of its predecessors had been to kindle this instinct. They were quite ashamed—perhaps even a little of each other. So much preparation, so much frustration: what indeed could be good enough for it all to lead up to? A mere meeting would be mere flatness. Did I see them at the end of years, they often asked, just stupidly confronted? If they were bored by the joke they might be worse bored by something else. They made exactly the same reflexions, and each in some manner was sure to hear of the other's. I really think it was this peculiar diffidence that finally controlled the situation. I mean that if they had failed for the first year or two because they couldn't help it, they kept up the habit because they had—what shall I call it?—grown nervous. It really took some lurking volition to account for anything both so regular and so ridiculous.

When to crown our long acquaintance I accepted his renewed offer of marriage it was humorously said, I know, that I had made the gift of his photograph a condition. This was so far true that I had refused to give him mine without it. At any rate I had him at last, in his high distinction, on the chimney-piece, where the day she called to congratulate me she came nearer than she had ever done to seeing him. He had in being taken set her an example that I invited her to follow; he had sacrificed his perversity—wouldn't she sacrifice hers? She too must give me something on my engagement—wouldn't she give me the companion-piece? She laughed and shook her head; she had headshakes whose impulse seemed to come from as far away as the breeze that stirs a flower. The companion-piece to the portrait of my future husband was the portrait of his future wife. She had taken her stand—she could depart from it as little as she could explain it. It was a prejudice, an *entêtement,* a vow— she would live and die unphotographed. Now too she was alone in that state: this was what she liked; it made her so much more original. She rejoiced in the fall of her late associate and looked a long time at his picture, about which she made no memorable remark, though she even turned it over to see the back. About our engagement she was charming —full of cordiality and sympathy. "You've known him even longer than I've *not,*" she said, "and that seems a very long time." She understood how we had jogged together over hill and dale and how inevitable it was that we should now rest together. I'm definite about all this because what followed is so strange that it's a kind of relief to me to mark the point up to which our relations were as natural as ever. It was I myself who in a sudden madness altered and destroyed them. I see now that she gave me no pretext and that I only found one in the way she looked at the fine face in the Bond Street frame. How then would I have had her look at it? What I had wanted from the first was to make her care for him. Well, that was what I still wanted—up to the moment of her having promised me she would on this occasion really aid me to break the silly spell that had kept them asunder. I had arranged with him to do his part if she would as triumphantly do hers. I was on a different footing now—I was on a footing to answer for him. I would positively engage that at five on the following Saturday he should be on that spot. He was out of town on pressing business, but, pledged to keep his promise to the letter, would return on purpose and in abundant time. "Are you perfectly sure?" I remember she asked, looking grave and considering: I thought she had turned a little pale. She was tired, she was indisposed: it was a pity he was to see her after all at so poor a moment. If he only *could* have seen her five years before! However, I replied that this time I was sure and that success therefore depended simply on herself. At 5 o'clock on the Saturday she would find him in a particular chair I pointed out, the one in which he usually sat and in which— though this I didn't mention—he had been sitting when, the week be- fore, he put the question of our future to me in the way that had brought me round. She looked at it in silence, just as she had looked at the photograph, while I repeated for the twentieth time that it was too preposterous one shouldn't somehow succeed in introducing to one's dearest friend one's second self. *"Am* I your dearest friend?" she asked

with a smile that for a moment brought back her beauty. I replied by
pressing her to my bosom; after which she said: "Well, I'll come. I'm
extraordinarily afraid, but you may count on me."

When she had left me I began to wonder what she was afraid of, for
she had spoken as if she fully meant it. The next day, late in the afternoon, I had three lines from her: she found on getting home the announcement of her husband's death. She hadn't seen him for seven years,
but she wished me to know it in this way before I should hear of it in
another. It made however in her life, strange and sad to say, so little
difference that she would scrupulously keep her appointment. I rejoiced
for her—I supposed it would make at least the difference of her having
more money; but even in this diversion, far from forgetting she had said
she was afraid, I seemed to catch sight of a reason for her being so. Her
fear, as the evening went on, became contagious, and the contagion took
in my breast the form of a sudden panic. It wasn't jealousy—it just was
the dread of jealousy. I called myself a fool for not having been quiet till
we were man and wife. After that I should somehow feel secure. It was
only a question of waiting another month—a trifle surely for people who
had waited so long. It had been plain enough she was nervous, and now
she was free her nervousness wouldn't be less. What was it therefore but
a sharp foreboding? She had been hitherto the victim of interference, but
it was quite possible she would henceforth be the source of it. The victim
in that case would be my simple self. What had the interference been but
the finger of Providence pointing out a danger? The danger was of
course for poor *me*. It had been kept at bay by a series of accidents
unexampled in their frequency; but the reign of accident was now visibly
at an end. I had an intimate conviction that both parties would keep the
tryst. It was more and more impressed on me that they were approaching, converging. They were like the seekers for the hidden object in the
game of blindfold; they had one and the other begun to "burn." We had
talked about breaking the spell; well, it would be effectually broken—
unless indeed it should merely take another form and overdo their encounters as it had overdone their escapes. This was something I couldn't
sit still for thinking of; it kept me awake—at midnight I was full of
unrest. At last I felt there was only one way of laying the ghost. If the
reign of accident was over I must just take up the succession. I sat down
and wrote a hurried note which would meet him on his return and
which as the servants had gone to bed I sallied forth bareheaded into the

empty gusty street to drop into the nearest pillar-box. It was to tell him that I shouldn't be able to be at home in the afternoon as I had hoped and that he must postpone his visit till dinner-time. This was an implication that he would find me alone.

When accordingly at 5 she presented herself I naturally felt false and base. My act had been a momentary madness, but I had at least, as they say, to live up to it. She remained an hour; he of course never came; and I could only persist in my perfidy. I had thought it best to let her come; singular as this now seems to me I held it diminished my guilt. Yet as she sat there so visibly white and weary, stricken with a sense of everything her husband's death had opened up, I felt a really piercing pang of pity and remorse. If I didn't tell her on the spot what I had done it was because I was too ashamed. I feigned astonishment—I feigned it to the end; I protested that if ever I had had confidence I had had it that day. I blush as I tell my story—I take it as my penance. There was nothing indignant I didn't say about him; I invented suppositions, attenuations; I admitted in stupefaction, as the hands of the clock travelled, that their luck hadn't turned. She smiled at this vision of their "luck," but she looked anxious—she looked unusual: the only thing that kept me up was the fact that, oddly enough, she wore mourning—no great depths of crape, but simple and scrupulous black. She had in her bonnet three small black feathers. She carried a little muff of astrachan. This put me, by the aid of some acute reflexion, a little in the right. She had written to me that the sudden event made no difference for her, but apparently it made as much difference as that. If she was inclined to the usual forms why didn't she observe that of not going the first day or two out to tea? There was some one she wanted so much to see that she couldn't wait till her husband was buried. Such a betrayal of eagerness made me hard and cruel enough to practise my odious deceit, though at the same time, as the hour waxed and waned, I suspected in her something deeper still than disappointment and somewhat less successfully concealed. I mean a strange underlying relief, the soft low emission of the breath that comes when a danger is past. What happened as she spent her barren hour with me was that at last she gave him up. She let him go for ever. She made the most graceful joke of it that I've ever seen made of anything; but it was for all that a great date in her life. She spoke with her mild gaiety of all the other vain times, the long game of hide-and-seek, the unprecedented queerness of such a relation. For it *was,* or had been, a relation, wasn't it, hadn't it? That was just the absurd part of it. When she got up to go I said to her that it was more a relation than ever, but that I hadn't the face after what had occurred to propose to her for the present another opportunity. It was plain that the only valid opportunity would be my accomplished marriage. Of course she would be at my wedding? It was even to be hoped that *he* would.

"If *I* am, he won't be!"—I remember the high quaver and the little break of her laugh. I admitted there might be something in that. The thing was therefore to get us safely married first. "That won't help us. Nothing will help us!" she said as she kissed me farewell. "I shall never, never see him!" It was with those words she left me.

I could bear her disappointment as I've called it; but when a couple of hours later I received him at dinner I discovered I couldn't bear his. The way my manoeuvre might have affected him hadn't been particularly present to me; but the result of it was the first word of reproach that had ever yet dropped from him. I say "reproach" because that expression is scarcely too strong for the terms in which he conveyed to me his surprise that under the extraordinary circumstances I shouldn't have found some means not to deprive him of such an occasion. I might really have managed either not to be obliged to go out or to let their meeting take place all the same. They would probably have got on, in my drawing-room, well enough without me. At this I quite broke down—I confessed my iniquity and the miserable reason of it. I hadn't put her off and I hadn't gone out; she had been there and, after waiting for him an hour, had departed in the belief that he had been absent by his own fault.

"She must think me a precious brute!" he exclaimed. "Did she say of me"—and I remember the just perceptible catch of breath in his pause— "what she had a right to say?"

"I assure you she said nothing that showed the least feeling. She looked at your photograph, she even turned round the back of it, on which your address happens to be inscribed. Yet it provoked her to no demonstration. She doesn't care so much as all that."

"Then why are you afraid of her?"

"It wasn't of her I was afraid. It was of you."

"Did you think I'd be so sure to fall in love with her? You never alluded to such a possibility before," he went on as I remained silent.

"Admirable person as you pronounced her, that wasn't the light in which you showed her to me."

"Do you mean that if it *had* been you'd have managed by this time to catch a glimpse of her? I didn't fear things then," I added. "I hadn't the same reason."

He kissed me at this, and when I remembered that she had done so an hour or two before I felt for an instant as if he were taking from my lips the very pressure of hers. In spite of kisses the incident had shed a certain chill, and I suffered horribly from the sense that he had seen me guilty of a fraud. He had seen it only through my frank avowal, but I was as unhappy as if I had a stain to efface. I couldn't get over the manner of his looking at me when I spoke of her apparent indifference to his not having come. For the first time since I had known him he seemed to have expressed a doubt of my word. Before we parted I told him that I'd undeceive her—start the first thing in the morning for Richmond and there let her know he had been blameless. At this he kissed me again. I'd expiate my sin, I said; I'd humble myself in the dust; I'd confess and ask to be forgiven. At this he kissed me once more.

In the train the next day this struck me as a good deal for him to have consented to; but my purpose was firm enough to carry me on. I mounted the long hill to where the view begins, and then I knocked at her door. I was a trifle mystified by the fact that her blinds were still drawn, reflecting that if in the stress of my compunction I had come early I had certainly yet allowed people time to get up.

"At home, mum? She has left home for ever."

I was extraordinarily startled by this announcement of the elderly parlour-maid. "She has gone away?"

"She's dead, mum, please." Then as I gasped at the horrible word: "She died last night."

The loud cry that escaped me sounded even in my own ears like some harsh violation of the hour. I felt for the moment as if I had killed her; I turned faint and saw through a vagueness that woman hold out her arms to me. Of what next happened I've no recollection, nor of anything but my friend's poor stupid cousin, in a darkened room, after an interval that I suppose very brief, sobbing at me in a smothered accusatory way. I can't say how long it took me to understand, to believe and then to press back with an immense effort that pang of responsibility which, superstitiously, insanely, had been at first almost all I was conscious of. The doctor, after the fact, had been superlatively wise and clear: he was satisfied of a long-latent weakness of the heart, determined probably years before by the agitations and terrors to which her marriage had introduced her. She had had in those days cruel scenes with her husband, she had been in fear of her life. All emotion, everything in the nature of anxiety and suspense had been after that to be strongly deprecated, as in her marked cultivation of a quiet life she was evidently well aware; but who could say that any one, especially a "real lady," might be successfully protected from *every* little rub? She had had one a day or two before in the news of her husband's death—since there were shocks of all kinds, not only those of grief and surprise. For that matter she had never dreamed of so near a release: it had looked uncommonly as if he would live as long as herself. Then in the evening, in town, she had manifestly had some misadventure: something must have happened there that it would be imperative to clear up. She had come back very late—it was past 11 o'clock, and on being met in the hall by her cousin, who was extremely anxious, had allowed she was tired and must rest a moment before mounting the stairs. They had passed together into the dining-room, her companion proposing a glass of wine and bustling to the sideboard to pour it out. This took but a moment, and when my informant turned round our poor friend had not had time to seat herself. Suddenly, with a small moan that was barely audible, she dropped upon the sofa. She was dead. What unknown "little rub" had dealt her the blow? What concussion, in the name of wonder, *had* awaited her in town? I mentioned immediately the one thinkable ground of disturbance—her having failed to meet at my house, to which by invitation for the purpose she had come at 5 o'clock, the gentleman I was to be married to, who had been accidentally kept away and with whom she had no acquaintance whatever. This obviously counted for little; but something else might easily have occurred: nothing in the London streets was more possible than an accident, especially an accident in those desperate cabs. What had she done, where had she gone on leaving my house? I had taken for granted she had gone straight home. We both presently remembered that in her excursions to town she sometimes, for convenience, for refreshment, spent an hour or two at the "Gentlewomen," the quiet little ladies' club, and I promised that it should be my first care to make at that establishment an earnest appeal. Then we entered the dim and dreadful chamber where she lay locked up in death and where, asking after a little to be left alone with her, I remained for half an hour. Death had made her, had kept her beautiful; but I felt above all, as I kneeled at her bed, that it had made her, had kept her silent. It had turned the key on something I was concerned to know.

On my return from Richmond and after another duty had been performed I drove to his chambers. It was the first time, but I had often wanted to see them. On the staircase, which, as the house contained twenty sets of rooms, was unrestrictedly public, I met his servant, who went back with me and ushered me in. At the sound of my entrance he appeared in the doorway of a further room, and the instant we were alone I produced my news: "She's dead!"

"Dead?" He was tremendously struck, and I noticed he had no need to ask whom, in this abruptness, I meant.

"She died last evening—just after leaving me."

He stared with the strangest expression, his eyes searching mine as for a trap. "Last evening—after leaving you?" He repeated my words in stupefaction. Then he brought out, so that it was in stupefaction I heard, "Impossible! I saw her."

"You 'saw' her?"

"On that spot—where you stand."

This called back to me after an instant, as if to help me to take it in, the great wonder of the warning of his youth. "In the hour of death—I understand: as you so beautifully saw your mother."

"Ah *not* as I saw my mother—not that way, not that way!" He was deeply moved by my news—far more moved, it was plain, than he would have been the day before: it gave me a vivid sense that, as I had then said to myself, there was indeed a relation between them and that he had actually been face to face with her. Such an idea, by its reassertion of his extraordinary privilege, would have suddenly presented him as painfully abnormal hadn't he vehemently insisted on the difference. "I saw her living. I saw her to speak to her. I saw her as I see you now."

It's remarkable that for a moment, though only for a moment, I found relief in the more personal, as it were, but also the more natural, of the two odd facts. The next, as I embraced this image of her having come to him on leaving me and of just what it accounted for in the disposal of her time, I demanded with a shade of harshness of which I was aware: "What on earth did she come for?"

He had now had a minute to think—to recover himself and judge of effects, so that if it was still with excited eyes he spoke he showed a conscious redness and made an inconsequent attempt to smile away the gravity of his words. "She came just to see me. She came—after what had passed at your house—so that we *should*, nevertheless at last meet. The impulse seemed to me exquisite, and that was the way I took it."

I looked round the room where she had been—where *she* had been and I never had till now. "And was the way you took it the way she expressed it?"

"She only expressed it by being here and by letting me look at her. That was enough!" he cried with an extraordinary laugh.

I wondered more and more. "You mean she didn't speak to you?"

"She said nothing. She only looked at me as I looked at her."

"And you didn't speak either?"

He gave me again his painful smile. "I thought of *you*. The situation was every way delicate. I used the finest tact. But she saw she had pleased me." He even repeated his dissonant laugh.

"She evidently 'pleased' you!" Then I thought a moment. "How long did she stay?"

"How can I say? It seemed twenty minutes, but it was probably less."

"Twenty minutes of silence!" I began to have my definite view and now in fact quite to clutch at it. "Do you know you're telling me a thing positively monstrous?"

He had been standing with his back to the fire; at this, with a pleading look, he came to me. "I beseech you, dearest, to take it kindly."

I could take it kindly, and I signified as much; but I couldn't somehow, as he rather awkwardly opened his arms, let him draw me to him. So there fell between us for an appreciable time the discomfort of a great silence.

He broke it by presently saying: "There's absolutely no doubt of her death?"

"Unfortunately none. I've just risen from my knees by the bed where they've laid her out."

He fixed his eyes hard on the floor; then he raised them to mine. "How does she look?"

"She looks—at peace."

He turned away again while I watched him; but after a moment he began: "At what hour then——?"

"It must have been near midnight. She dropped as she reached her house—from an affection of the heart which she knew herself and her physician knew her to have, but of which, patiently, bravely, she had never spoken to me."

He listened intently and for a minute was unable to speak. At last he broke out with an accent of which the almost boyish confidence, the really sublime simplicity, rings in my ears as I write: "Wasn't she *wonderful!*" Even at the time I was able to do it justice enough to answer that I had always told him so; but the next minute, as if after speaking he had caught a glimpse of what he might have made me feel, he went on quickly: "You can easily understand that if she didn't get home till midnight——"

I instantly took him up. "There was plenty of time for you to have seen her? How so," I asked, "when you didn't leave my house till late? I don't remember the very moment—I was preoccupied. But you know that though you said you had lots to do you sat for some time after dinner. She, on her side, was all the evening at the 'Gentlewomen,' I've just come from there—I've ascertained. She had tea there; she remained a long long time."

"What was she doing all the long long time?"

I saw him eager to challenge at every step my account of the matter; and the more he showed this the more I was moved to emphasise that version, to prefer with apparent perversity an explanation which only deepened the marvel and the mystery, but which, of the two prodigies it had to choose from, my reviving jealousy found easiest to accept. He stood there pleading with a candor that now seems to me beautiful for the privilege of having in spite of supreme defeat known the living woman; while I, with a passion I wonder at today, though it still smolders in a manner in its ashes, could only reply that, through a strange gift shared by her with his mother and on her own side likewise hereditary, the miracle of his youth had been renewed for him, the miracle of hers for her. She had been to him—yes, and by an impulse as charming as he liked; but oh she hadn't been in the body! It was a simple question of evidence. I had had, I maintained, a definite statement of what she had done—most of the time—at the little club. The place was almost empty, but the servants had noticed her. She had sat motionless in a deep chair by the drawing-room fire; she had leaned back her head, she had closed her eyes, she had seemed softly to sleep.

"I see. But till what o'clock?"

"There," I was obliged to answer, "the servants fail me a little. The portress in particular is unfortunately a fool, even though she too is supposed to be a Gentlewoman. She was evidently at that period of the evening, without a substitute and against regulations, absent for some little time from the cage in which it's her business to watch the comings and goings. She's muddled, she palpably prevaricates; so I can't positively, from her observation, give you an hour. But it was remarked toward half-past 10 that our poor friend was no longer in the club."

It suited him down to the ground. "She came straight here, and from here she went straight to the train."

"She couldn't have run it so close," I declared. "She never did that."

"There was no need of running it close, my dear—she had plenty of time. Your memory's at fault about my having left you late: I left you, as it happens, unusually early. I'm sorry my stay with you seemed long, for I was back here by 10."

"To put yourself into your slippers," I retorted, "and fall asleep in your chair. You slept till morning—you saw her in a dream!" He looked at me in silence and with sombre eyes—eyes that showed me he had some irritation to repress. Presently I went on: "You had a visit, at an extraordinary hour, from a lady—*soit:* nothing in the world's more probable. But there are ladies and ladies. How in the name of goodness, if she was unannounced and dumb and you had into the bargain never seen the least portrait of her—how could you identify the person we're talking of?"

"Haven't I to absolute satiety heard her described? I'll describe her for you in every particular."

"Don't!" I cried with a promptness that made him laugh once more. I colored at this, but I continued: "Did your servant introduce her?"

"He wasn't here—he's always away when he's wanted. One of the features of this big house is that from the street-door the different floors are accessible practically without challenge. My servant makes love to a young person employed in the rooms above these, and he had a long bout of it last evening. When he's out on that job he leaves my outer door, on the staircase, so much ajar as to enable him to slip back without a sound. The door then only requires a push. She pushed it—that simply took a little courage."

"A little? It took tons! And it took all sorts of impossible calculations."

"Well, she had them—she made them. Mind you, I don't deny for a moment," he added," that it was very very wonderful!"

Something in his tone kept me a time from trusting myself to speak. At last I said: "How did she come to know where you live?"

"By remembering the address on the little label the shop-people happily left sticking to the frame I had had made for my photograph."

"And how was she dressed?"

"In mourning, my own dear. No great depths of crape, but simple and scrupulous black. She had in her bonnet three small black feathers. She carried a little muff of astrachan. She has near the left eye," he continued, "a tiny vertical scar—"

I stopped him short. "The mark of a caress from her husband." Then I added: "How close you must have been to her!" He made no answer to this, and I thought he blushed, observing which I broke straight off. "Well, good-bye."

"You won't stay a little?" He came to me again tenderly, and this time I suffered him. "Her visit had its beauty," he murmured as he held me, "but yours has a greater one."

I let him kiss me, but I remembered, as I had remembered the day before, that the last kiss she had given, as I supposed, in this world had been for the lips he touched. "I'm life, you see," I answered. "What you saw last night was death."

"It was life—it was life!"

He spoke with a soft stubbornness—I disengaged myself. We stood looking at each other hard. "You describe the scene—so far as you describe it at all—in terms that are incomprehensible. She was in the room before you knew it?"

"I looked up from my letter-writing—at that table under the lamp I had been wholly absorbed in it—and she stood before me."

"Then what did you do?"

"I sprang up with an ejaculation, and she, with a smile, laid her finger, ever so warningly, yet with a sort of delicate dignity, to her lips. I knew it meant silence, but the strange thing was that it seemed immediately to explain and to justify her. We at any rate stood for a time that, as

I've told you, I can't calculate, face to face. It was just as you and I stand now."

"Simply staring?"

He shook an impatient head. "Ah! *we're* not staring!"

"Yes, but we're talking."

"Well, *we* were—after a fashion." He lost himself in the memory of it. "It was as friendly as this." I had on my tongue's end to ask if that was saying much for it, but I made the point instead that what they had evidently done was to gaze in mutual admiration. Then I asked if his recognition of her had been immediate. "Not quite," he replied, "for of course I didn't expect her; but it came to me long before she went who she was."

I thought a little. "And how did she at last go?"

"Just as she arrived. The door was open behind her and she passed out."

"Was she rapid—slow?"

"Rather quick. But looking behind her," he smiled to add. "I let her go, for I perfectly knew I was to take it as she wished."

I was conscious of exhaling a long vague sigh. "Well, you must take it now as *I* wish—you must let *me* go."

At this he drew near me again, detaining and persuading me, declaring with all due gallantry that I was a very different matter. I'd have given anything to have been able to ask him if he had touched her, but the words refused to form themselves: I knew to the last tenth of a tone how horrid and vulgar they'd sound. I said something else—I forget exactly what; it was feebly tortuous and intended, meanly enough, to make him tell me without my putting the question. But he didn't tell me; he only repeated, as from a glimpse of the propriety of soothing and consoling me, the sense of his declaration of some minutes before—the assurance that she was indeed exquisite, as I had always insisted, but that I was his "real" friend and his very own for ever. This led me to reassert, in the spirit of my previous rejoinder, that I had at least the merit of being alive; which in turn drew from him again the flash of contradiction I dreaded. "Oh *she* was alive! She was, she was!"

"She was dead, she was dead!" I asseverated with an energy, a determination it should *be* so, which comes back to me now almost as grotesque. But the sound of the word as it rang out filled me suddenly with horror, and all the natural emotion the meaning of it might have evoked

in other conditions gathered and broke in a flood. It rolled over me that
here was a great affection quenched and how much I had loved and
trusted her. I had a vision at the same time of the lonely beauty of her
end. "She's gone—she's lost to us for ever!" I burst into sobs.

"That's exactly what I feel," he exclaimed, speaking with extreme
kindness and pressing me to him for comfort. "She's gone; she's lost to
us for ever: so what does it matter now?" He bent over me, and when
his face had touched mine I scarcely knew if it were wet with my tears
or with his own.

It was my theory, my conviction, it became, as I may say, my attitude,
that they had still never "met"; and it was just on this ground I felt it
generous to ask him to stand with me at her grave. He did so very
modestly and tenderly, and I assumed, though he himself clearly cared
nothing for the danger, that the solemnity of the occasion, largely made
up of persons who had known them both and had a sense of the long
joke, would sufficiently deprive his presence of all light association. On
the question of what had happened the evening of her death little more
passed between us; I had been taken by a horror of the element of
evidence. On either hypothesis it was gross and prying. He on his side
lacked producible corroboration—everything, that is, but a statement of
his house-porter, on his own admission a most casual and intermittent
personage—that between the hours of 10 o'clock and midnight no less
than three ladies in deep black had flitted in and out of the place. This
proved far too much; we had neither of us any use for three. He knew I
considered I had accounted for every fragment of her time, and we
dropped the matter as settled; we abstained from further discussion.
What *I* knew however was that he abstained to please me rather than
because he yielded to my reasons. He didn't yield—he was only indul-
gent; he clung to his interpretation because he liked it better. He liked it
better, I held, because it had more to say to his vanity. That, in a similar
position, wouldn't have been its effect on me, though I had doubtless
quite as much; but these are things of individual humour and as to
which no person can judge for another. I should have supposed it more
gratifying to be the subject of one of those inexplicable occurrences that
are chronicled in thrilling books and disputed about at learned meetings;
I could conceive, on the part of a being just engulfed in the infinite and
still vibrating with human emotion, of nothing more fine and pure, more

high and august, than such an impulse of reparation, of admonition, or even of curiosity. *That* was beautiful, if one would, and I should in his place have thought more of myself for being so distinguished and so selected. It was public that he had already, that he had long figured in that light, and what was such a fact in itself but almost a proof? Each of the strange visitations contributed to establish the other. He had a different feeling; but he had also, I hasten to add, an unmistakable desire not to make a stand or, as they say, a fuss about it. I might believe what I liked—the more so that the whole thing was in a manner a mystery of my producing. It was an event of my history, a puzzle of my consciousness, not of his; therefore he would take about it any tone that struck me as convenient. We had both at all events other business on hand; we were pressed with preparations for our marriage.

Mine were assuredly urgent, but I found as the days went on that to believe what I "liked" was to believe what I was more and more intimately convinced of. I found also that I didn't like it so much as that came to, or that the pleasure at all events was far from being the cause of my conviction. My obsession, as I may really call it and as I began to perceive, refused to be elbowed away, as I had hoped, by my sense of paramount duties. If I had a great deal to do I had still more to think of, and the moment came when my occupations were gravely menaced by my thoughts. I see it all now, I feel it, I live it over. It's terribly void of joy, it's full indeed to overflowing of bitterness; and yet I must do myself justice—I couldn't have been other than I was. The same strange impressions, had I to meet them again, would produce the same deep anguish, the same sharp doubts, the same still sharper certainties. Oh it's all easier to remember than to write, but even could I retrace the business hour by hour, could I find terms for the inexpressible, the ugliness and the pain would quickly stay my hand. Let me then note very simply and briefly that a week before our wedding-day, three weeks after her death, I knew in all my fibres that I had something very serious to look in the face and that if I was to make this effort I must make it on the spot and before another hour should elapse. My unextinguished jealousy —that was the Medusa-mask. It hadn't died with her death, it had lividly survived, and it was fed by suspicions unspeakable. They *would* be unspeakable today, that is, if I hadn't felt the sharp need of uttering them at the time. This need took possession of me—to save me, as it seemed, from my fate. When once it had done so I saw—in the urgency of the case, the diminishing hours and shrinking interval—only one issue, that of absolute promptness and frankness. I could at least not do him the wrong of delaying another day; I could at least treat my difficulty as too fine for a subterfuge. Therefore very quietly, but none the less abruptly and hideously, I put it before him on a certain evening that we must reconsider our situation and recognise that it had completely altered.

He stared bravely. "How in the world altered?"

"Another person has come between us."

He took but an instant to think. "I won't pretend not to know whom you mean." He smiled in pity for my aberration, but he meant to be kind. "A woman dead and buried!"

"She's buried, but she's not dead. She's dead for the world—she's dead for me. But she's not dead for you."

"You hark back to the different construction we put on her appearance?"

"No," I answered, "I hark back to nothing. I've no need of it. I've more than enough with what's before me."

"And pray, darling, what may that be?"

"You're completely changed."

"By that absurdity?" he laughed.

"Not so much by that one as by other absurdities that have followed it."

"And what may *they* have been?"

We had faced each other fairly, with eyes that didn't flinch; but his had a dim strange light, and my certitude triumphed in his perceptible paleness. "Do you really pretend," I asked, "not to know what they are?"

"My dear child," he replied, "you describe them too sketchily!"

I considered a moment. "One may well be embarrassed to finish the picture! But from that point of view—and from the beginning—what was ever more embarrassing than your idiosyncrasy?"

He invoked his vagueness—a thing he always did beautifully. "My idiosyncrasy?"

"Your notorious, your peculiar power."

He gave a great shrug of impatience, a groan of overdone disdain. "Oh my peculiar power!"

"Your accessibility to forms of life," I coldly went on, "your command of impressions, appearances, contacts, closed—for our gain or our loss—to the rest of us. That was originally a part of the deep interest with which you inspired me—one of the reasons I was amused, I was indeed positively proud, to know you. It was a magnificent distinction; it's a magnificent distinction still. But of course I had no prevision then of the way it would operate now; and even had that been the case I should have had none of the extraordinary way of which its action would affect me."

"To what in the name of goodness," he pleadingly enquired, "are you fantastically alluding?" Then as I remained silent, gathering a tone for my charge, "How in the world *does* it operate?" he went on; "and how in the world are you affected?"

"She missed you for five years," I said, "but she never misses you now. You're making it up!"

"Making it up?" He had begun to turn from white to red.

"You see her—you see her: you see her every night!" He gave a loud sound of derision, but I felt it ring false. "She comes to you as she came that evening," I declared; "having tried it she found she liked it!" I was able, with God's help, to speak without blind passion or vulgar violence; but those were the exact words—and far from "sketchy" they then appeared to me—that I uttered. He had turned away in his laughter, clapping his hands at my folly, but in an instant he faced me again with a change of expression that struck me. "Do you dare to deny," I then asked, "that you habitually see her?"

He had taken the line of indulgence, of meeting me halfway and kindly humouring me. At all events he to my astonishment suddenly said: "Well, my dear, what if I do?"

"It's your natural right: it belongs to your constitution and to your wonderful if not perhaps quite enviable fortune. But you'll easily understand that it separates us. I unconditionally release you."

"Release me?"

"You must choose between me and her."

He looked at me hard. "I see." Then he walked away a little, as if grasping what I had said and thinking how he had best treat it. At last he turned on me afresh. "How on earth do you know such an awfully private thing?"

"You mean because you've tried so hard to hide it? It *is* awfully private, and you may believe I shall never betray you. You've done your best, you've acted your part, you've behaved, poor dear! loyally and admirably. Therefore I've watched you in silence, playing my part too; I've noted every drop in your voice, every absence in your eyes, every effort in your indifferent hand: I've waited till I was utterly sure and miserably unhappy. How *can* you hide it when you're abjectly in love with her, when you're sick almost to death with the joy of what she gives you?" I checked his quick protest with a quicker gesture. "You love her as you've *never* loved, and, passion for passion, she gives it straight back! She rules you, she holds you, she has you all! A woman, in such a case as mine, divines and feels and sees; she's not a dull dunce who has to be 'credibly informed.' You come to me mechanically, compunctiously, with the dregs of your tenderness and the remnant of your life. I can renounce you, but I can't share you: the best of you is hers, I know what it is and freely give you up to her for ever!"

He made a gallant fight, but it couldn't be patched up; he repeated his denial, he retracted his admission, he ridiculed my charge, of which I freely granted him moreover the indefensible extravagance. I didn't pretend for a moment that we were talking of common things; I didn't pretend for a moment that he and she were common people. Pray, if they *had* been, how should I ever have cared for them? They had enjoyed a rare extension of being and they had caught me up in their flight; only I couldn't breathe in such air and I promptly asked to be set down. Everything in the facts was monstrous, and most of all my lucid perception of them; the only thing allied to nature and truth was my having to act on that perception. I felt after I had spoken in this sense that my assurance was complete; nothing had been wanting to it but the sight of my effect on him. He disguised indeed the effect in a cloud of chaff, a diversion that gained him time and covered his retreat. He challenged my sincerity, my sanity, almost my humanity, and that of course widened our breach and confirmed our rupture. He did everything in short but convince me either that I was wrong or that he was unhappy: we separated and I left him to his inconceivable communion.

He never married, any more than I've done. When six years later, in solitude and silence, I heard of his death I hailed it as a direct contribution to my theory. It was sudden, it was never properly accounted for, it was surrounded by circumstances in which—for oh I took them to pieces!—I distinctly read an intention, the mark of his own hidden hand. It was the result of a long necessity, of an unquenchable desire. To say exactly what I mean, it was a response to an irresistible call.

Past a Year and a Day

Annette Covino

I sail on
In my paper boat.
Sail on cardboard waves
Painted midnight blue.

Sail on
Past the landscape
Of my dreams
Afraid to stop
And rest awhile
On my own night coast.

I send my albatross
To scout the shore
But he returns
And silently resumes
His watch
From my stooped back.

I would visit
That locked up king
In that deserted castle

If I were brave
And calm him
With Oreo cookies
And a paper doll queen.

But I am afraid
That morning would find me
Land locked
In that place.

So I sail on
Glimpsing shadow plays
Of my dreams.

How far north
Must I sail
Before I encounter
The long day
And bring my paper boat
To rest?

Ladies' Choice

Saralee Kaye

Dorothy Parker once wrote an amusing monologue called "The Waltz," in which a woman reveals her thoughts while dancing with a less-than-ideal gentleman. But what about wallflowers who never even get that far? "Ladies' Choice" gives one of them a chance to speak up . . . only to remind us there is a fine line between shyness and self-absorption. SARALEE KAYE's many pasts include acting, court reporting, teaching high school English, music contracting and textbook production editing. She is currently embarked on a new career as a physician assistant.

EIGHT MEASURES GONE on a ladies' choice. Couples began to fill the floor, and the gym became a mass of slowly circling heads. Ladies' choice—I felt my pulse quicken as the words rang in my ears, and it was hard to swallow with that tiny lump in my throat. "Now or never, now or never—ask him, *ask* him!" The words throbbed and pounded and echoed in my head.

All evening I had been waiting for this moment. From a purely practical standpoint I would truthfully be able to counter Mom's inevitable "Well, dear, did you dance tonight?" with a definite affirmative instead of the tired evasiveness of "Oh, nobody did very much—not really," or the defensive annoyance of "Can't I go to a stupid little dance without a cross-examination?!" I winced visibly at the thought of the latter response. Though I believed it was true that a fifteen-year-old didn't need to give a detailed rundown of each moment away from home, I also knew that I'd be only too ecstatic to unravel tales of my unrivaled success as the belle of the ball. Truly, I knew I'd be happy enough if I could only say, "Oh, yes, of course I danced," followed by the casual mention of two or three male names. Or one.

The one I was considering in particular was Walt Nelson. For about three weeks I had been secretly walking on a private cloud whenever Walt entered the chem lab or read the morning announcements in homeroom. And it had been just about too much for me the day before, when he was only one behind me in the cafeteria line. The thing was, he barely noticed me—until I spilled some soup from an overflowing bowl. Then he smiled sympathetically, and the smile remained imprinted on my brain through algebra, history and the long walk home. So that was another good reason to ask Walt for the ladies' choice. Walt would *have* to notice me if he were my dancing partner.

But as I took a step across the floor, that very idea made me tremble and stop. Yes, he will notice me, I thought, but what will he see? I *am* rather pretty, I told myself (and could really be attractive if my teeth were just a little straighter), and I spent hours fixing my hair, though it always manages to have that slightly frizzy look no matter how much effort goes into it, but oh—it *does* look extra nice tonight, doesn't it?

With each new notion and every panicky repetition, I could feel my heart beat faster and faster as the stream of frantic thoughts reeled through my mind. They picked up even more speed as I thought about my dress. It was new, and "just the right style to accent your slender figure," the saleslady had said, and I was sure she was right. But at that moment I wondered if it wasn't just a bit too dressy for such a casual dance, and maybe a little too long. And my eyes—large and green and so expressive, but if *only* I had tried just a dash of that eye makeup. Though surely those long, velvety lashes were lovely enough on their own. And, oh, those pantyhose *always* managed to gap at my ankles no matter what, and how could I be absolutely sure my slip wasn't showing? And on and on and on, right through the first stanza.

By the end of the first chorus, my knees were weak. Only half a record left. No one else had asked Walt to dance—that was an unusually lucky break. But what would he think when I asked him? Would he feel sorry for me—would he be embarrassed? He really couldn't say *no,* could he? What would he say to his friends after dancing with me? If he joked about it, I knew I'd just die. Worst of all, Walt might realize how I feel about him, and though he might find it amusing, he'd probably spend the rest of the night avoiding me. I shuddered at the various possibilities.

Finally, I steeled myself for the big moment. No matter what Walt does or doesn't think of me, he isn't about to come over and ask *me* to dance.

The second verse was well under way. I mentally reviewed the steps I would take, the words I would say. Fidgeting with the belt buckle on my new dress, I started purposefully across the floor. I saw Walt on the other side, and for an instant he grinned warmly. How perfect! Just the extra ounce of courage I needed!

But as the last chorus welled rhythmically over the sound system, my heart gave a sudden thud at a startling new notion. How could I ask Walt to dance *now,* when the selection for the ladies' choice was practically over? He might still dance with me, of course, for the five or six remaining measures, but it would be so short a time that he might feel *obliged* to ask me for the next dance. Or—even worse—he might *not.* And maybe by this time he'd even forgotten that this one was a ladies' choice.

The record ended. I was halfway across the floor, feeling a little dejected, a little relieved. I walked back into the other side to sit down for a while.

I've been sitting here for quite a while. There will probably be one more ladies' choice tonight, perhaps an hour from now, I figure. I'll have plenty of time to think, to plan. I'll walk right up to Walt, even before the music begins. Next time I'm sure I can do it—if only my dress doesn't get too wrinkled from sitting so long.

The Night People

Edward D. Hoch

Since May 1973, every issue of Ellery Queen's Mystery Magazine *has contained at least one new tale by the Mystery Writers of America's past president* EDWARD D. HOCH, *a Rochester, New York writer, who long ago lost count of how many stories he's written (by now, the number must be close to eight hundred). "You've been really digging into the old magazines to come up with 'The Night People,'" Ed says. "I'll be happy to have it back in print." It first appeared in the May 1961 issue of* Web Detective Story Magazine, *which I did almost literally dig out of a pile of old periodicals sold to me by a Broadway street vendor.*

"NOTHING EVER HAPPENS on Saturdays," the city editor complained, his yellowed teeth digging into the pipe stem. "That's why we have to use gimmicks to sell papers."

I cleared my throat and nodded in agreement, acting exactly like the cub reporter that I was. "Yes, sir," I mumbled, because it seemed the proper thing to say.

"Business closes down, Congress isn't usually in session, the government officials take the weekend off, and worst of all—there are fewer people downtown to buy our papers."

"You're right."

"On Sunday we can sell 'em ads and comics, but on Saturday afternoon it's rough. And that's goin' to be your assignment. You're goin' to dig me up a story—every Saturday—for the afternoon edition. A story that no one else has—a story that's big enough for front page headlines. Understand?"

"Yes, sir."

"Any questions?"

"No sir."

"Good. It's two-thirty now. You've got till ten A.M. to bring in your first big story, kid. Go to it."

"Thank you, sir . . . ," I mumbled.

"You'll get a by-line if it's any good," he called after me. "Remember, before ten o'clock. . . ."

I nodded silently to myself and went out, into the city. . . .

But where to find a story in the middle of the night, when Saturday's dawn was still so many hours away? The bars would have closed at two, and even the drunks would be well on their way home by this time. I stood in the doorway of the *Times-Chronicle* and lit a cigarette, thinking about it.

Perhaps an after-hours joint. . . . Sure, why not a story about what goes on during the night moments? But that would be feature-story stuff, not for front-page headlines. It wouldn't sell papers on a damp Saturday afternoon.

What would?

I started walking, turning up the collar of my raincoat against the soaking drizzle that drifted down over the city streets.

"Hello, mister. . . ."

I turned, barely able to make out the girl in the shadows. "Yes?"

"Lonely?"

I figured her for a street-walker and as she came into the light I had no reason to change my mind. She wore a raincoat open at the neck to reveal a dark sweater. Her lipstick showed signs of fast, irregular repair, and I guessed that she'd already had at least one customer tonight.

"Sorry," I said. "I'm not your type."

"I'm everybody's type," she answered, moving closer through the mist.

"Know any place where I can get a little action?"

"My apartment."

"Different kind. Cards, dice, that action."

"You a queer?" she asked, watching me more closely.

"I hope not. Come on, where's some action."

She sighed and made a motion of resignation. "Slip me five for my time and I'll take you to a place."

"It's a deal." I uncoiled a wrinkled fin from my wallet and passed it to her in the night. "How far?"

"Not far," she said. "Follow me," and she led the way down a side street where a broken streetlight added to the gloom of the dark. And as I followed her I felt like a hundred other men must have felt, perhaps following her down this same street, though with a different purpose.

I stepped cautiously around the streetlight's broken glass, half seen in the night's dimness, and ahead I saw the muted activity of a place that might have been a barber shop or a pool room. But wasn't.

We went in, and she nodded to the man at the door, a shifty little runt who looked as if he might not have seen the sunlight in twenty years. "I brought you a customer," she said. "Remember to tell the boss."

"Sure, sure," the runt told her.

Then she turned to me. "No poker tonight. Only dice—OK?"

"OK," I nodded.

She led me back further, into the bowels of the building, to a wide arena where an intent circle of customers crouched on the concrete.

"You're faded."

"Eight's the point."

I sneaked in between a bald middle-aged man and a younger fellow with a thin mustache, watching the shake and roll of the dice with almost hypnotic fascination. But the man who was rolling, a huge monster with a wicked, terrible face, stopped dead and stared at me. "Who let that guy in?" he said. "Does anybody know him?"

"I brought him," the girl said quietly but firmly. "He wanted action."

"Damn! Well, you can just take him somewhere else. This is a closed game. Take him somewhere else."

"Take him where?"

"To bed with you for all I care!" And a ripple of brief laughter passed over the circle of men.

"Come on," she told him. "Let's blow this lousy joint."

"OK," I nodded, following her once more into the outer dampness.

"Men!" she snorted. "I hate every damned one of them. I hate 'em!"

"That's an odd statement for a girl like you to make," I observed, falling into step beside her.

"Why, because of what I do?"

"Well, yes," I admitted.

"What am I supposed to say? That I love 'em all?"

"I don't know."

"Let me tell you sumthin'. Bud. Let me tell you the story of my life in one short chapter. My father got drunk one mighty night and beat my mother's head in with an ax. Then he did the same thing to my older sister. I was twelve at the time. I ran out of the house and hid behind the garage and prayed and cried all night, waiting for him to find me there. In the morning I crept back into the house and found him hanging from a beam in the basement."

"It must have been horrible."

"At first it was, but I got used to taking care of myself after that." She turned up her coat collar against the suddenly heavy rain. "Hell of a night, isn't it?"

"Yeah."

"Sure you won't come up to my place?"

"What for?"

"You gotta have a reason?"

"I'm working," I confessed. "I'm a reporter on the Times-Chronicle, after a story for the evening paper. Something big, the editor told me."

"Something big," she mused. "We could blow up city hall."

"Oh, I don't think. . . ."

"You take everything serious, don't you, kid?"

"Don't you?"

"Sometimes. Sometimes not. I take life as it comes. That's the only way."

"I suppose so." The rain was heavier now, and I steered her into a handy doorway.

"What time is it, anyway?" she asked.

"Must be close to four o'clock."

"What a stinkin' night."

"Why don't you go home and go to bed?"

"Just one more. I need just one more tonight. It's so damned cold in my room."

I was silent for a time, not knowing how to answer her. Then, finally, I mumbled, "I'll come up, just for a few minutes."

"Thanks, kid," she said, very quietly, and led the way through the rain once again. . . .

It was, I suppose, the kind of room I should have expected. Dim and damp and dingy, with a single naked light bulb swinging from the ceiling. With a couple of chairs and a table and a rumpled bed.

"Got anything to drink?" I asked her.

"Maybe. A bit of rum."

"Anything."

"Look, kid, you don't have to. . . ."

"Get me the rum, will you?"

"Sure, kid." And she poured me a stiff shot. "What's your story, kid? What are you running away from?"

"Got no story. If I did, I'd be a writer instead of a newspaper reporter."

"Everybody's got a story."

"Sure." I thought about it. "College for a couple of years, the army, and now a job on the Times-Chronicle. That's it."

"No girl?"

I nodded. "In college. She promised to wait for me, while I was in the army. Two months after I left home she married a football player."

"It's a story anyway."

"Sure."

"Would you like to sleep with me?"

"I. . . . I don't think so."

"It wouldn't cost you anything."

I felt sick. "No, I. . . . I appreciate it, but. . . ."

"But you're working."

"That's right. I'm working. Only a little over five hours to find that story."

"What if you don't find it?"

"What?"

"What if you don't find a story? Will the world end?"

"No, of course not. But he expects one. If he doesn't get it he'll have to run a story about the weather or something."

"So?"

"It's awfully tough to sell papers on Saturday afternoons. He explained it all to me."

"Yeah."

"Could I have another drink?"

"I guess so." There was a tapping on the door and she ducked the bottle out of sight. "Hope it isn't the cops," she whispered.

She walked to the door and opened it a crack, and saw what was apparently a familiar face. "What in hell do you want?" she stormed.

A creepy little guy slipped into the room. "Didn't want to interrupt you, but. . . . have you got a spoon I could borrow? It's real important."

She snorted and disappeared into the next room, returning in a moment with a spoon. "Don't bother to return it."

"Thanks. Thanks a lot. If you ever need anything. . . ."

"Just to be left alone, Mister, that's all."

"Well. . . . thanks again."

She slammed the door after him. "The stupid slob!"

"What the heck did he want with a spoon in the middle of the night?" I asked in innocence.

"He takes the stuff. Dope, you know. They warm it on a spoon or sumthin'."

I fumbled for a cigarette. "How can you live in a place like this, anyway? What kind of life do you find here?"

"What other kind of life is there? I could be one of those New York society dolls and only sleep with college boys, I suppose. Would that be better?"

I didn't answer, because I didn't really know what to tell her. She needed someone who'd lived a lot longer than I had. She needed a priest, or maybe just a good man. I surely wasn't a priest, and I was too young to know how good I was.

She poured herself a drink from the bottle and came over to where I sat. Suddenly, all at once, she was old—she might have been the oldest girl of twenty-five I'd ever seen. "I'm trapped," she told me, settling down on the arm of my chair. "Trapped in a life without beginning or end."

"I've got to be going," I said. "There's no story here."

"No," she agreed sadly. "Not here."

I started to get up, but she slid her soft weight down upon me. "I have to go," I repeated.

"How about a little kiss first?"

"No. . . ." I managed to break free, struggling to my feet. And then I was out the door, casting only a final backward glance at her sad, lonely face. As I went down the stairs I felt for my wallet, but it was still there. . . .

Outside, the rain had settled into an annoying pattern of early morning drizzle, with clouds that hung low over the dim buildings and blotted out the golden sunrise somewhere to the east.

I walked, because there was nothing else to do. No story, no nothing. It was Saturday morning and nothing ever happened on Saturday mornings. Nothing but sleep and regrets for the night that was past.

I stopped for coffee in a little fly-specked lunch counter just opening for the day's business, trading comments in a monotone of dull improbability with the sleepy-eyed counter man. And then back to the street.

With my footsteps carrying me back toward the apartment where she would be sleeping now, lonely after a damp night of wandering. Why not? Where else did I have to go? Why not go back to her, for a few minutes, an hour. . . .

And as I turned into her street I saw the first police car pulling up. And then another, almost as quickly from the opposite direction, its low siren splitting the morning quiet.

And before my running feet reached the house, I knew. I knew even as I pushed my way through the wakened tenants, up the stairs to her apartment. I didn't know how, but I knew what. . . .

"Where you goin', Mister?"

"Times-Chronicle."

"OK, take a look."

The little creep from downstairs was huddled in a corner of the hallway, sobbing and mumbling at the officers who crowded around him. I went into her room and saw what he'd done. Only one leg was visible, bare, hanging across the rumpled bed. The rest of her body had tumbled down between the bed and the wall, out of sight, mercifully. I saw the blood on the sheets and looked no further.

"He do it?" I asked one of the cops.

"Who else? He's all doped up. Must 'a killed him, seein' those guys goin' up to her room every night. Decided he wanted somethin' too," he said.

"Yeah."

I kept going, down the stairs to the street, walking, then running, away from there, back to the solid reality of the city room at the Times-Chronicle. I had my story.

All the way up the words tumbled about in my brain, sorting themselves into neat paragraphs of type. And the city room was buzzing when I reached it, clattering with typewriters, churning with words.

"You're back," the editor said, raising his head from a pile of wet galleys. "Get the story?"

"I got it. A murder."

His eyebrows went up and he motioned to the rewrite man. "Give it to me. From the beginning."

I gave it to him. From the beginning.

When I'd finished he frowned across the desk at me. "Well? Names, man, names!"

"Names?" I felt stupid.

"What were their names?"

"I. . . . I don't know. Do they need names?"

He sighed and shook his head at the rewrite man. "For a newspaper they need names. There's no story in a nameless drug addict killing a nameless prostitute."

"But it is a story," I insisted. "They were people, just like you and me."

He just kept shaking his head. "Not like you and me, kid. They belonged to a different world."

"But the story. . . ."

"Never mind. We've got a train wreck for page one. We don't need any local stuff."

He turned away from me then, and the rewrite man hurried away, and the buzzing of the city room rolled over me like a tide. And I went over to my little desk in the far corner of the room and sat there for a long time, staring at the typewriter and wondering what her name had been. . . .

Duet

Alexandra Elizabeth Honigsberg

A troubling woman is a key ingredient of "Duet," a sensual and sensuous drama set in the world of serious music—hardly surprising since ALEXANDRA ELIZABETH HONIGSBERG *is a concert violist, singer and conductor who has performed at Carnegie Hall, Lincoln Center and the Kennedy Center for the Performing Arts in Washington, D.C. Her stories appear in various genre publications, and one of her poems is featured in Edward E. Kramer's new anthology,* Dark Destiny.

PARTICIPANTS and spectators alike hung suspended for a moment, out of time, by the power of the master's hands. The air quivered with echoes in the aftermath of the conflagration, the hymn to the goddess, Love. The master's ecstasy-widened eyes narrowed, and he brought his stick down with a force like Thor's war hammer. The chords of the final chorus shattered the silence as voices exploded with cries to another goddess:

> O Fortuna,
> Velut luna
> Statu variabilis, . . .

Then the final mad headlong rush began, rose from a sudden tense pianissimo to the abandon of fortissimo. The maestro led them, leaping and slashing the air with his baton to whip his musicians and audience to ever greater frenzy. The relentless pagan drumbeats drove them on as he conjured controlled hysteria in the name of Carl Orff's *Carmina Burana.*

No matter how many times Arthur watched his mentor work, it never ceased to amaze him how the maestro could look so out of control but hold their very souls with a glance or gesture. He marveled at how Maestro Woodward, white-haired and leonine, could call composers back from the dead through the score. Mere mortals spoke of beat and structure, phrasing and cues, nuances of interpretation in every conservatory and café in the world. Bernard Woodward transcended all that to *essence,* embodied it, made it live. Arthur, as he thought back, realized that was what had made him decide that he must work with Woodward and no other, no matter what it took to win the position as his assistant. From principal horn player to doctoral candidate in conducting at Juilliard, to Tanglewood's summer program with the maestro, Arthur had been relentless until Woodward had noticed him.

Whenever Maestro Woodward conducted, Arthur felt himself there on the podium with him, and this night was no exception. They were linked. His heart raced, his breath quickened, and the blood surged through every part of his body, making muscles clench and thrum with life. Watching from the hidden observation window backstage at Carnegie Hall, Arthur felt the thrill of a voyeur, the visceral high of a lover. Power—raw, glorious power—filled him. And he knew that someday it would be his to wield as the maestro just did. The climax left him breathless. He barely heard the applause.

Arthur watched as the maestro stood frozen, arms raised, then turned slowly to face his adoring followers. An ache in Arthur's own fingers made him realize that he had been clutching at the window ledge. He steadied himself and took a few deep breaths before emerging from his inner sanctum to face the onslaught that was sure to greet him in the Green Room—and her. Like the consummate warrior, Arthur Godwin coolly strode off to meet the man who drove him toward greatness, and the woman who drove him toward chaos.

In the hallway Arthur politely greeted those around him, and they made way for the maestro's protégé. He remained outwardly austere, the performance fire just barely masked behind sable eyes which still smoldered. The applause from the hall was audible as Arthur slipped inside the quiet that was the Green Room.

Everything was ready for the small private reception—flowers, cards, telegrams, champagne. Within that brief silence, away from the spell of his mentor and the concert, Arthur's whole body ached with longing. He looked in the mirror at the dressing table, ran fingers through his hair, scrutinized every angle of his face. Yes, he still looked youthful, but hardened, like a shrewd Alexander. And just as ambitious, he laughed to himself.

For thirteen years, since the age of twelve, he had honed his skill and desire with a single-mindedness and fidelity that was fierce. Passions had come and gone—pleasures and playthings—but nothing had ever captured his heart like the maestro's music and the stage. Even now, he kept telling himself, Janine was just a diversion, a fascinating mental playmate of high spirits—his teacher's business manager, friend and youthful ex-wife. Love had nothing to do with it, no matter what she said.

"Arthur. You're here already. Good."

Arthur turned to see Janine closing the door behind her. The lights glinted off the rhinestones about her throat and warmed the depths of her black velvet evening dress. Sensory replays of the performance ran through him in distracting bits and snatches, but he silenced them. Control, business, he reminded himself.

Arthur flashed his most charming smile and said, "Janine. You look lovely," and lifted her offered hand to his lips. She locked eyes with him and gave him one of her sly-but-innocent half smiles, lingering a moment longer than he would have wished—which caused another sort of sensory replay to jolt his nerves. Damn her, he thought, and her raised eyebrow told him that his mental flinch had registered. She grinned with satisfaction. They had played this game before. Arthur turned her hand over and kissed her palm, giving her a jolt of his own, then turned toward the bar. Never let them see you sweat, he muttered to himself.

Before either of them could exchange another glance, the maestro entered the room and filled it with his presence. The buzz of admirers out in the hallway was abruptly cut off as the door closed. Arthur could swear that for a moment the maestro glowed. Then the man leaned against the wall, spent but sated. His mane was tousled and a few stray strands remained matted to his sweaty forehead.

Woodward walked over and embraced Janine, who kissed him. Then, still holding her hands, he fixed Arthur with his gaze. It made Arthur feel naked. Maestro Woodward gave a wry little smile and said, "So, Arthur, do you think we raised Orff's goddess tonight?"

Arthur shrugged. "Why bother to ask me? You heard it, you *felt* it." The words came out harsher than Arthur had intended them.

Woodward released Janine and reached out to clasp Arthur's shoulder. He chuckled and said, "Patience, Arthur, my proud falcon. You'll get your wings. But the more you want it, the longer you'll wait. It's all alchemy, the grand *coniunctio*."

Arthur hated when he did that, admonishing him with the words of some ancient magicians. "Talk score study, marketing, PR, orchestra relations, but *not* hocus-pocus. I'm no mystic," Arthur answered. "I'll wait, however long it takes—I've waited this long, after all, and you'd had your major orchestral debut by my age, don't forget. I just don't have to like the waiting." Arthur scowled.

"Arthur, above all, you are my legacy. Please don't rush things. Trust me. Trust yourself. It would make it easier if you didn't fight it so much, Arthur. You know that."

Arthur did know that—without children, Woodward was a relentless teacher. And the maestro had always been right in matters of his career.

"And now let me get to the bathroom, wash up, and have a cigarette. Then you can open the Green Room for visitors," said Woodward as he disappeared into his prep rooms. Both Arthur and Janine nodded. Janine set the table with the maestro's silver fountain pen and ink pot filled with silver leaf. When the maestro emerged, looking much refreshed, Arthur opened the door and drank in that moment of calm before the storm.

"You look like hell, Bernie. And with your birthday gala at the end of the week, you can't afford to run yourself into the ground," Arthur heard Janine say as he walked into Woodward's studio.

"Oh, you worry too much, Janine. I'll be fine. Sixty isn't quite venerable yet, you know," he replied, a wicked twinkle in his eye. He took a long drag on his cigarette, hacking, and shooed her away. Janine grunted her disapproval as she left and said over her shoulder to Arthur, "You talk some sense to him, will you?"

Arthur chuckled. "I'll do my best. But you know how he is."

"Too damn well," came her distant reply, both of them speaking in a tone that they knew the maestro would hear. Arthur watched, distracted, until she was out of his sight. He turned to catch Woodward's gaze lingering in her general direction as well. It was no secret that he missed her, even though he couldn't live with her—and it had little to do with the fact that Janine was half his age, as he could wear down a teenager, Arthur reminded himself.

Arthur shook himself from his musing and sat at the piano next to the maestro so they could work on the Verdi *Requiem* together for the gala. Woodward looked at him quizzically.

"Must I have both my business manager and my assistant plotting against me under my own roof?" he said with a smile.

"For your own good, maestro. Can't have you dropping from exhaustion in front of all those people, and don't want you getting run-down with this killer flu that's going around. Remember what happened to you in Vienna last season?"

"But I finished the concert!"

"And ended up in the hospital for your foolishness, right?"

"You all overreacted."

Arthur sighed. There was no talking to him when he was in one of these moods—imperious as ever. He would never understand how Janine could call this man, this icon, "Bernie."

Woodward took the break to turn to the score for the Verdi and opened, with reverence, to the finale, the "Libera me."

"Maestro, why perform a piece about death at a celebration of your life?" Arthur asked.

Woodward smiled indulgently, his eyes lit with excitement. "Because that's just it, Arthur—it's not about death. It's about facing death and awakening from our ideas about it. It's about breaking free, letting go, and finding peace in that—sort of a different side of the ideas of life and love in the *Carmina* we performed last week, no?"

Arthur shook his head, "I'm afraid I can't quite see it that way. I'm not the philosophical type."

"Then how do you see it, Arthur?"

Arthur stiffened and began to spout the usual about its form and structure. The maestro let him go on for a bit before interrupting him. "But what does it all mean, Arthur? Verdi was not a religious man, yet he had a certain faith and this is an operatic work. How do you see the drama?"

Good question, Arthur thought as he pondered it. But he could not quite put the ideas into words.

"Think about this staged as a sort of passion play. The lone soprano, speaking for all Creation, the Bride, the beloved Church, begging for deliverance from the Judgment. She pleads with her Savior for salvation —from eternal fear and loneliness. That plea is echoed by the entire stage. We need every soul in that hall involved in this drama by the end. Then we will make magic."

Arthur had never seen it in quite that way before. He often tuned Woodward out when he spoke of the mystical, the larger human struggle. But as a singular struggle, he could more readily understand it, and got an idea.

"If we take a short breath after the previous movement, 'Lux aeterna,' and kill all the lights but a single spot on the soprano opening in the 'Libera me,' we'll drive that point home." Arthur was surprised at himself, but he continued with the concept since the maestro had not flinched. "Then the lights are thrown up in time for the repeat of the 'Dies irae,' until the end of the piece."

Woodward grew thoughtful and nodded his affirmation. "Yes, yes, that could work. We keep the chorus seated until the lights come up— they can rise during the racket of the drums and brass. But the orchestra will need stand lights. Give the house manager at Carnegie a call about it, will you?"

"Sure thing," Arthur replied, and rose to make it so.

"Arthur, how do the trumpets sound from where you are?" Woodward called from the podium to the center of the parquet from where Arthur always listened. Arranged in the balcony and just below in the dress circle, on either side of the horseshoe, were four offstage trumpets to echo those in the orchestra—the trumpets of the Last Judgment, the "Tuba mirum."

"The ones in the balcony are behind, maestro—are their monitors set up?" Arthur replied.

Maestro looked to the stage manager, who gave him a sign in the affirmative. He looked up to the domed arch at the top of Carnegie Hall and said to them, "Please don't trust your ears. Watch me on the monitors or we'll have a train wreck—understand me, ladies and gentlemen?" The musicians waved to him from their perches. "Arthur, come up here and take it from their entrance at measure ninety-one, please. I want to go out into the house to listen myself."

An instant adrenaline rush hit Arthur as he grabbed his score and baton and mounted the stage. He closed his eyes for a moment to gather his wits, then gave the downbeat.

A lone trumpet gives its call and is answered from the four corners of the hall, one after another. Layer upon layer of sound is mixed until they play in unison, joined by a phalanx of horns and trombones—the instruments to shake the tombs and wake the dead from their long sleep.

When it was right, that section always gave Arthur chills—and it was almost right. Good enough for that afternoon. It was Wednesday, so they had two more rehearsals to perfect it before the gala on Saturday.

The maestro returned to the stage and thanked him, looking drawn and tired, but satisfied. Arthur hesitated a moment before he returned the podium to his mentor, then went upstairs to the Green Room to rest for a bit before the end of rehearsal. The next day would bring the soloists, and he wanted to take a careful look at those sections again. But he found a surprise inside.

"I didn't expect to see you here," he said to Janine, who lounged on the couch, scanning Woodward's datebook, looking not the least bit surprised.

"I had to rush to the agent's office and take care of some arrangements for Bernie. They needed a last-minute replacement in Vienna tomorrow night for Mahler's *Resurrection,* but he'll be back in time for the dress on Friday morning."

"Whoa," Arthur said, and whistled through his teeth, "nothing like cutting it close. But that's Woodward—as if he isn't pushing himself hard enough. I wonder when he would've told me?" He shook his head. "Is it me, or has this whole concert suffered from Chinese Interesting Times?"

Janine laughed. "Why, just because you can't control everything yourself?"

Arthur went cold. He didn't want to get involved with this familiar refrain. "That's uncalled for, Janine," he said. "It's the maestro's show, and I'm just his humble assistant."

"You, Arthur, have never been humble," she said, and he scowled at her. "But don't worry, I've never held that against you. I can appreciate a certain amount of arrogance. It's your control-freak routine that gets to me. When are you going to give it up?" She closed the datebook and got up from the couch, as if to leave without waiting for his answer.

Arthur reached out and grabbed her by the wrist as she tried to walk past him. "Give me a break, Janine—as if you don't like to control things, too? Look at the way you make the staff at every major hall in the world jump. Are you telling me you don't like that?"

She glared back at him and pulled her arm free. "Sure I like it. It makes my life a lot easier—it's very safe. Though I, personally, don't make them jump—it's the word of the king, from on high. I'm just his emissary." She paused and added quietly, "But I don't run my personal life the same way I do business, Arthur." Janine stared him down, but Arthur saw her gaze soften and he bit back the insult he had framed.

"Right. Whatever you say, Madame Woodward—and pigs can fly!" he finished under his breath.

Arthur glared at Janine as she walked over to the observation window, her back hard in his sight. He had meant to go into the other room, but he stood in the archway, transfixed.

As the orchestra worked its way through the final fugue in the "Libera me," Arthur remained agitated, distracted. He moved to watch some of the rehearsal, too.

Arthur came up behind Janine and watched from over her shoulder. They were not touching, but the sparks between them were all too palpable. The tension of their argument modulated to another refrain.

Before Arthur could stop himself, he wrapped his arms around her waist and nuzzled up behind her. He rested his chin beside her head, and the smell of her hair made him dizzy. It had been too long since they had been together, and it was more than an ache in his loins that made him want her.

Janine did not make a move to discourage him. With the distant music filling his ears, he pulled her hips even closer and she leaned back against him. They rocked together like that for a while as a chasm opened up inside him, one that Arthur feared might never be filled. All he felt was her, and he wanted to drink her in with every fiber of his being.

His hands slid over silk and lace, up to her breasts, and he sighed as each one filled his palms, pressed against his fingers. Janine's breathing urged him on, and he wondered if she knew just how much he wanted her, or needed her—hoped he could still keep that from her.

As the fugue rose to a crescendo, Janine guided his hands over her breasts and thighs, whispered encouragement. Arthur was overwhelmed. He hiked up her skirt to discover that she still wore garters and stockings. He slid her delicate lace panties aside—they felt warm and slick—undid his own pants, and prepared to enter her. Arthur paused only for a moment, and Janine reached back for him.

Her urgency was too much for him. Arthur pressed against her opening, her fragrance filling his head with wild visions of other lovemaking they had done. He slid home. Their strokes matched the music, Janine braced against the wall, driving back against him, her back arched. He plunged in deeply again and again.

Arthur reveled in their union, the power of it. He soared with each of Janine's new waves. She played him as he played her, until her most intense climax took him over the edge.

After their mutual shudders had subsided, Arthur slowly pulled away, turned Janine around, and kissed her with a passion he hadn't felt in months. Janine looked into his eyes, searching, her blue eyes full of icy sparks and questions. Then she smiled, a knowing smile, and Arthur turned away.

"You still love me, Arthur, don't you?" It was an accusation.

Arthur nearly groaned. "This was never about love, Janine. You know that and I know that. We're just friends who like to screw from time to time. Why can't you leave it at that?"

Janine maneuvered herself in front of him and hurled the words in his face. "Just friends, huh? Do you run out at three o'clock in the morning to buy roses for all your friends when they get back from a trip? Do you spend seven hours a day on the phone with all your friends when you're on the road?" She was in one of her quiet, cold furies, but he was not going to let her get away with that sort of blackmail. That was the past.

"That was infatuation, my dear—maybe even competition for what his majesty once had," he replied.

"Don't you dare degrade me, Bernie or yourself like that. You're a lousy liar, Arthur," she said, and grabbed him by the arm before he could slip by her. "You can't tell me all that never happened. You can't control emotions, Arthur. They come back to bite you."

"The hell I can't!" he said, not making a move to release himself.

"And since when are you privy to all my inner thoughts? Have you ever considered that you're dreaming, wrong?"

"No. I'm not wrong. That was no dream," she said. "I got past your defenses, and when you finally realized it, you ran like a coward. But you can't deny what we were—are. I won't let you turn twelve months of my life into a lie. We're in love—so why can't you just live with that?"

Janine let go of him and retreated to the bathroom. Sounds of the musicians packing up filtered upstairs in the brief lull and harmonized with the sound of running water.

Arthur continued through the bathroom door—"Give up the fairy tale, Janine. It doesn't become you"—as he straightened himself out and made to leave the room. But Janine poked her head from the bathroom for a parting shot.

"Arthur, you're an idiot. You'll die in that tomb you've built for yourself. Alone."

Arthur grumbled as he trotted down the stairs. "Like hell I will."

Arthur stands alone, naked, in a tight circle of light, surrounded by absolute darkness. He knows there are creatures out in that darkness, waiting for him, ready to rend his flesh at the slightest slip. The silence waits to be filled with life by his downbeat. But his arm is unresponsive, the baton as if made of stone. And all the while he feels the life draining from his limbs, bleeding out around the edges of the light.

"Death for life, Arthur. Let go. It is not as it seems," says a voice which resembles the master's.

Struggling to find a way out, Arthur focuses on a faint speck in the distance. It touches the darkness with its light. As if in response, it grows in size and intensity, getting closer.

Knees weak, Arthur's vision grays just as he makes out a lady in white—familiar but unidentifiable. He feels himself sink to the floor in the puddle of light. A long-fingered hand touches him and he jumps to life, crying out—

—and saw Janine's startled face hovering above him, her hand pulled back as if she had touched a hot stove.

"Jesus! Don't do that to me!" Arthur said, his breath still labored as he realized he was home and in bed.

Janine straightened, smoothed back her hair and opened the jacket of her linen suit. "I'm sorry, Arthur. But I used my key since you weren't answering your phone and your machine didn't pick up. I've been trying to get you for an hour."

Arthur kept staring at her, still dazed, so she continued. "We've got an emergency. I got a call from Montreal. It was Bernie—he sounds awful. His flight from Vienna had to land—engine trouble—so he's not going to get to Kennedy in time to make the downbeat of the dress rehearsal. You'll have to take it."

This woke Arthur up. He rolled over to look at the clock and realized that he had only thirty minutes to make a ten o'clock downbeat. "Damn!" was all he said before leaping out of bed. He ran around the apartment, Janine right behind him, clicking off instructions.

"The soloists will be in from the beginning. Bernie had planned to do spots in the first half, then run the piece in the second half. Do you have his notes? If not, he's faxed me the most important ones and you can go from there."

Arthur absorbed all she said and acknowledged it through various grunts and nods between eating, shaving, and brushing his teeth. He deviated from his usual rehearsal casual and donned a very proper black silk turtleneck and black trousers, but retained his bad-boy black boots and black leather jacket. He finished with his gargoyle sunglasses, and looked in the mirror.

"Let's go."

The quartet of soloists faced out into the nearly empty hall. Arthur took a deep breath and gave a downbeat. In response, ascending arpeggios from the celli floated out on the air, the lines gently punctuated by the upper woodwinds. On that cushion of sound, the mezzo-soprano and tenor entered for the "Offertorio."

Arthur loosened up a bit, though it was odd to conduct without Woodward's presence in the hall, without that link. Still, he was relieved. At least the musicians all seemed awake this morning, he thought. But they were a bit sluggish, as if he were dragging around a stubborn mule. And he knew why. As polite and professional as they were, they wanted their maestro, not him. They resisted his lead subtly, and that wall between them galled him.

The bass followed in the trio's entreaty to their maker to free them from the "profundo lacu," the deep pit, lest they be devoured and fall into darkness. Above that plea, soaring out into the stratosphere with two violins soli, Arthur supported the soprano's prayer to St. Michael to lead the souls to the "lucem sanctam," the holy light.

As the movement continued, Arthur listened and adjusted and they played their delicate game of tug-of-war. It was all together, quite neat and tidy for the first time that the total forces had joined—orchestra, soloists and chorus. But Arthur resented their resistance, and that distracted him.

The shadows of the dimly lit hall teased at the corners of his vision, and he felt as if he were being watched by the maestro himself—heard his voice saying, "Just relax with the music, Arthur." Outwardly calm, he could not settle his heartbeat, and snatches of his nightmare blended with his internal imagery of the text.

Arthur decided to just read through the rest of the movement—with all its lone voices giving praises and asking for salvation—and allow everyone to get used to each other.

With the opening fanfare of the "Sanctus," the chorus in full voice, Arthur saw Janine wave to him from the back of the orchestra. Maestro Woodward had arrived. He almost cut to turn the rehearsal over to his mentor, but the maestro stepped out beside Janine and motioned for Arthur to continue. Arthur settled into their familiar connection.

When the tempo began to rush and the entrances got ragged, Arthur stopped and Maestro Woodward ascended the podium next to him. The maestro took him into one of his bear hugs, and Arthur was struck by the uncharacteristic lack of strength in the man's arms, his shortness of breath. Major jet lag, he thought. But Woodward stepped back and beamed at him, patted him on the back, then leaned in and whispered, "Good job, Arthur. Just let go a little more next time," while the orchestra politely applauded. That tiny echo from his dream startled him. Arthur smiled, nodded and left the stage.

By the time Arthur got out into the hall, Woodward had had the stagehands get him a bass chair, and got settled down to work. Janine sat next to him, but he decided to shut her out and sulk, though the air momentarily crackled between them.

"Okay, folks. Let's take it from the top," intoned Woodward.

With the somber entrance of the celli, there was instant response, and Arthur knew that he had not matched the maestro's control—or magic.

• • • •

Surrounded by light, Arthur stands dressed in white tie and tails. The lady is out there in the darkness, coming closer, but still hazy. Arthur can hear voices, faintly singing in a language that is not his own, but familiar. He raises his baton, but his arm is stiff.

A long, slender hand reaches into the light and gently slips the tie from around his neck and unfastens the top button of his shirt. Arthur feels as if he can breathe again and looks up to thank his helper. It is the lady, in all her glory—like Janine, but not as he's ever seen her.

She is too brilliant, too beautiful to look upon and seems to sense this. Arthur watches the visage before him shift until it seems that Maestro Woodward is there with him, but a Woodward even more vital than he has ever known him. This Woodward smiles and reaches forward to embrace him, then steps back and begins to help Arthur shed the rest of his clothes.

Arthur bats away the hand, suddenly feeling under attack. Woodward looks very confused and his visage shifts again—to Janine's—naked, radiant, desirable beyond belief.

He reaches for her, and she for him, and they begin a slow lover's dance. As if in slow motion, Arthur sheds his clothing piece by piece until he stands naked before his beloved. He has never wanted her so much and moves with a fire in his groin that he is sure even weeks of lovemaking won't extinguish.

But Janine moves away and stares at him. Suddenly, Arthur is painfully aware of his nakedness—and the Janine-being has become dark and menacing. She reaches out to slash him with clawed hands. He runs for the darkness.

Arthur had a restless night. More ridiculous dreams, he grumbled as he went through his morning routine, though it was now afternoon. He could afford the luxury of sleeping in that morning, as he didn't have to get to the hall till six o'clock or so for the gala. Janine would be taking care of the other details, including making sure that the maestro would rest. He really hadn't sounded good since his return from Vienna— hacking and wheezing more than usual—thought Arthur. Always the workaholic, Arthur mused, and vowed to be more moderate when he reached Woodward's age.

After some food and a glance at the mail, Arthur took out the score to the Verdi. He lounged, wrapped in a silk robe, on his oversize sofa, sipping cognac. He knew the score, and it was out of his hands now. This night of all nights belonged to the maestro. But he couldn't help imagining what it would be like to take the stage in that legendary hall and hear the applause of a packed house. He wanted those soloists, that piece, the media coverage, everything. And he knew he might have it someday. But someday never seemed soon enough.

All afternoon, as Arthur puttered around through mundane tasks—grocery shopping, the post office, a haircut—he heard the trumpets, could feel the thunder of the drums as the *Requiem* played in his mind. Its call was seductive, relentless.

By five o'clock, when he had to dress before going to the hall, he was wound tight. And as he put on each piece of clothing, he was reminded of his odd dreams of late, but brushed those thoughts aside. Verdi. He would think only of Verdi.

In white tie and tails, Arthur arrived at the hall and headed for the Green Room. To his surprise, Arthur found it all ready but empty—no maestro, no Janine. By seven o'clock he began to worry and fidgeted with some pieces at the piano.

Finally, at seven-thirty, the elevator doors opened to reveal Maestro Woodward on Janine's arm. Arthur was startled by the fact that the maestro actually needed Janine's help to walk.

"Maestro!" Arthur exclaimed, and jumped up to help his mentor. They took off his coat and seated him on the couch. Woodward was flushed and sweating, his breathing labored. Janine, dressed in a white satin evening suit, took Arthur aside.

"He's had a bad night—a stomach flu or something—and refuses to see the doctor until after the gala, won't even let me call him. He insists he can get through the piece—you know he'd rather die than leave a thing unfinished. We've got the fever down and keep filling him with fluids. His blood pressure's okay, but I don't like this at all." Janine was breathless.

This was just what Arthur had feared when Janine announced that quick run to Vienna. But he'd seen the maestro conduct in worse condition than he seemed to be in at that moment.

What Arthur was even more startled by was the small voice in him that wanted the maestro to falter so he could take the podium and be a hero. What a Carnegie debut that would make! As he helped Janine make the maestro comfortable, he wrestled with his ambivalence.

When the stage manager announced that it was five minutes to curtain, Woodward rose and walked out, calm and confident, even though his hands shook. Arthur was at once relieved and disappointed as he followed Janine to their reserved box.

The lights slowly dimmed and the hall hushed as the concert master walked onstage. She nodded to the oboe to give the tuning A, winds and brass tuning, and finally the strings in a cacophonous ritual as old as music itself.

In the silence just before Maestro Woodward's entrance, Arthur borrowed Janine's opera glasses to scope out the crowd. Below him, above him, all around him was a sea of diamonds and glitter that was a rarity even among the concert world's elite. And near the back of the hall, in the parquet, was a row of cameras looking like ship's cannon ready for the bombardment.

As a wave overtook the audience, Arthur was swept up in it and turned to see his mentor taking the stage accompanied by wild applause. Woodward walked with a strength that Arthur hadn't seen upstairs. Arthur sat back and awaited the first sounds, confident that this would be a triumph. Before the first notes Janine took his hand and looked at him as if she might know what this meant to him.

From the audience he couldn't see the first downbeat, but Arthur could hear the hushed first tones of the celli, followed by the violins, and then joined by each section as they prayed together for eternal rest, "requiem aeternam." The sounds washed over him and seemed to strip him of any fears, doubts or preoccupations. Linked with his mentor, he became the music.

The entire piece went this way for Arthur—he nearly jumped from his seat in awe and fear during the "Dies irae," nearly wept with the tenor's "Ingemisco," rejoiced with the double chorus fugue of the "Sanctus" singing praises to the Almighty. And at the fringes of his perceptions was Janine, somehow urging him on to be more with the music, to live the drama.

The soprano and mezzo floated through their prayer to the Lamb of God, the "Agnus Dei," with rare poignancy. As the last notes faded, the hall was more silent than Arthur had ever heard it in his twenty years of attending concerts. It was a revelation and touched him to depths he never thought possible. He was not entirely comfortable with the things that were going through his mind during the concert, and even chastised himself again for his ambivalence toward the maestro's illness earlier in the evening.

The mezzo, tenor and bass rose for the "Lux aeterna," and Arthur stole a glance at the soprano sitting, waiting for the finale of what had indeed been a drama. The pause was longer than expected. The maestro removed a handkerchief from his pocket and mopped his brow, coughing. He seemed to be moving more deliberately than was his wont, but Arthur attributed that to the emotions and strains of a long piece.

The maestro finally gave an almost imperceptible downbeat that set the strings, in tremolo, to shimmering. It gave Arthur chills, as if he wore nothing but a thin nightshirt on a breezy winter's eve instead of his usually too heavy tailcoat.

The entire movement shifted back and forth between its sections of light and darkness. Suspended in time, the trio seemed to sing to Arthur of eternal light versus eternal darkness. Several times tears threatened at the corners of his eyes, and he felt the music with his mentor and longed to be even closer to it.

Janine squeezed his hand and he shut down, though she had obviously been sniffling through several sections of the piece. He still felt he had to hide such things from her, at least until he had control over his feelings for her. He did not want her to rule his emotions—not above himself, and not above his music.

The mezzo intoned the final plea for eternal light, accompanied by the tenor and bass asking for peace. The flutes spun out their arpeggios over it until a solo flute climbed to heaven and the strings echoed the final cadence. When the last notes faded, as planned, the hall was plunged into total darkness.

The cavern filled with people felt like a pit as Arthur could hear the muted gasps of surprise ripple up and down the aisles. His connection with the maestro snapped, and he heard a thud from the stage, followed by much commotion. This shook Arthur from his reveries just as the full house lights came up.

Everything was chaos. The audience went from shocked silence to severe agitation. Arthur finally saw what everyone else saw—Maestro Woodward had collapsed and stumbled from the podium. The concert master handed her violin over to her stand partner and helped him from the stage.

Arthur was horrified. So close to the end! They had to finish. He knew the maestro would not have it any other way. He turned to speak to Janine, but she had already left. He sprinted through the corridors to the backstage door.

Just inside the house manager's office, the staff had Woodward in a chair with a cold compress on his forehead. Janine held his baton, and nobody noticed Arthur until he was right beside the maestro.

Woodward looked up at Arthur and smiled. "Well, my dear boy, it seems that you will get your debut sooner than either of us expected. And this is not the first time I've wished to borrow your body, Arthur," he said with a wry grin, his voice raspy, as he turned to Janine. He took her hand, with the baton, and put it in Arthur's. "Go ahead, Arthur. Finish the drama. We can't very well leave it this way."

Arthur couldn't believe what he was hearing. He stammered. "But you can rest a few minutes and finish the last movement."

Woodward shook his head. "Don't be stupid, Arthur. Haven't I been foolish enough the past few days? Just do it." He then turned to Janine and said, "Make the announcement that the piece will be completed by Arthur Godwin in his Carnegie Hall debut, and calm them down before he goes out. I'll be fine and watching from the TVs in here. I'll be with you, Arthur."

They both hugged him and walked out. Arthur ran for a quick stop to the men's room, his bladder suddenly too active for comfort. Afterward, he straightened his hair and entered backstage. The hall was now eerily silent until the musicians tuned and awaited his arrival. Janine stepped toward him, her white suit shimmering dreamily in the work-lights backstage. She reached out and straightened his tie, then kissed him on the cheek and said, "Remember what he's always told you—just let go."

A memory from dream time flashed through his mind as he took a deep breath and nodded for the stage manager to open the door. Without fanfare, he entered the darkened stage and carefully ascended the podium. The faces of the musicians looked up at him, lit oddly by their stand lights. He nodded to them, tried to project an air of confidence and reassurance. The concert master nodded back at him.

Arthur looked to the soprano, and she stood, her white taffeta gown rustling like angels' wings. He raised his arms for the downbeat, the orchestra rose to attention and the follow spot hit the soprano in the darkness, dazzling. She began, alone—"Libera me, Domine, de morte aeterna, in die illa tremenda, quando coeli movendi sunt et terra"—and the orchestra rumbled at her words—"dum veneris judicare saeculum per ignem." After a silence the hushed chorus echoed her plea—save us from the dreadful day of judgment.

Arthur was split—inside and outside of himself. He was exultant and full of dread that at every beat he could lose it all with one slip and he, too, would be swallowed by the terrible conflagration of judgment. He did not know himself, had never known such fear in performance, and held on for his life, conducting in dream time.

The soprano sings, "et timeo." The lights blaze on as the chorus rises and the orchestra pounds through the hammer blows of the reprise of the "Dies irae."

Arthur could feel the chorus calm as it readied for the tremulous repeat of the opening "Kyrie" theme to the words "Requiem aeternam." They breathed as one, the group connection so real that Arthur swore he could feel all two hundred fifty of their heartbeats while the orchestra listened to them sing and awaited its next entrance.

He floated through each phrase with them, saw their visions as if with his own eyes—angels, demons, the glory of a world awaiting rebirth and a savior triumphant.

And then Arthur saw him—a specter in a pool of light off to the side of the stage. Woodward. Without considering the possible implications of this appearance, Arthur's resolve solidified. *No. The stage is mine now.* He flung his thoughts at his mentor.

Arthur rose to his full height, a maestro in his own right, and held the strings at bay, molto agitato, as the soprano intoned her final "libera me" chant in panicked frenzy. And with her final note, the mad chase began.

The cries of "libera me" are tossed between all the voices with more and more insistence as layer upon layer of instruments are thrown into the fray.

Trying to keep it from becoming a runaway chariot, Arthur went from tense to relaxed. He shifted back and forth and they followed him, obeyed him with supreme trust as they built a pyramid and climbed together with the music. And all the while Arthur felt Woodward trying to get inside him. He plunged deeper into himself and felt a vestige of their old link there. But this was different. He entered Woodward's world as he pleased, but he could not allow the all powerful Woodward into his without feeling consumed. *Let me finish with you, Arthur,* he heard Woodward say.

By the climax he could feel the audience swept away with him, and he let Woodward in as the maestro had with him so many times before. The link established, his fears slipped away, but not his own power.

With the percussive repeats of "Domine, do-mi-ne, domine, do-mi-ne, libera, li-ber-a-me" in the chorus and orchestra, the soprano surpassed even her most impressive rehearsals and climbed the summit to that high C with inspired strength and grace. He soared with her, to look down upon the magnificence he and Woodward had given birth to together. *Bravo, maestro,* came Woodward's voice in Arthur's head.

When the last fortissimo faded to softness, the soprano was there again, alone, to intone one last time, "Libera me, domine, de morte aeterna, in die illa tremenda," to fade with repetitions from all—"Libera me." Silence, then darkness.

Arthur froze, overcome with emotions—and alone again. The lights came up as the audience went wild. He looked up at his musicians—the singers, the soloists, the orchestra—and clasped his hands in thanks to them. Arthur didn't try to hide the tears running down his cheeks. He then turned to accept the standing ovation, awkward with motions that felt not quite his own.

As Arthur stepped back to allow the soloists their bows and the chorus master to take the stage, he saw Janine, who motioned that she was leaving. Over the din he heard the cry of an ambulance, soon engulfed by the rhythmic applause.

Arthur stood alone in the light.

The Wooden Damsel:

A Traditional Mongolian Tale that Parallels Pinocchio

Toby Sanders

TOBY SANDERS, *author of the definitive* How to Be a Compleat Clown, *is a teacher with the New York City public school system. A scholar of Chinese culture, language and literature, he is currently writing English versions of Asian folktales that have their counterparts in Western culture. In my 1993* GuildAmerica Books *collection,* Masterpieces of Terror and the Unknown, *"The Palace of the Mountain Ogre" corresponded to Hansel and Gretel. Now here is Mr. Sanders's rendering of the Chinese Pinocchio.*

L ONG AGO on the Mongol plain, there lived two craftsmen. Wood-carvers by profession, they managed to make a simple life for themselves. The elder was expert at wielding the blade and the younger was versed in the uses and applications of stains and colors. Neither was made rich by the profound knowledge they possessed. But, by the same token, they were not poor. Everyday they sat and worked by a small stream. Every evening they returned to their modest house and ate a modest meal before retiring.

All in all their life was not a bad one, although it could have been better. For one thing, neither man was married. They had no wives and no children. This didn't present a problem when they were young. But as they got older, they began to feel sad that no children would care for them in their declining years.

The elder woodcarver had just turned 60 years old when the loneliness of his life began to trouble him greatly. He went to the river to contemplate his barren existence. "This is the place where I work every day," he thought. "When I am gone, my friend, the painter, will be the only one left to work here. And he does not have too many years remaining to greet the dawn. Soon no one will come to the river bank to work. Soon we will be forgotten."

He was deep in thought when a log left the mainstream of the river and drifted lazily toward the shore. It was a sturdy piece of wood from a tree that must have been uprooted high in the mountains. On its journey to the plain, its branches probably broke away and settled at the sides of lesser tributaries while the trunk floated onward. The log drifted to the feet of the old man and came to rest. It remained there until the water lapping at its sides caught the old man's attention.

The elder looked at it with eyes practiced in the art of carving. "This is a perfect piece of wood," he thought, "perhaps the most perfect piece of wood I have ever seen."

He waded into the water and, lifting one end of the magnificent piece of timber, hauled it to the river bank where it could dry. For a long time he examined his discovery. Gently he ran his hands over its surface and caressed it with his eyes. To a woodcarver a piece of wood is never just a piece of wood. Before long the wood was offering up its secrets; the elder could see beneath the tattered scraps of bark still covering the trunk the object the wood concealed. He wasted no time in calling his friend. Together they carried the log further up the bank to a spot where it could dry properly.

"My friend," said the elder, "we may be old and alone, but I have a plan that will make us less lonely. My only children are the objects that I have carved during my long life. And none of them has ever been a suitable son or daughter. They have been too willing to leave when the price has been high enough. The fault has been mine because I have always used my skills with others in mind. I think now is the time to use my skill to serve myself. I plan to make a child of my own."

"And I can help," cried the painter. "Like a good father, I will make sure that the form you carve is dressed in beautiful colors that will bring it to life for all the world to see."

The two men returned to their work and waited for the wood to be ready. Every time they paused for rest, they stood by the log to admire its perfection. Before long the wood was dry enough for carving. The elder craftsman picked up a small sturdy blade. The skill he acquired during a lifetime of work guided his clever hands to lift the details of his new creation out of the smooth, curved face of the tree trunk. Gradually, a figure took shape. The elder deftly carved large eyes, a delicate mouth, and a small, loveable nose. The face of a beautiful young woman rose from the wood. The folds of the young woman's dress seemed ready to catch the wind, her hat rested at a thoroughly natural angle, and the braids that rested by her face looked as if they were ready to sway at her next step.

Once the carving was finished, the master painter stepped in to apply his craft. His brushes flattered the smoothed wood with color. Under his skillful hand the young woman's eyes acquired a luster, her mouth appeared about to release a pent up sigh, and her dress achieved the texture of real cloth.

The two men stepped back from their creation. They were both pleased. The figure of a young woman they had both created breathed life into the clearing by the stream where they worked. From that moment onward, she stood by their workplace to greet them. When they came to work in the morning, they bowed to her and at lunchtime they even prepared a light snack in her honor. Their lives seemed fuller and they were very happy. Life for the two men went on in this way for some time. The wooden maiden was the child they never had and, although wooden damsels generally do not require much attention, they doted on her.

One day the old men left their place by the stream to collect more materials for their work. They said their goodbyes to the damsel and reassured her that they would soon return. As they started on their way their faces were wreathed in smiles of contentment. No sooner had they gone than a young traveler rode up to the stream to rest his horse and take a refreshing drink. As he approached the clearing, he saw the maiden standing serenely looking out across the plain. She was the most beautiful creature he had ever seen. He instantly fell in love with her.

Quietly, he dismounted and took a few tentative steps toward the damsel. She did not seem to notice him, so he called out a polite, "Hello." Since she did not acknowledge his presence, he stepped closer.

"Good morning, little sister," he said to her. "I have traveled a long way and am very tired and thirsty. Could I have a drink from your stream?"

The young woman still did not answer him. He thought that this was very rude, but he was so taken by her beauty he could not hold her bad manners against her. He approached even closer. "I realize that my appearance is unseemly, but I have been riding many days," he said. "If I could use your stream, I am sure that I could make myself presentable to you."

The young woman continued to gaze out over the plain and refused to look at him. However, he noticed that the expression on her face did not change. She did not seem repulsed by his presence. "Maybe she is hard of hearing," he thought. He walked right up to her and positioned himself before her so that she could not fail to see him. "Young lady," he said. "I have traveled many miles. I do not wish to interrupt your meditation, but I respectfully ask permission to use your stream."

Again, the young woman did not speak. The young man examined her closely. For many moments he stood looking at her before he realized that this was not an ordinary damsel. She seemed perfectly natural as she gazed across the plain, but she did not blink. Hesitantly, he stretched out a hand and touched her. Under his hand he felt the un-yielding wood. Startled, he leapt back.

"What kind of trick is this," he thought. "Since I began traveling, I have never seen a woman of such beauty. Nowhere in the world can there be another young woman with such charming looks. How can I ever expect to find another so beautiful?"

Slowly, he sank to the ground by the wooden damsel. He felt cheated by the irony of life. He was sure he had found his one true love, and she was a block of wood. In a sad voice he began to sing.

> From the mountains the river flows 800 li.
> Yet it is something this beautiful maid can't see.
> You stand here alone through the rain and snow,
> And now that I've seen you, I cannot go.
> So I'll stay right here no matter how long
> And entertain you with my song.
> If only you'd come to life for me,
> I know how happy we would be.
> Please, come to life for me.

As the last note of the young man's song drifted away across the plain, the fringe of the young woman's dress ruffled in the breeze. Her braids began to sway. And with a sigh, she bent to place her hand on his head.

The young man jumped up and faced the damsel. He was surprised by the life that had been breathed into what he thought was an inanimate block of wood, but he was happy that he could be with the woman that had stolen his heart. He wrapped his arms around her. "I don't know how this happened," he told her, "but I will not argue with the luck fate sends my way. Let me show you the world you've only seen from a distance during the days you've spent standing here."

"I would like that," the wooden damsel agreed, "but please bring me back to this place before sunset. My fathers will worry if they find me gone."

The young man promised. Then, sweeping her off her feet he carried her to his waiting horse and the two rode away. During the rest of the day, he showed her the plains and all the animals that lived there. She marveled at the sun and the distant mountains. She was enchanted by the clouds and the wide variety of delicate flowers. Most of all, she was taken with the young man whose song brought her to life.

Meanwhile, the two old men returned and found their child gone. They were frantic. They searched high and low for her with no success. Finally, unable to hold back the tears of their grief any longer, they sank to the ground by the bank of the stream and sobbed uncontrollably.

This is how the two young people found them when they returned at sunset. Their sadness so upset the wooden damsel that she leapt from the horse before it was fully stopped and ran to the old men to comfort them. "Don't cry, fathers," she told them. "I am back. I would never leave you alone."

The old men looked at her without recognizing her. They had lost a wooden figure and the young woman standing before them was definitely not a wood carving. Suddenly, recognition dawned on the elder's face. "Can it be you?" he asked in disbelief.

"Yes, father, it is your little wooden child," she answered. "I am alive." She told the two craftsmen how the young man found her and brought her to life. "I didn't mean to worry you, but there was so much to see in the world that we couldn't come back sooner."

"Well," said the elder, "I suppose we shouldn't question our good fortune. Not long ago, we were childless with no one to take care of us in our declining years. Now we not only have a daughter but a son-in-law who seems to be a respectable young man. Who knows? Maybe one day we will even be blessed with grandchildren."

The two old men and the two young people happily began to make plans for the wedding. They were so engrossed in their plans that they did not hear the approach of the imperial chariot until it pulled into the clearing. Standing in the chariot was the Emperor himself. He looked toward the four people in the clearing, but only saw the young woman. Her beauty struck him at once and he immediately decided to have her for his own. Ceremoniously, he cleared his throat.

The four people chattering happily about the upcoming wedding paused and noticed the Emperor for the first time. They immediately fell to the ground to honor him. When they were finished offering the expected obeisance, the Emperor spoke. "I have never in my life seen a young woman of such perfection. I will reward you handsomely for her hand."

The two old men glanced at each other. They did not want their child carried off. How could they lose her so soon after she had come to life? The elder spoke respectfully, "Your majesty, although this young woman is beautiful, she would be unsuitable for an Emperor of your greatness. Besides, she is betrothed to this young man."

"Why would she be unsuitable for me?" asked the Emperor.

The elder quickly explained the nature of the young woman and how she came to life. "So you see," he concluded, "this young woman could be an embarrassment to a man of your greatness. She is only recently human."

"That changes matters," said the Emperor. "Both of you have lived on my land for a long time. You have taken advantage of my bounty. You eat food grown on my land. You have use of the sheep and goats that ultimately belong to me. All that you see around you is part of my domain. Even this beautiful maiden was grown from the soil of my empire. Therefore it is natural that both of you owe me a great deal for abundant lives you have led. I will take the maiden with me in lieu of the taxes you owe."

With that, he lifted the young woman into his chariot and drove away leaving the three men distraught in the clearing. He carried the maid to his palace where he installed her as his first wife. He was sure that her beauty would make him the most admired man in the kingdom. Nobody could deny that she was a jewel above all others.

However, from the first, the young woman did not act in a way the Emperor expected. For one thing, she would not talk. She would always respond dutifully, but she would not utter a single word. The Emperor watched her closely and discovered that she refused to respond verbally to anyone in the palace. It was almost as if she had forgotten how to speak. He was perplexed by this behavior, but supposed that her silence was a result of her separation from her family. He endeavored to surround her with other women in order to make her feel less lonely.

His careful plan did not meet with success. In fact, the young woman developed other peculiarities. She began to walk more slowly. Her motions became jerky. And she began to hold herself more stiffly. These peculiarities became more and more pronounced until at last the young woman ceased moving entirely. When the Emperor touched her, he only felt the hard, solid mass of the wooden block she had become.

The Emperor was furious. He sent soldiers to bring the old men to the palace. When they arrived and abased themselves before him, he rose to his full height and demanded, "Bring your daughter back to life for me!"

The elder craftsman humbly spoke to the Emperor. "Your majesty, we do not know how to accomplish this. We did not bring her to life. You must speak to the young man to whom she was betrothed."

The Emperor immediately sent more soldiers to find the young man. When the young man stood before him, he demanded, "How did you bring this young woman to life?"

"Your majesty," the young man answered, "I am not sure how I brought her to life. All I know is that I sang a song to her and she began to move."

"Teach me this song," demanded the Emperor.

The young man recited the words to the song, pausing so that the Emperor could repeat them. Then he taught the Emperor the melody. After an hour the Emperor was ready. In a clear voice, he sang to the wooden damsel. All eyes focused on the magnificent carving. It did not move.

The Emperor wheeled on the young man. "Why isn't she alive? Did you teach me the song properly?"

"I taught it to you exactly the way I sang it in the clearing," answered the young man.

"Then why doesn't she live?" screamed the Emperor.

"Perhaps she will not come to life because you really don't love her and she does not love you," answered the young man. "Why don't you let us take her home? She is no use to you like this."

"No," shrieked the Emperor. "She will not leave here. If I can't have her, neither will anyone else! Guards, build a large pyre!"

The young man tried to protest, but the two old men held him back. They did not want him to incur the Emperor's wrath. The three men watched as soldiers made a huge pile of wood in the center of the palace courtyard. They lowered their eyes when the wooden damsel was tied to a stake in the center of the pyre and they turned away when torches were brought to start the fire. Sadly, the three left the palace. None of them wanted to see the woman they loved destroyed. Slowly, they made their way to the woodcarvers' home.

In the palace, the Emperor watched as the pyre was lit. The torchlight reflecting in his eyes made his scowling countenance even fiercer. Gradually, the flames licked up the pyre until they flickered around the feet of the wooden damsel. As the fire burned hotter, the Emperor began to smile. But the Emperor did not realize the sap and tar inside the wooden damsel was beginning to bubble. It dripped to the earth and flowed from the pyre in all directions. One tendril stretched out to the feet of the Emperor. Finally, heat of the blaze became so great that the sap ignited. Miniature streams of fire shot out toward all the palace buildings and the Emperor himself. Bellowing loudly, the burning Emperor ran to the river while the palace servants attempted to put out the flames consuming the inner buildings. Unfortunately, the guards and soldiers were unable to keep even one pagoda from being completely destroyed.

Rushing through the main gate, the Emperor threw himself in the water to quench the flames. He turned dripping from the river. Angrily, he looked around at the ruin that had once been his magnificent mansion. The only thing left that was recognizable was the wooden damsel. Her paint had peeled away from the wood beneath. The wood itself was burnt and scarred, but her figure was little damaged and she seemed to be smiling at him through the smoke. Enraged, the Emperor grabbed the wooden figure, rushed to the river, and hurled the wooden damsel into the current far from the shore.

The wooden damsel floated for several days down the river before drifting toward the shore. When she finally came to rest, she was at the river bank in front of the clearing where the old woodcarvers worked. Sitting by the river were both old men and the young man that had been her suitor. The three had been consoling each other since they left the palace days before.

The water lapping against the sides of the wooden damsel once again attracted the elder craftsman's attention. As soon as he saw the figure resting on the bank, he rushed over to it. The painter and the young man quickly followed. Together they lifted the wooden damsel out of the water. The elder craftsman examined the damage.

"I think I can fix this," he said at last.

"And I can repaint her," said the other craftsman. "She will be even better than before."

The young man watched the old men work. They worked all night. The elder craftsman skillfully smoothed the scarred places. The other craftsman peeled away the remains of the scorched paint and began applying a new coat. None of them could sleep. Even the young man was restless. Sometime during the night he began again to sing his song. His voice was mournful as it drifted in the wind.

At last, the sun peeked over the horizon. The craftsmen put the finishing touches on the wooden damsel and the young man finished his song. As the painter applied the last brush of paint to the wooden damsel's cheek, the world became still. The fringe on the wooden damsel's dress fluttered in a puff of wind. Her braids swayed as she turned her head. She blinked, then slowly she stood and walked to the young man. Her fathers smiled happily. They were together again.

Love Song
from the Stars

Robert Sheckley

Back in the 1950's, when science fiction was beginning to develop in new directions besides so-called "nuts and bolts" tales of rockets and engineers, three essentially disparate authors were often grouped together for their refreshingly humanistic approach to the problems of SF: Ray Bradbury, the late Charles Beaumont and ROBERT SHECKLEY, *who went on to become the first fiction editor of* Omni *magazine. His many books include* Citizen in Space, Immortality, Inc.; Notions: Unlimited; The People Trap; Pilgrimage to Earth; Shards of Space *and* Untouched by Human Hands. *One of his stories was filmed as* The Tenth Victim. *Now here is another kind of victim, one whose domestic plight may well please ardent feminists.*

LOLLIA was a small, pine-clad cone of rock in the eastern Aegean. It was uninhabited, a difficult place to get to, but not quite impossible. Kinkaid rented an aluminum boat with outboard in Chios, packed in his camping equipment and, with a fair wind and a flat sea, got there in six hours, arriving just before sunset.

Kinkaid was tall and thin, with snubby features and fair, freckled skin, blotchy now in the fierce Greek summer sun. He wore a wrinkled white suit and canvas boat shoes. He was thirty-two years old. His hair was blondish-red, curly, and he was going bald on top. He was a member of an almost vanished species, the independently wealthy amateur archaeologist. He had heard of Lollia on Mykonos. A fisherman told him that the island was still visited from time to time by the old gods, and that people with any prudence stayed away. That was all Kinkaid needed to want to go there at once. He was in need of a respite from Mykonos's café amusements.

And there was always the chance he'd find antiquities. Many discoveries have been made in the open, or under an inch or two of soil. Not in the well-known places, Mycenae, Tiryns, Delphi, where scientists and tourists have been studying for hundreds of years. It was the less likely sites that yielded the lucky finds nowadays, places on the edge of a great culture. Like Lollia, perhaps.

And even if he didn't find anything, it would be fun to camp out for a night or two before flying on to meet his friends in Venice for the film festival. And there was always the chance he'd find something no one else had ever come across.

As for the fisherman's talk of the old gods, he didn't know whether to put that down to Greek love of exaggeration or Greek superstition.

Kinkaid arrived at Lollia just before sunset, when the sky of the Aegean darkens swiftly through the shades of violet into a deepening transparent blue. A light breeze ruffled the waters and the air was lucid. It was a day fit for the gods.

Kinkaid circled the little island looking for the best place to land. He found a spit of land just off the northern point. He pulled his boat ashore through light surf and tied it to a tree. Then he climbed the rugged cliff, through luxuriant underbrush scented with rosemary and thyme.

At the summit there was a small plateau. On it he found the remains of an old shrine. The altar stones were weathered and tumbled around, but he could make out the fine carving.

There was a cave nearby, slanting down into the hillside. Kinkaid walked toward it, then stopped. A human figure had appeared in the cave mouth. A girl. She was young, very pretty, red-haired, dressed in a simple linen dress. She had been watching him.

"Where did you come from?" Kinkaid asked.

"The spaceship dropped me off," she told him. Although her English was flawless, she had a faint foreign accent which he could not place, but which he found charming. And he liked her sense of humor.

He couldn't imagine how she had gotten there. Not in a spaceship, of course; that was a joke. But how *had* she come? There had been no sign of another boat. She was unlikely to have swum the seventy miles from Chios. Could she have been dropped off by helicopter? Possible but unlikely. She looked as though she was ready for a lawn party. There wasn't a mark of dirt on her, and her makeup was fresh. Whereas Kinkaid was aware that he looked sweaty and rumpled, like a man who has just finished a difficult technical rock climb.

"I don't want to seem inquisitive," Kinkaid said, "but would you mind telling me how you got here, really?"

"I told you. The spaceship dropped me off."

"Spaceship?"

"Yes. I am not a human. I am an Andar. The ship will return for me tonight."

"Well, that's really something," Kinkaid said, humoring her. "Did you come a long way?"

"Oh, I suppose it must be hundreds of millions of miles to our planet of Andar. We have ways of getting around the speed of light, of course."

"Sure, that figures," Kinkaid said. Either the girl was carrying a joke a long way or she was a loony. The latter, most likely. Her story was so ridiculous he wanted to laugh. But she was so heartbreakingly beautiful he knew he'd break down and cry if he didn't get her.

He decided to play along. "What's your name? Why did you come here?" he asked.

"You can call me Alia. This is one of the planets the Andar decided to look into, after the Disappearance forced us to leave our home planet and go out into space. But I'm not supposed to talk about the Disappearance."

She was crazy all right, but Kinkaid was so charmed by her that he didn't care.

"You wouldn't happen to be one of the old gods, would you?" he asked.

"Oh, no, I'm not one of the Olympians," she told him. "But there were stories about them in the old days, when my people visited this planet."

Kinkaid didn't care what she said or where she was from. He wanted her. He'd never made it with an extraterrestrial. It would be an important first for him. Aliens as pretty as this didn't come along every day.

And who knows, maybe she *was* from another planet. It was OK with him.

Whatever she was and however she got here, she was a beautiful woman. Suddenly he wanted her desperately.

And she seemed to feel something for him, too. He considered the shy yet provocative way she kept on glancing at him, then looking away. There was a glow of color in her cheeks. Perhaps unconsciously, she moved closer to him as they talked.

He decided it was time for action. Masterful Kinkaid took her in his arms.

At first she responded to his embrace, then pushed him away.

"You are very attractive," she said. "I'm surprised at the strength of my feelings toward you. But love between us is impossible. I am not of your race or planet. I am of the Andar."

The alien thing again. "Do you mean that you are not a woman in the sense we would mean on Earth?" Kinkaid asked.

"No, it isn't that. It's a matter of psychology. We women of the Andar do not love lightly. For us, the act of mating means marriage and a lifetime commitment. We do not divorce. And we *do* intend to have children."

Kinkaid smiled at that. He had heard it before, from the Catholic girls he used to date back in Short Hills, New Jersey. He knew how to handle the situation.

"I really do love you," he said. For the moment, at least, it was true.

"I have—certain feelings toward you, too," she admitted. "But you can't imagine what is involved when you love an Andar woman."

"Tell me about it," Kinkaid said, slipping an arm around her waist and drawing her to him.

"I cannot," she said. "It is our sacred mystery. We are not allowed to reveal it to men. Perhaps you should leave me now, while there's still time."

Kinkaid knew it was good advice: there was something spooky about her and the way she had appeared on the island. He really ought to leave. But he couldn't. As far as women were concerned he was a danger junkie, and this lady represented an all-time high in female challenges. He was no painter or writer. His amateur archaeology would never gain him any recognition. The one thing he could leave behind was his record of sexual conquests. Let them carve it on his tombstone: Kinkaid had the best, and he took it where he found it.

He kissed her, a kiss that went on and on, a kiss that continued as they dissolved to the ground in a montage of floating clothing and the bright flash of flesh. The ecstasy he experienced as they came together went right off the scale of his ability to express it. So intense was the feeling that he barely noticed the six sharp punctures, three on either side, neatly spaced between his ribs.

It was only later, lying back, spent and contented, that he looked at the six small, clean puncture wounds in his skin. He sat up and looked at Alia. She was naked, impossibly lovely, her dark red hair a shimmering cloud around her heart-shaped face. She did have one unusual feature which he had not noticed in the passion of lovemaking. There were six small erectile structures, three on each side of her rib cage, each armed with a slender hollow fang. He thought of certain female insects on the Earth who bite off the heads of their mates during the act of love. He still didn't really believe she was an extraterrestrial. But he didn't disbelieve it quite as strongly as before. He thought of different species of insect on the Earth which resemble other species—katydids that look like dry twigs, flies that imitate wasps. Is that it? Was she about to take off her body?

He said, "It was terrific, baby, even if it *is* going to cost me my life."

She stared at him. "What are you saying?" she cried. "Do you actually think I will kill you? Impossible! I am an Andar female; you are my mate for life, and life for us lasts a very long time."

"Then what did you do to me?" Kinkaid asked.

"I've simply injected the children into you," Alia said. "They're going to be so lovely, darling. I hope they have your coloring."

Kinkaid couldn't quite grasp it at first. "Are you sure you haven't poisoned me?" he asked. "I feel very strange."

"That's just the hibernation serum. I injected it along with the babies. You'll sleep now, my sweet, here in this nice dry cave, and our children will grow safely between your ribs. In a year I'll come back and take them out of you and put them into their cocoons and take them home to Andar. That's the next stage of their development."

"And what about me?" Kinkaid asked, fighting the desire to sleep that had come powerfully over him.

"You'll be fine," Alia said. "Hibernation is perfectly safe, and I'll be back in plenty of time for the birth. Then you'll need to rest for a while. Perhaps a week. I'll be here to take care of you. And then we can make love again."

"And then?"

"Then it'll be hibernation time again, my sweet, until the next year."

Kinkaid wanted to tell her that this wasn't how he'd planned to spend his life—an hour of love, a year of sleep, then giving birth and starting all over again. He wanted to tell her that, all things considered, he'd prefer that she bite his head off. But he couldn't talk, could barely stay awake. And Alia was getting ready to leave.

"You're really cute," he managed to tell her. "But I wish you'd stayed on Andar and married your hometown sweetheart."

"I would have, darling," she said, "but something went wrong back home. The men must have been spying on our sacred mysteries. Suddenly we couldn't find them anymore. That's what we call the Great Disappearance. They went away, all of them, completely off the planet."

"It figures they'd catch on sooner or later," Kinkaid said.

"It was very wrong of them," Alia said. "I know that childbearing makes great demands on the men, but it can't be helped; the race must go on. And we Andar women can be relied upon to keep it going, no matter what lengths we must go to. I *did* give you a sporting chance to get away. Goodbye, my darling, until next year."

Diesel Dream

Alan Dean Foster

Some years ago, the author-agent Richard Monaco asked me to contribute a column to Imago, *a science fiction magazine he meant to publish. Though the idea never quite jelled, I was one of a handful of people to read the galleys of the first issue, which included several excellent stories. One that continued to haunt me years afterward was "Diesel Dream," later to appear in* Solved. *Its author,* ALAN DEAN FOSTER, *penned the best-selling novelizations of many films, including the* Aliens *trilogy and* The Black Hole, *as well as the Spellsinger books and a series of tales recently collected as* Mad Amos. *Under the pseudonym of James Lawson Foster, he recently wrote* Montezuma's Strip.

WHATTHEHELL. I mean, I know I was wired. Too many white crosses, too long on the road. But a guy's gotta make a living, and everybody *else* does it. Everybody who runs alone, anyway. You got a partner, you don't have to rely on stimulants. You half a married team, that's even better. But you own, operate, and drive your own rig, you gotta compete somehow. That means always making sure you finish your run on time, especially if you're hauling perishables. Oh sure, they bring their own problems with 'em, but I'd rather run cucumbers than cordite any day.

Elaine (that's my missus), she worries about me all the time. No less so than any trucker's wife, I guess. Goes with the territory. I try to hide the pills from her, but she knows I pop the stuff. I make good money, though. Better'n most independents. Least I'm not stuck in some stuffy little office listening to some scrawny bald-headed dude chew my ass day after day for misfiling some damn piece of paper.

Elaine and I had a burning ceremony two years ago. Mortgage officer from the bank brought over the paper personal and stayed for the burgers and beer. Now there's a bank that *understands.* Holds the paper on our place, too. One of these days we'll have another ceremony and burn that sucker, too.

So I own my rig free and clear now. Worked plenty hard for it. I'm sure as hell not ready to retire. Not so long as I can work for myself. Besides which I got two kids in college and a third thinking about it. Yep, me. The big guy with the green baseball cap and the beard you keep seein' in your rear-view mirrors. Sometimes I can't believe it myself.

So what if I use the crosses sometimes to keep going? So what if my eyesight's not twenty-twenty every hour of every day? Sure my safety record's not perfect, but it's a damnsight better than most of these young honchos think they can drive San Diego—Miami nonstop. Half their trucks end up as scrap, and so do half of them.

I know when I'm getting shaky, when it's time to lay off the little mothers.

Anyway, like I was gonna tell you, I don't usually stop in Lee Vining. It's just a flyspot on the atlas, not even a real truck stop there. Too far north of Mammoth to be fashionable and too far south of Tahoe to be worth a sidetrip for the gamblers. A bunch of overinsulated mobile homes not much bigger than the woodpiles stacked outside 'em. Some log homes, some rock. Six gas stations, five restaurants, and one little mountain grocery. Imagine; a market with a porch and chairs. Lee Vining just kind of clings to the east slope of the Sierra Nevada. Wouldn't surprise anyone if the whole shebang up and slid into Mono Lake some hard winter. The whole town. The market sells more salmon eggs than salmon. Damn fine trout country, though, and a great place to take kids hiking.

Friendly, too. Small-town mountain people always are, no matter what part of the country you're haulin' through. They live nearer nature than the rest of us and it keeps 'em respectful of their humanity. The bigger the country, the bigger the hearts. Smarter than you'd think, too.

Like I was saying, I don't usually stop there. Bridgeport's cheaper for diesel. But I'd just driven nonstop up from L.A. with a quick load of lettuce, tomatoes, and other produce for the casinos at Reno and I was running on empty. Not Slewfoot: she was near full. I topped off her tanks in Bishop. Slewfoot's my rig, lest you think I was cheatin' on Elaine. I don't go in for that, no matter what you see in those cheap films. Most truckers ain't that good-lookin', and neither are the gals you meet along the highway. Most of them are married, anyway.

Since diesel broke a buck a gallon I'm pretty careful about where I fill up. Slewfoot's a big Peterbilt, black with yellow and red striping, and she can get mighty thirsty.

So I was the one running on empty, and with all those crosses floating around in my gut, not to mention my head, I needed about fourteen cups of coffee and something to eat. It was starting to get evening and I like to push the light, but after thirty years plus on the road I know when to stop. Eat now, let the crosses settle some, drive later. Live longer.

It was just after Thanksgiving. The tourists were long gone from the mountains. So were the fishermen, since the high country lakes were already frozen. Ten feet of snow on the ground (yeah, feet) but I'd left nearly all the ski traffic back down near Mammoth. U.S. 395's easier when you don't have to dodge the idiots from L.A. who never see snow except when it comes time for 'em to drive through it.

The Department of Transportation had the road pretty clear and it hadn't snowed much in a couple of days, which is why I picked that day to make the fast run north. After Smokeys, weather's a trucker's major devilment. It was plenty cold outside; cold enough to freeze your bvd's to your crotch, but nothing like what it would be in another month or so. It was early and the real Sierra winter was just handing out calling cards.

Thanks to the crosses I kind of floated onto the front porch of a little place called the Prospector's Roost (almost as much gold left in those mountains as trout), twenty percent of the town's restaurant industry, and slumped gratefully into a booth lined with scored Naugahyde. The window behind me gave me something besides blacktop to focus on, and the sun's last rays were just sliding off old Mono Lake. Frigid pretty. The waitress gave me a big smile, which was nice. Soon she brought me a steak, hash browns, green beans, warm rolls with butter, and more coffee, which was better. I started to mellow as my stomach filled up, let my eyes wander as I ate.

It's tough to make a living at any one thing in a town the size of Lee Vining. If it don't take up too much floor space, some folks can generate an extra couple of bucks by operating a second business in the same building.

So the north quarter of the Prospector's Roost had been given over to a little gift shop. The market carried trinkets and so did the gas stations, so it didn't surprise me to see the same kind of stuff in a restaurant. There were a couple racks of postcards, film, bare necessity fishing supplies at outrageous prices, Minnetonka moccasins, rubber tomahawks for the kids, risk-kay joke gifts built around gags older than my Uncle Steve, Indian turquoise jewelry made in the Philippines. That sort of thing.

Plus the usual assortment of local handicrafts: rocks painted to look like owls, cheap ashtrays that screamed MONO LAKE or LEE VINING, GATEWAY TO YOSEMITE. T-shirts that said the same (no mediums left, plenty of extra-large).

There was also a small selection of better-quality stuff. Some nice watercolors of the lake and its famous tufa formations, one or two little hand-chased bronzes you wouldn't be ashamed to set out on your coffee table, locally strung necklaces of turquoise and silver, and some woodcarvings of Sierra animals. Small, but nicely turned. Looked like ironwood to me. Birds and fish mostly, but also one nice little bobcat I considered picking up for Elaine. She'd crucify me if I did, though. Two kids in college, a third considering. And tomorrow Slewfoot would be thirsty again.

The tarnished gold bell over the gift shop entrance tinkled as somebody entered. The owner broke away from his kitchen and walked over to chat. He was a young fellow with a short beard and he looked tired.

The woman who'd come in had a small box under one arm which she set gently on the counter. She opened it and started taking out some more of those woodcarvings. I imagined she was the artist. She was dressed for the weather and I thought she must be a local.

She left the scarf on her head when she slipped out of her heavy high-collared jacket. I tried to look a little closer. All those white crosses kept my eyes bopping, but I wasn't as sure about my brain. She was older than I was in any case, even if I'd been so inclined. Sure I looked. It was pitch black out now and starting to snow lightly. Elaine wouldn't have minded . . . much. A man's got to look once in a while.

I guessed her to be in her mid fifties. She could've been older but if anything she looked younger. I tried to get a good look at her eyes. The eyes always tell you the truth. Whatever her age, she was still a damn handsome woman. Besides the scarf and coat she wore jeans and a flannel shirt. That's like uniform in this kind of country. She wore 'em loose, but you could still see some spectacular countryside. Brown hair, though I thought it might be lighter at the roots. Not gray, either. Not yet.

I squeezed my eyes shut until they started to hurt and downed another swallow of coffee. A man must be beginnin' to go when he starts thinking that way about grandmotherly types.

Except that this woman wasn't near being what any man in his right mind would call grandmotherly, her actual age notwithstanding. Oh, she didn't do nothin' to enhance it, maybe even tried hiding it under all those clothes. But she couldn't quite do it. Even now I thought she was pretty enough to be on TV. Like Barbara Stanwyck, but younger and even prettier. Maybe it was all those white crosses makin' gumbo of my thoughts, but I couldn't take my eyes off her.

The only light outside now came from gas stations and storefronts. Not many of the latter stayed open after dark. A few tourists sped through town, fighting the urge to tromp their accelerators. I could imagine 'em cursing small towns like this one that put speed limits in their way just to keep 'em from the crap tables at Reno a little longer.

I considered the snow. Drifting down easy, but that could change. No way did I need that tonight. I finished the last of my steak and paid up, leaving the usual good tip, and started out to warm up Slewfoot.

The woman was leaving at the same time and we sort of ended up at the door together, accidental-like. Like fun we did.

"After you," she said to me.

Now I was at least ten years younger than this lady, but when she spoke to me I just got real quivery all through my body, and it wasn't from the heavy-duty pharmaceuticals I'd been gulping, either. She'd whispered, but it wasn't whispering. I knew it was her normal speaking voice. Now I've had sexier things whispered to me than "After you," but none of 'em made me feel the way I did right then, not even those spoken on my fourth date with Elaine which ended up in the back of my old pickup truck with her telling me, "Whatever you want, Dave."

Somebody real special has to be able to make "After you" sound like "Whatever you want." My initial curiosity doubled up on me. It was none of my business, of course. Here I was a married man and all, two kids in college and a third thinkin', and I oughtn't to be having the kinds of thoughts I was having. But I was running half an hour ahead of my schedule, and the snow was staying easy, and I thought, well hell, it don't hurt nothing to be friendly.

"You local?"

She smiled slightly, not looking up at me. It got darker fast when we stepped outside and those damn crosses were making like a xylophone in my head, but damned if I didn't think she was so pretty she'd crack, despite the fine lines that had begun to work their way across her face. She pushed her jacket up higher on her body and turned up the sheepskin collar.

"It's cold, and I've got to go." I shivered slightly, and it wasn't from the snow. "Nothing personal. I just don't believe in talking to strangers."

What could I say, how could I reassure her? "Heck, I don't mean no harm, ma'm." I think maybe that got to her. Not many folks these days say heck and ma'm, especially truckers. She glanced up at me curiously. Suddenly I wasn't cold anymore.

"Where are you from?"

"I asked you first."

"All right. I live here, yes. You?"

"L.A. right now, but me and my wife are from Texas. West Texas. The back o' beyond." Funny how Elaine had slipped into the conversation. I hadn't intended her to. But I wasn't sorry.

"Nice of you to mention your wife." She'd picked up on that right away. "Most men don't. That's why I try to come into town around dark. You'd think an old lady like me wouldn't have that kind of trouble."

"No disrespect intended, ma'm, but I've never set eyes on an old lady looked like you do." I nodded toward the cafe/gift shop. "You do those woodcarvings?"

"Yes. Do you like them?"

"I've seen a lot of that kind of stuff all over the country, and I think yours stack up real well against the best. Real nice. Good enough to show in a big gallery somewhere."

"Willie's place is good enough for me." Her voice was honey and promise. "This is my home now. The people up here leave you alone and let you be what you want to be. I'm happy."

"You married?"

"No, but I have friends. It's enough that they like me for what I am. I've been married before, more than once. It never worked for me."

The snow was coming down heavier.

"I'm sorry." She must have seen the concern on my face. "Got far to go?"

"Reno and on to Tahoe. Groceries for them folks that are trying to make it the easy way. Can't let the high rollers go hungry." Her smile widened slightly. It made me feel like I'd just won a new rig or something.

"No, I guess you can't." She tossed her head slightly to her left, kind of bounced a little on her feet. "It's been nice talking to you. Really."

"My name's Dave."

"Good meeting you, Dave."

"You?"

She blinked away a snowflake. "Me what?"

"What's your name?"

"Jill," she said instantly. "Jill Kramer." It was a nice name, but I knew it was hollow.

"Nice meeting you too, Jill. See you 'round, maybe."

"See you too, Dave."

That's what did it. She didn't so much say my name as sort of pucker her lips and let it ooze out, like a little hot cloud. She wore no lipstick. She didn't have to.

White crosses. White crosses and bennies and snow. Damn it all for a clear head for two lousy minutes!

I tried to think of something to say, knowing that I had to glue my eyes to the blacktop real soon or forget about driving any more that night altogether. I couldn't afford that. Nobody pays a bonus for brown lettuce and soft tomatoes.

"I thought you were dead," I finally blurted out. I said it easy, matter-of-fact, not wanting to startle her or me. Maybe the crosses made me do it; I don't know. She started to back away, but my country calm held her.

"I knew I shouldn't have talked to you this long. I try not to talk to anyone I don't know for very long. I thought by now. . . ." She shrugged sadly. "I've done pretty well, hiding everything."

"Real well." I smiled reassuringly. "Hey, chill out. What you've done is no skin off my nose. Personally I think it's great. Let 'em all think you're dead. Serves 'em all right, you ask me. Bunch of phonies, the lot of 'em."

She still looked as if she wanted to run. Then she smiled afresh and nodded. "That's right. Bunch of phonies. They all just wanted one thing. I spent all my time torn up inside and confused, and nobody tried to help. Nobody cared as long as they were making money or getting what they wanted. I was just a machine to them, a thing. I didn't know what to do. I got in real deep with some guys and that's when I knew that one way or another, I had to get out, get away.

"Up here nobody cares where you come from or what you did before you got here. Nice people. And I like doing my carvings. I got out of it with a little money nobody could trace. I'm doing fine."

"Glad to hear it. I always did think you were *it*, you know."

"That wasn't me, Dave. That was never me. That was always the problem. I'm happy now, and that's what counts. If you live long enough, you come to know what's really important."

"That's what me and Elaine always say."

She glanced at the sky and the light from the cafe fully illuminated her face. "You'd better get going."

"How'd you work it, anyway? How'd you fool everybody?"

"I had some friends. True friends. Not many, but enough. They understood. They helped me get out. Once in a while they come up here and we laugh about how we fooled everyone. We go fishing. I always did like to fish. You'd better get moving."

"Reckon I'd better. You keep doing those carvings. I really liked your bobcat."

"Thanks. That one was a lot of work. Merry Christmas, Dave."

"Yeah. You too . . . Jill."

She turned away from me, knowing that I'd keep her secret. Hell, what did I have to gain from giving her away? I knew how she must feel, or thought I did. About the best thing you can do in this mean world is not step on somebody else's happiness, and I wasn't about to step on hers. It's too damn hard to come by and you might need somebody else to do you a similar favor sometime. It doesn't hurt to establish a line of credit with the Almighty.

I watched her walk away in the falling snow, all bundled up and hidden inside that big western jacket, and I felt real good with myself. I'd still make Reno in plenty of time, then pop over to Tahoe, maybe get lucky and pick up a return load. My eyes followed her through the dark and white wet and she seemed to wink in and out of my sight, dream-like.

White crosses. Damn, I thought. Was she real or wasn't she? Not that it really mattered. I still felt good. I sucked in the sharp, damp air and made ready to get back to business.

That's when she sort of hesitated, stopped, and glanced back at me. Or at least, whatever I saw there in the Sierra night glanced back at me. When she resumed her walk it wasn't the stiff, horsey stride she'd been using before but a rolling, rocking, impossibly fluid gait that would've blasted the knob off a frozen thermometer. I think she did it just for me. Maybe it was because of the season, but I tell you, it was one helluva present.

Not knowing what else to do I waved. I think she waved back as I called out, "Merry Christmas, Norma Jean." Then hurried across the street to the parking lot to fire up Slewfoot.

Distaff Darkness

If Life and Death's relief
Were ours to command
Then parting were no grief.
   —patterned on a haiku by the Lady Eguchi
   (c. 890)

The Strange Voyage of Dr. Morbid

Jessica Amanda Salmonson

One of the most erudite scholars in modern fantasy is JESSICA AMANDA SAL-MONSON, *poet* (The Ghost Garden), *publisher of* Fantasy Macabre *and other periodicals, author of* A Silver Thread of Madness, The Golden Naginata, Tomoe Gozen *and* The Swordswoman, *and World Fantasy Award winning editor of* Amazons!, *as well as* Heroic Visions *and* Tales by Moonlight. *Jessica's idiosyncratic short fiction includes such unforgettable tales as "Atrocities," "Carmanda," "The Trilling Princess" and "The Strange Voyage of Dr. Morbid," which even by Jessica's standards is truly bizarre . . . and wonderful. At the end of the tale is added "Bone Wings," a poem by Ms. Salmonson which, though distinct from "The Strange Voyage of Dr. Morbid," strikes me as a fitting aftermath.*

DR. MORBID combs her long black hair and sits in her cramped cabin. Beyond the porthole, glimmering violet waves heave upward then downward, upward then downward, up and down, hypnotizing the vessel.

In her smoky, gossamer dress, Dr. Morbid strides upon the deck, dark tresses lifted by the wind. She unhinges a mask and throws it in the sea.

The ship is made of a fleshy substance. Dr. Morbid's footsteps make no sound, although her heels are sharp and cleated. Where she steps, blood-blisters well.

The engine of the mighty ship does not rumble or vibrate. It breathes.

At night, Dr. Morbid hears the vessel sighing. She feels its beating heart. Suddenly, the doctor sits up in her bed, surprise upon her face. The vessel's heart is fibrillating! Its breath is as raspy as an old man with pneumonia.

Flinging a black knit shawl about her shoulders, she hurries from the cabin in her bed-gown. She meets the captain in the hall. His face is pale but he hides his worry. "Can I help?" says Dr. Morbid. She adds, "I'm a doctor."

In the engine room, she administers penicillin. The crew sits up the whole night, as does Dr. Morbid, hoping the ship will pull through. At dawn, it breathes its last; a sorrowful exhalation, and the pump gives out.

The passengers know nothing. They play shuffleboard and remark how the deck is firmer and better for the game. Someone mentions how the sound of wheezing in the distance kept him up all night, but now it's nice and quiet. Dr. Morbid glides among the passengers, her visage severe with disapproval. Around the motionless ship, the violet waves have grown still.

TWO

Dr. Morbid is shunned by her colleagues, perhaps because she is a woman, or because she is beautiful, or because she makes so little effort to conform to their imagined scheme of things. It is difficult for older men, though liberal, to invite a woman to their yachts in the same way they invite each other.

One day, they are in the cafeteria together. The men drink coffee. Dr. Morbid has green tea in a styrofoam cup. Above their heads, neon tubes of green and red are twisted into the shape of interlacing stethoscopes. "I disagree," says Dr. Asp, a distinguished neurosurgeon, but Dr. Morbid persists: "Consider Dr. Scatter's specialty. What is the rate of success in your surgical arena, doctor?"

"Ninety percent success," says Dr. Scatter proudly.

"And five months later?" she asks.

Dr. Scatter squirms and winces. The green and red lights glisten against the moisture of his face.

"In follow-up," ventures Dr. Morbid, "less than two percent have survived the first half year after duodenoduodenechtomy. Curiously, the rate of remission in untreated patients is slightly higher."

"Dr. Scatter's specialty is a delicate one," says Dr. Asp, in defense of his friend of many years.

"Quite so," says Dr. Morbid, faintly smiling. "Yet it reinforces my premise that we trade in death, not health. If the world were strictly healthy, we'd be unemployed. We are all personifications of Death, gentlemen. Some of us more so than others."

"I disagree," says Dr. Asp, a strange cloudy substance half materializing at his shoulders, then dissipating.

"As do I," says Dr. Scatter, his manner increasingly nervous. "It is our mission to battle death at every turn."

"As well to say we're here to stop the tides," says Dr. Morbid. "Well! Do pardon me, gentlemen. I've a patient waiting. A friend of yours, I believe: Dr. Rotario. A bad way."

Dr. Morbid leaves. The others sit silently. Serpents cling to the ceiling's neon stethoscope. Then Dr. Scatter says into his dissolving cup, "She's an odd one."

"She's young," says Dr. Asp. "She'll learn." His wristwatch peeped, reminding him to take his medication. He washed it down with coffee. Dr. Scatter watched him, infinitely sad.

THREE

"Is there nothing you can do, doctor?" the grieving husband pleads. He clings to Dr. Morbid's blouse of black lace. She tries to calm the man but must be firm. "She was dead when you brought her in. If she'd come sooner . . ."

The husband wails. He was the one who wouldn't believe his wife's pain was as bad as that, kept her from the doctor, complained about their lack of medical insurance, his unemployment, their desperate straits, his insistence that she absolutely not be sick.

"There has to be something!" he whines, falling to his knees, clutching Dr. Morbid pathetically. He never loved his wife but the guilt is awful. How dare she die, leaving him these feelings of terror! He sobs and gasps in such agony that his shouting turns to dull, wracking grunts. Dr. Morbid pries his fingers from her clothing and says, "There may yet be something."

Immediately she regrets herself. But the man is instantly silent, gazing upward as to a god, hope glinting in his reddened eyes.

The corpse reposes on a wheeled bed in a hallway, awaiting the morgue. Dr. Morbid goes to the dead wife's side and bends to her ear and whispers, "Your husband wishes you to come back." In a moment, the wife's eyes begin to move back and forth beneath the lids. Dr. Morbid shouts for aides and the woman is wheeled to intensive care. Later, the husband sits by his wife's side. He's been crying the whole day. His eyes are swollen. Yet he smiles as he says, "I thought you were dead. Everyone thought you were dead." He puts his forehead on her shoulder.

The wife has not yet recovered enough to speak. Her eyes are wild and full of fright. When Dr. Morbid arrives to see how she is doing, the wife glowers at the doctor with malevolence.

The husband clings to his wife's arm.

FOUR

These are the children of Dr. Morbid, orphans with terminal diseases, abandoned by parents who could not or would not cope or care. Each child seeks to be loved. The doomed children wish to live, yet have no fear of death. They are stoic and horrifically beautiful.

They understand that they will not live long. They will settle, therefore, for being loved. But who will love them? They have nothing, only pity. Medical staff harden themselves lest their emotions suffer. But Dr. Morbid holds the oozing infants. Each thin or swollen child is her treasure.

"I love you, Dr. Morbid," says the bald and dark-eyed boy.

"I love you too," she answers, and shows him the needle.

"Will it hurt, Dr. Morbid?" he asks, deep eyes beacons of fear.

"Doesn't it hurt already?" she says.

"Yes it hurts, here and here," he says.

After the injection there is no more pain. The boy bucks up and smiles. The morphine opens his awareness. "Oh, Dr. Morbid!" he says.

"Yes, 'oh,' " she agrees, and pulls the sheet around his shoulders.

"There are angels," he says. "There are angels and pretty flowers in the sky!"

"Yes," says Dr. Morbid and leaves the boy to rest in the gloomy sterile room.

Across the hall a skeletal girl gasps, her blue lips opening and closing like the gills of a fish. Sunken eyes see Dr. Morbid. Thin arms raise, expecting a hug. "Angels?" she gasps, and Dr. Morbid promises, "Angels, yes." She strokes the girl while a fat nurse prepares the needle. After her injection, the child grins hideously. The nurse, horrified, looks the other way.

At the doorway to the little girl's room a humming electric wheelchair stalls. A wobbling head with hairless pate turns to see Dr. Morbid sitting by the girl's bed.

"Hello," he says, his voice a squeak. "Hello," Dr. Morbid replies; and he says, "Hello." Five or six times they say hello. His bony, spotted, quivering hand moves upon the wheelchair's button and he hums into the room.

"Hello," he says, and the weirdly smiling girl says, "Hello."

"Hello," he says, and Dr. Morbid says, "Hello."

Then all of them giggle, gasping squeaking giggles from the children, a musical refrain from Dr. Morbid, and a choking sound of disgust from the fat nurse who flees the room. Then everyone is silent.

"Dr. Morbid," says the thin bald boy with the thin high voice, "will you come to my funeral? I would like to invite you to come."

"I'll be there," Dr. Morbid promises.

"I want songs at my funeral and flowers, too, and I'll invite anyone I please. It'll be fun."

"That's right," says Dr. Morbid.

"Afterward we can go somewhere and have ice creams," he suggests.

"How are you feeling today?"

"I'm okay," he says, as Dr. Morbid takes the wheelchair's handles and moves out into the hall. As the boy rides along, he says, "The angels are with me always now. I don't need shots."

He looks over his shoulder at her, smiling, and there is a weird sad beauty to his face. Then he looks straight down the hall, leans his head forward, and makes a rattling sound in his throat. Dr. Morbid stops the wheelchair, kneels at the dead child's side, and murmurs in his ear, "Yes, angels."

FIVE

At times Dr. Morbid finds it best to wear a mask to see her patients. "What is underneath the mask?" asks a ghastly ill man. He wonders, "Is it Lady Death?" At such a moment she reveals her face to be beautiful and serene. The patient invariably feels better, although his case is hopeless, for whoever knows what lies beyond the mask is comforted.

Other times she thinks it better not to wear the mask, but to keep her mask nearby. A child in the advanced stages of this or that, hairless and emaciated with the deepest eyes you can imagine, asks, "Are you unhappy, pretty doctor? Don't feel bad," and Dr. Morbid places the mask just so and the dying child will laugh.

Some say the mask is made of glass, others that it is wood, while others insist it is fashioned out of lacquered paper. If her patients are asked the color of the mask, they always disagree. "It's a black mask," says one, another, "White," while someone else is convinced the mask is violet. If asked to describe the mask's expression, they'll say, "A harlequin's sad smile," or "a newborn's gaping confusion," or that it is a monster from Africa, a bird devised by Native Americans, a puckermouthed whistling peasant from a Japanese comic play.

Some have decided, "Dr. Morbid has a lot of masks—a big collection."

But where does she keep them? She seems to have them with her at the exact moment they are needed, to fit the occasion.

The old woman, a thousand years old and finally dying, is hardly able to speak. But other patients gather near to hear the last of her wisdom as the weary voice tells them, "Dr. Morbid—has no mask at all."

In this moment of enlightenment, she dies.

Bone Wings

Jessica Amanda Salmonson

"And so he passed into the place where faded rainbows are."
—THOMAS LOVELL BEDDOES

I saw Cupid as a skeleton,
child-death with bird wing-bones
and crookèd arrows made of thorn.
"I give thee love of ashes,"
he said, as fletched thorn flashes
through the dismal, rainy morn.
"I give thee love of crumbled flowers,
of regrets and tragic, final hours;
of all that's tortured, sad, and worn."
(Arrows pierced my tattered laces.)
"I give thee love of silent places:
graveyards, caverns in the sea,
glaciered wastes where endless night
glimmers sable over white,"
said the wingèd sprite to me.

On that garden path of stone
Cupid as a skeleton

held me in his infant embrace,
clung as children will to mother's knee,
then left me dreaming of worlds otherly—
the clatter of bone wings his only trace.

The Gift

Susan C. Stone

SUSAN C. STONE *was born in Buffalo, New York, and now makes her home in the warmer climes of New Jersey. "After college," she writes, "I deferred admission to law school when I realized that if I became an editor instead, people would actually pay me to read books." Currently a freelance editor and writer as well as an enthusiastic gardener, she adds, "I still enjoy reading." Her romantic ghost story, "Lady of Shadows," appeared in Mary Elizabeth Allen's 1992 anthology* All Hallows' Eve.

THOUGH NO ONE DARED to speak, the anteroom was anything but silent. The room was filled with people and so with sounds. Stiff formal clothing scraped against skin, shoes echoed on the marble floor, and a multitude of objects, large and small, soft and brittle, brushed, rattled and clanged against each other.

There were three things that all those present had in common—we bore gifts for the queen, we and our gifts had been carefully searched to make certain no weapons entered the royal presence . . . and we waited.

Others fidgeted, paced, or preened like peacocks. I did not. I had learned patience in a school even less tolerant of errors in judgment and decorum than the current royal court. Nothing would be allowed to cost me this opportunity. The queen, not one of her degenerate courtiers or

larcenous councilors, would be the recipient of what had been so carefully prepared.

I occupied a bench in a shadowed alcove, near the massive carved
door that gave access to the great audience chamber. From that vantage
point, I was able to observe, without appearing to, the guards at the
door, as well as my fellow would-be gift givers.

Though we obviously represented many different guilds and crafts,
and none present were courtiers, some instinct for self-preservation
seemed universal. We had all tried to mimic to some degree the current
formal court styles. The high collar of my own tunic was not, perhaps,
the height of fashion, but it suited my needs and was neither startling
nor remarkable enough to be dangerous.

To pass the time, I surveyed what I could of the other gifts. They
were a varied and costly lot, intended to tempt the queen's jaded taste.
Luminous jewels sparkled among gay wrappings. The rich glow of or-
nately carved wood vied with the glint of finely worked metal. Glimpses
of bright feathers and the subtle sheen of lustrous fur revealed the rare
birds and exotic animals that joined their raucous cries and menacing
rumbles to the myriad sounds of human origin. The air was heavy with
scents, animal musk mixed with rare spices, foods and perfumes, all
added to the sharp tang that betrayed human fear.

My own offering was in a box of stiffened cloth, as long as my arm
and half again as wide. It was unwrapped, unbound, and in the shadows
of my alcove, seemed unadorned. But its fabric was as extravagant as
what I knew it contained, dyed a costly indigo, woven thin and fine and
given form by stiff embroideries worked in thread of gold, forming the
symbol of the royal house. It was a subtle masterpiece, designed with the
torchlight of the royal audience chamber in mind.

"Next is Gethe of the Guild of Weavers." The functionary's voice
rasped with impatience and fatigue. Many had come before, and I could
see there were many more yet to follow.

I moved immediately, not wishing to risk provoking his temper, ru-
mored to be even more capricious than the queen's own.

The great door swung open silently as I approached, and closed with
an echoing thud after I had passed through.

A remarkable carpet, woven all of a piece and worked in a multi-
hued design of fanciful creatures, muffled the sound of my footfalls as I
walked the length of the audience chamber. I held my gift before me,

hands carefully placed both to reveal its glistening ornamentation and to avoid alarming the queen's ever zealous guards.

When I was still slightly more than a spear's length from the throne I stopped. I knelt, carefully set down the box, and pressed my forehead to the carpet, awaiting the queen's permission to continue.

When the signal came, I took my first breath since passing through the door and began my carefully planned speech. "Your Majesty, I humbly beg to offer a gift from your loyal Guild of Weavers and Dyers."

I paused to set aside the top of the box and withdraw the carefully folded contents. Like the box that had contained it, the gift seemed to catch fire from the light of the torches, and a muted murmur of amazement, almost awe, issued from the nearest watchers.

"Continue," urged the queen.

I draped the radiant fabric against my unadorned sleeve. "This was crafted for you by our finest artisans, Majesty," I said, though the quality of the workmanship stated that without words. At court the forms had to be observed. "It attempts to reflect, on this the anniversary of your birth, some small part of the glory of your reign." As I spoke, I rose and shook the cloak to its full length. The thin leather gloves I wore kept my work-roughened fingers from catching against the fabric, protecting both the gift and the giver.

In a single, much-practiced movement, I set the cloth in motion. It slipped through the air with a sighing sound, like that of the wind over fields heavy with grain, and settled gracefully over my shoulders, as flattering to my form as it would be to her majesty's. The finely-crafted, entwined dragons that stiffened the collar and cleverly concealed the fastening were unfortunately overwhelmed somewhat by the high neck of my tunic. It was no accident that the cloak had been designed to show to its best advantage when worn with the more revealing style favored by the queen.

I turned slowly, to reveal the cloak in all its glory. The midnight blue of the rich silk, and the sinuous paired dragons embroidered upon it in gold, echoed the banner hanging above the throne—the banner of the royal house. The last mutterings and shufflings of bored courtiers stilled at the sight. It was truly a majestic gift. "May my guild hope that it has pleased you, Majesty?" I asked softly.

The queen's, long, elegant fingers twitched covetously and she nodded once.

I took that as my signal, slipped the garment off, cradled it in my arms, and took three slow, careful steps forward.

The queen signalled her guards to hold their ground and permitted me to assist her. I took care to see that the collar settled smoothly against the soft skin at the back of her neck, and that the heavy cloth of the garment draped smoothly across her bare shoulders. Then I stepped back and awaited judgement.

"You may convey my appreciation to the leaders of your guild," the queen said, her tone uncharacteristically gracious.

"You may be sure I will, Your Majesty," I responded with absolute sincerity. Then, carefully observing all the forms of court courtesy, I withdrew from the chamber.

It was not until I had passed out of the palace grounds that I took my first totally unguarded breath of the day. My commission was completed and I was safely away. Now it was only a matter of time. The poison impregnated in the collar of the cloak would do its work, even if Her Tyrannical Majesty never wore it again after today.

Before the next full moon we would have a new sovereign—one who owed that position solely to me and my equally well-concealed fellows in the Ancient and Worthy Society of Assassins, Spies and Entrepreneurs. With such a ruler, surely all our enterprises would prosper.

Vanishing

Hope Manville

My friend and former student HOPE MANVILLE *is currently hard at work on a young adult fantasy novel, but she took time out to draw on her own dark experiences of chemotherapy and produce "Vanishing," a harrowing deathbed vignette whose theme is psychosexual symbiosis. Hope's first story, "The Bones of Faerie," was published in* All Hallows' Eve *(Walker and Co., 1942).*

SHE LIES ALONE in the wide bed they once shared, her sweating palm turning the worn twist of paper into grayish pulp. She found it only a few hours before, hidden between the mattress and the bed frame of the narrow white cot in which her husband now spends his days and nights. Inside are thirty green-and-white sleeping capsules.

He must have been planning this for months.

The first alarm clock goes off, interrupting her thoughts. It is five A.M. Despite the fact that they could afford a housekeeper, cook, even a round-the-clock nurse, she does it all alone, all the work of tending to him, ignoring frequent offers of help from his children and grandchildren (they are all the sons, daughters and grandchildren of his dead first wife, Marthe, this, his second marriage being without issue).

"Why won't you let me help you with Grandfather?" Nini often pleads. Just thinking of it, Gerda shakes her head. What good could a girl like that be?

Besides, Nini tires her grandfather out. With her endless talk and smiles she is too much for him. *Too much.*

Now, as he lies, dry-skinned, hairless, hopefully asleep in the small room they call the library, Gerda rises to begin her day. As always, she dresses from head to toe facing the blank wall, despite the fact that there is a large mirror on the back of the closet door.

This done, she starts pressing the sheets that she laundered by hand the night before.

Again she thinks of the cache of sleeping medication, noticed by accident, confiscated the moment he'd slipped into fitful slumber. She'd stolen back eagerly to see what he was hiding, only to realize, the minute she looked at the pills, what he planned to do.

In her heartsickness she forgets, and applies the starch twice. The finished sheets are cardboard to the touch, but she does not notice.

Entering his darkened room, she stands in the doorway. He groans and moves his head from side to side. He is talking. To the untrained ear he speaks gibberish; however, if you wait a few minutes, you can make out the sense of the words. He is talking to the ghosts who he says live in the corners of his room.

"I remember you, I remember you now!" he calls to them. "I am so sorry I did not make them stop the train, that I did not ask why—I should have guessed—I shall make it up to you, I promise! I promise!"

"Good morning darling!" She pitches her voice high and keeps her tone light, noticing how his eyes dart toward the former hiding place of the pills, then instantly away.

"How are you, darling?" she asks. Instead of waiting for the answer which will not come, she lifts his naked head to turn his pillow, making him wince.

"How are you?" she asks again.

"I am well." His tone belies his words.

She puts the fresh sheets down on the corner of the table that holds bottles of medicine, and a *Daily News,* the only paper she allows now, since she fears his favorite *Times* would be too wearing.

She grunts as she half carries, half drags him to the worn dark couch. He whimpers briefly as a dog might, then is silent.

Gerda tears the sheets off the bed to replace them with the fresh ones. The armpits of her thick brown knit dress are now stained with large half-moons of sweat.

"All right, darling, now I'll put you back to bed and we'll have break-fast." She plants a kiss on his cheek that leaves no imprint of lipstick. (Cosmetics are for trash.)

She works so hard to cure him, and make him well with nourishing food, even though those doctors want to starve him to death. The doctors insist that the chemotherapy treatments he receives make eating agony for him. *Light, dry foods!* the doctors say. So she nods and smiles at them when they talk, but as soon as they leave she works like a ditchdigger, spooning food into him—chopped liver, stewed fruit, strained carrots, beef boiled for hours and put through the blender and mashed potatoes. She places him on the bedpan like clockwork. She cleans him, tends to him. She cares for him as if he were the baby he never wanted her to have. He was, after all, forty-five when they married, more than twenty-five years older than she was. At his age, a second young family would be a strain.

She shakes her head, remembering. How strong and wise he was then.

"No more schooling for you," he'd told her. "You are not so bright that it will do you much good. The training you need is done here at home."

She knew he was right. Stupid she had always been. Besides, a wife's job, after all, is to be a wife.

The training was hard, though. He believed in getting things right the first time, and she almost never did. Which meant the punishments, always. They were to make her better, and were hard on him, she knew. He did not like to hit her, or pinch or slap, or humiliate her in front of people, he made this clear. A smart girl would never require so much teaching. This, of course, made her feel even worse.

She tried to be better, she tried, but she was so ignorant, and from the old country.

The slaps and the hits were for when she failed to look attentive in company. Or when she behaved in a manner he considered too hesitant or shy. But there were other punishments, too.

Once she yawned in front of a client. It was late, and she had had too much to drink (refusing wine was always punished, because not to take it made the others at the table feel uncomfortable), and she did cover her mouth, but she could see the way his eyes narrowed how bad she was.

When the company was gone, he made her strip down to her slip and lie facedown on the bed . . .

She sighs. It was hard. It might have been easier if she had a friend who could tell her how a lawyer's wife should act and behave; however, he did not believe she should have friends until she was properly trained, and that time never came.

But she was so lucky, so young and stupid, barely knowing the language, to have caught his eye. She and her sister and father had just come over here with a letter referring them to *Herr Doktor,* for help getting their simple business affairs established here. *Herr Doktor* did all that for them admirably.

"And he wants to marry you, too!" she remembers her father marveling.

As time went on, she only got stupider, suggesting that a perfectly good piece of furniture was shabby when there was plenty of wear in it after all. She was made to lie facedown on the very couch she had thought to replace while he wondered aloud. "A belt? A stick?"

She shakes her head at herself. Stupid. Stupid and willful. He wanted her hair cut only for her own sake, for people might easily think that the bright blond color was out of a bottle, like a tramp.

She'd wept, crying harder because she was distressed, knowing that the sounds of her sobs irritated him. He worked hard. He needed quiet at home. It was two days before she was able to calm down enough for the trip to the hairdresser.

Over the years she found that it was best to simply accept what she was too ignorant to understand. If she could not comprehend it, well, someday she would be rewarded.

But surely someday must be here by now?

She walks into the kitchen to start the meat boiling and to cut up the broccoli.

How to bring him back?

Despairing, she chops onions. It is as if there were less of him every day. But surely without the food she gives him it would be worse.

The pills. The pills. How could he, when her entire life was given over to his. What would happen to her without him?

Her life was worth barely five minutes of his, she knew.

But that did not make it any easier to let him go.

For with him she was nothing, but without him, she would be even less . . .

She finds herself remembering the wedding day, the old priest in the small chapel, the rustle of papers and documents, her birth certificate from her little town. An unceremonious lunch at an elegant restaurant that frightened her.

The second alarm clock goes off, and she returns to the sickroom again. It is time for the midmorning battle of wills that involves the bedpan.

After washing her hands she goes back into the kitchen, where the pots boil merrily on the stove. She takes out dried apricots, prunes and raisins to make a compote. Fruit. He needs fruit but the fresh fruit is full of germs.

She tries to recall if he kissed her on their wedding day and cannot.

She hurries in with the lunch tray, for the nurse comes for his chemotherapy today and she wants to tidy him up before Miss Frost arrives.

He groans softly at the sight of the tray and tries to keep his mouth closed, but she grips his head in the crook of her arm and holds his nose tight until he is forced to open his mouth to breathe.

Because of the pills, she feeds him twice as much as usual.

"I know it's hard, darling, I know it's hard. But when you are well you will thank me."

Tears come to his eyes as he tries to swallow. Food dribbles down his chin and she spoons it back up and into his mouth. He heaves slightly, but the gray-brown mush that comes back up is so similar to the form the meat and the vegetables take once they are blended together that she simply spoons it back into him.

"One, two, buckle my shoe." She smiles as she tucks puréed broccoli between his narrow lips.

"Three, four, shut the door."

He is particularly slow today, and it takes three rounds of "One, Two" and four choruses of "London Bridge Is Falling Down" before lunch is all gone.

Gerda forces herself to smile. "Our nurse comes today."

He blinks in acknowledgment, but nothing more.

The doorbell rings, and Miss Frost, with her tubes and needles, comes in. The chemicals are bright yellow and red. They shimmer in sunlight as Miss Frost pushes the plunger of the injection slowly, firmly down.

Gerda holds him while he shivers and cries that it is liquid ice, that it burns.

The nurse has a calm face and smooth, capable hands. She tells Gerda the same stupid instructions again and again each week, how he should eat lightly or not at all, how people with infectious diseases must stay away, how if he develops a rash or fever they must call the hospital immediately.

Again Gerda nods and smiles, but she knows better. If he went into the hospital, they would leave him to lie in the bed and starve him, letting him waste away, and perhaps one of those doctors who wants to kill him would come in with a long, long needle . . .

No, you have to be careful.

That Miss Frost, always talking about fresh ginger to suck for the nausea. Everyone knows a raw vegetable is bad for you. It has germs and must be cooked and cooked. Two weeks ago, Gerda bought a piece of ginger at the store and took it home. It was dirty like an onion from the bin. It tasted of dirt.

When Gerda showed Miss Frost the ginger, Miss Frost said no, you have to peel it. With a small knife, Miss Frost peeled back the ginger skin to reveal fruit as white as an apple. Before Gerda could protest, Miss Frost popped a piece into Gerda's mouth. The astringent, burning freshness was a reproof.

Miss Frost always offers to stay and help give him a bath, help her change the linens. Gerda always says no.

When they do not think she is listening, the family talks of how much easier Gerda's life would be if he died. Not so old really, and all that money. She could travel. But Gerda feels old. A thousand years old. And she has never been anywhere but this apartment and a few other places since she came here. They are so dumb, all of them, to think such!

Miss Frost is still speaking.

"And, of course, a pill at night for sleeping."

"A pill at night!" Gerda hears a voice speaking. She is startled when she realizes it is hers.

"A pill at night! Is that what you think happens here? Are you stupid?"

Suddenly, Miss Frost looks a great deal younger.

"I tell you what happens! He takes the pill and pretends to put it in his mouth and drink water, but then when I am not looking he takes it out of his mouth and puts it in paper to save up and take all at once! And I wash him and I bathe him and I wash sheets and I clean house and he treats me like the maid, the maid THE MAID THE MAID THE MAID—"

"Please, Mrs.—Gerda." The nurse puts her hands on Gerda's shoulders, for two arms wave like a windmill, and they are Gerda's.

"You think I am stupid? You try it. You try it. Try it! Just try! . . ." Gerda is sobbing.

"Please, please! You're very upset!" The nurse guides Gerda out of the sickroom into the living room. She forces Gerda onto the couch.

Gerda is unable to stop crying.

"Do you want me to stay?"

Gerda does not answer. The two of them sit in the fading light for a while. The next alarm goes off.

"What's that?" Miss Frost looks around.

"Medicine time," Gerda answers mechanically.

"Oh." Miss Frost looks at her watch. "I have another patient over on the East Side, but . . ."

"Fine," says Gerda. "Good-bye."

"No." Miss Frost goes over to the phone. "I'm going to call your granddaughter. Maybe she can come over for a while." The nurse begins dialing.

"She's not my granddaughter," Gerda says.

Nini is apparently not home, for Gerda hears the nurse talk in that mechanical way that people do when they reach an answering machine.

The walls of the living room are a faded mud color. When the paper was new, it was a dark beige, chosen by Marthe. The couch, chairs, carpet and all other furnishings were all hers. Gerda has lived in this apartment for over twenty years and has not been allowed to change a single thing.

For years she suffered as she struggled along on the same household budget on which Marthe used to manage so beautifully, wearing the ugly dresses and shoes for an old lady on which he insisted.

Then one day it became clear to her. She must accept his will as law. Her slavery would become her freedom. She let down the hems of the already dowdy skirts even farther. The hair (what was left of it) she got rid of herself with a nail scissors. Her world, never large, became smaller.

There were, she knew, those who argued, kissed and shouted and flew in planes and danced. But such was not for her.

"I can stay," the nurse sits down on the couch next to Gerda and puts her hand on Gerda's arm. "I'll call my next patient and say I'll be late. That way I can stay until your granddaughter gets here."

Gerda looks at the woman. All of a sudden it dawns upon her what she must do. But first she must get rid of Miss Frost. "You can go."

"I don't think you should be alone now," the nurse says. "Besides, what if your granddaughter doesn't get the message? I really don't want—"

"No, you go," Gerda says firmly. She forces herself to smile confidently. "I'll be fine." It's almost four-thirty. Nini gets home around five. That means there isn't much time.

"I really don't mind—"

"No, go," Gerda says. "They'll be waiting."

The nurse leaves reluctantly.

Gerda swallows hard as she walks into the sickroom. Again he is talking to the ghosts.

"I always gave you something, a dime, a quarter. It was not enough, I know that now. I apologize. I apologize." It must be the ghost that was once the beggar who lived on the corner near 103rd Street. The one with no eyes.

He is slipping away. He is going. He is all she has, but he does not wish to stay. She must try to make him stay.

"Darling," she says. She smiles. Taking his hand, she places it under her skirt, places a fold of stockinged thigh between his fleshless fingers.

"I was bad in front of the nurse. Punish me."

His eyes widen, then close.

"I was bad."

"Darling?" She places her own hand around his, forcing him to bear down on her skin.

His eyes narrow in disgust. *He?*

And if she had not found the pills, would he even be here now to despise her?

She runs into her room. Her first thought is to take the pills herself. She could show him. She lies on the bed supine, her flat, broad face ground into the spread.

The downstairs bell rings. *Nini.*

Gerda rings Nini in, takes Nini's blue ski parka from her.

"The nurse said to come over as soon as possible, that you needed me. Is something wrong?"

"No," says Gerda. "The nurse wants you to help me. I can't do it all anymore."

Gerda waits for Nini to go into the old man's room. She waits a beat before she speaks.

"Nini, you are going to give your grandfather a bath," Gerda announces. Nini does not look directly at Gerda or say anything. But the old man wheezes with pain as he turns toward them.

"Gerda . . ." he says. It must be the first time in years he has used her name. "Don't . . ." He begins to cough.

"Uh," Nini says. "I kind of have this cold?"

"I will get the water running," says Gerda.

She turns the water on full force. Over the noise of the rapidly filling tub, Nini's sneeze is a bullet of sound.

For the next twenty minutes Gerda directs, checks, inspects and insists that Nini perform the simple but humiliating actions again and again.

He sits on the aluminum bath stool motionless, unresisting, his face a mask. Nini keeps her reddened eyes lowered, and sometimes holds the back of her hand over her mouth for a genteel cough, but Gerda urges the girl on, with washcloth and Cuticura soap. Gerda will never be happy, she knows that now. But at least he can be as miserable as she.

He is broken. But when Nini leaves, he still catches the hand of his favorite grandchild and kisses her fingers.

Three days later, the dark room is empty at last of bottles, sheets and pain. In tears, Gerda flings the window open wide, still unbelieving, but forced to see that her love and her boiled beef and her alarm clocks were no match for the doctors, or anything else for that matter.

The doctors hid the truth within their lies, and she was too stupid, too stupid to see what was fact and what was false. Trying to beat them at their own game was useless anyway, for he has finally vanished into the world of his beloved ghosts.

Those chemicals really did make him helpless before the slightest germ.

That Nini, lying at home in bed now with the flu.

Gerda shrugs. She is still glad she did not take him to the hospital when his fever went up and his lungs filled, for he would have died starving. Here on his last day, nobody could say she, Gerda, did not try, for she stuffed him with casseroles, rich with cream.

As she raises the window of the former sickroom for a final airing, she is unaware of the gently twisting ribbon of gray smoke that touches her cheek, perhaps in apology, perhaps only in farewell.

The smoke escapes out the window, leaving Gerda alone.

A Room with a Vie

Tanith Lee

Beauty and the macabre mingle hauntingly in the award-winning fiction of TANITH LEE, *British author of* The Birthgrave, Companions on the Road, Dark Dance, East of Midnight, Drinking Sapphire Wine, Red as Blood *and many other novels. Her highly original ghost (?) story, "A Room with a Vie," is one of the most chilling I've ever read. Distaff darkness, indeed!*

"THIS IS IT, then."

"Oh, yes."

"As you can see, it's in quite nice condition."

"Yes, it is."

"Clothes there, on the bed. Cutlery in the box. Basin. Cooker. The meter's the same as the one you had last year. And you saw the bathroom across the corridor."

"Yes. Thank you. It's all fine."

"Well, as I said. I was sorry we couldn't let you have your other room. But you didn't give us much notice. And right now, August, and such good weather, we're booked right up."

"I understand. It was kind of you to find me this room. I was lucky, wasn't I? The very last one."

"It's usually the last to go, this one."

"How odd. It's got such a lovely view of the sea and the bay."

"Well, I didn't mean there was anything wrong with the room."

"Of course not."

"Mr. Tinker always used to have this room. Every year, four months, June to September."

"Oh, yes."

"It was quite a shock last year, when his daughter rang to cancel. He died, just the night before he meant to take the train to come down. Heart attack. What a shame."

"Yes, it was."

"Well, I'll leave you to get settled in. You know where we are if you want anything."

"Thank you very much, Mrs. Rice."

Mr. Tinker, she thought, leaning on the closed door. *Tinker*. Like a dog, with one black ear. Here, Tinker! Don't be silly, she thought. It's just nerves. Arrival nerves. By-the-sea nerves. By-yourself nerves.

Caroline crossed to the window. She stared out at the esplanade where the brightly coloured summer people were walking about in the late afternoon sun. Beyond, the bay opened its arms to the sea. The little boats in the harbour lay stranded by an outgoing tide. The water was cornflower blue.

If David had been here, she would have told him that his eyes were exactly as blue as that sea, which wasn't at all the case. How many lies there had been between them. Even lies about eye colour. But she wasn't going to think of David. She had come here alone, as she had come here last season, to sketch, to paint, to meditate.

It was a pity, about not being able to have the other room. It had been larger, and the bathroom had been "contained" rather than shared and across the hall. But then she hadn't been going to take the holiday flat this year. She had been trying to patch things up with David. Until finally, all the patching had come undone, and she'd grasped at this remembered place in a panic—I must get *away*.

Caroline turned her back to the window. She glanced about. Yes. Of course it was quite all right. If anything, the view was better because the flat was higher up. As for the actual room, it was like all the rooms. Chintz curtains, cream walls, brown rugs and jolly cushions. And Mr. Tinker had taken good care of it. There was only one cigarette burn in the table. And probably that wasn't Mr. Tinker at all. Somehow, she couldn't imagine Mr. Tinker doing a thing like that. It must be the result of the other tenants, those people who had accepted the room as their last choice.

Well now. Make up the bed, and then go out for a meal. No, she was too tired for that. She'd get sandwiches from the little café downstairs, perhaps some wine from the off-licence. It would be a chance to swallow some sea air. Those first breaths that always made her giddy and unsure, like too much oxygen.

She made the bed up carefully, as if for two. When she moved it away from the wall to negotiate the sheets, she saw something scratched in the cream plaster.

"Oh, Mr. Tinker, you naughty dog," she said aloud, and then felt foolish.

Anyway, Mr. Tinker wouldn't do such a thing. Scratch with a pen-knife, or even some of Mrs. Rice's loaned cutlery. Black ink had been smeared into the scratches. Caroline peered down into the gloom behind the bed. *A room with a view,* the scratching said. Well, almost. Whoever it was had forgotten to put in the ultimate double-"u": *A room with a vie.* Either illiterate or careless. Or smitten with guilt nine-tenths through.

She pushed the bed back again. She'd better tell the Rices sometime. God forbid they should suppose she was the vandal.

She was asleep, when she heard the room breathing. She woke gradually, as if to a familiar and reassuring sound. Then, as gradually, a confused fear stole upon her. Presently she located the breathing sound as the noise of her own blood rhythm in her ears. Then, with another shock of relief, as the sea. But, in the end, it was not the sea either. It was the room, breathing.

A kind of itching void of pure terror sent her plunging upwards from the bed. She scrabbled at the switch and the bedside light flared on. Blinded and gasping, she heard the sound seep away.

Out at sea, a ship mooed plaintively. She looked at the window and began to detect stars over the water, and the pink lamps glowing along the esplanade. The world was normal.

Too much wine after too much train travel. Nightmare.

She lay down. Though her eyes watered, she left the light on.

"I'm afraid so, Mrs. Rice. Someone's scratched and inked it on the wall. A nostalgia freak: *A room with a view.*"

"Funny," said Mrs. Rice. She was a homely woman with jet black gipsy hair that didn't seem to fit. "Of course, there's been two or three had that room. No one for very long. Disgusting. Still, the damage is done."

Caroline walked along the bay. The beach that spread from the south side was packed with holidaymakers. Everyone was paired, as if they meant to be ready for the ark. Some had a great luggage of children as well. The gulls and the children screamed.

Caroline sat drawing and the children raced screaming by. People stopped to ask her questions about the drawing. Some stared a long while over her shoulder. Some gave advice on perspective and subject matter. The glare of sun on the blue water hurt her eyes.

She put the sketchbook away. After lunch she'd go further along, to Jaynes Bay, which she recollected had been very quiet last year. This year, it wasn't.

After about four o'clock, gangs of local youth began to gather on the esplanade and the beach. Their hair was greased and their legs were like storks' legs in tight trousers. They whistled. They spoke in an impenetrable mumble which often flowered into four-letter words uttered in contrastingly clear diction.

There had been no gangs last year. The sun sank.

Caroline was still tired. She went along the esplanade to her block, up the steps to her room.

When she unlocked the door and stood on the threshold, for a moment—

What?

It was as if the pre-twilight amber that came into the room was slowly pulsing, throbbing. As if the walls, the floor, the ceiling were—

She switched on the overhead lamp.

"Mr. Tinker," she said firmly, "I'm not putting up with this."

"Pardon?" said a voice behind her.

Caroline's heart expanded with a sharp thud like a grenade exploding in her side. She spun around, and there stood a girl in jeans and a smock. Her hand was on the door of the shared bathroom. It was the previously unseen neighbour from down the hall.

"I'm sorry," said Caroline. "I must have been talking to myself."

The girl looked blank and unhelpful.

"I'm Mrs. Lacey," she said. She did not look lacy. Nor married. She looked about fourteen. "You've got number eight, then. How is it?"

Bloody nerve, Caroline thought.

"It's fine."

"They've had three in before you," said fourteen-year-old Mrs. Lacey.

"All together?"

"Pardon? No. I meant three separate tenants. Nobody would stay. All kinds of trouble with that Mrs. Rice. Nobody would, though."

"Why ever not?" Caroline snapped.

"Too noisy or something. Or a smell. I can't remember."

Caroline stood in her doorway, her back to the room.

Fourteen-year-old Mrs. Lacey opened the bathroom door.

"At least we haven't clashed in the mornings," Caroline said.

"Oh, *we're* always up early on holiday," said young Mrs. Lacey pointedly. Somewhere down the hall, a child began to bang and quack like an insane automatic duck. A man's voice bawled: "Hurry up that piss, Brenda, will you?"

Brenda Lacey darted into the bathroom and the bolt was shot.

Caroline entered her room. She slammed the door. She turned on the room, watching it.

There *was* a smell. It was very slight. A strange, faintly buttery smell. Not really unpleasant. Probably from the café below. She pushed up the window and breathed sea.

As she leaned on the sill, breathing, she felt the room start breathing too.

She was six years old, and Auntie Sara was taking her to the park. Auntie Sara was very loving. Her fat warm arms were always reaching out to hold, to compress, to pinion against her fat warm bosom. Being hugged by Auntie Sara induced in six-year-old Caroline a sense of claustrophobia and primitive fright. Yet somehow she was aware that she had to be gentle with Auntie Sara and not wound her feelings. Auntie Sara couldn't have a little girl. So she had to share Caroline with Mummy.

And now they were in the park.

"There's Jenny," said Caroline. But of course Auntie Sara wouldn't want to let Caroline go to play with Jennifer. So Caroline pretended that Auntie Sara *would* let her go, and she ran very fast over the green grass towards Jenny. Then her foot caught in something. When she began to fall, for a moment it was exhilarating, like flying. But she hit the ground, stunning, bruising. She knew better than to cry, for in another moment Auntie Sara had reached her. "It doesn't hurt," said Caroline. But Auntie Sara took no notice. She crushed Caroline to her. Caroline was smothered on her breast, and the great round arms bound her like hot, faintly dairy-scented bolsters.

Caroline started to struggle. She pummelled, kicked and shrieked.

It was dark, and she had not fallen in the grass after all. She was in bed in the room, and it was the room she was fighting. It was the room which was holding her close, squeezing her, hugging her. It was the room which had that faint cholesterol smell of fresh milk and butter. It was the room which was stroking and whispering.

But of course it couldn't be the damn room.

Caroline lay back exhausted, and the toils of her dream receded. Another nightmare. Switch on the light. Yes, that was it. Switch on the light and have a drink from the small traveller's bottle of gin she'd put ready in case she couldn't sleep.

"Christ." She shielded her eyes from the light.

Distantly, she heard a child crying—the offspring probably of young Mrs. unlacy Lacey along the hall. "God, I must have yelled," Caroline said aloud. Yelled and been heard. The unlacy Laceys were no doubt discussing her this very minute. The mad lazy slut in number eight.

The gin burned sweetly, going down.

This was stupid. The light—no, she'd have to leave the light on again.

Caroline looked at the walls. She could see them, very, very softly lifting, softly sinking. Don't be a fool. The smell was just discernible. It made her queasy. Too rich—yet, a human smell, a certain sort of human smell. Bovine, she concluded, exactly like poor childless Sara.

It was hot, even with the window open.

She drank halfway down the bottle and didn't care any more.

"Mr. Tinker? Why ever are you interested in him?"

Mrs. Rice looked disapproving.

"I'm sorry. I'm not being ghoulish. It's just—well, it seemed such a shame, his dying like that. I suppose I've been brooding."

"Don't want to do that. You need company. Is your husband coming down at all, this year?"

"David? No, he can't get away right now."

"Pity."

"Yes. But about Mr. Tinker—"

"All right," said Mrs. Rice. "I don't see why I shouldn't tell you. He was a retired man. Don't know what line of work he'd been in, but not very well paid, I imagine. His wife was dead. He lived with his married daughter, and really I don't think it suited him, but there was no alternative. Then, four months of the year, he'd come here and take number eight. Done it for years. Used to get his meals out. Must have been quite expensive. But I think the daughter and her husband paid for everything, you know, to get a bit of time on their own. But he loved this place, Mr. Tinker did. He used to say to me: 'Here I am home again, Mrs. Rice.' The room with his daughter, I had the impression he didn't think of that as home at all. But number eight. Well, he'd put his ornaments and books and pieces round. My George even put a couple of nails in for him to hang a picture or two. Why not? And number eight got quite cosy. It really *was* Mr. Tinker's room in the end. My George said that's why other tenants'd fight shy. They could feel it waiting for Mr. Tinker to come back. But that's a lot of nonsense, and I can see I shouldn't have said it."

"No. I think your husband was absolutely right. Poor old room. It's going to be disappointed."

"Well, my George, you know, he's a bit of an idiot. The night—the night we heard, he got properly upset, my George. He went up to number eight, and opened the door and told it. I said to him, you'll want me to hang black curtains in there next."

Beyond the fence, the headland dropped away in dry grass and the feverish flowers of late summer to a blue sea ribbed with white. North spread the curved claw of Jaynes Bay and the grey vertical of the lighthouse. But the sketch pad and pencil case sat on the seat beside Caroline.

She had attempted nothing. Even the novel lay closed. The first page hadn't seemed to make sense. She kept reading the words "home" and "Tinker" between the lines.

She understood she was afraid to return to the room. She had walked along the headlands, telling herself that all the room had wrong with it was sadness, a bereavement. That it wasn't waiting. That it wasn't alive. And anyway, even sadness didn't happen to rooms. If it did, it would have to get over that. Get used to being just a holiday flat again, a space which people filled for a few weeks, observed indifferently, cared nothing about, and then went away from.

Which was all absurd because none of it was true.

Except, that she wasn't the only one to believe—

She wondered if David would have registered anything in the room. Should she ring him and confide in him? Ask advice? No. For God's sake, that was why she was imagining herself into this state, wasn't it? So she could create a contact with him again. No. David was out and out David would stay.

It was five o'clock. She packed her block and pencils into her bag and walked quickly along the grass verge above the fence.

She could walk into Kingscliff at this rate, and get a meal.

She wondered who the scared punster had been, the one who knew French. She'd got the joke by now. A room with a vie: a room with a *life*.

She reached Kingscliff and had a pleasantly unhealthy meal, with a pagoda of white ice cream and glacé cherries to follow. In the dusk the town was raucous and cheerful. Raspberry and yellow neons splashed and spat and the motorbike gangs seemed suitable, almost friendly *in situ*. Caroline strolled by the whelk stalls and across the car park, through an odour of frying doughnuts, chips and fierce fish. She went to a cinema and watched a very bad and very pointless film with a sense of superiority and tolerance. When the film was over, she sat alone in a pub and drank vodka. Nobody accosted her or tried to pick her up. She was glad at first, but after the fourth vodka, rather sorry. She had to run to catch the last bus back. It was not until she stood on the esplanade, the bus vanishing, the pink lamps droning solemnly and the black water far below, that a real and undeniable terror came and twisted her stomach.

The café was still open, and she might have gone in there, but some of the greasy stork-legs she had seen previously were clustered about the counter. She was tight, and visualized sweeping amongst them, ignoring their adolescent nastiness. But presently she turned aside and into the block of holiday flats.

She dragged up the steps sluggishly. By the time she reached her door, her hands were trembling. She dropped her key and stifled a squeal as the short-time automatic hall light went out. Pressing the light button, she thought: Supposing it doesn't come on?

But the light did come on. She picked up her key, unlocked the door and went determinedly inside the room, shutting the door behind her.

She experienced it instantly. It was like a vast, indrawn, sucking gasp.

"No," Caroline said to the room. Her hand fumbled the switch and the room was lit.

Her heart was beating so very fast. That was, of course, what made the room also seem to pulse, as if its heart were also swiftly and greedily beating.

"Listen," Caroline said. "Oh God, talking to a *room*. But I have to, don't I? Listen, you've got to stop this. Leave me alone!" she shouted at the room.

The room seemed to grow still.

She thought of the Laceys, and giggled.

She crossed to the window and opened it. The air was cool. Stars gleamed above the bay. She pulled the curtains to, and undressed. She washed, and brushed her teeth at the basin. She poured herself a gin.

She felt the room, all about her. Like an inheld breath, impossibly prolonged. She ignored that. She spoke to the room quietly.

"Naughty Mr. Tinker, to tinker with you, like this. Have to call you Sara now, shan't I? Like a great big womb. That's what she really wanted, you see. To squeeze me right through herself, pop me into her womb. I'd offer you a gin, but where the hell would you put it?"

Caroline shivered.

"No. This is truly silly."

She walked over to the cutlery box beside the baby cooker. She put in her hand and pulled out the vegetable knife. It had quite a vicious edge. George Rice had them frequently sharpened.

"See this," Caroline said to the room. "Just watch yourself."

When she lay down, the darkness whirled, carouselling her asleep.

In the womb, it was warm and dark, a warm blood dark. Rhythms came and went, came and went, placid and unending as the tides of the sea. The heart organ pumped with a soft deep noise like a muffled drum.

How comfortable and safe it was. But when am I to be born? Caroline wondered. Never, the womb told her, lapping her, cushioning her.

Caroline kicked out. She floated. She tried to seize hold of something, but the blood-warm cocoon was not to be seized.

"Let me go," said Caroline. "Auntie Sara, I'm all right. Let me go. I want to—please—"

Her eyes were wide and she was sitting up in her holiday bed. She put out her hand spontaneously towards the light and touched the knife she had left beside it. The room breathed, regularly, deeply. Caroline moved her hand away from the light switch, and saw in the darkness.

"This is ridiculous," she said aloud.

The room breathed. She glanced at the window—she had left the curtains drawn over, and so could not focus on the esplanade beyond, or the bay: the outer world. The walls throbbed. She could *see* them. She was being calm now, and analytical, letting her eyes adjust, concentrating. The mammalian milky smell was heavy. Not precisely offensive, but naturally rather horrible, under these circumstances.

Very carefully, Caroline, still in darkness, slipped her feet out of the covers and stood up.

"All right," she said. "All right then."

She turned to the wall behind the bed. She reached across and laid her hand on it—

The *wall*. The wall was—*skin*. It was flesh. Live, pulsing, hot, moist— It was—

The wall swelled under her touch. It adhered to her hand eagerly. The whole room writhed a little, surging towards her. It wanted—she knew it wanted—to clutch her to its breast.

Caroline ripped her hand from the flesh wall. Its rhythms were faster, and the cowlike smell much stronger. Caroline whimpered. She was flung backwards and her fingers closed on the vegetable knife and she raised it.

Even as the knife plunged forwards, she knew it would skid or rebound from the plaster, probably slicing her. She knew all that, but could not help it. And then the knife thumped in, up to the handle. It was like stabbing into—into meat.

She jerked the knife away and free, and scalding fluid ran down her arm. I've cut myself after all. That's blood. But she felt nothing. And the room—

The room was screaming. She couldn't hear it, but the scream was all around her, hurting her ears. She had to stop the screaming. She thrust again with the knife. The blade was slippery. The impact was the same. Boneless meat. And the heated fluid, this time, splashed all over her. In the thick unlight, it looked black. She dabbed frantically at her arm, which had no wound. But in the wall—

She stabbed again. She ran to another wall and stabbed and hacked at it.

I'm dreaming, she thought. Christ, why can't I wake up?

The screaming was growing dim, losing power.

"Stop it!" she cried. The blade was so sticky now she had to use both hands to drive it home. There was something on the floor, spreading, that she slid on in her bare feet. She struck the wall with her fist, then with the knife. "Oh, Christ, please die," she said.

Like a butchered animal, the room shuddered, collapsed back upon itself, became silent and immobile.

Caroline sat in a chair. She was going to be sick, but then the sickness faded. I'm sitting here in a pool of blood.

She laughed and tears started to run from her eyes, which was the last thing she remembered.

When she woke it was very quiet. The tide must be far out, for even the sea did not sound. A crack of light came between the curtains.

What am I doing in this chair?

Caroline shifted, her mind blank and at peace.

Then she felt the utter emptiness that was in the room with her. The dreadful emptiness, occasioned only by the presence of the dead.

She froze. She stared at the crack of light. Then down.

"Oh no," said Caroline. She raised her hands.

She wore black mittens. Her fingers were stuck together.

Now her gaze was racing over the room, not meaning to, trying to escape, but instead alighting on the black punctures, the streaks, the stripes along the wall, now on the black stains, the black splotches. Her own body was dappled, grotesquely mottled with black. She had one white toe left to her, on her right foot.

Woodenly, she managed to get up. She staggered to the curtains and hauled them open and turned back in the full flood of early sunlight, and saw everything over again. The gashes in the wall looked as if they had been accomplished with a drill or a pick. Flaked plaster was mingled with the—with the—blood. Except that it wasn't blood. Blood wasn't black.

Caroline turned away suddenly. She looked through the window,

along the esplanade, pale and laved with morning. She looked at the
bright sea, with the two or three fishing boats scattered on it, and the
blueness beginning to flush sky and water. When she looked at these
things, it was hard to believe in the room.

Perhaps most murderers were methodical in the aftermath. Perhaps
they had to be.

She filled the basin again and again, washing herself, arms, body, feet.
Even her hair had to be washed. The black had no particular texture. In
the basin it diluted. It appeared like a superior kind of Parker fountain-
pen ink.

She dressed herself in jeans and shirt, filled the largest saucepan with
hot water and washing-up liquid. She began to scour the walls.

Soon her arms ached, and she was sweating the cold sweat of nervous
debility. The black came off easily, but strange tangles of discoloration
remained behind in the paint. Above, the holes did not ooze, they merely
gaped. Inside each of them was chipped plaster and brick—not bone,
muscle or tissue. There was no feel of flesh anywhere.

Caroline murmured to herself. "When I've finished." It was quite
matter-of-fact to say that, as if she were engaged in a normality. "When
I've finished, I'll go and get some coffee downstairs. I won't tell Mrs.
Rice about the holes. No, not yet. How can I explain them? I couldn't
have caused that sort of hole with a knife. There's the floor to do yet.
And I'd better wash the rugs. I'll do them in the bath when the ghastly
Laceys go out at nine o'clock. When I've finished, I'll get some coffee.
And I think I'll ring David. I really think I'll have to. When I finish."

She thought about ringing David. She couldn't guess what he'd say.
What could *she* say, come to that? Her back ached now, and she felt sick,
but she kept on with her work. Presently she heard energetic intimations
of the Laceys visiting the bathroom, and the duck-child quacking happily.

She caught herself wondering why blood hadn't run when the nails
were hammered in the walls for Mr. Tinker's pictures. But that was
before the room really came to life, maybe. Or maybe the room had
taken it in the spirit of beautification, like having one's ears pierced for
gold earrings. Certainly the knife scratches had bled.

Caroline put down the cloth and went over to the basin and was sick.

Perhaps I'm pregnant, she thought, and all this is a hallucination of
my fecundity.

David, I am pregnant, and I stabbed the room to death.

David.

David?

It was a boiling hot day, one of the last-fling days of the summer. Everything was blanched by the heat, apart from the apex of the blue sky and the core of the green-blue sea. Caroline wore a white dress. A quarter before each hour, she told herself she would ring David on the hour: ten o'clock, eleven, twelve. Then she would "forget." At one o'clock she rang him, and he was at lunch as she had known he would be, really.

Caroline went on the pier. She put money into little machines which whizzed and clattered. She ate a sandwich in a café. She walked along the sands, holding her shoes by the straps.

At half past four she felt compelled to return.

She had to speak to Mrs. Rice, about the holes in the walls.

And then again, perhaps she should go up to number eight first. It seemed possible that the dead room would somehow have righted itself. And then, too, there were the washed rugs drying over the bath that the unlaceys might come in and see. Caroline examined why she was so flippant and so cheerful. It was, of course, because she was afraid.

She went into the block, and abruptly she was trembling. As she climbed the steps, her legs melted horribly, and she wished she could crawl, pulling herself by her fingers.

As she came up to the landing, she beheld Mr. Lacey in the corridor. At least, she assumed it was Mr. Lacey. He was overweight and tanned a peachy gold by the sun. He stood, glowering at her, blocking the way to her door. He's going to complain about the noise, she thought. She tried to smile, but no smile would oblige.

"I'm Mr. Lacey," he announced. "You met the wife the other day."

He sounded nervous rather than belligerent. When Caroline didn't speak, he went on. "My Brenda, you see. She noticed this funny smell from number eight. When you come along to the bathroom, you catch it. She was wondering if you'd left some meat out, forgotten it."

"No," said Caroline.

"Well, I reckoned you ought to be told," said Mr. Lacey.

"Yes, thank you."

"I mean, don't take this the wrong way, but we've got a kid. You can't be too careful."

"No. You can't."

"Well, then." He swung himself aside and moved a short way down the corridor towards the Lacey flat. Caroline went to her door. She knew he was watching her with his two shining Lacey piggy eyes. She turned and stared at him, her heart striking her side in huge bruising blows, until he grunted and went off.

Caroline stood before the door. She couldn't smell anything. No, there was nothing, nothing at all.

The stink came in a wave, out of nowhere. It smote her and she nearly reeled. It was foul, indescribably foul. And then it was gone.

Delicately, treading soft, Caroline stepped away from the door. She tiptoed to the head of the stairs. Then she ran.

But like someone drawn to the scene of an accident, she couldn't entirely vacate the area. She sat on the esplanade, watching.

The day went out over the town, and the dusk seeped from the sea. In the dusk, a police car came and drew up outside the block. Later, another.

It got dark. The lamps, the neons and the stars glittered, and Caroline shuddered in her thin frock.

The stork-legs had gathered at the café. They pointed and jeered at the police cars. At the garden pavilion, a band was playing. Far out on the ocean, a great tanker passed, garlanded with lights.

At nine o'clock, Caroline found she had risen and was walking across the esplanade to the holiday block. She walked right through the crowd of stork-legs. "Got the time?" one of them yelled, but she paid no heed, didn't even flinch.

She went up the steps, and on the first flight she met two very young policemen.

"You can't come up here, miss."

"But I'm staying here," she said. Her mild voice, so reasonable, interested her. She missed what he asked next.

"I said, what number, miss."

"Number eight."

"Oh. Right. You'd better come up with me, then. You hang on here, Brian."

They climbed together, like old friends.

"What's the matter?" she questioned him, perversely.

"I'm not quite sure, miss."

They reached the landing.

All the way up from the landing below, the stench had been intensifying, solidifying. It was unique. Without ever having smelled such an odour before, instinctively and at once you knew it was the perfume of rottenness. Of decay and death.

Mrs. Rice stood in the corridor, her black hair in curlers, and she was absentmindedly crying. Another woman with a handkerchief to her nose, patted Mrs. Rice's shoulder. Behind a shut door, a child also cried, vehemently. Another noise came from the bathroom; someone vomiting.

Caroline's door was wide open. A further two policemen were on the threshold. They seemed to have no idea of how to proceed. One was wiping his hands with a cloth, over and over.

Caroline gazed past them, into the room.

Putrescent lumps were coming away from the walls. The ceiling dribbled and dripped. Yet one moment only was it like the flesh of a corpse. Next moment, it was plaster, paint and crumbling brick. And then again, like flesh. And then again—

"Christ," one of the policemen said. He faced about at his audience. He too was young. He stared at Caroline randomly. "What are we supposed to do?"

Caroline breathed in the noxious air. She managed to smile at last, kindly, inquiringly, trying to help.

"Bury it?"

Babchi's Drawer

Gina M. Angelone

The following hard-to-classify, hard-to-forget vignette reminds me of the Joycean "epiphanies" that sometimes appear in The New Yorker. GINA M. ANGELONE, *an independent film and video producer/writer, says: "I began writing short stories somewhere between Massachusetts and Malaysia, Paris and Patagonia . . . a writer of polar extremes drawn to twisted personal topographies and marginal family encounters."*

BABCHI STUCK HER FINGERS in a dirty ashtray, then wiped them on her robe and whispered, "I'm not wearing anything under this." She took a swig of the certified-for-sacrament wine that the Polish priest brought her the day before and fell back into her lounger.

Cecelia could feel the gentle thud of her grandmother's old body against the crackling leatherette cushions and woke from her sleep. She found her grandmother alone in her room, trying to stuff a big wooden drawer into a small dresser slot. Cecelia stared at the old drawer where a confusion of household objects were kept when she was a child and grinned. To the other members of the family, nothing special was in there. Some unpolished spoons, one or two outdated kitchen utensils, and some receipts from old purchases—expensive ones that should be remembered. That, and maybe an old sweet or two stuck in the back corner that would never get eaten.

The handle on the drawer was broken before Cecelia could even remember, and never repaired. Whenever anyone wished to open it, they had to take a big knife from the kitchen, give a good stab into the soft wood, and yank. The old drawer had lots of nicks in it, and was much abused from far too many mistaken jabs

Every time someone was missing some important thing, and the whole small house had to be turned upside-down, the drawer would get a quick verifying poke. It was one of the places that had a lot of forgotten things in it. Nobody ever found anything that they were looking for in there. Nobody but Babchi.

"He wanted me to die, so I died . . . ," Babchi muttered, and a strand of old hair from her balding gray head forced its way into her sad discourse as she recalled some misplaced souvenir.

Relatives in the next room spoke in loud hushes about Babchi as if she'd lost her hearing and not her wits. Chochia Stefania was chortling in a loud affected voice about who was getting Babchi's collection of Royal Doultons. Milk-fed cousins browsed around the room, practicing teary good-byes and licking their lips in anticipation of what token might be bestowed on them by the bereft old woman. Exchanged glances of discomfort and insincerity made Cecelia swear that if she heard them one more time, she'd scream. That would make four times that day.

The smell of fresh cut grass, sweet and thick, and the sound of mowers at dusk accompanied Cecelia around the block. A group of Polish women with flouncy skirts and flubbery thighs were in front of the church doing folk dances and selling galumpkes. Native flags and old flesh fluttered in the wind to the beat of a polka as Cecelia waded by.

Neighbors outside raced against sunset to finish washing the cars and trucks that advertised their function in the community: *Joseph Pulowski Lumber; Stanislaus Dobek Plumbing; Jaju Sicowitz & Sons Aluminum Siding.* Cecelia wondered why her uncle Jaju kept *"& Sons"* printed on his truck, even when everyone knew that all five sons only agreed to work for their father *after* he died.

Cecelia recalled the strange day eleven years ago when Jaju first expired. After being pronounced deceased, Jaju saw an archetypal white light, heard the voice of the Lord, and dutifully came back to the world of the living. When he did, he realized how much his children disappointed him and set them all to work. After all, the next time he died would probably be the real thing, and all he'd have left to show his good name were his five miserable sons and a town full of aluminum siding.

Cecelia headed across the old school yard towards the Catholic cemetery. "Talk about being born again," she muttered as her memories of the old town accelerated with the diminishing speed limit.

Cecelia wandered around in the fading light and cooling summer air. She found a fresh burial mound that had not yet been sodded and sat down next to it. It was comforting to have the earth so close to her skin. Cecelia always found the stillness of cemeteries quite calming and settling.

She sat atop a small, brown mound and stuck her hands into the fresh earth. The finer grains slipped through her fingers while the small stones accumulated in her palm. She rubbed the pebbles together between her fingers and examined the specks of brownish black dirt on her hand. "Moles," she said, and tucked them all into her pocket.

Cecelia had inherited Babchi's moles. Blackish-brown speckled outgrowths, popping up here and there on her soft young body. "Remove them," she thought, and imagined swift, painless razor cuts to the right and to the left.

Babchi always called them beauty marks. And Babchi had beauty marks all over her entire body. Hundreds of them. Mountains more than mole hills. Cecelia would often stare at her grandmother in sudden disgust and repulsion.

Slice. She'd imagine the same swift, sharp, gesture pruning her grandmother's body, smoothing out the protrusions, leveling the wobbly, flesh-filled growths sprouting from her wrinkled neck and back and from the soft part under her arms.

Whack. Cecelia suddenly remembered the time she had a mole taken off her back when she was a child. When the doctor finished injecting her with non-feelings, he lopped the mole off and stuffed it into a plastic container which he showed her before she went home for dinner.

She couldn't eat anything that night, or for several days thereafter. The small container with her old mole floating in it kept swimming around in her head, cutting off her appetite.

Cecelia went back to her grandmother's tidy little home to find that the old woman was still searching around for something.

"Those pills . . . those pills are throwin' me," Babchi mumbled. "I'm just gone flyin'."

"Are you okay, Babchi?" Cecelia reached for her grandmother's hand. "I'm 80 years old. I get woozy sometimes. . . . Wait! I won't be 80 till October." Then a sudden look of happiness.

Cecelia looked at her fragile little grandmother perched on top of the lace-covered bed with her night gown drooping and her wig on the floor. The sight reminded her of the tiny figurines that Babchi would use to decorate the tops of her birthday cakes. Cecelia had seen years and tiers of cakes—single-layered pound, double-layered chocolate, strawberry short, pineapple cheese.

She recalled all the roses and garlands that would twine around in thick sweet bunches up the smooth white slopes. Little ceramic maidens in flowery dresses that reigned over cream-frosted landscapes. Delicate demoiselles, armless now, or wearing chipped dresses, packed away on top of dusty old shelves, in cardboard boxes or slipped into miscellaneous drawers.

Cecelia helped her grandmother down from the bed. "Time to go to sleep, Babchi."

"They asked me to be the Chairwoman of some committee. But I can't remember which. If I'd known this was gonna happen to me so suddenly, I wouldn't have accepted. I think we have a meeting soon. I don't remember."

Babchi continued to scan through her possessions, pulling things apart, looking for something her memory had lost. Cecelia tried to stop the search by distracting her with funny memories. But at the end of each account, Babchi would just shake her head and mutter, *"Sad. . . ."*

She burrowed through a dusty pile of passbooks and photographs. Photos kept her bedside vigil: a favorite dead cousin in Krakow; a family vacation in Zakopany. Her drawers were all crowded with dime-store jelly jars and condiment containers that she found for a song. Old trinkets and baubles, words and things she gathered for no reason. Things she kept with no intent. But Babchi seemed to treasure them as age-old family heirlooms.

Though Babchi could not name what she was looking for, Cecelia knew that her grandmother had left something precious behind. Something she needed to dig out . . . something she never got a handle on . . . and that Babchi was just waiting for the day she could chip away at the old wood, take a good stab, fling it all open, and get to all the good stuff inside. She seemed to remember an old sweet or two stuck in the back that nobody ever tasted.

Babchi finally settled on an old photograph and began to smile. "Do you miss your father?" she asked Cecelia, who had her father's chin and often thought of him when she washed her face at night. But before Cecelia could summon up the words to respond, her grandmother had fallen fast asleep.

It was a cool autumn day, and rain clouds flirted with the sun. Cecelia lifted her numbed legs and stood motionless graveside in the cemetery behind the old school. Yes, she missed her father. She missed Babchi too. Missed the way she used to turn red when she got excited and sometimes bump her thick leg in sudden haste.

Cecelia stuffed a handful of stones and dirt from the adjacent graves into her pocket and said good-bye to her grandmother and father, to mother and son.

A rain cloud broke as she walked away and turned the earth into soft brown mounds of mud. "Beauty marks," Cecelia thought. And as she headed back through the familiar streets of her childhood, the sound of thunder resounded in her heart like an old wooden drawer being shut on some sweet memory.

Untitled

Morgan Llywelyn

Born in New York and raised in Dallas, "where I became horse crazy,"
MORGAN LLYWELYN *is equally passionate about Ireland, where she now lives.
She is the author of many international best-selling historical fantasy novels,
including* Bard, The Horse Goddess, Lion of Ireland *and* The Ele-
mentals. *Her short fiction is so strikingly different that no two tales ("Me,
Tree," "Princess," "The Mistletoe Bough") seem remotely alike, and the
following sexually explicit horror story is no exception.*

STRETCHED AND SIZED, the canvas waited. He had been staring
at it for a long time with that particular listening expression that
effects an artist waiting for inspiration. He waited in vain. None came.

At last, with a deep sigh, he turned to the pallet waiting on the three-
legged stool to his right, and ran his eyes lovingly over the glass tumbler
holding fresh brushes, the unopened bottle of turps, the tubes of pigment
aligned in a neat, waiting row. He murmured names to himself. "Rose
madder, chrome yellow, prussian blue." He loved everything about
working in oils except the terrible moment when he must face the blank
canvas and try to wrest life from it.

As a man constructs the cross upon which to crucify himself, Bart
Elgin had chosen to be a portrait painter in the full knowledge that it
was demanding, extremely difficult, and would mean dealing with subjects who would never be totally pleased with the result. A sitter's inner

image of him or herself would never conform to the painter's view, and was always coloured by ego.

There had been some very frosty scenes on occasions when Elgin presented a client with the finished work. But he kept on painting, willing himself to believe that talent would triumph and one day he would be vindicated.

On this sultry Tuesday morning, triumph seemed far away.

Pinned around the edges of his easel were half a dozen preliminary photographs of the subject he meant to paint, a thin woman in her late forties, the wife of a prominent businessman. She had explained, "I can't possibly come in and sit for you every day. My committee meetings, you know. I'm on the Board of this and I'm a Trustee of that . . ."

So he had taken photographs and promised to do the first sketching from them, only requiring her valuable time after the composition began to take shape. It had seemed simple enough. He would show her sitting in a chair by a window, gazing out as if rapt in thought. She had the sort of goldfish face with bulging hyperthyroid eyes that was better shown in half-profile.

But now, as he tried to force the first outline to form in his mind, nothing came. Even looking at her photograph did not summon an image of her for him to build upon.

Nothing.

He got up, paced the room, drank half a cup of coffee, returned to his easel. Perhaps the problem was physical. Not enough sleep last night. An uncomfortable heaviness in the groin, an unfocussed sense of desire and no woman, not since the argument with Peggy. She had slammed out of his apartment complaining that he preferred his work to her, which was true. But sometimes he needed a woman.

Physically needed a woman, as any healthy male in his thirties would.

He was too fastidious for a prostitute, or a one-night stand with a casual date. And masturbation, that refuge of the solitary provided only the most temporary relief, so that desire returned not reduced but amplified. No, he needed a woman, all right.

But more than that he needed to paint Mrs. Randolph Hathaway's portrait so he could collect the money for the thing. His rent was due. The day when his talent was sufficiently recognized still lay too far in the future to provide any degree of economic security, if it ever would.

With a sense of increasing depression as heavy as the hot day, he selected a charcoal pencil and forced himself to begin sketching the woman in the chair. As he worked he tried to ignore his physical symptoms and lose himself in his art, but what he was doing was not art. It was commercial labour and his soul knew it.

The desire remained, leaden at the bottom of his lap.

At last he snapped the pencil in two between impatient fingers and hurled the two parts across the room with an oath.

"Hopeless. It's hopeless. How can I paint that damned woman. I don't like her, I don't like anything about her, her flat chest or her frizzled hair or her bright red fingernails like claws dipped in blood . . ."

In his mind a different image began forming of its own volition, a female figure the exact opposite of Mrs. Randolph Hathaway. This woman was also seated in a chair, but instead of gazing out the window, her face was turned toward Bart. He could almost see it.

He snatched up another pencil and began to draw.

She came to life under his fingers as if she had always been there, embedded in the canvas and waiting for him to bring her out. "That's more like it," he muttered to himself. "That's what an inspiration is."

She had a waterfall of smooth hair pouring over her shoulders. Her figure was rounded without being plump, her breasts and belly soft, tempting, the triangle of flesh below her belly equally rounded and strangely smooth, his fingers leaving it devoid of hair. The mound of Venus lay like a hill of secret delights between the tops of her thighs.

A thin film of sweat began to form on the artist's forehead. "Come on, baby," he murmured. "Come to me."

A few sure strokes of the pencil shaped her body. When he turned his attention to her face it appeared with equal ease, as if he was sketching a living woman sitting six feet away.

She had a diamond-shaped face with narrow forehead and chin, and slightly slanted eyes. Her lips were thin but her mouth was sensuously curved.

There was no doubt of her sensual appeal. Before he had been sketching for five minutes, Elgin felt something like real heat radiating from the image. Into its creation was going a composite of all those female features which, in the depths of his subconscious, he found most desirable.

No love went into the image. Love was for women like Peggy, who could evoke tenderness and confusion and jealousy and pride. The figure on the canvas demanded only lust.

She sat curiously slumped in her chair, gazing out at him as his fingers invested her with an aura of sexuality and danger.

Danger?

Surprised, Elgin stopped drawing and stepped back to inspect the figure. "Are you dangerous, baby?" he asked, half-amused.

But she was. He could see it now. Those slanted eyes, huge and deep in great hollow sockets. That expression of intense watching almost . . . predatory.

And the way her mouth curved. As if she was just about to open it, to reveal a plump red tongue inside. Inside that hot, sweet mouth.

She looked . . . hungry.

"Me too, baby," Elgin told her, unaware that his hand had drifted to the front of his jeans. When he realized what he was doing he jerked the hand away. "Hey now, none of that!" he warned himself. "Not at ten o'clock in the morning on a work day!"

Angry with himself for his lapse of discipline, he reached for a rag and the turps, intent on wiping away the entire image and starting over. Did no good to let your imagination run away with you.

Something stopped him. He stood with the rag in his hand, gazing at the canvas for an immeasurable time. Then he removed it from the easel, unpinned the photographs, covered the sketch with a towel and leaned it against the wall, and began preparing a new canvas for Mrs. Hathaway's portrait.

The sketch of the naked woman waited behind the towel, like a promise, as he worked feverishly throughout the day, forcing himself to keep his mind and his fingers on the commissioned portrait.

Nightfall found him still working. His eyes were red-rimmed and his hand beginning to tremble with exhaustion, but he was satisfied. The figure was complete, the background filled in. All he really required was an hour or so of Mrs. Hathaway's time to get the colouring of her face right, and he would be able to collect his money from her husband once the painting was dried and varnished.

He'd be able to pay his rent.

The rent covered the studio with its skylight and an adjacent apartment with a shabby sitting room, a bedroom, bath, and kitchenette hidden behind louvered cupboard doors. Sometimes he didn't even use the bedroom, but fell asleep on a couch he had purchased for the studio, a couch he had bought in anticipation of dalliance with voluptuous models who had never appeared.

For Bart Elgin, the glamourous world of the artist had proved to be pretty prosaic. Painting portraits that were ego-trips for the sitters was a long way from the life he had once envisioned. The dreams . . .

Before going to bed, he tossed back the towel and took one last look at the dream on the first canvas, just to enjoy that moment of freedom her creation had represented for him.

He got quite a shock.

While Elgin laboured over Mrs. Hathaway, it was as if the picture under the towel had been creating itself. The figure was much more developed than he remembered. The arms and hands, which he had indicated with only a couple of lines, were now arranged so that one arm, bent at the elbow, rested on the back of the chair, while the other hand lay, palm up, on one thigh, with the fingers slightly curled, knuckles resting almost against the plump swelling of the pudenda. The eyes that seemed to be meeting Elgin's held a distinctly startled expression.

He had the sudden, profound conviction that she had been touching her sex in the moment before he removed the towel, and had only drawn her hand away at the last instant.

Was he mistaken, or was there also a certain defiance in that startled gaze?

Shaken, he dropped the covering back over the canvas. "I don't remember doing that much work on it," he said aloud. He was grateful for the sound of his own voice in the room.

His sleep that night was troubled. Half a dozen times he awoke abruptly, sweating, each time with an enormous erection. He stumbled to the bathroom, waited agonizingly for the erection to subside enough to allow him to empty his bladder, then groped his way back to bed only to fall into a feverish sleep that brought a repetition of the process. The last time, he wakened abruptly out of a dream in which he could feel a woman's hot mouth closing around his penis, sucking sweetly . . .

"Jesus!" Elgin sat bolt upright in bed, his heart pounding. He was very close to orgasm.

Compelled by an impulse he could not explain, he got out of bed and made his way to his studio. When he clicked on the overhead light he was briefly blinded by its radiance, and turned it off again. He could find his way without it. He crossed the room to the covered sketch of the nameless woman and removed the towel that covered it. Enough light seeped in through the skylight from the sickly neon glow above the city to illumine the figure on the canvas.

She was waiting for him. He saw it in her eyes.

And her mouth was open.

He groaned. "It's you and me, baby," he told her. "There isn't any other woman here and sometimes a man just has to."

This time when his hand sought his own flesh he made no effort to stop himself. A shudder of pleasure ran through him as he began the long, slow stroking. For as long as he could, he kept his eyes open, watching her watching him.

He could have sworn she licked her lips at the exact moment the convulsion seized him and his spine arched with passion, sending the hot semen spurting out to drench the canvas.

When it was over he slumped, shaken by the intensity of the experience, leaning against the wall for support. Sex had never been that good with a woman. Hell, it had never been that good, period.

At last he was able to go to the small sink at the end of the studio, where he washed his brushes, and clean himself. Then he turned on the light again and went back to the canvas to clean it off too.

"How do you get semen stains off canvas?" he asked as he reached out with a rag.

Then he stopped. There were no stains on the canvas. It was bone dry, as if all the liquid had been absorbed.

The expression on the woman's face was one of utter satiety.

Elgin had a sudden, shocked sense of invasion, of being the victim of rape.

His most precious body fluid taken from him, tricked out of him . . . !

"No!" he cried aloud in the silent studio. "That's crazy, stop thinking like that! It's just a picture, for Godssake, a picture I drew myself out of my own head! She's not real. She couldn't be . . ."

It must be some crazy nightmare, brought on by stress and overwork. Perhaps. He switched off the light and fled back to his bedroom, only to lie naked and wide-eyed on the bed, hating himself for the anticipation he felt whenever he remembered the dream of her mouth on him.

But the dream did not come again that night. And when the dawn came, it found him sleepless and exhausted.

He dressed and went down to the coffee shop on the corner for a breakfast he was unable to eat. Three cups of coffee and he was back in the studio, staring fixedly at the Hathaway portrait and trying not to let his eyes wander toward the covered canvas. He managed to resist until almost noon.

During that time he played perverse, tantalizing games with himself. Five more minutes. I'll hold out for five more minutes. Then I'll look. Now five minutes more. Just five minutes more. Now I'll wait until ten o'clock. Ten thirty. Eleven. Five minutes more, that's all . . .

Shortly before noon his thread of will power snapped and he abandoned Mrs. Hathaway for the woman of the sketch.

When he threw back the cover she was waiting for him.

In the interim since he last saw her a delicate sort of cross-hatching had been added to the drawing, rounding her thighs and arms, her belly, her shoulders, giving her dimension. Her face was full of life in spite of being only rendered in black and white. The eyes burned with a cold fire that contained nothing of intelligence but everything of lust. Highlights had been added to her long hair, making it look glossy.

He found himself wondering what colour it was.

"Colour!" He snapped his fingers. "That's it, you need colour."

But what colours?

She was his own creation, he could invest her with any hues he chose. Why not . . . his own?

Elgin smiled. It was no longer a totally sane smile.

He went to the palette that waited beside the incomplete portrait of Mrs. Hathaway and stared down at the crumpled tubes of pigment, the smeared stains of burnt umber and vermillion. Not colours he wanted for his woman. He rummaged restlessly among the other tubes, cast them aside. Looked vaguely around the room, seeking.

His gaze fixed on the small cracked mirror over the washbasin.

Step by step, he approached it. Peered in. Smiled.

Returning to his workplace, he prepared a fresh palette. With a bemused expression he plucked several hairs from his own head and placed them on the palette. Then he glanced over his shoulder.

In her eyes he read approval.

Encouraged, he took up a palette knife and scraped at his forearm until he had tiny flakes of skin which he added to the hairs. Then he went to the kitchenette and got a steak knife. He sawed at his arm, ignoring the pain, until a drop of blood welled. This too went into the mix. He moistened it with his saliva and carried it to her like a priest bearing an offering.

She watched, waiting.

Taking the Hathaway portrait off the easel, he replaced it with the woman of the sketch.

Neither brush nor knife would do. He smeared the substance made from himself over the canvas with his naked fingertips. As he worked, he could feel increasing warmth in the canvas. He worked as one inspired, following the flow and curve of line and idea, caressing her body with his strokes, pressing every last particle of his own atoms into the figure on the canvas. Only when the palette was absolutely wiped clean did he stand back to study the effect.

He gasped.

The original sketch had been rounded but not plump. The figure was now decidedly plump. There was a little roll of fat around her waist that he had never drawn there. The texture of her skin was incredibly real, satiny across the breasts and thighs, slightly coarser, almost grainy, on shoulders and clavicle.

Though there had been no blue tints on his palette, her eyes were now a deep, slumberous azure, set in violet shadows.

And though his hair was dark, hers was now glittering gold.

Elgin heard himself moan. It should have been a moan of fear, the despair of a man faced by some supernatural agency.

Instead and to his shame, it was the sound of uncontrollable desire.

As if his body had a will of its own apart from his rational mind, it pressed against the painting on the easel. The heat of her flesh came to him through his clothes. Frantically, he ripped the cloth barriers away until his bare skin was touching hers.

Hers felt like skin. There was no sensation of rough canvas, only of hot, soft flesh, writhing against him as he was writhing against her.

Aghast, his mind crouched in his skull and jibbered at him, divorced from what was happening. But it had no power to stop him.

Elgin closed his eyes.

In darkness she grew, became lifesize. Became a living woman naked in his arms, eagerly accepting the desperate thrusts of his swollen penis against her soft belly. He could not control himself enough even to guide his organ between her legs and into the waiting opening, the deep wet luscious waiting . . .

The orgasm exploded through him, threatening to pulverize his very bones with its force.

He came to some time later, lying, damp and sticky, on the floor in front of the easel. When he dragged himself to his feet he tried not to look at the painting. Gathering his discarded clothes, he staggered from the studio.

The sound of a shower running soon issued from his apartment. The water ran for a very long time.

Over the sound of running water Elgin did not hear his doorbell. When Peggy abandoned ringing and resorted to pounding on the door with one small, determined fist, he did not hear that either.

She went downstairs and found the manager of the building. "I know he's in there, I can hear water running in the bathroom. But he won't answer me."

The man shifted his weight from one foot to the other and scratched himself in one armpit. "Didn't you used to come here a lot?" he asked impudently.

She felt her face redden. "I did."

"But not lately. You have a fight or somethin'?"

"I don't see that that's any of your business. Just let me in. I'm afraid something's wrong."

The super sneered. "What's wrong is, you want him to take you back and he don't wanna. Go away, find yourself somebody else. When it's over it's over, y'know?"

Part of her knew he was right. Yet another part, a deep visceral sense that had nothing to do with reason, kept insisting that Bart Elgin was in trouble and she must go to him. She held her ground until at last the super wearied of the argument and fetched his passkey.

It opened, not directly into Elgin's living quarters, but into the studio. Peggy strode in first, then stopped and stared.

The building manager almost bumped into her. Then he stared too.

The figure on the easel was more than arresting. It was so lifelike it was hard to believe it had been created from paint and canvas. A plump, sleek, glossy woman with the face of a satisfied cat stared back at them, her eyes glittering, her fingers lightly touching her sex in unmistakeable invitation.

The super swallowed. Hard. "Jaysus," he whispered, feeling a surge of lust rise in his withered loins.

Peggy's eyes were wide with incredulity. "Bart never painted anything like that in his life!"

"Do you mean, never painted anything that good in his life?" asked a sharp voice. She whirled around. Bart Elgin stood in the doorway to his living quarters.

Peggy's hand flew to her throat. "I didn't say that."

"You thought it though, didn't you? Remember our last quarrel when you told me I should give up trying to paint because I'd never be more than a commercial hack? Do you call that hack work?!" he asked triumphantly, gesturing with a flourish toward the canvas and its compelling figure.

"You're a bloody genius, that's what you are," the building manager was muttering.

Elgin advanced toward them, interposing his body between theirs and the woman on the easel. Suddenly he did not want their eyes on her any more. Whatever she had, whatever life or magic, was for him and him alone. He began urging them toward the door.

"But Bart . . ." Peggy protested.

Clenching his jaws, he shoved her backward. He drove the pair of them through the open door and then slammed it after them, shoving home the bolt so they could not return.

Peggy called to him from outside but he did not answer. He turned back toward the easel. His eyes met those of the seated woman, and she smiled.

It took Peggy several days to convince the police there was anything seriously wrong with Bart Elgin. At first, like the building manager, they attributed her worries to a lovers' quarrel. But when at last it was impossible to ignore the mountain of bills and letters piling up outside the studio door—or the unpleasant smell seeping from beneath the studio door—they agreed to break in.

Fortunately for Peggy's health and sanity, they did not allow her to enter the room. She was spared the sight that sent one burly policeman into premature retirement and several others into mental hospitals for varying lengths of time.

No one would ever be able to explain how Bart Elgin had created his untitled masterpiece—if that is the appropriate term for something unique in the world of art. The canvas on the easel in his studio depicted a naked man, with his back turned toward the observers and his face seen in near profile as he embraced a seated nude woman. The female was all but hidden by his upper torso in the painting, so no one would ever know what she looked like.

But no one who saw it would ever forget the naked lower half of a very dead man, a flesh-and-blood man, which was emerging from the painted figure on the canvas. The corpse's buttocks and legs, decomposing, projected into the room, dangling below the easel.

And on what could be seen of the painted face atop the upper portion of the body was an expression of insane rapture.

A Child's Game

Maryellen B. Wanderer

It's only a child's game,
   she pushes on my shoulders with small hands
I'm in the blue pool water
Suddenly, the bottom level drops too quickly,
I'm completely submerged,
       light penetrates the crystal-clear water,
     my lungs cannot breathe
       I fight wildly for air,
         for life
    my lungs scream and I struggle,
     but small firm hands push me down
I manage to get my eyes above the water's surface
  and a mouth full of water,
         little hands think it's air
   down the little hands playfully push

I see the pool bottom,
         my lungs cry for air
Will I die?
In what are moments,
     but seem like years
I reach the side and pull myself up,
  Little hands on my shoulders come up too

Little hands realize my deep, ragged breaths
as my lungs gather air,
like precious gems.
Are you all right?
It was just a game

The Wake of Reddy

Barbara Gallow

BARBARA GALLOW *is a Connecticut actor and writer whose critically acclaimed story "Jane" appeared in* Ghosts, *my first Doubleday anthology. Barbara's earlier tale was partly true, and so, apparently, is the deadpan comedy described in "The Wake of Reddy."*

THE WAKE was Sandy's idea. I had planned to bury Reddy on the low clay hill across the street from my house, but Sandy said we should give him a real funeral. Since I was, at seven, ignorant of funeral proceedings, and since Sandy seemed to know what she was talking about, I agreed to let her take charge. After all, Reddy had been my favorite turtle and I wanted to do the right thing for him.

"You hafta get him a coffin," Sandy explained.

I already had a coffin for Reddy. My mother had put him in a shoebox because I was afraid to see him dead. I thought he'd be ugly and feel hard and wet.

"He's in a shoebox," I told Sandy.

She considered. "Yeah, that's good. Let's go make him a grave."

So Sandy and I brushed away the twigs and loose dirt on top of the clay mound and dug a shallow hole. We patted the walls of the grave smooth and firm, making a neat little pile of the extra earth. When we finished, Sandy said, "First we hafta give him a wake before we bury him."

I had never heard of a wake, but I didn't want to admit it, so I said, "Yeah, I know. But how will we do it—I mean, for a *tur*tle?"

Sandy looked shocked. "We *hafta* give him a wake! You don't want him to go to *Hell*, do you?"

I certainly did not! I wondered why I hadn't been taught about wakes in Sunday school.

Sandy was explaining that her brother and sister and anyone else we could round up would be the mourners. I would be the widow.

"Can Mitzi be a mourner?" Mitzi was my dog.

Sandy thought it over. "Yeah, I guess so. There's supposed to be wailing anyway."

I was glad. Mitzi and Reddy had been friends.

Sandy told me that as widow I had to wear black and have a veil. I nodded and ran into my house to change clothes. I rummaged through my drawers, but I didn't have anything that was black. Instead, I put on a pair of navy blue dress-up shorts and wrapped a scarf of my mother's around my head.

Mom saw me when I went into the kitchen to get Reddy, who lay in his shoebox next to the sink.

"Why are you wearing my scarf?"

"I have to," I said. "We're giving Reddy a wake and I'm the widow."

Mom looked at me. "You're kidding," she said. "Whose idea was that?"

"Sandy's. She knows all about funerals." I took Mitzi's leash from the closet and gingerly picked up the shoebox.

"Sandy's Catholic," Mom said.

"I know."

"Well, we're Jewish."

"So?" I was in a hurry. I didn't want Reddy to have a chance to go to Hell.

"Jews don't have wakes," Mom said.

I halted. What was this? Did that mean we all went to Hell? I tried to ignore that thought. "This is a Jewish, turtle-kind of wake," I mumbled. There must be some special ways Jews go to Heaven, but I wasn't taking any chances with Reddy.

As I went out the door, Mom called, "Just bury that thing, will you?"

"I'm taking Mitzi," I answered, snapping the leash on the dog.

When I banged through the screen door, Sandy was waiting in the driveway with six other kids, including her brother and sister, Timmy and MaryBeth. Timmy and the other boys carried empty soda bottles and some of the girls had collected bunches of flowers and weeds from the surrounding woods.

"This is the processional," Sandy announced.

Confused, I stood clutching Mitzi and the shoebox. "What do we need a procession for?" I asked.

"We hafta process to the cemetery."

"It's across the street."

"No, we hafta have a long one, all around the block, so everyone can see. That's respectful."

"Oh, yeah. That's right." I wanted to show respect for Reddy.

"I'll walk Mitzi," Timmy offered, taking the leash from me.

"You walk in front," Sandy commanded. "We hafta walk slow, everyone. This is a funeral."

I led the way, holding the box straight out in front of me like an offering to God. I didn't want to know that I was carrying Reddy's dead body. I pretended there was a rock or something in the box. I threw my head back and marched stiffly, hoping I looked dignified.

We processed up the dirt road at the end of Mather Drive, and onto Wilkins Street, the boys blowing into the soda bottles, the girls scattering flowers. Mitzi strained at her leash and yipped.

When we passed the playground, Sandy gave the order: "Okay, start mourning." The girls began a long, keening wail, "Ooooohhh, ooooowww, oooohhhhhh," and dropped their heads. The boys tried to blow "Taps" into the soda bottles. I sniffled—the bereaved widow. I was beginning to enjoy myself. It was like playing Queen Esther in a Purim pageant.

Some kids in the playground jumped off the swings and rushed over to gawk at us, openmouthed. "What the heck are you *doing?*"

I gave them a tragic look out of the corner of my eye and kept marching. I didn't know if I was supposed to talk.

"Marcy's turtle died," Sandy said solemnly. "This is his wake." I winced a little at that word. This was a *processional.*

Then Mitzi, who had been yapping at another dog across the playground, broke loose from Timmy and darted away.

"Mitzi got away, Mitzi got away!" Timmy shouted, racing after her. The funeral procession halted mid-wail. We looked at each other, at the

flower petals mashed along the road, at Timmy and MaryBeth screaming, "Mitzi! Mitzi!" at two boys from the playground laughing hysterically. I felt silly in my scarf. I took it off slowly and stuffed it into my
pocket.

Timmy ran back, panting. "I couldn't catch her. She jumped over the
hedge."

"She'll come back," I said. "She always does."

I looked at the shoebox. Reddy's beautiful . . . procession had been
ruined by a stupid dog.

"Come on, everyone," Sandy was saying. "We gotta finish. We hafta
bury Reddy."

"I hafta go home, I think," mumbled one of the girls, dropping her
handful of weeds.

"Yeah, Mr. Softy'll be here soon," said someone else.

Sandy and I looked at each other. I shrugged and started walking
toward home.

"Wanta bury him anyway?" she asked.

"Yeah, I guess."

"Wanta have another wake tomorrow?"

"No. My mother'd be mad. She doesn't want me carrying a dead
turtle around." I wondered if I was bad for giving a Jewish turtle a
Catholic wake. Reddy rattled dully in the shoebox. We went back to the
clay hill, Sandy and I and a few stragglers from the processional.

"I guess I'll just bury him." I tried to place the shoebox in the grave
Sandy and I had dug, but it didn't fit.

"You'll hafta take Reddy out," Timmy said practically.

"Yeah." I couldn't let them know I was afraid, so I opened the box,
turned my head, grabbed Reddy and dropped him in the hole. I looked
down. He didn't look any different. Raising my head, I briskly patted
the dirt over the grave and smoothed it.

"We hafta pray for him," Sandy said. I agreed. I prayed that Reddy
would go to Heaven even if he wasn't supposed to have a wake. I prayed
that I wouldn't go to Hell for being a widow in a Catholic wake.

At the end of our prayers Sandy crossed herself. I started to do the
same, but had a feeling that it was wrong. I made the Star of David in
front of myself.

We walked away from the hill, and as I headed toward my house,
Sandy called, "Do you wanta put a cross over him?"

The Other Mother

Lisa Tuttle

Without sacrificing one jot of originality, LISA TUTTLE *manages to evoke the, well, ghost of Henry James in the following nightmarish novella. Its mysterious woman haunting the other side of the lake is linked in more ways than one with Miss Jessel, the dreadful governess of James's classic "The Turn of the Screw." Ms. Tuttle is a popular, award-winning fantasist perhaps best known for her novels* Windhaven *and* The Storms of Windhaven *(with George R. R. Martin).*

ACROSS THE LAKE, on the other shore, something moved: pale-white, glimmering. Tall as a person.

Sara looked up from her work, refocusing her eyes. She realized how dark it had become. It had been too dark, in the rapidly deepening twilight, to paint for the past half-hour, but she had been reluctant to admit it, give up and go in.

There, again. A woman in a white gown? Gone again.

Sara frowned, vexed, and concentrated on the brushy land across the narrow expanse of dark water. She waited, listening to the crickets and frogs, and she stared so intently that the growing shadows merged, reforming in strange shapes. What had she really seen? Had that pale glimmer been a trick of the fading light? Why did she feel as if there was a stranger lurking on the other shore, a woman watching her who would let herself be seen only in glimpses?

Sara realized she was tired. She arched her back and exercised her aching arms. She still watched the other shore, but casually now, hoping to lure the stranger out by seeming inattentiveness.

But she saw nothing more and at last she shrugged and began to tighten lids on tubes of paint, putting her supplies away. She deliberately avoided looking at the painting she had been working on. Already she disliked it, and was annoyed with herself for failing again.

The house was stifling after the balmy evening air, and it reeked of the pizza she had given the children for dinner. They had left chunks of it uneaten on the coffee table and were now sprawled on the floor in front of the television set, absorbed in a noisy situation comedy.

"Hello, sweethearts," Sara said.

Michael gave a squirming shrug and twitched his mouth in what might have been a greeting; Melanie did not move. Her mouth hung open, and her eyes followed the tiny moving images intently.

Sara put her painting and supplies back in her bedroom and then began to clean up the leftover pizza and soft drinks, wanting to turn off the set and reclaim her children, but too aware of the tantrums that would ensue if she interrupted a program.

At the next commercial, to catch their attention, Sara said, "I just saw a ghost across the lake."

Michael sat up and turned to his mother, his expression intrigued but wary. "Really?"

"Well, it looked like a ghost," Sara said. "You want to come with me and see if she's still there?"

"Not *she;* ghosts aren't girls," Michael said. But he scrambled to his feet. Melanie was still watching the set: a domestic squabble over coffee.

"Why can't ghosts be girls?" Sara asked. "Come on, Melanie. We're going outside to look for a ghost."

"They just can't be," Michael said. "Come *on.*"

Sara took hold of Melanie's sticky little hand and led her outside after Michael. Outdoors, Michael suddenly halted and looked around. "Did you *really* see a ghost?"

"I saw something," Sara said. She felt so relieved to be outside again, away from the stale, noisy house. "I saw a pale white figure which glided past. When I looked more closely, it was gone. Vanished, just like that."

"Sounds like a ghost," said Michael. "They float around, and they're all white, and they disappear. Did it make a noise?"

"Not that I noticed. What sort of noise does a ghost make?"

Michael began to produce a low moaning sound, gradually building in intensity and volume.

"Mommy, make him stop!" Melanie said suddenly.

"That's enough, Michael."

They had reached the water's edge now and they were quiet as they looked across the dark water. Almost nothing could be seen now of the opposite shore.

"Did you really see a ghost?" Michael asked, yet again. Sara felt his hand touching her blue-jeaned hip.

She put an arm around his shoulder and hugged him close. "Maybe I imagined it. Maybe it was an animal of some kind. I just saw something from the corner of my eye, and I had the impression that it was, well, a woman in a long white gown, moving more quickly and quietly than any living person should. I felt she wasn't ready to let me really see her yet. So when I tried to find her, she had disappeared."

Sara felt the hairs on the back of her neck prickle and was suddenly ashamed of herself. If she had made herself nervous, what must the children be feeling?

Melanie began to whimper for the light.

"She can't turn the light on here—we're outside, stupid," Michael said. Sara suspected a quaver in his voice.

"Come on, kids. There's nothing out here. Let's go inside, and I'll tell you a story before you go to bed."

Michael broke into a run towards the safe harbor of the lighted house, and Melanie let go her mother's hand to chase him.

Sara turned to follow her children but then paused, feeling that she was being watched. She turned and looked back across the lake. But even if someone were standing on the opposite shore, it was now much too dark to see.

After the children had bathed and were in their pajamas, Sara told a story about a tricycle-riding bear, a character both the children had loved, but which Michael was beginning to outgrow.

Melanie was good about going to bed, snuggling sleepily under the bedclothes and raising her round, sweet face for a goodnight kiss.

"Now a butterfly kiss," Melanie commanded, after exchanging several smacking kisses with her mother.

Sara, kneeling by the bed, bent her head and fluttered her eyelashes against her daughter's downy cheek. The sound of Melanie's sleepy giggle, her warmth, the good, clean smell of her inspired a rush of love, and Sara wanted to grab her daughter and hug her suffocatingly tight. But she only whispered, soft as a breath, "I love you, sweetie," before she drew away.

Michael was waiting for her in his room with a deck of cards. They played two games of Go Fish and one of Crazy Eights before his uncontrollable yawns gave him away. He agreed to go to bed, but insisted upon hearing a story first.

"A short one," Sara said.

"A ghost story," he responded, nodding impatiently.

"Oh, Michael," Sara sighed, envisioning nightmares and demands for comfort later.

"Yes. A ghost story. About that ghost you saw across the lake today."

Had she frightened him? Sara couldn't be sure. But this was her opportunity to make up for what she'd done, to remove the menace and mystery of that unseen figure. She tucked him under the covers and settled herself at the end of his bed and then, in a low voice, began to weave a comforting sort of ghost story.

The ghost was a sad but friendly figure, a mother eternally searching for her children. They had run off into the wilderness one day without telling her and had become lost, and she had been looking for them ever since. The story had the moral that children shouldn't disobey their mothers or run and hide without telling her where they were going.

Michael was still too young to protest against stories with morals; he accepted what he was told, smiling sleepily, and gave his mother a warm hug and kiss goodnight.

But if Sara had protected Michael against nightmares, she had not been able to protect herself.

That night Sara dreamed of a woman in white, gliding along the lake shore, heading towards the house. She was not a ghost; neither was she human. Her eyes were large, round and protruding, like huge, milk-white marbles. The skin of her face was greyish, her mouth narrow, her nose almost nonexistent. She wore a long, hooded, all-enveloping gown.

Sara saw then that Michael and Melanie were playing in the yard, unaware of the ghastly figure gliding steadily toward them.

Where is their mother? Sara wondered. Where am *I*? She could only watch helplessly, powerless to interfere, certain that she was about to see her children murdered before her eyes.

Dreaming, Sara sweated and twitched and finally cried out, waking herself.

She sat up in the dark, hot room, feeling her heart pounding. Only a dream. But she was still frightened. Somewhere in the darkness those dead white eyes might be staring at her.

Sara turned on the light, wishing for comfort. She wanted a lover, or even her ex-husband, some male figure whose solid, sleeping presence would comfort her.

What a baby I am, she thought, getting up and putting on her robe. To be so frightened by a dream. To have to make the rounds of the house to be sure everything is normal.

Michael was sleeping on his back, the covers kicked away, breathing through his mouth. Sara found his snores endearing and paused to pull the sheet up to his waist.

As she reached the doorway to Melanie's room, something white flashed by the window. Sara stopped breathing, feeling cold to the bone. Then she saw the bird. It was just a white bird, resting on the window ledge. A second later it had flown away. Sara felt weak with relief and annoyed with herself for overreacting. Just a bird at the window, a white bird.

Melanie was sleeping soundly, curled into a ball, her fists beneath her chin. Sara stood beside the bed looking down at her for a long time. How infinitely precious she was.

The next morning the children were particularly obnoxious. They were up early, spilling milk and cereal on the floor, slapping each other, fighting over television programs, complaining of boredom and asking questions without pausing to hear the answers. Their high-pitched voices repeating childish demands affected Sara like a cloud of stinging insects. Her skin itched. She felt raw and old, almost worn out with the effort of keeping a lid on her anger.

Sara suggested new games and answered questions in a level voice. She cleaned up their messes and promised the children ice-cream cones at Baskin-Robbins if they were good and quiet in the car and the grocery store. They were neither good nor quiet, but she bought them the ice-cream anyway, to avert a worse outburst. She longed for Thursday, when a neighbor would take Michael into town for a birthday party, and looked toward Sunday—when the children's father would have them both all day—as to her hope of heaven.

After lunch Melanie blessedly fell asleep, and Michael occupied himself quietly with his plastic dinosaurs. Almost holding her breath for fear the spell of peace would be broken, Sara went to get her canvas.

But at the sight of it her tentatively building spirits plunged. The painting she had spent so much time on the previous day was dreadful, labored, flat and uninspired. She had done better in high school. There was nothing to be done about it, Sara decided. She had done too much to it already. She would wait for it to dry and paint over it with gesso, she decided. She felt despairing at all the time she had wasted—not only yesterday, but all the years before that in which she had not found time to paint. Perhaps it was too late now; perhaps she had lost whatever talent she once had.

But she would lose this afternoon, too, if she didn't snap out of it. Sara turned the canvas to the wall and looked around. Water colors, perhaps. Something quick and simple, something to loosen her up. She had been too stiff, intimidated by the oils and canvas. She would have to work up to them.

"Can we go to a movie tonight?" Michael asked as she emerged from her room with the big, spiral-bound pad of heavy paper and her box of water colors. He was marching a blue dinosaur across the kitchen table and through the fruit bowl.

"We'll see," Sara said absently.

"What does that mean? Does that mean yes?"

"It means we'll see when the time comes."

"What will we see? Will we see a movie?" He followed her outside.

"Michael, don't pester me."

"What's *that?*"

There was a tone in his voice . . . Sara turned to look at him. He was staring in the direction of the lake, astonishment on his face. "Is that the ghost?"

Recalling her dream, Sara felt a chill. She turned, shading her eyes against the sun, and looked in the same direction. There was a large white animal walking on the farther shore, too oddly shaped to be a dog, too small for a cow.

"It's a pig," Sara said. She had never seen such a large, white pig before, and she wondered where it had come from. What was some-body's prize pig doing so far from the farm?

The pig had stopped its purposeful walk and turned towards the water to face them. Now it stood still and seemed to watch them. Sara took an involuntary step backward, her arm moving down and to the side as if to shield Michael.

"It sees us," Michael said. Sara couldn't tell from his voice if he was frightened, pleased, or merely commenting.

"It can't get to us," Sara said. "There's all that water in between." She spoke to comfort herself. She had never heard that pigs were dangerous, but it was a very large animal, and there was something uncanny about its presence there, and the way it stood watching them.

Then, just as abruptly as it had come, the pig turned away from the water and began to trot away, following the shoreline until it was out of sight.

Sara was relieved to see it go.

That night, Sara painted. She got out her oils and a new canvas; she felt inspired. She was excited; she hadn't felt like this in years. The picture had come to her, a vision she felt bound to paint. She was in no mood for sketches or exercises, or "loosening up" with water colors. This was her real work, and she needed no more training.

The main figures in the painting would be a large white pig and a shrouded human figure. Sara hoped to express some of the terror she'd felt during her nightmare, and to recapture in the painting the unease she had felt upon seeing the pig on the shore in the midday sun. She planned to keep the robed figure's face hidden, fearful of painting some-thing merely grotesque instead of terrifying.

She worked for hours, late into the night, until she realized that weariness was throwing off her sight and coordination. Then, pleased, exhausted, and looking forward to the next day's work, she went to bed.

The children let her sleep no later than they ever did in the morning, but Sara didn't mind. The hours spent painting seemed to have invigo-rated her, enabling her to thrive on less sleep.

When Mary Alice arrived to pick up Michael, she offered to take Melanie for the day, too, as company for her youngest. Sara gazed at her in mute gratitude, seeing her blond, smiling friend as a beneficent goddess, the personification of good fortune. With both the children gone, she would be able to work.

"Oh! Mary Alice, that would be wonderful! Are you sure you don't mind having her along?"

"What's one more kid? Kelly needs someone to play with. And besides," she patted Sara's shoulder, "it will give you some time to paint. Are you working on anything right now?"

It had been Mary Alice, with her ready sympathy and praise, who had encouraged Sara to take up painting again.

Sara smiled. "I started something new last night. It's different. I'll show you what I've done when you get back."

But despite her words and easy manner, Sara felt her stomach fluttering nervously when she went to bring out the uncompleted painting after the others had left. She was afraid of what she would find; afraid it would be clumsy or stiff or silly, and not at all what she remembered working on.

To her own surprise she was pleased by the sight of it. She felt a rising excitement, and a deep satisfaction at the thought of having uninterrupted hours to work on it.

The pig and the shrouded woman stood on a misty shore. Nearby was a bush in which nested a large white bird.

Sara painted all day with an easy authority she had not known in years. She felt light and free and intensely alive. She didn't have to think about what she was doing; the work had its own existence.

"Unusual."

Sara turned with a start to see Mary Alice. She felt as if she had been abruptly awakened. The children—her own, and Mary Alice's three—were roaring through the house like a hurricane. She looked back at the painting and saw that it was finished.

"Would you like some wine?" Sara asked.

"Please." Mary Alice slumped into the old armchair and continued to study the canvas. "I've never seen you do anything remotely like it. The white goddess, right?"

In the kitchen, pouring wine, Sara frowned. "What do you mean?" She brought the two glasses back into the family room.

"Well, it reminds me of Welsh mythology," Mary Alice said, accepting the wine glass. "Thanks. You know, the pig, the bird, the hawthorn bush. The hooded figure could be Cerridwen. White goddess of death and creation."

Sara shivered and looked around. It was as if a door had been opened and shut quickly, letting in a chill wind.

"I don't know about any of that," Sara said. "I never heard of . . . what's-her-name. But I had a dream about this terrifying white figure, and then I saw this huge pig across the lake. I just . . . they fit together into a painting, somehow. The bird's just there to balance out the composition."

"A dream," said Mary Alice. She glanced at her watch and stood up. "I suppose you don't have to know what a symbol means, to pick up on it."

Sara also stood. "Look, why don't you and the kids stay for dinner? It's just spaghetti, but there's lots of it."

"Thanks, but Bill's expecting me back. He hates having to fend for himself."

"Some other time, then," Sara said, feeling oddly bereft. She wanted adult conversation, adult companionship. It had been so long since she had eaten a leisurely meal with other adults.

Mary Alice touched Sara's arm and said, "You'll have to come for dinner some night soon—a late meal, after the kids have been put to bed. There's a friend of Bill's from the university that I've been wanting you to meet, and I could cook something really elaborate, and make a party out of it."

"That sounds marvelous," Sara said. She glanced at the painting again, then away, oddly disturbed. "You know, I had no problems with this painting. I never had to stop and think, and I've never worked so fast and surely in my life. It was odd, coming right after so much discouragement. For months I haven't been able to finish anything I liked."

"The muse takes her own time," Mary Alice said. "She's the White Goddess too, you know—at least for poets." She raised her voice to call her children.

Company gone, Michael and Melanie buzzed around Sara, tugging at her arms and reciting unintelligible stories about the adventures of the day. They were tired and hungry but keyed up to such a pitch by the events of the day that Sara knew she would have a hard time calming them. She put her completed but still-wet painting back in her bedroom, out of reach of flailing arms and flying toys, and resigned herself to being a mother again.

Sunday morning Sara rose even before the children. She felt as if she'd been in hibernation for the past 48 hours, dozing as she tended her children, cleaned the house and ran errands, and only now was she awake again.

In a few hours the children's father would come for them, and Sara would be free to paint and live her own life until Monday morning. She had found a few moments to sketch, and she was bursting with the urge to take up brush and paints and turn her grey preliminaries into color.

Not even pausing for her usual cup of tea, Sara pulled on a bathing suit and rushed outside. The air was a blessing on her bare skin and smelled of honeysuckle. The grass was cool and slippery beneath her feet, and there was a special taste in the air that exhilarated her. She began to run, her thoughts streaming out behind her until she knew nothing but sensation.

She plunged into the water as she had plunged into the morning and began swimming vigorously toward the other shore. She was panting so hard she felt dizzy when she arrived, but she grinned with delight.

"Come on out, oh Pig or Ghost or whatever you are!" she called as she walked ashore. "I'm not afraid of you—show yourself!"

She began to shake herself like a dog, simply to feel the droplets of water flying off of her. Then, somehow, she was dancing: a wild, primitive, arm-waving dance.

Finally, tired, she dropped to the rocky beach and rested. She gazed northward to where the narrow lake began to widen. Then she looked across the narrow stretch of water to her own house and to the others like it which dotted the shore. This early on a Sunday all was still and quiet.

Sara drank it all in: the sun, the clean, warm air with the scent of cedar in it, the songs of the birds, the solitude. Everything was as it should be.

She was cheerful when she returned, telling the kids funny stories and making blueberry-and-banana pancakes for breakfast. It was a special morning; even the children felt it.

"You're our good mommy, aren't you?" said Melanie, hugging Sara's bare legs.

"Of course I am, sweetie." She put the butter and syrup on the table and dropped a kiss on her daughter's head.

Feeling the promise in the air, Michael said, "Could we maybe rent a sailboat and go sailing today like you said we maybe could someday?"

"That will be up to your father," Sara said blithely. "Did you forget he's picking you up this morning? I'm going to stay home and paint."

Michael's face was comical as he absorbed this: the conflict between the pleasure of going out with his father and disappointment that he couldn't make use of his mother's good mood was clearly written there. Sara laughed and hugged him.

After breakfast had been eaten and the dishes washed, Sara began to feel impatient. Where was Bruce? He always liked to get an early start, and the children were ready to go.

The telephone rang.

"Sara, I'm not going to be able to make it today. Something's come up."

"What do you mean you're not going to be able to make it? Sunday's your day—you know that. We agreed."

"Well, I can't make it today." Already annoyance had sharpened his tone.

Sara clenched one hand into a fist, wishing she had him in front of her. "And why not? One day a week isn't so much. The kids have been counting on seeing you."

"I haven't missed a week yet and you know it. Be reasonable, Sara. I just can't make it."

"Why? Why can't you make it? What's so important on a Sunday? You've got a date? Fine, bring her along. *I* don't care. Just come and take the kids like you're supposed to."

"Look, put the kids on and I'll explain it to them."

"Explain it to *me,* damnit!"

A silence. Then he said, "I'm in Dallas."

Sara was too angry to speak.

"Tell the kids I'm sorry and I'll try to make it up to them next week."

"Sorry! You *knew*—why'd you wait until now to call?"

"I don't have to explain myself to you. I'll be by to pick up the kids next Sunday, 9 a.m." He hung up.

Sara held on to the phone, still facing the wall. There were tears of frustration in her eyes, and her back and shoulders ached as if she'd been beaten. When she had regained some control she went to look for the children.

They were outside on the driveway, eager to catch the first glimpse of their father's car.

"Sweethearts," Sara said. Her throat hurt. "Your father just called. He's . . . he's not going to be able to come today after all."

They stared at her. Melanie began to whine.

"Why?" Michael asked. "Why?"

"He's in Dallas. He couldn't get back in time. He said you'd all do something extra-special next weekend to make up for missing this one."

"Oh," said Michael. He was silent for a moment, and Sara wondered if he would cry. But then the moment passed and he said, "Can we go sailing, then?"

Sara sighed. "Not today. But why don't you two put on your bathing suits and we'll go for a swim?"

To Sara's relief they accepted the change of plans without fuss. For the next hour Michael showed off his skills in the water while Sara gave Melanie another swimming lesson. Afterwards, she got them started playing a board game and went off to her room to be by herself.

She felt exhausted, the euphoria of the early morning faded into the distant past. She sat on the bed and paged through her sketchbook, wondering why she had been so excited and just what she had intended to make of these rather mediocre sketches of a woman's face and details of tree branches. With a part of her mind she was still arguing with her ex-husband, this time scoring points with withering remarks which left him speechless.

Finally she stood up and took out her paints and the fresh canvas. As she set up the work in the bedroom, she could hear the children running in and out of the house, laughing, talking and occasionally slamming the screen door. The children seemed occupied and might not bother her until they grew hungry for lunch. After that, with luck, she might still have the afternoon to paint while Melanie napped and Michael played quietly by himself. She'd had such days before.

But it didn't matter: Sara didn't know what to paint. She was afraid to make a start, so sure was she that she would only ruin another canvas. Her earlier certainty was gone. She stared at the blank white surface and tried without success to visualize something there.

Then, from the other room, Melanie screamed.

It wasn't a play scream, and it didn't end. Melanie was screaming in terror.

Sara went cold with dread and ran into the family room. She saw Melanie cowering against a wall while Michael shouted and leaped around. At first Sara could not make out what was happening. Then she heard the mad fluttering of wings and saw a pale blur in the air: a bird had somehow blundered inside and was now flying madly around the room.

Poor thing, thought Sara. It can't find the way out again.

Her relief that the crisis was nothing more dangerous than a confused bird which had blundered into the house turned her fear into irritation with the children. Why were they being so stupid, carrying on so and making matters worse?

"Calm down!" she shouted. "Just shut up and keep out of the way. You're scaring it."

She gave Michael a firm push and then opened the door, keeping it open by lodging the iron, dachsund-shaped foot-scraper against it.

"Melanie, be quiet! You're making things worse," Sara said in a loud whisper.

Melanie's screams trailed away into noisy sobs. She was still cowering in a corner, head down and hands protecting it.

The bird flew three more times around the room, finally breaking out of that maddened, fluttering pattern to soar smoothly and surely out through the open door. Smiling, Sara gazed after it. Then she turned back to her children.

"Oh, Melanie, what *is* the matter? It was only a bird and it's gone now." Annoyed but obligated, Sara crossed the room to crouch beside her youngest child. "Now, what's this all about?"

Gently she raised Melanie's face away from her hands and the tangle of her hair, and saw that she was covered with blood.

"My God!—oh, sweetheart." Sara hurried the little girl down the hall to the bathroom. So much blood . . . was her eye hurt? She'd never forgive herself if. . . .

A wet washcloth, carefully used, revealed no great damage. There were two small cuts, one just above Melanie's left eye and the other on her left cheek. Melanie snuffled and breathed jerkily. She was obviously content to have her mother fuss over her.

Michael peeked around the door-frame as Sara was applying Band-

Aids to Melanie's face. "That bird tried to kill Melanie," he said in a tone of gleeful horror. "He tried to peck her eyes out!"

"Michael, *really*." Sara sighed in exasperation. Melanie would be nervous enough about birds without his stories. "It was an accident," she said firmly. "Birds aren't mean or dangerous—they don't try to hurt people. But that bird was frightened—it was in a strange place. Unfortunately, Melanie got in the way while it was trying to get out. If you'd both been more sensible, instead of jumping around like that—"

"It flew right at her," Michael said. "I saw it. It tried to get me next but I wouldn't let it—I kept waving my hands around over my head so it couldn't get at my face like it wanted." He sounded very self-important and pleased with himself, which annoyed Sara still more.

"It was an accident. The bird felt trapped and didn't know how to respond. It's not something you have to worry about, because it's not likely ever to happen again. Now I don't want to hear any more about it." She hugged Melanie and lifted her down from the sink ledge. "Feel better?"

"Hungry," Melanie said.

"Glad you mentioned it. Let's go eat lunch."

Monday morning Sara took her children to play with Mary Alice's children. It was a beautiful day but already stiflingly hot. Sara felt lethargic and faintly sad. After Michael and Melanie had joined the other children in the safely fenced-in yard, she lingered to drink ice tea and talk with Mary Alice.

"I hope you got a lot of work done yesterday," Mary Alice said, settling onto a brightly cushioned wicker couch.

Sara shook her head. "Bruce copped out. He called at the last minute and said he couldn't come—he was in Dallas."

Mary Alice's eyes went wide. "That . . . creep," she said at last.

Sara gave a short laugh. "I've called him worse than that. But I should know by now that he's not to be counted on. The kids are starting to learn that about him, too. The worst thing about it is what I lost—or what I felt I lost. I woke up feeling great—I was ready to conquer the world, or at least to paint it. I felt so *alive*. I felt—I don't know if I can explain how I felt. I think of it as my "creative" feeling, and I haven't had such a strong one since Michael was born—or maybe even since I married Bruce. It's a mood in which everything has meaning, everything is alive, everything is possible."

"There's a girl who sits for us sometimes," Mary Alice said hesitantly. "She's very young, but responsible—she doesn't charge much. You could have her over some afternoons to take care of the kids while you. . . ."

Sara shook her head, discarding the suggestion impatiently. "They'd still be around. They'd still be—oh, calling to me, somehow. I don't know how to explain it. Sometimes I feel I'm just looking for excuses not to paint, but . . . there's just something about being both a mother *and* an artist. I don't know if I can manage it, not even with all the good examples, and all the babysitters, in the world.

"Art has never been a part-time thing for me. Art was all I cared about in school, and up until I met Bruce. Then the part of me that was an artist got submerged. For the past five years I've been a full-time mother. Now I'm trying to learn how to be a part-time artist and a part-time mother, and I don't think I can. I know that's very all-or-nothing of me, but it's how I feel."

The two women sat quietly in the bright, sunlit room. The high-pitched voices of their children, playing outside, floated up to them.

"Maybe it's just too early," Mary Alice ventured at last. "In the fall, Michael will be in school. You could put Melanie in a nursery, at least during the mornings. Then you could count on having a certain amount of time to yourself every day."

"Maybe," Sara said. She did not sound hopeful. "But even when the children aren't around, the pull is there. I think about them, worry about them, have to plan for them. And my art makes as many demands as a child—I can't divide myself between them. I don't think it can ever be the same—I'll never have all my energy and thoughts and commitment to give to my art. There are always the children pulling at me." She sighed and rubbed her face. "Sometimes . . . I wish I had it to do all over again. And I think that, much as I love them, I would never have chosen to have children. I would never have married."

Silence fell again, and Sara wondered if she had shocked Mary Alice. She was rousing herself to say something else about her love for her children, to find the words that would modify the wish she had just made, when the clamor of children filled the house, the sound of the kitchen door, opening and slamming, the clatter of many feet on hard-wood floors, and voices raised, calling.

Sara and Mary Alice both leaped to their feet as the children rushed in.

Melanie and Kelly were both crying; the boys were excited and talking all at once.

"It was the same bird!" Michael cried, tugging at Sara's arm as she knelt to comfort Melanie. "It came and tried to kill us again—it tried to peck her eyes out, but we ran!"

Melanie seemed unhurt; gradually, bathed in her mother's attention, her sobs subsided.

The children all agreed with Michael's story: there had been a white bird which had suddenly swooped down at Melanie, pecking at her head.

"Why does that bird want to hurt us?" Michael asked.

"Oh, Michael, I don't think it does. Maybe you were near its nest; maybe it was attracted by Melanie's hair." Helpless to explain and trying not to feel frightened herself, Sara hugged her daughter.

"Me go home," Melanie muttered into Sara's blouse.

Sara looked up. "Michael, do you want to go home now, or do you want to keep on playing here?"

"You kids can all go play in Barry's room," Mary Alice said.

The other children ran off. Sara stood up, still holding Melanie and staggering slightly under her weight. "I'll take this one home," she said. "You can send Michael by himself when he's ready, unless . . . unless he wants me to come get him."

Mary Alice nodded, her face concerned and puzzled. "What's this about the bird?"

Sara didn't want to talk about it. As lightly as she could she said, "Oh, a bird got trapped in the house yesterday and scared the kids. I don't know what happened in the yard just now, but naturally Michael and Melanie are a little spooked about birds." She set Melanie down. "Come on, sweetie, I'm not going to carry you all the way home."

Keeping her head down as if she feared another attack, Melanie left the house with her mother and walked the half-mile home staying close by her side.

At home, Sara settled Melanie in her room with her dolls, and then, feeling depressed, went back to her own bedroom and stretched out on the bed. She closed her eyes and tried to comfort herself with thoughts of the children in school, a babysitter, a silent house and time to work. It was wrong to blame the children, she thought. She could be painting now—it was her own fault if she didn't.

Thinking about what she would paint next, she visualized a pale, blond woman. Her skin was unnaturally white, suggesting sickness or the pallor of death. Her lips were as red as blood, and her long hair was like silvery corn silk.

The White Goddess, thought Sara.

The woman drew a veil over her face. Then, slowly, began to draw it back. Sara felt a quickening of dread. Although she had just seen her face, she was afraid that another, different face would now be revealed. And then the veil was removed, and she saw the grey face with dead-white, staring eyes.

Sara woke with a start. She felt as if she had dozed off for less than a minute, but she saw from the bedside clock that she had been asleep for nearly an hour. She sat on the edge of the bed and rubbed her eyes. Her mouth was dry. She heard voices, one of them Michael's, coming from outside.

She stood up and walked to the window and pulled back the heavy drapes, curious to see whom Michael was talking to.

Michael was standing on the edge of the lawn near the driveway with a strange woman. Although there was something faintly familiar about her, Sara could not identify her as any of the neighbors. She was a brassy blonde, heavily made-up—even at this distance her lips seemed garishly red against an unnaturally pale face. Something about the way they stood together and spoke so intently made Sara want to intrude.

But by the time she got outside, Michael was alone.

"Hi," he said, walking toward her.

"Where'd she go?" Sara asked, looking around.

"Who?"

"That woman you were just talking to—who was she?"

"Who?"

"You know who," Sara began, then stopped abruptly, confused. She had just realized why the woman seemed familiar to her—she'd seen her first in a dream. Perhaps she had dreamed the whole incident?

She shook her head, bent to kiss Michael, and went with him into the house.

·   ·   ·   ·

In the middle of the night Sara started up in bed, wide awake and frightened. The children? She couldn't pinpoint her anxiety, but her automatic reaction was to check on their safety. In the hall, on the way to their rooms, the sound of a muffled giggle reached her and made her turn aside, into the family room. There she saw Michael and Melanie standing before the window, curtains opened wide, gazing into the back-yard.

Sara walked slowly towards the window, vaguely dreading what she would see.

There was a white pig on the lawn, almost shining in the moonlight. It stood very still, looking up at them.

Sara put her hand on Melanie's shoulders, and the little girl leaped away, letting out a small scream.

"Melanie!" Sara said sharply.

Both children stood still and quiet, looking at her. There was a wari-ness in their gaze that Sara did not like. They looked at her as if expecting punishment. What had they done? Sara wondered.

"Both of you, go to bed," Sara said. "You shouldn't be up and roam-ing around at this hour."

"Look, she's dancing," Michael said softly.

Sara turned and looked out the window. The pig was romping on the lawn in what was surely an unnatural fashion, capering in circles that took it gradually away from the house and toward the lake. It wasn't trotting or running or walking—it was, as Michael had said, dancing.

On the shore of the lake it stopped. To Sara's eyes the figure of the pig seemed to become dim and blurred—she blinked, wondering if a cloud had passed across the moon. The whiteness that had been a pig now seemed to flow and swirl like a dense fog, finally settling in the shape of a tall, pale woman in a silver-white gown.

Sara shivered and rubbed her bare arms with her hands. She wanted to hide. She wanted to turn her gaze away, but she could not move.

It's not possible, she thought. I'm dreaming.

The harsh, unmistakable sound of the bolt being drawn on the back door brought her out of her daze, and she turned in time to see Michael opening the door, Melanie close behind him.

"No!" She rushed to pull the children away and to push the door shut again. She snapped the bolt to and stood in front of the door, blocking it from the children. She was trembling.

The children began to weep. They stood with their arms half-outstretched as if begging for an embrace from someone just out of their reach.

Sara walked past her weeping children to the window and looked out. There was nothing unusual to be seen in the moonlit yard—no white pig or ghostly woman. Nothing that should not have been there amid the shadows. Across the lake she saw a sudden pale blur, as if a white bird had risen into the air. But that might have been moonlight on the leaves.

"Go back to bed," Sara said wearily. "She's gone—it's all over now."

Watching them shuffle away, sniffing and rubbing their faces, Sara remembered the story she had told Michael on the first night she had caught a glimpse of the woman. It seemed bitterly ironic now, that story of a ghostly mother searching for her children.

"You can't have them," Sara whispered to the empty night. "I'll never let you hurt them."

Sara woke in the morning feeling as if she had been painting all night: tired, yet satisfied and hopeful. The picture was there, just behind her eyes, and she could hardly wait to get started.

The children were quiet and sullen, not talking to her and with only enough energy to stare at the television set. Sara diagnosed it as lack of sleep and thought that it was just as well—she had no time for their questions or games today. She made them breakfast but let the dishes and the other housework go and hurried to set up her paints and canvas outside in the clear morning sunlight.

Another cool nighttime painting, all swirling greys, blues and cold white. A metamorphosis: pale-colored pig transforming into a pale-faced, blue-gowned woman, who shifts into a bird, flying away.

The new creation absorbed her utterly, and she worked all day, with only a brief pause when the children demanded lunch. At a little before six she decided to stop for the day. She was tired, pleased with herself, and utterly ravenous.

She found the children sitting before the television set and wondered if they had been there, just like that, all day. After putting her unfinished painting safely away and cleaning her brushes, she marched decisively to the television set and turned it off.

Michael and Melanie set up a deprived wailing.

"Oh, come on!" Sara said, scoffing. "All that fuss about the news? You've watched enough of this pap for one day. How would you like to go for a swim before dinner?"

Michael shrugged. Melanie hugged her knees and muttered, "I want to watch."

"If you want to swim, say so, and I'll go out with you. If you don't, I'm going to start cooking."

They didn't respond. So Sara shrugged and went into the kitchen. She was feeling too good to let herself be annoyed by their moodiness.

The children didn't turn the television set back on, and Sara heard no further sound from the family room until, the chicken broiling and a potato salad under construction, Sara heard the screen door open and close.

She smiled and, as she was going to check on the chicken, paused to look out the window. What she saw froze her with terror.

The children were running toward the lake, silently, their bare arms and legs flashing in the growing twilight. Michael was very much in the lead because Melanie ran clumsily and often fell.

Across the lake on the other shore stood the pale woman in white; on her shoulder, the white bird; and at her side, the pig. The woman raised her head slightly and looked over the children, directly at Sara. Her blood-red lips parted in a gleaming smile.

Sara cried out incoherently and ran for the door. Ahead of her she saw Michael leap into the lake with all his clothes on. She caught up with Melanie on the shore and grabbed her.

"Go back to the house," she said, shaking the girl slightly for emphasis. "Go on back and stay there. You are not to go into the water, understand?"

Then, kicking off her sandals, Sara dived in and swam after Michael.

She had nearly reached him when she heard a splashing behind her, and her courage failed: Melanie. But she couldn't let herself be distracted by her worries about Melanie's ability as a swimmer. She caught hold of her son in a life-saver's neck-grip. He struggled grimly and silently against her, but he didn't have a chance. Sara knew she could get him across to the other shore, if only she didn't have to try to save Melanie as well.

"Michael," Sara gasped. "Honey, listen to me. It's not safe. You must

go back. Michael, please? This is very dangerous—she'll kill you. She's
the one who sent the bird!"

Michael continued to thrash and kick and choke. Sara wondered if he
could hear her at all. She looked around and saw Melanie paddling
slowly in their direction. And on the other shore the White Goddess
stood, making no sound or motion.

"Michael, please," Sara whispered close to his ear. "Don't fight me.
Relax and we'll all be safe." With great difficulty, Sara managed to pull
her son back towards the home shore.

Melanie swam with single-minded concentration and was within
Sara's grasp before she could try to avoid her. She thrashed about in
Sara's armlock, but not as wildly or as strongly as her brother.

Sara had them both, now, but how was she to swim? She was treading water, just holding her own against the children's struggles and
hoping they would soon tire, when she felt a rush of air against her
cheek, and Melanie shrieked.

It was the bird again. Sara caught sight of it just as it was diving for
Michael's head. The sharp beak gashed his face below one eye. Michael
screamed, and the bright blood streamed down his cheek.

Trying to help him, Sara relaxed her stranglehold on Michael. At once
he swam away, kicking and plunging below the water.

"Michael, go back to the house—you'll be safe there!"

She swallowed a mouthful of lake water as she spoke and choked on
it. Letting go of Melanie, she managed to catch hold of Michael's flailing
legs and pull him back close to her. Melanie, trying to avoid the bird
which was still flapping around, was screaming and crying and barely
keeping herself afloat. Sara had no trouble catching her again.

Shouting at the bird and wishing for a spare hand to strike at it, Sara
pulled her children close to her, pressing their faces tightly against her
chest. They struggled still to get away, but they were tiring and their
struggles grew weaker. Sara knew she would win—she would save
them from the bird and from the goddess; she would protect them with
her own body.

Finally, the bird flew away. In the sudden calm, Sara realized that her
children were much too quiet, much too still. She relaxed her tight hold,
and their bodies slipped further into the water.

She stared down at them, slow to understand. Their eyes were open,
looking up through a film of water, but they did not see her. She looked

up from their sweet, empty faces and across the silver water to where the white-faced figure still stood, her pale eyes staring out at death, her favorite offering.

Sara saw it all as a painting. The pale figure on the shore glowed against the deep blue twilight, and the water gave off its own shimmering light. The woman in the water, also dressed in white, was a terrible, pitiable figure with her two drowned children beside her, their hair floating out around their heads like fuzzy halos; an innocent murderess.

I was the one they were afraid of, thought Sara.

She threw back her head and howled her anguish to the empty world.

A Dozen Roses

Jean Paiva

During her tragically brief career, JEAN PAIVA *(1944–1989) edited and cofounded* Crawdaddy *magazine, wrote two novels published by New American Library's Onyx Books division,* The Last Gamble *and* The Lilith Factor, *the latter nominated for the Horror Writers of America's Best First Novel Award. Her short story "Just Idle Chatter" was printed in Kathryn Ptacek's anthology* Women of Darkness II. *A friend and former student, Jean was public relations director of my readers theatre company, The Open Book, which bestows an annual Jean Paiva Memorial Award for promising new writers. The posthumous story "A Dozen Roses" was deeply important to Jean.*

IT WAS THAT FIRST, perfect rose that signaled the beginning of the wedge that divided us.

Coo and I probably never would have connected if we hadn't been the only two women under sixty, make that closer to thirty, in the grief therapy group. Though my desolation was every bit as wrenching as hers, when she introduced herself as Coo I actually smiled and stifled a giggle. My brief mirth went unnoticed. Her pain was still too new, too raw a wound, to admit anything or anyone past her protective shell.

A month later, when we had our first coffee together, I apologized and got, in return, a tentative smile back. That brief cup of coffee led to dinner the next time, and soon we found ourselves meeting regularly after therapy. We had been warned by the counselor that new "relation-ships" formed in the group could rebound and might not pan out in the long run. But our friendship was just that—a friendship, not a relation-ship in quotes as the counselor cautioned. It wasn't long before we decided to pool our limited widowed resources, join households and live together.

The first few months went smoothly. I had my career as Marketing Director for Sansworth Electronics where the more work I assumed, the fatter my paycheck grew. Taking extra responsibility was my way of filling a void, but the reward was immediate and tangible. It helped support my habit of charging small fortunes at chic stores. Coo, on the other hand, lived simply. She'd never been bitten by the fashion bug, yet always managed to look comfortably right. Her "associates" at work agreed, but Coo was co-founder of the neighborhood day-care center and her associates were all under three feet tall.

The Tuesday the first rose was delivered I was home. Unusual for me on a weekday, but I'd been at a convention half-way around the world from Thursday through Monday. Between jet lag and some minor para-sitic intestinal dysfunction, I felt no qualms about hitting the couch with a totally irrelevant paperback book. It was mid-day and Coo was home on break—easy for her to manage with the day-care center only a half block away. The rose arrived promptly at one o'clock.

Coo tipped the delivery man and brought the slender cylinder of paper into the living room. She directed a faintly questioning look at me. I rested the book on my chest and managed my first cohesive sentence of the day.

"What's that?"

"I don't know," Coo answered, her puzzled look deepening. "I thought you might have some idea."

Raising myself, I looked over the back of the couch and out the picture window. "The van is Pete's Florist. It must be flowers."

Coo shook her head in obvious awe at my astute observation. "I'm aware it comes from the florist, Claire. It's a rose, and it's for me. But there's no card."

"Ummm." My mind, still on Hong Kong time, refused to rise to the occasion. Expressing my interest in the situation with one, succinct grunt, I lifted the book back to my tired eyes.

The rustling as Coo unwrapped the cone of paper barely distracted me from my unfolding fantasy quest, and her soft gasp was no more noticeable than the sound of a page turning. But her groan did get my attention.

I looked up and saw her holding a single pure white rose, still in bud. She raised a finger to her lips.

"I pricked it," she said.

By the next morning, I'd recovered enough to go to work. On my groggy trek to the front door, the rose caught my eye. It was still tightly budded, a fat, heavy blossom already threatening to bend its deceptively slender stem. A heady fragrance, so intense it seemed impossible that a single flower could be the source, reached me. The rose, displayed in my silver bud vase on the fireplace mantel, reflected itself in the elaborate, gilt edged mirror behind it. Its pale petals were rimmed with a thin, ragged border of red.

Bending close, I shut my eyes and inhaled its sweet essence. Coo, I murmured, surprising myself. But the rose smelled, no—*radiated* the name Coo.

I grabbed my purse and attaché and hurried for the commuter train. I got my favorite seat and closed my eyes. The scent of that rose lingered in my memory and I thought about the way Coo's name had sprung to my lips. I thought about names.

Coo, whose given name is Colleen, was aptly named. I, on the other hand, am not truly a Claire. An appropriately named Claire would have some of Coo's softness, but I was all lean angles, from my short sculpted auburn hair to my tailored suits, a style *very* appropriate to my corporate position. Claire was pleasant, but I should have been a more sophisticated Sybil or, preferably, a Diane.

Coo was definitely a Coo, though. From the very first she struck me with her freshness and innocence; a clean, simple appearance, gentle and undeniably feminine with a fuzziness to her edges, but whether this blurring was a physical effect caused by the furry sweaters and full skirts she always wore and the halo her fine blond hair became in the sunlight, or whether it was a metaphysical projection of her complacent and accepting nature is still unknown to me. It was a great part of her charm; her charges at the day-care center related well to the fairy tale aura that surrounded her.

I worked late that day, catching up on paper work and returning calls.

I ate both lunch and dinner at my desk so, once home, my only real need was to slip into my night shirt and go to sleep. With the fullness of accomplishment, I slept well and late—so late that, in rushing to catch the last train that would get me to the city on time, I barely noticed the second, pale rose.

The early commute home Thursday was welcome. Coo had called that day and we planned a simple dinner together, complete with a rented video. Even on weekends we tended to live separate lives, but a weekly dinner kept us in touch. We each knew we had the strength to find our own way because of our supportive friendship. An evening once a week helped cement that bond.

The perfume greeted me as soon as I opened the door. Roses, a room full of roses. As I entered the living room, I expected a sight to match the scent. The silver bud vase had been replaced by a smoked crystal vase. Three tall roses held their heads high.

"Coo," I called, "these roses are charming. Who sent them?"

Emerging from the kitchen, wiping her hands on a small terrycloth towel, Coo looked first at me and then at the roses.

"I don't know," she said simply. "You were here when the first arrived. There's been one each day. They *are* lovely, though, aren't they?"

"Yes, they are." I walked towards the mantel, instinctively drawn to the roses. One, a cloud of soft petals, glowed pink in the setting October sun. It was the first to open and its deep, red border flowed outward from an even deeper red heart.

"They're definitely not tea roses or 'American Beauties'," I said, reaching out to touch the velvet smooth flower.

"Be careful, Claire. They have thorns. Somehow I've managed to prick myself on each one."

"Do you know any botanists?" I asked, following Coo into our dining room. "They might be a new species. They have more layers than I've ever seen. Even their coloring is unique."

She'd laid the table with mats instead of a cloth and the gleaming silver reflected elegantly in the dark wood.

"No, I don't know any botanists," she laughed. "Other than calling a lawn service, I don't even know anyone who gardens. They are beautiful, but I *have* seen variations on the colors before." Her voice became a murmur. "Nicolas is the only one who ever sent me roses. It's our fifth anniversary next week."

"Coo, do I have time to change?"

She looked in my direction, but more through than at me. "Change, of course. Dinner in five minutes."

Comfortably clad in soft jeans and a well-worn shirt, I detoured to the basement for a bottle of Sauvignon Blanc, a California Bordeaux I'm particularly fond of. "Can I help?" I called into the kitchen, wary of intruding on what was unquestionably (thank whatever powers there be) Coo's domain.

"Carry the casserole," she suggested, "I've got the salad and bread." The casserole smelled wonderful, rich with home grown herbs. The salad, while scant to the eye, contained a myriad of ingredients—a taste treat that wouldn't infringe on the waistline.

Half the meal went by with conversation directed at the quality of the food and irrelevant anecdotes about the day-care center and my trip. But as I poured our second glass of wine, I reflected on Coo's brief, but unnerving reference to the flowers.

"Coo, those roses—" Her eyes met mine. "Have you called the florist to ask who's sending them?"

"No," she answered, sitting back with her wine. "I hadn't thought of that. I'll call first thing in the morning." Somewhere inside Coo's head, the same switch as before was thrown. Her eyes dimmed and unfocused. "I saw him today," she said in a monotone.

As I watched Coo's slack face, I felt small icy fingers clutching at my insides. "Who?"

A smile played at the corner of her mouth. "I saw him when I changed vases. I needed a larger one to fit today's roses. There'll be more, you know. He always sends a dozen."

The cold fingers firmly gripped and twisted my gut. I swallowed the acrid bile that rose to my throat.

"When I put the vase back on the mantel," Coo continued, "Nicolas was in the mirror, smiling, reaching out for me. I was so happy. But when I turned, he wasn't there."

Without excusing myself, I dashed to the downstairs toilet and relieved myself of dinner.

The chill I'd felt melted into a pool of fear. Coo was slipping.

. . . .

Her brother Michael had warned me. I met him soon after I moved into Coo's house. During his "welcome" afternoon visit, he waited until she left the room for refreshments before speaking to me.

"Watch her," he'd pleaded. "Her hold on reality has always been tenuous, at best. Nicolas was everything to her. If you ever—well, sense a change, call me." Michael pressed his card into my hand, and I'd stuck it in some corner of my desk, convinced I'd never need it.

Maybe I still don't, I prayed. I'd keep an eye on her for awhile. This was sure to pass.

Dashing cool water on my face, I took a few deep breaths and went back to the dining room.

Coo was stacking plates, her face animated, again flushed and lovely. She greeted me with a grin. "Claire, did I tell you about our nature trip today, and how the McKenzie boy decided to inaugurate the girls into the wonders of male anatomy?"

I smiled back, reassured. With the mood noticeably lightened, we cleared the table in record time, put the dishes in to soak and took our frozen tofuti to the living room. A choice of video tapes awaited me: last year's missed Woody Allen hit, an unknown gory grade-D horror (which I knew Coo got for me) and a Deborah Kerr haunted house classic, *The Innocents.* The gore could wait, I decided, and chose the Woody Allen cassette. My hand briefly touched the third tape, but Coo pulled it aside. No explanation was given, but then, between friends, none is needed. We paused only once, to microwave some popcorn.

After rewinding the tape, I retired to sort the files I'd brought home for next week's trip. From my room I heard the video machine being fed another cassette. I thought, but wasn't sure, that I heard a muffled sob.

Fridays before a business trip are traditionally hectic for me, but Friday nights are also traditional. I shrug off my robe of responsibility, slip on high heeled sandals and kick up those heels until it's time for the last train home. Some nagging concern over Coo tried to dissuade me from relaxing, but by the time I reached my third party, I stopped trying to remember.

Sleeping late Saturday morning is part of my religion and I gratefully observed it comfortably cuddled under my light quilt. By the time I woke, the fifth rose had been delivered.

The snow white bud, as heavy on its delicate stem as the others, nested with its four mates in the smoked crystal vase. I glanced past them to the clock on the mantel and then to the gilded mirror, but my eyes hypnotically returned to the roses. There were five in gradient shades, from the pure white bud that just arrived to one of the deepest reds I'd ever seen. The red rose's head drooped from its own weight, but it still looked fresh and vibrantly alive.

Their perfume reached out and enveloped me. The house had been sweetly permeated ever since the first one arrived, but today their scent was cloying, heavy and intrusive.

I moved closer. Looking at them from the newest rose to the first was like watching a time-lapse frame by frame portrait of a rose unfolding to perfection. I didn't hear Coo enter the room.

"Good afternoon, Claire, or good morning, as the case may be." Her voice behind me was gentle on my slowly waking senses. "A fresh pot of coffee is on. I heard you shuffling about and thought you'd head for the aroma."

"I didn't smell the coffee, not over these roses. Their scent is overpowering." I turned round to face Coo and gasped.

Her creamy skin was as porcelain smooth as always, but instead of her usual healthy flush she was pale, almost drawn. Her misty grey eyes that usually sparkle bright and alive under feathery lashes were sunken.

Coo's fixed smile was still directed at me and right now coffee seemed like a good idea. "Did you find out who's sending them?" I asked, heading for the kitchen. Meeting her blank stare, I added, "The roses."

"They didn't know," she answered quietly, looking past me to the mantel. "They said they had instructions to deliver a rose every day for twelve days."

My morning mathematical skills were limited but this was easy. "That's a dozen roses."

"Just like Nicolas sends me." Coo moved close to the five roses. Minutes passed before she glanced back at me. "I'm going out for awhile, Claire, but I'll be home to put dinner together."

I nodded. I wanted to spend some time at home this weekend before jetting off to London on Monday. Not only did I have work to do, I wanted to watch Coo. I made a mental note to look for her brother's number, though not to call him. *Yet.*

The day, devoted to chores, passed much too quickly. Saturdays should go on forever. After putting away the groceries, I went to my room to sort my travel clothes. Noises from the kitchen told me Coo had returned. She called upstairs and said food would be on the table in half an hour—a quick meal of spaghetti a la carbonara and salad that would have taken me hours to prepare.

When I came downstairs at the appointed time, I asked Coo if she'd be willing to forgo wine for bottled water. She answered with a shrug, looking past me. Long moments later she said, "Water will be fine."

Dinner was silent. Every time I opened my mouth to say anything, I had to stop myself from bringing up the roses. Their powerful fragrance penetrated the taste of the food, spoiling that as well.

"Let's spend Sunday together," I said. "We haven't had a whole day together in months."

No answer. I raised my eyes to hers. They were lifeless, sightless; they could have been made of glass.

"Coo, where are you?" I demanded. "Talk to me!"

Her eyes swam back into focus. "I'm here, right here," she whispered. Her hands, holding cutlery, shook noticeably.

"I'll clear and wash tonight."

She nodded. "I'd like to go to my room. I'm rather tired." Her face masked and totally unreadable, Coo left the table.

The dishes were a welcome distraction and focus for my confusion. I finished up, retrieved the paperback I'd just begun, the next in a series I'm wholly addicted to, and headed for my room. With the door closed, pillows plumped high, I settled into bed for the night. A delicious drowsiness soon overcame me.

I woke. Quietly, suddenly, confused. There was no sound, no breeze, no reason . . . then I realized it was the air that woke me; it was strangely heavy and my breathing was labored. As I lay there, the room got cold. An oppressiveness grew and pressed on me. The moonlight dimmed, as if blotted by heavy clouds.

Moving my eyes to the door, I saw it now stood open. Across the hall the door to Coo's room was also open and a dim glow shone from within, a pale prism of light that grew and pulsed with stolen energy. The colors intensified, slowly strobing to a primitive rhythm.

A gentle sigh sounded faintly from her room. Alarmed, I tried to rise but the weight of my quilt held me firmly to the bed. I half-convinced myself that I was dreaming, but then her moans began.

It was the unmistakable sound of a woman being loved.

Her murmured words, carrying through the thinned night air, sounded clearly in my room. "Nicolas, oh my darling Nicolas."

I pressed my face into the pillow, feeling each thread in the weave rub into my tightly-closed eyes. I never wanted to cross that hall again.

Sleep once again mercifully found me.

By the time I woke, Sunday had dawned bright and clear, yet the house was strangely quiet. Coo's normal clatter was all the more noticeable for its absence. No crackle of bacon frying, the spicy odor sinuously wafting up to my room to tease me to consciousness. No coffee smell mingled with the promise of eggs or pancakes to lead me out of bed. Just the damned scent of roses.

Coo was in the kitchen and, yes, there was coffee, but that was all. Withdrawn and even paler than yesterday, she sat quietly at the kitchen table toying with the handcrafted mug in front of her. The dark smudges under her eyes had deepened.

I opened my mouth, but found I couldn't mention last night. "Are you feeling all right?" I asked, instead.

She looked up at me. "I'm fine. Just a little tired, that's all," she said so softly I had to lean forward to hear her. Her eyes again returned to her coffee mug, held by hands scabbed with small wounds.

"What happened to you?" I asked. "Your hands are all torn!"

She looked slowly at each hand, turning them over, carefully studying each finger; palms up to palms down to palms up to palms down. "Nothing, Claire. I've just caught them here and there. The children, you know. And the roses."

I moved to the sink to dispose of my coffee cup, then turned back to begin a heart-to-heart talk with Coo, but she was gone. The kitchen door stood wide open from her silent departure.

There were now six roses. Half a dozen, half way to the dozen. Six perfect roses: one white bud; one pale with a red edge on its unopened petals; one pink; another pinker still; one red and opening its face to the world, and one last incredibly voluptuous red rose.

My mind suddenly clicked on a detail. This fully-opened rose, the first to be delivered—how had it turned such a brilliant red? It was pale when it arrived: white or, at the most, pink. The next day I'd seen the red edges and asked about the botanist. Were these an amazing new strain or could Coo be switching roses?

That Sunday was the longest day I'd ever experienced. Watching the clock on the mantel—next to the roses reflecting back their number— the minutes barely passed. I read the paper and glanced at the clock and the roses. I'd finish one section and look at the clock, and the roses. I finished the paper, my eyes returning to the clock . . . and the roses. I picked up my book, looked back at the mantel and saw a dozen roses, half here, half in reflection. Disquiet possessed me—a gnawing with no name, no direction, no outlet.

"Not true," I said aloud. Shaking off my growing lethargy, I reached the mantel in three quick strides. I felt my anger rise, tightening my muscles, feathering the hairs on the back of my neck. I wasn't sure if I wanted to crush or caress, but as my hand neared the vase, all energy ebbed from my arm. My fingers uncurled. I reached out to a single flower and gently ran my fingertip around the soft edge of the outer petals. The curve of the rose was delicate. A tissue-thin petal was just beginning to separate from the heart of the flower. Following the out-line, my finger reached the stem, long and firm, rising majestically from the vase. How dark the water looked.

Seeing the single thorn, jutting thickly off the slender stalk, I continued to trace its silhouette. My finger paused at the thorn, then continued around to its needle point. Testing.

Piercing.

A drop of my blood pooled and transferred to the christened point, slipping quietly down the rose's stem. I remembered the growing cold the night before, but now the air grew torrid and humid. I've always been squeamish when I bled, but this sudden warmth alarmed me. The room dimmed and slipped out of focus.

Darkness. The heart of the shadow, now tangible, enveloped me. A soft, tender pressure on my breast stirred longings I wasn't ready for. Or so I thought. I saw myself in the mirror; my head thrown back, my lips moist as the shadow embraced me. Hazy arms circled my waist, stroked my hair, held me close. The touch of gentle lips on my throat, a hardness pressed against me. I let the fever grow, opening my eyes only when the pleasure reached a bittersweet pitch.

The mirror reflected my passion and my lover.

"Nicolas!"

The shock in his empty eyes matched my own. Drawn to the roses and the essence of woman, he had been called by my need. "No," I sobbed, abruptly pulling myself away. I threw myself on the couch and curled into the smallest space I could fill. Whether to keep him out or myself in—it didn't matter.

Coo found me there, still sobbing. Her eyes searched mine for an answer to my heartbreak. How could I tell her it was the mourning I'd neglected months ago and, even worse, how could I hurt her by revealing I'd been with Nicolas?

I think she knew. She brought me a glass of water and left me, going to her room. Quietly closing the door behind her, she locked herself in—and me out.

Filled with guilt, consumed with doubts for my own sanity, I went to pack for my trip. I found her brother's card and slipped it into my passport case. But how could I call him now? I was the one slipping.

I found a rarely-used sedative prescription and used it. My early morning flight demanded unbroken sleep. Besides, I don't think I could have listened—*not tonight.*

Friday night. After traveling a whole day longer than planned, I let myself in. Tired from waiting for closed airports to open, sleepless from time changes, I nonetheless felt good. I was home.

When I knew I'd be a day late, I called Coo. She sounded fine. Far, far away, but fine. Overseas connections are like that. You can sound as if you're right next door or—like this time—as if a million miles and countless echoes separate you.

Coo's door was slightly open. I dropped my luggage inside my room and looked in on her. She was sleeping peacefully, her breathing regular, her arm thrown across the double bed she once shared.

The raw, now almost acrid, essence of roses hit me full force. I closed her door, then mine as well and, stripping clean, fell into my welcome, freshly-made bed. She was fine, I was fine. The call to her brother had not been necessary. I fell fast asleep.

Two business trips, back to back, had left me even more paralyzed than usual. An early Saturday morning pee, a sip of tap water, then back to bed and it was afternoon. Once I'd heard the doorbell ring, but drifted back to sleep when Coo's footsteps padded down the stairs.

When I finally woke up, I recognized the late afternoon sun by the angle from which it shone through my windows. Now or never, I told myself, and slid my feet into waiting slippers.

The house was completely still. Downstairs, dust motes danced in the living room windows and only the *whirrr* of the dated refrigerator broke the otherwise total quiet. A band of pressure I hadn't realized was there loosened its grip on my head. My temples relaxed and I breathed deeply. Cool, crisp, autumn air. I looked around the neat living room. Something was out of place, or missing.

The roses. The scent. Of course . . . they were with Coo. The pressure I'd felt was from their perfume upstairs. The clean air in the living room was a relief. How, I asked myself, could she stand it? But I thought no further than my coffee. As I brewed the pot, I remembered the one errand I had to run, going to the cleaners. Almost inhaling the restoring beverage, I shuffled back through the living room to go upstairs and unpack.

A torn florist's wrapping tissue lay on the vestibule floor, a small piece of delicate fern still clinging to its folds. Scooping up the green paper, I crumpled it into a ball and tossed the wad toward the waste basket. It was then I saw the first drop of blood.

And the second drop and the third and the fourth leading up the narrow stairway to our rooms. Each single drop evenly spaced from the drop before it. Each single drop no larger than the one before or the one after. Each drop leading closer and closer to Coo's bedroom door.

I followed the trail. Trying to suppress my alarm, I called Coo's name, but got no response. I pushed open her door.

She lay on her bed holding a single rose, the last of the twelve. Its deep bloom and color was equal to the eleven other roses spread gloriously full in the smoked crystal vase. Each as perfect as wax. Each blossom as red as the flower Coo held in her bloodless hands.

Stunned, I moved closer. Closer still. I touched her cold forehead. As I moved numbly back, the vase tipped, spilling the roses and the clotted blood which fed them onto Coo's sheets, pooling in the still-warm indentation surrounding her lifeless body.

•   •   •   •

The memorial service was as she would have wanted it. Strains of Chopin drifted through the chapel. I avoided her brother's eyes, but he was the first to embrace me.

Sitting there in the chapel, I fully realized for the first time what I'd missed in my own marriage. Coo had never really been apart from her Nicolas; she'd always been with him and he with her, but as much as we had loved each other, Michael and I lived two separate lives; we inhabited the same space but rarely shared it. The hollowness inside me grew even as the loss of Coo ebbed. She, at least, now had what she wanted. Nicolas. What did I have?

The answer was waiting for me when I got home.

A single, tissue wrapped, pure white rose bud.

Propagation of the Faith

Joan Vander Putten

JOAN VANDER PUTTEN, *a Long Island, New York, mother of five, left bank-ing to become the author of a series of remarkable stories—"In the Shadows of My Fear," "Just a Little Thing," "Remember Me"—that are alternately horrifying, humorous and/or touching. But "Propagation of the Faith" is neither amusing nor tender. Reader, beware: Its horrors are sadomasochistic and* very *explicit.* . . .

I WATCHED THE ANGER blossom red, like drops of blood, on Momma's cheeks. With fists pressed into hips, she tried to bully Gram into coming to church with us. As usual, Gram didn't give an inch. Stubborn old heathen, Momma called her. Behind her back, of course. Not even my feisty mother would dare insult Gram to her face. Not even Uncle Bryce would, and he was the eldest of Gram's nine children.

"God is love, Mom," Momma argued. "Wayne and I want to have Benny christened in church, so he starts life knowing that. You'd think you'd at least come to your newest grandchild's christening."

Gram slowly lifted one fuzzy gray eyebrow. It looked like an old caterpillar inching its way through the wrinkles on her forehead. "What makes you think I'd go to Benny's christening when I never went to any of the others?"

The way Gram said *christening,* it sounded like a dirty word.

She made a shooing motion with her hands. "Get along now! Go find love, or God, wherever you want. But don't you try to tell me church is the only place to find love, or that God is the only one who gives it. I know better."

She looked at me and smiled then, showing spots in her gums lonely for missing teeth. A secret smile, a smile that made my skin feel like it was covered with slugs. As if we shared a secret. Which we didn't.

Not then, at least.

Momma sighed, and I knew she'd given up. Since she and all her brothers and sisters had found God in the words of a passing preacher, none of them had succeeded in getting Gram to even step foot inside a church, much less have something they all called a "conversion." "C'mon, Naomi," she said to me. She turned and gave Gram the look *I* usually got when I did something bad. "We'll see you later, Mom."

Gram smiled, knowing she had won. "The party fixings are ready whenever your God decides Benny knows he's loved." Her black eyes gleamed with the taunt. Momma opened her mouth, then clamped it shut so hard I saw the muscles in her jaw twitch.

Daddy shook his head when we got in the car, and Aunt Lula, who sat in back with me and was holding Benny, snorted. "Told you it wouldn't do any good, Sally. She's as stubborn as mold on a ceiling."

"Seems more so since Pop died," Momma said, turning to look at her sister.

"Probably because she's not getting it anymore. The way she and Pop would go *at* it, remember? The way they screamed, you'd think—"

"Lula!" Momma jerked her head at me, and I knew that would be the end of gossip about my grandparents' sex life. Did they think I was stupid enough not to know what Aunt Lula was talking about? Why, I was thirteen, and some of my friends were already "getting it." I myself was still a virgin, but open to the possibility that that might change at any time. My fourteen-year-old cousin Oren, Aunt Lula's son, had, on more than one occasion, offered his services in that area. Made me giggle, he did. I don't think he was serious, but with Oren, you never knew. He'd never been with a girl as far as I knew. Leastways he didn't brag, and I guessed that was probably because he didn't have anything to brag *about*.

"I baptize thee Benjamin, in the name of the Father, and of the Son, and of the Holy Spirit, Amen." The minister poured holy water over my baby brother's head as he held Benny over something that looked like a toilet bowl with a tall base and no handle for flushing. Benny wailed, and I didn't blame him He'd been sleeping. It occurred to me that Benny'd had no say in whether or not he wanted to be christened. Neither had I, for that matter, or my other two younger brothers, or Oren, or his younger sister and brother. Our parents had decided that all of us were gonna be Christians, like it or not, and that was that.

I wasn't positive sure what a Christian was—we never went to church except for christenings of one kid or another—but I knew Christian meant believing in God, and that I did. I figured somebody must've put this whole world together and kept on holding it together, else we'd all be off and spinning in the universe like ants brushed off a picnic table. So if everybody wanted to call that person God, well, I wasn't about to argue. But how God could be love, like Momma was always saying, was a mystery to me.

Back at Gram's we ate till we near burst. Turkey and ham, sweet potatoes, biscuits, beets, greens, and three kinds of dessert. Gramps, who had been dead near six months, would've said, "It was a feast fit for a king." He'd always said that after a meal, no matter what Gram cooked. Then he'd go up to her and pinch her nipples till she cried out, and they'd kiss afterward. The grown-ups always tried to scoot us kids out before Gramps got up from the table. Most times they were quick enough so we wouldn't see. Sometimes they weren't.

While everyone was helping clean up, Gram came over to me. "Do you believe God is love?" she asked. I didn't rightly know how to answer, because as I said before, I didn't have that one quite figured out yet, and before I could open my mouth, she asked me another question. "Do you believe love is God?"

"Must be, if the two are the same," Oren piped up from behind me. I hadn't known he was standing there.

Gram laughed. She motioned for the two of us to follow her into the living room, where nobody was. We did.

"Gramps and I had our own religion, different from the one your namby-pamby folks believe in," she whispered as she bent closer to us. "Gramps was *my* God and I was his, and I think it's time for me to do some propagatin' of the *true* religion in this here family, before my grandkids turn as namby-pamby as their folks. You two are old enough to read the bibles."

Now, reading anything was something I hated more than pea soup, and I guess Gram could see that by my face, because she quickly added, "Not the Bible your folks have. Gramps and my bibles. There's a lot of 'em, but they're skinny, not much to read at one time. I want the two of you to go downstairs and open the chifforobe, the long cabinet way back in the corner of the basement." She produced a key from somewhere between her heavy breasts and tucked it into Oren's palm, closing his fingers over it. "Now, go on, you two, and do as your gram says. You go on down there and open that cabinet, and you'll find a stack of bibles in the top left-hand drawer. Don't you come up until you've read at least one of them . . . but you can read more if you've a mind to. I'll tell your parents not to come down and bother you. When you're done, just come up and tell me." Gram's black eyes had a funny sparkle to them, but it didn't look like she was about to laugh.

Oren and I had felt her switch on our behinds more than once when we'd disobeyed her, and neither of us had a hankering to feel it then. We shuffled over to the basement door slowly, ready to make a run for it when Gram turned her back, but she crossed her arms over her chest and planted herself on the flowered rug like she was a stubborn weed growing right up out of it, bound and determined not to be uprooted. We went.

The basement wasn't finished except for a small bathroom in one corner by the washer and dryer. Gramps had put that in, intending to finish the rest . . . one day. A naked bulb dangled at the base of the stairs, and there was another one in the corner by the chifforobe. To get to that piece of furniture, though, was like walking through a jungle blindfolded. Broken furniture littered the way, and old moth-eaten rugs that smelled so bad of mold I thought I'd see it growing right before my eyes, and black plastic bags that bulged with God-only-knew-what. Oren and I pushed aside what we were willing to touch, and stepped over what we weren't.

The key *snicked* in the lock and the door swung open. On the right side hung clothes, but Oren and I paid them no mind. We wanted to do what we had to and get out of there before mold started growing on us, too, which we weren't positive sure *wouldn't* happen for real. We opened the left-hand drawer and pulled out . . . a stack of magazines.

"Bibles?" Oren and I said together. I shrugged my shoulders, and we slid the top magazine off the pile before replacing the others in the drawer. The magazine had no cover, and it smelled like the rest of the basement. Mold speckled the top right-hand corner of the first page, and I shivered in disgust. Oren held it, and turned the page.

There was these two pictures, side by side, of a naked man and woman. Now, I'd seen girlie magazines before. Oren had sneaked some into his room, and one time when I was in there alone, I found them. There were all these pictures of men and women *doing* it, in every position I could think of, and some I couldn't have imagined even if I'd stayed up all night trying. But this picture was different.

The man was *peeing* on the woman! And in the next picture she was squatting over him, doing the same. "The Golden Shower" the title read. Oren and I gasped right about at the same time, and Oren flipped the page real fast. Both of us were red as the beets we'd eaten for dinner.

The next page was even worse.

Another man and woman, with *things* attached to their privates, things that looked painful as all get out.

With one hand the man was pulling a little ring clamped to the woman's breast. "Look at her tit!" Oren whispered. "It looks like a Sno-Kone!" It didn't look like a Sno-Kone to me, and I felt a twinge of sympathetic pain in my own budding left breast.

With his other hand the man held something that looked like a long, pointed tweezer. The woman was spreading herself *down there,* as if she was waiting for him to grab something else. I'd done a little exploring of my own down there in recent months, and I had a pretty good guess what it was.

"Jeez!" Oren exclaimed. "Look at *that!*" He pointed to a weird looking thing at the base of the man's dick, something that seemed to make it swell up like a giant . . . well, *sausage,* all plump and juicy. Something fluttered just below my belly, a feeling I was only lately starting to have since I'd begun exploring, a feeling I knew was connected to "doing it." My cheeks felt hotter than tar roads in July, and I couldn't bring myself to look at Oren. But then, he didn't seem to be able to look at me, either, so I figured something was going on for him, too.

As we studied the magazine page by page, we got an education we'd never get from our teachers at Four Corners High, which I had just started. *This* was Gram and Gramps *religion?* We pulled out more bibles, and each and every one was more or less like the first. One of them was titled "Love Hurts." Oren hadn't spoken since his first comment, but I noticed he was breathing funny. My own breathing was a little strange, too—like I couldn't get enough air in fast enough, and that feeling below my belly was stronger now.

Oren pulled over a rug that didn't look too moth-eaten. We plopped down, the stack of bibles next to us. Sitting opposite him like I was, I couldn't help but notice. His dick was trying to poke out of his pants. He saw me looking, and had the decency to blush. I did, too, being caught and all.

"How can Gram call these bibles?" I asked, trying to ignore Oren's crotch, which wasn't easy to do for some reason. "They're just a bunch of dirty books!"

Oren looked thoughtful. "Did you notice the faces on the people in these magazines?" he asked. "They sure as hell looked like they were having a conversion. I went to a revival meeting once with Ma, and people were dropping like flies. Slayed in the spirit, they call it, and their faces looked just like these." He pointed to a couple who were dressed in leather, with holes cut out for their privates. I wasn't sure what exactly it was they were doing to one another with things that looked like branding irons, but their faces looked like they were seeing the Lord himself. "Umm," I said, unable to disagree. "But what kind of religion could it be?"

Oren thought another minute, then said, "Love, like Gram said. These people are feeling love, and that's God, right? Gram said so. Even our folks say God and love are the same." I couldn't disagree with him there, either. His next words, though, hit me like a punch in the stomach.

"It's the religion Gram wants us to follow," he said, so serious he sounded as reverent as the minister had today. I know I gulped. He stood, and went over to the chifforobe again.

In the second drawer he found them—most of the things we'd seen in the pictures, and others, besides. Clamps, tweezers, branding irons, things with spikes, leather straps, more than I could name. When we had them all spread out on the blanket, I could see Oren trembling. But then again, so was I. He looked at me, and said in a hoarse voice, "Let me love you, Naomi, and then you can love me." All I could do was nod. I felt all warm, and I knew my panties were wet, although I hadn't peed myself. It was a strange, wonderful feeling, and I took off my clothes shyly but willingly.

Oren stared at me a minute, and I could see the bulge was back in his pants. "You, too," I said, not wanting to be the only one naked. I mean, fair is fair, right? I'd never seen a real dick up close and in person before, and although Oren's wasn't as big as some I'd seen in the bibles, it was bigger than others. I told him that. He told me my tits were "getting there," but I wasn't hurt because I knew he was only telling true. They were still only about the size of a half-scoop of ice cream. "Now what?" I asked. Seeing as how he was older, and a boy, I figured I'd leave this whole thing up to him.

He tapped his finger against his teeth a minute, then said, "Since this is our new religion, I guess we should start with a baptism." He took my hand and led me into the bathroom. "You can go first," he offered. He knelt in front of the toilet bowl, facedown.

"Oh, yuck, that's gross!" No way did I want to do *that.*

"We have to, Naomi, if we're gonna do the rest of the stuff. No religion takes unless you get baptized into it." I made a face, but I straddled him. If this was gonna be a christening, at least we should make up a prayer, I thought, so I did when I let go. "I baptize you Oren, in the name of Gram, and of Gramps, and of . . . 'Love Hurts.'" He didn't whimper or gag, not once. I wish I could say I was as brave when it came my turn. There wasn't any soap by the sink, so we had to make do with plain water to wash our heads. We'd have to think up something to explain to our folks why our heads were wet.

We went back to the blanket. He told me to lie down, and I obeyed. He took two of the rings and figured out how to pinch my nipples with them. They hurt, yeah . . . but the hurting felt good, in a way I can't describe. My insides twittered, down there. Then he took the long, pointy tweezers, spread my thighs, and grabbed the exact same thing I'd discovered. My body jerked a few times, and I felt the wet run out of me. I was suddenly, totally relaxed. After a minute I sat up and leaned over to give Oren an awkward kiss on the lips. It was the least I could do, after the way he had loved me.

Then I looked through the books, wanting to find an extra-special way for me to love him back.

It made a logical kind of sense to me at the time. If love was God and God was love, then the way Oren had loved me made him God. Now I understood why Gram said she and Gramps were God to one another! Like I said, it made a logical kind of sense. I found a picture and showed

Oren the way I wanted to love him. It reminded me of the way Jesus had loved us, according to Momma, although it wasn't exactly the same.

And the man with the woman's face buried in his crotch didn't look like he was suffering at all.

Oren's eyes grew wide, but he nodded, trusting me. This was making more sense all the time. You were *supposed* to trust God; and if Oren and I were gonna be God to one another, we had to trust each other. I set about gathering the stuff I needed, and prepared his neck with the collar I'd found.

When everything was set, I kicked the chair out. His kicking legs made it hard to keep my mouth on his dick, but he finally stopped.

It wasn't until I looked up to see if he was enjoying how I was loving him that I noticed the collar around his neck had slipped.

He just hung there, not enjoying anything.

Angelica

Jane Yolen

JANE YOLEN's *prolific imagination—she has written more than seventy books — is surpassed only by her delightful sense of humor and personal charm. In addition to teaching and writing essays on children's literature, she has penned many volumes of engaging fantasies for all-age children, including* The Witch Who Wasn't, The Princess Who Couldn't Sleep, The Wizard of Washington Square *and* Tales of Wonder. *"Angelica," though its protagonist is a little boy, is not meant for children. I've never read a story quite like it—and I'm not sure I want to ever again.*

Linz, Austria, 1898

THE BOY could not sleep. It was hot and he had been sick for so long. All night his head had throbbed. Finally he sat up and managed to get out of bed. He went down the stairs without stumbling.

Elated at his progress, he slipped from the house without waking either his mother or father. His goal was the river bank. He had not been there in a month.

He had always considered the river bank his own. No one else in the family ever went there. He liked to set his feet in the damp ground and make patterns. It was like a picture, and the artist in him appreciated the primitive beauty.

Heat lightning jetted across the sky. He sat down on a fallen log and picked at the bark as he would a scab. He could feel the log imprint itself on his backside through the thin cotton pajamas. He wished—not for the first time—that he could be allowed to sleep without his clothes.

The silence and heat enveloped him. He closed his eyes and dreamed of sleep, but his head still throbbed. He had never been out at night by himself before. The slight touch of fear was both pleasure and pain.

He thought about that fear, probing it like a loose tooth, now to feel the ache and now to feel the sweetness, when the faint came upon him and he tumbled slowly from the log. There was nothing but river bank before him, nothing to slow his descent, and he rolled down the slight hill and into the river, not waking till the shock of the water hit him.

It was cold and unpleasantly muddy. He thrashed about. The sour water got in his mouth and made him gag.

Suddenly someone took his arm and pulled him up onto the bank, dragged him up the slight incline.

He opened his eyes and shook his head to get the lank, wet hair from his face. He was surprised to find that his rescuer was a girl, about his size, in a white cotton shift. She was not muddied at all from her efforts. His one thought before she heaved him over the top of the bank and helped him back onto the log was that she must be quite marvelously strong.

"Thank you," he said, when he was seated again, and then did not know where to go from there.

"You are welcome." Her voice was low, her speech precise, almost old-fashioned in its carefulness. He realized that she was not a girl but a small woman.

"You fell in," she said.

"Yes."

She sat down beside him and looked into his eyes, smiling. He wondered how he could see so well when the moon was behind her. She seemed to light up from within like some kind of lamp. Her outline was a golden glow and her blonde hair fell in straight lengths to her shoulder.

"You may call me Angelica," she said.

"Is that your name?"

She laughed. "No. No, it is not. And how perceptive of you to guess."

"Is it an alias?" He knew about such things. His father was a customs official and told the family stories at the table about his work.

"It is the name I. . . ." She hesitated for a moment and looked behind her. Then she turned and laughed again. "It is the name I travel under."

"Oh."

"You could not pronounce my real name," she said.

"Could I try?"

"*Pistias Sophia!*" said the woman and she stood as she named herself. She seemed to shimmer and grow at her own words, but the boy thought that might be the fever in his head, though he hadn't a headache anymore.

"Pissta. . . ." He could not stumble around the name. There seemed to be something blocking his tongue. "I guess I better call you Angelica for now," he said.

"For now," she agreed.

He smiled shyly at her. "My name is Addie," he said.

"I know."

"How do you know? Do I look like an Addie? It means. . . ."

"Noble hero," she finished for him.

"How do you know *that?*"

"I am very wise," she said. "And names are important to me. To all . . . of us. Destiny is in names." She smiled, but her smile was not so pleasant any longer. She started to reach for his hand, but he drew back.

"You shouldn't boast," he said. "About being wise. It's not nice."

"I am not boasting." She found his hand and held it in hers. Her touch was cool and infinitely soothing. She reached over with the other hand and put it first palm, then back to his forehead. She made a "tch" against her teeth and scowled. "Your guardian should be Flung Over. I shall have to speak to Uriel about this. Letting you out with such a fever."

"Nobody *let* me out," said the boy. "I let myself out. No one knows I am here—except you."

"Well, there is one who *should* know where you are. And he shall certainly hear from me about this." She stood up and was suddenly much taller than the boy. "Come. Back to the house with you. You should be in bed." She reached down the front of her white shift and brought up a silver bottle on a chain. "You must take a sip of this now. It will help you sleep."

"Will you come back with me?" the boy asked after taking a drink.

"Just a little way." She held his hand as they went.

He looked behind once to see his footprints in the rain-soft earth. They marched in an orderly line behind him. He could not see hers at all.

"Do you believe, little Addie?" Her voice seemed to come from a long way off, further even than the hills.

"Believe in what?"

"In God. Do you believe that he directs all our movements?"

"I sing in the church choir," he said, hoping it was the proof she wanted.

"That will do for now," she said.

There was a fierceness in her voice that made him turn in the muddy furrow and look at her. She towered above him, all white and gold and glowing. The moon haloed her head, and behind her, close to her shoulders, he saw something like wings, feathery and waving. He was suddenly desperately afraid.

"What are you?" he whispered.

"What do you think I am?" she asked, and her face looked carved in stone, so white her skin and black the features.

"Are you . . . the angel of death?" he asked and then looked down before she answered. He could not bear to watch her talk.

"For you, I am an angel of life," she said. "Did I not save you?"

"What kind of angel are you?" he whispered, falling to his knees before her.

She lifted him up and cradled him in her arms. She sang him a lullaby in a language he did not know. "I told you in the beginning who I am," she murmured to the sleeping boy. "I am Pistias Sophia, angel of wisdom and faith. The one who put the serpent into the garden, little Adolf. But I was only following orders."

Her wings unfurled behind her. She pumped them once, twice, and then the great wind they commanded lifted her into the air. She flew without a sound to the Hitler house and left the boy sleeping, feverless, in his bed.

Walking Aunt Daid

Zenna Henderson

The closing spot in my anthologies is always reserved for the story I consider the most remarkable. It was an especially difficult decision this time; Angels of Darkness contains many first-rate candidates. I finally chose "Walking Aunt Daid" because of its unique wedding of nameless terror and radiant beauty. The late ZENNA HENDERSON *was an Arizona writer and schoolteacher best known for her science fictional stories of "the People," collected in* Pilgrimage: The Book of the People *and* The People: No Different Flesh. *NESFA Press recently announced its plan to issue the complete series in one volume.*

I LOOKED UP in surprise and so did Ma. And so did Pa. Aunt Daid was moving. Her hands were coming together and moving upward till the light from the fireplace had a rest from flickering on that cracked, wrinkled wreck that was her face. But the hands didn't stay long. They dropped back to her saggy lap like two dead bats, and the sunken old mouth that had fallen in on its lips years before I was born puckered and worked and let Aunt Daid's tongue out a little ways before it pulled it back in again. I swallowed hard. There was something alive about that tongue and *alive* wasn't a word I'd associate with Aunt Daid.

Ma let out a sigh that was almost a snort and took up her fancy work again. "Guess it's about time," she said over a sudden thrum of rain against the darkening parlor windows.

"Naw," said Pa. "Too soon. Years yet."

"Don't know 'bout that," said Ma. "Paul here's going on twenty. Count back to the last time. Remember that, Dev?"

"Aw!" Pa squirmed in his chair. Then he rattled the *Weekly Wadrow* open and snapped it back to the state news. "Better watch out," he warned, his eyes answering hers. "I might learn more this time and decide I need some other woman."

"Can't scare me," said Ma over the strand of embroidery thread she was holding between her teeth to separate it into strands. " 'Twon't be your place this time anyhow. Once for each generation, hasn't it been? It's Paul this time."

"He's too young," protested Pa. "Some things younguns should be sheltered from." He was stern.

"Paul's older'n you were at his age," said Ma. "Schooling does that to you, I guess."

"Sheltered from what?" I asked. "What about last time? What's all this just cause Aunt Daid moved without anyone telling her to?"

"You'll find out," said Ma, and she shivered a little. "We make jokes about it—but only in the family," she warned. "This is strictly family business. But it isn't any joking matter. I wish the good Lord would take Aunt Daid. It's creepy. It's not healthy."

"Aw, simmer down, Mayleen," said Pa. "It's not all that bad. Every family's got its problems. Ours just happens to be Aunt Daid. It could be worse. At least she's quiet and clean and biddable and that's more than you can say for some other people's old folks."

"*Old* folks is right," said Ma. "We hit the jackpot there."

"How old *is* Aunt Daid?" I asked, wondering just how many years it had taken to suck so much sap out of her that you wondered that the husk of her didn't rustle when she walked.

"No one rightly knows," said Ma, folding away her fancy work. She went over to Aunt Daid and put her hand on the sagging shoulder.

"Bed time, Aunt Daid," she called, loud and clear. "Time for bed."

I counted to myself. ". . . three, four, *five,* six, seven, eight, nine, *ten,*" and Aunt Daid was on her feet, her bent old knees wavering to hold her scanty weight.

I shook my head wonderingly and half grinned. Never failed. Up at the count of ten, which was pretty good seeing as she never started stirring until the count of five. It took that long for Ma's words to sink in.

I watched Aunt Daid follow Ma out. You couldn't push her to go anywhere, but she followed real good. Then I said to Pa, "What's Aunt Daid's whole name? How's she kin to us?"

"Don't rightly know," said Pa. "I could maybe figger it out—how she's kin to us, I mean—if I took the time . . . a lot of it. Great-great-grampa started calling her Aunt Daid. Other folks thought it was kinda disrespectful but it stuck to her." He stood up and stretched and yawned. "Morning comes early," he said. "Better hit the hay." He pitched the paper at the woodbox and went off toward the kitchen for his bed snack.

"What'd he call her Aunt Daid for?" I hollered after him.

"Well," yelled Pa, his voice muffled, most likely from coming out of the icebox. "He said she shoulda been 'daid' a long time ago, so he called her Aunt Daid."

I figured on the edge of the *Hog Breeders' Gazette*. "Let's see. Around thirty years to a generation. Me, Pa, grampa, great-grampa, great-great-grampa—and let's see, for me that'd be another great. That makes six generations. That's 180 years—" I chewed on the end of my pencil, a funny flutter inside me.

" 'Course, that just guessing," I told myself. "Maybe Pa just piled it on for devilment. Minus a generation—that's 150." I put my pencil down real careful. *Shoulda been dead a long time ago.* How old *was* Aunt Daid that they said that about her a century and a half ago?

Next morning the whole world was fresh and clean. Last night's spell of rain had washed the trees and the skies and settled the dust. I stretched in the early morning cool and felt like life was a pretty good thing. Vacation before me and nothing much to be done on the farm for a while.

Ma called breakfast and I followed my nose to the buttermilk pancakes and sausages and coffee and out-ate Pa by a stack and a half of pancakes.

"Well, son, looks like you're finally a man," said Pa. "When you can out-eat your pa—"

Ma scurried in from the other room. "Aunt Daid's sitting on the edge of her bed," she said anxiously. "And I didn't get her up."

"Um," said Pa. "Begins to look that way, doesn't it?"

"Think I'll go up to Honan's Lake," I said, tilting my chair back, only half hearing what they were saying. "Feel like a coupla days fishing."

"Better hang around, son," said Pa. "We might be needing you in a day or so."

"Oh?" I said, a little put out. "I had my mouth all set for Honan's Lake."

"Well, unset it for a spell," said Pa. "There's a whole summer ahead."

"But what for?" I asked. "What's cooking?"

Pa and Ma looked at each other and Ma crumpled the corner of her apron in her hand. "We're going to need you," she said.

"How come?" I asked.

"To walk Aunt Daid," said Ma.

"To walk Aunt Daid?" I thumped my chair back on four legs. "But my gosh, Ma, you always do for Aunt Daid."

"Not for this," said Ma, smoothing at the wrinkles in her apron. "Aunt Daid won't walk this walk with a woman. It has to be you."

I took a good look at Aunt Daid that night at supper. I'd never really looked at her before. She'd been around ever since I could remember. She was as much a part of the house as the furniture.

Aunt Daid was just so-so sized. If she'd been fleshed out, she'd be about Ma for bigness. She had a wisp of black hair twisted into a walnut-sized knob at the back of her head. The ends of the hair sprayed out stiffly from the knob like a worn-out brush. Her face looked like wrinkles had wrinkled on wrinkles and all collapsed into the emptiness of no teeth and no meat on her skull bones. Her tiny eyes, almost hidden under the crepe of her eyelids, were empty. They just stared across the table through me and on out into nothingness while her lips sucked open at the tap of the spoon Ma held, inhaled the soft stuff Ma had to feed her on, and then shut, working silently until her skinny neck bobbed with swallowing.

"Doesn't she ever say anything?" I finally asked.

Pa looked quick at Ma and then back down at his plate.

"Never heard a word out of her," said Ma.

"Doesn't she ever *do* anything?" I asked.

"Why sure," said Ma. "She shells peas real good when I get her started."

"Yeah." I felt my spine crinkle, remembering once when I was little. I sat on the porch and passed the peapods to Aunt Daid. I was remembering how, after I ran out of peas, her withered old hands had kept reaching and taking and shelling and throwing away with nothing but emptiness in them.

"And she tears rug rags good. And she can pull weeds if nothing else is growing where they are."

"Why—" I started—and stopped.

"Why do we keep her?" asked Ma. "She doesn't die. She's alive. What should we do? She's no trouble. Not much, anyway."

"Put her in a home somewhere," I suggested.

"She's in a home now," said Ma, spooning up custard for Aunt Daid. "And we don't have to put out cash for her. Besides, they'd never walk her and no telling what'd happen to her."

"What is this walking business, anyway? Walking where?"

"Down hollow," said Pa, cutting a quarter of a cherry pie. "Down to the oak—" he drew a deep breath and let it out—"and back again."

"Why down there?" I asked. "Hollow's full of weeds and mosquitoes. Besides it's—it's—"

"Spooky," said Ma, smiling at me.

"Well, yes, spooky," I said. "There's always a quiet down there when the wind's blowing everywhere else, or else a wind when everything's still. Why down there?"

"There's where she wants to walk," said Pa. "You walk her down there."

"Well," I stood up. "Let's get it over with. Come on, Aunt Daid."

"She ain't ready yet," said Ma. "She won't go till she's ready."

"Well, Pa, why can't you walk her then?" I asked. "You did it once—"

"Once is enough," said Pa, his face shut and still. "It's your job this time. You be here when you're needed. It's a family duty. Them fish will wait."

"Okay, okay," I said. "But at least tell me what the deal is. It sounds like a lot of hogwash to me."

There wasn't much to tell. Aunt Daid was a family heirloom, like, but Pa never heard exactly who she was to the family. She had always been like this—just as old and so dried up she wasn't even repulsive. I guess it's only when there's enough juice for rotting that a body is repulsive and Aunt Daid was years and years past that. That must be why the sight of her wet tongue jarred me.

Seems like once in every twenty-thirty years, Aunt Daid gets an awful craving to go walking. And always someone has to go with her. A man. She won't go with a woman. And the man comes back changed.

"You can't help being changed," said Pa. "When your eyes look on things your mind can't—" Pa swallowed.

"Only time there was any real trouble with Aunt Daid," said Pa, "was when the family came west. That was back in your great-great-grampa's time. They left the old place and came out here in covered wagons and Aunt Daid didn't even notice until time for her to walk again. Then she got violent. Great-grampa tried to walk her down the road, but she dragged him all over the place, coursing like a hunting dog that's lost the trail only with her eyes blind-like, all through the dark. Great-grampa finally brought her back almost at sunrise. He was pert nigh a broken man, what with cuts and bruises and scratches . . . and walking Aunt Daid. She'd finally settled on down hollow."

"What does she walk for?" I asked. "What goes on?"

"You'll see, son," said Pa. "Words wouldn't tell anything, but you'll see."

That evening Aunt Daid covered her face again with her hands. Later she stood up by herself, teetering by her chair a minute, one withered old hand pawing at the air, till Ma, with a look at Pa, set her down again.

All next day Aunt Daid was quiet, but come evening she got restless. She went to the door three or four times, just waiting there like a puppy asking to go out, but after my heart had started pounding and I had hurried to her and opened the door, she just waved her face blindly at the darkness outside and went back to her chair.

Next night was the same until along about 10 o'clock, just as Ma was thinking of putting Aunt Daid to bed. First thing we knew, Aunt Daid was by the door again, her feet tramping up and down impatiently, her dry hands whispering over the door.

"It's time," said Pa quiet-like and I got all cold inside.

"But it's blacker'n pitch tonight," I protested. "It's as dark as the inside of a cat. No moon."

Aunt Daid whimpered. I nearly dropped. It was the first sound I'd ever heard from her.

"It's time," said Pa again, his face bleak. "Walk her, son. And Paul . . . bring her back."

"Down hollow's bad enough by day," I said, watching, half-sick, as Aunt Daid spread her skinny arms out against the door, her face pushed up against it hard, her saggy black dress looking like spilled ink dripped down. "But on a moonless night—"

"Walk her somewhere else, then," said Pa, his voice getting thin. "If you can. But get going, son, and don't come back without her."

And I was outside, feeling the shifting of Aunt Daid's hand bones inside my hand as she set off through the dark, dragging me along with her, scared half to death, wondering if the rustling I heard was her skin or her clothes, wondering on the edge of screaming where she was dragging me to—*what* she was dragging me to.

I tried to head her off from down hollow, steering her towards the lane or the road or across lots or out into the pasture, but it was like being a dog on a leash. I went my way the length of our two arms, then I went her way. Finally I gave up and let her drag me, my eyes opened to aching, trying to see in the dark so heavy that only a less dark showed where the sky was. There wasn't a sound except the thud of our feet in the dust and a thin straining hiss that was Aunt Daid's breath and a gulping gasp that was mine. I'd've cried if I hadn't been so scared.

Aunt Daid stopped so quick that I ploughed into her, breathing in a sudden puff of a smell like a stack of old newspapers that have been a long time in a dusty shed. And there we stood, so close I could touch her but I couldn't even see a glimmer of her face in the darkness that was so thick it seemed like the whole night had poured itself down into the hollow. But between one blink and another, I could see Aunt Daid. Not because there was any more light, but because my eyes seemed to get more seeing to them.

She was yawning—a soft little yawn that she covered with a quick hand—and then she laughed. My throat squeezed my breath. The yawn and the hand movement and the laugh were all young and graceful and —and beautiful—but the hand and the face were still withered-up old Aunt Daid.

"I'm waking up." The voice sent shivers up me—pleasure shivers.

"I'm waking up," said Aunt Daid again, her soft, light voice surprised and delighted. "And I *know* I'm waking up!"

She held her hands up and looked at them. "They look so horribly real," she marveled. "Don't they?"

She held them out to me and in my surprise I croaked, "Yeah, they do."

At the sound of my voice, she jerked all over and got shimmery all around the edges.

"He said," she whispered, her lips firming and coloring as she talked, "he said if ever I could know in my dream that I was just dreaming, I'd be on the way to a cure. I *know* this is the same recurrent nightmare. I *know* I'm asleep, but I'm talking to one of the creatures—" she looked at me a minute "—one of the *people* in my dream. And he's talking to me —for the first time!"

Aunt Daid was changing. Her face was filling out and her eyes widening, her body was straining at the old black dress that wasn't saggy any more. Before I could draw a breath, the old dress rustled to the ground and Aunt Daid—I mean *she* was standing there, light rippling around her like silk—a light that cast no shadows nor even flickered on the tangled growth in the hollow.

It seemed to me that I could see into that light, farther than any human eyes ought to see, and all at once the world that had always been absolute bedrock to me became a shimmering edge of something, a path between places or a brief stopping place. And the wonder that was the existence of mankind wasn't unique any more.

"Oh, if only I *am* cured!" she cried. "If only I don't ever have to go through this nightmare again!" She lifted her arms and drew herself up into a slim growing exclamation point.

"For the first time I really know I'm dreaming," she said. "And I know this isn't real!" Her feet danced across the hollow and she took both my numb hands. "You aren't real, are you?" she asked. "None of this is, is it? All this ugly, old, dragging—" She put her arms around me and hugged me tight.

My hands tingled to the icy fire of her back and my breath was tangled in the heavy silvery gleam of her hair.

"Bless you for being unreal!" she said. "And may I never dream you again!"

And there I was, all alone in the dark hollow, staring at hands I couldn't see, trying to see the ice and fire that still tingled on my finger tips. I took a deep shuddery breath and stopped to grope for Aunt Daid's dress that caught at my feet. Fear melted my knees and they wouldn't straighten up again. I could feel terror knocking at my brain and I knew as soon as it could break through I'd go screaming up the hollow like a crazy man, squeezing the black dress like a rattlesnake in my hands. But I heard Pa saying, "Bring her back," and I thought, "All my grampas saw it, too. All of them brought her back. It's happened before." And I crouched there, squinching my eyes tight shut, holding my breath, my fingers digging into my palms, clutching the dress.

It might have been a minute, it might have been an hour, or a lifetime before the dress stirred in my hands. My knees jerked me upright and I dropped the dress like a live coal.

She was there again, her eyes dreaming-shut, her hair swinging like the start of music, her face like every tender thing a heart could ever know. Then her eyes opened slowly and she looked around her.

"Oh, *no!*" she cried, the back of her hand muffling her words. "Not again! Not after all this time! I thought I was over it!"

And I had her crying in my arms—all that wonderfulness against me. All that softness and sorrow.

But she pulled away and looked up at me. "Well, I'll say it again so I won't forget it," she said, her tears slipping from her face and glittering down through the dark. "And this time it'll work. This is only a dream. My own special nightmare. This will surely be the last one. I have just this one night to live through and never again, never again. You are my dream—this is all a dream—" Her hands touched the wrinkles that started across her forehead. The old black dress was creeping like a devouring snake up her and her flesh was sagging away before it as it crept. Her hair was dwindling and tarnishing out of its silvery shining, her eyes shrinking and blanking out.

"No, no!" I cried, sick to the marrow to see Aunt Daid coming back over all that wonder. I rubbed my hand over her face to erase the lines that were cracking across it, but the skin under my fingers stiffened and crumpled and stiffened and hardened and, before I could wipe the feel of dried oldness from the palm of my hand, all of Aunt Daid was there and the hollow was fading as my eyes lost their seeing.

·　·　·　·

I felt the drag and snag of weeds and briars as I brought Aunt Daid back—a sobbing Aunt Daid, tottering and weak. I finally had to carry her, all match-sticky and musty in my arms.

As I struggled up out of the hollow that was stirring behind me in a wind that left the rest of the world silent, I heard singing in my head, *Life is but a dream. . . . Life is but a dream.* But before I stumbled blindly into the blare of light from the kitchen door, I shook the sobbing bundle of bones in my arms—the withered cocoon, the wrinkled seed of such a flowering—and whispered,

"Wake up, Aunt Daid! Wake up, *you!*"

Acknowledgments